Dedications

To my parents, Les and Della, thank you for love provided, knowledge imparted and wisdoms taught.

To Michael Molden and all at Cauliay Books – thank you so much for all your belief and support.

To Susan Watson, the scourge of the 'That's'. You didn't get them all though.

To Joey Cremin, the poser of questions and spotter of plot-holes and also the hairiest bald man I've ever known

Acknowledgements

As always, all my love to my darling wife Marian, my Sightless Queen.

To my sons, Ben and Jack – the Motionless Student and the Fleshless Drummer, still making me proud each and every day.

To Happy - normally blondes who know how pretty they are really get on your nerves, but I'll make an exception in your case.

To Frankie, the Mufasa of Buckie - if they ever do a live action remake of the Lion King, you'd be the star!

To my friends and colleagues in the Community Support Service of The Moray Council, you take the 'b' out of job and replace it with a 'y'.

To everyone who bought the first book, I hope you enjoy this one just as much.

The Flawless Knight

By

Phil Williams

Published by

Cauliay Publishing & Distribution
PO Box 12076
Aberdeen
AB16 9AL
www.cauliaybooks.com

First Edition
ISBN 978-0-9571330-2-0
Copyright © Phil Williams 2012
Front cover painting: **Chivalry** By Sir Frank Dicksee
Back cover photo: **Howling Wolf** By Retron

The Warriors Of Camelot Odyssey

The Knights of The Round Table, a body of men so valiant and well-famed that, over a millennium after myth and legend first recorded their gallant deeds, they still retain their place within the lexicon of heroes who have bestrode these blessed lands.

Twelve men, pure of spirit and stout of heart, noble in their every thought and brave in their every endeavour, their names embodied all that was good and just in the harsh, inhospitable times in which they lived.

Led by the archetypal 'knight in shining armour', King Arthur Pendragon, they ruled the demesne of Camelot wisely and without favour, each of them acutely aware of their responsibilities as leaders among men, each of them scrupulously trustworthy and honourable.

There was Sir Galahad, the chaste and pure, second only in valour to King Arthur himself.

Sir Kay, King Arthur's foster brother and seneschal to the court of Camelot.

Sir Bedivere, Duke of Neustria and one of the first knights to join the Round Table fellowship.

Sir Gawain, eldest son of King Lot of Orkney.

Sir Gareth, Gawain's younger brother and impeccable exemplar of chivalry

Sir Gaheris, most steadfast of King Lot's sons, the level headed brother of Gareth and Gawain.

Sir Geraint, heir to the kingdom of Dumnonia and knight of Devon.

Sir Bors, King of Gannes and cousin to the disgraced Sir Lancelot.

Sir Lamorak, son of King Pellinore and one of the foremost jousters in the land.

Sir Tristan, son of Meliodas and heir to the kingdom of Lyonesse

and completing the duodecad, Sir Percivale, the only member of the fellowship to actually be ennobled by King Arthur in recognition of his battle prowess.

These were the Round Table Knights. These were the Warriors of Camelot.

Their courageous deeds under Arthur's leadership have been documented on numerous occasions but the stories of their lives after King Arthur fell upon the field of Camlann and Camelot's power began to wane have languished in the mists of antiquity for too long and demand to be told, and be told they will, in the Warriors of Camelot Odyssey.

The Flawless Knight is the story of Sir Galahad.

Prologue

The woman ran.

Her shoulder-length blonde hair streamed out behind her as she vainly tried to negotiate the uneven terrain without injury. Sheer naked terror had lent her feet wings when her initial flight had begun, but now a combination of fatigue, the gusty, snow-laced wind which had blown in from the north and the spongy, boggy ground left her all but spent.

A heartfelt sob escaped her as she surveyed the wilderness in which she found herself. There was no hope of shelter within sight, a few scrubby trees, singularly dotted across the bleak landscape, offered no succour and would only add seconds at most to the time it would take her pursuers to find her.

As if the mere thought of her hunters had called them into earshot, she heard the sounds of pursuit on the wind. Whether it was a trick of the breeze or not, they sounded mind-freezingly close.

Daring a glance behind, she squinted into the twilit murk, hoping against hope that she still had enough time to somehow engineer a miraculous escape. That hope was strangled at birth.

She could clearly see them, three to the left of her, two to the right. The knowledge of her capture turned her legs to jelly and she collapsed to the ground. She had expected her unclothed body to shiver uncontrollably as it came into contact with the damp earth, but it was almost as if the realisation of her impending fate had detached her mental self from her physical self and so she simply lay catatonic, in the foetal position, as the animals closed in. She felt no pain as their jaws began to rip and rend her flesh and she made no sound as she died, savaged beyond recognition by razor-sharp claws and row upon row of jagged fangs.

The pack of wolves continued their feeding frenzy long after their prey's last breath had issued unseen into the darkness. Their scarlet-stained muzzles were spattered with gore and the fur of their front paws was reddened and matted.

Two of the ravening beasts each took a bite at the same piece of meat, resulting in a snapping, snarling confusion of teeth and talon. Within seconds, what had started as a mere dispute over food had spilled over into a fight to the death as the two wolves became engulfed in a berserk melee of rage and brutality.

"Enough."

Though the word issued from a human mouth, there was a definite wolven bark contained within it, one with enough authority to cause the two animals to halt their struggle and the rest of the pack to cease their feast of flesh.

A massively muscled warrior strode with languid assurance over to the chaos of bones and organs that constituted the remains of the fleeing woman. He dropped to his haunches and surveyed the carnage with strikingly green eyes. With one hand, he stroked the long, drooping strands of the blonde moustache which framed his full-lipped mouth and, with the other, absent-mindedly scratched behind the ears of one of the now placid wolves.

The only area of the woman's carcass that remained relatively untouched was her delicate, pale face. The man placed a fur-booted foot down upon the corpse's chest, ignoring the splintering of the rib cage, and trod on the spinal column which had been picked nearly clean of tissue by the beasts' hunger. With a dispassionate gaze at the woman's deep-blue eyes he took hold of her chin and forehead and wrenched the head clear of the shoulders.

For the briefest of moments, her eyes seemed to lock with those of her defiler. The warrior's own flared for a moment in shock then, just as quickly, hooded whilst his mouth twisted into a cruel smile as he realised it had been a trick of the light. Almost tenderly, he cradled the head in his hands and planted a kiss on the rapidly bluing lips.

"Nowhere to run now, bitch," he said softly, "Nowhere to run now."

With a lack of ceremony that belied the previous show of gentleness, he plunged the head into a sack and began to walk back to his home.

He gathered his wolf-skin furs about his immense shoulders and, with a snap of his fingers, indicated that the pack should follow.

He had walked barely ten feet when a pathetic whimpering came to his ears. He turned and squinted into the gloom. One of the wolves who had been involved in the two-way fight for the hunk of meat was limping towards him, its left hind leg trailing uselessly behind it.

The giant's eyes showed a touching depth of pity for the wounded animal for he knew at once that nothing could be done to save her. He advanced towards the creature, its fur seeming to glow like mercury in the moonlight. In a similar manner to the slaughtered woman, the wolf accepted her fate and dropped her proud head. Deep down in her bones, she knew that the pack could not support a member as crippled as she, any more than she would if the position was reversed and another wolf in the pack was gravely harmed.

One final mournful howl fled her throat and headed for the stars as the man withdrew his dagger from its oilskin sheath and plunged it into her heart.

The she-wolf slumped against him. He withdrew the dagger, throwing it to the ground and held her to his breast, eyes closed, feeling the rhythm of the creature's chest falter, slow then finally stop.

He held her even as the body elongated, the fur receded and the muzzle withdrew into a human face.

With a tell-tale catch in his voice, the man whispered a prayer into the night, "May you stalk the sky for eternity, at one with Hati and Skoll."

In a unisonic burst, the wolves gave vent to their anguish, the eerie atavistic hymn carrying for miles on the strengthening wind.

The man retrieved his knife from the damp ground and resumed his walk, effortlessly carrying the corpse in his arms, though in truth the additional burden did weigh him down physically as well as mentally.

As he walked, he reflected on the path his life had taken ever since he and his kith and kin had been banished from their native land.

Since arriving on these shores, a destination determined by no more than the whim of tide and sea, the pack had thrived beyond all imagining. Food was plentiful as was the sport, he reflected, remembering the exhilaration of the recent chase, which momentarily lifted the grief from his fearsome countenance.

It had been nearly a year now since his band had come upon the domain that they now called home. They had descended on the island-folk in a hurricane of ferocity and power, driving inland from their landing point like a knife piercing flesh, slaughtering the native farmers and their livestock and leaving a trail of bloodshed and terror for mile upon mile. Many a local chieftain had been besieged in their broch with their clansmen gathered about them, watching helplessly as their life, territory, livelihood and property were remorselessly pillaged and devastated by the rampaging horde of beasts.

It was clear to the tribesmen and women that they would not be able to breathe the air of their mother country for many years, given the manner of their banishment, yet they regretted nothing. They were the exalted, the chosen and though their path had been one of initial hardship and sacrifice, the glory that would be theirs at the conclusion of their odyssey would be a reward a thousand times more valuable than any price paid upon the journey.

With that thought of ultimate salvation re-igniting the zeal in his eyes, the warrior's walk became more purposeful and his gargantuan strides began to eat up the ground beneath his booted feet.

After a time, the giant and his brood of lycans came upon their homestead. Dun Varulfur, they had christened it. It was, formerly, a crannog inhabited by one of the native chieftains, who had resisted the wolven rampage for more than a week before finally succumbing to the rabid assault of the vicious beasts. It had been the first place since their incursion that the pack had come up against any sort of organised defiance and, out of some sort of twisted respect for their fallen victims, the wolves had decided to make the island-based roundhouse their domicile.

The crannóg itself was a circle of oaken stakes with axe-sharpened bases that were driven into the ground, forming a circular enclosure of about two-hundred feet in diameter. The stakes were then joined together by interlaced branches and wattle. The interior surface was built up, first with wooden logs, then with branches, rocks and other earthen materials. At the centre, a large stone hearth had been built with flat stones, and the wooden home was constructed around it. The structure was accessible only by a causeway cunningly wrought just below the waterline which enabled those approaching the dwelling to appear to walk upon the surface of the surrounding water.

The colossus continued his walk across the shores of the loch and onto the wooden path, ignoring the cold water that lapped about his boots, approaching the wooden construction with a sureness of foot that belied his size. The wolves followed him, transforming into their human forms as they came within the penumbra of the two sconces that stood to either side of the entrance to the dwelling, illuminating the pitted, wooden surface of the twin gates. One or two of the beasts had chosen to swim across the space between mainland and island, remaining in their vulpine guise as they loped into the crannog, a pink trail of intermingled water and blood marking their passage.

Due to his burden, the giant who, through deference from his pack was always the first to enter the building, was forced to kick the door open. The loud report of his boot coming into contact with the wood caused all activity within the dwelling to cease momentarily as the returning members of the pack entered.

They walked into a scene of nightmare.

Where before the pack had arrived on the island, the crannog had borne witness to the domestic goings-on of the tribe of farmers and their families who had inhabited the surrounding pastures, now it was an unkempt, uncared-for den of wickedness and vile practices.

Torture and death had become ingrained in the walls and the stones in the hearth were now liberally scattered with skulls and gnawed bones. Blood spattered the boards of the mud-strewn wooden floor and the stench of decay and ruin permeated the air. As the man stood on the threshold, the grunts and wails of the drug-addled denizens resumed, as their orgiastic fervour began to reach a crescendo.

The leader of the Ulfhednar clan stood silently, drinking in the sight of his clan's debauchery, all thought of the distressing burden in his arms forgotten. Breathing deeply, he began to stride through the room towards the roaring hearth.

The flames erupted from the centre of the confusion of debris that was used as fuel for the fire. He edged as near as he could to the conflagration and deposited the body of the fallen pack member upon the blaze, then returned to his perusal of the iniquity that was occurring all around him.

His initial woe at the wolf-bitch's demise had now thoroughly departed as had the brief, ice-cold thoughts of revenge upon the perpetrator of the deed. In this form, it was easy to get caught up in the petty insignificances of humanity, easy for the mind to be cluttered by the anarchy of emotion, easy to forget the beautiful simplicity of life as one of wolvenkind.

The Ulfhednar chief cast the merest of backward glances towards the dancing light of the fire, then, as an afterthought, reached into the sack that hung at his side and casually tossed the escapee's head towards the orange glow, ignoring its trajectory as it flew through the flames and skittered drunkenly to a halt yards from the seat of the firestorm.

With muzzle, teeth, fur and claws lengthening, Varga Hrolfsson, self-proclaimed leader of the clan Ulfhednar, privileged warrior of Fenrir HelMouth, favoured supplicant of Hati and Skoll, swung round, pushed past a tangle of arms and legs as it writhed in a sweaty heap on the floor and made his way to a table which remained miraculously unscathed in the bedlam that surrounded it. He retrieved a cup from its scuffed surface and drained the contents, shivering as the bitter liquid cascaded down his throat.

Breathing sensually, he reached out towards a passing figure. His claws bit into the flesh of the devotee, raking at her flank as a heat which had nothing to do with the roaring fire in the centre of the room came upon him.

Oh yes, he sighed, as the last vestige of his humanity slipped from him, life as a wolf was beautifully simple.

Chapter 1

The skies wept.

In concert, Sir Galahad of Camelot, temporary wielder of the Holy Grail, occupier of the Siege Perilous, most vaunted Knight of The Round Table, wept with them.

He was utterly bereft and alone. The other knights and their retinues had long since retreated into Camelot Castle, the massive crenellated edifice that dominated the skyline for miles around.

Through a cascade of water, part rain, part grief, he extended his gaze across the calm waters of the lake to where his captain, mentor and friend had been taken into the ethereal embrace of the Lady.

Long after the floating bier had been consumed by the mist that had appeared almost instantaneously as the boat was launched onto the ever-moving meniscus of the water, Galahad remained, as still as the grave, staring at the point where King Arthur's body had disappeared into the haze with an intensity borne of denial, loss and a huge unbearable burden of guilt.

For now Galahad found himself the major player in a theatre of nightmare.

His slumber was routinely haunted by the last few seconds of the King's life. Whenever he closed his eyes, he could picture the expression of confusion and horror on Arthur's face as, momentarily distracted by Galahad's warning shout, he had been run through by his traitorous cousin Mordred, upon the field of Camlann. Had Galahad not bellowed that warning, Arthur would have been fully concentrating on his adversary and would still be alive.

Through the shock of the moment, he could not recall Arthur locking eyes with him, the wordless accusation held within his stare as vivid as the gore of the killing wound in his side, but now, when sleep overwhelmed him and the night terrors took hold, it was unfailingly there, its fierceness growing second upon second until Galahad felt he would be incinerated by the heat of it. It was always at that point that he awoke, bathed in sweat, heart hammering an uneven tattoo within his heaving chest, gulping in ragged breaths as he fought for calm and wished for an end to his torment.

Within the space of hours, his reputation, standing and life had been utterly obliterated. Where he had once been second only to the King in renown for his exploits, most notably the retrieval of the Holy Grail, now he felt tainted beyond redemption. Despite protestations from his fellow knights, he felt himself unworthy of their forgiveness.

Though he had found the Grail and delivered it to the Round Table in Camelot, he had also been charged with its stewardship and it was there that he had been found wanting. In his arrogance and pride, he had removed it from the sanctuary of the castle walls and nearly delivered it into the hands of a demon made flesh.   It was only through sheer, blind luck and a desperate lunge with Whitecleave, his famed blade, that he had prevented the creature from possessing the Cup of Christ and warping it to its own foul designs. And even then, he had not regained possession of it, merely sending the Grail and the creature which held it within its twisted talons to a watery grave in an unnamed lake.

His despair at the loss had led him to fall upon his sword, only to be saved at the last by Merlin, the awe-inspiring wizard of Camelot. As the two had locked horns on innumerable occasions prior to that, what with Merlin's dalliances with the dark arts being a constant source of unease to the chaste and pious knight, Galahad had been deeply touched by the compassion that the magician had displayed in his darkest hour.

From the cliff overhanging the Grail Lake where both hell-spawned fiend and heaven-forged cup had plummeted, the pair had flown, propelled through the wintry air by Merlin's mighty skill to the blood-soaked meadow of Camlann. From the clouds above the battlefield, they had descended like angels with wings aflame, their unheralded appearance causing exultation in the ranks of the King and consternation in the defeated soldiery of the usurper, Mordred.

At that point in the conflict, the balance had been tipped in Arthur's favour and he faced his familial adversary in a one-to-one sword-fight to the death which, given Arthur's legendary prowess with the well-renowned Excalibur, was, everyone thought, a foregone conclusion.

That was until Galahad's untimely intervention.

His shrill warning, robbed of its hoped-for volume by the howling wind that buffeted him and Merlin as they barrelled headlong towards the site of the duel, was enough to momentarily divert Arthur's attention from his foe, enabling his nephew to seize the initiative and skewer the King upon the point of his blade.

Blinking back tears of grief and shame, he was jerked back to the present as he became aware of a presence next to him. It was Merlin, standing resplendent in his ever-present dark-blue cowl, silver circlet snaking around his head, meeting in an elaborate coil upon which was depicted a stylised M.

The wizard cut an imposing figure as he too stared across the lapping waters of the Lake, his features unreadable as he contemplated the events that had occurred scant days before but had rocked the very foundations of the lives of all who dwelt within the insurmountable walls of Camelot.

He stood well over six feet tall and, though he had the slender build of an ascetic which was emphasised by his close-cropped greying hair and beard, he radiated an aura of authority that hinted at bottomless reserves of power and influence which extended far beyond the mundanity of this world and far into the fantastical realms of enchantment and magic.

His angular face betrayed nothing that he did not wish it to, though when someone found themselves pinned by a stare from his pitiless ice-blue eyes, they were left in no doubt as to the mage's mood.

He laid a strong hand upon the shoulder of the grieving knight and spoke in a deep, rumbling timbre, "Shed no more tears, Sir Knight, it is unbecoming in one of your standing."

Galahad's eyes flared and his hand flew to his shoulder, ripping the magician's fingers from it. Without taking his gaze from the Lake, through gritted teeth he spat, "You think I care what others think of me? You think that others will view me with more ignominy than I view myself?" For the first time in hours, his gaze moved from the constantly shifting surface of the Lake and fixed on the aquiline features of the wizard. In a hoarse whisper, he said, "The King lies dead and his blood stains my hands as much as they stained his bastard nephew's."

Merlin regarded the broken man who stood before him, inwardly taken aback at the change that had come over him since the demise of King Arthur. Where before the knight had walked the environs of Camelot with his battle-honed shoulders thrown back and broad chest thrust outwards, inflated with a self-importance and arrogance that was nearly as massive as the magician's own, now he was a shrunken shadow of his former self. He appeared to physically shrivel day by day, his hazel eyes were red-rimmed and puffy, seemingly forever pointed at the floor, as if unwilling to face the scrutiny of any who crossed his path. His face had the pallor of the insomniac, grey and drawn, the black rings that encircled his eyes standing out in stark contrast to the paleness of his skin. The sorry picture was topped off by his usually scrupulously neat hair hanging in unkempt rat-tails upon his shoulders.

Since King Arthur's death, to the wizard's knowledge, he had only emerged from his rooms within the castle to attend the monarch's funeral. Indeed, his harsh response to Merlin's statement had been the first time in days that his voice had displayed any sort of emotion or passion beyond that of self-pity and despondency.

Seeing this as an opportunity to try and jerk Galahad free from his depression, Merlin pressed the point. "Nonetheless, after the King's demise, whether you wish it or not, you are now the face of Camelot. If you show weakness, then Camelot shows weakness. Would you have the King's death be nothing more than a preamble to the fall of all that he laboured to build?"

Galahad pushed past the magician, nearly knocking him from his feet. "Did you not hear me, wizard? I care nothing for it. I could cast myself into the waters of the Lake and sink to the bottom and Camelot would still endure.

My face need never darken the walls again and it would make not one jot of difference."

Merlin smoothed down his robe and, with a great effort, subdued his rage at being jostled in such a way. With a controlled anger ablaze within his stare, he stated calmly, "Then you must renounce your place at the Round Table, Galahad. Ever have you been the warrior to whom the other knights have looked to for leadership in Arthur's absence. Now, though I have no doubt you would wish the circumstances different, there is a seat resting under the Round Table that demands to be filled and there are too few candidates worthy of such an honour." He advanced upon the distraught knight, this time resting both of his hands upon the slumped shoulders. "Aside from that consideration, I am unsure as to whether the Siege Perilous will suffer your presence any more."

Galahad nodded slowly. The Siege Perilous had been his privileged seat ever since he had returned to the Table with the Grail in his possession, for Merlin had placed it under an enchantment, rendering it fatal to all who sat upon it, save those able to bear the Grail.

Merlin regarded the knight dispassionately, though he was secretly delighted by the ease with which he was manipulating the sorry figure before him. "Please, good Sir Knight, I have no wish to further distress you, I merely wish to point out that your honoured seat was designed to do great harm to any who sat upon it who were not pure of heart. In the normal course of events, I would have no doubt you could assume your customary place without incident. However, it is plain for all to see that your heart is currently besieged by thoughts and feelings of the darkest hue, and I am not sure my spell will recognise them for what they are, guilt and grief rather than hatred and evil."

Galahad sneered, "What miracle is this? The esteemed conjuror of King Arthur's court unsure of his own talents? I would have thought that you would be enthused at the prospect of my removal from the forthcoming power struggle."

Merlin's eyes immediately hooded and his face froze. "Have a care, Sir Galahad. I understand your need to lash out at something or someone, but pick your targets with more deliberation in the future." He took a deep breath. "Think on my words, Sir Knight. The only power struggle that exists is between your heart and your head. Do not bear a burden that is not yours to carry."

Galahad's face remained twisted in an unprepossessing snarl for a moment longer before his resolve crumbled, "I apologise, Merlin." He remained silent for a moment then let forth a shuddering sigh that rippled through his whole being. "I know not what to do. I have always lived my life according to the highest motives. I have opted for a life of chastity and purity, placing those virtues above all else, in the hope that it would reap reward in this life and the next. After what has happened, I..." Again, the façade disintegrated and the tears came. However, despite his protests to the contrary, he was mindful of Merlin's words and so regained his composure faster than he had before. With a deep breath, he continued, "After what has happened, I wonder if that lofty ideal in itself has brought about this fall from grace."

Merlin suppressed a sigh at the thought of yet another debate with the devout knight on the nature of pride and piety. Unable to keep the irritation out of his voice, the magician snapped, "Does the origin of your grief really matter? Does there even have to be a reason for what happened to the King?" Merlin shook his head and continued, "Time and again, you examine events and seek to place your own particular perspective upon them." Merlin jabbed a thin finger toward the grieving knight. "I accept that you have no patience with the idea of fate, dismissing it out of hand, yet you fall to your knees and look to the sky, accepting that your life is subject to the machinations of a god you cannot see or hear. Forgive my indifference but the question you pose is one that I see no reason to answer. Where is the sin in having pride in ones' achievements if they are worthy of such?" He continued relentlessly, invading Galahad's personal space, driving him back both mentally and physically. "Think of the deeds that you have accomplished throughout your life, think what justice has been meted out by Whitecleave, all in the name of God. On the battlefield, can you honestly say that all of the men you have faced have fallen due to God guiding your sword-thrust? Has your grip never slipped as you made the killing stroke? Has there never been a time when you have run a man through in error as your boots have slipped in the mud and blood?"

Galahad retreated before Merlin's verbal onslaught, his eyes wide and his breath ragged as the commanding mage bore down upon him.

Merlin loomed above the cowed knight, sudden shadows dancing across his face, lending it a ghastly aspect and, for the first time in days, Galahad saw the omnipotent wizard of towering wrath rather than the thoughtful, considered spell-weaver of recent times. However, Merlin ceased his remorseless advance and suddenly assumed a defeated pose, knowing that his argument would fall on deaf ears but needing to say his piece nonetheless. He sighed loudly and resumed speaking in a much quieter voice, "You cannot, on the one hand, live your life worshipping one intangibility yet, on the other hand, dismiss all others."

At this, Galahad stiffened and drew himself up, all hint of his previous recoiling from Merlin forgotten. He stood proud and erect, and seemed to transform in front of the magician's eyes. Gone was the snivelling wreck of a man who had cried like a babe-in-arms as the King's body began its final journey to the shores of Avalon. Now, in place of that poor wretch, once again stood the valiant warrior of Camelot, the armoured hero of the Round Table and, perhaps most famously, the Steward of the Holy Grail. His face took on a steely hardness and his words issued forth as sharp as knives. "Of all your faults, magician, your penchant for casual blasphemy is by far the worst. How can you call Him an intangibility when all around you stands evidence of his glorious works." With an extravagant gesture, Galahad waved a gauntlet-clad hand towards the landscape that stretched off into the distance, "Even in the depths of my despair, I have drawn comfort from the simple peace of the fields and hills that surround us. In the last few days, I have walked these pastures in solitude, alone with my thoughts, untroubled by the clarion call of battle or the vapid warblings of court. I have prayed in quiet contemplation posing questions both of myself and of God."

Merlin attempted to force an expression of polite interest but could not quite manage it, "And did you receive answers?" he asked, the sneer of disdain evident in both his face and his voice.

"Aye, I did, wizard. His guidance led me to one who showed me the path that I must now follow," Galahad said simply.

Scorn gave way to intrigue in Merlin's gaze and he indicated for the now tranquil knight to continue.

The Grailbearer's gaze swept across the countryside. He breathed deeply and, in that profound, cleansing exhalation, shed the burden that had dogged him since the demise of King Arthur. Staring at some random point in the middle distance, with restrained dignity, he began to speak.

Galahad strode through the ankle-length grass, as if on a mission of the utmost importance which, in his own mind, he was.

Since the loss of the King upon the blood-sodden field of conflict, he had been a man bereft, dislocated from all that was familiar to him. Where before Camelot had been a haven of comfort and constancy, indeed the nearest thing he had ever had to a home, now it was a cold, bleak place of woe and misery, as empty to the knight as the royal throne that now sat unoccupied in the chamber of The Round Table.

He had absented himself from all company no matter what the station, be it serving staff or fellow knight, and had not spoken a word to anyone since the King's death.

He had taken to traversing the rolling hills which surrounded the castle in an attempt to escape the accusing eyes that bore into him as he moved around Camelot's corridors and the susurration of accusatory whispers that seemed to assail his ears during every waking moment.

He would slink from his chambers as the first crimson wisps of sunrise caressed the horizon and not return until the sun had long since retreated behind the hills and shadow had engulfed the land.

Intellectually, he was aware that his behaviour was bordering on the madness of the recluse but he found his mood so black that he was unable to bring himself to care enough to break its all-consuming cycle.

On this day, the day before the King's funeral, he followed a well-trodden path which had felt his footsteps on many occasions since Arthur's death. The morning had transformed itself from fog-wreathed dimness to one of unexpected brightness. The sun had climbed high in the deep blue sky and the few clouds that scudded across it were insubstantial and feathery.

Galahad paid little heed to where he walked, his eyes fixed on some distant point on the vista of hills. He was vaguely aware of the shadows of the clouds moving across the grass like mobile blots of ink and the chirruping of the birds as they sang their appreciation of the unseasonably warm day, but he was ostensibly oblivious to everything outside his own miserable self-contained world.

Despite this self-induced isolation, as he walked, he felt an inexplicable tugging at his consciousness, as if a note in the music of the universe was slightly off-key. The wrongness resolved itself as he crested the brow of the hill. As his eyes adjusted to the sunshine, he saw a hunched female figure kneeling before a pile of collapsed stones. The discordant noise that had disturbed his contemplation came from her. She was sobbing uncontrollably. Galahad could see little of the woman but he could discern that she was young, dressed in peasant garb and, judging by the heartbreaking sound of her torment, utterly, utterly grief-stricken.

The knight's first instinct had been to leave the woman to her anguish, as the guilty thought that her suffering was nothing compared to his own flashed across his mind but, after hearing her wails of pain, the unworthy notion left him instantly.

He stood and regarded her pityingly as she tried to pile the stones into some sort of order but her attempts were doomed to failure and the rocks toppled to the rich grass. Seeing this, Sir Galahad, bravest of the brave, did one of the most courageous things of his life. Through sheer strength of will, he forced himself to put aside his depression and offer the woman succour.

In a deep, reassuring voice, he said, "Lady, may I be of help?"

She had not seen him approach and jumped in shock, nearly dropping her burden upon the knight's right foot. She shuffled back from him, clasping her tattered robes to her body as if to protect herself. Her face was reddened and puffy from the tears and her eyes stared wildly at him.

Galahad took a step back as his gallantry came to the fore. With hands spread wide in a conciliatory pose, he said, "I apologise if I startled you." He nodded at the stones with his head and slowly stooped to pick up the one that had come within inches of injuring him. "Would you like me to help you?" he repeated.

The woman peered at him through eyes as wide as saucers. As he stood waiting for a response, Galahad studied the woman closely. His gaze took in the tanned skin of her face, darkened by months spent out working the land in all weathers and streaked from the flood of tears she had cried. His eyes moved to her individual features, the light blue eyes with their colour heightened by the sky, the slight upturn of the end of her nose, her mouth open wide in surprise with bottom lip trembling, before finally settling on the blonde shoulder-length hair, savagely cut in a jagged line that partially exposed her sleek neck.

Galahad blinked as the woman covered herself even further and shrunk from his gaze.

His stare had been more intense than he had intended but nevertheless he felt a surprisingly strong surge of anger at the notion that this peasant thought herself special enough that he could not contain his carnal urges and sully himself with the pleasures of her flesh. With a bitter harshness in his voice, he spat, "Do not flatter yourself, wench. I have no interest in you."

He stalked off across the grass away from her, angry at the woman's reaction, angry at the disturbance of his directionless journey, angry at the shunning of his offer of help. He continued down the hill, his strides picking up pace as the gradient became steeper. Just as the weeping woman was about to disappear from his view, Galahad ceased his flight and turned round, squinting into the sun at the indistinct figure upon the slanted horizon.

As he watched her struggle with the heap of stones again, his mood swung back to that which it had been when he had first happened upon her and he was visited with a near overwhelming sense of shame.

Composing himself, he returned to the woman and her labours. With the same caustic scorn that he had poured upon her now turned upon himself, he merely started piling the rocks up without a word, unsure of how to break the incredibly awkward silence that had been created by his insensitivity and intemperate words.

The woman, for her part, flinched away again and crouched on her haunches, watching the muscular knight go about his work. When it became apparent that no threat was being offered, she resumed the construction of the cairn, though she still watched him owlishly.

For long minutes, they worked on the structure, the only sounds being the whizz and whirr of insects enjoying the summer sun and their grunts of exertion.

At length, they reached an impasse, for they had run out of stones. Casting a look about the surrounding ground, the knight of Camelot finally brought his eyes up to meet the woman's once again. With an overly florid bow, he sighed, "My lady, I apologise for the hot-tempered words that I cast in your direction. You were merely the unfortunate recipient of days of festering guilt and towering grief." His eyes fell to the floor again, "I am sorry."

The woman said nothing, but continued to look at Galahad until he began to shift uncomfortably under her gaze.

He was about to speak again when the woman finally broke her silence.

"Come," she said, in a lilting rural accent that cracked a little, betraying the brittleness which still lay just below the surface. "The stones lie at the bottom of the hill."

As the pair of them walked down the slope, with the silence between them now one of peace rather than tension, Galahad found himself re-appraising the woman's fortitude. She had brought the stones up from a large stream that babbled along the base of the hill. The site of the cairn was a full three hundred paces from there and the knight estimated that it consisted of at least fifty rocks.

They both dropped to one knee and began searching the stream-bed for suitable stones to add to the construction. Galahad inhaled sharply as the cold water penetrated his leggings but the woman bore the chill without reaction. "Tell me," the knight asked quietly, "why do you take the stones from here? There are rocks dotted about the grass upon the slope that would suffice."

The woman regarded him seriously. "It is tradition that the stones of a cairn are brought from the bottom of a hill."

Galahad nodded, "So the cairn is closer to God."

To the knight's disgust, the woman hawked and spat into the stream. "It has nothing to do with God," she hissed, her voice positively dripping with contemptuous venom. "It is so the departed spirit may watch over the lands that it worked upon and tended. God has no interest in the likes of us peasant-folk." She stared for a long time at the man kneeling next to her. "I take it from your look that you do not agree," she murmured, an unprepossessing curl to her lip marring the prettiness of her face.

Galahad hefted a stone and began to trek back up the hill. "God watches over all of us," he said calmly. "He cares for all without favour, rich or poor, vital or sick," he stared pointedly up toward the cairn, "alive or dead."

The woman, who had also resumed the walk back to the site of the stones, suddenly threw her burden to the ground and launched herself at the knight. She screeched like a banshee, clawing at Galahad's face, kicking his shins and yanking at his hair, with her face twisted into a contorted personification of hate.

Stunned by the unexpected assault, at first Galahad tried to defend himself whilst still clutching the rock he had unearthed. As he retreated though, he too relieved himself of his load and, at the third attempt, managed to grasp the maddened woman by the wrists. "What is the matter with you?" he snarled, still dodging her flying feet.

The adrenaline of the initial fury drained away and she ceased to struggle, pulling away from his grip and running past him up to the half-built cairn. There she fell to her knees and returned to the position that Galahad had found her in when he first saw her, weeping uncontrollably and beside herself with grief.

"Damn it," Galahad snapped as he raised his hand to his face. He could feel three distinct scratches running down his cheek, two of which were bleeding. He re-examined his words and found nothing there to have caused such an extreme reaction. Once again, the urge to harangue the woman over her attitude and behaviour rose up and he stalked over to her, the words piling up upon his tongue ready to burst forth in a tidal wave of derision. As it was, the woman beat him to it.

Her head shot up and the look she bestowed upon him caused Galahad, the knight who had stood his ground against all the enemies that fate had thrown at him, to take a step back.

She advanced purposefully, jabbing her finger at him. "Don't you dare preach to me, you pious fool. My man lies dead in some forsaken field, no more than food for the crows, because his head had been turned by promises of God-given glory from those bastards in yonder castle." She jerked her thumb over her shoulder in the general direction of Galahad's home. "I begged him not to go, because I have seen what God's favour means for the farmers and villagers who live in the shadow of Camelot."

Galahad tried to interrupt her, but the woman's wrath was relentless. "It is strange, is it not, that God's favour is in short supply when it comes to the winter and food is scarce yet it prospers in abundance when wars are to be fought and blood is to be spilled. Is it now God's favour that my bairns are to grow up without their father? Is it God's favour that I now have to work the land by myself and struggle to put food in my children's mouths? For that is what God's favour means to the likes of me. Starvation and hardship. So spare me your sermon, stranger, I have no use for it."

With that, she spun away and went back to the cairn, though this time, she stood proud and erect, her blonde hair billowing behind her in the breeze.

The knight from Camelot stood swaying in both the gale of the woman's words and the wind that suddenly seemed to have picked up from nowhere. He wanted to remonstrate with her, to point out the error of her blasphemy, but he could not. He could not because, after Arthur's death, he had questioned God's existence himself, albeit in the privacy of his own head, but questioned it nonetheless.

He remained there for a while, embarrassed and alone, unsure what to do or say. After a while, without another word passing his lips, he began to walk back to Camelot.

On the journey back, he pondered all that had happened on this day and came to a decision.

Merlin's face was unreadable as his gaze roamed across the knight's features, trying to gauge some sort of inkling as to what news Galahad was about to impart. It rested briefly on the still vivid wound that scarred him, the three red lines running parallel to each other across his right cheekbone, a pointed piece of evidence as to the truth of Galahad's tale.

Without any preamble, Galahad announced, "You will get your wish, wizard. I cannot allow myself, in all good conscience, to resume my seat at The Round Table after what has transpired. I leave Camelot at dawn."

Merlin blinked in surprise. He was not sure what he had expected to hear but it certainly was not this. He had never known the knight to run from anything in his life, yet here he was, about to ride off over the horizon.

It was no secret that, for the most part, he found Sir Galahad an insufferable prig but the knight's exploits in battle had earned Merlin's grudging respect as well. He puffed out his cheeks in a long drawn-out breath. The magician, who was not used to being caught off-guard in such a manner, saw the look in Galahad's eyes and knew that it would be a waste of words to try and deflect him from his choice.

With a shrug, designed to disguise the shock which was caroming inside his head, he muttered, "I can see your mind is made up and I will not attempt to dissuade you from your chosen course. There is one thing I would ask of you however," he raised his eyebrows as if seeking permission to continue.

"Say on, Merlin," the knight gestured vaguely with his hand, "if you will forgive me saying, you are not normally so reticent."

The magician's face twisted into an expression that might have been a smile but then again, might not. "Do you have a destination in mind? Or will you merely wander the landscape as the most richly dressed vagrant the land has ever seen?"

21

Galahad nodded emphatically, "Seeing the distress of that lady at the loss of her loved one made up my mind for me." Again, he broke off eye contact with Merlin and stared into the distance, "I will go north to Joyous Garde."

The wizard had thought the revelation of Galahad's departure was staggering enough, but upon hearing his ultimate intention, he was flabbergasted. "Well, what better way to honour your dead king's memory than to go and pay a visit to the woman who ripped his heart out and stamped it into the ground."

Galahad's head whipped round from his contemplation off the horizon, "It is not like that, magician. I am well aware of the wrongs she visited upon Arthur, however, I am also well aware of the joy and happiness that they brought each other when they were betrothed." Through gritted teeth, he hissed, "Guinevere has a right to know that Arthur has fallen."

Merlin regarded Galahad for some time then shrugged again, "If that is what you think is right." He began to walk away from the famed warrior of the Round Table, back towards the looming edifice of the castle. After a few paces, he turned and said simply, "You will be missed, Sir Galahad of Camelot," before leaving the knight alone, standing statuesque in the gathering shadows, pondering his future away from the walls that he had come to know so well.

Chapter 2

Sir Galahad, erstwhile knight most valiant of Camelot, tightened the cinch upon the saddle of his battle-steed, Farregas, a Destrier of seventeen hands stature, which had accompanied him for more years than he cared to remember. Though his mount was not really suited to everyday riding, being trained from foalhood in the art of war, the horse was one face that he could not bear to be departed from when he left Camelot for his cathartic journey north.

He was clad in a white doublet and red hose which corresponded with the dual colours of his coat of arms. To counteract the coolness of the season and the brightness of his garb, he also wore a substantial bearskin cloak, clutched about his neck by an intricate brooch with a depiction of the Holy Grail upon it, a gift from King Arthur, presented to him days after his return to Camelot with that most holy of vessels.

As he adjusted his pack and baggage upon the grey's broad back, Galahad could feel the bunched muscles underneath the smooth, dew-damp skin, tense and twitchy, ready for the off. He patted the horse on its thick neck and leant into him, feeling comforted by the warmth of the beast and the familiar smell of his sweat. "Quiet yourself, my friend. We will ride soon, though not into battle. Today will be no more than a leisurely stroll through God's own country."

The animal let forth a snort to show his disgruntlement at that. Galahad smirked at his mount and patted him fondly, "Well, for myself, I am tired of the blood and the screams of the wounded and dying, so I am looking forward to a pleasing ramble along the highway. I cannot remember the last time I was able to sit upon horseback and drink in the scenery of the kingdom without fear of a sword at my throat or an arrow in my breast."

At length, Galahad finished his preparations for the journey north and mounted his horse with more difficulty than usual as there was usually a page at hand to help him astride the saddle.

The white, insubstantial clouds of his breath drifted upwards to join their more significant counterparts in the scarlet-tinged sky as he set off for Sir Lancelot's remote stronghold, leaving behind the comfortable life of privilege and pampering that he had experienced within Camelot's walls and, for the first time in his life, striking out into the wider world.

As Farregas loped languidly down the path leading from the drawbridge, the former Steward of The Grail reflected on his still young life. As he did so, he was visited by a profound sense of sadness. So much of his youth and short adulthood had been spent sword in hand, visiting pain and death upon the enemies of his King and his God. Even what should have been the proudest moment of his life, when he had brought the Cup of Christ to Camelot and basked in all the reflected glory which that deed had bestowed upon him, was now forever tainted with the nightmare of Arthur's death and the part he had played in it, indirect though it was.

In a brutally stark moment of self-recognition that cannoned into him like an oaken ram splintering a wooden door, Galahad realised how much of his life had been awash with blood and the words of the embittered woman on the hill came back to him.

How many of his victims had the misfortune to feel the caress of Whitecleave for no other reason than 'because their heads had been turned' by their betters?

How many had faced him in battle at the behest of others who had beguiled them with words of glory and honour?

How many men had died by his hand?

With a numbness that reached deep into his marrow and chilled him to the bone, he stared at the expensive gauntlets holding the reins loosely in their grip and reflected on whether his conduct had been appropriate for a man so quick to preach to others of God and all his works. Why, he found himself thinking, if he had kept himself chaste and pure enough to be able to take the Holy Grail into his possession, did the thoughts that now hammered into his head make him feel dirty and sullied?

Galahad was discomfited beyond measure by the route upon which his contemplation was leading him.

He had long ago chosen to deny himself the pleasures of the flesh, thinking that he was above such wanton, base desires yet he had excelled and, at times he guiltily admitted to himself, gloried in the raw energy of the arena of battle as he had dispatched innumerable foes to the cold embrace of death.

How could that possibly render him pure and close to his God? Unless his God was a bloodthirsty savage who celebrated carnage and revelled in agony?

Galahad's mind roiled at the revelations which seemed to be enveloping his brain like a horizon-spanning storm, its thunder rocking the foundations of his beliefs and its lightning splitting them asunder.

The reins fell free from his hands as he clamped them to the side of his head before giving vent to an ear-splitting wail of frustration and torment as he tried to drown out the voice in his head that was repeating phrases mantra-like,

Your life is a lie. You are a harbinger of death. You are a force of corruption, not purity. Your God is a travesty of all that is good and right with the world.

24

Galahad opened his eyes to find himself staring up at the sky. He lay on the cooling grass for a while, disorientated and nauseous. Slowly, equilibrium reasserted itself and he struggled to his elbows, wondering what had happened. The shriek that he had spat towards the sky seemed to have banished the insidious whispers from his mind and he felt strangely liberated and energized. Staring left and right, he tried to find the whereabouts of his mount.

Farregas stood in shin-high greenery, his noble profile that of a proud beast put-upon and hard done by. He had been chewing upon the lush grass but took the time to look up from his meal and nicker sarcastically at Galahad's prostrate form.

The supine knight struggled to his feet, massaging his back. He assumed that his scream had unsettled the horse and he had been thrown to the ground. He approached his steed awkwardly, a gnawing pain in his rump causing him to wince with each step. With a supreme look of indifference on his face, Farregas went back to his food.

Galahad's right hand snaked out and caught hold of the reins that had draped themselves over the horse's dappled neck. With a yank more severe than he intended, he jerked the horse's head around to face him, "I hope that was not some sort of repayment for the disappointment of not riding into battle."

The grey stallion went to nip at Galahad's nose to reproach him but the knight leaned in towards him, almost challenging him to do it. "I tell you now, Farregas, if it was then I hope you have got it out of your system because the miles will be long beyond endurance if I have to fight you all the way."

Farregas held Galahad's eyes for a few seconds then looked away, faking unconcern and returning to his repast.

"Alright then," the knight nodded emphatically, certain that he had got his point across. He turned round to leave his mount to fill his belly for a moment. With a start, he found himself being watched.

The man lay, casually sprawled on the opposite side of the track, head pillowed on his arm and his peaked cap perched jauntily atop it. He was dressed well, if not as richly as the warrior from Camelot, for his hose were dusty and stained, presumably from his journey. As he stood, it became clear that he was powerfully muscled, although in a slightly inferior way to Galahad.

He strode across the road purposefully, a look of undisguised anger on his face. His blue eyes fixed upon Galahad and his mouth twisted into a menacing snarl as he hissed, "If there is one thing I hate, it is a man, and I use the term loosely, who berates others for their own mistakes."

Galahad raised an eyebrow at the newcomer, choosing to stand his ground as a gale of stale air issued from the stranger's mouth and washed over his face. The man stood before him, clenching and unclenching his fists with an uncompromising quality in his stare which suggested to Galahad that the confrontation would not end peaceably.

The knight tutted, affecting bored indifference whilst, in reality, he was sizing up his adversary and readying himself to strike the first blow. He sighed and said, "And one thing that I hate is people poking their bulbous, misshapen noses into matters that do not concern them." With the insult spoken, Galahad's right hand reached down with finely-tuned accuracy to withdraw Whitecleave from its leather haven. However, he noted that the interloper had glanced past him over his right shoulder. He ceased his movement and, with uncommon agility for a man of his size, threw himself to the left, narrowly missing Farregas with his dive. He regained his feet quickly and found his peril trebled as he was confronted by the man and two of his cohorts.

Fully alert now, he judged, by the fetid appearance of the man's companions, that the richly dressed one was a decoy designed to hold the victim's attention while the other two crept up behind and dispatched their unsuspecting target. Using all his battle-honed intuition, within seconds, Galahad had sized up the situation and launched his attack. That, in itself, put him at an advantage, because the trio of robbers were more used to their prey cowering in terror as they relieved them of their money and their lives or, as had happened on more than one occasion, simply not reacting at all due to the element of surprise.

Whitecleave sliced through the air and took the hapless robber on the left of the three in the throat. As he fell to the grass, frantically scrabbling at his sundered neck, the other two circled the knight, licking their lips nervously. They had both produced blunt dirks from their boots but the way they held them told Galahad all he needed to know about their prowess. On top of the obvious mismatch in terms of skill and weaponry, the remaining pair were unable to shut out the bubbling sounds of their comrade's demise and could not prevent themselves chancing glances at him as he died his agonising death.

That was all the opportunity Galahad needed. When his original assailant flicked his gaze one too many times towards the fallen man, the knight from Camelot struck. Whitecleave slid through the man's ribs like a hot knife through butter. The vagabond's eyes looked as if they were about to burst from their sockets in shock as he felt the pain of the thrust bloom in his chest. As he slipped off Galahad's blade with a sigh, the knight turned to face the remaining bandit.

The man looked from Galahad's grim smile to his companions, one slain, one mortally wounded. In a futile attempt to stop this Death in human form's onslaught, he threw his knife at the knight and turned tail, scampering away like a hare across the fields.

Galahad batted the flying blade away with a contemptuous flick of his wrist, ignoring the surprisingly fat spark that leapt from the two weapons as their edges met. He eyed the brigand's retreating form dispassionately as he whistled to his horse. "Farregas, to me," he barked in command.

His tone of voice told the now attentive beast of his master's purpose and his answering whinny possessed a nearly joyous quality as he reared then cantered over to him.

With practiced ease, as Farregas rode alongside him, in one massive gauntlet, Galahad took hold of the reins and used the horse's momentum to swing himself in place upon the saddle.

The feel of the beast underneath him and the exhilaration of the gallop invigorated the knight and, whereas before his face had been a mask of anger and bile, now it cracked into a dazzling smile as, for a few seconds, he found himself able to forget the recent burdens which had dragged him down into the abyss of despair and concentrate on the simplistic pleasures of the hunt.

With a feeling of guilty elation, he ran the thief down and, with an agricultural swipe of Whitecleave, removed the man's head from his shoulders. The body continued to run for two or three paces as the head flew in front of it, bouncing erratically to a halt a full ten yards away from the collapsed cadaver.

Galahad brought Farregas to a stop, reining the powerful beast in with an effort, for the thrill of the pursuit and the lightening of the knight's mood had somehow communicated themselves to the horse and he yearned to gallop over the horizon and beyond.

"Ho there, boy," Galahad chuckled, smiling crookedly at the Destrier's playfulness. They both returned to the scene of the original attack, Farregas trotting like a colt at the unexpected distraction of the attempted robbery.

The first to fall to Galahad's blade stared sightlessly up at the sky, but the second victim still lived, weeping pitifully as the crimson stain slowly spread across his off-white tunic. It was not until his killer's shadow fell across him that he managed to peel his eyes away from the wound. With difficulty, he managed to focus on the man standing before him. The ragged gasps that spoke so eloquently of his agony quickened still further as Galahad moved within touching distance of him.

The knight's glare had been stony and unforgiving but, as he knelt beside the poor unfortunate, he could not prevent the sympathy from showing on his face.

A gout of blood erupted from the dying man's mouth as he coughed but, with a huge effort, he forced himself to speak. Unable to do anything other than nod towards the knight, he muttered, "My, that is a fine blade to be stuck upon."

Galahad blinked, the words taking him off-guard, "I...well, thank you," he managed to say. He went to his saddlebag and extracted a wineskin, unstoppered it and trickled some liquid over the man's mouth.

"That is a fine brew," the man sighed, smacking his lips together. "Not bad for a final sup."

The man from Camelot shuffled uncomfortably, evoking a pained laugh from the injured party. "You do not have to sit my death-watch, stranger. You set my feet upon the road but I can manage the final few steps all by myself." The words were spoken without rancour, just a wistful hint of regret.

Galahad wiped the neck of the skin, took a swig and sat himself down on the grass. "With respect, outlaw, your actions in waylaying travellers upon the King's highway were what set your feet upon the path of destruction."

"Maybe, maybe," the man accepted. "Not that it really matters, but my name is Romney."

Ignoring the unspoken question, Galahad asked one of his own. "Your clothes are rich for a thief. I take it you were more successful on your previous escapades?" Though he held the man in distaste for his chosen career, given the thoughts that had unseated him from Farregas' back, Galahad saw no reason to labour the point, especially as he could see that the man would be facing a far stricter judge than himself in the very near future.

Romney shook his head. "Not really. Believe it or not, these clothes are my own. I have been wandering these roads for about a month or so. Those two were no more than itinerants that I picked up along the way. We had no food, no money, naught but the clothes in which we stood. Again, if you believe me or not it is of no matter, but for myself, I became a bandit for no other reason than to put food in my mouth. I suspect that that pair were not so unused to a life of thievery but, as they say, misery acquaints a man with strange bedfellows."

The knight's expression spoke volumes about his opinion of that. Whether Romney noticed or not was unclear but he continued talking, his voice becoming slurred, his eyes losing the sparkle of life and growing ever more distant, not really speaking to Galahad now, simply revisiting his memories of the events that had led him to an untimely death on an unknown road at the hands of an unknown stranger.

"I had a barony away up north near York. Reports of banditry upon my estates had come to my notice and I rode out to the utmost border of my lands with my retinue at my back to try to quell the activity. As we rode through a forest, we were ambushed by the bastard baron from the neighbouring demesne." Romney's voice became hoarse, though whether it was through the agony of the wound or the agony of the memory, Galahad did not know. "I saw my retainers, my guards cut down before my eyes. They came on so suddenly that we were overwhelmed within seconds." A shuddering sigh escaped him. "It was obvious that to survive, we had to flee." With surprising strength, he grabbed Galahad's arm and pulled him close. "There were too many of them and my men were slaughtered like lambs. We had to flee." He repeated, his voice trailing off into the wind.

Galahad wrapped his cloak tighter about his shoulders against the sudden biting cold. In reality, he was beginning to wish he had simply left Romney to die by the side of the road, but now that the man had begun his story, he felt compelled to see his decision through to the end. An end that was approaching very rapidly now. In apparent response to his imminent mortality, Romney began to speak more quickly, tripping over his words, leaving Galahad struggling to understand him. "We were chased for miles. We looked for a place to stand but there was none. They picked us off one by one. It was only due to my exceptional mount that I escaped their clutches. I lay hidden for a couple of days, slowly but surely making my way back to my stronghold. I managed to return there and I was about to approach through the gates but something stayed me, so I slunk across the grounds, my own grounds, keeping to the shadows, gripped by a nameless feeling of dread." Romney's eyes closed and his head slumped to the side.

Galahad realised that he had been holding his breath in anticipation of what Romney was about to impart. He let it out in a huge gasp, taken aback by the surprising strength of sadness that he felt at the man's death. He made to move away from him when...

"She was with him. In his arms. My Rosa. In his arms." With that, Romney died.

Galahad bit his lip, wanting with all his might to turn away from the body, but unable to. The look in Romney's eyes, the insurmountable anguish, the haunting, hollow pain, the pure acid agony mirrored almost exactly King Arthur's face when he had learnt of Guinevere's adultery. Before his eyes, the prostrate form of Romney transformed into the King, laid to rest upon the bier on the boat travelling across the Lady's Lake to Avalon.

"Damn me," Galahad cuffed away the tears that had sprung unbidden to his eyes. He stumbled blindly over to Farregas and mounted him. As he gained the horse's back, he caught sight of the topmost towers of Camelot on the horizon, tiny flags fluttering in the breeze. For long minutes, he stared across the miles, grateful for the solitude that his flight from the castle had brought.

Time and again, he had seen the damage caused by allowing oneself to be open to others, be it by way of friendship, love or even the simple camaraderie of a military campaign.

How many had been brought to their knees by the acts of those in whom they had placed all their trust and love?

How many had professed their love to another when, in reality, they were merely infused with lust?

How many men had he come to know and trust only for them to fall in battle?

How many parents lost to children and children lost to parents?

His gaze moved from the crenellations of the castle to the now peaceful corpse of Romney. Two names sprang to mind quite readily. One just met and one known for many years. And both now dead.

He wheeled Farregas around to the right, sparing one last glance at Camelot. Not for the first time, he found himself reflecting on his choice of chastity and aloofness, a lonely life choice to be sure, he acknowledged as a raven landed on Romney's belly and began worrying at the fabric of his tunic, but, on the whole, infinitely more preferable than ending up as fodder for the birds.

*

Aside from the initial excitement of their encounter with the trio of crooks, the journey to Joyous Garde was largely uneventful. True to Galahad's word, over the course of three weeks, he had treated the trek as no more than a ramble in the countryside.

He had been mildly concerned about being challenged by Romney and his gang so close to the walls of Camelot, praying that it was not an augury for the rest of the journey.

However, aside from an attack by another trio of ill-fated outlaws in the forests of Nottingham and an unexpected assault from a wyvern close to Doncaster that he had easily turned away, the three-hundred-and-seventy-five mile expedition had passed with so little incident that even Galahad, jaundiced though he was with conflict and battle, found himself wishing for some sort of relief from the boredom.

As he had not been in any particular hurry, the journey had taken him the best part of a month, during which time he had seen the leaves on the trees shade from a lush green to a veritable riot of oranges, yellows and reds and the temperature begin to render the fallen ones rigid and brittle. Galahad now found himself bitterly regretting his languorous progress, for the weather had turned from autumnal pleasance to wintry vindictiveness.

When the knight and his steed had set out, the winds had been, in the main, warming and pleasant aside from the odd inclement day which hinted at the coldness that was to come. Now though, it chased Galahad and Farregas along the roads and through the woods like a pack of wolves harrying them, wearing them down, leaving them constantly on edge and praying for respite.

For the umpteenth time, Galahad pulled his cloak around him, fumbling at the fastening with numbed fingers and silently cursing the weather. On this day, as he had traversed the countryside atop Farregas' proud back, he found his eye constantly drawn to a roiling, turbulent thunderhead of slate grey that had been slowly building to his left, seemingly rising in height with every stride of their trek like a foreboding tidal wave poised to swamp him and his horse in whatever was contained within.

Its ever-growing shadow blotted out the watery sunlight and lay across the surrounding meadows like some sort of dread being, bleaching away the brightness of life and draining everything it touched of vitality and energy, leaving the landscape wan and ugly.

The first snowflakes began to fall then, thick but soft little pillows of frozen water that almost seemed to fizz under Farregas' hooves as he plodded along, head down against the wind, the sodden blanket across his back adding an extremely unpleasant burden to the many that he already had to contend with. However, after so many years of bearing the gallant warrior of Camelot upon his back, he had inherited many of his characteristics, one of which was the stoicism of his rider and, as such, he accepted the woeful conditions without complaint.

Other than the muted hiss of the horse's passage, the silence was all-encompassing with the snow, which was becoming heavier by the second, drowning the land in a picturesque ocean of white with the occasional wind-blown boulder or barren tree breaking the surface like an isolated island.

The featureless path began to insinuate itself upwards and Farregas' breath came in great clouds as he tapped new reserves of energy to accommodate the change in gradient.

Galahad gazed despairingly at the summit of the hill they now climbed, for it seemed that the land fell away into nothingness as great swathes of powdery snow were whipping across it, blotting out the landscape beyond absolutely.

As he contemplated what confronted him over the crest of the hill ahead, he caught the murmur of something on the breeze, penetrating the mournful sough of the wind. Though his senses were inevitably dulled by the conditions, he tried with all his might to will himself into alertness and, consequently, his eyes narrowed as he attempted to breach the sheets of snow which battered him. Farregas' ears flickered as he too raised his head, his bestial senses more alert to the unknown presence than Galahad's would ever be.

The knight's head snapped to the left as the unmistakable mutter of conversation became audible in clipped snatches as the wind's direction undulated erratically. However, though he strained his ears to hear them, no clear words could be discerned.

His right hand strayed without conscious thought to the intricately wrought pommel of Whitecleave, his fingers sculpting themselves around it as if a glove was affixed to the grip. Though his hand was numb, nearly to the point of uselessness, the warmth of familiarity was enough to provide him with the reassurance to enable him to resume his journey. He touched his heels to Farregas' flanks and they began to move off, mindful of the proximity of the unknown persons but not unduly troubled by them.

With gimlet eyes sweeping the road before them, Galahad and his mount breasted the hill.

As they began their descent, mercifully the wind eased slightly and visibility increased, though it was still uncomfortably close to a white-out. The snowflakes were whirling like dervishes in the heart of the blizzard and the continual squinting against the brutality of the storm was beginning to develop into a gnawing ache in Galahad's temples.

Then, he saw a light to the left. A disembodied lantern, miraculously still ablaze despite the wintry tempest, cast a dull penumbra mere yards from where Galahad rode. Bizarrely, the guttering flame appeared to bob along in the air of its own accord, because, try though he might, Galahad was unable to apprehend any semblance of the person who carried it. There was a mere suspicion of a dark shape, momentarily silhouetted by the snow, but no more than that. To Galahad's fatigued eyes, the black mass seemed to bulge obscenely until his vision adjusted and he found himself chiding his overactive imagination. It was simply that the man holding the flame had companions with him, huddled into the feeble warmth that the fire generated and they had now begun to move away from the glow.

Farregas was beginning to get skittish, dancing from side to side like a dressage horse and, though he ceased the movement when Galahad murmured reassuring words in his ear, the knight could still sense the tension emanating off him like steam rising from his flanks after a gallop across a battlefield.

"Quiet, boy, quiet. Hold…" The wind was sucked out of Galahad's lungs as Farregas reared. His shrill neigh cut through the darkness like an archer's arrow and suddenly the silence was shattered by shouts from all quarters. Lights had now appeared to the right of the man from Camelot and the lanterns on the left had also started to approach him, warily bobbing across

32

the unbroken surface of pure white, wanting to find the source of the sudden noise but aware that the blanket of snow was, in reality, a mass of uneven ground eminently able to snare the incautious in an unexpected dip or hole.

For his part, Galahad fought with the reins as Farregas bolted for the gap between the two groups of torches that now approached from either side. The knight knew that fleeing blindly in such conditions would end with Farregas dead, either from a broken leg or neck, and himself, injured or worse, prostrate on the cold, hard ground and unable to defend himself against whoever it was that had come upon them out of the night.

By the time he had righted Farregas, doing so without chastisement because he had rightly guessed that the horse's uncharacteristic behaviour was due to a healthless mixture of fatigue, numbing cold and the all-encompassing darkness, the torches and their bearers had them surrounded and the pair would have been unable to break through the encircling ring of flame without injury.

With a great effort, Galahad straightened his back and dramatically threw back the cloak from his left shoulder, allowing him to free Whitecleave from its scabbard. He drew the sword and pointed it straight at the torch that stood flickering in front of him. Manfully trying to keep the chatter from his teeth, Galahad's deep, rolling voice boomed across the intervening space, "Who deems themselves important enough that they may bar a weary journeyman from travelling the King's Highway?"

Silence greeted the question, a silence that grated on Galahad as his weary gaze swept from figure to figure. He counted at least ten featureless forms before him and, for all he knew, there could be any amount of others out of reach of the lantern's illumination.

He was also painfully aware of the effort that it was taking to maintain Whitecleave's equilibrium and, on more than one occasion, a muffled grunt escaped his grimly set mouth as he willed the strength down his arm to keep his blade on an even keel.

With the slightest hint of a challenge in his voice, he continued, the words issuing from his mouth in a harsh bark. "If you are unwilling to spare me the courtesy of an answer, then I am unwilling to spare you any more of my time." His hand tightened around the pommel of his sword as he spurred Farregas into a walk.

The circle closed in and Galahad was forced to halt. "Look," he began, and this time he was unable to keep the pleading from his voice, "both I and my horse are weary beyond measure. We have ridden for weeks to deliver a message to Joyous Garde. I request leave for safe passage through these lands. I have no quarrel with your good selves but I warn you now, I *will* fight you, all of you if I have to, if you continue to baulk my journey." He

33

knew that the threat was an empty one, given the disproportionate numbers on each side but he could not, indeed would not, reduce himself to begging for his own safety.

Still not a sound issued forth from the surrounding shadows and a creeping uneasiness began to leech into Galahad's bones. The blizzard had relented to an extent and the forms began to define themselves into something more substantial. The knight from Camelot blinked hurriedly, trying to concentrate, trying to calm the nauseating waves of exhaustion that were inexorably eroding his thought processes. He knew to the very depths of his soul that there was a massive incongruity before him and in his head, something battering at his consciousness, beseeching his brain to work, to identify the anomaly, but he might as well have tried to grasp hold of his breath as it ballooned up in ragged clouds towards the stars.

All the while, his eyes continued their measured sweep of the force arrayed before him, the ten statuesque shapes, unmoving, as silent as death itself. Momentarily, Galahad wondered why that notion had appeared in his head then, with a suddenness that caused his heart to skip a beat, he realised what was wrong with the tableau before him.

His was the only breath that entered the frigid air of the Northumbrian winter. Where there should have been clouds of white issuing from the cowled heads of the men before him, there was nothing.

With great ceremony, the central choreographer of this sickening, motionless dance lifted the hood back from his head.

Farregas' eyes rolled wildly and he pawed nervously at the frozen ground beneath him, the only thing preventing him from bolting being his years of battle training. Galahad fought to keep from retching as the leering face beneath the covering was revealed in all its horror.

Green skin hung in flaccid folds beneath blood-red eyes. The mouth was an irregular gash just below the nose, its shape perverted by a slash that ran from the right side of the lips to the pulped remains of an ear. It opened in a gross approximation of a smile and began to laugh. Even from yards away, Galahad could apprehend the stink of its breath and it was the stench of catacombs, the reek of the grave, the gut-emptying foulness of death.

He wanted to turn away because he found the sight before him offensive to the very core of his being, yet he could not drag his hypnotised gaze from it. The seductive power of the beings before him was staggering. Join us, they seemed to say, come to a place where there is no pain, no problems, no emotional anguish, no soul-searching, no right, no wrong. Who would not want life lived in such a manner?

From the depths of his soul, a voice cried out, sounding thin and reedy amidst the all-enveloping tumult that engulfed him.

"That is not life lived, that is death."

Galahad sat entranced by the scene before him. The pleading voice in his head decreased in volume, retreating into a bottomless void from which no sound could escape. The knight from Camelot knew without doubt that he was destined to follow it, destined to be lost in the black, depthless nothingness.

As his mind toppled on the brink, Farregas bucked, sending his rider crashing to the ground. The impact saved Galahad's life, for it left him winded and concussed and broke the hex which held him in its thrall.

With his eyes rolling in his head, Galahad felt rather than saw the hideous spectres slither across the surprisingly hard blanket of snow towards him, readying themselves to drag him into their false existence, forever imprisoning him in a depraved imitation of life. He tried in vain to fight the waves of unconsciousness that rolled over him, knowing in his heart that to sleep was to die.

However, his valiant efforts were of no use and, with despair gripping him, he fell into oblivion, feeling certain that once there, he would never return.

Chapter 3

Wakefulness came in short, painful bursts.

Faces of dreadfulness, green and fetid. A pretty face amidst the revulsion, framed by long brunette hair.

Skin hanging from exposed bone. A smile that lifted the mood of whomsoever it was bestowed upon.

Maggoty eye sockets, black and puckered. Hazel eyes, hidden momentarily behind overlong, fluttering lashes.

Gnarled fingers with broken nails, beckoning, clawing, grabbing. The soft caress of healing, caring hands.

The cold, unyielding snow reminiscent of the slab. The warmth of human contact and luxurious bedding.

The forbidding sky, midnight black and bereft of stars. Flamboyant tapestries, rich in colour and detail.

The sweet smell of perfumed hair. The cloying, sickly stench of the pit, of purgatory, of hell, of **death...death...death!**

Sir Galahad of Camelot jerked violently awake as the nightmare fled from before his eyes and transformed into something infinitely more pleasing.

A slender arm was draped across his chest which now slid down towards his lap as he sat up in the bed. Confusion crashed into his brain at almost the same time as his much-abused bones and muscles shrieked protest at their recent treatment. He slumped back onto the capacious, downy pillows and closed his eyes. The pain began to ease as the initial shock of his awakening and the surroundings he found himself in subsided.

As he lay there, he began to shiver, for his naked frame was clothed in sweat which had dried, cold and clammy on his body. Weakly, he pushed the arm that lay across him away, evoking a muffled protest from its owner as she turned her back to him.

After a second or two, his mind registered the implications of that and, despite the protest from his battered joints, he leapt from the bed as if scalded, startling its other occupant into wakefulness.

The confused knight made a grab for the luxuriant bed-coverings, yanking them off the bed and wrapping them around himself. To his horror, the woman that had been sharing the bed was as naked as he was. Moreover, as she stretched languidly with her large brown eyes never leaving his, she made no attempt to cover herself.

"Dear God, woman," he screeched with a voice strangulated by embarrassment, spinning round so that he was unable to look at her.

36

She laughed at him, a rich, surprisingly deep sound, then slid elegantly off the bed and retrieved her clothing from the floor.

Her merriment at his humiliation only served to anger him and he spat, "Cover yourself, strumpet. I have no use for the likes of you."

Silence followed his outburst and Galahad assumed that the woman, because even in his thoughts he could not bring himself to call one so brazen a lady, had used the moment to hurriedly gather her clothes together and depart in shame.

He began to turn and instantly regretted his inaccurate assumption, for he suddenly found himself in the midst of a chaotic, brutal tornado of scratching nails, anatomically accurate kicks and ear-splitting invective. "Who are you that you feel able to dismiss me in such a way?" she roared, launching herself off the edge of the bed at the astonished knight. He half-caught her and they tumbled to the hardwood floor in a tangle of limbs and bedding. This was not enough to still the onslaught, however. Fearing serious injury, Galahad relinquished his vice-like grip on the linen and raised his arms, warding off the frenzy of blows as best he could.

The woman continued her attack regardless. "I have tended you when your brow was dripping with fevered sweat and comforted you when your nightmares left you rigid with fear. I have lain beside you when the shivering of your body threatened to collapse the bed and I held you when your fevered nightmares left you sobbing like a newborn ripped from the breast. How dare you label me a whore when I have been naught but a wet-nurse to you for the last three days."

Breathing heavily, the woman's anger subsided and she ceased straddling her victim, stood up, then stretched her lithe body once more, again whilst pointedly holding Galahad's gaze. "Why would you assume that I would demean myself by bedding you anyway? Are you so accomplished in the bedchamber that women form lines outside your door, panting and impatient to enjoy the benefit of your erotic talents."

Galahad regarded her dispassionately, though a hint of distaste still played around his lips. Ignoring her now, he glanced around the room that he found himself in. The walls were bedecked with fabulously appointed tapestries which he rightly identified as the draperies he had seen when floating in and out of consciousness. The spacious canopy bed, supported on four sturdy yet exquisitely fashioned legs of oak, was situated against the only unadorned wall in the room. The curtains which surrounded it to keep at bay the draughts that were inevitable in a room so large were all tied back, yet even when unopened, the quality of the fabric was obvious to one who was used to the privileged life of the gentry. The colours of the material were a deep blue with some sort of design depicted upon them which Galahad could not distinguish due to the material being gathered together by the tasselled fastenings attached to each post of the bed.

The coat-of-arms upon the opposite wall facing the bed was unmistakable though. Three golden lions passant on a field of azure. The blazon of Sir Lancelot du Lac.

With his body now beginning to ache once more from his injuries and his recent exertion, he let forth a huge sigh and sat back on the side of the mattress. He turned to the woman with whom he had recently shared his bed. "I am in Joyous Garde then?" he said simply.

The woman, who had taken the opportunity during Galahad's appraisal of the room to re-dress, turned to him with a thunderous look. Curtseying floridly and with a voice dripping with sarcasm, she said, "Oh my lord, how would I know that? I am but an easy harlot who shares her bed with anyone and everyone, taking no note of my surroundings or my whereabouts."

Quickly pulling on a pair of scarlet hose that had been left on one of the ornate chairs which were placed on either side of the bed, the knight turned to her and his mouth quirked into an apologetic smile. With huge exaggeration, he mimicked the woman's supplication. "I crave your pardon, lady. I can only prostrate myself before you, beseech your forgiveness and express thanks to you for your ministrations. The shock of finding you next to me was the fuel for the fire of my heated words. If you crave a boon from me to appease your wrath, then you have only to ask and, if it is in my power, I will grant it."

The woman re-appraised the man before her with a very direct look that ignited the beginnings of a blush in the knight's face. "Hah," she chortled, "I guessed from your initial reaction that you have little experience of the bedchamber and all its inherent delights." She moved towards him, the hem of her daffodil-yellow gown swishing sensually across the uncarpeted floor. Gazing into Galahad's eyes, her forefinger began tracing a line down his chest where she momentarily tousled the black hairs that sprouted in the middle of it. "Your honeyed words are of some consolation to me, however, so I believe I will accept the bonus that is on offer." She leant into him with lips parted.

With a force considerably more gentle than that employed by the woman when she assaulted him, Galahad propelled her backwards. "My lady, I did specify that the boon had to be within my power to bestow."

The lustful look was replaced by one of nonplussed confusion. "It is a rare man indeed whose thoughts are not governed by his loins, yet for some reason, I do not feel that I should be offended by your refusal," she muttered as she walked round him, studying him as if he were an exhibit in a museum. "I fancy my looks are not the problem, for I can see the passion writ large in your gaze." She halted, pursing her lips as she pondered the muscular enigma before her.

The knight shifted uncomfortably under the examination. In an attempt to bring the scrutiny to an end, Galahad began to explain. "You are right not to take offence, lady, for you are certainly a fine example of womanhood." She nodded slightly at the compliment and gestured for him to continue. "My quandary is one of a spiritual nature. I am committed to a life of celibacy, you see." He said simply.

The intrigued look in the woman's eyes gave way to an open expression of puzzlement that Galahad found almost comical.

"By remaining chaste, I am no longer enslaved by the shackles of the corporeal world and have taken the first small step upon the stairway to heaven so that I might gain entrance to His kingdom." He continued to explain rather pompously.

The woman scoffed loudly. "What nonsense is this?" she spluttered. "Why on earth would God wish you to deny yourself in such a way?" She breathed huskily, moving into him again. Whispering in his ear, she began stroking his upper body once more. "To not experience that white-hot feeling building inside you, bubbling under the surface yearning to burst forth like a volcano, to not feel the soft, yielding press of flesh upon flesh, to not perceive the sensuousness of intimacy afforded by the act of coupling seems cruel in the extreme."

The disbelief in her voice was as apparent as the effect of her words upon the knight. His knuckles became whiter as he clutched the knot of bedding to him as if it was a shield against all the sins of the world.

"Do not seek to tempt me," Galahad cautioned, the warning edge returning to his voice. "Though I cannot deny the feast you place before me is one of undoubted delicacy, I regret I cannot partake."

"But…" she protested.

"Woman, I will not repeat myself again." And this time, there was no mistaking the threat contained within his tone. "I thank you for the care you have taken in my recovery but I do not have time to tarry. I have tidings of the utmost importance to impart to Lady Guinevere and Sir Lancelot, though I doubt they will thank me for them."

Pouting childishly, she slunk away from him, returning to the edge of the bed. "So you know the Lord and Lady of the manor yet remain willing to stay ignorant of the name of the one who has shared your bed these three nights past."

Almost mirroring the actions of his unexpected bedfellow, Galahad returned to his chair and clothed himself without further words. When fully dressed, the knight walked over to the opposite side of the bed, took the woman's hand in his and placed a delicate kiss upon it. "Lady, now I have my wits about me once more, it would please me greatly if you would be my guide around this stately castle. Could you take me to Lady Guinevere? I must see her as soon as possible."

Sighing hugely, with wistful regret permeating every word, she acceded to Galahad's request. "I will, good Sir Knight."

As they left the room and began their tour of the house, the woman who had nursed the injured warrior back to health finally introduced herself. "I am Lady Joanna Dubin, one of the ladies-in-waiting in Lady Guinevere's court. May I enquire as to the nature of your news? From the comment you made moments ago, I guess it is information that will not endear you to the Lord or Lady of the house."

Galahad shook his head slightly, though he softened his refusal with a smile. He found that, despite her scandalous antics, he liked the woman walking beside him. Despite his years of self-denial and restraint, practicing the disciplines of mind-calming prayer for hours each day, Lady Joanna had still fired his passion in a way he would not have thought possible. Though he knew he would not act upon the base impulses that had set his blood pounding as she had paraded naked around the bedchamber, the fact that she had awakened any desire at all was, for Galahad, a potent testament of the maiden's beauty.

After introducing himself and being secretly gratified by the excited gasp of recognition at his name, he linked arms with her as they proceeded down the corridor at a leisurely pace. In spite of his repeated protestations, now that he was safely within the confines of the keep, Galahad's need to inform Guinevere of her former husband's demise had become less urgent and, as he strolled down the passage which led into the main body of the fortress, he found himself taking the time to appreciate his surroundings, for Joyous Garde was renowned as the nearest equivalent to the magnificence and grandeur of Camelot in the whole of the land.

He walked along captivated by hefty wall-hangings depicting fantastical creatures doing battle with warriors in golden armour. Also, many elaborately carved plinths stood, supporting earthenware vessels of both local and distant origin.

As Galahad was guided through the hallways by Guinevere's lady-in-waiting, he was visited by an unexpectedly powerful pang of melancholia for Camelot. His recent memories of it as a place of personal recrimination and painful condemnation had diminished the further north he had travelled to the point that, as he negotiated the splendid halls and passageways which were so reminiscent of his former abode, he found himself steeped in the nostalgia of his time with the Knights of The Round Table and King Arthur in particular.

As he contemplated this, a boy of approximately seven years of age came barrelling round the corner, laughing heartily as he sped past them, intent on his imaginary adventure and oblivious to all else.

Lady Joanna chuckled at the youngster as he swerved past them without breaking stride. She turned to her companion saying, "Ah, that boy is like a breath of air in a deserted room." However, upon seeing the knight's face, she stopped short. "What on earth is the matter, Sir Galahad? You look as if you have seen a ghost."

"That boy. Who is that boy?" he stammered, whipping round to face her. The lady-in-waiting had to stop herself taking a step back from him, for the torture in his eyes was an alarming thing to behold. "Who is he?" he repeated, his voice coming out in a stifled shriek.

Lady Dubin stared after the child who had, by now, disappeared into one of the many rooms leading off the corridor. "That is Robert, the Lord and Lady's son," she replied, her face a studied mask as she pondered the reason for the knight's reaction to the boy.

Though his eyes betrayed little, Lady Joanna sensed that Galahad only brought his emotions under control by dint of a Herculean effort. "Come," he managed to say, "let us find Lady Guinevere."

The two of them set off along the arched corridor at nearly the same speed as the child who had just flown past them, the lady-in-waiting's skirts fluttering behind her chaotically as she strove to keep up. Between that moment and their arrival in the castle's Great Hall, they shared no more words. Lady Joanna had seen something in the knight's eyes which left her in no doubt that should she probe further into Galahad's reaction, she would receive, at best, a curt response or, at worst, a repeat of the venom directed at her before they had become properly acquainted.

Galahad's silence, however, was born of a hundred feelings that he thought buried when he had left Camelot behind him. As he had peered at that familiar face, magically shorn of its beard and approximately forty-five years of age, he knew with a certainty as rock-solid as the walls on either side of the passageway that the child who had run past them, so carefree and so innocent, was not Sir Lancelot's progeny, but instead, a surviving remnant of a love that had, at one time, seemed as eternal as the sea but now lay in derelict ruin, the memories tainted forever by infidelity and betrayal.

At length, they arrived at a gargantuan pair of doors, upon which had been expertly carved the three lions of the master of the house. There were two guards, one positioned on either side of the door, standing statue-still, their pikes creating an X of steel through which none would pass without permission.

Upon seeing the Lady Dubin, however, they stood down their weapons and the one on the left, his grey eyes impassive and unblinking, pushed open one of the doors to allow them admittance to the Great Hall of Joyous Garde.

As the pair of them strode into the room, Galahad found his breath stolen as he contemplated the sumptuousness of the chamber. Even though he was well used to the finery and grandiosity of Camelot, the opulence of the décor and furnishings left him open-mouthed.

The first thing that struck the knight was the three massive arches arcing up towards the roof. They swept up in the direction of the thick rafters and overhung a raised dais that held pride of place in the centre of the far wall. They dominated the room, leaving any who came before the lord of the house dwarfed and cowed by their sheer immensity.

Upon the platform, a gilt throne sat. It was shaped as a high-backed chair with plush arm rests and deep blue cushions that afforded the occupant ample padding against the hard oak of the frame. The back was an exquisitely rendered scrollwork adorned with ivory plaques intricately carved with mythological, heraldic and biblical scenes and the arms flared out into roaring lion's heads at the end. The legs of the throne continued the leonine motif, ending as they did in four thick-set paws, so cunningly wrought that they seemed poised to leap into life at any moment.

To the left of this was a similar chair, slightly smaller in size but just as ornate. However, whereas the throne in the centre radiated authority and command, this one was, in some indefinable way, less threatening and more welcoming. Galahad suspected that it was due to the more pastoral scenes which decorated its back and the softer edges that had been fashioned for the arms and legs.

Behind the thrones hung substantial curtains of azure suspended from a golden pole that ran between the columns of the arches.

As the knight from Camelot approached the platform, he scanned the guards who stood unmoving in a mirror image of their fellows outwith the chamber. Though they stood at ease, his heightened battle sense detected a tension in their stance as though they expected some sort of difficulty to manifest itself.

His eyes left them then, becoming hypnotised by the dancing flames of the blistering fire that burned in the hearth of a huge fireplace which was dug deep into the right-hand wall. Whether it was a primal urge from his ancestral past or simply the warming blaze of the fire he did not know, but Galahad always found the mesmerizing leaps and flickers of a wood fire to be a singularly comforting experience. With an inward sigh, he continued his walk towards the seat of Lancelot du Lac, permitting himself only the most cursory of glances at the remaining wall as the distance to the dais closed.

At some point during Galahad's contemplation of the hall, Lady Dubin had melted away from his side and he now stood rather self-consciously before a vacant throne.

With great ceremony, a herald appeared from behind one of the curtains that screened the lower half of the wall behind the throne. Holding a weighty sceptre which looked much too hefty for his spindly arms, the man walked down the stairs that led to the floor of the chamber.

As Galahad beheld him, he was amused to see the flames from the fire dancing in a writhing, indistinct mass atop the man's bald head. Whilst the herald cleared his throat to announce his tidings, the knight found his gaze wrenched back to the blue curtains as they parted once more. Through the billow of the rich fabric emerged one of the most potent figures of his recent past. A man whom he had once counted a brother but one who had chosen to turn his back on his leader, his home, his friends, all for another who had also let her selfish immorality override any considerations of decency and propriety.

The herald banged the base of the sceptre on the floor three times and proclaimed in a surprisingly strong voice for one so slender, "Sir Lancelot du Lac, Lord of Joyous Garde."

With his eyes never leaving Sir Galahad and an unreadable expression on his face, Sir Lancelot strode across the platform and took his seat.

As he was a guest in the man's home, Galahad bowed deeply, though he hated himself for doing so. In the instant that he had locked stares with the disgraced former champion of Camelot, all of Merlin's words about dishonouring King Arthur's memory with his quest crashed into his mind in a deluge of recrimination and shame. With a masterful effort, he kept his face neutral and took to studying the changes which the last seven years had produced in his host.

The head of curly, blond hair still nested on top of his head, though it was streaked with grey lines at the temples. He still had the look of a man who was totally sure of himself, but now there were other facets to his aspect that Galahad felt may possibly explain the uneasy atmosphere in the court. Lancelot had always been a vainglorious creature but now there was an unpleasant arrogance to his movements and expression and, since his appearance, his mouth had been permanently set in a thoroughly disagreeable smirk which irked Galahad beyond measure. However, it was the ice-blue eyes that captivated the knight although not for a good reason. Though Lancelot was, to all intents and purposes, smiling, the look had a predatory quality to it and there could be no doubt that beneath the veneer, a smouldering anger lay, banked at the moment, but ever present and ready to erupt at a moment's notice.

Lancelot got himself comfortable upon his throne, arranging his flamboyant golden robes so that he could sit down without creasing them. He rested his elbow on one of the arms of his throne and regarded Galahad through hooded eyes.

An uncomfortable silence grew, its all-encompassing nature ratcheting up the pressure of the encounter to near breaking point. Finally, the host spoke, his voice dripping with boredom bordering on contempt. "Well, Galahad, did you come all this way to stand before me like a startled deer or did you have some news to impart?" he drawled.

Galahad blinked in surprise at the sheer malice in his former friend's voice. He had prepared himself for a measure of hostility but nothing on the scale of the malevolence emanating from the man before him. "My lord," he stammered, again despising himself for putting his manners before his emotions, "is the Lady Guinevere joining us? The tidings I have will be of great moment to her."

At the mention of the name, Lancelot's eyes narrowed even further. His lips peeled back from his teeth and he appeared to be about to launch into a diatribe but, at the last, he subsided and murmured in a barely audible voice, "No, the lady will not be joining us."

Even if Lancelot had not been acting so objectionably, Galahad's interest would have been piqued now, for the way that his host had pronounced the word 'lady' spoke volumes.

Galahad was about to say something else when the curtains drew back again in a flurry of material and Robert emerged, giggling uncontrollably. His sweet voice tore the baleful atmosphere to shreds as he taunted his would-be pursuer. "You can't catch me, Frederick. I'm too fast for you."

Behind him, a sheepish looking page peeped through the crack in the curtains. The colour leeched from the older boy's face when he realised where his charge had chosen to escape to. He emerged fully from behind the drapery, blinking owlishly at his master's thunderous face. "Come, Robert," he quavered, "we should not be...."

"Papa!" Robert squealed in delight, bounding across the space between him and Lancelot and launching himself onto the knight's lap before roughly hugging him.

The Lord of Joyous Garde gently disentangled the boy's stick-thin arms from around his neck and spoke quietly. "Frederick is right, boy, you should not be here. Be off with you."

Robert wrinkled his freckled nose and reluctantly got down from his father's lap. For long seconds, Lancelot regarded his son's face, as if searching for something he knew he would not find.

Despite the hatred that his host's manner had engendered in him, Galahad found the anguish which flared momentarily in Lancelot's stare a horror to behold and hurriedly turned his own face away.

When Lancelot spoke again, his voice was thick with emotion. "Please, Robert, you must go." He waved the boy away with his right hand as he drew his left hand down over his face. To all who observed him, it was as if Lancelot's hand had wiped away all the agony that had been so apparent only seconds before, for, after his dismissal of the child, his face reset itself into its previous aspect of sneering derision.

Frederick darted across the stage and dragged the protesting youngster from sight. Aside from another momentary trace of torment flickering in Lancelot's eyes as the boy's voice became more distraught at his ejection, his mask of indifference held fast.

The knight from Camelot was caught hopelessly off-guard by what was transpiring before him. "Lancelot, I..." he began, but once again he was stopped from finishing his statement as a susurration began around the hall. Unnoticed by all, another figure had made its way out of the shadows and into the guttering light provided both by the fire in the massive hearth and the torches that danced and fluctuated in the sconces which lined each wall.

The words died in Galahad's throat as he beheld the familiar features of Lady Guinevere, former wife and cuckoldress of King Arthur Pendragon.

He was surprised that his first instinct upon seeing her was one of pity, given his violent reaction to the sneering face of her husband. However, when his head caught up with his heart it was easy to see why his thoughts had been thus. Guinevere's movements were that of a woman many years older than her age. Though she maintained a straight-backed dignity, it was clear to all who watched that every step extracted an agonising toll from her. Visibly wincing, her hand unwittingly flying to her ribs in an attempt to stem a lancing pain, she assumed her seat next to her spouse. It was noticeable, however, that Lancelot made no move to aid her, indeed, he could not even bring himself to spare her a glance.

All is not well in the house of Joyous Garde, Galahad observed dryly to himself.

He wanted to return his gaze to Lancelot and continue their confrontation, but there was something horribly compelling about the appearance of Lady Guinevere. Now that she had made her way into the full light of the room, her haggard appearance became even starker. Her face was drawn and thin and her skin bore the sickly pallor of poor health. Her eyes were red and puffy with the beginnings of a bruise starting to discolour her left cheek. Where her fabulous low-cut turquoise dress of blue dashed with streaks of saffron yellow should have been curving in harmony with her once perfect figure, now it hung upon her uncomfortably and the flesh which was visible was stretched taut over jutting bone.

Once again, the silence returned, but this time it was a silence of unspoken questions and damning accusation. Finally, Galahad blurted, "It is…good to see you again, my lady." He cringed inwardly, aware of the inadvertent pause that had slipped into his greeting.

"As it is you, good Sir Knight." She replied breathily, her words coming out in measured tones though her expression spoke eloquently of her relief. She threw a fleeting look sideways at her husband, who pointedly ignored her once again. Her gaze travelled down to his hands, noticing that the knuckles were white upon the left as he gripped the arm of his throne as tightly as he could, and that the right was bunched into a fist which clenched and unclenched fitfully. Closing her eyes and breathing as deeply as her injuries would allow, she continued, "My Lady Joanna informs me that you have urgent news which you wish to share with us all."

Galahad bowed deeply and rather than facing the throne directly, came forward to the lowermost step of the dais. He then dropped to one knee before the Lady of Joyous Garde. His act was petty in the extreme but he felt he had to show his distaste at Lancelot's manner and felt that marginalising the Lord of the House in this manner was the best way to go about it.

"My lady, I have the gravest of news, I…" It would be nice, Galahad thought as he was shoved to the floor, to be able to finish a sentence once in a while. He looked up at the apoplectic face of Sir Lancelot looming over him. Sputum flicked from the knight's mouth as he shrieked, "When you are present in my court, you will address me and me alone!"

Galahad's eyes narrowed as he regained his feet. Though he had expected hostility, this was hatred bordering on madness. The flames from the fire danced in Lancelot's eyes, giving him the look of a demon. For a split second, as the flames accentuated the shadows of Lancelot's cheekbones lending him a skeletal appearance, Galahad was wrenched back to his spectral encounter in the blizzard scant days ago and he gasped involuntarily.

Lancelot's anger dissolved into an unpleasant smirk as he misunderstood Galahad's reaction, thinking it to be fear. However, the smile soon disappeared and he took a step back as Galahad advanced upon him mercilessly, until they stood nose to nose. "If that is your wish, Lancelot, then so be it." Holding the knight's gaze unblinkingly, Galahad stated calmly. "I am sorry to be the bearer of such grievous news, Lady Guinevere, but King

Arthur", he paused as Lancelot grimaced at the mention of the name, "is dead."

For a second, it seemed as if everyone in the Great Hall held their breath awaiting some sort of response to the tidings, either from the towering presence of the Lord of the House or from the fractured shell of his wife, sitting upon her throne. Then after a final look at Galahad, Lancelot spun round, ascended the steps in one bound and re-seated himself upon his throne. "I had thought that, from your solemnity, the intelligence you had was of some import." He shrugged. "I fail to see what the death of a distant rural monarch has to do with the house of Joyous Garde?"

Galahad looked pityingly at his past companion from the Round Table at Camelot. He saw no point venting his spleen at Lancelot, it would only ensure more angry words and violence and he concluded, after seeing the effect of his news upon Guinevere that, despite Lancelot's dismissal of the tidings, she still had to come to terms with it.

"Is that all, Sir Galahad?" Lancelot sneered. "If so, do not let me detain you. I'm sure you cannot wait to return to the bosom of your hero-worshipping lackeys at Camelot, especially now that their esteemed leader has fallen." He tapped his fingers on the arm of his throne, as if pondering something. Suddenly, his face lit up. "Or did they drive you from the castle? Perhaps that is why you have fetched up here, so far from your home. Perhaps they found your unending sanctimony insufferable and took the opportunity to eject you from the premises, once your chief apologist was no longer around to protect you." The Lord of Joyous Garde stared from face to face around his court, seeking others who would join him in his mockery of the knight.

Galahad stood impassively, saddened beyond measure by the bitterness exuding from the man who sat before him. With a huge sigh, he nodded, "Yes, Sir Lancelot, that is all. Such a small amount of words to convey such a large amount of pain." Shaking his head, he continued, "I cannot deny that your response to what I have told you is nearly as much of a tragedy as the news itself. The knight, no, you were more than just that, the *friend* I knew from our days at Camelot would never talk of another human being in the way you have, especially one to whom you were once bonded so closely. What has become of you, Lancelot? Where is your nobility, your gallantry, your humanity?"

Sir Lancelot du Lac, late of Camelot, aristocrat of Joyous Garde, hung his head and, for a brief moment, Galahad thought his speech had breached whatever wall Lancelot had erected between himself and his memories of King Arthur. He was wrong.

When Lancelot's head came up, Galahad had to consciously stop himself stepping back from the expression that disfigured his former companion's face. "Who do you think you are to talk to me in such a manner in my own home? Get out of my sight. I will allow you to remain under the roof of this house for one more night, but then you have until the sun reaches its apex tomorrow to remove yourself from these walls, never to darken them again." He stood and roared, "Did you not hear me? Begone! Begone from here lest I reconsider my decision and order you thrown into the bitterness of this winter night."

Galahad coloured and looked about to challenge his host's words, but a beseeching yet almost imperceptible look from Lady Guinevere caused him not to.

He turned on his heel and stalked from the hall. As he strode across the intricate mosaic that decorated the floor, his mind pondered what he had seen in the Great Hall. Why had Lancelot reacted in such an objectionable manner?

However, his main concern was reserved for the Lady Guinevere. Whatever could be ailing her? Obviously, there was some sort of tension between her and Lancelot but, even taking that into account, her appearance had shocked the knight from Camelot. To see her beauty so dimmed and her demeanour so dispirited was dreadful but, unfortunately, he could not bring himself to view it as anything other than just another horrendous aspect of the torrid time he had experienced since leaving Camelot.

He was scant yards from the door when his gaze, which had hitherto not really been concentrating on anything, was wrenched to the tapestry that dominated the wall to his right. All of the splendid surroundings seemed to dissolve into the background and Galahad felt as if he was being sucked toward the fabric that hung upon the wall. He struggled for breath as he was transported back to the blizzard three nights ago and his encounter with the hideous parodies of non-life which had so nearly claimed him as one of their own.

Sir Galahad…

He shivered as he imagined the snow and wind enveloping him once more and he began to sway as he again smelt the aroma of decay.

Sir Galahad…

His legs began to buckle and darkness rushed towards him, an all-engulfing vacuum of nothingness beckoning him forward into blissful oblivion.

Sir Galahad…

With a hideously unnerving sense of dislocation, his headlong descent ceased abruptly and he was dragged violently back into the grandiose reality of the Great Hall of Joyous Garde. He was unable to focus and simply allowed himself to be forcibly ejected from the hall, collapsing in a heap just beyond the entrance. He lay on the cold stone floor, struggling for calm as the last remnants of the sickeningly sweet perfume of death vanished from his nose.

With a clang of death-knell finality, the two doors hammered shut.

He felt hands upon him again and, after much furious head-shaking and blinking, managed to steady his vision.

Lady Joanna Dubin was trying in vain to get the knight from Camelot upright and walking. After several false starts, verticality was achieved and the pair began to wend their tremulous way back to Galahad's rooms.

They shared no words on their journey, for Galahad was still recovering from his flashback to the encounter in the blizzard and Lady Joanna was concentrating all her efforts on getting the both of them to the relative sanctuary of the knight's bedchamber.

At length, they returned to Galahad's quarters and both slumped over the threshold, relieved that they could now achieve some modicum of rest.

Galahad crawled over to the bed and feebly heaved himself on to it, lying on his back and numbly staring at the fabric draped over the bed whilst his mind feverishly roiled with what he had seen. Lady Dubin poured them both a goblet of wine, placed it on the bedside table next to the prostrate knight and perched herself daintily on the edge of the bed.

She spoke in a voice that brooked no argument, "Galahad, you must tell me what happened to you."

His eyes darted nervously from side to side and sweat beaded upon his forehead. In an exhausted voice, he moaned, "I am sorry. I cannot. It is a horror that I have no compulsion to revisit. It haunts me as I sleep, I have no wish for it to haunt me in my waking hours as well."

"Yet it is clear that it does, good Sir Knight. I took you for a man touched by madness as you swayed gibbering and drooling in the Hall." She lowered her head. "Please tell me. Why did you take such a fit of hysteria?"

Galahad did not acknowledge her plea, he merely continued staring at the bed's canopy.

"Godsdammit, man," she threw her half-full glass to the floor and stood looming over him with hand raised as if to strike him, "why must you be so prideful? What are you afraid of, brave Sir Knight? He who is so pure and close to his God that he has clasped the Holy Grail to his chaste and untainted bosom? He who has fought demons and dragons and slain scores of unholy villains?" Her voice became softer and her face lost its sarcastic snarl, "Why, when you have shown your valour and courage a hundred times over when other men would quail and hide, are you afraid of something as insubstantial as a dream?"

Galahad slowly, painfully, propped himself up on his elbows but could not bring himself to look Joanna in the eye. Instead, he stared silently at the gradually spreading pool of wine that insinuated itself across the wooden floor and looked like nothing more than a bloodstain, but one that was somehow obscenely animate and aware. Without conscious thought, words began to flow from him and before he knew it, the candles had burned low and a scarlet dawn had begun to peep over the horizon and he had told Lady Joanna Dubin his thoughts, his fears and everything else which had assailed his life ever since King Arthur Pendragon had been impaled upon his treacherous nephew's sword mere weeks, but what seemed like a whole lifetime, ago. "And then, seeing those hideous faces again on the tapestry, it was more than I could bear." He bit back his emotions as tears threatened to well up in his eyes once more, but even as they did, by simply unloading his feelings to another person, he was amazed that now they seemed to lack the potency which they once had.

With a slightly ashamed look on his face, he finally brought his head up to meet Lady Joanna's gaze, their eyes met and an understanding passed between them. Galahad took a deep breath and said simply, "Thank you for listening."

For her part, Lady Dubin reached out and tenderly stroked his beardless cheek. She shook her head and gazed out of the window for a moment at the startling shade of pink that wreathed the morning sky. "How I wish you had told me this before, Galahad," she sighed, turning to face him again. "You are not the first to have borne witness to this nightmarish phenomenon. I myself have seen it."

At this, Galahad sat upright and stared at his companion intently.

"When I arrived here in the retinue of the Lady Guinevere. What you saw, what we have both seen, is the Dolorous Guard. That tapestry you saw is a representation of the story of where the castle gets its name," she explained.

The look of confusion on Galahad's face was so exaggerated that Lady Joanna stifled a most unfeminine guffaw before continuing, "Do not forget, Galahad, you only actually saw but a small part of the whole. To understand what has haunted you these last few days, I must tell you the full tale." She smoothed down the front of her dress and cleared her throat demurely.

"After Sir Lancelot and Guinevere left Camelot in disgrace, they travelled north, wanting to put as much distance between themselves and Arthur's wrath as they could. We traversed the lands for nearly a month, directionless and lost. We came across the castle one gorgeous summer's day," her eyes glazed as she revisited memories that she had not explored for many years, "only to find it occupied, guarded by a man who identified himself as The Copper Knight. For some reason, he thought us an invading force and rather than welcoming us, bellowed a challenge from the ramparts. Well, you know yourself, about the immense vanity of Sir Lancelot du Lac. It ate at him, you see, the fact that he had been forced to leave his comfortable life in Camelot, but, at that moment in time, he would have walked to the ends of the earth for his lady and she had begged to absent herself from Arthur's baleful eye. Anyway, without thought, he accepted the challenge of this Copper Knight. Well, the Copper Knight had an elite force, the Dolorous Guard, a band of twenty murderous brigands who did their master's wicked bidding. Lancelot fought them all. He had to do battle with ten knights at the first wall, ten knights at the second wall, and then finally with the Copper Knight himself. However, after defeating the twenty knights, he discovered that the Copper Knight had fled.

As you can well imagine, the Copper Knight had been found wanting as a liege lord and used the Guard to rule the surrounding countryside with harsh cruelty. The townspeople were overjoyed to be free of his stewardship. They led Lancelot to a cemetery, where they stood him before a metal slab. The slab stated that only one knight could lift it and that this knight's name was written beneath the slab. Well, Lancelot lifted it and discovered that the name underneath was indeed his, though it was spelt Launcelot." She shrugged diffidently. "It may be that some element of fakery was involved, some ruse that the serfs employed to rid themselves of an unpopular nobleman, but whatever the circumstances, Lancelot and Guinevere used the opportunity to install themselves in the castle and christened it Joyous Garde, after the mood of victory following the defeat of the Copper Knight."

Galahad took hold of Lady Joanna's hand and stroked the soft, flawless skin. "That is an interesting tale, yet I still do not understand what your point is? Are you saying that those atrocities I saw are the spirits of the twenty slain knights?"

Joanna nodded, her hair falling across her face momentarily. "So the legend says. They appear to those who have the miasma of death about them, they are black thoughts personified, they themselves were taken before their time after a life of debauchery and sin and they live, though that may be too strong a word for their existence in the shadows of perpetuity, to consume good souls, good souls like yourself, who find their minds thrown off-kilter by misfortune and tragedy."

"So you are saying that only those on the verge of insanity bear witness to these beings?"

Lady Joanna waved away the remark with a gentle peal of laughter. "No, Sir Galahad, you misunderstand me. I do not think you mad. Any man who has been through what you have would have seen the Dolorous Guard, though I am bound to say that most would have emerged from the experience with their minds wrecked beyond repair. No, the foundations of your life and your beliefs had taken a fearful pounding and you were ripe for the Guard's pernicious mischief. Do not be ashamed of your fears, Sir Galahad. A lesser man would surely have fallen in the face of such crushing setbacks."

Galahad moved off the bed and took Lady Dubin's head in his hands. He surprised himself by planting a passionate kiss upon her lips. In her shock, she did not respond immediately and, before she could, he disengaged himself. With a dazzling smile upon his face, he resumed his position back on the bed. She stared at him for a moment then began to crawl across the blankets towards him. Galahad held up his hands to indicate she should go no further. "Please, Lady, that kiss is all you will obtain from me so do not seek anything more. I know it is what you wish for but you would not want me besieged by doubts once again, would you?" he asked, a quirky, toothy smile smeared on his lips to soften the rebuff.

A look of irritation passed over her face like a cloud in front of the sun but, after an awkward moment, she shrugged again and sat back.

The knight from Camelot stared out onto a patchwork of inky darkness that the dawn sun had not quite reached and sighed, "I am afraid that I must leave here soon. There cannot be more than four hours before the sun reaches noon and, if I am to accede to his lordship's request, then I must make preparations to depart."

His mouth gaped in shock at the obscenity that Lady Dubin spat out. "Now that is a man who will receive a visit from the Guard soon and good riddance too."

Galahad ceased gathering his belongings together and stared at her, "Yes, I must say I had prepared myself for some hostility but his behaviour was unconscionable. He is not the man I fought alongside for so many years when we were brethren of the Round Table."

Her face twisted into an unprepossessing snarl as she hissed, "He has always been an arrogant, narcissistic man but he is as a man possessed now, possessed by demons, evil demons." As she spewed these words, her resolve broke and she began to sob, the scene made all the more touching because of the way she had been so strong for Galahad.

He came over to her then and held her shuddering body within his arms until the tears subsided. "He will kill her, you know. I had not seen her for the three days that you lay in your fever dream. I had known something was wrong ever since he came back but it was only today after I left you in Great Hall that I met with her and saw her injuries. She broke down and told me that ever since he returned he has been in turmoil, hitting out for no good reason, yet he would not say why. She said that the only language he uses now is the language of cruelty and violence."

Sir Galahad struggled to choke back his astonishment. "You think Lancelot did that to Lady Guinevere? But he loves her, does he not?"

52

"I thought so, but..." Joanna turned away and strove to compose herself again.

The knight's brow wrinkled, "You said that he has been this monster ever since he came back. Do you know where he came back from?"

She shook her head. "Not for certain. I did hear rumour that the king's usurper nephew had been sighted moving in this direction. It may be that Lancelot took it upon himself to harry his forces, but it was court gossip, no more than that."

Galahad was quiet for a time, pondering Joanna's revelation. What on earth could have caused such a momentous transformation in Sir Lancelot's attitude to his ill-gotten bride? Then in a flash of insight, he asked, "Tell me, has his demeanour changed towards the boy?"

"Robert, you mean?"

Galahad nodded solemnly, the seed of suspicion beginning to flower in his mind.

Lady Dubin chewed upon her lower lip. "I am Guinevere's lady-in-waiting. I do not really have a great deal to do with him, but now you mention it, I have heard the other maids mention that he does not seem to visit the boy as often as he did. Why?"

"Joanna, I think you should sit down." She did so and he took her hand in his again. "You remember my reaction when I first saw him out in the corridor." She nodded, intrigued by what she was about to hear. "Well, the reason was that he, Robert, is the mirror image of Arthur. I thought I had been catapulted back in time when he came charging around that corner."

Joanna's mouth was agape. Had the situation been less fraught, Galahad probably would have burst out laughing at her expression. He continued sombrely, "My guess is that Lancelot did indeed harry Mordred and, in the course of that action, met up with Arthur. After all, Arthur rode from Camelot for that very reason, to apprehend his bastard relative and make him pay for his betrayals, so it was highly likely their paths would converge at some point. Obviously, given their history, it is unlikely that they met on good terms. Assuming that is what happened, Lancelot would have been dismissed from Arthur's sight in quick time, returned here in the foulest of humours and then been confronted by the undeniable fact of Robert's parentage." He paused for a moment then stared pointedly at his new-found confidante. "Believe me, if you had known Arthur, you would agree there is no mistaking the father of that lad." A distant look quirked his features, "It would seem that the terms on which Guinevere left Arthur all those years ago were more amicable than was first thought."

Lady Joanna let out a booming exhalation of amazement. "That would certainly explain a great deal." Shaking her head, the fierceness returned to her face and she said, "That does not condone what he has done to Lady Guinevere. What right has he to vent his anger upon her?"

This time it was Galahad's turn to shrug. "It is said that you reap the harvest which you sow."

She rounded on him with eyes narrowed and teeth bared, "What is that supposed to mean? She has wronged her man and so deserves to feel the fury of his fists upon her?"

Galahad stood calmly, unmoved by her vehemence. "I was merely pointing out that, considering the manner in which their hearts became entwined, perhaps Lancelot should not be completely shocked that his lady was not entirely true to him in the months after they first met."

When she began to advance threateningly towards him, he held up his hands conciliatorily and backed away. "Do not misunderstand me, Lady Joanna, I do not seek to excuse his actions, I am simply saying that as his, or who he thought was his, son comes to manhood, it will be painfully obvious to all that he bears no resemblance to his presumed father and, as you said, Lancelot is and always was such a vainglorious peacock that his pride will compel him to hit out as savagely as he can at the ones whom he feels have made a fool of him." He shook his head and looked down at the floor. "I fear that life will not be particularly pleasurable for Guinevere from here on in, or indeed for poor Robert."

A look of naked frustration settled on Lady Joanna's face. "This is unfair, so unfair."

"As one who has observed rather than experienced the ups and downs of romance, I will forbear to comment."

Her face changed then, taking on a predatory aspect that the knight found rather unbecoming. "Sir Galahad, you have built your reputation by stepping forth when gallantry was required." She walked towards him and embraced him. With her head laid upon his chest, she said huskily, "I would say that, at this moment, Guinevere is very much a damsel in distress." She withdrew from the embrace and looked up at the muscular knight, her hazel eyes brimming with moisture and the calculating look upon her face collapsing into heartfelt distress. "Please, Sir Galahad. I truly fear she will die by his hand."

Galahad held Joanna's tormented gaze for as long as he could. He had guessed that the conversation would begin to lean in this direction but, even with that suspicion in his head, he was unable to decide on a definite course of action. How could he ride to Guinevere's rescue like a shining warrior of righteousness when she had committed an act of such staggering emotional violence herself by betraying the King in such a callous, calculating manner?

He did concede that, as Joanna had pointed out, his reputation was one of dauntless bravery and he had triumphed in situations with worse odds than this but, inextricably entwined with his renowned chivalry, was undying loyalty and integrity and he suspected that, were he to accede to Lady Dubin's request and intercede on Guinevere's behalf to release her from the largely self-inflicted punishment she had sentenced herself to, then there would be an extra layer of accusation in the white-hot glare that King Arthur would direct toward him when next his tortured slumbers sent him to revisit the hellish fields of Camlann. He knew, with a certainty as unyielding as the buckler he bore upon his fist in battle, that his mental state was still fragile enough to fracture with even a slight increase of the pressure upon it and he was unwilling to risk his sanity for the sake of one so undeserving of his sympathy.

An uneasiness lurked at the back of his mind however, that he was being too harsh in his treatment of her because the wretched figure that Guinevere had cut upon entry to the throne room did cause him considerable pangs of sympathy.

Speaking with an assuredness he did not feel, he shook his head, "It is not my way to turn my back on suffering and distress, but neither is it my way to betray the faith and trust placed in me by my friends and brothers." He held a hand up to quash the protest which had started to erupt from Lady Dubin's mouth. He did not look at her however, merely fixing his eyes on some point in the middle distance and picturing memories of countless conversations, conversations which had lasted through the night, conversations filled with recrimination, regret and discomfiting poignancy.

Blinking furiously, he returned to the present, "I reached an accord with King Arthur that, should I come upon...those who wronged him so grievously, whilst I would not offer them hostility unless they first offered it to me, neither would I offer them succour, no matter how pressing the need." Now his eyes did come up and meet hers and the expression of dismay upon her face told him that she had recognised the resolve in his voice and the steel in his gaze. In short, she knew he would not be swayed.

Her shoulders slumped and her head drooped to face the floor. "You had better make ready and take your leave. If Lancelot is prepared to harm someone as beloved to him as Guinevere then he will certainly not hesitate in doing you injury," she murmured.

Galahad reached out to her, gently placing his hand upon her shoulder. "What of yourself? I cannot thank you enough for the care and attention which you have shown me during my stay and I could not, in all good conscience, leave you in any sort of peril. Will your closeness to Guinevere endanger you in any way?"

She smiled then, inclining her head in mute thanks for Galahad's solicitude. "Would it make a difference if I told you it did?"

Galahad was at a loss as to how to respond for the question was a highly pertinent one. Could he walk away from Joyous Garde knowing that he had left his newfound associate at risk from Lancelot's cruel temper? After all, Joanna was in no way part of Guinevere's perfidy.

In the end, Guinevere's lady-in-waiting resolved the knight's dilemma herself. She reached up to him and stroked his jaw-line, stopping when her index finger alighted upon his lips. "You can leave the castle with your principles intact, good Sir Knight. I do not believe that Lancelot's ire will extend beyond his lady and I certainly will not leave her in her hour of need." She smiled warmly to soften the slight reproach that her voice hinted at. "Though the lie would slip easily from my mouth, I would not stoop to mislead you, especially after you have bestowed such glowing praise on my recent behaviour."

Galahad bowed deeply and went back to his travel bags. Lady Joanna stared at his back for long seconds then turned towards the door. She stopped as she was about to exit the room and murmured, "Goodbye, Sir Galahad of Camelot."

The knight continued thrusting his undergarments and tunics into Farregas' saddlebags, to all intents and purposes oblivious to her departure. However, when he heard the door close, he stopped for a moment, "Goodbye, Lady Joanna" he whispered.

Chapter 4

Sir Galahad of Camelot, ex-champion of King Arthur Pendragon of the Britons, rode proudly atop his battle horse, Farregas. He had departed from Joyous Garde before noon under the malevolent glare of Sir Lancelot Du Lac. As he had rode from the castle, he had returned the glare with interest, deliberately keeping his reproving gaze fixed upon the former knight of the Round Table, challenging him to react and give Galahad a reason to exact some sort of redress for his inexcusable treatment of Lady Guinevere. Even as he passed under the portcullis, trusting in the surefootedness of his Destrier steed to keep him in place, he held Lancelot's vision, the unspoken challenge wrought large in his manner.

Of Lady Dubin, there was no sign and the pang which Galahad felt at that surprised him with its strength. Whether it was lust or something deeper, he did not know. He could certainly recall every curve and sweep of her nakedness with startling clarity and was also fairly certain that four days, three days of which were spent in varying stages of delirium, was not a particularly ample amount of time in which to fall in love, so, given those two facts, he came to the conclusion that his experience with the Dolorous Guard had weakened him mentally to such an extent that it had allowed thoughts of a sordid nature to inveigle their way into his head.

He did acknowledge how much he had enjoyed her company however, and was prepared to accept that he would have enjoyed continuing their acquaintance, but Lancelot's decision to oust him from the castle had taken the choice out of his hands.

His preoccupation had taken him out of the shadows of the crenellations, though he was still in sight of the massive edifice. For the first time he took stock of the building in which he had stayed for the best part of a week. The manner in which he had gained entrance to the castle had meant that he did not have any real idea of what it looked like from the outside.

His sharp battle-honed knowledge came into play as he stared up at the imposing structure and he could not help but be impressed by its defensibility and design. The castle dominated the immediate area, standing in magnificent splendour atop a massive outcrop of rock, a forbidding structure which seemed to offer defiance to any who came with conquest in mind.

The so-called Copper Knight must have felt so secure within his domain, despatching his henchmen to do his dirty work for him, thinking himself untouchable. Galahad reflected that he could not have been much of a tactician if he had let the castle fall so easily to Sir Lancelot.

Its positioning on the pinnacle of Bamburgh Hill afforded its occupants panoramic views of the surrounding countryside, which meant that concealed approach by anything more than a few people was nigh on impossible.

Facing south, Joyous Garde looked out over the village that had, for decades, skulked in the shadows of its stones. Also called Bamburgh, it was home to farmers, blacksmiths, tanners and various other trades that had languished under the despotic rule of the Copper Knight, but were now thriving under the less demanding stewardship of Lord Du Lac.

However, the industry that kept the township economically buoyant and in the good humour of its ruler was the fishing. The gatherers of Neptune's harvest found plentiful pickings in the surrounding waters and returned daily, nets bulging with bountiful catches of mackerel, cod, haddock and whiting as well as lesser amounts of saithe and herring. As well as these, many crustaceans also found themselves subject to the attention of the seafarers and prawn and shrimp were regularly farmed from the ocean floor along with lobsters and mussels in abundance.

Indeed, as Galahad and Farregas plodded along the road away from Joyous Garde, they could both see a flotilla of boats bobbing and swaying in the tidal currents. The sands that stretched along the coast as far as the eye could see were flat and featureless, save for a few rocks and boulders carried to their unlikely resting places by the relentless power of the North Sea. At the moment however, the sea was as flat as the beach it lapped upon.

Inland from the sands, in the direction that Galahad was heading, dunes stretched away like golden waves, undulating erratically and studded with clumps of stubby grass and gorse. It was a bleak but beautiful scene which found Galahad once more appreciating the beauty of the land he lived in. However, the quickening wind reminded him of the brutality of the winter months which this part of the kingdom was subjected to and concentrated the knight's mind as to where his meanderings would carry him now. Though there was a pleasantness to the temperature that was more than bearable, Galahad was all too aware that, when the sun disappeared over the horizon, the temperature would plunge and he had no wish to be caught in the biting cold of night without shelter.

He brought Farregas to a gentle halt and dismounted, patting the great beast upon the neck and staring into the expressionless brown eyes. "Well, old friend, where away shall we head?" he asked rhetorically. Farregas looked as if he was considering the question for a few seconds before his head dropped and he began to chew at a patch of dry grass. Galahad chuckled and left him to it, striding to a grassy knoll, scanning the horizon intently, hoping for some sort of sign, an omen with which to justify whichever direction he and his steed chose to travel in. None was forthcoming. With a sigh, he returned to his horse's side. He adjusted the saddle and rummaged in his bags whilst his mind pondered the question of where their next destination would be.

He had fulfilled his need for freedom from the cloying suffocation he endured at Camelot and had done his duty to Lady Guinevere by informing her of her ex-husband's demise, but beyond the task of imparting the tragic tidings to Guinevere, he had thought little of what he would do after the deed was done.

Though he had absented himself from Camelot for well over a month now, he certainly had no wish to go back there. He did not even know if he would ever feel the pang of homesickness and return there. A timely gust of wind caused him to shudder and he decided that it was more pressing for him to decide where he did want to go rather than where he did not.

He was in the process of remounting Farregas when the beast looked up with a questioning whinny. The knight's head whipped round and he immediately saw six soldiers rocketing forth from the distant castle.

Instinct took over and Galahad leapt onto his mount. His heels jabbed into Farregas' flanks and the grey Destrier was off, his long, galloping gait eating up the ground beneath him. As his steed settled into its stride, Sir Galahad chanced a fleeting look over his shoulder. The warriors which were bearing down upon him wore the blue and gold tabards of Sir Lancelot, an insignia which he had become heartily sick of in the last few days. Knowing now that his show of bravado as he left Du Lac's dwelling had been misjudged at best, he turned to the vista before him, hunting for the right course to take in order to successfully flee his unwanted followers.

Farregas' swift progress had taken him over the crests of the dunes immediately in front of him and he was heartened to see that the sands were not as extensive as he had first thought. The land dropped away steeply down a rocky slope into multiple stands of trees which would afford one as experienced as Galahad in the art of conflict ample opportunity to evade his pursuers.

Attempting to put all thoughts of the chase from his mind, he concentrated his efforts on navigating Farregas down the treacherous slope. Though it was well within the horse's capabilities to negotiate the incline, the knight was aware that one false move could result in all sorts of problems for him and his beast, so he took his time as he had no wish to end up bloodied and broken in the jagged scree that had accumulated over the years at the base of the slope.

He was two-thirds of the way down when the first arrow deflected off the stones within feet of where he rode, sending up a puff of dust before it ricocheted away.

Galahad cursed inwardly, hunched over Farregas' neck and began to hiss urgent commands into his horse's ear. In response, his mount sped up, less intent now on picking his way down than on surviving the descent without being wounded.

The knight's eyes flared as he felt Farregas' back legs begin to slide out of control. He jerked on the reins to try and halt the unwanted momentum, but as he did so, he felt the breeze of another projectile whistle past his ear and in unconscious panic, yanked them too hard.

The horse reared, balancing on back legs that were already sweeping out from underneath him. The world spun as Galahad was thrown to the ground. The wind was punched from his lungs and he lay helpless, bracing himself for the crushing weight of his mount to fall upon him. Miraculously, Farregas seemed to dance to the side before he fell in sickening slow-motion. Galahad watched as the steed that had borne him for a decade or more collapsed onto the jagged stones, whinnying in fear and terror. Gaining his feet, the knight from Camelot made a grab for the reins just as a heart-rending shriek invaded his ears. His gorge rose as he looked to his horse's face. The shaft of an arrow protruded from Farregas' eye. Galahad watched in catatonic horror as a thin trickle of blood slid in an obscene stream from the wound into one of the stricken beast's nostrils.

A stinging sensation wrenched him from his contemplation of the fallen horse and he found himself staring at the tri-coloured fletching of an arrow that had sliced across the flesh of his thigh but, mercifully, had not pierced any deeper. As it hung uselessly from the material of his britches, he reached down and tore it free with an atavistic howl. Without thinking, he began to run back up the slope, his face set in a fearsome grimace of hatred.

After seeing Galahad thrown, the warriors had begun advancing slowly down the slope towards him. They were caught totally unprepared by his sudden change of direction. As with Farregas mere seconds ago, the riders' uncertainty communicated itself to the horses and they began to fight against the commands being given to them.

One of the soldiers had already been catapulted out of his saddle to land with a nauseating crack on the stones of the hillside. Galahad ignored the injured man's screams as he closed on the remaining hunters.

The other five quickly discovered that trying to aim bows whilst wrestling with unsettled horses required more dexterity than they possessed and found themselves faced with a dilemma which was becoming more desperate with every passing second.

The next few minutes passed for Galahad as if he was in a dream. He felt as if a part of him, his dispassionate rational self, was floating over proceedings below, watching as the five who pursued him dithered over whether to dismount and face their approaching nemesis or stay atop their steeds and regroup at the edge of the valley. Watching as their indecision cost them their lives. Watching as he fell upon them like he was possessed by a demon which gorged on mayhem and blood. Whitecleave's sweeps were so fluid and well-balanced that the blade seemed to be an extension of the knight's arm, perfectly in tune with his body as it tore through flesh and bone. The first to engage with the marauding berserker was rendered headless within seconds. He was swiftly followed by another warrior, dispatched after a balletic leap from Galahad which dodged the man's own blade and left him defenceless against an unstoppable backward thrust.

The knight from Camelot continued his remorseless attack, fuelled as it was from a bottomless pit of adrenaline consisting of frustration and grief. The third warrior had his nose splattered across his face by Galahad's buckler as he punched it forward into the man's face. As his hands flew to his ruined features in blind agony at the injury, the knight from Camelot ran him through.

An unexpected concussion forced Galahad back a pace or two, but it was a momentary distraction as the two remaining able-bodied attackers opted for flight rather than fight. The decision made, they desperately rode for the sanctuary of the open ground at the summit of the headland. However, the uneven terrain of the slope meant that their escape was by no means as assured as it would have been in most environments, so a painfully disjointed and scrambling race began with all the participants slithering and scrabbling for purchase on the ever shifting ground.

The rage which had propelled Galahad through the quintet with such explosive efficiency was beginning to fade and his progress was starting to become laboured. This was balanced out by the panic of his assailants' horses as the whiff of blood assailed their nostrils and a primal, bestial fear began to claim them. They danced and slid as they made their gradual way back up the slope, responding as best they could to the frantic pleas of their riders.

With his sanity beginning to reassert itself, the red mist began to lessen and Galahad started to examine his predicament with a more considered view. He could see that, even though the horses were struggling to climb the slope, they would gain even ground before he could stop them and then he would be an easy target for their arrows.

Without slowing his progress, Galahad sheathed Whitecleave and stooped to the right, casting his eyes about for a large stone to hurl at the retreating backs of the two soldiers. His hand closed about a sharp, flat piece of rock and he brought it up. Trusting his instincts, he sped up and flicked the missile out without aiming, then ducked almost instantaneously to pick up another projectile before the first had found a target. In this manner he continued to run after the cavalrymen who fled before him.

The first stone had flown wide of the pair. The second one bisected the space between the two almost perfectly. However, the third one flew straight and true, catching one of the riders just behind the ear. He flopped to the left and his mount continued on for a few steps before he fell from the saddle. He hit the ground hard but with one foot still caught in the stirrups. This meant he was dragged underneath the horse, tripping the animal and causing it to tumble on top of him. If the impact of the stone had not killed him, then the crushing weight of the horse surely would.

With a grim set to his features, Galahad continued his onslaught towards the one remaining enemy rider. He was dimly aware of a growing bloom of pain in his side and upon examination, found himself staring down at an arrow protruding from his tunic and a slowly growing pool of scarlet tackiness that stained his clothing and leggings.

Shaking this off, his eyes flared as he saw that the final rider had breasted the summit and had climbed down from his horse, confident in his skill with bow and arrow. Galahad was within twenty yards of the man and was, for the briefest of seconds, lost in indecision. His adversary was moments away from letting loose his first shot and Galahad took the time to stare about the scene. Four bodies lay in various states of repose, sleeping a sleep from which they would never waken, whilst their horses milled about uncertainly, eyes rolling and wild, ears flat to their heads, terror leaving them on the brink of bolting, battle-honed discipline preventing them from doing so. The combatant who had first been thrown had ceased his screaming but was rendered immobile by his injury. Galahad quickly noted that his bow had been thrown clear and he was incapable of retrieving it so he dismissed the wounded man as no threat and turned back to the bowman on the brow of the hill.

The knight's sixth sense for battle situations had allowed him to assess all this in mere seconds and, as the remaining soldier drew a bead on him, he opted for attack, instantly aware that his withdrawing back would present a far greater target than his advancing front, even though it was only afforded minimal shielding by his buckler and his own survival instinct. As well as this, he hoped that the murderous prowess he had shown moments ago would instil a rising sense of panic in the archer and cause him to rush his shot, certain in the knowledge that if he failed to stop the killing machine before him with his arrows, he would follow his fellows on the road to oblivion in the blink of an eye.

The first arrow sang through the air, only to be batted aside by Galahad's shield.

The second flew forward at a lower trajectory, punching home in the knight's right shin, causing him to stumble and nearly lose his footing on the shale.

The third missed Galahad by pure luck. He had planted his foot down but the pain of his wound had caused his leg to buckle, sending him sprawling to the jagged ground, which, though it was horrendously painful and evoked a shriek of agony, actually saved his life, for the arrow was making a beeline straight for the knight's forehead.

Now it was the bowman's turn for hesitancy because, in his pride, he had not expected Galahad to make it this far under the hail of arrows he had unleashed. However, he suddenly realised that he was faced with a stark choice. He could either give up trying to kill the knight and gallop back to Joyous Garde, there to face the towering wrath of his ever more unpredictable liege lord or use his final shaft to try and halt the remorseless advance.

With Galahad mere feet from him now, both attacker and attacked knew that the bowman had mere seconds to make the most important decision of his life.

As the archer stared at his target, looming ever closer, he licked his lips and saw no mercy in the inhuman warrior before him. And so, locked in an agony of vacillation, the pressure of the moment cost him both the opportunity and his life. Too late, he opted to stand his ground but, in his haste, he set the arrow incorrectly upon the string so, when he let fly, the hemp snapped against his wrist and the arrow cart-wheeled off to the left, yards wide of its intended target.

Whimpering with pain, the archer threw the now useless bow at the oncoming knight and drew his sword.

Galahad swatted the weapon aside as if it was nothing more than a bothersome insect and continued his remorseless advance, the pain of his injuries set aside as he finished off his bloody work.

The man, not much more than a teenager in fact, dropped to his knees, whimpering, "Please, no…"

Without a word or change of expression, Galahad separated his head from his shoulders.

A part of him, the holy warrior of God who prayed twice daily to his Lord, who had held the Cup of Christ to his breast as he delivered it into the hands of the Round Table Knights and had slain numerous enemies all in the name of his faith, was appalled beyond measure by the casual slaughter of these men who, when all was said and done, had only been following their master's orders but the other part of him, the angst-ridden, tormented knight of recent months revelled in the catharsis of killing, rejoiced in the simplistic choice of kill or be killed, celebrated in the triumph of victory, no matter what the cost had been to his soul.

A noise jerked him from his bifurcated thoughts and he turned quickly, Whitecleave still blood-soaked and sodden in his grip.

The surviving soldier had vomited onto the rocky ground and was sitting awkwardly, propped up on a makeshift pile of rocks, shaking violently in shock at both his injuries and the ease with which his comrades had been sent to their deaths.

His breath came in short, sharp gasps as the grimacing vengeful killer began to stalk towards him. He saw no point in pleading for clemency. He could see no quarter would be given and licked lips that were suddenly as dry as a desert, trying to prepare himself for death in as dignified manner as possible, but unable to stay the fear which erupted from his innards like a volcano.

In silence, Galahad stalked towards the whimpering man, watching dispassionately as the man evacuated his stomach once again. The knight was spattered with blood from head to foot and his weapon was still dripping crimson fluid onto the stony floor. The two arrows which had found their target jerked erratically as he approached and he shut out the pain with a will of iron. His mind was awhirl with conflicting emotions, anger at Lancelot for his gutless behaviour and for hiding behind his soldiers when he should have been man enough to challenge Galahad himself, shame at the exhilaration he had felt at the moment of victory over the hapless guardsmen, helplessness at the downward path that his life seemed to be taking, hopelessness at ever leaving the bloodshed that had tainted his life behind, confusion as the face of the incapacitated soldier metamorphosed into the reproachful features of King Arthur's...*he blinked furiously*...Merlin's pompous smirk stared back at him...*what is happening*...Mordred, the bastard nephew who tried to usurp Arthur's throne at Camelot sneered at the knight, his rat-like face wrinkling distastefully...*what is happening to me*...other faces from both Galahad's recent and distant past seemed to appear before him in a visual cacophony of memories, each perfectly fitting the pallid face of the fallen warrior, there was Lady Joanna Dubin, Sir Bors from the Round Table, Guinevere as she was when still wed to King Arthur, then, as she was now, anguished and pale, wracked with pain. He staggered, dropping Whitecleave to his side as the remaining strength fled his arms. He was left kneeling awkwardly, head down, staring uncomprehendingly at the widening pool of blood that crept revoltingly across the rocks. With a huge effort, he lifted his head, gasping as he found the lead knight from the Dolorous Guard smirking his hideous grin at him. Unconsciousness rose up like water from a geyser and he fell prostrate, instinct causing him to twist his body at the last moment so as not to push the arrow that spiked from his side further into flesh. The very end of the fletching still caught a jag of rock however and Galahad's scream echoed over the stones and took flight into the gathering clouds overhead. His head lolled to the side and his gaze ended up resting on the dying knight from Joyous Garde who had, by then, transformed back into the man who had plummeted from his horse when Galahad had made his surprise attacking move.

As their gazes locked, a moment of sparkling clarity passed between them and they exchanged mutual nods. Galahad passed out.

The fallen warrior called out to his attacker, wanting to speak to someone, wanting some distraction from the numbness that crept inexorably up his lower body but Galahad would not be roused. Moments passed and the warrior from Joyous Garde began shuddering violently in shock. A crow perched itself within feet of the man and cawed raucously in his ear, perhaps advising his fellows that a feast was but moments away.

The warrior grabbed a stone and pitched it at the black harbinger. The throw was weak and the bird barely moved to avoid it, all the while keeping its beady eyes fixed on the large, animate lump of carrion that promised ample pickings very soon.

The knight howled as the white-hot agony tore up his leg, the anguished screech yanking Galahad back into wakefulness. Unbeknownst to the both of them, the movement required to grasp the stone had caused a razor-sharp shard of bone to come away at the point of breakage and pierce the femoral artery. Blood started to spurt in great gouts from the man's leg and he knew death was mere moments away. Galahad fought in vain against the disorientation that assailed him but, try though he might, he could not move from his supine position and could only watch as the man's screams petered out in volume and his lifeblood ejaculated itself onto the stones. With a final rasping sigh, the man died.

The crow, which had now been joined by two of its feathered companions, regarded him for a few moments, gingerly walking closer and closer to the corpse until it finally plucked up the courage to nip and peck at him.

Galahad shouted to scare the avian parasites away, but it was an incoherent, slurred warning and only succeeded in drawing off one of the trio, which now began to make its inelegant way over towards him.

Angrily regretting his seemingly cursed run of luck, Galahad briefly reflected that he really must stop losing consciousness when faced with mortal danger. With that bitterly ironic thought caroming around his skull, darkness engulfed him and he passed once more into the realm of dreams, unsure whether he would ever return to the world of waking.

When Galahad awoke, he found himself squinting into the dancing flames of a fire that crackled and hissed in its hearth. A raging headache announced itself to him with a rampant tattoo which battered at his temples, eliciting a low growl of pain.

"So you have awakened then?"

The question came from over his shoulder and, without thinking, he attempted to raise himself up on his elbows and jerk his head round to see its originator. The weakness caused by his injuries defeated even this simple task and he slumped back onto the cushions with a resigned sigh. Shutting his eyes against the stars that swirled and skipped across his vision, he heard soft footsteps behind him and tentatively opened his eyes as they came to a halt before him.

"My apologies, good sir." The silhouette in front of the flames dropped down to his haunches so that his guest could better apprehend him. "How are you feeling?"

Blonde hair hung to the man's shoulders framing a face that was open and friendly. A dusting of stubble surrounded a mouth which looked ready-made for smiling and the blue eyes held the sparkle of one who viewed life with the emphasis very much on the positive. The one incongruity in the man's otherwise sunny visage was a grossly malformed nose which squatted in the middle of his face like a boulder in the middle of an ornamental garden.

The man laughed and unselfconsciously stroked the warped appendage in response to Galahad's gaze. "The result of a misspent youth, I am afraid."

Galahad stared dubiously at his apparent rescuer. The man looked barely older than the knight himself. "Though you undoubtedly brought out the caring side in me when I found you lying down on the rocks, I was not always so solicitous to strangers. This," he explained, pointing to his nose, "was the result of a disagreement between me and another drinker at the Castle Tavern in town. I was well in my cups and took it upon myself to announce that I was the most accomplished fist-fighter in Bamburgh and I would take on all-comers." He adopted the classic fighter's pose and did a dainty shuffle to demonstrate his footwork skills. "The other fellow disagreed. Took me down with his first punch." The man stopped his frenzied dance and regarded Galahad mischievously, "Proved my point though. Never has a fall into unconsciousness been so accomplished and pleasing to the eye." He let forth a booming laugh and extended his hand. "I am Marcus and this is my humble abode." He swept his arm expansively around the room. "It's not much but it keeps the rain from my head and the wolf from my door. Broth?"

The knight nodded. His head was starting to clear and his appetite had begun to attack his stomach with a vengeance. Despite the travails of recent weeks, Galahad could not help but smile crookedly at his host, finding the man's enthusiasm for life surprisingly infectious. He cast an eye about the room in which they dwelt. Now his eyes had adjusted to the fire he espied a cauldron suspended above it, from which issued a juicy bubbling noise and a mouth-moistening aroma. From there he took in the walls, which were pine logs expertly lashed together, the crudely fashioned window-holes covered with the stretched skin of some poor unfortunate beast, a deer he guessed. It was not much but, after the attack on the hill, it seemed like the most luxurious mansion imaginable to Galahad.

The only other section of the house was separated from the main room by a ragged curtain that moved slightly due to an unseen draught.

Marcus handed his visitor a bowl of thick, steaming broth. "Have a care, it is still piping hot," he warned.

The much-abused warrior from Camelot stared longingly at the bubbling mish-mash of vegetables and meat, blowing on it periodically to try and hasten the moment at which it would become edible.

"Sir, please accept my apologies for my rudeness. You have taken me into your home and now fed me, yet I have not even given you my name. My name is Sir Galahad of Camelot and I am forever in your debt." The knight blinked in surprise at his own candour.

Marcus studied the man before him closely, reacting to the sudden hooding of Galahad's eyes after he had given his name and, for the first time since Galahad's return to consciousness, losing the omnipresent grin. "You need not fear honesty in this house, Sir Galahad. You can be as open or as guarded as you wish, it matters not to me. I will extend the same hospitality to you as I would my own brother. All I will ask is that you conduct yourself as you would in your own house, although, as a former denizen of the well-famed Camelot, I suspect you may find the habitation uncomfortable at best."

Galahad nodded acknowledgement at his host's frankness. "Believe me, Marcus, it is a thousand times more comfortable than the coldness of the shale on that hillside." He shook his head and fixed Marcus with a pointed stare. "I must apologise once again. There have not been many new people in my life recently who have not wished me ill so your kind-heartedness is rather a novelty."

The big booming laugh broke through the atmosphere like a refreshing wind blowing away a fog. "Most eloquently put, good Sir Knight. From the predicament I found you in, I am guessing that one of those people is the Lord High Muck-a-muck at the castle."

An ironic smirk flashed across Galahad's face momentarily. "I doubt if I would be top of the list of people he would choose to break bread with. I took it upon myself to bring him tidings which did not prove welcome in his court."

Marcus nodded slowly. "It must have been a highly controversial piece of news for him to seek your death?"

Again, Galahad found himself divulging events in far greater detail than he normally would have done, a fact that, on an unconscious level, the usually guarded knight felt he should be concerned about, but he was finding Marcus' company so agreeable that he could not bring himself to be overly worried about it.

During Galahad's discourse of events, Marcus had pulled up a chair and seated himself opposite his suddenly verbose guest. He leant back on it and let forth a grunt of understanding. "It seems that your association with King Arthur before his death was of great profit to you, but since he fell at Camlann, he has been the bane of your existence."

The former champion of Camelot frowned at that. Objectively, he could see Marcus' point, but to have it put in so forthright a manner did not sit comfortably with him. He had never been able to see beyond his own feelings of guilt at the King's death but Marcus' brusque summary of his current situation seemed to bring a new lucidity to his feelings. Before, he had felt that to blame anyone else for his misfortune, especially the King, would be nothing more than a feeble attempt to assuage his conscience by false means but now, whereas Lady Joanna had been nothing more than a shoulder to cry on, Marcus had verbally challenged his self-pitying words with insightful questions and caused him to study events afresh.

Pondering this, Galahad finished his broth and, feeling reinvigorated by its wholesome contents, started to get up, looking for a place to clean his bowl.

Swiftly, Marcus jumped from his chair to relieve him of the soiled earthenware. Walking over to a bucket of water that stood within the penumbra of heat emanating from the fire, he plunged the wooden basin into it and began worrying at it with his fingers. As he cleaned the utensils, he said, "I hope you do not think me presumptuous, picking apart your mindset like this. In my experience, I find that men such as yourself, who set themselves up as paragons of virtue and warriors of justice, often seek to shoulder burdens which are not theirs to carry when the outcome of events is not what they wish it to be." He finished scrubbing the bowls and placed them in an uneven pile in the corner of the house. Turning back to his guest with a sombre look on his face, he re-seated himself in his chair with a tired sigh.

Sir Galahad sat up straighter, wincing slightly at the pain, but gritting his teeth until it slowly dissipated. "If you'll pardon me saying, Marcus, I could say that you have the same air about you."

For the first time during their brief acquaintance, the knight from Camelot felt that his new-found associate's expression became cautious and he was being less than candid with him.

For a long moment, Marcus held Galahad's gaze in silence, then nodded. "Perceptive of you, Galahad," he murmured.

To avoid any possible animosity, Galahad immediately held up his hands. "Please, Marcus, your treatment of me has gone far and above any reasonable measure and I would certainly not wish to put your nose out of joint by prying into your private business."

Almost as soon as he said it he grimaced inwardly at his faux-pas, for Marcus' hand had immediately flown to his ruined nose and his eyes had flared.

"I...I'm sorry, I..." Galahad babbled, as Marcus jumped up from the chair and stood facing the fire, arms folded and head bowed.

The knight's cheeks flamed with embarrassment. He swung his legs off the pallet and walked painfully over to his host, laying a sympathetic hand on the man's shaking shoulder.

With a suddenness that caused Galahad to jump back and up-end a rickety table, Marcus snorted out a hearty guffaw. "I'm sorry. The look on your face was a pleasure to behold." Marcus ceased his hilarity and tried to assume a look of seriousness, but it dissolved instantly when he saw the mixture of anger and humiliation on the knight's face. Though he still chuckled expansively, it was now Marcus' turn to hold his hands up in apology. "You will have to forgive me. I find humour in the strangest places. I do not seek to poke fun at you, it is merely my way. Please...." He gestured at the pallet, indicating that Galahad should resume his seat.

With his irritation still bubbling under the surface, Galahad did as he was bid.

Marcus also retook his chair, mirth still alive in his eyes. "As I said, you are an observant man. There are not many people who, having been through such torment, would still have the empathy to recognise the same pain in others. I have found that the majority of men, when faced with great anguish, will seek to make out that they are the only ones who are capable of suffering in such an exquisite way and, as such, will shut themselves off from others, rendering themselves selfish, distant and incapable of help." His gaze grew in intensity and he leant forward to the point of nearly touching his guest's nose with his own, the flickering flames lending him an almost infernal appearance. "I know this because I used to be in that majority." For a moment his head dropped, as if the weight of the words which he was about to speak was dragging it down, then he began to talk slowly and carefully, as if the memories he was sharing were being resurrected from the deepest of burials. "I used to live in the environs of Bamburgh," he began, staring at his hands, "a tanner by trade, I was. Well renowned too. I used to command the business of whomsoever resided at the castle, both Copper Knight and Sir Lancelot after him. I was happy, in my way, trade was good. I did not want for anything, well, save someone to keep me warm on the cold Northumbrian nights." He laughed bitterly.

Galahad watched in silence, intrigued by the complete change of demeanour in his host.

"I found that though, oh how I found that," Marcus continued. "Damn me, talking about it again makes it seem like only yesterday but it must be fully three years ago now. I can still see..." his voice trailed off, only to return more forcefully than before, "she was stunning. At the time, I counted myself an articulate man but she reduced me to a dribbling child unable to string two words together. I swear, Galahad, I can see her, as clear as I can see you now, I can see her walking into the tannery, so proud, so wondrous, so beautiful. Yet there was no disdain for the stench of the hides or indeed myself. She simply came over to me to place her order and melted me with her dazzling smile. I very nearly sliced off my fingers scraping clear the hair from the hide as I watched her disappear from the shop. She must have known, must have seen the effect she had on me, for as she left, she bestowed another smile upon me with the added spice of a wink. I threw the stinking skin to the floor and ran after her like a besotted youth in the first flush of spring. I mean, I was young then, but I wasn't inexperienced in the ways of the world. Just one glimpse of her though, that was enough to reduce me to a graceless idiot. Anyway, I ran out into the road but there was no sign of her. It sounds insane but my heart ached when I saw she was not there, even though I had been in the company of this woman for little more than a minute, I was bereft that she had gone."

With a shrug, Marcus continued, the dam of remembrance opened, the torrent of words tumbling from him unabashed. "So I sought her out. I tried to calm myself, to return to my craft, but I did not work any more that day, or indeed the day after that. I trawled the town for news of her, I must have walked every inch of Bamburgh, visited every home, every shop, every tavern for the slightest news of her. No-one knew her. I was beside myself, tortured beyond endurance by my inability to see her again. After nearly a week's fruitless searching, I had retired to the Castle Tavern to drown my sorrows. When it finally closed, I began to weave my way home. Then I saw her on the outskirts of town, walking across the dunes. I ran to her, crying with elation and joy. When I caught up with her, I got down on bended knee and proclaimed my love for her, shouting it across the sand and the waves. We made love then and it was so pure, so...so right. It was without a doubt the most precious moment of my life. We lay there for I don't know how long, together in the sand, revelling in each other, drinking in the wonder of the turn that both our lives had taken. When the tide began to come in, I swept her up in my arms and carried her here and we fell asleep in each other's embrace."

Galahad's breath came in short gasps. The intensity of Marcus' recitation of the tale had been so passionate that he had been holding his breath in anticipation of the denouement. Though he had never felt the white-hot, wrenching emotion of such love, the ferocity with which Marcus spoke of his lost sweetheart was sufficient to give him more than enough of an inkling as to the sort of fervour that such feelings could provoke. He whispered hoarsely, almost unwilling to break the spell woven by Marcus' florid words. "What happened?"

Marcus held his gaze then and the agony in his eyes was the same as Arthur's when he learnt of Guinevere's infidelity, the same as Romney's when he spoke of his Rosa in the arms of another. "I awoke the next morning. I awoke in my bed and she was gone, the curve of her body was still imprinted on the blankets, the smell of her hair was still present on the pillows, but there was no sign of her." Tears ran unashamedly down his cheeks. "That one night, just that one night is all I have of her and it haunts me, Galahad. It tortures me to the bottom of my soul that I will never feel her caress again, never hold her in my arms again, never see her again." With that final pronouncement said in a jumble of garbled sobbing, Marcus leapt from his chair, knocking it to the floor. He ran from the room, out into the cold night.

Galahad gathered the coarse blankets about him against the sudden blast of cold air caused by Marcus' rapid exit and stared in embarrassment around the room. It was as if a switch had been flipped inside his host, for the man had gone from a carefree confidante to a tortured melancholic within the time it had taken to recount the story of his lost love.

The force of Marcus' departure caused the door to rebound off the wall and close itself again, leaving the room silent save for the popping and crackling of the fire. Galahad pushed back the warming covers and pushed himself painfully to his feet. At a snail's pace, he traversed the room, acutely aware of the raging throb in his lower leg and the slightly duller ache in his side. He pulled back the hide from the window and peered outside to see if Marcus was still within sight. His eyes took a few moments to adjust to the murk, though whether it was dawn or dusk he did not know.

Galahad had no memory of his journey to Marcus' home so, when he failed to spot the distraught man immediately, rather than actively seeking him out, he took the chance to survey his place of refuge.

From what he could see, the house stood in a clearing surrounded by huge, forbidding pines that provided a modicum of protection from the harsher aspects of the Northumbrian climate. Galahad watched breathlessly as, on a path which had been cleared through the trees, a proud stag strutted, stopping momentarily as the mournful sound of an owl echoed hauntingly through the silence of the night.

The man from Camelot found himself revelling in the peace that seemed to exude from the glade and simply stood at the window, staring at the soothing rhythm of nature and drinking in the tranquillity.

With a suddenness that made Galahad jump and sent a rasping streak of pain along his side, the beautiful beast bolted down the path, its grace of movement all the more astounding due to its powerful build.

Marcus emerged from the trees on the other side of the path from where the male deer had disappeared. Where he had been Galahad could only guess, but wherever it was seemed to have restored him to a semblance of his former ebullient self. As he strode onto the path that led into the house, a spring seemed to reappear in his step.

As the knight transferred his gaze to the door, it flew open and Marcus burst through it with a grin on his face which seemed to suggest that everything was right with the world. As Galahad marvelled at the second transformation of his host in a matter of minutes, he noticed the slightest suggestion of puffiness around his eyes, the only indication of the emotional wreck which Marcus had been not long ago.

Unsure of what to do, Galahad maintained his position near the window and waited for Marcus to initiate the conversation.

Marcus stopped in his tracks when he saw the knight standing by the open gap in the wall. The smile stayed in place but uneasiness flickered about his eyes. "Up and about, I see. That's good." He said slowly.

The knight hesitated, then plunged on, encouraged by the openness that Marcus had said was part and parcel of life in his household. "I was...concerned when you left in the manner you did. Being only a visitor in your home, I was at a loss as to what to do. I thought to look for you to try and offer some sort of comfort in the same way that you have to me."

Marcus nodded his appreciation of that. "That is good to know. I had an inkling that you were a good man despite the circumstances in which I found you," he breathed heavily, "I am glad my instincts were correct. However, you have no need to worry on my account. It is the anniversary of that night in a couple of days and I am always beset by these irrational outbursts at this time of year."

Galahad shrugged. "Who is to say what is irrational? To have lost something so precious to you after such a short period of time would leave most men angry and hollow inside."

"Thank you for your understanding." Marcus went over to the ragged curtain that separated his room from the rest of the house. "Now, if you will excuse me, I will bid you good night. These…episodes tend to leave me quite drained." Without further word, he departed behind the curtain and left his guest standing alone.

A fleeting thought came to the knight that he could go outside and enjoy the seclusion but it was swiftly followed by a gnawing pain in his shin caused, Galahad supposed, by being on his feet more in the last few moments than he had since his encounter with Lancelot's soldiers. With a resigned grunt, he returned to the pallet upon which he had recuperated and settled himself down to a mercifully dreamless sleep.

Chapter 5

The next few weeks were ones of unsophisticated bliss for the knight. Used as he was to the luxury of existence at the castle of Camelot, he found an unexpected pleasure in the simple life of the woodsman and the days soon settled into a routine of sorts.

From one of the other windows, Galahad had discovered that the cottage was slightly more open than he had first thought and the view through the sparse trees stretched for miles over beauteous countryside.

As the first tinges of dawn began to colour the sky they would both arise, whereupon Marcus would prepare breakfast, usually of porridge or toasted bread. They would then set about the tasks of the day. At first, Galahad could do little as he was still laid low by his injuries, but gradually, despite Marcus' protestations that he should recover fully before contributing to the household duties, the knight began to rebuild his strength.

It was not long before the hut which housed the wood for the fire was stocked to the gunwales and the wheat straw thatch upon the roof repaired where the weather had caused damage. Galahad found that the uncomplicated chores allowed his mind time to view recent events without the hot passion that the initial emotional fallout had infused them with.

Marcus and he would talk long into the night, Galahad about life in Camelot, especially the exploits of the Round Table Knights. Naturally, Marcus pressed him on the Holy Grail and all its wonders but Galahad was reluctant to speak of it and only gave a very broad and sketchy account of his association with this holiest of vessels. Given his initial speech with regards to the openness or otherwise of the household, Marcus acknowledged Galahad's reticence and did not press the point.

The knight found Marcus' life story far more intriguing, as it opened a whole new area of existence to him. He found himself feeling vaguely uncomfortable that he had never really taken much interest in the various tradesmen and craftsmen who had worked within the walls of Camelot. Save for the armourers and squires whom his life had depended upon when in battle and who kept Farregas in such fine condition, the other denizens of the castle had been mere shadows in his consciousness. When he tried to recall the men and women who had attended him during the near decade he had spent at King Arthur's castle, he found himself confronted by a succession of nameless, faceless silhouettes, men and women who, he supposed, were little different from the former tanner who sat in front of him, staring into the fire, recounting his life story to a man whom, under normal circumstances, would probably not have bothered to pass the time of day with him.

The past few months aside, by no stretch of the imagination could Sir Galahad's life have been described as anything approaching a struggle and therefore he had never really given any thought to the travails of everyday folk, how their very existence often hung on the whim of the landowner upon whose domain they were forced to live. As Marcus' narrative wound on, the discomfort he felt at his lack of interest in his fellow castle-dwellers transformed into a surprisingly acute sense of shame.

When he heard of the life that Marcus had led and the matter-of-fact way he described the everyday deprivation and squalor that was endured by the majority of the Kingdom's populace, he felt hugely ill at ease.

If Marcus noted his visitor's discomfort then he did not show it. He was too immersed in the tide of nostalgia that the recounting of his life story had evoked.

In actual fact, unbeknownst to the knight from Camelot, Marcus' existence had not been as disadvantaged as most. He had resided in Bamburgh all his life. His mother was a maid in the castle when the Copper Knight first came to the town and she had brought him up until her untimely death when he was a mere stripling of seven years. The identity of his father was unknown to him. Being an orphan, he would normally have been thrown out of the castle to fend for himself. However, fortunately for him, one of the saddlers in the stables housed next to the castle had recently lost a son to influenza and saw in Marcus a surrogate child with which to try and ease the pain of his grief.

For his part, Marcus seized the opportunity with both hands, the unknown need for a father figure blossoming under the kindly gaze of his adopted family. Even at that early age, he had been eager to pay back the faith that the saddler, Daniel by name, had shown in him. To that end, he put himself forward for any and every job which Daniel required doing, even to the point where Daniel was inventing tasks for him to undertake, simply to get him out from under foot. Marcus did not see it like that of course. He was too busy revelling in all the attention he was receiving, for, whilst he had loved his mother, she had never been the most caring of women. On the other hand, Daniel and his wife, Annalese, were not ones to stint on the affection that they lavished upon their substitute son.

It was through one of the regular tasks which Daniel gave the boy that he came into contact with the tannery situated on the edge of the town. Though most people steered clear of the odiferous sheds that housed Bamburgh's tanneries, Marcus found them a whole different world compared to the cleanliness and sometimes stifling atmosphere of the castle. He was after all only a young boy and, like most young boys, was not the least bit phased by being caked in mud and filth. He soon began finding excuses to go there, not least because he earned himself a few precious pennies for gathering dung or collecting the piss-pots which sat on the street corners. Once at the tannery, he found himself glorying in the pungent smells, the freedom of not being supervised and enjoying the gruff, brusque manner of the tanners, finding it wholly refreshing compared to the strangled, careful tones of those in the castle.

He was too young to realise that the difficult, stilted ambience which he experienced within the walls of Bamburgh Castle was due to the all-encompassing trepidation that surrounded the Copper Knight and his Dolorous Guard and not, as he saw it, adults trying to stifle the adventures and escapades of a young lad.

As he grew older and the tanners became more and more accustomed to his presence, they began to properly introduce him to the trade, discussing among themselves the boy's potential as an apprentice.

Then disaster befell his father, as he had come to consider Daniel. Annalese, his wife of fourteen years, walked out, having been seduced by one of the travelling players who had attended the Copper Knight's fortieth birthday celebrations.

It ripped the heart from Daniel and he died within the year, a hollow husk of the man he once was. So wrapped up in his own misery was he that his relationship with Marcus faltered and, to all intents and purposes, disappeared from Marcus' life, leaving the orphaned teenager once more bereft of parental guidance and love.

To mask the hurt and abandonment that he felt, Marcus threw himself into his duties at the tannery, working long into the night, hours after the other tanners had taken to their beds. As he had shown previously when life had contrived to bring him low, he was nothing if not a fighter and he thought nothing of working from dawn till dusk, soaking the untreated skins in water to soften them or scraping the urine-soaked hides free of hair. He was quite often to be found, knee-deep in a large vat of water mixed with dung, patiently kneading the hides into suppleness with his bare feet. As this task could last for anything up to three hours and the various other jobs were very physical in nature, he soon began to bulk up, his physique transforming from callow youth to well-muscled man in the space of months.

This brought him to the attention of the women of Bamburgh, both married and unmarried. He was surprised to find that the low standing of his profession in the general scheme of things was overcome by his good looks and he soon found his company in demand with the womenfolk of the town.

However, the behaviour of his adopted mother led him to spurn most of the advances that he received, especially from the married women. Some of the more persistent females did manage to breach his defences however and he soon became renowned in the town for his prowess.

As the tanners were unused to vying for the attentions of women, being in a trade which rather left them at a disadvantage with the opposite sex, they paid little heed to any goings-on of that nature as long as it did not affect their apprentice's work ethic.

And it did not. The tannery at Bamburgh soon gleaned a reputation for itself which stretched well beyond the narrow confines of the Northumbrian settlement and soon demand began to come from as far afield as Gateshead to the south. Marcus did not deal with the large, bulk orders but, if the landowners and liege lords had sons who required any speciality hides with a bit of individuality, as he was the youngest member of the tannery, they found themselves automatically gravitating to him.

Marcus soon became a man of means with the added income of all the speciality hides which he was asked to produce, but he began to find the work tedious and unfulfilling, finding his clients over-demanding and impatient. With the money he had accrued and still being young enough for the brashness of youth to lend him misplaced bravado, he resolved to go to the Copper Knight and pleaded leave to purchase some land from him and build his own home upon it, though he did not know exactly where.

His workmates counselled him against such a course of action but Marcus was beginning to feel out of place in the hustle of the overly busy tannery and yearned to have his own space, because, at this time, not only was he working there but he was also living in one of the outbuildings.

To the surprise of all, given the Copper Knight's reputation, the request was granted with raised eyebrows being the order of the day.

For the next few days, Marcus looked around the town for a suitable location for his home, but everywhere he went, he found himself besieged by amorous women or customers agitating for their goods to be completed. Thoroughly disenchanted with this, he took himself off for a week into the surrounding countryside, striking out across the dunes and disappearing into the widespread woodland which stood within a day's ride of the settlement. It was during the fourth day of his sojourn that he came upon the home where he and Galahad now sat, emerging breathless through the trees and gazing upon the wondrous vista of the Northumbrian hills.

Finishing off any outstanding business that he had with the local landowners, he retired to the woods, camping under the summer stars whilst, over the course of the next six months, he built the cabin using only the sweat of his back and the materials provided by the woodland around him.

After the complete break from civilisation, he felt re-energised and came back to Bamburgh, there to find the tannery's business faltering. Two of the tanners had died unexpectedly, victims of the ravages of disease which was a fact of life of the times, and the two remaining were starting to feel the depredation of old age and infirmity. He soon got back into the work, but now refused all the specialised items and instead concentrated on restoring the business to its former heights.

The trio were well on the way to doing that, mainly through work commissioned by the new lord of Joyous Garde, when the fateful meeting with the mysterious lady occurred. After the devastation of the woman's desertion of him, he became a recluse, remaining in his cabin, ignoring all pleas to return to his vocation and only venturing into Bamburgh when the need for human contact overrode the need for isolation. However, he now found the busyness of the town unsettling and normally ended up inebriated and incoherent, making his painful, hung-over way back to his lodge the next day, vowing never again to return to the township.

It was nearly a month after one of these ill-advised expeditions that he met a man who changed his outlook on life irrevocably.

By this time, the moon was beaming down upon the cabin and the dawn was mere hours away but, whether it was Marcus' skill as a storyteller or for some other unnamed reason, Galahad was gripped by the tale and urged his host to continue the narrative until its conclusion.

Marcus went on, "The itch to trek into Bamburgh was upon me again and I was preparing to set out when an itinerant appeared at my door. I tried the best I could to divest myself of the beggar's company politely but he would not be shifted. Well, as you can imagine, I was unwilling to leave my home whilst he was in such close attendance so I threatened him, I mean, I was at such a low ebb that I was ready to kill him. I struck out at him but he grabbed my hand and I could not move." He paused momentarily, before continuing, "He fixed me with the most fear-inducing gaze I had ever seen and said in a ringing voice, 'You stand at a crossroads, Marcus. You have taken many steps on the road to purgatory already, perhaps you may even have walked too far upon it to return, that part of your future is closed to me, but my future is not and my destiny is not to die by your hand'. To say I was taken aback would be a gross understatement. I had not told him my name and, as far as I was aware, had never set eyes on him before. And as for his comments about the road to purgatory, well, they meant nothing to me. I mean, I would be the first to admit that my life is by no means whiter than white, but to suggest that my acts had somehow condemned me to the pits of hell…I had no idea what he meant."

Marcus stopped talking and regarded Galahad with an enigmatic eye.

Galahad returned the gaze, trying to interpret it, intrigued by what was being left unsaid, "Can I take it from your expression that that was not the full extent of his words?"

Marcus nodded slightly with a hint of reluctance.

The knight from Camelot leant forward, "What is it, Marcus?"

"He spoke of you, Galahad. He told me of your coming."

The knight's brows knitted in confusion as Marcus began to intone:

'First the Copper, then the White, then the chaste yet troubled Knight
Save him from the blazoned blue and he will do the same for you
Treat him as you would your kin, and he will help atone your sin
Your deed's the harvest that you sow, for reasons you don't even know
The mind wiped clear of conscious guilt, but stained by all the blood that spilt
The Table's loss may mean you're saved, yet also walk you to your grave
Look inside and search down deep, the truth will not remain asleep
But when your act is laid out bare, pray the Flawless Knight is there.'

"What a piece of uninspiring doggerel," Galahad observed. "Do you have any idea what it means?"

"There you have hit the nail on the head, my friend. I have not the slightest idea," Marcus shrugged. "After that little gem of poetry, his look transformed into one of absolute contempt and he walked off without a backward glance, his cracked laughter echoing through the glade. As you can imagine, my appetite for visiting Bamburgh had waned somewhat, so I took myself off through the forest, to try and make some sort of sense of his gibberish." He pointed at Galahad. "And that is when I came upon you, bleeding to death upon the hillside, carnage all about you. If I am honest, I had no interest in becoming involved in whatever the dispute was between you and Sir Lancelot, but with those words still resonating so powerfully through my mind, I could not leave you there. I had to save you else I would have driven myself mad pondering the old man's riddle. So, I chased away the crows, scrofulous bastards that they are, and brought you here."

Not for the first time, Galahad expressed his concern as to whether his biding in Marcus' home would bring about reprisals from Joyous Garde, given the circumstances and the events immediately after his ejection from the castle.

Marcus spread his hands, as he had done when the knight from Camelot had posed the question before. "That is a bridge which we will cross should it confront us," he repeated. "It may be that they do not even know you are here. Perhaps when they came upon the butchery, they assumed that you had taken yourself off somewhere to die or any number of other scenarios, it matters not."

"Why did you not speak of this before, Marcus?" Galahad asked. He felt decidedly uncomfortable that his coming to Marcus' home had been foretold, finding the mystery uncomfortably reminiscent of the complex scheming of Merlin. "When I first awakened, you spoke of honesty and openness being watchwords in your home, yet you have chosen, until now, to keep this from me. I do not seek to sit in judgement, I am just interested as to the reasoning behind your reluctance to divulge this?"

For the first time since Galahad's unceremonious arrival in the man's home, Marcus showed real anger towards him. "I did not take you for a dullard, Galahad. Did you not hear the words I recited? On the one hand, you are supposed to be my saviour yet, on the other, you may be the man who 'walks me to my grave'."

Galahad spread his hands in a conciliatory fashion. "Do not take your confusion out on me, Marcus. I am just as much a pawn in this supposed prediction as you are." He leant forward and placed his elbows on his knees. "However, I ask again, why now? Why are you telling me now?"

Marcus' anger rose further and his cheeks coloured. He looked murderously at Galahad and the knight shifted his weight to fend off an attack but, at the last, Marcus deflated with a huge sigh and slumped down into his seat. "Truth be told, I could not shoulder the burden of it myself anymore. I have been turning it over and over in my mind for too long. I had to tell someone." A quick smile flashed across his face. "And who better to tell than the chaste yet troubled knight?"

Galahad was not convinced, but held his peace. As he did not want to antagonise the man who rescued him from a cold death in the Northumbrian countryside, he changed tack. "Well, as you have unburdened yourself of this, or at least shared it with me, perhaps a fresh analysis of the words from a different viewpoint may shed some light upon the enigma?"

Again, Marcus shrugged, "I have had that infernal verse reverberating around my brain for far longer than I would wish." He looked out of the window at the encroaching night. "You are welcome to try and pick it apart if you wish, but I think it unlikely you will reach any definite conclusion."

Ignoring Marcus' understandable lack of enthusiasm, Galahad began pondering, "Well, the first line is obvious, though I have never heard of Lancelot being called the White."

"That was a monicker that the villagers bestowed upon him when he drove out the Copper Knight. To do with his lustrous blonde locks, I believe," Marcus drawled, ironically stroking at his own mane, which was lank and sweaty from the day's labours.

"Then the second line…"

Marcus held up his hands. "Hold hard there, Galahad. We have not finished examining the first line yet? I guessed from our conversations that you were troubled, but perhaps the reason for your trouble is that you are chaste?"

The knight from Camelot regarded him coolly. "I think not. When I consider the pain and distress which I have witnessed as a direct result of such goings-on, I count myself fortunate that I have avoided such difficulties in my life. So poke fun if you wish, but having seen the agony on your face when you spoke of your vanished sweetheart, well, let us just say I have no wish to experience that."

Marcus had been raring to unleash any amount of mischievous jibes at Galahad's expense, for he found the conscious decision to lead a celibate life profoundly bizarre, yet he bit his tongue, in part due to the absolute solemnity of Galahad's reasoning and also because the fact was that his love's disappearance *did* still roar painfully like an open wound whenever he thought of it.

Galahad stared pointedly at his host, seeing from his reaction that his point had hit home. "The second line, then?"

Marcus nodded silently.

"Again, fairly obvious. You saved me from Lancelot's men."

Marcus shook his head. "I disagree. You had saved yourself. I merely came upon you after you had routed your tormentors. It is true I brought you here and tended your injuries but to say I saved you from Lancelot's men, well, that is stretching things a tad."

"Yet were we not just discussing what would happen should reprisal come from Joyous Garde? You cannot deny that by bringing me here you have certainly stayed the hand of vengeance at least, for if I had been found upon the rocks where I had fallen, there is no doubt they would have slaughtered me like a hog."

Marcus held his hands up in a gesture borne of irritation. "Do you see now how maddening it is? We are but a quarter of the way through this bloody ode to idiocy and we are at each other's throats."

Galahad reached across and supped at his cup of water, taken from the well that was itself fed by the snowmelt and rainfall which was as much a part of the climate as the bitter wind. With a deep breath, he plunged on, feigning no notice of Marcus' exaggerated eye-rolling. "Now, perhaps we come to the crux of the puzzle. You have indeed treated me as you would your kin and for that I thank you, but I cannot see how I would be able to save you from sin, if you do not know or acknowledge what that sin is." He leant forward with an intensity of gaze which held Marcus pinned like a butterfly on a collector's page. "Is there nothing in your past that can possibly account for these words? Perhaps an act you may have perpetrated in a drunken stupor of which you have no memory?"

"If I have no memory of it, how can I recall it?" Marcus spat, fairly launching himself out of his chair and walking over to the window, where he stood in silence, staring into the impenetrable darkness of the surrounding trees.

Galahad chose to hold his counsel, for an inkling of suspicion had wormed its way into his mind and, whilst he certainly wished no ill upon his newfound acquaintance, his interest was piqued to the extent that he would not be deflected from uncovering the conundrum, especially if it turned out that the suspicion which had been growing steadily day by day in his head contained even a morsel of truth.

Suddenly Marcus bolted, mumbling his apologies and exiting the house at a goodly rate. Galahad followed him quickly, rightly guessing if he did not stay within sight of him, he would very soon lose his trail in the blackness of the night.

"Marcus," he shouted, but the man was gone, the merest hint of his passage caused by a rustling to the knight's right. For one of the first times in Galahad's life, he employed his finely-tuned natural intuition for his environment to stalk a prey that was not for killing. He closed his eyes and let the plethora of background noise wash over him, immersing himself in the surprisingly loud clamour of the forest.

He filtered out the natural soughing of the wind and the graceful swish of leaf on leaf as well as the ferreting activity of various unseen nocturnal creatures going about their business in blissful ignorance of Galahad's eavesdropping.

There. The knight's head snapped round and he was off, covering the ground lithely, not so fast that he would lose his footing if confronted by an unseen obstacle, but fast enough that he could easily keep pace with his fleeing quarry.

As he set off, he quickly turned to the cabin, where the flickering fire provided what scant light there was and fixed its direction in his mind so he did not become too disorientated. However, having ascertained which path Marcus had set off on, Galahad was certain he knew where his unhappy host was heading. Sure enough, after a bare five minutes of following the man's spoor, Galahad found himself peering at the statue-still form of Marcus as he stood, head bowed in a glade which was ostensibly the same as several others within easy walking distance.

And so we return here, Galahad thought.

He had first come upon Marcus' chosen place of contemplation by accident. Though he was confident his hunting abilities were second-to-none, he was not arrogant enough to believe there was nothing else he could learn, especially in such an unfamiliar environment as this. For that reason, Marcus and Galahad had begun going into the forest, incorporating humanity's never-ending quest for sustenance into their rota of daily tasks. Galahad let Marcus take the lead, more through politeness than anything else as well as an obvious acknowledgement that he was more familiar with the territory.

During the previous week they had painstakingly made their way between the improbably thin trunks of the pine trees which made up the vast majority of foliage in this part of the woodland. As the wind increased in force and the conifers began to sway, Galahad was astounded by how far the trees were able to bend without breaking.

Marcus nodded, "Aye, it is something of a mystery," he bent close to Galahad's ear and whispered, "especially," pointing at a tree which had been ravaged by the sometimes brutal conditions and had toppled to its final rest, "as the roots do not seem to stretch very far beneath the earth. You would think that they would topple with the slightest puff of breeze. However, we are not here to ponder the puzzles of the forest." He jerked his head to the left, "We are here for that."

Galahad followed the trajectory of Marcus' finger as it moved with glacial slowness from pointing at the ground to pointing at the magnificent stag which was making its stately way through the undergrowth.

As they were upwind from the proud beast it did not detect their presence immediately and momentarily forgetting their homicidal purpose, the two hunters found themselves captivated by the wondrous sight.

After a few seconds, with a deep but quiet breath and a considered step into the open, Marcus came up in a fluid movement and let fly with his crossbow. The sinewy string clicked loudly against the yew bow as the bolt tore straight and true across the intervening space. The stag barely had time to move before the metal projectile punched through its skull, killing the beast almost before it had hit the ground.

Galahad nodded in appreciation at the economy of Marcus' technique as they both made their way over to the bow's victim. As Marcus shouldered the animal, Galahad said, "As the larder is stocked full well, I would like to try and bring home the bacon tomorrow," he eyed the deer roguishly, "or the venison anyway. I still feel like an interloper in your house and would like to take some of the pressure off you, after all, my mouth is the extra one you have to feed so it seems only right that I should provide some of the food which goes in it."

"No reason why not," Marcus smiled lazily as he shifted the dead weight to a more comfortable position. "One condition though," he puffed.

Galahad raised his eyebrows quizzically.

"You have to carry it home," Marcus chuckled.

The knight from Camelot smirked at the hunter and then his burden before clapping his hands together, "Rabbit it is, then."

Marcus' laughter echoed through the woods.

The next day, Galahad had bidden Marcus goodbye and made his way into the woodland. Despite his joke of the previous afternoon, he was not definite as to what his preferred quarry would be, deciding straight away that he would leave it to the vagaries of the forest as to what his trophies would be from the expedition.

He was armed with a crossbow, upon which he had practiced every day since he had been able to stand without support, and a sling, not a weapon with which he was particularly proficient, but one which he wished to hone his skills in and he reasoned that there was no better environment for improvement in his technique than his prey's own habitat.

He set off at a slow pace, determined to get a feel for his surroundings before he even attempted any sort of aggressive move. As he moved through the woods, he began to realise just how full of activity the forest was.

There seemed to be a wealth of red squirrels scampering and playfully leaping among the branches above his head. Galahad ignored them, for whilst their pelt was highly prized, even at times being used as currency for bartering, they did not make good eating. From his trips with Marcus, he knew that the woods were populated with far better fare than that. During the course of their joint hunting trips, they had come upon deer, hare, rabbit and, on the odd occasion, an errant pheasant which had blundered across their path and any one of these would make a fine meal given Marcus' culinary knowledge of herbs and flavourings. Cooking had been the one task which Galahad had found beyond him, his two abortive attempts resulting in an undercooked chicken that, given the harshness of the winter and the paucity of food available, they decided to risk eating and which gave them both severe bouts of the stomach flux, and a vegetable-based soup that Marcus managed to choke down two mouthfuls of before depositing the rest of the contents of his bowl out of the window.

From that time on, it was decided by mutual consent that Marcus would have sole control of the cooking duties.

Galahad forced the smile from his face as the memory of Marcus' pained gurning at the appalling taste of his concoction rose up in his mind's eye. He dismissed the image from his mind and mentally shook himself, intent on displaying his huntsman's skills through deed rather than word.

He had been out for approximately two hours, or so he judged by the occasional glimpses of the sun that dappled the needle-strewn ground. Since leaving the cabin, he had ghosted through the forest in a vague semi-circle.

After a couple of abortive attempts with the sling on a brace of rabbits that had bounded unsuspecting into his range, Galahad decided on a change of tactic. He had scaled a sturdy larch and was settled into a fairly comfortable nook created by the trunk and a thick branch that erupted from the tree at a height of about ten feet from the ground.

He had been sat there for ten minutes or so, trying to move as little as possible, to become a part of the tree, when he spotted movement to his left. Remembering his newfound companion's words, he calmed himself and shifted position slowly, not wanting to lose sight of his unsuspecting victim but not wanting to warn it of his presence either. He blinked in surprise as he saw the figure of a man walking aimlessly through the wood. Instantly, he recognised the familiar form of Marcus as he picked his way through the undergrowth, mainly keeping to the well-trodden trails but sometimes high-stepping through the scrubby bushes which clung to life in the shadows of the pines. Though he had immediately identified Marcus as the lumbering figure, it was also blatantly obvious that something was very wrong with him. Gone was the ubiquitous smile and erect gait and, in its place, was a hunched, shambling mess of a man. His hair hung lank and unkempt and, though he did not stumble once, his head remained bowed and his gaze clung to the ground.

Galahad was about to announce his presence when a stab of curiosity assailed him. He decided to follow Marcus through the forest, telling himself that he was merely testing his tracking skills against a worthy opponent, arguing that if he managed to successfully track him on his home territory without giving himself away then it would be a worthwhile exercise and considerable accomplishment.

He slipped gently to the ground, having convinced himself that Marcus was unaware of his presence. With catlike stealth, he pursued his quarry, his controlled movements to avoid detection so exaggerated they would have looked highly comical to anyone unaware of his ultimate purpose.

Thrilled by the passion of the chase, Galahad's breath came in short sharp bursts as he began to raise his pace in an effort to keep Marcus in sight. However, his hastening speed came at a cost to his concealment and, twice in quick succession, he winced as his boot came down upon the brittle leaves and twigs that carpeted the earth, making an excruciatingly audible crack, leaving Galahad inwardly cursing his haplessness. To his amazed disbelief, Marcus continued walking without apparent heed to the knight's clumsy attempts at clandestine pursuit.

Startled that he still appeared to be undetected, Galahad continued to follow, caught halfway between his quest for secrecy and his wish to find out exactly where Marcus was heading because, by now, he was sure his host was heading away from his home and, though he was far from certain, he was also fairly positive that he was not heading towards Bamburgh either.

For a brief moment, he lost sight of his host, who was wearing a nondescript tunic of green and grey coupled with leggings of a similar hue.

In his eagerness to glimpse Marcus again and in light of his host's seeming indifference to his presence, Galahad picked up the tempo.

Within seconds, he burst into a clearing that was bathed in wintry sunlight, cold, clear and eye-wateringly bright after the relative dimness provided by the canopy of the pines.

Luckily for Galahad, Marcus was standing statuesque on the far side of the glade, head bowed in silent contemplation facing a stand of trees which, to the knight, looked much the same as any other.

As Galahad gazed upon the scene, he was struck by two things almost simultaneously. Firstly, though Marcus had never shown any sort of religious observance in the period that Galahad had been under his care, he felt sure that the man who stood so still and quiet before him was praying and secondly, he was beginning to experience an overwhelming feeling that he was an interloper on a scene which should have remained intensely private.

Feeling inexplicably sick to his stomach, he retreated from the open space and tried to resume his hunt. However, after the unexpected encounter he found himself unable to concentrate fully and so returned to Marcus' home empty-handed, where he took his host's sarcasm at his lack of success stoically and without comment, inwardly amazed at Marcus' transformation from the pallid, distracted fellow he had seen wandering trance-like through the trees.

That had been three weeks past and, where he had not really noted Marcus' frequent unexplained disappearances before, now every time that his host left the immediate confines of the house and garden, Galahad had to fight down the urge to follow him surreptitiously to see if he returned to the clearing.

Now, as he slunk through the moonlit forest with the revelation of the old man's cryptic words ringing loudly in his ears and Marcus' dramatic and, Galahad thought, rather over-exaggerated reaction to his probing, the knight decided that there was definitely something not right with his housemate. On the other hand, Marcus had taken him into his home, cared for him whilst he recuperated and had proved to be a very agreeable companion at a time when Galahad had been sorely in need of such. Not normally one for dithering, Galahad held his ground, torn between wanting to play out his part in the old man's riddle and not wanting to show ingratitude to his new-found friend.

His indecision was brought to an end by a calm voice cutting through the eerily supercharged silence, "Show yourself, Galahad."

With an uncomfortable look on his face, Sir Galahad of Camelot emerged into the uneven moonlight, blinking furiously because Marcus had ignited a branch which he had retrieved from the leaves on the ground. Returning the tinderbox to his pocket, he rounded on his unwanted guest. "I do not wish for company, Sir Knight," he hissed, an ominous warning note in his voice, "I told you that examining the old fool's rhyme would cause naught but friction between us but you would not let it lie, would you?" Marcus shook his head. "Why would you not let it be?" he whispered plaintively, though Galahad was unsure if the comment was directed at him or not.

"I apologise, Marcus. If you wish me to return to the house, I will. If you wish me to leave your house, never to return, I will, but I suspect that what you actually wish for is to be free. Free of whatever it is that eats away at you day and night." Above Marcus' heated protestations, he ploughed on, determined now to say his piece. "Please do not think of it as spying, but I have watched you, Marcus. You are a master of disguise when it comes to your emotions. When we speak, you come across as a genuine, personable man, open and honest in your dealings and provider of a sympathetic ear when required and I do not doubt that you possess all of those qualities in abundance, but when you are alone..." he faltered, trying desperately to frame his words correctly, "you are a shadow of yourself, introverted, unhappy and bereft of peace. I have heard you in the night sobbing pitifully though I would hazard that you were still asleep." Galahad let forth a huge sigh. "You are a good man, Marcus. It would not sit well with me if I did not try my utmost to unburden you."

"How lucky I am to have taken such a saintly guest into my house." Marcus observed acidly as he fixed his guest with a hate-filled stare. "I need neither your pity nor your aid. I managed to survive before you took refuge in my house and, though your absence will leave a hole in my life that I will labour for the rest of my days to fill, I am sure I will manage to struggle on after you leave." He turned his back to Galahad and resumed the pose in which the knight had found him moments before. "Now you are fit enough to track me through the woods, I judge you are sufficiently recovered to make your way in the world once more and so bring to an end your overstayed welcome."

Shaking his head, Galahad stood his ground. "Your torment will not end, Marcus. You can bluster all you wish, my friend, but I beseech you, let me stay until we have unravelled the puzzle. If you still wish me to leave, then that is your wish and of course I will respect it, but you said yourself that you have been maddened beyond endurance by the man's words. Will you find peace if I vanish into the night with the issue unresolved?"

"Has it occurred to you why it tortures me so? That I am torn between wanting to understand the verse and scared witless by what the answer will be?" Marcus whispered hoarsely, his voice barely carrying across the intervening space. "If, as you say, I am a good man, then how do you explain the words, Galahad? What sin? Clear of guilt but stained by blood that's spilt? Walk me to my grave?" He held his hands out plaintively and the acid agony of his words cut the knight's soul with their poignancy. "What have I done, Galahad?"

The former champion of Camelot advanced across the glade towards the flickering torchlight and placed a hand on Marcus' shoulder. "I think that is what we need to find out." He looked around, unable to see anything because of the lateness of the hour but instead taking the opportunity to blink away the dancing after-image of the flame from his vision. "And I think the place to start is here. Why do you return here so readily? It is undoubtedly a picturesque spot but you seem to spend an unusual amount of time here."

Marcus had calmed down a little and, rather than biting Galahad's head off, actually took the time to ponder the observation. "I…don't really know. I feel drawn here for some reason. Despite what you say, I feel at peace here, perhaps here more than anywhere else."

"May I?" Without waiting for an answer, the knight took the torch from Marcus' unresisting hand and began to walk back and forth, sweeping the clearing with the penumbra of the flame.

Suddenly he stopped and leant forward slightly, peering intently at the base of one of the trees that surrounded the glade. He was struck by a recent memory of a blonde woman determinedly pacing a hillside bearing stones and raging against the injustices of life.

"Marcus," he beckoned the man over and stepped back, letting him look at what was before him without comment.

"It is a heap of stones." Marcus shrugged. "What of it?"

"They do not remind you of a cairn?" Galahad said quietly, a chill settling on him that had nothing to do with the plummeting temperature of the night. The silence stretched into the darkness. When Marcus spoke, Galahad nearly jumped out of his skin. "What are you saying? It is a grave that I am returning to at every opportunity? You think me some sort of murderer?"

"I think nothing of the sort. As you say, it could just be a pile of stones or, alternatively, it could be a cairn. I just find it intriguing that you are, in your own words, drawn here. I repeat, I make no accusation, but perhaps we may excavate it to remove all doubt?"

"Doubt of what, Galahad? Do not hide behind your florid little speeches, speak your mind. Do you think me a killer or not?"

Taking a step back as Marcus advanced, the knight was all too aware that he had left Whitecleave biding in its scabbard at Marcus' house. "I merely wish to fathom the puzzle, Marcus." He spoke guardedly whilst weighing up which way the conversation might play out.

"You ungrateful bastard," Marcus sneered.

"Please…" Galahad's placating words went unsaid as, for once, his battle instinct failed and Marcus lunged at him unexpectedly, bowling him over. His host's normal countenance of amiability and warmth was twisted into a snarling, bestial contortion as he spat incoherent imprecations at his accuser.

The torch had been knocked from the knight's hand and Marcus lunged at it, scooping up the burning brand triumphantly. The victorious smirk dissolved to be replaced by a murderous stare as he beheld the prostrate Galahad.

Reading the man's intentions, the knight dug both heels into the ground, straightening his legs and propelling himself backwards, out of range of the brandished torch which Marcus had thrust at his face.

Frantically, Galahad scrambled to his feet and spun to face his erstwhile friend. Unfortunately his foot found a patch of ice, still intact under its cover of leaf litter and shade, and he slipped, falling forwards as he fought for balance.

An explosion of light and heat hit him and he shrieked in shock and pain. Marcus had pursued his retreat and had driven the torch into the knight's face. Staggering drunkenly, Galahad clawed at his agonised eyes, forgetting the danger he was in, just wanting to do something, anything to relieve the all-encompassing pain.

He felt hands upon him and lashed out with an animalistic roar. The grasp remained however and he found himself propelled through the woods, lost in waves of agony though, on occasion, the outside world did momentarily intrude. Mumbled sobs intermingled with words of apology and regret clashed together in an incoherent melee which only added to the knight's disorientation.

After an indeterminate time, he ended up back at Marcus' home or so he guessed, for the little he could make out through the blinding stain that blotted his vision, looked vaguely familiar.

The iron grip left him and he heard Marcus' voice retreating into the distance as he fled the scene. "I am sorry, Galahad. I did not think…I cannot believe…I am so sorry…"

The knight sat upon his pallet, staring blindly at the far end of the house, unaware of the tears running down his much-abused face, trying to calm the maelstrom which swept around his mind. His head turned this way and that, trying without success to peer through the misshapen splash of impenetrable colour that dominated his sight. How long he sat there he did not know, rocking back and forth, crying a river of tears, while he beseeched the edges of the ugly bulge to shrivel and reduce.

Sweat dripped down his face and his heart felt like it would hammer through his ribs, as the realisation that his sight loss could be permanent blasted through him like a hot summer sun through the final snows of winter. He began to convulse and, with unseeing eyes rolling up in his head, he fell back unconscious.

He awoke hours later, squinting against the brightness of the unspoilt sunshine that bathed Marcus' home in a wonderfully golden hue. However it took him a few seconds to fully comprehend the significance of that. The searing pain, which had caused his lapse into catatonia, had dulled to a barely bearable ache. Once more, unbidden tears sprung to his eyes as he contemplated what had occurred and how close he had come to blindness. He made his way over to the wall where a basin had been affixed. Above this, Marcus had attached a crude mirror of blown glass coated with molten lead. Gingerly, fearing what damage he was about to behold, he peered at it intently. He bit his lip as he surveyed the raw scarlet rings around his eyes and the dry, cracked skin of his face where the torch had bit into him. His eyebrows had been singed into nothingness and his fringe had been all but obliterated by the heat which had left an ugly mark disfiguring his face. Never one to be overly concerned with his looks, he shrugged this off and breathed another sigh of relief that he had escaped with only superficial injury.

As his eyes roamed across the polished surface once more, he caught sight of Whitecleave, propped against the wall nearest his pallet. A cold ball of ice immediately appeared in his stomach as he contemplated what to do regarding Marcus.

How did he balance out what had transpired between the pair of them? Marcus had saved his life, although, after the disclosure of the old man's cryptic verse, it could not be said he had done it for entirely altruistic reasons. On the other hand, despite Galahad's battle-hardened demeanour, he could not help but shudder at the memory of the homicidal look on Marcus' face as he had lain helpless at his feet. There was no doubt in Galahad's mind that Marcus would have committed cold, bloody murder without thought, had he not taken the evasive action that he did.

Still unresolved as to what action he would take when the two of them met again, the knight from Camelot sheathed his blade and exited the house.

So intent was he on confronting the man who had all but disabled him, he paid no heed to the rustle of leaves and the crack of dry twigs at his back as he progressed through the forest.

He approached the glade where he and Marcus had fought, with a fluidity that belayed the anger which had begun boiling inside him almost as soon as he had set foot on the path to the clearing.

With Whitecleave unsheathed and ready to do its gory work, he bounded into the open with an atavistic roar, all pretence of uncertainty stripped away. Galahad was there to visit murder upon his attacker.

Narrowed, predatory eyes scanned the woodland for their quarry, darting from tree to tree, seeking out the tell-tale movement of a man in hiding. Fighting against the rampaging aggression which threatened to tip him into the rage of the berserker, he coldly noted the disturbance of the earth at the base of one of the thicker pines that encircled the ground. His head jerked up in surprise as something dropped from the branches above the pile of upset soil. Just as suddenly as the thoughts of reconciliation had evaporated from Galahad's mind when he had first sought Marcus out, so did the white-hot feelings of revenge as his erstwhile host plunged from the branches of the tree, jerking to a sickening halt as the rope snapped taut and his neck cracked like a twig made brittle by the harsh frost on a winter's morning.

Though Galahad threw Whitecleave to the ground and scuttled up the tree in a vain attempt to loosen the knot which constricted Marcus' airway, he knew immediately that he was too late. The man's neck was sitting awkwardly upon his shoulders with the jutting bones of his shattered upper spine protruding against his skin, seemingly on the brink of punching through its thin layer of flesh.

Galahad nearly lost his balance as a dry, elderly voice carried up to him. "He finally did what was right, then?" wheezed the old man who stood at the base of the tree.

The former knight of Camelot ignored the newcomer, worrying at the knot that bound the stricken victim to the tree. Finally, he freed it and Marcus dropped to the ground like a stone, raising a cloud of dust as he hit the floor.

Sweating freely, Galahad descended the pine tree, all the while holding the gaze of the old man, as if challenging him to comment.

Before Galahad could reach his fallen companion, the ancient had shuffled over to Marcus and spat upon his corpse. In one movement, Galahad swept up Whitecleave and levelled it at the stranger, who regarded it with an unfazed eye. "You had better explain yourself else you will be joining him on his final journey," he said in a flat voice, devoid of emotion.

A tired sigh whistled from the man's mouth. "There is no threat in that, believe me. Now that this scum has finally done the decent thing, there is nothing to live for anyway. Though, before you dispatch me to the Lord, I would appreciate it if you stepped off my daughter's grave."

Taken aback by that statement, Galahad looked down and nearly gagged as he saw a skull, riddled with maggots and half-shorn of skin grinning up at him. For a few stomach-emptying seconds, he was revisited by memories of the Dolorous Guard and their hideous leers, but then he recovered himself and jumped to the side.

"What is this?" he managed to blurt through gritted teeth.

The old man looked hunched and broken as he began to speak, "This is what remains of my wonderful daughter, Tereza. And this," he flicked his head contemptuously at Marcus' body, "is the bastard who took her from me."

As there was obviously no threat from the old man, Galahad lowered his weapon and beckoned for him to continue.

Seating himself down tiredly on a twisted bole, the old man rubbed a rheumatic leg and began to tell his tale and, even though he related it in a monotone, that very fact and the man's manner was enough to convince Galahad there was no duplicity in his words.

"Myself, my wife and my daughter came to Bamburgh just over three years ago now. We were part of a travelling troupe of tumblers and acrobats who toured the country." The man spread his bony arms and, for the briefest of moments, a twinkling smile shone through the dirt caked on the man's scrubby white beard. "I realise that might be hard to believe, but I used to be reckoned one of the finest exponents of my art. My daughter was a dancer, by the gods, she moved with an elegance and grace that could set the angels singing. To be honest, I suspect they only tolerated my presence to ensure that Tereza remained with them, but anyway, we travelled as a family, myself, Tereza and my wife, Mairead." Tears stood in his eyes as, without a pause in his re-telling, he revisited his wife's passing. "Twas the pox that claimed her within days of arriving," he shook his head and his voice shrunk to a whisper, "No-one should have to see a loved one go through what my Mairead endured." With a huge sigh, he seemed to regain his strength and held Galahad's gaze with a hellfire of pain raging in his eyes, "Tereza had not wanted to come so far north, she had long tired of the nomadic nature of our lives and wanted to put down roots but, to my shame, I pushed her into it again and again. She swore to me that this would be the last time she would join us on our travels and I could see she meant it. Then, of course, she saw her mother perish in the most heinous of circumstances and she blamed me. Blamed me for not letting her live her life, blamed me for killing her mother by forcing her to follow the troupe as well." He shook his head and stared blindly at the ground. "She said she hated me." His body began shuddering as gulping sobs began to escape him. "Her last words to me were ones of spite and bile...and my memories are...I try to remember her smile and her warmth, but all I see in my mind's eye is the snarl on her face when she parted from me."

Galahad could not bear to look upon the man's torment and found himself staring mutely from the bleached-white skull of Tereza to the fresh corpse, wondering, as his gaze alighted on Marcus' unruly mop of blonde hair, if he had misjudged yet another so-called friend.

The man had regained his composure when the knight looked back and continued his recounting. "I thought she had fled from me, fled and begun to make her own way in the world. Anyway, after a few weeks as the resident entertainment at Joyous Garde the time came to move on once more. They were good to me, the troupe, holding onto the engagement at the palace for as long as they were able, allowing me as much time as possible to search for my Tereza but, eventually, they had to leave, as did I. I am an old man, sir, and they feared I would not survive left to my own devices in the countryside." He shrugged expansively, the gesture all the more pronounced due to his stick-thin physique. "I wrestled for days and nights with the decision to leave my daughter, but, to my eternal regret, I let my pride override my instinct and left. I did not think she would want to lay eyes on me again, such was the bitterness of our goodbye, so I left, condemning her to this." He stared at the patch of disturbed earth which had become his daughter's last resting place.

Galahad was at a loss as to how to respond. In fact, he was not even sure that the old man was expecting a reaction from him, he was simply using him as a sounding board upon which to offload his pent-up grief and angst. "Not a day went by when I did not think of my gorgeous child, wondering what she was doing, what opportunities she was making with her life." Again he lapsed into near silence as he contemplated the grisly sight before him. "I never thought for a moment that I would never see her dance again, never see her auburn hair flowing behind her as she twirled, never..." his voice trailed off, unable to control his emotions.

The knight from Camelot laid a comforting hand on the broken man's shoulder. With a surprisingly violent jerk, the man wrenched himself free from Galahad's solicitous gesture. "Little more than six months ago, the troupe was joined by a man who claimed he could speak with the dead. The older amongst us counselled caution and wished nothing to do with such black arts, but the younger heads won out and he wheedled his way into our group."

"A necromancer?" Galahad started back from the man, as if he would somehow be tainted by associating with one who had consorted with such a person. After the last few months, he was surprised by the sudden vehemence of his feelings. Perhaps, he mused, his religious zeal had not been squashed as completely as he had thought.

Unmoved by the knight's disgust, the old man continued, "I had as little as possible to do with him. But one night, he sought me out. He said he had a message for me." Sighing hugely, he spat the words out quickly as if wishing them as far away from his mouth as possible. "I was expecting…well, to be honest, I was expecting little or nothing. I had no truck with such things but if anything was to come of it, I was expecting a message from my dear, sweet Mairead. As you can imagine, I was beyond comfort when he spoke the name of Tereza. I heard little of what he said after he spoke her name, but one thing did stand out. She wanted vengeance. Vengeance upon the man who had robbed her of her life," he jerked his head to the side, "vengeance upon him."

Galahad shook his head, open-mouthed. The suspicion about his host's continued return to this spot had resembled something along these lines from the moment he had first heard the verse which the old man had recited to Marcus, but he had not envisaged anything as dreadful as this.

"It was you," he blurted, "You were the old man Marcus spoke of."

Tereza's father fixed him with a withering look. "Yes, I was. After I had regained myself somewhat, the soothsayer, as he styled himself, told me what had happened to her. Your friend raped her, you see, raped her then killed her."

Galahad shook his head lamely. "But he spoke of her with such love, such compassion."

The man leapt up and advanced upon the confounded warrior. His words came out in short, clipped tones, each one fired out like a crossbow bolt. "I do not wish to hear what that bastard had to say about my little girl."

The champion of Camelot suddenly felt an overwhelming urge to explain himself, to justify why he had spent time in the company of a rapist and murderer. Though he had no evidence of Marcus' crimes beyond Tereza's father's testimony and a few circumstantial clues, the old man before him seemed so sincere and so haunted that he could not believe he would tell such a monstrous lie. He was also aware that his record of judging character in recent times would not hold up very well to scrutiny, but the man's tale made too much sense, particularly in light of Marcus' bizarre behaviour when questioned too closely about a relationship that, even by his own admission, had lasted less than a day.

"Sir, I swear to you I had no idea of this. If I had known, I would have brought him to justice without a moment's hesitation!"

For the first time, the man actually seemed to take stock of what Galahad was saying. He looked him up and down, as if weighing up the honesty of his words. "You would be the chaste, yet troubled knight then, would you?"

Nodding slowly, Galahad struck out for a change of subject, hoping to deflect any blame, however unjust, that the man might bestow upon him. "The soothsayer provided you with the verse then?"

The balding fellow returned the nod. "Yes, he told me that if it was recited to the one who committed the crime, it would drive him mad. I don't know if there was some sort of spell or incantation housed within the words, but he assured me it would torture him to the brink of insanity and, believe me, there was nothing more in the world that I desired, save seeing him face down in the dirt, lifeless and dead."

Galahad regarded Marcus once more, the man with whom he had shared his innermost thoughts and musings over the last few months and found his initial feelings of abhorrence waning and undertook a swift re-examination of the man who would now never breathe the sweet pine-scented air of the forest again.

The more he considered Marcus' actions in a dispassionate light, the more he became convinced that, whether through denial of the deed or some trick of the mind, Marcus had been ignorant of what he had done. He did not have the air of one troubled by such a black act, for surely he would not have been inviting strangers into his house, no matter what dark portents had been spoken to him. He would have been in hiding, not wanting to draw attention to himself if he had done what he had been accused of. His life story had certainly sounded plausible enough right up until he met the mysterious woman whom Galahad now knew as Tereza. Perhaps that one action, inexcusable though it was, had been so out of character that Marcus' psyche had rebelled against it, not wanting to admit that its host was capable of such an atrocity and had shut it out of his memory, but, on another subconscious level, his mind had been drawing him to the glade where he had buried his victim, trying to scream its message through the self-induced wall that his waking mind had built between that night three years ago and his life since.

"Well, you have got your wish, old man. Here he lies dead before you. Does it gladden your heart to see it so, for it does not bring your daughter back?" Galahad said quietly.

The grizzled fellow nodded emphatically whilst searching Galahad's face to see if he sought to try and chide him for his loathing of the fallen fellow. When he saw no sign of this, he spoke, "Yes, it does. It is true that my Tereza is still just as far away from me as she was before this cowardly whoreson took his own life, but I hope now she will have some semblance of peace. I know that I will."

The knight from Camelot weighed the man's words and shrugged. "What will you do now? I would offer you hospitality where I have been lodging but I would assume you would not wish to spend any time there?" He let the question hang in the air.

"I will bide here tonight and decide what to do when I awaken. There is nothing here for me now. I may return south to warmer climes, for this northern winter does manage to seep into my bones."

"I mean no offence, but will you be alright out here? Your clothing is barely sufficient and, as you say, your age does you no favours."

For the first time, a semblance of colour came to the man's pallid face. "I have survived for many weeks out here searching for this bastard, so I think I can manage one more night." He said stiffly then his face softened as he gazed upon his child's grave. "I will sit vigil and say my final goodbyes to Tereza."

Galahad held up a placating hand, "As you say. I will remove Marcus from your sight though as I am sure his continued presence, dead or not, is unwelcome in the extreme."

The old man said nothing as he got up and began gathering sticks and branches for a fire. Galahad watched for a brief moment then hefted Marcus' corpse onto his shoulder and left the glade. His thoughts were confused as he made his way back to the cabin he had called home for the last half-year. Whatever the rights and wrongs of the situation, Marcus had saved his life and he felt it his duty to give him a decent burial at least. As he walked, he wondered at what had occurred. He still found himself wondering if Marcus had duped him and had indeed been a callous, lying fiend, but he could not pinpoint anything in the man's character to suggest it. Was it possible for the human mind to perform such tricks of illusion upon itself? He did not know. He had seen men upon the battlefield suffer terrible injuries, yet before they died, they had seemed oblivious to the pain, numbed by shock and in blissful ignorance of their impending doom. Was the mind capable of the same feat?

Such imponderables rebounded to and fro through his head as he went about the monotonous task of interring Marcus' body in a patch of ground that lay just to the left of the vegetable patch which Marcus had cultivated over his years of residence in the woods.

With that job done, Galahad retired inside the cabin, having already resolved to return to the clearing with spare blankets and a tinderbox to help with the blaze.

Almost as if bidden by some outside agency, he found his gaze drawn to the curtained-off area of the house in which Marcus had spent his nights. Galahad had respected his privacy and, despite it being the only other room in the house, had not succumbed to the urge to break his host's trust and sneak a quick look behind the partition. After a guilty glance outside to where Marcus now lay at rest, he told himself that, with his host's demise, it did not matter whether he broke the confidence now. With that dubious reasoning arrived at to justify his inquisitiveness, he stalked quickly over to the curtain and pulled it back.

For a few moments, he simply stood in the entrance, not venturing in, merely analysing what was before him. However, to his surprise, there was not really much to analyse. The room resembled nothing more or less than the ordinary sleeping quarters of a normal man. Galahad was not sure what he expected to see after the old man's revelations, but all there was to see was a straw stuffed mattress with animal skins laid haphazardly over it, tunics and hose strewn over the floor and a few personal possessions dotted about the room. One of these was a small box, no more than a hand-span wide, which sat on the floor by the bed. The lid was propped up against it and, without quite knowing why, the knight from Camelot, despite his discomfort at what he was doing, stepped into the room properly so that he could look inside. With a sudden lump in his throat, he found himself staring at a ringlet of auburn hair lying in a tight curl in the middle of the box's base.

He felt his features tighten grimly as he replaced the lid, then stowed it in his pack. Though it would be convenient for him to stay in Marcus' home, after what he had learnt he knew he would never find peace there, knowing what had occurred under the thatch. He decided he would return to Tereza's shallow grave, deposit the lock of hair within, then offer help to the old man in whatever he chose to do now that his mission of retribution had achieved its goal

Galahad left Marcus' home without looking back, forced to reflect on yet another shattered friendship, riven by lies and betrayal.

He tramped through the woods without incident, coming upon the open ground just as the first thick flakes of snow began to fall, dulling the pale-blue sky to an inky grey as the clouds began to build.

He espied the man, sitting upon a fallen trunk by his offspring's tomb. "Please do not be offended, sir, but I have brought you blankets and tinder and if you do not mind, I will…." He began, forcing a levity into his voice that he did not feel. Immediately though, he knew something was wrong.

Tereza's father was staring off into space with a thin line of drool besmirching his beard. Galahad waved his hand in front of two unseeing eyes, one which had, Galahad noticed, a bigger pupil than the other. Gently shaking the man, he tried to rouse him but only succeeded in dislodging him from the log where he sat, sending him crashing to the ground, as limp and lifeless as Marcus had been, scant hours before. It was only then that Galahad spotted the red stain of blood which had trickled from his ear and matted the straggly hair on the left hand side of his face.

With a heartfelt sigh at the cruel vagaries of life and death, Galahad unshouldered his pack and set about digging his second grave of the day.

He laid the old man to rest next to his daughter, shovelling the last few piles over the wrinkled face with his hands. For an eerie moment, the knight thought he noticed a flush of colour appear and the merest glimpse of a grateful smile play upon the rapidly bluing lips, but it was gone as soon as he apprehended it.

Galahad stood and stretched the tiredness out of his back. Though he was now fully recuperated from the injuries sustained in the duel with Lancelot's men, this day he had undertaken more work and expended more energy than he had in a long time and he felt it. However, he had resolved not to return to Marcus' home and vowed to stick to that.

Stifling a yawn, he began to trudge towards the outskirts of Bamburgh, there to purchase a horse and strike out upon an unheralded path once more, ignorant of a destination but trusting that his luck could not continue in the same vein for much longer. Though he had spat his dismissal of such notions of fate and the like at Merlin all those months ago, he took the view that, at the moment, he was bereft of purpose and floundering in a sea of chaos. However, from some untapped well within himself, he felt the first stirrings of belief that this state of affairs would not continue and soon he would experience an epiphany which would steer his life back onto the right path.

He had no basis for this, save a vague recognition that, barring death itself, he had faced down the harshest things life could throw at him and emerged from them, if not unscathed, then at least a better person for the experience.

With that thought warming him as the temperature dropped and the snowflakes started to perform their stately descent with quickening frequency, he set off for Bamburgh, hoping that he would avoid any further trouble from Joyous Garde and be able to slip away from the Northumbrian village unmolested, but accepting that, if that was not the case, then it was simply one more hurdle to overcome.

Chapter 6

Howls rent the night.

The Pictish chief peered keenly into the darkness, fancying that he could see the surrounding enemy and wishing he had a better idea of their numbers, wishing he had more tribespeople to call upon, wishing that the pack had not chosen his clan to pick on, wishing that his life was not on the brink of ending. That last wish was unlikely to come true though. The wolves of Dun Varulfur had been a plague of unstoppable ferocity which had rampaged across the Outer Hebrides in a whirlwind of death.

There was however one last vestige of hope available to him and he spun round, ceasing his watch upon the surrounding fields and fixing one of his tribe with a pointed gaze.

"Does he come?" hissed Duncan Mackendrick, chief of the Venicones, a tribe whose territory, until the beasts had descended upon them, had extended to over a hundred square miles of the islands. Now though, in the space of little more than six months, the wolves had decimated them and they were left, bloodied but proud, making a last hopeless stand in the chieftain's halls of Dun Eiledon, facing extinction in the only way they knew how, with backs as straight as their blades and hearts as strong as their shields.

The one to whom Duncan had spoken continued his contemplation of the seven stones arrayed before him, scattered seemingly haphazardly but all within the confines of a beautiful concave glass bowl, which was inlaid into the floor of the broch. Without looking up, he nodded and spoke in a whispery, gravelly voice that was somehow suggestive of the rugged country in which he had been raised. "Aye, Duncan, he comes," he held up a warning hand as a look of relief rushed across his leader's face, "too late for us, mind, but he comes." A crooked smile that peeked through an abundance of red-haired beard brought further wrinkles to an already lived-in face, though the twinkling of the green eyes held hints of mischief favoured by those of a much younger vintage.

"I fail to see where the humour is in this situation, Jameson. I am sure that a seer's flesh is just as tempting to the wolf as a chieftain's."

"Or indeed a washerwoman's," Jameson shrugged. "We have passed beyond the point of salvation, Duncan. Perhaps if Monkshood had come before the winter bit hard we may have endured but not now. He will overcome this pestilence but not for months, maybe years."

Mackendrick ran a filthy hand through the sweaty blonde hair that sprouted unevenly from his head. He peered around the wooden construction, taking in each and every one of the frightened faces which stared back at him, looking to him, their chieftain, for hope at a time of hopelessness. He had not really taken note of the dwindling numbers of his people until now, but here before him, huddled in petrified groups, were barely more than fifty Venicone, the final remnants of a clan which had resided upon these lands for centuries. Any of the group which had not managed the last desperate scramble to the ultimately ineffectual protection of Dun Eiledon were now undoubtedly dead, victims of the ravening monsters who were, even now, closing in all around the broch.

A loud concussion on the main doors ripped everyone's heads round and caused what muted conversation there was to cease instantaneously. The silence that followed was worse, an all-encompassing breath waiting to be exhaled in response to what was to follow.

Something sailed through the square opening out of which Duncan had been looking moments before. He saw the movement before anyone else, as all eyes were still upon the doors and the sturdy beam which lay across them. His eyes flared as he realised what the projectile was and he raced across the wooden boards in a frantic attempt to disguise its nature, though he guessed it would be a futile effort.

"Papa!"

Mackendrick's heart sank as the near-incoherent shriek of the child raked agonisingly across everyone's ears. He had managed to smother the severed head on its first bounce and hurriedly thrust it underneath his sweat drenched jerkin, but not before the poor youngster had seen her father's pallid face, blood spattered and gored, staring sightlessly at the floor. Within seconds, more shouts and wails began to erupt as a further obscene deluge began.

As the chief of his clan, McKendrick was used to the loneliness of leadership and all the difficulties inherent with that responsibility, but these circumstances and the storm which he knew was about to descend on the last of the Venicones left him feeling helpless like never before. He cast a beseeching eye towards the seer, who remained squatting over the stones he had cast, to all intents and purposes, oblivious to the rain of death that fell all around and about him, but he gave no indication of action.

Duncan became aware that silence had fallen once more. The heads of the departed lay dotted about the wooden floor, all staring accusingly at their distraught leader, the man who had failed them.

Mackendrick felt a hand upon his shoulder. "There was nothing more you could have done, Duncan. The time of the Venicones is at an end, that is all. Everything must end, Duncan. Everything must end."

The chieftain nodded appreciation at Jameson's sentiments, whilst acknowledging the emptiness of the gesture. An uncharacteristic tear appeared in his eye as he heard the stout timbers begin to split on the door as they threatened to, then actually did, give way to the fearsome beating they were taking.

A massive figure stood framed in the doorway. The aura of power that emanated from him was almost tangible as he stood, surveying the naked terror of the men, women and children who cowered before him with deliberate slowness to ratchet up the level of dread to even greater heights.

Two wolves slunk in on either side of the blood-sodden warrior and began loping around the room, stopping at each and every occupant, snuffling at them as they shrunk away from the leering grins and dripping jaws, mottled as they were with both fresh and dried blood.

To Mackendrick's horror, one of the very young children, Ffiona McKintosh who was barely three years old had, oblivious to the danger, broken away from her petrified mother's grasp and went to stroke one of the beasts, babbling inconsequential niceties in the manner of one her age.

The wolf's eyes narrowed then the muzzle snapped open, ready to rend the little girl's flesh.

With one harsh word, the man growled an order and all in the room saw the animal's bunched muscles relax as the planned attack died before it had begun.

After completing a circuit of the close, fear-soaked room, the pair returned to the giant's side and sat, resembling nothing more than two faithful hunting hounds returning to their master.

It was Mackendrick who broke the silence, thoroughly ashamed of the quaver in his voice but unable to prevent it nonetheless. "Why have you come here?" he asked.

Though the goliath's dead, green eyes rested upon him, he got no answer.

"Why are we cursed to suffer your presence here?" Mackendrick asked again through clenched teeth.

Without changing expression, the massive warrior walked across the room with surprisingly soft footfalls. He looked down upon the Venicones chief with an expression of arrogance and disdain. Leaning down so his mouth came within inches of the chieftain's ear, he whispered a single word, "Ragnarok".

Duncan's brows wrinkled in confusion at the unfamiliar word, but quickly re-focussed as he beheld the huge back of the warrior as he began to return to his station in the doorway.

Without thinking, Duncan unlooped the wicked looking battleaxe from his belt and swung it, bracing himself for the impact as it bit into the giant's shoulder blades.

At least, that was what he expected to happen.

Instead, a colossal arm snaked out with a speed which seemed impossible for one so huge and grabbed the shaft of the weapon. With a jerk, he wrenched it from Mackendrick's grasp, reversed it then brought it down in a bone-shattering arc that cleaved the chieftain from left shoulder to right hip. As the dead clan-leader slid to the floor with an obscene sigh, all hell broke loose within the broch. Whatever spell of fear the wolves had held over the frightened folk was destroyed by the unspeakable violence of Mackendrick's death and suddenly the room was a chaos of fleeing humans and feeding wolves.

Through the centre of it all, the man walked as if he had not a care in the world. As he reached the ruined entranceway, he stopped, peered at the carnage which he and his family had wrought and, with a lazy smile playing upon his lips, exited Dun Eiledon.

He stood upon the threshold of the homestead, breathing in the night, relishing the frigid air as it sighed against his skin, feeling the thrill of the blood, alive in a way he found hard to describe, though he always experienced this rush after the ecstasy of killing.

He cupped his hands to his mouth and bellowed, "Feed, my family, feed. Fenrir's teeth, there's enough to go round."

As one, the howls erupted into the starry sky and the werewolves which had waited patiently outwith the domicile of the Venicones galloped into the house, there to add their presence to the mayhem within.

Varga Hrolfsson regarded the pack with affection as they all rushed past him. With a hearty laugh, he retreated from the scene to stand in the middle of the pasture that surrounded the chieftain's home. He peered towards the cloudless sky, fascinated as ever by the silver moon which dominated the vista, its grey and black shadows playing tricks on the eye as they seemed to fashion themselves into the gaping maw of Fenrir, the great wolf of slaughter from the eschatological mythology of his ancestors.

As he did so, a vivid memory returned to him.

He remembered sitting rapt upon his father's knee in the longhouse of their village as the bearded colossus recounted the events of the first Ragnarok, the final battle waged between the *Aesir*, the Norse gods led by Odin, and the various forces of the giants or *Jötnar*, which immediately preceded the destruction of the world. He recalled his open-mouthed excitement as saga after saga was told, of how the majority of the gods, giants and monsters involved had perished in the apocalyptic conflagration and how almost everything in the universe was sundered and destroyed.

The passion and fire of these tales were what formed the backdrop of his formative years, these were the words that shaped his destiny, these were the myths and tales which had first set his feet upon the path which he now trod.

Varga had idolised his father and was devastated when, after departing his home for the first time to partake in the pillage and plunder of which his sire had spoken so fervently, he returned to find the giant of a man who he worshipped as a god, withered and dying, riven by a cancer which seemed to consume his very soul. Dying of illness or old age was considered ignominious by the Viking people and was reputed to earn the victim an afterlife in Hel, so Varga beseeched the gods to save the old man.

To his distress, his prayers remained unanswered and his father perished, his last words a reedy plea for salvation, for he too feared his destiny of forever patrolling the Corpse Shore in the Hall of Hel.

The Hall of Hel itself was said to be large and woven from serpents like a wattled house. The heads of these snakes all faced inward and spat venom so that rivers of poison flowed along the hall. Floundering in these caustic streams were the souls of murderers, oathbreakers and seducers and all others denied entry to Valhalla. On the shores of the rivers, the hideous dragon Nidhogg tormented the bodies of the dead and Fenrir himself tore at the corpses of the damned.

Remembering the sagas of Ragnarok and in particular of Fenrir, the ferocious wolf-son of Loki, Varga's grief at his father's passing transformed into an obsession with sparing his father from the torment he was fated to suffer for the rest of eternity.

To this end, he resolved to find favour with Fenrir and began practicing rites of sacrifice and violation in His honour, believing that the more lives he took and the more sacrifices he offered, the more he would be able to influence Fenrir both in his prayers in life and when he too came to walk the Nastrond in death, to intercede on his father's behalf and quell the Wolf-God's bloodlust for he knew the rituals he had enacted and participated in were heinous atrocities which would undoubtedly condemn him and the other perpetrators to Hel.

However, such was the power of his fervour that followers soon began to flock to the black and silver wolf's-head banner of the Ulfhednar clan and before long he held the village where he grew up, Ulfsgaard in the Petty kingdom of Rogaland, in his thrall.

The area soon became known as a hellish place of damnation and death and outsiders knew to avoid it at all costs. Due to this, once the homesteads in the immediate vicinity had been desecrated by the pack, Varga's disciples began to spread themselves into the wider countryside, brushing the borders of Agder in the south and Hordaland in the north.

Soon tales started to seep into the other kingdoms and the tribes of the Skagerrack coast of the Agder kingdom and the Etne and Odda tribes in

South Hordaland began to find evidence of the Ulfhednar's notorious deeds in their territories.

Though the Viking clans had long been renowned for their viciousness when confronting their enemies, they could not condone what was occurring in their own backyard and so a meeting of the clans was convened at the Mead Halls of Skien, a settlement consisting of a number of longhouses specifically designed for such important matters. The community was overseen by Harald Sandhair, so named for the shock of fair hair which cascaded over his ears and down his shoulders.

Harald had proclaimed himself King of Telemark over a decade ago but, as the legitimacy of Telemark as a kingdom was itself a hotly debated topic with approximately half of the petty kingdoms recognising it and the other half not, perversely it was also seen by all as the most neutral place in the area, so it was here that the problem of the Ulfhednar clan was debated and decided.

Around the oaken tables of Skien was the fate of Varga Hrolfsson and his minions determined.

Death was the verdict. Many were the voices who called for the denizens of Ulfsgaard to experience the justice meted out by sword and axe and even those who felt that sentence harsh could only suggest banishment as an alternative.

The tribes all agreed that Hrolfsson's deification of Fenrir was an affront to all the gods who had perished during the end-times and it was this blasphemy which sealed his and his tribe's fate.

'According to the legends of the Viking people, it was Fenrir who had slain Odin, chief God of the Aesir during the final battle of Ragnarok and his two sons, Hati and Skoll, who had first precipitated the events of the Norse Armageddon, pursuing the sun and moon across the cloudscape in a perpetual chase that ended with them devouring both, causing the stars to burn out and vanish from the sky, plunging the earth into darkness.

This caused Garmr, the monstrous hound, imprisoned in the cave of Gnipahellir, to bay loudly. In response to that, three cockerels began to crow: Fjalar in Jotunheim from the forest of Gallows-wood, Gullinkambi in Valhalla who woke the einherjar or battle-dead, and Daemonful, who crowed in Hel and roused the sinful dead. To add to the tumult, the giant Hraesvelgr sat on the edge of the heavens in eagle form and shrieked with anticipation at the holocaust to come.

This catastrophic turn of events caused the earth to tremble so violently that trees were uprooted and mountains began to fall. The concussion freed Loki, god of mischief and strife, from the fetters imposed upon him by the Aesir along with his afore-mentioned ferocious son, whose slavering mouth gaped wide open with his upper jaw against the sky and his lower one against the earth.

Likewise, Garmr's bonds were broken and the ravener began to run free.

At the same time, the oceans surged up, drowning the land in a great flood as Jörmungandr, the Midgard Serpent twisted and writhed in fury, making his way onto the shore. He stood shoulder to shoulder alongside his brother Fenrir, spewing venom and spattering the sky and earth with his poison.

Then, in the upsurge of waters, the great ship Naglfar, the ship of the giants, which was made from the nails of the dead, was released from its moorings in Jotunheim. Set free by the catastrophic flooding and tsunamis caused by the serpent, it was carried along from the east, captained by the giant Hrym and transporting the legions of Jotnar toward the battlefield of Vigrid.

From the north Loki sailed in a ship which carried a great army of evil people who were named the Heljar sinnar, to fight against the einherjar.

Amid that turmoil, the sky opened and, from it, rode the fire giants of Muspelheim, led by Surtr who brandished a flaming sword. They advanced from the south with fire before and behind them, tearing the sky apart as they closed in on Vigrid. As Surtr and the others rode over Bifröst, the rainbow bridge that separated the mortal world from the realm of the gods, it broke behind them and fell to the earth, whilst the mountains themselves cracked open, releasing hordes of troll-wives upon the land.

Thus, all the forces of the Jotnar arrived on three fronts to storm Asgard, the home of the gods, and gathered in battle formation upon Vigrid. They all but filled the plain, even though it stretched for over one hundred leagues in every direction.

Heimdall, the guardian of the gods, was the first to see the enemies approaching and blew mightily on Gjallarhorn, sounding such a blast that it was heard throughout all worlds. All the gods awoke and at once met in council. Odin then rode to the well of Mímir astride his mighty steed Sleipnir, consulting him for guidance on his own and his people's behalf.

Yggdrasil, the World Tree, groaned and shuddered, shaking from root to limb, and all became afraid on the earth and in the heavens and in Hel. The dwarves lamented before their doorways of stone and all the Aesir and einherjar donned their war gear and advanced onto the field to meet the giants. Odin rode in front of the vast host wearing a golden helmet, a shining coat of mail and brandishing his spear, Gungnir. He made straight for Fenrir, and, though Thor was standing at his right hand, he was unable to help because his old enemy Jörmungandr, the Midgard Serpent, fell upon him.   Freyr fought the fire giant Surtr but, after a harsh conflict, became the first of all the gods to fall as he had given his own sword to his servant Skírnir. Tyr battled Garmr and each slew the other.

Thor killed Jörmungandr with his hammer Mjolnir but, with the fatal strike, unleashed a torrent of the serpent's poison upon himself and fell to the ground dead.

Odin continued to fight valiantly against Fenrir but was swallowed by the wolf. However, Odin's son Vidar immediately advanced against the beast of slaughter and stepped with one foot on the wolf's lower jaw. On this foot he wore the heavy shoe which he had been making since the beginning of time, consisting of all the leather waste pieces which men pared off at the toes and heels of their own shoes. With one hand he grasped the wolf's upper jaw and tore his mouth apart, killing him at last and avenging his father.

At the climax of the war, Heimdall fought Loki but neither survived the evenly matched encounter. Seeing a stalemate looming, Surtr raised his hand and loosed his flame over the earth, burning the entire world. The conflagration leapt high against the heavens, and Surtr himself was consumed by his own fiery destruction along with all the other beings who dwelt upon the earth.

Unable to cope with the upheaval, the land sunk completely into the sea and thus ended the reign of the Aesir over the world of the Norsemen.

Yet somehow the earth endured and life was not extinguished.

After a time when the fire of Surtr had died down and the smoke and steam had dispersed, a new earth rose up from the sea. It was green and fair with crops and fields prospering without the need for a seed to be sown.

All ills were healed as a waterfall plunged from the sky and an eagle soared above it.

A daughter born to the sun goddess also rose from the ocean to continue her mother's solar journey across the sky.

In a place called Hoddmimir's Forest a man and woman named Lif and Lifthrasir miraculously survived the cataclysm, having found refuge from the fire. Together they became the progenitors of a new race of humans and the world was inhabited once again.

And so the mortal realm continued, as did the immortal, for not all the gods perished. Odin's sons Vidar and Váli, neither of whom was harmed by the flames or the deluge, dwelt in the temples of the gods on the field of Idavoll where Asgard, now destroyed, had previously been. Thor's sons Magni and Modi, the inheritors of their father's hammer, then arrived, bringing Mjolnir with them. Baldr and his brother Höd who had both died prior to Ragnarök were reborn, fully reconciled, and ascended from Hel to dwell in the former halls of their father Odin in the heavens.

From then on, the new generation of mortals worshipped the new pantheon of gods, led by Baldr, the legitimate heir of Odin.'

These were the legends which Varga had learnt in his infancy and had stayed with him to this very day.

With Fenrir having slain the chief of the Norse pantheon, Odin, head of all the gods who had failed Varga and his father, the wolf-god was the obvious choice to be the deity to make the Aesir suffer for their indifference to his father's fate.

As the depravity of his followers and himself plumbed ever-lower depths, Varga began to be visited by dreams, at first no more than a jumbled cascade of disjointed images; chains torn and destroyed, a set of manacles flung far beyond sight, a bloody hand freshly ripped from its owner's arm and still spurting its scarlet contents as pain upon pain erupted within, a sword falling to the ground with a death knell finality, an old man dying in agony, a mighty boot and a blinding light of darkness.

On the night of this last vision, he had jerked awake, sodden with sweat, convinced in his bones that he was dead beyond retrieving. He pushed himself from the bed, glancing dispassionately at the man and woman with whom he had rutted hours before and strode into the cold night air, shivering at the bite of the winter upon his naked skin.

He stretched languorously, scrunching his eyes tightly shut as various muscles worked their way back into place from the exertions of the night. As his eyes opened, he stepped back in astonishment for he now found himself facing the gaping mouth of a massive cave, the roof of which rose fully fifty feet above him. Though his mind reeled with a thousand questions, primal instinct cut in and he spun round, fearing he knew not what, gripped by a nameless dread made all the more keen by the fact that he had not felt the emotion for a long time.

He was greeted with a sight that stole the breath from his lungs. He was standing atop a mountain which reared through a grey, insubstantial carpet of cloud, thus robbing Varga of any point of reference from which he could get his bearings.

With a dry mouth and now acutely aware of his nudity, he padded very slowly into the yawning mouth of the cave, all of his senses reaching out, questing for any sign of life, be it friend or foe.

An eldritch light allowed the huge man to pick his way across the pitted stone floor of the cave, but still he trod stealthily, for he did not wish to forewarn whoever or whatever bided within the gloom of his presence.

As he proceeded, he began to relax, or at least lose the edginess to his movements. The place through which he now crept felt dead for ages past. It put him in mind of a crypt for the air was dry and still and he was surprised to find himself feeling uncomfortable, but in an unexpected way. Normally possessed of a calm assurance of place which came from the absolute leadership and authority he held over the Ulfhednar, he felt belittled and almost blasphemous by being in this place that had been bereft of life for so long.

Shaking off his uneasiness, he saw something lying on the floor of the cave. Stopping for a moment to make sure he was not about to spring a trap, he strode quickly over to it, gathering it up in his powerful hands and turning it this way and that to try to puzzle out what he had found.

It was a silvery, silken rope that glowed eerily in the dimness. Varga fingered it and wondered at the texture, for it was unlike anything he had ever touched before.

"'Tis forged by dwarven trickery," a voice growled behind him.

Varga dropped the object and immediately backed against the wall of the cave, shuddering as the coolness caressed his spine.

"Be not afeared, Varga Hrolfsson. It is I who am in your debt."

The immense Viking from Ulfsgaard realised he had sucked in a huge breath and let it out explosively for what he saw before him defied belief.

A gargantuan wolf crouched upon its haunches, regarding him with ice-blue eyes which peered out from a face of blackest fur. The mouth briefly opened for a long pink tongue to flick out and Varga found his gaze irresistibly drawn to the razor-sharp teeth that were exposed by the movement.

A gravelly sound came from the beast and the leader of the Ulfhednar clan suddenly realised that the animal was laughing at him, though whether it was affectionate or mocking he could not tell.

Then, in a blinding flash of understanding, he knew. In an instant, he was supplicant on the cold, hard floor, ignoring the probing rock as it pressed against him painfully.

"Arise, son of Kraaken," Fenrir, wolf-son of Loki and Angrboda, brother of Jormungandr the Midgard Serpent and Hel, she who presided over the Nine Worlds of Viking myth, spoke slowly. "You and your people have thrilled my being with your rites and ceremonies in a way I had hitherto thought impossible. What you have done for me and my get has earned you the right to stand before me unbowed and full of pride. Each drop of blood you spill in my name infuses me, each unbeliever you slay in my name empowers me. Without you and what you have achieved, I would still be fettered on the Nastrond, feeding on the bodies of the damned."

Varga regained his feet and, with the knowledge that he stood before a god made flesh forming an icy ball in his stomach, simply accepted that if he was to die here, then there was none at whose bidding he would rather perish than the deity who he had worshipped so deeply and absolutely.

As he stared dumbly at the impossibility confronting him, he saw that the enormous animal seemed to be insubstantial, its fur writhing and swimming as though it was fashioned of smoke.

As if reading Varga's mind, the wolf said, "It is the souls of all the dead I have consumed. I have used my arts to create this illusion to concentrate your mind else your senses would be floundering in chaos at my real form."

"How is this possible?" the Viking clan-chief managed to stammer. He had to resist the urge to reach out and stroke the ethereal pelt of the massive wolf.

Fenrir grinned, again exposing his yellowed teeth. "I am a god," he stated simply.

"What is this place?" Varga whispered.

For the first time since he appeared, Fenrir's expression changed from its hitherto benign state to one of anger. He bared his teeth and snarled, "This is the place where the Aesir duped me into captivity, binding me to the rock and leaving me to rot."

Hrolfsson tried to shrink further into the cave wall, scared half to death by the malevolence of the voice. His eyes widened and fell to the glowing cord that he had dropped to the cave floor. "Then..."

"Aye, it is Gleipnir, the rope of magic, fashioned by the bastards of dwarvenkind to render me captive in the remotest cave on the barest mountaintop. Distant though I was from the snivelling, cowering Aesir who tricked me into imprisonment, I screamed my defiance day after day, ensuring that those who deceived me would never forget their treachery and would always be warned of what terrible fate would befall them once I was free."

During this tirade, Fenrir's growl grew deeper and deeper and the guttural tones shook dust from the ceiling of the cavern.

Varga gaped fearfully at the motes of dirt that fell upon him and frantically sought to calm the savage anger of the wolf.

He scooped the cord from the floor and fingered it inquiringly, "It must be of a special material to bind you, Lord."

The God's eyebrow arched at the honorific and, for a heart-stopping second, Varga thought he had insulted Fenrir in some way.

However, when the wolf spoke again, his voice was no longer infused with anger. "Yes Varga, very special. The gods of Asgard knew that nothing human-made would confine me, so the black dwarves of Svartalfaheimr created that at the behest of the Aesir. It is said that it was shaped using the sound of a cat's footfall, the beard of a woman, the roots of a mountain, the sinews of a bear, the breath of a fish and the spittle of a bird."

Despite his situation, Varga could not contain the snort of derision as it escaped him. "Such things do not exist."

"Yet nonetheless it bound me here, did it not? So there was certainly something about it that is suggestive of magic. And what is more magical than that which does not exist?"

Varga dropped the rope to the gritty surface at his feet and commanded himself to calmness. "What would you have of me, my Lord Fenrir?"

The wolf's teeth bared again, "Enough of the sycophancy, Hrolfsson. It bores me." The pitiless eyes fixed upon the massive Viking, looking him up and down, measuring him, pondering whether he would be up to the task which was about to be placed before him.

"I would have you free me, Varga Hrolfsson. Free me from the ties which moor me to the banks of the River of Poison in Hel, free me to assume my place at my father's right hand as we stand bestriding the world of men, my father above, my sister below, my brother ruling the seas and myself ruling the land."

Once again, Varga dropped to his knees in an instant. "If it is in my power, then it will be done."

Fenrir rolled his eyes impatiently. "Get up, will you, man."

When the slightly shamefaced chieftain regained his feet, Fenrir shuffled his position slightly, captivating Varga as the flimsy film that was his ghostly skin rippled and shifted.

"How can this miracle be performed?" The clansman stammered.

"There is only one way to free me from my sister's domain. The same way that I was freed from my imprisonment on the island of Lyngvi."

Varga chanted the answer like a mantra, as the full weight of what the wolf-god was confiding to him became apparent. "The earth will shake violently, trees will be uprooted, mountains will fall, and all binds will snap."

"Aye, Varga Hrolfsson, my get will swallow the sun and moon once more and the stars will disappear from the sky." Fenrir smiled slowly, an evil smirk that chilled the Viking to his very marrow. "And Ragnarok will be upon us again."

"How...?"

"All that you must do is finish what you have begun, Varga. If you do this thing for me, rest assured, as my family return to godhood from the ashes of Hel, so will your family ascend too. Your father will be reunited with you and you and he will be honoured by all."

The wolf's eyes lit up with a repugnant zeal that transfixed Varga. "Harken to me, for you now have a new purpose. Search deeper in this cave and you will find two skulls. They are what remains of my two sons. You must take them with you back to the world of mortal men. There is one other thing that you must also bear." The wolf's head described a circle as he stared around and about, taking in all that surrounded him. "This glow, this light that you can see by but appears to have no origin, it comes from an ever-burning shard of Surtr's flaming sword. It is housed in the same room as the skulls. Again, you must take it with you."

Varga's mouth was dry as he stared at the massive beast before him. "How may I bear it if it is of Surtr's fire? It will burn me to nothing if I touch it."

"You will be rendered immune to its heat."

"How, Fenrir?" Varga quavered, apprehension etched in every feature.

Without hesitation, Fenrir's mouth darted forwards and bit down on Varga's right hand.

The chieftain of the Ulfhednar screamed in horror, steeling himself for the agony which he was sure was about to tear into his consciousness. The sweat poured off him as he stared at the glimmering roof of the cave, unwilling to look at the dreadful injury that had been inflicted upon him by the vulpine monster.

"Cease this embarrassing display, Hrolfsson, and behold the honour which I have bestowed upon you."

Varga's appalled rictus travelled downwards from the canopy of stone, past the grinning countenance of the wolf-god, then down to what he fully expected to be a bloodied, ruined stump gouting its scarlet contents onto the ages-old dust.

His eyes widened in shock as he saw his hand was, to all appearances, untouched. He turned it over, scrutinising the back of it first then returning his gaze to the palm, tracing the lines as they threaded across his skin. "I am sorry, Fenrir, I cannot see ..." As he spoke to the supernatural being, he became aware that the wolf was not looking directly at him but at his hand.

In the same instant, a crippling pain slashed up his forearm and he dropped to one knee, whimpering. In horror, he watched as coarse silver fur began to sprout through his skin, thrusting out in clumps and then smoothly joining together to form a velvety pelt which crawled up his arm and started to envelop his body. As this was occurring, to the accompaniment of bones popping and crunching, his fingernails began to elongate even as his hands retreated into his wrists, the fingers inexorably folding into half clenched fists which disappeared under the fur, until they emerged, having transformed themselves into razor-taloned paws designed for rending flesh and cleaving bone.

He screamed as his cheekbones changed shape, feeling as if they were racing away from his eyes. For a terrible moment, he struggled for breath. He then began to hyperventilate as his nose flattened against his tortured skull and started to extend into a muzzle.

Pain touched every inch of his being as the transmogrification reached its climax. As his screaming continued, his voice began to modulate in pitch, beginning with the high-pitched shriek of a human on the brink of death and ending in a harsh growl of bestial ferociousness.

His eyes snapped open and a wolf stared out.

Fenrir's smirk was evil incarnate. "Go deeper into the recesses of the mountain, Varga, return my sons to me and the blade that burns eternal, then will I impart to you the reason that our fates have become so inextricably intertwined."

A blind obedience gripped Varga Hrolfsson, born of the even deeper affinity he now had with the wolf-god. Despite the enormous changes which had wracked his body seconds before, all pain had now fled and he found himself immediately appreciative of the vast potential that his new form granted him. Though he was still able to walk upright, he was also able to drop to all fours and so, with an overwhelming eagerness to test his new bodily structure, he did so and padded off into the semi-darkness with the purpose conferred upon him by Fenrir emblazoned across his brain to the detriment of all else.

As he loped along, getting used to the unfamiliar feel of the stone on the pads of his paws, he noted how much his senses were heightened by the shape-shift that he had undergone. Even with the light of Surtr casting its muted luminescence, details of the terrain had been lost upon the Viking but now, through these eyes, even though his vision had become monochrome, he could pick out every single rut and crevice that lined the forbidding walls of the grotto. He could see layers of dust, untouched for aeons as well as skeletons of both man and wolf, bleached white and petrified in grotesque attitudes.

As he proceeded further down the noiseless avenues of stone, he felt a heat begin to grow before him. Feeling sure that he was approaching the final resting place of Hati and Skoll, he picked up the pace, his panting echoing loudly around the tunnels.

He came to a left hand curve in the passageway and followed its arc, emerging into a place which positively stank of bloodletting and brutality.

As he stared around the pitted floor, he felt his whole being begin to infuse with an irresistible zeal. This place called to him like none other ever had, but even though he had never set eyes upon it before, he simply knew it was a part of him, a part of his past, a part of his present and a part of his future.

He strode reverently over to the raised pile of stones which dominated the centre of the room and along which ran gutters stained black with the blood of sacrifice. He so yearned to reach out, to touch it, to run his claws down the darkened ruts that the need was an almost physical thing. As he caressed it, an eerie howl came to his ears, echoing distantly yet still powerful enough to reverberate for minutes after the contact was broken. Varga sat statuesquely, listening to the call, which hovered on the cusp of his hearing. As he sat rapt by the emotion of the last few moments, Fenrir's voice replaced the howl, also echoing in the same unnatural manner, mesmerising him still further.

"Behold my *horgr*, Hrolfsson. The shrine upon which my children slaughtered hundreds and hundreds of unbelievers, the unbelievers who worshipped those that bound me. The tides of blood that were shed in this room kept me vital for many a long year whilst I was incarcerated in this hellish prison of unyielding rock and stone. The lifeblood of all the cowards and traitors invigorated me, enabling me to hoard my strength and power against the day that Ragnarok came to pass once more."

The wolf-god paused, allowing the howl to seep back into Varga's ears. "See how the cry of Garmr still resounds in this place. Bring me the skulls of my sons and the splinter of immortal iron and that cry will flee from its confines and be heard around the world once more."

The Viking chief looked about the room, which had now lapsed into the silence of the grave. He stalked from one side to the other, occasionally glancing at the eye-watering glyphs which were etched into the rock walls but mainly concentrating on his quest for bone and blade.

With a mounting unease, he began searching amongst the plethora of skeletal detritus that was arrayed across the cold floor, wondering which of the innumerable skulls were of the wolf-god's progeny.

When he had been charged with the task, he had imagined that it would be the work of but a moment to find the requested items, reasoning that a shard from a sword which had created the biggest conflagration in all the world would be an easily identified object, as would the mortal remains of two demi-gods.

But now, in this place of holiness and worship, under the pressure of knowing that if he was to fail he was to die, he found himself becoming more and more frantic as the objects he sought remained hidden.

Varga found himself caught in a life-or-death dilemma, for the human part of his mind was overwhelmed by the need to satisfy Fenrir's lust for these artifacts but the wolven part was unable to reason out a better method of searching for them. On one level, he was aware that he was becoming more beast than man and the simplicity which went with that was as liberating as anything he had ever felt before but he was also very conscious of the expectation that he had been burdened with. Ever since his father had been enslaved upon the Corpse Shore, Varga's life had been geared towards engineering an escape for him and now, through the rites he had performed and the largesse of the deity which he had performed them for, he had the opportunity to do just that.

With a tongue-swallowing suddenness the wolf-god's voice came loudly back into his head, "Learn to control the wolf within, Hrolfsson, for make no mistake, if you are found wanting in the undertaking which I have placed upon you, then your life will be forfeit."

The tone was so chillingly matter-of-fact that it focussed Varga's mind sufficiently for him to cease his crazed hunt and properly ponder the problem. Immediately, his thought processes began to slip again and he recognised the root of his difficulty. With a regretful sigh, he cast his thoughts through the deadened air of the caves back to the wolf-god. "I am sorry, my lord, the sheer glory of this form is too heady a tonic for me to contain. I must return to my human body so I may find your sons and the flaming sword."

He heard a non-committal grunt and braced himself for the pain of transformation.

To his surprise, the return to humanity was not fraught in the least and, in a matter of seconds, he found himself upright and back in a world of multi-coloured hues. In an instant, he saw a peculiar emanation glowing from the centre of the altar-stones. What he had taken, in his lycan form, to be nothing more than intriguingly shaped stains intermingled with all the other bloody evidence of the shrine's use, could now be seen for what they were, shimmering veins of heat, radiating gently as they glowed from the soft pink of a sunrise at dawn to the violent orange of a belching volcano.

He stood, enjoying the sensuous feel of it as it bathed his naked flesh with its warmth. He remained there for a time, hypnotised by the pulsing rainbow which caused the walls of the room to throb with ever-changing shadows. Mentally shaking himself, he returned his thoughts to the task at hand, for he still had to overcome the conundrum of how to retrieve the sliver of sword from the rock and transport it to Fenrir without being utterly consumed by its ferocity.

He circled the much-used altar like the wolf he had so recently been, determined to solve the riddle. Though he had no further communication with the wolf-god, he began to sense a mounting impatience, not only from within himself but also from Fenrir. Again, the bond he had forged with the supernatural being leant him an insight which he would otherwise have lacked and he found himself contemplating the fact that, no matter how impatient he felt at his lack of progress in finding what he sought, it was nothing compared to what the wolf-god had endured in the years, centuries, aeons during which he had bided in the prison of Hel. How long had Fenrir yearned for a return to his previous exalted station? How long had he festered upon the shores of the toxic river remembering what he had been and how far he had fallen?

Too long.

Varga steeled himself and sent forth his thought to the wolf-god as he climbed atop the altar and began dismantling it, exposing more and more of the luminescence of the eternal flame to the consecrated walls that had been denied its brightness for so long. "Fenrir, forgive this blasphemy but I see no other way to recover the blade."

...and in the cavern where Varga had first happened upon the ghostly form of Fenrir, the wolf god breathed a huge sigh of contentment and closed his eyes as if to go to sleep...

The massive Viking continued scrabbling at the mighty pile of stones, his muscles writhing and his body sweating with the effort of his labour. For the first time in centuries, fresh blood spattered upon the shrine as Varga's knuckles were shredded by the jagged, unyielding rock, yet still he worked away like a man possessed, squinting as the intensity of the light grew as he moved more and more stones from the sacred altar.

For how long he laboured, he did not know but finally the *horgr* was no more, laying before him in countless pieces. Heat vapour wended its way up to the ceiling as the full power of Surtr's weapon was loosed into the altar-room, seemingly warping the walls on the opposite side from where Varga stood, doubled over, breathing heavily and trying to ignore the ache in his shoulders.

Shielding his eyes, he tried to make out the thin slice of metal that held within it so much potency, but try though he might, the glare became too much and he was compelled to look away.

He growled in frustration because, every time he seemed to make any progress in fulfilling what was asked of him, another obstacle was placed in his way.

Inside his mind, he became aware once more of Garmr's baying reaching him across the mists of time and of Fenrir's warning to 'control the wolf within'. He breathed deeply and closed his eyes.

When he opened them again, he was wolf once more. Varga smiled toothily as his unnaturally enhanced vision enabled him to pick out the small triangle of metal at the seat of the bloom of radiance.

However, despite the wonder he felt at being chosen by Fenrir to perform His works, he still hesitated when it came to reaching forth and grasping the prize, for he was still gripped by the numbing fear of what would happen when he attempted to remove the super-heated weapon from its age-long resting place.

An agony of indecision beset him as his body automatically positioned itself to pounce whilst his mind recoiled in anticipation of the pain that would result if he did. Such was the dichotomy he found himself in, he did not immediately realise that his whole form was quivering uncontrollably.

His embarrassment at this shameful display was what finally tipped the balance and drove him to action. Here he was, in the presence of his God and in a position to rescue his adored father from an infinity of torment and all he could do was shake and shiver like one of the victims of the rampage which the Ulfsgaard clan had unleashed on Rogaland and beyond.

With an atavistic growl of rage, he thrust his paw into the heat, bracing himself for the pain that he was certain would course up his arm, searing his fur in an instant and incinerating his foreleg into ash.

Varga nearly overbalanced as nothing more than a gentle wash of heat ruffled the pelt upon his arm. So surprised was he that he did not even claim the shard straight away, instead he remained poised, entranced by the play of light upon his fur and the manner in which his arm cast mighty shadows across the walls of the newly lit cave.

At length, he reached forward to scoop the blade up in his paw. As his claw touched it and closed around it, his eye was drawn to the direction where the tip of Surtr's sword pointed. He inhaled sharply. Directly in the path of the arrow-like treasure were the top halves of two skulls, each facing the other.

He nearly laughed as he realised that it had taken him what seemed like an age to get to this point, but now, he had found all three objects within the space of minutes.

His discovery was confirmed when, after stalking across the grotto, he awkwardly lifted the skulls up one after the other. Under the first one, there were runic carvings spelling out the legend *"Devourer of The Sun"* and beneath the other, *"Devourer of The Moon"*.

He breathed reverently as the thrill of handling the final remnants of the offspring of Fenrir swept through him, evoking a shiver of excitement that extended from head to toe.

With the uncovering of the skulls now accomplished, with a flick of his right paw, Varga batted the tip of the luminous sword to a place where it was visible to the human eye, for he knew his paws would not be able to manipulate all three objects sufficiently well to enable him to return them to Fenrir.

He winced as he touched it, for the temperature of the sword was beginning to build and the doubts about transporting the weapon safely back to the wolf-god flared within him once more. He sat back on his haunches and considered his next move. He found himself staring blankly at the skulls, at a loss as to what to do. The bark of Garmr was roaring in his ears once more and he realised his thought processes were beginning to fail, the siren call which signalled it was time for him to resume his human form.

He found that, the more he effected the change, the easier it became and so within seconds he was upright once more.

He reached out to pick up the metal point, shrinking back at the last moment as the heat bit at his hand. He cast about for anything in which he could carry the incandescent cargo, a piece of hardy cloth, a bowed section of wood or rock, anything. Nothing presented itself.

...and in the recesses of Gnipahellir, Fenrir, strengthened by the presence of his most worshipful acolyte, sent forth his will...

Varga gasped in shock as the two skulls began to pulse in his hands. He tried to drop them to the cold stone but found he could not. With a surprising lack of concern, he watched as the two top sections of Hati and Skoll's craniums began to fuse themselves to his hands, raising his eyebrows slightly as the unyielding bone expanded fluidly over his fingers and wrists, leaving him grotesquely malformed. He was not disturbed by this however, for he had felt the thrill of connection with his god once more and knew it was His desire that he should be so.

Confident in his new form now, he reached down and used the teeth of Hati's skull to flick the burning shard of sword into the bony mass of his brother-wolf's skull cavity. As soon as the point of the long-unused weapon touched the smooth bone, an irresistible pull gripped him and his two misshapen limbs snapped together to ossify into one large lump of white, the eyeholes shrinking and disappearing totally and the teeth interlocking and meshing into a form so pure and complete that the surface was flawless.

The gargantuan Norseman cocked an ear as he became aware once more of Garmr's eternal baying, though it seemed to him that now it was possessed of an exultant quality, a joyful tone which sang infectiously in Varga's head, causing a grin to slowly smear itself across his sweat-drenched face. With a whoop of joy somewhere between human and vulpine, Varga began to jog back to where he had left Fenrir, elated beyond imagining at his success in retrieving the long-lost artifact and desperate now to find out what plans the wolf-god had for him.

His long strides ate up the ground as he returned to Fenrir's scrutiny. When he found himself before the massive beast again, he could not bring himself to speak, so overwhelmed was he at completing the task.

As the huge animal beheld him, Varga's hands morphed back into their human form and he returned to the man he had been when he had entered the dream. He proffered the trophy he had obtained to Fenrir, bowing low as he held out the two skulls, inside one of which was held the tip of Surtr's sword.

The wolf-god of the Norsemen nodded slightly at the bounty and he began to speak. If he felt any pleasure at the reclamation of the sword and the skulls it did not transmit itself in his voice. Instead, Fenrir's proclamation positively dripped of menace. "Curb thy elation, Hrolfsson. You have taken but one small step upon the path on which your life has now embarked. You have many trials and obstacles to conquer before my re-admittance to the ranks of the gods is to occur and each test must be overcome without exception."

The wolf-god's foreboding words had the desired effect and Varga's zeal began to diminish immediately. Once again, he pushed aside the fantastical nature of his current situation and paid heed to Fenrir's words, hanging on them with rapt attention.

"Then say on. What is it you require from me, Fenrir, son of Loki, for I am yours to command?"

The mammoth wolf rolled its narrow-slitted eyes, but otherwise showed no reaction to the rather incongruous sycophancy, coming as it did from a man who had been either directly or indirectly responsible for hundreds upon hundreds of deaths.

"What you hold in your hands is the key which will unlock the door to our immortality," Fenrir sighed. "It is true that my body is still to be found upon the shores of the Poison River, but I merely exist, I do not live." He fixed the Viking with a ferocious gaze, steeped in an elemental power yet tinged with something else, though whether it was a desperate sadness at his current situation or the excitement of fortune finally beginning to favour him once more, Varga was unable to tell. "There are those who seek to thwart my designs, servants of the treacherous ones who bound me here all those aeons ago. Even as you lie in your bed dreaming this dream, they approach, ready to lay siege to your enclave and end your life."

Varga found himself rather taken aback by the defeatist tone present within the god's voice. He had geared himself up for a blood-and-thunder diatribe railing against the deceitful Aesir and their underhand ways. "Then they will be faced down and routed. Slaughtered just as you slaughtered Odin on the plain of Vigrid," he countered, hoping his words would awaken some sort of resistance in Fenrir's voice.

"Whose son then tore my jaws apart and despatched me to Hel," the wolf roared, his lips peeling back in a terrifying snarl. "Make no mistake, Hrolfsson, you may have a deity on your side but no destiny, not even one as blessed as a god's, is ever written in stone. Trust me, the multitude who march upon you are too many in number for you to best in battle. You must retreat from their wrath, so that you may face them down in future days."

The Viking's face betrayed his confusion for Fenrir barked a guttural laugh. "Do you question my commands, Varga? My powers may be lacking in most ways but I still have the gift of foresight. I can penetrate the mists of the future and apprehend the series of events which are required to happen for my plans to be achieved, but they are as much subject to the winds of change as a leaf separated from a branch by the advance of autumn."

The wolf continued regarding his disciple for a time, allowing him to ponder his words then he continued. "You must flee from Rogaland, Varga, and you must do it soon. I can snuff the first stirrings of the second Fimbulvetr in my nostrils and, if you do not leave the shores of your Petty Kingdom within the month, the seas will become impassable and you will be left stranded in Ulfsgaard, contemplating the imminent death of all your hopes and dreams."

Varga licked lips that were suddenly bone-dry. "Where should our heading be? I have only raided once and..." His voice tailed off as he saw the wolf's massive hackles begin to rise.

"You are Viking-born," screeched Fenrir Hel-Mouth. "Do not dare stand before me and snivel your excuses. If you do not think yourself worthy of my trust then I will strike you down where you stand and find another to take your place."

"I am sorry, Fenrir. It is just not in my nature to leave my enemies at my back. I would rather them bloodied and bowed before me, pleading for their miserable lives."

The wolf-god nodded curtly, "That is the kind of language I had expected to hear from you, Varga," he smiled warmly. "I have had word enough of your deeds that I should not doubt you. Excuse my heated words, they are fuelled by the impatience of an eternity spent thirsting for release."

"So where then?" Varga pressed. "Where will you send me and my cohorts?"

"In all honesty, I do not know." The wolf shrugged. "Such is the nature of prophecy, I am afraid. You will be subject to the whims of Njord as much as any other seafarer and will end up where you may."

The Norseman's face revealed little of his thoughts but the vagueness of Fenrir's words troubled him.

"There will be a place, a place not in these lands, that will call to your soul as no other place ever has or ever will. It is there that you must take my children's skulls and the eternal heat of Surtr's sword."

Scepticism was writ large in the chieftain's voice as he said, "Please do not misunderstand me, Fenrir, but I find it impossible to believe there can be another location upon the earth that will captivate me like Ulfsgaard. It is the home of five generations of Hrolfssons and their family. I was born there and my father and mother are interred there, along with their parents and their parents before them."

The wolf-god seemed to accept the clansman's words in the spirit they were intended, merely nodding graciously. "Nonetheless, Varga, it is your fate to find this place. You will be free once there to establish a permanent home from which you will be able to accomplish our ultimate goal of resurrection and redemption." The light had returned to Fenrir's eyes as he said this and the sheer brute power pulsing from the god flooded into Varga's being like fire in his veins.

"Do not make the error of assuming that our foes will not still seek your destruction even though you no longer bide upon these shores. You must be forever vigilant against them but here you will have an advantage, provided to you by my sons and Surtr."

Though he had not thought it possible, Varga began listening even more intently to the god of wolves, for here was the crux of why he was here, here was the reason he had been chosen, here was the beginning of the solution to his father's never-ending torment.

"You must use the skulls to transport Surtr's sword away from here. Once you have discovered your ultimate destination and laid down your roots, place the skulls in the centre of your house on either side of the blade and use the weapon as the spark to light a fire. It will be a flame that must be fed with the fuel of blood and bone. You must take the skulls of a hundred thousand enemies and see them consumed by its fire. Then and only then will the flame have burned hot enough and long enough to burn through the earth and downwards into Hel, there to create a gateway through which I and my minions may rise again and visit misery upon misery to all who confounded us all those centuries ago."

Varga Hrolfsson stood agape, now fully in possession of Fenrir's scheme and also the enormity of the undertaking which had been laid before him.

"Go now, Varga. Seek out your fate across the waves," Fenrir nodded. With that, he began to howl, the sound building in volume from an eerie moan to a spine-tingling crescendo of anguish that caused Varga to drop the skulls and sword to the floor of the cave and clamp his hands over his ears in an effort to shut out the nearly physical force of the wolf-god's lament. He shut his eyes and, as an instinctive release, joined in the call, screaming until he felt his lungs would burst.

With a start, he felt hands upon him and jerked upright.

Shivering and with sweat pouring from him, he looked down to see the woman whom he had left naked and spent in his bed before the vision of Fenrir had come to him, stroking the tousled hair of his chest, her green eyes wide and her blonde hair falling across her face. "What is it, Varga?" she gasped loudly as he turned to her with hellfire ablaze in his eyes.

Without a word, he sprung from the bed, startling the other male occupant into wakefulness. He threw the door aside and stalked out into the night, casting suspicious looks into the pre-dawn gloom.

He became aware of the woman's hand again, this time stroking him more intimately. "Come back to the bedchamber," she purred, "Myself and Henrik will chase your nightmares away."

Without thought, he lashed out, viciously backhanding the woman to the floor. "Put your clothes back on, Ingemara," he spat contemptuously. "Then pass the word around the village. We are to leave Ulfsgaard as soon as we may."

Ingemara snaked a tongue across her rapidly swelling lips, tasting the acid tang of blood and shivering both in fear and excitement at the sheer magnetism exuding from the clan chief. "Leave," she stammered, "but..."

Varga's right hand snapped out and grabbed her around the throat. "Do not make me ask twice." He released her. "Go."

That had been three years past.

Within a week, Ulfsgaard had become a ghost town, populated only by the scavengers of the animal world who had descended upon the deserted homesteads, gleefully accepting the plentiful bounty on offer.

From there, the denizens of that forsaken place had set sail across the German Ocean on a voyage of unknown destination, leaving the tribes dispatched from Skien to obliterate them impotently furious at being robbed of their target.

The Ulfhednar had endured dreadful conditions as they traversed the sea in their longship and it was only through the skills of the more grizzled veterans that they survived the crossing at all.

They had been blown to the north into the Norwegian Sea almost immediately by strong winds and driving rain, although initially this had seemed like a blessing as, within weeks, they had beached upon the northern shores of what was to become the Shetland Islands, tearing through the unwelcoming terrain like a scythe through wheat as, at Varga's behest, the tribe began to set about their bloody god-given task.

After a matter of weeks, it became clear to Varga that this was not the place which Fenrir had alluded to in his vision and so the clan embarked once more across the waters, despite the fact that, as the prophecied eternal winter of Fimbulvetr had begun to increase its grip on the northern seas, the showers were now more often than not flecked with snow and sleet.

The whims of Njord, Norse God of the sea, took them north and they once again found themselves marooned upon a desolately bleak coastline, this time the southern coast of the Faroe Islands, though again they were not known as such. This time it took even less time for Hrolfsson to conclude that Fenrir's scheming would perish at birth were the clan to settle there, for the lands seem to consist of little more than sheep and birds.

After this ill-starred sojourn, the clan finally began to drift on a southerly heading, eventually arriving on the North Ronaldsay coastline after nearly half a year at sea.

As Varga Hrolfsson stood upon the prow of the ship, he suspected that, at last, he was nearing the ultimate destination which Fenrir had spoken of, for the Ulfhednar had been sorely tested ever since they had left the uninhabited Faroes. Though they had stocked up as far as they could with meat for their voyage, it was meagre fare and rumblings of discontent had begun to emanate from some of the crew. The clan-leader moved swiftly to quell the disruptive mood by the simple expedient of killing the perceived ringleaders and sharing their remains among the surviving tribes-people, thus solving two problems in one fell swoop, but privately the beginnings of doubt were starting to play on his mind and he knew that his violent solution to the immediate difficulty was a stop-gap measure at best.

Therefore when land was sighted once more, Varga's relief was as heartfelt as any man or woman aboard.

Over the next year, the Ulfhednar clan became a blight upon the Pictish people who inhabited the hitherto blissfully paradise-like islands.

As with most peoples in the north of Europe, the Pictish life was one of farming centred around small communities and, though they were blessed with the usual characteristics of toughness and stoicism that the vagaries of their existence had bred into them, they were completely unprepared for the ferocity of the Viking clan's onslaught and they were routed within weeks, a fate which then befell several of the other islands within the archipelago.

Sanday, Eday, Stronsay and Shapinsay all felt the taint of blood spilt and death dealt as the hordes of Norse warriors swept across them. Still though the call of the soul, which Varga braced himself for day after day proved elusive and, once again, the need to move on, to find that perfect place which would become the new shrine to Fenrir, tugged at him and he had uprooted his people once again, this time adopting a more placatory approach to his reasoning, trying to accomplish with words what he had hitherto only managed to achieve with violence and intimidation. To his surprise and pleasure, the passion of his words and vision seemed to find favour with the tribe and they were more than willing to do as they were bid.

This time though, after they had embarked upon the next leg of their journey, they found themselves inexorably drawn towards the coastline of mainland Caledonia, the tides propelling them west then south as they left the waters of the North Atlantic Ocean and found themselves traversing the body of water known locally as The Minch. However, the apparent attraction to the mainland began to dissipate and they began to float away from the mainland towards the Hebridean islands.

Inauspiciously, the Ulfsgaard Vikings first found themselves upon the beaches of the uninhabited Shiant Islands, finding only a plethora of seabirds to keep them company. It took the clan less than four days to ascertain the absence of people upon the breathtaking vistas and so they struck out across the water once more.

It was on this stage of the voyage that Varga Hrolfsson received the omen which he had been praying to see for so long. The longship was hugging the awe-inspiring jagged cliffs of the eastern coast of the island of Lewis, allowing the currents to take them where they would. The massive leader of the Ulfhednar was standing as close to the prow of the *Varulv* as he dared, staring intently at the beauteous mountainsides that graced the land which they drifted by. The moon, so huge and stirring in its magnificence, lit the wave-tops and rocks with an almost supernatural brilliance and the stars glistered in the cloudless sky, stretching away over the land and sea and out of the Norseman's sight away beyond the horizon.

The whole night had a breathless quality to it which teased at Varga's senses, tantalizing him into a restless frenzy of expectation. He had prowled around the front of the ship for hours, taking up his position as the sun had briefly broken through the all-pervasive cloud and begun its descent into evening, then on through the slate-grey of dusk as the banks of snow-clouds reclaimed the sky once more.

He remained unmoved as the thick flakes began to fall, sending the less hardy seafarers to seek some shelter, still staring across the ever-changing seascape, eyes fixed on some unspecified point alone with his thoughts. The appearance of his beloved moon changed the trajectory of his gaze from the constantly roiling surface of the water to the immutable changelessness of the island's cliffs.

The unexpected incandescence of the moonlight seemed to burn the clouds away and it was not long before the last shreds had dispersed from the sky, leaving the moon and stars as the only occupants of the heavens above.

The moon was positioned in such a way that it seemed to be rolling along the summits of the cliffs as the *Varulv* made its graceful progress through the waters of the Minch. Varga's head came up as if he had apprehended something on the wind, though no wind was present on this most peaceful of nights. Then, with a heart-stopping suddenness that sent a frisson of excitement racing up and down his spine, the sound of a wolf's mournful baying came to his ears. His head spun round seeking the source of the magical sound and there upon the headland was the authoress of the lament.

The magnificent beast was silhouetted perfectly by the silver orb and Varga felt a surge of honour that he was able to bear witness to such a display. The lithe female wolf sat with her back proudly erect, perched on her haunches, narrow chest thrust out majestically, muzzle to the sky, baying from the depths of her soul.

As the call echoed over the waves, Varga felt the ship begin to shift towards the shore. He briefly flicked his gaze away from the she-wolf towards the clansmen operating the oars and, even though he could not make out all of their faces, he knew that they too were enthused by the spectacle and nodded appreciation.

Whilst the Viking chief had been transfixed by the splendid animal, the longship had struck out for a break in the imposing coastline which cleaved its way into the main body of the island but, even as the cliffs reared above the *Varulv*, blotting out the moon and stars, those upon the deck were still able to follow the progress of the beast as she mirrored their course deeper into the Hebridean countryside, for the bitch was surrounded by an otherworldly glow, an ethereal radiance that bathed her in a cool, clear light.

A startled shout jerked Varga from his appreciation of the she-wolf's effortless grace and he made his way down towards the stern of the ship, picking his way through the lines of sea chests which acted as both seats and storage to the Viking warriors, though he still took the time to glance up at the rocks to ensure that the silver sentinel continued to accompany them. However, taking into account the timing of the beast's appearance and the manner in which it had announced its presence, he felt sure that the wolf would be a constant companion for the remainder of their journey, showing them the way to their new home.

As Varga gained the stern, he saw a burly warrior standing back from his oar with a shocked expression on his face. Following the man's wide-eyed gaze, Varga inhaled sharply. The oar was crawling with the same mercurial aura as the wolf upon the headland. With a lazy smile breaking upon his face, the chief laid a comforting hand upon his fellow Ulfhednar's shoulder and said, "Do not be afraid, Jorgen. See, the spirit-light shares the same hue as our guardian upon the bluff. This is a blessing from Fenrir, something to be thankful for, not to cower from. It will not harm you."

Though he was certain of his safety, Varga's reach was still tentative as his fingers quested forward, eventually touching the oar and silently marvelling as the silver shimmer engulfed him, wrapping him inside a cocoon of flickering brilliance.

With orgiastic pleasure, he changed into his lycan form and bellowed a reply to the fantastical creature upon the promontory. As she answered him with her own eerie call, like a ripple from a stone dropped in a pond, the crew of the *Varulv* began to transform, first in ones and twos and then in groups, joining their leader in his bestial form and roaring their exultations to the ends of the earth and beyond.

The oars and sails remained bathed in the ghostly luminescence and moved of their own accord, continuing along the waterway which they had begun to navigate when the wolven bitch had first appeared.

For the remaining span of the night, the *Varulv* drifted along its ordained path, shadowed all the while by the watcher upon the hill. As the Viking vessel was moving along under its own supernatural power, the majority of the Ulfhednar remained in their lycan form, revelling in the animalistic straightforwardness, whilst those who chose to embrace their humanity once more gave voice to the unspoken joy they all felt at Varga's proclamation that the wolf upon the hill had appeared to usher them to their new home.

And so it was that, after nearly two years of life upon the water, though it was unknown to them at the time, the Ulfsgaard clan were scant hours away from gazing upon the crannog that they would name Dun Varulfur, for the first time. The Vikings had espied many villages and isolated farmsteads within view of the shores of the loch but, unlike before where they had plundered without stint, Hrolfsson resisted the temptation of further brutality because their vulpine escort showed no inclination to cease her long, loping strides and the war-chief feared that, should they lose sight of her, Fenrir would visit woe upon woe on the tribe as the wolf-god would take offence at their blasphemous indifference to the miracle he had provided them with.

With a rumbling voice that stayed the hands of even his most rabid disciples, he said, "Do not forget, we will soon establish our new home hereabouts. We will have more than ample time to introduce ourselves to the local livestock."

That had evoked uproarious laughter amongst the clan and they had resumed their waiting without further complaint.

Just as the dawn began to lighten the endless Hebridean sky, they beached upon the north-western shore of Loch Seaforth and struck out across the meadows of heather as ever following the trail of the wolf. The ingenious design of the *Varulv*, indeed the design of all Viking longships, was such that the ship's light weight enabled it to be carried over portages as well as its shallow draft allowing navigation in waters as little as one metre deep.

Therefore, the sunrise was greeted with the rather bizarre sight of the *Varulv* apparently floating across the idyllic pastures of the isle of Lewis.

By the light of the sun, the she-wolf which had led the party inland lost some of her enigmatic power but there was still a feeling about her of elemental energy which both thrilled and chilled Varga in equal measure.

At length, after carrying the *Varulv* nearly five miles across the fertile grassy plains, they arrived at the shores of another loch, this one bathed in a deadening fog that had increased in its thickness as they had travelled further west.

Varga peered around the countryside, unable to see very much at all. He fancied that it was near noon, for the fog burned brightly directly above the exhausted crew. Though they were, to a man, powerfully built, this had been by far the longest distance which they had ever shouldered the *Varulv*.

He stared at the wolf which had stopped at the threshold of the water and sat upon her haunches regarding him coolly.

"We have followed you across water and earth, where away are we bound now?" he asked respectfully.

The wolf looked over her shoulder and jerked her head in a surprisingly human way.

Varga looked in the vague direction of the animal's nod then returned his gaze to the wondrous creature. His eyes flared in shock, for the elegant beast had disappeared, the only suggestion that she had ever been there being a slightly deeper silvery tint to some of the tendrils of fog which drifted around the Viking tribe.

As the last vestiges of the she-wolf dissolved, shouts erupted from the crew and the clashing of sword upon shield rang through the murk. Varga's hand flew to his Langsax, the long-handled knife which was the weapon of choice among the Ulfhednar. With an evil fervour lighting his stare, he traced the intricate engraving of a wolfshead, which had been cunningly formed upon the wicked blade, with narrowed eyes then lightly kissed the keenly edged weapon, "Come, Varkolak, it is time for you to dance."

As he advanced towards the fighting, the miasma began to thin out and he saw a number of wooden constructions stretching out across the peaceful waters of the loch. He could clearly see five of the domiciles and was surprised that more were becoming apparent as the sun began to burn off the mist. However, Varga had no time to further ponder this strange set of dwellings because, in the matter of a few strides, he found himself amongst a chaotic mass of struggling bodies, each enthused with murderous intent.

Battlecries from the native tribesmen were bellowed into the air, their words not meaning anything to the Viking invaders, but their intent clear.

Hrolfsson lay about himself, slicing through the throat of a wild-eyed defender who looked little older than a child, then swung around to thrust his blade into the unprotected guts of a woad-daubed bare-chested giant, whose self-assured expression rapidly disintegrated into undisguised agony, as the pain from the killing wound tore through him.

As Varga searched for his next victim, wiping the stickiness of the blood from his weapon upon the fallen man's woollen kilt, he found himself gazing into the dead eyes of one of his fellow Ulfhednar, Ranald Asketill, one of the first of Varga's villagers to pledge his fealty to the green-eyed war-chief.

A fleeting sensation of pity visited him as he looked into the lifeless grey eyes and the matted, blood-spattered beard and face of his former disciple. Varga considered the possibility that a re-evaluation of their newfound foes might be prudent because, even though they had inevitably lost members of the clan on their bloody voyages around the seas and islands of Northern Europe, they had merely been the victims of natural selection, new to the calling of the wolf and more vulnerable than the more seasoned lycanthropes.

Ranald, on the other hand, was a veteran of the clan and had, at times, even acted as confidante to the younger man, though the divine guidance under which Varga believed himself to be meant that those times were few and far between. Shaking himself free of the momentary melancholia, Varga re-launched himself into the fray, quickly dispatching another three of the Picts to their graves.

During another temporary lull, he counted seven more of his comrades lying prone amongst the slaughtered. Further shouts came on the wind as a host of nearly a hundred Pictish tribesmen hoved into view from behind a small barrow, bellowing curses as they crested the shallow hill.

"Ulfhednar! To me!" Varga bellowed, "Make for the ship."

Though he was not unduly worried by the natives' superiority of numbers, he judged it wise to withdraw to the relative safety of the *Varulv* and thus remove the element of surprise that the Picts had managed to achieve.

As the majority of the Vikings gained the deck and shouldered the oars, Varga led a ruthless blitzkrieg through the front ranks of the native clansmen, cleaving and hewing with his beloved Varkolak, scattering them and allowing the launch of the *Varulv* onto the loch. Like the battle-honed machine that they were, at Varga's barked order, the Norsemen who had joined him in his maniacal onslaught withdrew from the massacre, wading into the corpse-strewn water, stained pink by the blood of the dead and dying and were hauled onto the vessel, seeming to fly out of the water as they gripped the ropes which had been thrown to them before being pulled clear of the loch by those already aboard.

The two groups eyed each other across the rapidly growing space which had opened between them as the *Varulv* floated out into the main body of the lake.

Though they spoke no words, the Picts began to bang their shields and swords together in a solemn wordless hymn to the fallen, emboldened by their triumph yet filled with sorrow at the loss of their fellows.

For their part, the Ulfhednar nodded grudging respect towards the native clansmen. Though Varga's men had no doubt that this was no more than a temporary setback, it was the first time they had even come close to being bested and, in a strange way, it cemented the initial certainty he had felt that this place, the place which the ethereal she-wolf had led them to, was their new spiritual home.

As the leader of the Vikings lost sight of the Picts in the hazy sunshine, he turned from them and studied the many wooden constructions which dotted the edge of the loch, stretching away along the shoreline as far as the eye could see. He counted ten of them extending off into the distance and found himself wondering how the native folk reached them, for he could see hate-filled faces regarding him from every window of the dwellings.

"Varga," Leofric, a blond-haired warrior born blind in one eye, tapped his chief on the shoulder and pointed across the water, stroking his drooping horseshoe moustache with the other hand.

"Interesting" was all Varga said.

The pair rested their elbows on the side of the ship and watched as a goodly amount of villagers followed the stately progress of the *Varulv* through the limpid waters, ostensibly by walking atop the surface of the loch between the crannogs.

"That is ingenious," Leofric observed, "How do you think they do it? Do they number volvas amongst their ranks?"

Varga peered over his shoulder at his counterpart with a look of disgust upon his face which suggested he thought Leofric may have got a bang on the head during the recent skirmish. "Either that or they have simply erected platforms just below the waterline."

"Maybe," Leofric acknowledged with an impish grin on his face.

Varga dismissed him with a clipped "Idiot" and returned his scrutiny to the network of wooden houses.

As he stared appreciatively at the construction, he found himself picturing a new Ulfsgaard being birthed in this place. A volcano from which the destructive might of the Ulfhednar could erupt at will then return with the spoils of their plunder to enjoy at their leisure, in an eminently defensible position.

He snuffed in a huge lungful of the pure, refreshing air and exhaled expansively, "We are home, my children." He turned to address the assembled multitude of his people upon the wooden deck of the *Varulv*, looking from face to face, slightly unsettled by the lack of response to his proclamation. "I see misgivings in your eyes. Do you doubt my judgment?" he said calmly, his voice dangerously quiet.

Still not a word was forthcoming, which, in itself, was an all-too-clear answer to Varga's question.

The Viking chief's face twisted into a bestial grimace and he could feel the wolf behind his eyes, straining at the leash, still at bay but barely. "So this is the next chapter of the saga of the Ulfhednar, is it? The all-conquering horde cowed into silence and licking their wounds at the first instance of real resistance they meet? Fenrir's teeth, you are a pathetic bunch. What is the matter with you all? Have you grown fat and lazy, lulled by the unending decadence and debauchery which you have indulged in?"

He vaulted athletically down from his station at the prow, stalking through the ranks of oarsmen and women, his temper plain for all to see. Like a ripple of energy emanating from him, as he walked, those whom he walked past shrunk back from his rage.

"Well? What do you say? Why do you visit such dishonour upon your Viking heritage?"

He whipped round as a cracked voice spoke behind him. Varga was momentarily caught off-guard by the speaker's identity, for it was the one of the oldest residents of Ulfsgaard, Beyla the Seeress.

She was regarded by most of the villagers with a healthless mixture of awe and fear, for she had bided in the Rogaland area for generation upon generation. She was part of the fabric of Ulfsgaard's history, a walking, talking threat used by parents upon their errant children to cow them into frightened obedience.

She had always seemed wizened with age for as long as anyone could remember. Even Varga himself had vivid memories of sitting on his father's knee and being warned that 'old Beyla's evil eye' would seek him out if he did not do as his parents wished.

In his formative years, Varga would shrink from her sight when he saw her shambling about the dusty streets of Ulfsgaard, thrilled by a frisson that was half fear, half excitement as he and the other village children ran from her, hiding as she passed by and whispering hurtful insults at her retreating back.

Then, as he grew into a young man, according her a modicum of respect for reasons he was not altogether sure of, simply aping his father's deference towards her.

He then had little to do with her for a number of years after that, for the carousing, rambunctious life of his tribe was at its height and he cared little

129

for the homespun banality of Ulfsgaard, preferring to muse as to what was beyond the horizon, not remain concerned as to what he had left behind.

The folly of Varga's arrogant disdain towards his roots came back to haunt him as he returned from his first voyage to the horror of his father's illness.

Beyla had been there then, as she had from the moment the old man had first taken sick.

Beyla had mopped his brow when he was burning from the inside out and lain with him to warm him when his fevered dreams imagined him into the grip of the hardest winter.

Beyla had cleansed him when he had soiled himself and taken his foul-mouthed abuse in mute resignation, recognising it for what it was, the acidic ramblings of a scared, dying man.

For those bottomless acts of kindness, Varga had, from then on, always treated her with veneration above and beyond the esteem in which a seeress was usually held.

To have done all she did for his father even though her gift, or curse in this case, must have revealed that all her efforts would be for naught, was something Varga would never forget.

That reverence for the old woman made him bite off the stream of bile which he had readied to unleash upon the first to speak and, instead, he merely glared at the author of the interruption.

"Varga Hrolfsson," her cracked voice hissed, "do not assume you or indeed any here are invincible. It is undeniable that you are touched by the Gods but as Fenrir himself cautioned you 'no destiny, not even one as blessed as a God's, is ever written in stone'."

Outwardly, the only indication of the clan chief's surprise at the fortune-teller quoting directly from his dream of so long ago was a slight narrowing of his emerald eyes. Inwardly, however, he was rocked by the unexpected revelation and he could tell from the hag's gap-toothed smirk that she knew it.

"Aye, Varga, never underestimate what Beyla knows. Just be warned that once the fire you bear is hearthed, you take care not to let the flame inside you extinguish."

"Your meaning, Beyla?" Varga asked, his voice possessing its usual harsh edge but slightly tempered by curiosity at her riddle.

"Even now, your purpose is becoming clouded. A hundred thousand skulls you need to unleash Fenrir HelMouth, yet you do not even know how many you have already hoarded aboard the *Varulv* or how many heads have gone begging when the battle-lust is upon you." She advanced upon the huge Norseman and would have cut a comic figure as she jabbed a misshapen finger at the Viking's massive chest, had it not been for the fey light which blazed in her eyes. "Will your appointed task fall by the wayside as you rape and pillage your way through the native folk of these islands? Think on, Hrolfsson, when you have a shrine to return to day in and day out and are robbed of the urgency of the nomadic life, it might well be you who ends up lulled by the decadence and debauchery."

"What have you seen, Beyla? Do you warn me of this after something you have perceived through the mists of the future?"

The ancient shook her head causing her long white hair to flutter strangely in the suddenly cold wind. "Just some words to keep in mind, Varga." She gesticulated at the rest of the tribe, who were sitting open-mouthed, wondering which of the two egos would come out on top of the debate. "All who abide upon this boat have given up their homeland for you to follow you on your blessed quest. Do not cast accusations at them when you know they are well aware that to argue with you is to die at your hand. Perhaps the questions you pose are aimed at yourself as well as them? It is said that a bad blacksmith blames his tools. Well, they are your tools, Varga Hrolfsson. Who then is to blame if they do not work as wished?"

A dangerous smile appeared on the lips of the Ulfhednar clan-chief and all who had seen it before were visited with the certainty that blood would be spilt before it disappeared. "What makes you think I will not kill you for questioning my authority, harridan?" he hissed, his deference to the seeress being overridden by what he saw as the undermining of his leadership by the withered crone.

Beyla shrugged, "You will do what you will. You will listen if you wish. It makes no difference to me. I am long overdue to depart from this life. If this is my time, then it is my time." She sighed, as if resigned to the fact that Varga was about to kill her where she stood, but, at the last, she turned and the power which emanated from her crackled almost tangibly in the intervening space between her and Varga. "I will say one more thing to you, esteemed leader of the Ulfhednar. If you kill any aboard this ship at this moment in time after what you have accused them of, you had better be absolutely sure that you do not succumb to all the worldly pleasures which will undoubtedly follow if you create this shrine to Fenrir because, if you do, then all who survive your wrath on this day will remember what you have done and your hypocrisy will be laid bare for all to see and, in that moment, you will have lost them. Lost them and lost your father to the Nastrond forever. And how do you think Fenrir will treat him then, Varga? What punishments will Fenrir visit upon your father if you, his great hope for a return to godhood, fail in your endeavours?"

"What is your point, Beyla?" Varga sighed.

"You cannot do this on your own, Varga. You will have a need of allies before this journey comes to an end."

The chief said nothing but his face twisted into a disbelieving sneer.

Beyla's eyed flared in anger at the supercilious response but, as they roamed his face, they softened and she shook her head. "Your arrogance will be your downfall, Varga Hrolfsson. You believe that none can stand in your way but there is one who will come, one who will be the bane of you and your kin. Best him and you will fulfil your destiny. Fall to him and you will see out your days as Fenrir's plaything, living for eternity upon eternity of torment and agony."

"What have you seen, Beyla?"

The old woman leant into him and whispered in his ear, "I have seen Monkshood."

"Monkshood?" Varga repeated, the native word feeling strange on his tongue.

Beyla merely raised her eyebrows and walked away.

Varga stared at the back of her head with an unwavering gaze for a long moment, then he too turned away without a word, re-assuming his place at the rail, staring out across the ever-moving water of the loch, the set of his shoulders communicating to any whom approached that he wished for solitude.

The leader of the Ulfhednar blinked, taking a moment to remember where he was, because the memories and images had been so vivid and powerful even though they had occurred many moons ago.

As he stared at Dun Eiledon, the Ulfhednar chief wondered why that particular memory had resurfaced at this time. Had Beyla's words come to pass? Had the sacred purpose which had propelled Hrolfsson down this path been washed away by the oceans of blood that had been spilt upon its altar, drowned into oblivion by the depravity and self-indulgence of his and his tribe's lives?

Varga shook off the unfamiliar feelings of uncertainty which suddenly consumed him, fighting down an involuntary shudder that he tried to convince himself was due to the quickening breeze. A blood-curdling howl jerked him from his contemplation. To add to his doubts, his finely-tuned senses marked it out as one of the pack. With gargantuan strides, he loped across the corpse-scattered field, pausing at the threshold of the Dun.

Once again, a tremble ran down the length of his spine and this time he was unable to pass it off as a sudden drop in temperature. He found his fearful eyes inexorably drawn to the moon, high in the star-pocked sky above him. They widened in shock and his mouth gaped open as a single cloud passed across its cratered face. A cloud in the shape of a cowled man in battle stance, sword held above his head, as if poised to deliver a death blow. As Varga reeled, a word insinuated itself into his psyche, echoing in and out of the dark recesses of his mind, tearing away at the walls of his towering self-assurance and exposing them as wafer-thin facades ripe for destruction. "Monkshood," it whispered.

Varga's unsteadiness of resolve only lasted for scant minutes before being obliterated by the wolf within. With an animalistic bellow, he kicked in the door of the broch, removing it from its hinges.

He scanned the room through narrowed eyes, his gaze settling on the naked body of one of his tribe. Stalking over to the corpse, he saw it was one of the newest converts to the tribe, Malcolm or Martin something, Varga could not bring himself to be bothered to remember the name, but was aware that he could not let the death go unpunished, especially with the recollection of Beyla's warning still so fresh in his mind.

"What has occurred here?" he barked, his deep voice rasping through the sudden silence that his dramatic entrance had caused.

A metallic clatter dragged his gaze to the left as a bloody dirk skittered across the wooden floorboards. It had fallen from the hands of a wide-eyed, petrified tribeswoman. Her long brown hair was matted and sticky with blood and had half-fallen across her face. Her homespun woollen dress had been torn to shreds by both human nail and wolven claw. A mass of cuts and bruises showed through the rents in the fabric and exposed her chest to Varga's lascivious look. She caught the dangerous light blazing in his eyes and backed away from him, gathering her garment about herself in a fruitless attempt to cover up her partial nudity.

It was to no avail. In two massive strides, Varga was before her. He grabbed her wrist and wrenched her to her feet. She hung from his iron grip like a broken marionette whose strings had been severed. The Ulfhednar chief roughly groped her uncovered breast without ever taking his leering eyes from her face. Throwing her to the floor, he began to lower his breeches, licking his lips and grinning hugely.

The world seemed to contract into a bubble for the Pictish clanswoman. The murderous chaos and gory horror all about her seemed to fade into greyness and all there was in the world was the heart-stopping knowledge of her immediate fate and the massive, sickening smirk of Varga Hrolfsson.

She slowly became aware that the Viking had scooped up the knife with which she had stabbed the inexperienced Malcolm Fergusson when he had tried to violate her, and was weaving it in a figure of eight in the air before her. Transfixed by the glinting blade, she jumped when Varga's guttural voice cut through the breathless quiet. He pointed at the prostrate form of the dead man, "You kill?" he asked.

Dana Mackendrick, eldest daughter of the recently slaughtered Chief of the Venicones, nodded hesitantly.

Again, the arrogant sneer appeared, "If I take you, you kill me too?" he scoffed.

She looked at the bunched clumps of muscle on the giant's arms and his mammoth chest, knowing that she would be powerless to stop him if he did choose to force himself upon her. However, she still nodded because the manner of her father's demise demanded that she offer as much resistance as she was able.

Varga threw back his head and laughed, the sound dying on his lips as he felt an impact on his right hand. He hissed as the limp form of Dana Mackendrick slid off the knife and collapsed to the ground.

Robbed of the opportunity to release the complicated build-up of emotions which had surfaced after his remembrance of Beyla and the eerie shadow which had blighted the moon, the heat of lust became the heat of fury and he kicked the dead woman against the bloodstained walls of Dun Eiledon.

For a moment, he stood statuesque, even though a raging volcano caromed around within him.

The young woman lay dead before him but he still yearned to violate her, to demonstrate the strength and virility which had characterised his leadership to all who bore witness, be they invader or native but, try thought he might, he was unable to keep the passion kindled, which enraged him even further.

As his teeth began to sharpen, nails began to lengthen, spine began to reconfigure itself as had happened hundreds of times before, he lashed out, eyes tight shut, uncaring whether lycan or innocent fell victim to his killing frenzy.

Both Ulfhednar and Venicone shrank from him as he tore about the room, ripping throats and dealing death in a scarlet tornado borne of impotence and frustration.

To all outward appearances, Varga Hrolfsson had become lost in the uncontrolled red mist of the berserker but, as the transmogrification was now second nature to him, he found that he still retained a good deal of humanity in his mind at least, though not in his physical form.

He had just despatched another newcomer to the tribe, this time a raven-haired beauty named Ailsa, who had attached herself to the Ulfhednar when they had overrun the Pictish resistance at the village of Mullochry. She had been condemned to burn as an adulterous witch and was about to be put to death when the wolven horde had descended upon the village and she had been both quick to show her gratitude and her willingness to adapt to the Ulfhednar way.

However, she had attached herself to one of the Krieghund, an elite group of five who were, to all intents and purposes, the deputies of the clan, although the inherent disorganisation of the Vikings meant that the title was simply an unspoken recognition of their place in the tribe rather than an actual position in an official hierarchy.

As Ailsa died at the feet of the ravening clan-chief, Olof Sigurdsson, her confederate in the Krieghund, rounded on his leader, snarling insults at him. "Varga, cease this now."

"You dare speak to me like that?" Varga roared in answer, launching himself across the space between them.

They both went down in a blur of claw and fur, rolling around on the dirty wooden floor of the Dun.

After a minute or so of mindless violence, they broke away from each other, circling, taking note of one another's wounds, looking for the split second of opportunity which would mean triumph for the victor and death for the defeated.

Hrolfsson's lips were peeled back, baring his razor-sharp teeth. "So it comes to this, Olof?" he hissed. "What misguided notion makes you think you can best me? Honeyed words from your dead bitch?"

The Krieghund cuffed away some of the free-flowing blood that poured from a nasty wound above his left eyebrow. "It is not a matter of besting you, Varga," Olof snarled back, "It is a matter of what is best for the clan."

The Ulfhednar leader feinted to swing with his right paw, then hit out with his left, his claws coming within inches of his challenger's face, "And what makes you think you know what is best for the clan, Sigurdsson?"

"I know that trawling aimlessly about the countryside or indiscriminately killing our kith and kin is not." Olof countered.

Varga's eyes narrowed. "How else are we..." In mid-sentence, he leapt at his former second-in-command, putting him off balance. His outstretched paw punched through Sigurdsson's stomach, shredding the werewolf's intestines as he moved in closer, raking the claws from left to right and up and down, relishing the horrified look on Olof's face and breathing sensuously as the warmth of the gouting blood drenched his arm and torso. In a voice which carried more impact for its quietness, he muttered in the dying lycan's ear, "How else are we to collect the skulls of our enemies to add to the pyre at Dun Varulfur?"

The gurgling answer died in Olof Sigurdsson's throat as he joined the recently deceased Ailsa in death's eternal embrace.

135

Varga let the body fall from his bespattered arm then stared all around Dun Eiledon, drawing an urgent satisfaction from the fetid atmosphere of death and chaos that his tribe had brought about. As his gaze returned to the shattered bodies of Olof and Ailsa, he resumed his human form. "Kill those still alive, gather the skulls then return to the Dun," he muttered quietly to the remaining four Krieghund.

When they failed to move, his voice dropped even lower and positively dripped with menace. "Do you seek to supplant me as well, Jordis? What of you, Morten? Do you wish to join Olof on the Nastrond?"

Without a word, the four remaining beasts removed themselves from his sight, though their demeanour suggested that the murder of their compatriot would be an issue which would raise its head in the future.

To the accompaniment of the remaining victims' shrieks and the splintering of bone as heads were rent from bodies, Varga walked ponderously from Dun Eiledon. Reluctantly, he forced himself to stare skyward at the moon, readying himself to roar defiance at the enigmatic figure described upon its surface. He was pleasantly surprised to find the cratered exterior completely free of shadow so he closed his eyes and drank in the majesty of the night. For long moments he stood, confidence restored, for this was his domain and the moonlight was his friend.

A footfall behind him robbed him of the perfection of the moment and he sighed heavily.

A hesitant voice intruded on his consciousness, "Varga?"

He turned to face the reticent interrupter of his reverie with a raised eyebrow.

"There is one who will not die, Varga. He is some sort of spellweaver I presume." The bearer of the news, one called Strogen, who had stood with Varga from the beginnings of the odyssey in Ulfsgaard, followed his clan-chief back into the tribal home of the Venicones, babbling hurriedly, trying to ensure that the failure of the Ulfhednar to do as they were bid did not rebound upon him. He had long ago recognised that the best way to steer clear of Varga's towering rages was to blend into the background and immerse himself in the pack, which meant he was unused to addressing the massive Viking on a one-to-one basis. "He seems immune to our attacks. He simply stands, eyes closed and no matter what we do, he continues to live without a mark upon him." Strogen yammered nervously, disquieted by the silence with which Varga had received his tidings.

Hrolfsson's eyes blazed irritably which was enough to quieten the constant stream of Strogen's justification of the clan's failure to wipe out the last remaining native.

As he entered, his eyes instantly spotted the one thwarting the wolves. Four beasts were attempting to maul the man but, as Strogen had described, they might as well have been trying to rip the air in two.

Varga barged them out of the way and immediately raked his claws across the face of the man, but his powerful stroke was met with no resistance and he nearly overbalanced. Despite feeling the onset of another berserk rage starting to build, Varga forced himself to consider the problem. The first thing he noticed was the man's mouth, though it was hard to discern through the unkempt tangle of his red beard. It was constantly moving, mouthing silent words or a magical incantation, perhaps even a prayer, Varga thought.

His eyes travelled down the man's body. An unclothed torso wrapped loosely by a filthy mish-mash of furs, matted with old dirt and fresh blood, thin, pale legs spattered with mud, and leather boots, discoloured through age and an inhospitable climate. He dropped to his haunches and stared intently at the man's feet.

Slowly, a broad smile appeared upon Varga Hrolfsson's face.

A couple of miles away in a large stand of trees, two men stood facing each other, one old and despondent, the other vital and spry, though both were utterly drained by despair.

The older man was speaking urgently, "You must flee from here, Craigan. Go before the horde tire of the slaughter and hie along this trail. It will take them seconds to overcome you and then the Venicones will truly be extinct. You are our people's last hope. You must seek out Monkshood, for he is the only one who may bring a halt to the pestilence that so blights these lands."

He stared beseechingly at the younger man, hoping against hope that his words would hit home and steer him towards doing the right thing.

Craigan shifted uncomfortably from foot to foot, trapped in an agony of indecision. His voice cracked and, as he spoke, it became clear he was on the brink of weeping. "I cannot. I must stand and fight this evil. I am Venicone. How would I be able to look any of my kin in the eye ever again if I run, Jameson?"

The grizzled seer of Dun Eiledon resisted the urge to berate the youngster because he knew he would be torn in exactly the same way, were he faced with the dilemma. He laid hands of forced gentleness upon Craigan's shoulders and spoke softly, pitching his voice in a way that demonstrated his sympathy for the situation but would also brook no argument. "You have to, Craigan. They are all dead. I saw Duncan cut in two and..."

The colour drained from Craigan's face as he tried to speak, the words choking him. "Not Dana."

"I'm sorry, lad," Jameson hung his head for a moment but, when he looked up again, his face was set in a grimace of ferocious pride, "damn me if she didn't die a death befitting the daughter of a chief, though. She killed one of them then looked that massive bastard square in the eye as she died." He glowered at the youthful tribesman. "You owe it to her to seek help, boy."

Craigan McIntyre cuffed away the tears from his cheeks and tried to quell the urge to empty his stomach. "But where do I go, Jameson? Where will I find this Monkshood? How will I even know I have found him?"

"You will find him on the mainland, Craigan. I…" Jameson began to say, but the words died in his throat. Without ceremony and, with the adolescent Venicone looking on in abject horror, his head toppled from his shoulders.

The young man's hands flew to his face, covering his eyes in an effort to erase the hideous spectacle.

When he had plucked up the courage to remove them, there was no trace of Jameson to be seen.

Varga poked at the three stones in the palm of his hand, tracing the random pattern of lines and ruts which swirled around their surface. He then stared down at their four fellows, which were now spread out on all four sides of the glass bowl upon which the native spell-weaver had been standing.

With no more than a sidelong glance at the decapitated corpse, he rounded on the wolves who he had charged with the mopping up of the last remaining victims. "Did you fools not see the circle of stones in which he stood? Did it not occur to you that magic was afoot?"

His eyes flared as he watched the copious amount of blood begin to pool in the base of the bowl. When Varga had ripped his head from his shoulders, Jameson's neck had been left, hanging over the edge of the glass vessel and so, his lifeblood was gushing into the bowed bottom. It ebbed and flowed in a disconcerting manner, forcing Varga to avert his gaze as the erratic movement unsettled him for reasons he could not explain.

Sharp intakes of breath reverberated around the hushed Dun. The clan chief of the Ulfhednar stared in curiosity at the faces of his cohorts then forced himself to look back towards the elaborate glass basin.

What he saw chilled him to the marrow.

The blood, despite it having been spilt mere seconds before, had dried into a warped stain that spread over the surface of the bowl. However, in defiance of all logic, it had congealed into the self-same shape as the shadow which had passed over the moon and had so perturbed the Viking warrior.

Again, Varga endeavoured to convince himself that it was a million-to-one coincidence, but he knew with dreaded certainty it was not. Beyla's words echoed around his mind once more, *'there is one who will come, one who will be the bane of you and your kin'.*"

Shaking off the sudden coldness that enveloped him, Varga yanked Jameson's head from the floor by the hair and curtly signalled that the tribe was to begin the trek back to Dun Varulfur.

He led the werewolf-pack across the killing fields where the Venicones had stood and died, ignorant of all that went on around him, completely and utterly self-absorbed by the events and omens of the night just past.

Chapter 7

Craigan McIntyre ran as if the very hounds of hell were pursuing him across the heather which, if he was to believe Jameson's warnings, was not very far from the truth.

In the silence of the night, he could still make out the yowling of the wolves as they continued to go about their bloody business in Dun Eiledon. Drenched in sweat and trying desperately to marshal his thoughts into some sort of coherence, the sixteen-year old ceased in his flight and doubled over against the trunk of a Scots pine, gasping for breath and grasping for sanity. He closed his eyes and found that all he could see was Jameson's head falling from his shoulders. Unable to stop it, his stomach heaved and he was copiously sick.

He hawked and spat then wiped his mouth as best he could, smacking his lips together in distaste at the abysmal tang which now pervaded his tongue.

As he regained a modicum of control over his emotions, he found himself musing over the dead seer's revelations. Could he really be the last of his clan? Did the fate of the Venicones really rest upon his shoulders? All these questions and more rebounded around the youngster's head as he resumed his flight from the carnage that had befallen his tribe.

He had little sense of where he was heading, crashing through the scrubby undergrowth, ignoring the punishment which his lower legs were taking from the bushes and shrubs that carpeted the floor of the wood. His headlong flight began to take him into terrain which he was unfamiliar with and he slowed down in an attempt to get some sort of idea of where he was. The first blush of dawn had begun to tinge the sky to his left, which at least told him the direction he was moving in. South.

He knew he had to begin veering towards the red sky in the east, but the landscape was still too dark for him to be able to locate any landmarks by which he could navigate. With many a nervy glance over his shoulder and straining his ears to the limit for any sign of the Ulfhednar, he resumed his escape.

As the sun began to peek over the horizon, the landscape began to resolve itself into more identifiable parcels of land. Craigan stared intently across the undulating countryside, frantically searching for something to jog his memory and give him a sense of which direction he should be going in.

He had to squint against a sparkling glare which was beginning to appear on the horizon. He knew with certainty that there was only one body of water to the east which would cover such a large expanse of the landscape.

"Loch Seaforth," he whispered excitedly, because, to the scared youngster, the light of the glimmering sun upon the glassy water was like the first flicker of flame after an eternal night.

Though he was young, the hard life and climate of the country in which he had been raised meant Craigan was well versed in the behaviour of animals as the Picts were, by and large, an agricultural race living in small communities. Though he had little experience of cattle and horses, sheep and pigs were kept in large numbers and where there were sheep, there were dogs, which Craigan knew were closely related to wolves. He prayed that, if he could get to the far side of the loch then, as he had witnessed the working dogs of the clan do on many occasions before, the werewolves would lose his scent and he would be free from the constant pressure of the chase.

With the immediate goal of dodging his pursuers uppermost in his mind, he struck out for what he saw as the protection of the loch.

Craigan did not know how long he ran for. The sun which had shown him the way towards the loch was soon lost behind an angry group of storm-clouds that had blown in from the west. The wind began to cut through the woollen robes which he had pulled tightly about his shoulders when the clouds had first blotted out the sun and, to Craigan's disbelief, large flakes of snow began to fall. The optimism forged from his sighting of the loch quickly gave way to despair at the weather change. He began to shiver and stared miserably at his surroundings. He was bone-tired from the terror-filled sleepless night, the exertions of his escape and the constant stress of not knowing how far behind him his hunters were. Craigan was certain that to stop running was to die, so he pushed himself on once more, ignoring the cold, draining liquid which began to weigh down his clothing. He made it another hundred yards until the uneven terrain began to gently slope upwards once more. At first, he stumbled, his exhausted legs unable to do what his brain commanded. With a gargantuan effort, he forced himself to his feet once more only to fall to the soaking wet grass again within seconds.

His mind's eye began to populate the nearby meadows and hills with slavering, bestial wolves powering across the ground like speeding arrows, all converging on the point where he now lay.

With a desolate whimper, he started to crawl up the incline, gaining what purchase he could on the slippery pasture, cutting a pathetic figure as the snow began to fall in thicker flakes.

With a jerk, Craigan opened his eyes. His fatigue had overcome him halfway up the slope and he had lapsed into unconsciousness. In panic, he sat up, his aching limbs protesting at the cold conditions.

The cloud cover was still absolute and, if anything, darker than when he had fallen asleep, so he had no way of knowing for how long he had been comatose.

He cocked an ear at a nearly inaudible sound off to his left. His brain was still groggy from a debilitating mix of weariness and the wintry conditions so he struggled to recognise the noise for what it was, though he knew it was important.

There it was again. This time though, as he came to full wakefulness, a clarion call of alarm tolled in his head. The wolves!

He staggered to his feet, the terror of discovery delivering a jolt of energy which had him on his feet before he had time to think. He crested the top of the slope and, with a sob of relief, saw that the expanse of Loch Seaforth was a mere few hundred yards ahead of him. Once again though, circumstances contrived to snatch the mood of hopefulness from him within seconds of attaining it.

Craigan shot one last glance over his shoulder before descending the slope to the shores of the loch and was eternally grateful he did, though, in that instant, he did not feel that way.

A grey shape bounded over the last hill which Craigan had traversed before he had collapsed. It was all the young lad could do not to scream as he saw the wolf effortlessly change direction and make a beeline towards him.

He was lost and he knew it. His shoulders slumped as the full weight of what was about to happen came crashing down upon him. He was the last prospect of salvation for his clan and he had been found wanting. Here he would die and the Venicones with him. His memory flicked through images of the tribesmen and women who, only weeks before, had been living in a blissful, pastoral peace with nothing more than the normal vagaries of farming life to contend with.

He remembered Duncan MacKendrick, the chief of the clan, a fair and just leader whose manner and bearing evoked respect and warmth in equal measure. And then, always at his right hand, Jameson the seer, the ancient soothsayer, whose unparalleled wisdom and knowledge of the tribal lands and clan history provided the keystone of Duncan's rule.

Unabashed tears began to run down his cheeks as the beauteous face of Dana MacKendrick then appeared to him. The translucent eyes, as blue and depthless as the waters of a loch, the wondrous waterfall of red hair cascading down her back or flowing behind her like the after-image of a flame in the night as she ran through the heather. He tried to hold onto that face, a face blessed by a smile which used to light up the Dun with its kindness and joy, but he found it slipping away from him, only to be replaced by that of a deathly, pallid corpse painfully robbed of life.

142

Craigan froze. He could feel the despondency begin to transform inside him from a cold lump of ice in his stomach to a raging inferno of anger which began to spread through his entire being. Though it pained him beyond measure to imagine Dana MacKendrick dead on the floor in Dun Eiledon, he held tenaciously on to the mental picture because it was this image which, once conjured, had banished the desolation of defeat from his mind.

Although every fibre in his body screamed at him to flee, he held his ground for a few seconds. He was relieved to see that it appeared he was only being pursued by a lone wolf rather than the pack and the flame of relief burned yet brighter. However, he was still under no illusions as to his chances against the predatory beast, so he turned and ran for the shores of Loch Seaforth.

Through the machair he flew, occasionally risking a quick look behind him to gauge the position of his hunter.

Then he was there, the lucid water lapping at the toes of his boots. He shivered, partially from the cold burn of the liquid and partially due to the closeness of his pursuer.

The grey shape crested the final hill and continued on, a streak of silver against the whiteness of the newly fallen snow which blanketed the plain that bordered the loch.

Craigan had hoped he would not be so hard-pressed when he came upon the shore. He cursed his ill-luck and cast about for a method to defend himself because, though he was well versed in the ways of animals, he was uncertain how well wolves were able to swim and he was an indifferent swimmer at best. With one last brief look across the water at the relative sanctuary of the far shore, he turned to face his four-legged foe.

In the seconds he had taken to glance longingly at the squat huts on the other side of the loch, the werewolf had halved the distance between them. Craigan tensed in anticipation of the animal's attack but instead, the beast slowed itself, padding to a halt before him and regarding him with cold, dead eyes.

Unknown to Craigan, Varga had instilled in his warriors a keen sense of psychological warfare, though he did not identify it as such, providing them with yet another weapon in their already formidable arsenal. The Ulfhednar clan-chief had not just sat enraptured as he heard the tales of yore, he had learnt from the sagas of his people, absorbing the knowledge and wisdom of his race like a sponge.

He realised that, if the exploits of his countrymen, which had fired his blood with such a feeling of fervour, had that effect on him then they would undoubtedly put the fear of the Gods into the potential victims of the Viking's rampage.

And so it proved. Even before Fenrir's warning that his enemies were approaching Ulfsgaard, the Viking village became surrounded for miles on all sides by potent emblems of the tribe's brutality. Throughout the Scandinavian pine forests which bordered the outer reaches of the settlement and even further afield, severed heads with faces forever frozen in various aspects of horror could be found rammed atop spears dotted amongst the deceptively peaceful trees.

Once the Ulfhednar had determined to spread themselves beyond Rogaland and needed means of travelling the fjords, they had built the *Varulv* and Varga had ordered the figurehead fashioned into a slavering wolf's head, teeth and muzzle drenched in scarlet gore, leaving any who gazed upon it in no doubt as to its purpose and the ferocity of its occupants.

Taking his lead from the way of the lone wolf, he had also hit upon what he called 'the power of silence', which was the tactic that Craigan's tormentor was now employing.

Hrolfsson drummed into his minions that, in his experience, the lone wolf, which usually preyed on solitary victims separated from their fellows, would normally face down their target rather than charging into the fray and leaving themselves open to an unlucky blow. They would merely make themselves visible to their quarry and then stalk them, causing the tension in their victims to rise intolerably until they hurriedly chanced fight or flight, inevitably making a fatal error of judgment in their eagerness to escape.

The wolf sat primly upon its haunches, eyes never leaving the pale face of the Venicone lad. Slowly, the beast's mouth opened to reveal two rows of wicked looking teeth. Craigan tensed in preparation to defend himself, but the wolf did not move. It took him a few moments to realise the silver animal was grinning at him and, once that insight had hit him, he wondered how he had not comprehended it before. The bastard creature was taunting him, playing with him as a cat would a mouse.

Craigan was caught in a half-crouch, licking bone-dry lips and breathing in short, sharp gasps of what the wolf took to be terror but were, in fact, the beginnings of a cataclysmic eruption of anger. To Craigan, the wolf suddenly represented everything evil which had befallen his tribe. That languid smile was not only mocking him but mocking all those who had died at the hands of the wolf pack, Duncan, Jameson, sweet, sweet Dana, all the men, women, sons, daughters, brothers and sisters, kith and kin that now lay cold and lifeless in Dun Eiledon and the surrounding fields.

His lips peeled back, unconsciously mirroring the wolf's expression and he shifted position slightly. His boot touched something and he knelt down further, never taking his eyes from the wolf, keeping it directly in front of him.

The branch which Craigan's fingers closed around came as a pleasant surprise to the youth, as he had expected to face his foe unarmed. He had no time to ponder his luck at finding such a weapon when there was not a tree within sight, he simply assumed it was just a rather substantial piece of driftwood, a piece of the usual flotsam washed in from the seas that the whim of the tides had chosen to deposit upon the shores of Loch Seaforth.

Craigan's eyes narrowed as he brandished the wooden club. He weaved it in a figure of eight, deriving strength from the fact that perhaps the odds against him emerging victorious from this encounter had just shortened somewhat.

The Venicone youngster noted that, where before the werewolf's eyes had been unblinkingly fixed upon him, they now skipped between the movement of the wood and Craigan's determined gaze. Unexpectedly, he chanced a quick step forward and was gratified to see the wolf rock back from the feigned blow. Resuming his ready stance, he challenged the beast with an atavistic snarl. "Come on then, fiend. What are you afraid of? Not so sure of yourself, are you, when you do not have the rest of the flea-riddled scum with you."

Still the wolf made no move, though a low growl began from its throat. Its pitch caused a frisson of fear to shudder down the lad's spine, because it cast his racial memory back to more primal times.

Craigan hefted the tree-limb again, hoping that the act would instil confidence back in him once more, but it did not.

The wolf stood and Craigan froze, preparing himself for the attack.

Suddenly, the wolf was leaping, teeth bared, claws extended. Craigan McIntyre fell back in shock, but not before swinging blindly at the oncoming beast and getting a satisfactory contact which contained enough force to sting his fingers.

A yelp of pain was his reward and gave him inspiration to try and press the advantage. He gained his feet as quickly as possible, but was knocked to the ground again as the wolf charged, taking his legs out from underneath him. The somersault he turned was too violent for him to be able to hold on to the branch and it flew from his hands onto the ebbing surf. Craigan was groggy from the impact with the pebbly sand and struggled to regain his wind. Luckily for him though, the branch had caused a considerable amount of damage to the wolf's right hind leg and the beast could not repeat its initial attack. It tried to leap at him again, but collapsed as its leg gave way with a nauseating crack. The animal's breathing was ragged as pain coursed through it but, try though it might, the wolf could not regain its paws and it fell to the surf, whimpering pathetically, ears flattening against its head.

The young clansman did not hesitate. He waded into the water, grabbing the branch as it began to follow the outgoing tide. Then he was there, looming over the prostrate wolf, branch upraised, ready to mete out the vengeance which all the Venicone clansmen and women who had died at the hands of the Ulfhednar, demanded from him.

Again and again, he brought the club down, screeching incoherently at the obscenity beneath him. How many times he hit it, he did not know but, when fatigue finally robbed him of his vengeful thirst, there was little left which could be recognised as either wolf or human.

Craigan had been so blinded by his rage, so consumed by his need for revenge he did not immediately register that, at some point during the thrashing, the wolf had returned to its human guise.

As the red mists parted, the gorge rose in his stomach as he beheld the dead body of the woman he had just murdered, her head lolling obscenely to one side where his blows had shattered her spine and neck.

No, a voice in his mind shot back. Not murder. Do not dare think like that. That woman had been party to and, for all you know, participated in the vile acts which culminated in the bloodbath at Dun Eiledon. Do not waste your pity on her. She deserved the justice you gave her. Do not think for a moment she would not have torn you to pieces, given the chance.

The thoughts were there in his head and he knew they made sense, he knew that all the words echoing in the privacy of his mind were true, but all those facts paled into insignificance against the one which loomed largest in his head. He had killed a living, breathing being in cold blood and the bloodlust, which had awakened within him as he perpetrated the act, could still be tasted upon his tongue.

The way of life of the Picts meant that most, if not all of the clanspeople, were accustomed to the continual ebb and flow of life and death. The sometimes brutal routine of farming always resulted in the loss of a few of the weaker animals of the flock or herd and, from a very early age, it was made clear to youngsters such as Craigan that there was no room for emotion when they came upon a dead lamb or calf, it was merely the natural way of things.

However, there was nothing natural about the abomination which lay ruined at his feet and that was why it affected him so much, though his conscience still tried to convince him he had no other choice.

With a final look at what he had done, he waded out into the bitter waters of the loch, gasping at the abrupt change in temperature but determined to brave it out, thinking it would cleanse him of the sullied feeling which cloaked him like a suffocating shroud.

Though the expanse of water was little more than a mile wide, Craigan found himself struggling to cross it. His chest was inexplicably tight and he was unable to draw anything but the shallowest breath. Fighting against the rising panic, he tried to will the far shore closer to him but, if anything, it seemed to be receding into the distance. He blinked furiously but could not focus. He opened his mouth, moaning for help that his fear told him would not come. As he did so, some of the water which he had disturbed with his desperate thrashing, looped into his mouth and he choked on it, unable now to take any sort of breath, shallow or not.

The water then enveloped him completely and he began to sink.

As he was sucked towards the bottom of the loch, his mind seemed to detach itself from his body and a pleasant calmness began to lull him. He was shocked to see how clear things became to him, all the bubbles which floated from his mouth up to the surface became pristine before his eyes, every one a perfect little transparent ball reflecting all the colours of the rainbow until they began fading to black....

The breath exploded out of Craigan's lungs as he was wrenched upwards, erupting through the water like a leaping salmon, and pulled roughly into a small boat.

He was indelicately turned onto his side and retched up a goodly amount of water. Forceful hands laid him on his back and he found himself staring into the face of a wolf. After the abuse that both his mind and body had taken in the last few moments this scare was the last straw and he fainted, passing from consciousness with his final view being an elongated maw full of pointed teeth and passionless yellow eyes regarding him like a falcon about to pounce upon its prey.

Craigan groaned as he awoke, still trapped in the moment of when he had lapsed into sleep. His lungs burned and his ribs ached as he tried to sit upright. A throaty voice commanded, "Sit still, else you'll capsize the boat."

With vegetable slowness, scared witless by what he would see, Craigan turned his head to see whom had spoken. The being which returned his gaze brought even more memories crashing down upon him and, forgetting the warning which had been issued seconds ago, he tried to retreat from it as much as possible.

"Damn it, lad, I won't tell you again."

Craigan had not picked up on it before, but the caution had been delivered with a distinctive burr which served as a poignant reminder of his recently desecrated home and actually put him slightly more at ease.

The man, if that's what he was, returned the open-mouthed gaze with interest. "Do not be afeared, boy, I'll not hurt you."

"I...What...." Craigan stammered.

The creature which, whilst the exchange had been going on, was rowing the little currach across the loch, laid down the oars and stared pointedly at his half-drowned passenger. "I am Taiga." He said, extending his hand which, aside from being covered with a profusion of brown fur, possessed fingers and nails rather than claws and pads. Craigan looked at it as if it was a leprous, palsied horror which he would not touch for all the treasure in the world.

Taiga did not seem overly offended by the reaction. "I would think you would be rather more solicitous to the person who just saved your life but...." He shrugged and went to retrieve the oars from the floor of the boat.

Finally Craigan's curiosity took on larger proportion than his fear and he found his tongue. "I apologise, Taiga. It is just your appearance reminded me of..." he trailed off, staring distantly towards the shore where an indistinct red and pink mass could still be seen lying.

Taiga's eyes hardened but he managed to keep his voice even. "I am not...of that kind."

Craigan looked again at the creature before him, "Then what are you?" he asked, taking in Taiga's appearance more closely. To the Pictish youth, he looked like nothing more than a very hairy human with a wolf's head. His physical form below the chin was that of a medium-sized, muscular man with the requisite two arms, legs, hands and feet. It was just that he was covered from head to toe with short, brown hair. His head was a different matter though and that was what had frightened Craigan so much. It appeared identical to the beast which had attacked him at the edge of the loch, though now he was able to study it closely, subtle differences began to become apparent. There was a softness around the eyes which had been completely absent from the wolf-bitch on the shore and somehow the facial expressions seemed more human, although whether that was because the head was attached to a human body, Craigan was unsure.

The only clothing he wore was a leather loincloth, unlike the wolf on the shore which, when she had transformed back to her dead human form, had been completely nude.

"I am a wulver," Taiga said. When it was clear the word meant nothing to his passenger, Taiga expanded, "I concede we are similar in appearance to the nightwalkers, but it is a physical similarity and nothing more. They feed on death and woe and evil trails them wherever they walk. Rest assured, we wulvers are a different breed. We bided far to the north where we have lived alongside you and your brethren for centuries, surviving off the land, keeping ourselves apart as much as we could from all others. And so it would have remained, had it not been for those accursed lycans."

Taiga picked up the oars and began to row once more, the gentle bob of the currach a soothing contrast to the savage anger which seared through his words as he spoke of the coming of the Ulfhednar to the Shetlands. "For myself, I and my family used to stay upon an idyllic isle called Unst. We bade in peace until they came." Taiga's head dropped and his voice receded to a hoarse whisper, "They destroyed all before them, leaving nothing untainted by their foul deeds. They appeared suddenly upon the beach one angry, raw morning, emerging out of an impenetrable fog and sweeping across the islands for weeks. Then, just as suddenly, they disappeared to who knew where.

Sadly, by then, the damage was done. My clan fell prey to the same prejudice you displayed when you first awakened. The islanders, those which had survived the rampage, began actively hunting us out rather than just letting us be as they had done before. We tried to protect ourselves, tried to lie low and weather the storm, for my kind have never revelled in aggression and intimidation like the nightwalkers have, but it was to no avail. The islanders drove us from our territory, harrying us until we fled. It soon became clear that, if we did not leave the islands, we would be hunted to extinction, so we struck out across the sea in our currachs." He gestured hopelessly at the small boat in which they sat. "These were designed for lochs, not the open ocean."

He fixed Craigan with a look which was worryingly reminiscent of the wolf he had just slaughtered upon the loch's edge. "We subsisted on the most meagre diet of fish, caught as we crossed the sea, for we had not time to pack provisions, but it was not enough. I watched my kith and kin die, either through their craft's sinking or from starvation." Taiga openly wept now and Craigan steeled himself to extend a comforting hand upon the wulver's shoulder. The wolfman composed himself and nodded thanks for the gesture. He shrugged, "By some miracle, my boat stayed intact and I survived. How, I do not know, though in these past few months it has come to be more of a curse than a blessing. For all I know, I am the last of my kind, doomed to live out my life, friendless and bereft."

Those last few words struck a powerful chord with Craigan and, this time, he extended his hand for Taiga to shake. "We are two of a kind, Taiga. The wolven scum have obliterated the rest of my tribe and I too am the last of my people." He took a deep breath, for even the act of saying the sentence was like a knife through his heart. "I apologise. I have not even thanked you for saving my life. I am forever in your debt."

The wulver acknowledged the thanks, surprised at the strength of the handshake and the strength of feeling which blazed like an inferno behind Craigan McIntyre's eyes.

The Venicone turned away from the bank where the dead wolf-bitch lay, in a deliberate attempt to put the events which had happened there behind him and stared at the far bank, wondering what the next step would be in his quest to find the distant enigmatic figure of Monkshood.

The silence stretched out between them, the only sounds being the gentle lap of the water against the boat and the swish of the oars as they broke the surface of the loch.

The wulver sighed, "The whim of the tides brought me to this place, but I believe that fate has been just as much of a player in this journey."

The clansman's stare was drawn from the seemingly deserted cluster of huts on the distant shore, "Fate? What makes you say that?"

Taiga sighed again. "My people were driven from their homes and cast adrift on unforgiving seas and I watched as they died one by one, unable to do anything for them. I was kinless, purposeless and bereft of hope and I was ready to die," Taiga's head dropped, as if the weight of his words was too much for him to stare Craigan in the face, and his voice fell to a volume which the clansman struggled to hear, "yet I lived. At first I viewed my continued existence as a punishment for sins I had perpetrated, though I knew not what they were." Taiga's voice regained its strength and his head came up once more to fix Craigan with a look of intractable purpose. "But, as the days and weeks went on and I showed no signs of illness or deprivation, I began to re-examine that thought and it occurred to me that perhaps I was being kept alive for a reason."

Craigan nodded, certain now he had found an ally in his search for Monkshood, "You seek to avenge your people?"

Taiga continued to speak and Craigan was unsure if he had even heard him. "Then something happened which set my thoughts in stone. During what I presumed was going to be another interminable night drifting aimlessly on the waves, I heard the siren call of a wolf in the darkness. It was on the cusp of my ears but it was unmistakeable. It was so exquisite that it filled me with joy, an emotion I had all but forgotten during the crossing. I grabbed the oars and struck out for the source of it, intrigued beyond measure, for I did not know how close I was to landfall. I found reserves of energy which I did not know existed and ate up the distance, with the baying sounding louder all the while. Then I saw her, and what a sight she was to behold, her fur aglow with a radiant silver sheen and a voice to light up the sky with its glory. I was enchanted by her, so much so that I was nearly crushed in the wake of a big ship which had hoved silently into view whilst I was hypnotised by the call of the she-wolf.

I barely managed to manoeuvre the boat clear of the ship's bow but as I did, I saw him. I saw the massive bastard who leads those who have caused you and I so much grief and anguish. Luckily for me, he too was entranced by the wolf upon the cliff, else I am sure he would have ordered my boat destroyed, such is his cruelty.

It was in that moment, when I saw he found the wolf-song as captivating as I did, that the baying began to sound discordant in my ears. It was almost as if my mind could not bring itself to appreciate something which that monster also enjoyed. But then with that realisation came another. I pondered my fortune at coming upon him and his pack again and the purpose I had wondered about previously was suddenly crystal clear. I was being kept alive so I might bring about the demise of him and his clan of thugs. So, since that day, I have been following them, trailing in the wake of their violence, in the hope of bringing an end to their murderous reign of terror."

"I have been charged with the selfsame task, Taiga. Will you accept me as your ally? It could serve to act as part repayment for your rescue of me."

Taiga looked sceptical as to what level of help such a young stripling could provide him with. "I watched you on the shore slaying the shapeshifter," he said carefully.

Craigan hawked and spat over the side, "So you know I am able to kill, then?"

Taiga's expression remained unchanged. "And I also saw your reaction afterwards."

The youngster's bravado diminished somewhat. "It was the first time I have slain in cold blood. I was merely...overwhelmed by my strength of feeling for a moment."

"And the loch? Are you that poor a swimmer you could not even cross such a small area of water?"

Craigan deflated visibly. "Usually it would not have posed a problem...I don't know what happened. I..."

The wulver chewed upon his lip. "Do not misunderstand me. I do not doubt your heart, Craigan, nor your wish to wreak revenge upon the werewolves, it is just that I look at you and I see a child bearing a burden which you have no hope of fulfilling."

The youngster's eyes flared in anger. "And when I first laid eyes on you, I thought you the same as them, a ravening, rabid beast bereft of morals and steeped in evil," he snapped back.

Taiga laid the oars down once more, a slow deliberate gesture which positively oozed menace.

Craigan held up his hands placatingly. "Look, Taiga, I am sorry I..."

The wulver's face lost its anger. "Do you not see, that is the problem, lad," he sighed. "You cannot spit out words of rage one minute and then backtrack on them the next when they lead you into danger. The werewolves will give you no quarter. If you challenge them, they will fight you and they will kill you. They will not listen to your pleas; they will not spare you any pity. Are you truly prepared for that, Craigan?"

"What have I got to lose, Taiga? I have nothing, no home, no family, no friends. The only thing I have is a score to settle. And to be honest, if you are not willing to help me, then I will thank you once again for your rescue and be on my way."

"Yet the Ulfhednar lie in that direction, do they not?" The wulver pointed out, extending a fur-covered arm in the direction where Craigan had appeared on the shores of the loch.

"I go to seek one who may be able to end the tyranny of these monstrosities. One whose identity was vouchsafed to me in the dying words of my tribe's seer."

Taiga raised an eyebrow at this. "Then he must be a special man indeed, if he is capable of such a feat. I must say, though I have followed them for a goodly span of months, I am no nearer to finding a cure to this most heinous of diseases. They are possessed of such numbers and strength. I have no wish to pour scorn upon the words of your tribe's wise man, but I find it very difficult to believe that one man will be enough to halt the wolves in their rampage."

Craigan shrugged, "Yet that is where I am bound."

For long moments they simply continued their leisurely progress towards the bank. The adolescent Pict kept transferring his gaze from the ever-nearing huts to Taiga, then to the ominous storm-clouds which seemed to encircle the water.

At the other end of the boat, the wulver found himself wondering if his rescue of this young pup was yet another unforeseen twist in the path which his life had taken in the last year. He had convinced himself that his reason for living was to visit death upon the werewolf tribe but, as he had just admitted to Craigan, he had made no progress towards achieving that goal. Perhaps this young man was offering him a chance to exact his vengeance.

Both of the occupants of the boat were so engrossed in their thoughts, they were both jolted in surprise by the currach beached upon the sand. The youngster moved first, propelling himself out of the small vessel. As his foot hit the gritty surface, Taiga came to a decision.

"Wait, lad."

The Venicone tribesman halted in his tracks.

"Listen, Craigan, just now you said you had no home, no family, no friends. Well, if you will excuse the jest, we find ourselves in the same boat. We both have nothing."

Craigan McIntyre stared intently at the wolfman as he got out of the boat.

Taiga continued, "However, I think you are wrong on one count at least," he extended his hand, "You now have a friend."

This time, without any semblance of hesitation, Craigan McIntyre, last surviving member of the Pictish tribe of the Venicones, grasped the proffered hand and shook it vigorously.

"Thank you, Taiga. That means a lot."

The wulver nodded in acknowledgment then assumed a serious look, "It is only meaningful if we end this blight. Where will we find this superman you spoke of in the boat?"

Craigan stared off into the distance, hoping that Monkshood would appear as if by magic, marching towards them across the countryside. "Unfortunately, Jameson did not supply me with that knowledge."

"Then where are we to begin our search?" Taiga asked in exasperation.

Craigan shrugged, "The mainland is all he managed to say before he died."

The wulver rolled his eyes and looked at the vessel in which they had traversed Loch Seaforth. Though currachs had little or no reputation for being seaworthy, the craft had great sentimental value to Taiga, as it had carried him much further than he had any right to expect. However, he had warned Craigan about the need for absolute focus on their ultimate goal and, if he was honest, the boat of wicker and cowhide did not look in very good shape. Though it had no actual leaks, he could see that the covering was wearing thin in several places and could not hope to survive crossing the Minches.

"Well, we will need a bigger boat, that is for sure." Taiga sighed.

Just then, a bitter wind scythed across the loch sending a shiver down Craigan's spine. The wulver bore it stoically, his pelt obviously giving him a modicum of protection against the chill. The gust soughed mournfully and sounded eerily like the cry of a wolf to the still fatigued youth and his stare shot across to the far bank, though the twilit clouds did not provide enough light for him to see anything. "Do you think it safe to bide here for the night or will we need to put more distance between us and them?"

The wolfman shook his head. "They hunt by night, lad. I think it would be a mistake for us to tarry here. We need to keep moving, at least until the sun comes up again, anyway."

Craigan stifled a moan. He was bone-tired due to the exertions of the last few hours and the thought of no rest for another night caused him no little distress.

Taiga eyed the young lad, noting the brief flicker of misery which flashed across his face. He could see Craigan was tired. He was standing bent over with his hands upon his knees and, when he looked up, Taiga saw that his eyes were shrunken inside his head and encircled with dark rings. He also recognised that the tribesman was mentally drained as well. Not only was his face pallid and drawn, but the deep hazel eyes were dreadfully haunted and, on the crossing over the loch, in the moments of silent contemplation they had both experienced, the wulver had noticed that the lad was ever staring downwards at the floor of the boat, eyes tearing and forehead frowning.

"How old are you, Craigan?" he asked gently.

"I turned sixteen just a month past," he answered.

Taiga drew a hand down over his face, for the first time acknowledging how tired he was. "Perhaps we will be safe here. It was only the one werewolf after all and we have the loch in between us and them." He left the question hanging as they both looked around the settlement in which they found themselves. It was a motley collection of roughly ten wattle and daub huts that, to all intents and purposes, were deserted. No light emanated from any window openings and all that could be heard was the zip and sizzle of the clouds of insects which always appeared around dusk. Craigan instinctively ducked as a shape shot past his ear but it was only a bat taking advantage of the rich pickings that the time of day was presenting it with.

Taiga smiled toothily. "I think perhaps we should hole up here for the night. Neither of us is in any fit state to go further and, with fatigue and terror accompanying us at every step, we are likely to injure ourselves in our haste to flee." He gingerly approached the nearest construction and pushed open the door. Craigan watched tensely as he disappeared inside, re-emerging a minute later shaking his head and ushering the youngster over the threshold. "I think we'll be safe here, lad," he sighed heavily.

Frowning, the Venicone entered the squat, dark building. At first, he did not understand what Taiga was getting at but, within a few seconds, the sickly sweet smell of death assailed his nostrils and he gagged. Through gritted teeth, he hissed "They've already been here." It was a statement, not a question.

"Aye, they have," Taiga nodded, pointing to a filthy curtain which partitioned one section of the house from the other. "Behind there," he breathed heavily, still perversely glad that the sickening acts of the Ulfhednar could still inspire such feelings of rage within him. Though he had protested vehemently that werewolves and wulvers were only alike physically, he was painfully aware that all of wolvenkind, whether fully animal or partly bestial and partly human, had within them the potential to be killers and, though he had never experienced the need to indulge in such behaviour beyond the normal fish diet of his kind, it was a huge fear to him that one day he would become desensitised to it and give in to his carnivorous urges.

After the initial grisly discovery, they went from house to house hoping to find one which had not been visited by the violence of the werewolves. It was only when they came to the furthest house from the loch's edge that they found one untouched.

"I will keep watch. My eyes are keener than yours in the darkness." Taiga said in a flat, emotionless voice.

Craigan offered no argument and immediately retreated to the far side of the room, flopping down on the rickety pallet which served as a bed without a word. Within minutes, an amused grin quirked briefly on the wulver's face as the youngster began to snore.

Having followed the clan of werewolves for so long, Taiga was confident that the havoc which had blighted this little community was down to them and meant the likelihood of them returning was highly doubtful and so his mind wandered, pondering the chance of finding this hero of whom the boy had spoken. He began reflecting on his newfound acquaintance as he took up station in the shadowy doorway of the house, allowing his mind to wander from the Ulfhednar for a while. He knew Craigan was hopelessly unprepared for the forthcoming quest, but he also saw that he would not be swayed from it. He also knew he could not blame the lad. He well remembered how ashamed and impotent he had felt when he had been unable to halt the persecution that his kind had suffered after the Ulfhednar's exploits had left their homeland devastated. As the wulvers were forced to flee across the sea, he had sworn revenge upon both the werewolves which had decimated the islanders and also the islanders themselves, who had turned on his kind with such blind rage. It made him ponder whether his alliance with Craigan bordered on hypocrisy after the curses he had spat at the humans but, having had time to reflect on their actions during his enforced isolation, he conceded that, though their harassment of his kind was undoubtedly unfair, it was also entirely understandable.

Taiga then took to wondering about the man upon whom Craigan was pinning all his hopes. Had the dying seer simply spoken of him as a sop to the youngster to try and soothe the rawness of the situation or was there actually a chance that this man would possess the wherewithal to rid the islands of this inexorably spreading cancer?

The wulver shrugged, knowing there was no point wasting his time on imponderable questions which would only be answered in the fullness of time. He shifted position and stared into the darkness, straining his ears for any out-of-place sounds but thinking it unlikely he would hear any. No, the night was calm and peaceful and Taiga fully expected it to remain so.

"Taiga."

The wulver jumped, startled by the whisper. To his embarrassment he had fallen asleep, lulled by the quietness of the night. "Craigan," he stammered, "I am sorry, I…"

The youngster waved away the attempted apology. "I am hardly in a position to judge, my friend. I was asleep within seconds of lying down. I am sure you kept watch for much longer than I would have been able to."

"Yes, but..."

Craigan shrugged, again impressing the wulver with his maturity. "Nothing untoward happened so do not concern yourself over it." The tribesman pulled over another rickety stool and sat next to the wolfman, joining him in his perusal of the loch and surrounding fields. For a few moments they sat in silence, watching the dawn become brighter then Craigan broke the peace.

"Why have they come, Taiga?" he asked simply.

The wulver rested his elbows on his knees and his chin in his hands, "The short answer to that is I don't know, lad." He tugged at an untidy tousle which sprouted from his cheek, twiddling it absently as he framed his answer. "The nightwalkers were evil legends in our culture, tales used by one generation to scare the generation below, warning them of the importance of controlling the inner wolf. We wulvers are an unassuming lot on the whole and not very populous. The elders of our race realised long ago that we must co-exist with humanity rather than challenge it, or else we would be hunted down like the wolf which attacks the flock and so that is precisely what we did. And it proved a successful strategy for us until the Ulfhednar." He shook his head. "We did not even know that such creatures existed. As I said, they were known to us as nightmares of the mind, not beasts of the flesh."

"Well," Craigan asked reasonably, "what did your legends say of them? Presumably they were based on experience rather than stories."

"Presumably," Taiga agreed. "Our legends say that, originally, they were humans which came upon the ability to shape-shift into a wolf, either purposely or being bitten by another werewolf or by being placed under a curse."

"They are magic, then?" Craigan spluttered.

Taiga nodded. "So it is said. The stories also speak of many ways to become wolven. Rubbing magic salves upon oneself, for example, or drinking water out of the footprint of a wolf, drinking from enchanted streams."

Craigan seemed to shrink in size and the wulver was again struck by the boy's immature appearance. "Then what hope do we have, Taiga?" he muttered.

"You must not give in to despair so easily, lad." He chided. "As there are many ways to become a werewolf, so there are some weaknesses as well, albeit not as many. Wolfsbane. That is known as the commonest antidote but it is bizarre. When humans eat it, it induces the transformation into becoming a werewolf but, if a werewolf eats it or smells it, it is a lethal poison. They also have a vulnerability to silver blades, the metal burns them inside apparently. Iron as well, if you are fortunate enough to have some about you. Depending on the severity of the wound, it does not always kill the beast but it does remove the lycan form from them if it comes into contact with their skin. Other than that, they must be decapitated before they can truly be counted as dead. If you are bitten yourself then the curse may be removed by receiving three blows on the head with a knife or kneeling in the same place for a hundred years."

Craigan's scepticism was apparent and he puffed out his cheeks. "It is not much, is it? Do you know what Wolfsbane looks like or where it occurs?"

"Yes, I do, though if we find it I may not handle it. It would do harm to me just as much as it would to a nightwalker. It is chiefly found in mountainous parts, growing in the lofty meadows. It has dark green leaves and a tall, erect stem crowned by petals of large, eye-catching blue, purple, white, yellow or pink flowers."

The young tribesman tried to remember if he had seen anything even remotely resembling Taiga's description but could not call anything to mind. He shrugged, "Perhaps that is something we can keep an eye out for then, as we search out Monkshood."

"Monkshood?" Taiga asked.

"Aye, that is the name of the one we are seeking."

"A strange name."

Craigan shrugged, "That is the name Jameson gave me."

"Not exactly helpful information, is it?" Taiga's mouth quirked into a brief smile.

"Damn it, Taiga. He has just seen all he knew and loved slaughtered without mercy. He knew he was moments from death. Would you have been any more forthcoming?" he hissed, standing up so suddenly that the stool he was sitting on crashed backwards to the floor. Without another word, Craigan ran from the hut.

The wulver cursed his tactlessness. Concerned they were about to embark on a wild goose chase, he was guessing that Craigan was pinning all his hopes on this Monkshood and, if that was the case, what would happen if they were unsuccessful in their pursuit? How long could they devote to the search before giving it up and returning to try and thwart the werewolves in another way? Where would they even start looking? The more that Taiga thought about it, the more unanswerable questions came into his head and the more certain he was that the task before them was nigh on impossible. But then what if Monkshood really was the one hope left to them? Looking out across the deserted village, he saw Craigan standing immobile, digging his thumb and forefinger into his eyes to try and stem the tears which were flowing freely.

157

He crossed over to where the boy had stopped and laid a kindly hand upon his shoulder. "I am sorry, lad. One of the troubles with being alone for as long as I have is that you don't need to engage your brain before you speak. It was a throwaway observation which I should have kept to myself."

Craigan cuffed away the moisture from his eyes. "Do you need sleep?" he said tersely.

Taiga nodded despite himself. He was feeling safe and felt attuned well enough to the environment that he felt confident he would be aware of any imminent threat. "Aye, I will rest my head a while, but wake me if anything happens and I mean anything, Craigan. We are of no use to anyone dead."

"I will," the boy said solemnly. They walked back to the hut and both went inside, Craigan stopping at the undisturbed stool and planting himself down heavily upon it, pointedly sitting with his back to the wulver. Once again, Taiga silently reproached himself for his unguarded comment. Shaking his head with equal measure at both himself and at the intransigence of youth, he lay down and, like Craigan, fell immediately to sleep. However, his dreams were tortured and his slumber troubled.

His legs wrapped themselves in the coarse fabric of the bed coverings...*as he ran from ranks of rapacious werewolves with his family by his side, hoping against hope that some sort of miracle would prevail to save them from death at the hands of the fearsome horde. In quick succession, his life-mate fell, followed by his two sons and one daughter. He tried to cease his headlong flight but, even though his legs were no longer moving, the pack of wolves which had descended upon his stricken kin were retreating into the distance and, try though he might, he could not get near to them. With an ear-shattering scream, he tried to launch himself forward. An unsettling jolt of dislocation overtook him and he shot forward, careering into the melee of feeding beasts. The concussion of his arrival knocked him unconscious and the last thing he saw was two of the blood-drenched monsters detach themselves from the heap of animals which snapped and jostled at each other in their determination to feast and begin stalking towards him.*

When his eyes re-opened, all he could see before him was a massive open wound and a mess of guts and organs pumping blood and fluids. Before he realised what he was doing, his tongue had snaked out, licked his mouth dry and he thrust his head back in to the gore. Almost immediately, he shrunk back in horror, hawking the taste from his throat and rubbing vigorously at his sticky mouth.

Craigan spun round as Taiga's howl obliterated the tranquillity of the night. In a moment, he was at the wulver's side shaking him awake. "Taiga, what is it?" he shouted urgently.

The adolescent tribesman leapt back as the wulver's hand swiped at him and his eyes seemed to blaze red.

"What are you doing?" Craigan bellowed.

The wolfman looked to be on the brink of attacking the youngster but, as if coming out of a spell, Taiga blinked and his face lost its bestial snarl. "I was...dreaming, it was a nightmare," he stammered, his face fur matted with sweat and tears.

Craigan slumped onto the floor, distressed by what had happened. The look on Taiga's face as he had woken up was eerily reminiscent of the wolf he had killed on the shores of the loch and, not for the first time, he found himself wondering if he was truly safe in the wulver's company.

A measure of his concern must have transmitted itself to his expression because Taiga felt an overwhelming need to justify his actions. Though he had only known the Venicone for less than a day, he had found the recent months of solitude to be the lowest period of his life, mainly because of the circumstances of his isolation, but also due to a hitherto unrecognised need for social contact which had never before surfaced in his life. The thought of going back to the eremitic existence was not one to be relished and, besides that, he found himself genuinely liking Craigan's youthful vigour and wide-eyed optimism.

"Please do not fear me," he moaned. "I will not harm you, Craigan. I..." he wanted to explain, wanted to elaborate on what had caused him to nearly attack his companion but the words would not come. He screwed his eyes tightly shut, trying to stop the tears flowing again, but snapped them open when he found that the image emblazoned upon his brain was a frozen tableau of his life-mate's face as she lay dying, beseeching him to stop feasting upon her.

With a haunted look towards Craigan which took the tribesman's breath away, Taiga stumbled from the hut and threw up copiously outside.

Craigan hesitated before following him into the rapidly lightening outdoors. He so wanted to believe that the wulver was a trustworthy cohort but the ferocity of Taiga's attempted assault and the needless cruelty of his comment about Jameson roused misgivings within him which he could not banish very easily.

Shouts sounded from outside and Craigan was up, barrelling out of the hut before he had time to think about it.

Taiga was standing with his back to the mud-splashed wall of the hut, hands stretched out placatingly before him.

He was facing three clansmen who stood arrayed in a semi-circle, their hunting spears levelled at the wulver. Each of them, at various times, stared around in open-mouthed horror at the ruin which had been visited upon their village.

The one on the right immediately pointed his spear at Craigan as he emerged from the hut.

All three were dressed in simple brown woollen tunics spotted and smirched with the dirt of the trail and leather shoes which displayed the same marks. However, the one who addressed Craigan in a deep gravelly brogue also wore a tartan cape which was pinned in the middle with an ornate fibula made of bone.

"Who are you, boy? What has happened to our home?" he spat in an accusing voice.

Craigan's mouth was dry with fear as the caped one stalked over to him and rested the point of the spear on his chest, "I asked you a question?" He then cast a withering glance at Taiga. "And what creature from the Otherworld is this?"

The young Venicone racked his memory trying to recognise the tartan of the cape, but he could not. Surprising both himself and Taiga with the steadiness of his voice, he said calmly, "I am Craigan McIntyre of the Venicones, my home is…was Dun Eiledon and my clan-chief was Duncan Mackendrick."

The man's beard bristled wildly from his face and his pale-blue eyes sparkled dangerously. "What is this talk of 'was'?" he snarled. "And you still have not told me what this is."

Taiga visibly bridled at being addressed in such dismissive terms and snarled back, "I am Taiga Haas of the wulver clan Kurtadam, late of the island of Unst, far away to the north of this benighted collection of hovels."

The two men covering the wulver with their weapons thrust them forwards and he barely dodged the rough points of the spears, "Damn it, Taiga." Craigan snapped. "Hold your tongue."

The wulver glared at him as the apparent leader of the trio smirked, "Your pet, is he?"

"Look…" McIntyre began.

The leader looked back at the youth and any trace of humour which had appeared around his eyes when he had mocked Taiga, vanished in an instant. "No, you look, boy. We left our homestead four days ago on a hunting expedition to the south and we come back to find our village deserted and razed to the ground. Now tell me what happened, you little bastard, or I will gut you like a fish." James McChirder, clan-chief of the Taexali hissed.

"When we came upon the village, it was as you see it now. None of what has transpired here is of our doing."

"James," A strangled cry emanated from the Taexali to the left of the two who menaced Taiga. He pointed to the hut nearest to the one where Taiga and Craigan had slept. There were copious amounts of dried blood, now visible due to the dawning of the new day, both on and around the door-hanging and frame which the two refugees from the Ulfhednar's rampage had missed when they had first come into the village. For their part, the Taexali had been so surprised by Taiga's appearance that, it was not until the situation had calmed somewhat, they were able to actually take in what they were seeing.

McChirder's eyes flamed with murderous intent and Craigan knew the quest for Monkshood would assuredly die at birth if he did not explain what had happened to the chief's satisfaction.

"It was the Ulfhednar," Taiga said through gritted teeth, for he was also aware of the precariousness of their circumstances.

With huge steps, James strode over to Taiga and backhanded him across the face, sending him crashing to the floor. "I do not to speak to monsters. I was speaking to the boy."

Taiga wiped away the blood which dripped from his muzzle as McChirder came back to stand before Craigan, his face within inches of the younger man's.

"If you think Taiga a monster, then there are no words to describe the Ulfhednar. They are a pack of murderers and cut-throats imbued by some sort of magic which can transform them into wolves." Craigan spoke quickly. "I have seen them, they came upon the Dun the night before last after raping the countryside and all that bided within it." Once again, he found his voice become thick with emotion as he spoke of what he had seen in the fields around Dun Eiledon the previous night. "They are unstoppable and they feed on death. I am all that is left of the Venicones who lived at Dun Eiledon."

McChirder took a step back as he found himself staring at eyes which had gazed into hell.

"The Ulfhednar did this to your homestead, not us." Craigan finished.

The Taexali chief recovered himself and scoffed at Craigan's story. "Yet you, a callow boy barely out of swaddling, managed to survive these awesome killers? And, on top of that, we find you in the company of a creature which, let's be honest, looks like a bloody wolf. What do you take me for, lad?"

Craigan hung his head. "I escaped because I was asleep in the branches of a tree."

The three Taexali tribesmen and Taiga waited to see if the youngster was going to expand upon this and, after a few seconds of breathless silence, he did.

"I was supposed to be tending one of the tribe's herds but it was hardly the most stimulating job in the world and I grew bored. I shinned up a broad oak and rested in the nook of a bough and the trunk. For how long I slept, I do

161

not know, but it was dusk when I came to. I was awakened by the distressed lowing of the cattle as the werewolves came upon them. I made to drop down to find out what was causing them such upset but, as I was about to, the Ulfhednar began to pass under the tree and I shrunk back, frozen in place by fear."

"Cowardice, more like." McChirder spat.

Craigan's head came up slowly and his eyes blazed with fury, though once he had spoken it was clear his anger was directed at himself as much as the Taexali chief. "Do not think I am not ashamed of my actions." His eyes lost their intensity as he remembered, "They all seemed so immense, thundering past beneath me, blood dripping from their jaws." Craigan's voice tailed off and he stared at the ground.

The chieftain's expression clearly showed that he thought the youngster was lying but the two who still levelled spears at Taiga looked uncertainly at each other.

With a huge sigh, Craigan continued, "I remained rooted to the branch until long after the wolves had finished passing. When I finally found the courage to get down, it was nearly dark. I staggered out into the field where the herd were kept and there was nothing left except bones. There were fully thirty head of cattle in that field and they had been picked clean in less than an hour." He shook his head. "When I saw what the wolves had done, I wandered around aimlessly, lost in a nightmare which I could not wake from. It took a while but suddenly it dawned on me that they were heading for the Dun. That jerked me into action and I began to run back towards my home. I reached the stand of trees where I had hidden and was passing through them when Jameson appeared before me."

McChirder's eyes narrowed at the mention of the name, "The seer?"

Craigan nodded, "He told me to flee, that I was the last hope of the Venicones and, if I was to fight the beasts, I would die. He told me of one who may be able to end the domination of the wolves. He begged me to go and seek him out."

"So is McKendrick dead too?" Warren McLeish, one of Taiga's guards, asked quickly.

"Sliced in two, so Jameson said. Dana, his daughter, is dead also." He turned his eyes back to McChirder. "You must let us go. The future of my people rests on my shoulders."

Gradually, James lowered the point of the spear and spoke. "Assuming I believe this fantastical tale of yours, you still have not explained who or what this is?" He sneered at Taiga, "Seems strange company for someone who is petrified of wolves."

"He saved my life," Craigan said simply. "I managed to kill one of the bastard creatures on the far shores of the loch, but I got into difficulty as I swam across towards your homestead. I was sinking like a stone and he fished me out."

"But he looks like a wolf," McChirder persisted.

The chief's incapability of getting past this point gave Craigan a moment's pause to reflect once more on the steadfast leadership which Duncan McKendrick had provided to the Venicones, because the way McChirder was tenaciously holding on to the blindingly obvious was suggestive of one not used to thinking on his feet, and Craigan wondered what this wholly shocking turn of events would do to such a man.

Taiga surged up from his prostrate position, taking Warren McLeish and his brother, Tavish, completely by surprise. He grabbed the long haft of each spear and jerked it out of their hands. The two brothers did not have a chance to stop him, so powerful and fluid were his movements. With deliberate slowness, his hands closed around the hafts and squeezed. To the astonishment of all who watched, the wood splintered and Taiga dropped the spears, which were now broken completely in two.

"I am a wulver," Taiga seethed.

James McChirder stood open-mouthed at this totally unexpected display of strength, as did Craigan. When he had got his temper under control, Taiga spoke with forced calmness, "I have already told him he has nothing to fear from me." He snarled, indicating Craigan with a nod of his head. "I will tell you once and once only. I am not as the Ulfhednar. Do not make me repeat myself."

The Taexali chief looked from Taiga to the brothers. He was about to say something but his shoulders slumped and he withdrew his spear from Craigan's chest. "Is there no-one left?" he asked beseechingly.

Both Craigan and Taiga shared a glance as they were both visited once again by the memories of their own lost kin. "We came here during the hours of darkness and searched all the huts, trying to find somewhere to rest. There were bodies in all of them." The wulver explained, his voice now truly calm.

"It's possible we may have missed survivors in the gloom," Craigan ventured, though the words sounded hollow even as he said them.

The two companions watched in sympathy as the three Taexali left them to search the ruins of their desecrated home.

"You should not have given them false hope. You know as well as I there were none left alive." Taiga murmured gently.

Craigan could think of nothing to say as the anguished cries of James McChirder and the McLeish brothers began to tear the silence brutally apart.

"What should we do?" the youth asked.

163

Taiga shrugged, "What can we do?"

"I think the best thing we can do for these people, indeed for all the people of these blighted islands, is to find Monkshood and bring him back so this evil can be stopped."

The pair walked off into the fields surrounding the picturesque settlement without as much as a backward glance towards the trio of Taexali frantically searching for any surviving remnants of the life they had left behind just four days previously.

They walked on an easterly course, striking out for the edge of the island, setting a steady pace as they were unsure how far they would have to walk. "We should be able to find some sort of boat in one of the villages along the coast."

"We have no coin, Taiga."

The wulver's face was fixed in an attitude of determination. "We need a boat, Craigan. If we cannot pay for it, we'll steal it."

This did not sit well with the youngster, but he held his peace as they made their way through a small wood consisting of some scrubby pines and spruces. For the most part, they walked in silence once more. On a couple of occasions, Craigan demonstrated his skill with the sling which he carried at his belt at all times, bringing down a brace of scrawny rabbits which, after being skinned and cooked in a bowl that Taiga had fashioned from thin strips of bark, barely touched at the hunger they were both feeling.

They now both sat in the scant shelter afforded them by the overhanging branches of a large spruce as freezing rain, which had mercifully held off until they cooked their meal, began to fall more heavily. Craigan shivered in the miserable, damp conditions and found himself marvelling at Taiga as the wulver sat, in no apparent discomfort, staring out at the clumps of trees which were slowly being swallowed up by an inexorable fog, which had begun to insinuate itself among the trunks of the trees.

Despite the tribesman's discomfort, he felt his eyes drooping as an inexplicably warm feeling began to ooze over him. He jolted awake as Taiga grabbed his arm, "Someone comes." The wulver pointed a furred hand towards the trees directly over where they had laid their cooking fire.

For long moments, Craigan heard nothing and was tempted to put it down to the wulver's imagination as, once again, he began to feel enveloped by a warm fuzziness and nearly fell asleep.

Taiga nudged him and moved out of their cramped shelter with rather more stealth than Craigan thought necessary. He forced himself to his feet clumsily and almost fell over at the base of the tree, his stumble creating a cacophony of broken twigs and rustling leaves.

The wulver threw him a vicious look and motioned for him to be quiet. In a distant way, Craigan knew something was wrong because his body was not responding correctly. He slumped to the wet ground and tried to rise, but the wood was spinning all about him now and, despite the warmth he felt, he could not stop shivering.

Taiga's expression changed from rage to concern when it dawned on him that his young companion was in some sort of distress but, just as he was about to go and minister to him, there was a crashing from the trees and the three Taexali came charging into the clearing.

They were all stained scarlet from finger to elbow and each held a wicked looking dirk in their right hands. They stopped momentarily to take in the scene then advanced purposefully towards the unarmed wulver, who spread his arms placatingly whilst trying to keep all three intruders in view.

"You murdering scum will regret the day you wronged James McChirder," the chief spat, the hatred twisting his face into a horrible sneer.

Taiga said nothing. He could see there was no point in proclaiming their innocence once again. He was also surprised to feel something akin to sympathy for the trio. He knew the insane thoughts which ran through a mind when its world had been suddenly thrown off-kilter for no good reason. The need to lash out at something, anything, when faced with a life-changing shock was by no means restricted to humans only.

His eyes flicked back and forth between the three, trying to keep all of them within sight, all thoughts of Craigan's mysterious collapse forgotten. Taiga had to keep his concentration on them because he knew this would be a fight to the death. The wulver cursed silently as they began to fan out, edging ever closer to the limits of his field of vision. He knew he had to make a move quickly to reduce the odds. In an instant, he decided to go for the chief who, as it happened, was the middle tribesman, reasoning that, were he to kill one of the brothers, then the other would redouble his efforts to slay him. With lightning quickness, he leapt at McChirder with hands extended and teeth bared. He targeted the dirk hand, grasping the wrist with a grip of iron and snapping it back with all his might. The loud concussion of ligament and bone echoed sickeningly around the clearing. The chieftain fell back screaming in pain and, in one fluid movement, Taiga was upon him. In that single bound, Taiga had seized the dirk which had fallen from the stricken man's grip and stepped past him, wheeling round to grab him from behind, putting the chief between himself and the McLeish brothers, who had, by now, recovered themselves and were approaching menacingly.

"Don't make me kill him." Taiga hissed, fighting against McChirder's struggling as well as his own fear.

A low moan came from Craigan and the brothers shared a look. One began to move towards the youngster with a nod whilst the other remained where he was.

Everything went red for Taiga at that point and instinct took over. All the pent-up rage at what had happened since the Ulfhednar had tainted his life came roaring up from the lowermost depths of his mind and he had no hope of quelling it.

He smashed the dirk into McChirder's throat and dropped him to the ground. In three loping strides, he crossed the intervening space, ducked under a wild slash from the tribesman and slammed his shoulder into his midriff, winding McLeish and rendering him useless for a few precious moments. He rocketed away from the sprawling twin and descended upon his brother in a whirlwind of violence which, in a matter of seconds, had the man moaning in pain and nursing at least two broken ribs, as a consequence of an exquisitely executed roundhouse kick.

With the imminent threat considerably diminished, Taiga's anger-fuelled insanity began to wane.

Tavish McLeish painfully regained his feet, puffing hard from the winding he had received, as the wulver, who now stood guard over Craigan, found his attention returning to his companion.

He kicked Warren's dirk away into a drift of leaves and stared coolly at the grunting Taexali. "Life is all about choices. I had no choice but to kill your friend and I made a choice not to kill you. Or him." Warren McLeish had managed to get onto his knees and was doubled over, wheezing heavily.

For a moment, the balance between peace and violence teetered uncertainly in the hands of the tribesmen but, in a move which left Taiga blinking in shock, Tavish moved over to the fallen body of his chief and kicked it so hard that the corpse ended up on its side.

"He was no friend of ours," he said witheringly before striding over to aid his brother. "We pleaded with him not to come after you but he would not be swayed. He drew his dirk upon me and my brother when we hesitated over following you. He was sure you were responsible for what happened back in the village, you see."

"Hardly a reason to warrant kicking his corpse," Taiga pointed out.

Tavish shrugged, "He was a bully as well. Always used to pick on me and Warren when we were young." He hung his head, unwilling to look the wulver in the eye. "We were always too cowed to stand up to him." He stared at the dead body of the Taexali chief. "Funny, he looks a lot smaller now."

One of the wulver's eyebrows arched up in distaste, trying to marry his knowledge of the proud Pictish people with the craven coward who stood before him. "And you? What do you believe?"

"I believe that the look in your eyes when you were accused of ransacking our village and murdering our folk was not the look of a guilty man."

Taiga nodded in acknowledgement, "And does your brother feel the same?"

"Aye" came a strangled voice from the needle-strewn floor. "Damn me, you've got a kick like a bloody war-hammer."

Taiga looked at the two of them then down to Craigan. He dropped to his knees and laid a hand on the Venicone's forehead. It was as cold as ice. To add to Taiga's concern, there was the beginning of a blue tinge starting to appear around Craigan's lips and his breathing was slow.

"He doesn't look very well," Tavish pointed out over the wulver's shoulder.

Taiga's head whipped round, "Strip him." He barked, pointing at James McChirder's lifeless body. "Strip him and bring the clothes here."

Tavish strolled over to the fallen tribesman. "Come and help me, Warren," he said over his shoulder.

"Hurry yourselves, damn you." Taiga snarled.

At that, the two brothers fairly raced over to the side of their fallen former chief and began divesting him of his garments.

Taiga spared them a brief glance of disdain at their lack of backbone then began rubbing Craigan's arms and legs vigorously. He swore under his breath that he had not identified the signs earlier. As he continued his ministrations, Taiga shook his head as thick, sizzling snowflakes began to fall and found himself wondering whether the winter was ever going to end. In his forty years, he had never known such a dismal period of weather as this one. For months now, the sky seemed to have been stained a permanent slate-grey and, on the very few occasions the sun had managed to break through, it had been weak and watery, almost as if it was struggling to project its heat as far as the earth.

Putting his thoughts to one side, he felt the boy's forehead again but there was no change in his temperature. He noted that the violent shivering was beginning to subside but, in Taiga's experience, that was not necessarily a good sign, because he had seen something like this happen before.

Once, when he was a lot younger, almost Craigan's age, he realised with a nostalgic sigh, he and his younger sister had taken themselves off to practise the fishing techniques which their father had taught them, in one of the plethora of salmon streams which criss-crossed their island home. It had been a cold winter's day and, though it was sunny, the bite of the water as they waded into the middle of the river had caused them no little discomfort.

On her first attempt, Haida had been successful in catching a wonderful specimen but, as she had stood there marvelling at the play of sunlight on the fish's scales, she had inexplicably slipped, falling completely under the water and losing hold of her catch. She had been drenched from head to toe but would not go back to the bank, instead choosing to remain in the water intent on replacing her lost trophy. As the older one present, Taiga should have insisted that they returned to their settlement, but he had been childishly jealous of Haida's immediate success and did not want to return without claiming some sort of prize for himself.

They had continued for a time without replicating their initial luck when a fine, plump fish began circling around Taiga. Resisting the urge to reach for it straight away, he kept himself as still as possible, breathing slowly and rhythmically, head down watching the beautiful creature describe a figure of eight as it slipped between and around his legs.

It stopped to feed at the bottom of the stream right in between his feet and he knew that he would never have a better chance. Tensing himself to reach down and claim his trophy, he was surprised by an almighty splash to his left. His eyes came off the fish and glanced over to where Haida should have been, but she had once again fallen into the water.

"Damn it. What are you doing? I was about to..." His voice tailed off when he saw her kneeling down in the water, struggling to hold her head above the surface. "Haida?" he whispered. He waded over to her just as she pitched forward again. They managed to get to the bank with Taiga having to drag his sister most of the way. She was shuddering and mumbling incoherently and her lips were thin and turning blue. Without a second thought, Taiga's fraternal instinct took over and he scooped her up in his arms and began the most important walk of his life. As his lungs burnt and his muscles strained, he kept looking down at his unconscious sibling, willing her to show some sign of life, scared to death that he would never see her smile again. After what seemed like an eternity but was, in fact, just over fifteen minutes, he crested a rise and there before him was Hermaness, home of the Kurtadam clan.

Though he was exhausted from his efforts, his fear for his sister lent his voice strength and he screamed for help as he began to move downhill towards the settlement.

Three or four figures emerged from the rude huts which were dotted about at the base of the slope. Intrigued cries quickly gave way to urgent shouts as they realised something was very amiss. Taiga felt a huge wave of relief as one of the distant shapes resolved itself into his father.

Demas Haas accelerated up the slope when he saw who it was creating the commotion. He reached his son's side and relieved him of his burden immediately, turning sharply and running down the slope seemingly without effort. "Come, lad. Let's get her inside and you can tell me what occurred."

Taiga did as he was bidden, wanting to get closer and help his sister, but not wanting to get in the way of his father's attempts to save her.

"Tell me," Demas gestured frantically. "Tell me what happened?"

Taiga recounted what had occurred at the stream whilst his father listened intently. His immature reason for staying at the water now seemed ridiculously juvenile and he hung his head as he finished.

"Get blankets," his father said quietly in clipped tones.

Taiga did so and was sent off immediately afterwards to brew an elderberry tisane. When he returned, Haida was enwrapped tightly within the blankets and had a modicum of colour starting to flush her pallid cheeks once more. He placed the brew upon the floor next to Haida's sleeping pallet and looked at his father. "I am so sorry," he said quietly.

Demas gently lifted Haida's head and poured some of the drink into her mouth. She murmured something, which Taiga did not catch, then laid her head back down. For long moments, Demas said nothing, staring with undisguised love at his daughter. "You only need to be sorry if you do not learn from this, boy." He said suddenly, turning to face Taiga. "Pride has been the downfall of many and the salvation of none. Think about what you would have gained had you stayed at the stream for longer? A fish, good for a meal or two, fine to taste and pleasant in the stomach?" He laid his large hands upon his son's shoulders and held his gaze, the old wulver's sapphire blue eyes standing out amongst the grey-flecked fur on his face. "But consider, Taiga, what would you have lost?"

Tears started in the boy's eyes but, with a huge effort, he kept his voice even. "Will she be alright?"

With a kindly gesture, his father rubbed his son's cheek. "Aye, she'll be fine. Once the warmth of the infusion starts running through her veins, she should start to come round. Her body had gotten too cold to work properly from being drenched through to the skin then standing too long in the winter wind."

Out of the corner of his eye, he studied his son, wondering if he should have been harder on him for endangering his sister in such a foolhardy manner. However, the concern on the boy's face was enough to show the old wulver that the point had hit home. "That was pretty impressive, you know," he smiled. "Carrying Haida all that way, I mean. It probably saved her life. If you had left her on the bank and ran here alone, we might not have made it back to her in time." The reaction he got from that remark only served to illustrate Taiga's appreciation of the lesson he had been taught.

He shrugged, "She was in my care. She was my responsibility. I could not have left her there alone."

The face he turned upon his father was as determined a look as Demas had seen on anyone, let alone a young boy who had not yet reached adulthood. "I will keep her safe, father. I'll never let harm come to her again."

"I do not doubt that for a second, lad. Not for a second."

The old wulver's face dissolved into the dancing flames of the fire which Warren and Tavish had lit whilst he had watched over Craigan. The boy's breathing was more regular now and he had a healthy colour about him.

Taiga's face was grim. He had not reflected on the promise he had made to his father on that day for a long time. Haida had recovered but at a cost to her health. One of her lungs had taken in water when she plunged beneath the surface and she had developed pleurisy, which debilitated her to the point that she was rarely well enough to leave the confines of Hermaness.

When the Kurtadam clan had been forced to flee their homes, she was hopelessly unprepared for the journey and had perished just as Taiga had sighted the Hebridean coast. With her dying breath, just as she had done on innumerable occasions before when Taiga had apologised for being the cause of her suffering, she had placed her finger on his lips and shook her head, telling him that she had made the choice to stay at the stream and he had to stop blaming himself. He knew in his heart he would never be free of the guilt he felt but, when Haida bestowed one of her dazzling smiles upon him, as she always did when they spoke of the incident, he found that he could not disappoint her and so he promised he would try. He suspected she knew he was merely paying lip service to her wishes but he also knew that she truly did forgive him and that, in itself, caused him to cherish his sister even more than he would have done in the normal course of events.

Though he had only known Craigan for a matter of days, he felt the same twinge of responsibility which he had felt towards Haida, although it was by no means as powerful.

After the experience with his sister, he was aware that he should have been more awake to the danger signals, but there had been so many different things going on and, if he was honest, he had been far too wrapped up with his own thoughts to pay much attention to anything other than gaining vengeance against the ultimate architects of his clan's demise, the ravening hordes of the Ulfhednar.

Craigan stirred and murmured something sleepily.

Taiga was at his side in an instant. When he was sure he was awake, he asked, "How do you feel, lad?"

The youthful tribesman ventured a tired smile and nodded slowly, "Better, I think." He breathed deeply as if trying to summon up energy to speak further. "What happened?" he asked.

"You had hypothermia, Craigan. Your body got too cold from when you plunged into the water in the loch. Add that to the lack of rest and the mental stress which you have been under, well, that's a potent combination. You lapsed into some sort of shock or suchlike."

"So you saved my life again then, Taiga? This is getting to be a habit." The Venicone chuckled weakly.

The wulver brushed the observation aside and placed another couple of twigs upon the pile of flaming wood.

Craigan jumped as the harsh brogue of Tavish McLeish intruded on the conversation. "Don't belittle your efforts, wulver. The lad's right. You saved his life." The Taexali walked into view, his ferocious appearance of ginger beard bristling and heavily bruised face made all the more frightening by the odd angle from which Craigan saw him. "You should have seen him, laddie. Worked like a farmer harvesting crops in a rainstorm he did. Rubbing you up and down and feeding you this hot brew that he conjured up from leaves and plants. It was nothing short of miraculous."

Craigan turned back to Taiga in time to see an embarrassed look of exasperation cross his face. For some reason, the look on the wulver's face was one of the funniest things he had ever seen. He started to laugh then laughed even more when Taiga threw him a black look. The wulver shook his head and stomped away from the fire, leaving Craigan and the two McLeish brothers dissolved in fits of amusement.

As he stood away from the flames, staring out into the fog-wreathed forest, Taiga found that, despite himself, he too was smiling at the infectious sounds of laughter pealing through the deadened air of the woodland. It was an unexpected moment of levity which, for Taiga, suddenly shone out like a beacon in the darkness of the events of his recent life. He found himself wondering how long it had been since he had laughed like this. Not since the nightwalkers had entered his life, that was for sure. With that realisation, the laughter died in his throat and, with a sigh, he turned back to the three Pictish tribesmen huddling around the fire. The McLeish brothers sat on the far side of the flames, two shadowy figures obscured by the brightness of the fire which contrasted starkly with the overcast weather and the ethereal fog which shrouded all about in its unmoving cloak.

The wulver viewed the addition of the two Taexali with ambivalence. On the one hand, he was pleased the siblings had joined them because, after all, there was safety in numbers and, on top of that, it meant there were would be more people seeking out Monkshood. However, on the other side of the coin, if

171

Taiga was frank with himself, he could really not bring himself to like them. The revelation that they were so crippled by their cowardice, they had refused to hunt down the assumed perpetrators of the devastation which had been visited on their homes and families was wholly anathema to the wulver, especially when contrasted with his own overwhelming compulsion to exact revenge on the werewolves. Added to that, their breathtakingly casual disregard of James McChirder's death and mute acceptance of his leadership grated on him like an itch which he was unable to scratch.

No, Taiga decided as he walked back to the trio, the brothers were useful up to a point, but he certainly could not bring himself to trust them. At least, not yet.

As he sat down within the penumbra of the fire, the McLeishs' shared a look and ceased talking. Taiga looked down at Craigan and saw that he had fallen asleep.

"Sorry for laughing," Warren muttered warily. "It's just that..."

"Dammit man, you don't have to explain yourself to me." The wulver growled, the irritation at being laughed at returning with surprising force.

"Alright, alright," Warren held up placating hands and lapsed into silence once more.

Taiga sighed, "Excuse my shortness of temper, I am tired."

Again, a fraternal look was shared. "Well," Tavish shrugged rather exaggeratedly, "if you wish to sleep, we will stay awake to keep the fire lit and the beasts at bay."

Though the wolfman yearned to rest, his feelings of distrust would not leave him and so he changed the subject. "Did Craigan tell you of our quest?" he asked.

"A quest, is it?" Warren raised an eyebrow at that. "Intriguing" was all he would offer beyond that.

"We are seeking to bring an end to the Ulfhednar. We are looking for a man who is prophesied to vanquish them."

"So what are these Ulfhednar?" Tavish asked. "They must be savage creatures to have done what they did to our village."

Taiga nodded, "Up until a couple of years ago, they were nothing but myths. My people knew of them only as legends to share around a crackling fire on a dark winter's night. Then they actually arrived on our shores in a fury of claw and fang."

Warren and Tavish leant in towards Taiga as his voice dropped to a hoarse whisper. "By day, they walk as men, not unlike yourselves, but with a larger build, but by night," Taiga shook his head, "they are able to shape-shift, turning themselves into wolves. Our legends say it was only when the full moon bulked in the sky they were able to effect the change but that does not appear to be the case with these monsters. They are able to transform at will but, worse than that, on top of the wolven cunning inherent in them, they also seem to retain a great many of humanity's crueller traits. In short, they are a formidable force of both nature and supernature."

The two Picts shifted uncomfortably, adding perfunctory twigs to a roaring fire which did not really need any more fuel. They both kept looking sidelong at Taiga and it was clear they wanted to say something but neither was prepared to do it.

As if reading their thoughts, Taiga continued, "Do not concern yourselves. My people are not the same as the Ulfhednar and their ilk. We have lived in the north since the reign of King Cennalath and his forebears in harmony with the Picts and Gaels of Dal Riata. It was the home of my father's father and many generations before that." Taiga broke eye contact with the McLeishs and stared blankly into the fire, "But all that is lost now." He went on to describe what had happened to the Kurtadam clan after the werewolves had swept through Unst and the surrounding islands.

"From what you have said it was the Picts who drove you away from your homeland, not these Ulfhednar. It's surprising that your thirst for vengeance does not involve them rather than the werewolves."

Taiga sighed, "It is true to say I do not exactly hold your kind in the highest regard but I have seen the terror and horror which the nightwalkers inspire. What I try to keep uppermost in my mind is that the people who harried us from our lands had just had their lives completely destroyed before their eyes, perhaps had loved ones killed or their homes and livelihoods obliterated in a matter of hours. After many days of lonely contemplation, I found I could not really blame them for their reaction to my clan. Believe me, it causes me almost physical pain to acknowledge my kind's similarities to those butchers but, unfortunately, we are alike and, in the rawness of those grief-stricken moments, the islanders could not bring themselves to see past the muzzles and fur. I do not deny that, whilst my clan and I drifted across the water and I watched friends and family whom I had known for decades perish one by one, I railed at the injustice of it all and wished great harm upon the islanders who had committed this crime against my people but, with the weeks and months of isolation, came a realisation that the catalyst of all the hurt and pain was not the tribesmen, but the werewolves. So that is why I do not bear a grudge towards your kind. You are as much victims in this as I. That is why I saved Craigan. It was merely the unselfish act of one living thing helping another living thing and look what has come out of it." He gestured towards the slumbering Venicone. "I was wandering the countryside aimlessly, hanging on the blood-matted tails of the werewolves, hoping that, in the face of all the evidence, I could find some sort of weakness in them which would bring about their demise and send them snarling and snapping back to the pit which spawned them but, up until I fished Craigan out of Loch Seaforth, I had just been flailing in the dark. Now I can see a light at the end of a long dark tunnel which, on more than one occasion, I thought I would never emerge from." With that said, he stared down almost tenderly at Craigan.

"And this one man is the key to overcoming the werewolves, is he?" Tavish tried to keep the incredulity from his voice, but failed miserably.

The wulver's head whipped round and he hissed menacingly, "He has to be."

It was all that Warren and Tavish could do not to jump back at the sheer venom in Taiga's voice.

The silence seemed to close in around them as Taiga turned back to look at Craigan and whispered plaintively, "He has to be."

Chapter 8

"What is it, my lord?"

The question came from the direction of the ground, forcing Varga to lift his wearied head from its resting place on the back of his throne, which was an ebon monstrosity of tortured wood and eldritch patterns.

He tried to remember the name of the blonde-haired, blue-eyed woman who stared up at him but his drug-addled mind could not recall it. "It is nothing that concerns you," he waved a hand at her, "Leave me."

"But, my lord, I..."

Her protest was cut short by a thunderous punch, which sent her sprawling across the floor. "I said, leave me," he repeated in the same monotone voice.

As she stumbled tearfully through the door out into the harsh winter's afternoon, Varga slumped back against the throne, let out a massive sigh and closed his eyes. Immediately, he snapped them open again and cursed effusively. The shadow was still there, as it had been ever since he had seen it besmirching the perfect argent surface of the moon. Would he ever be rid of the silhouette which appeared to be indelibly emblazoned upon his inner eyelids?

He dragged himself from his seat and shuffled over to a pitted, rickety table and poured himself a goblet of red wine, uncaring that he spilt half of its contents onto the uneven surface. He stared numbly at the rivulets of blood-red liquid as they oozed themselves into the grooves and dribbled onto the bloodstained floor. Draining the vessel in one huge gulp, he slammed it down and refilled it, swilling the wine around in the cup as he weaved unevenly back to his lofty perch.

His eyes were drawn to the walls of the Dun, entranced by the play of light upon the wood. The many dots of flamelight which spotted the walls all around put him in mind of the glister of stars in a clear night sky. He turned his attention to where the captivating display originated from, the mountain of skulls heaped in the middle of the room.

The flame of Surtr still burned as brightly as it had when the Ulfhednar had first established themselves in Dun Varulfur, its unquenchable power methodically melting away the skulls which were situated at the root of the mound. These were the remains of those who had first perished before the ferocity of the werewolves and the bottom of the mound was now a twisted, ossified plinth upon which the more recent victims' heads rested. It had been an unexpected glory to Varga when he had first noticed the wondrous show emanating from the pile and also a source of amazement that the orange glow was incandescent enough to penetrate the labyrinthine path from the base of the stack of bones and shine through the decomposing heads onto the four walls of the Dun.

Despite this, ever since the unsettling whisper of Monkshood had reached his ears at Dun Eiledon, the light had become somehow muted and not so vivid. Initially he had shaken it off, supposing that his eyesight had simply become used to the radiance but the concern still persisted, gnawing away at his mind like a dog worrying at the last morsel of meat on a bone. He began to try and drown the doubts out with ever-increasing amounts of wine and narcotics, but even that was insufficient to quell his insecurities and he now lived as a virtual recluse, housed within the Dun, seeming to be in permanent station upon the throne atop the dais on the wall opposite the main entrance.

Now the only time most of the tribe had any contact with their leader was when the various raiding parties returned from their sojourns across country and entered the Dun to empty the sacks of their obscene cargo onto the fire.

There were only now a privileged few among the clan who were still able to gain audience with Varga and, even then, he would not stand their presence for very long. The four remaining Krieghund and the ancient, seemingly immortal, seeress Beyla were the only ones who were able to get any sort of sense from the Ulfhednar leader now.

Varga watched dispassionately as another sack of heads was emptied onto the floor. One of the skulls rolled away from the others, coming to rest on its side, the red hair sprouting from its crown at crazy angles, the face caked in dried blood and the lifeless eyes fixing the clan-chief with an unblinking stare.

He found his eyes drawn to it as those Ulfhednar who had brought the skulls to the Dun left the benighted den.

"Monkshood"

The chief's jaw dropped and he knuckled at his eyes vigorously, dropping the now half-empty goblet to the floor. Leaning forward and acutely aware of the thunderous thumping of his heart, he stared intently at the disembodied head.

"Monkshood"

A pathetic whimper escaped Hrolfsson's lips and he ran over to the pallid face, stopping a couple of feet from it. He fell to his knees, ignoring the splinters jabbing into his shins and crouched down, gingerly moving his head towards that of the corpse.

"Monkshood"

Varga nearly swallowed his tongue as he watched the mouth open and the lips move. With a terrified hiss, the Ulfhednar leader gained his feet and kicked the head across the floor as hard as he could.

His head swam and he struggled to maintain equilibrium, taking a couple of staggering steps before pitching forward and cracking his head against the wall.

As he lay unconscious, confusing images raced across his psyche, both comforting and unsettling. In the space of an instant, his mind's eye returned him to the dream-rendered cavern where he had first stood before Fenrir HelMouth and basked in the comforting nearness of his god. Then the image wavered and he watched in horror as the god's head began to shade from the supernatural grey ghostliness of the wolf's spirit form to the absolute pitch darkness of a night bereft of moon and stars, making the individual features utterly intangible. The inconstant billowing of the roiling blackness stopped so suddenly that Varga almost persuaded himself it made a noise. Rooted to the spot by sheer terror, he looked aghast as the hooded figure which Fenrir had become, began to grow and expand, towering above him with its massive sword poised to shear him into pieces.

With overwhelming helplessness he watched as the blade began its arcing descent towards him. He closed his eyes and braced himself for the bite of the monk's weapon. Calmness enveloped him and he was surprised at how unconcerned he felt that his life was about to end.

He sighed sensually and opened his arms to embrace death.

"Varga"

The chief struggled to open his eyes as rough hands shook him awake.

The vulpine faces of Jordis Rasmussen and Morten Jawrender, two of his elite Krieghund generals, loomed over him. They both stood resplendent in their wolf-fur capes, bound at the throat by an ornate brooch upon which were depicted the runic symbols ᚠᛗᛏᚱᛁᚱ, in honour of the god they revered above all else.

Rasmussen was an archetypal Viking warrior with eyes the bright, limpid blue of the fjords among which he grew up and his meticulously braided blond hair brushing against his huge muscular shoulders as he walked.

Morten Jawrender, on the other hand, was a smallish man, wiry and quick, but with a towering temper and pugnacity which more than compensated for his slighter stature. His hair was dark to the point of blackness and close-shaven to his head. His skin had a swarthy tint to it, which was uncommon in the Viking race.

Varga stared up at them, his uncomprehending bloodshot eyes meeting theirs without any flash of recognition present within. It was clear they had both noted their leader's vulnerable state because, even through the drug-induced fug of Varga's mind, the contrast between the two figures was plain to see. Jordis' thick brows were deeply furrowed and concern was etched on his face, whereas Morten's yellow eyes were narrow and calculating, lending a predatory look to his appearance that had very little to do with his blood ties to the Ulfhednar and everything to do with his own innate personality.

The clan leader backed away from them, gaining his feet unsteadily and shambling back to the throne, trying desperately to regain some sort of cohesion to his thoughts.

The two Krieghund followed him to the bottom step of the dais, where they bowed perfunctorily. Jordis spoke first, fidgeting uncomfortably as he looked up at his distressed chieftain. "Varga, what ails you?" He stared sidelong at Morten, who nodded quickly, urging his compatriot on. "We heard...sounds of misery." He finished lamely.

Warning bells had begun to ring their clarion call in Hrolfsson's brain as soon as he had registered Jawrender's look and now, as he stared down at the two of them, in a sudden moment of paranoid clarity, he became sure that they were both weighing him up, gauging his behaviour and searching for weakness, though it was clear to him that Morten was approaching the task with far more relish than Jordis, for the blond warrior was struggling to look Varga in the eye.

Hrolfsson slumped onto the chair and tried vainly to frame an answer to the question. He was saved from that ignominy by a commotion at the far side of the room. It was Beyla the seeress. Despite the frailty brought on by her advancing years, she crashed the door back against the wall of the Dun and strode purposefully over towards the two who awaited Varga's response, her misshapen staff of beech rapping an angry tattoo upon the dirty floor. "What mischief are you stirring here, you two?" she hissed.

As Jordis swung round to address her, Varga noted the look of absolute hatred that flickered across Morten's face before he too turned to confront the elderly witch.

"We were concerned, Beyla. Londara came to us in tears and said that Varga was not himself, so we came to check on him." Jordis said calmly.

"What business is it of yours anyway, harridan? Since when did we need your permission to enter the Dun?" Morten snapped.

As she walked slowly up the steps of the raised platform upon which Varga sat, Beyla locked glares with the two, holding them in her unblinking gaze until they began to shift uncomfortably under the scrutiny. Her eyes, white but for the slightest tinge of blue in each, roved back and forth from one to the other. "If it affects the leader of the Ulfhednar then you can be damned sure it affects each and every one of us." She responded hotly. "I might equally ask you why you feel so able to offer care and guidance to him?"

Neither replied as they both looked beyond her, for Varga had sat up straight and began to speak. The two Krieghund blinked in surprise, because whilst they had been quarrelling with Beyla, Varga's eyes had lost their vacancy and his voice had regained most, if not all of its forbidding timbre. "Jordis, I thank you for your anxiety over my welfare. I had simply over-indulged and lost my balance. Whilst I was unconscious, I must have fallen into some sort of dream-state, which is why I was so confused when you awoke me."

Whether Jordis was fooled by the rather weak lie Varga neither knew nor cared, but he continued to speak regardless. "Go and pass on my thanks to Londara also."

The Krieghund took this to be his dismissal, nodded and made for the door. As he was on the brink of leaving the chieftain's presence, Varga hailed him with a leering grin. "Tell her she may attend to me later where I will proffer a more personal gift of gratitude."

Rasmussen kept his face neutral as he exited.

The leader of the Ulfhednar re-focussed his attention back onto the pair before him.

Morten was standing in an attitude of insolent contempt, hand resting on the pommel of the seax which was tied to his belt, glowering with barely disguised antipathy at the wizened old woman.

Beyla drew herself as erect as her elderly bent back would allow and returned the fierce look with a defiant stare of her own. Varga coughed loudly, partially to attract their attention and partially to cover up the boom of laughter which was on the brink of escaping him.

He composed himself then stood up purposefully, his massive form looming over them, shrouding them in the flickering shadow cast by the flame of the torch mounted in the sconce, positioned on the wall behind the throne for that very purpose.

Beyla and Morten both turned away from each other at the same time and bestowed their full attention on their leader. "Is there a root cause to your enmity towards each other or is it a mere clash of personalities?" Varga asked, slightly intrigued as to whether they would speak the truth or not.

"I have nothing but the best interests of the Ulfhednar at heart," Morten responded quickly.

"That does not really answer the question, Morten. Do you mean you do not believe Beyla has the same noble cause at the forefront of her mind as well?" he drawled sarcastically.

Morten shot a baleful look at the seeress before continuing, "I do not doubt she sees her machinations as essential to our ultimate goal but..." Varga's lieutenant hesitated, trying to word his reply as he wished.

To Varga's surprise, rather than being provoked by Morten's prevarication, Beyla's face split into a gap-toothed smile and she laughed heartily, "You dislike me for no other reason than my age, Jawrender. You hate the fact that poor old grizzled Beyla has been held in such high esteem by the clan for so long, yet you, a mere pup to my eyes, must scrap and fight for respect and admiration." Her voice lost its joviality and dropped to an ominous hiss, "I have been holding the ear of the Ulfhednar clan-leader for decades. I have been at the right hand of Varga's predecessors for more years than I care to remember. I knew his father and his father's father. I have seen leaders come and go. Jakan Anderssen, Grigori Razortooth, Connevar Larsson. All have sought my wisdom, all have heeded my words, yet I am bound to say that none had the stuff of greatness about them like Varga Hrolfsson. My one regret is that I am too old and ancient to properly enjoy the glories which Varga's leadership have brought to the tribe." Her milky eyes took on a distant look and her voice dropped to a poignant sigh. "Alas, the days of decadence are naught but memories for Beyla now." Then, she stepped towards Morten and the venom in her voice returned. "But I have never acted for personal gain, beyond that which I will accrue as an eminent member of the clan. The Ulfhednar are always first and foremost in my thoughts and I am sickened to my stomach that a mewling bastard barely free from his mother's teat would dare suggest otherwise. What have you done for the Ulfhednar, Morten Jawrender? Aside from conspiring with your cohorts to overthrow its leader?"

Jawrender bristled at the accusation, batting the staff which Beyla had jabbed at him aside and advancing towards the old woman. "So you accuse me of treason now?" he raged. "I will not waste my breath bandying words with a lap-dog when I can speak to its master." He turned back to Varga and ascended to the second step of the platform. "This is the cause of my hatred, Varga. Her words are poison to your mind. She fears the loss of her position in the great scheme of things and will stop at nothing to ensure she is the only one able to command your attention."

Varga sat and listened as the pair started arguing again, by turns half amused and half wearied by the puerile bickering. His dilemma was that he was fairly certain the words of both were true. Beyla had proved herself totally committed to both the tribe and himself personally on innumerable occasions and had often put clan interests before Varga's. He did not doubt that the defence of her deeds was indeed true but, as Morten had pointed out, she had been a confidante for decade upon decade and, in Varga's experience, people in exalted positions who had held them for so long did not relinquish them without a fight.

That knowledge made Varga leery of taking her totally at her word, but he did not accept that the motive for her actions would bring harm upon the tribe. Therefore, he felt he had no choice but to heed her warning.

On the other hand, in Morten's defence, Varga knew only too well that it was the nature of the pack for its leader to become subject to challenges from time to time and it was one of the misgivings which he had considered when he had formed the Krieghund. He had reasoned that, by diluting the power between five, there would be too much in-fighting amongst the quintet for them to focus their efforts on ousting him. Also, as a further back-up, he had hoped that, if he had misread their level of loyalty, then one or more of the appointees to the elite force would prove grateful enough to him that they would, at least, provide some sort of warning were a coup to be attempted.

The Krieghund had been in existence for over two years now and, so far, the idea behind the group had more or less borne fruit, save for the unfortunate demise of Olof Sigurdsson at Dun Eiledon.

After they had become settled at Dun Varulfur, they had set about counting the skulls which they had amassed on their sojourns over sea and land. The total had been a respectable twenty thousand, but was far from the final figure required. Varga knew that the flow of skulls had to be speeded up otherwise it would be decades before the ascension of Fenrir HelMouth would come to pass.

With that in mind, he had handpicked five of his most able warriors and split the clan, assigning each section to a Krieghund general. Four of the generals were then sent forth, charged to take their battalions into the countryside and unleash their bloody harvest of mayhem and death, whilst the other general remained behind with his troop as security for the Dun and its surrounding homes. This group of wolves would then depart as soon as the first pack from the four which roved the land returned.

Initially, the plan had worked spectacularly well and the amount of skulls gathered to reside in their final resting place atop Surtr's pyre began to increase with a pleasing regularity. Within the first year of the Krieghund's formation the total of skulls had reached thirty thousand and, within ten months of that milestone, the figure had doubled again to sixty thousand.

Now, however, the groups were being forced to cast their nets further afield as they had laid waste to the areas within close proximity to the Dun and the first murmurings of discontent had begun.

Olof Sigurdsson had been the first to vocalise the Krieghund's misgivings, his guttural voice grating on Varga's ears as he listed the concerns of the werewolf troop. Varga had sent him away with a promise that he would consider the problem.

Jawrender had been next, a mere two weeks later, requesting to talk immediately upon his section's return. As his troop began depositing their macabre trophies upon Surtr's flame, Varga granted him audience, struggling to hold his temper in check as Morten put his points across with a highly unprepossessing whine.

With depressing regularity, the Krieghund, minus the now absent Sigurdsson, whose section had been split between the surviving quartet, continued to gripe whenever the opportunity presented itself, usually when a pack returned from the hunt, although the first time Andrakhan Steinsson raised his voice in dissension had been when his section of the clan were about to embark upon their latest killing spree.

Finally, after hearing the same argument put in the same way for the umpteenth time, Varga snapped. The unfortunate recipient of his wrath was Futhark Vermaelen, who was sent from the Dun with his metaphorical tail between his legs, the harsh curses of his leader echoing loudly in his ears.

Within days of this, runners were sent out to find the hunting packs and bring them back to Dun Varulfur, there to convene a meeting of the clan where all issues were to be addressed.

As he watched Beyla and Morten continue to argue, his memory flew back to that day.

He had sat atop his forbidding throne, surveying the seething, sweating mass of his wolven kin, trying to catch the mood of the room as various snatches of conversation became temporarily clear amidst the general buzz of expectancy. This was something which had not occurred since Varga had ascended to the head of the tribe. Aside from fleeting moments such as Beyla's heated argument with him upon the deck of the *Varulv*, Varga Hrolfsson's authority over the Ulfhednar had been unquestioned and absolute, but now a change in the wind could be detected, faint and intangible at the moment, yet with the possibility that it might grow into a savage tornado which could devastate the accepted order of things and usher in a revolution which would rock the tribe to its very foundations.

As Varga scanned the heaving Dun, it became clear how much his power over his underlings had waned. Where before his glare was enough for them to bow their heads and avert their gaze, now they held his eyes, not overtly challenging him but not being cowed by him either.

The four remaining Krieghund had made their way to the bottom stair of the dais and the milling throng had arranged themselves into their sections behind them. Recognising the danger of the moment, Varga realised that they were, at the current time, four troops of a finely-honed attack force ready and willing to do his bidding but, if the gathering turned against him then, in the blink of an eye, they would become four armies flanking their generals, ready to fight for overall command of the tribe.

He stood ready to address the quietening crowd, hoping that the trepidation he felt was not apparent in his eyes. With a deep breath, he began to speak, "Hear me now, Ulfhednar, for the words I am about to say to you will not be repeated. I do not think I need to remind you all of our sacred purpose. You all made the choice to leave our homeland to follow me in my quest and you all know the depth of gratitude I have for that is bottomless. Know though that my desire to fulfil the mission I was charged with by Fenrir HelMouth himself is also bottomless and eternal and there is no-one either within or without this room who will steer me from it."

He ceased his discourse for a moment and let the now-silent atmosphere in the room build steadily. He stared unwaveringly at the carefully neutral eyes of the quartet of his supposedly trustworthy deputies and wondered what they were thinking. Shrugging the thought aside, he continued, "Where we have walked before, we have cleansed the land of unbelievers. We have travelled across uncharted waters and undisturbed earth in our pursuit of immortality and all who thought to arrest our progress have shrunk before us knowing that they would be unable to withstand the god-given power of the Ulfhednar. Unfortunately, in a way, we have been too successful in our endeavours and we are now the victims of our own accomplishments, having left the country hereabouts as barren as the tundra of our homeland when it is in the grip of the hardest winter. Therefore we have no choice, but to extend our domain. After all, that was the compelling reason which convinced me of the need to form the Krieghund in the first place. We *must* look beyond the familiar confines of Dun Varulfur and strike out into the unknown once more, otherwise we will fall short of what our god expects of us. We have already achieved a stunning amount in an amazingly short time, yet the horizon still contains nothing more than a path without a destination. However, if we keep walking along that straight and true course, the destination will appear in due time. It may be hazy and intangible at first but, over the days to come, it will resolve itself into the place which we seek. I, Varga Hrolfsson, pledge to you that I will lead the Ulfhednar to the halls of Hel and throw the doors wide open to allow Fenrir HelMouth to unleash his fury upon the world. And as He vents his lethal passion upon those who tricked him and trapped him and those poor fools find the second coming of Ragnarok upon them, there the Ulfhednar will be, bathing in the glory of a god renewed, standing proud in the teeth of the gale, reaping the rewards which our efforts will have brought us. That is why we must continue to look outwards towards new horizons and gather our harvest from pastures as yet untouched. Think not of the hardships which assail us here and now. Think of the triumphs and

183

gratitude of your god when He is the ruler of the world." Varga's arms swept out towards the multitude, "I do not condemn you for voicing your misgivings. The shadows of doubt shrink once they are brought into the light but, if left in the dark, they will fester and bloat, growing ever larger until they can be contained no more."

With that said, he threw his head back and started to howl, the eerie modulations echoing strangely off the walls of the Dun. As the Ulfhednar took up the ululation, he narrowed his eyes and stared at his four deputies, noting with quiet satisfaction their fidgeting discomfort. Only one of the Krieghund returned his stare. Jordis Rasmussen's moustache turned up at the edges as he smiled and nodded at his leader with genuine warmth. Hrolfsson also saw that Jordis' troop was not looking towards him with distrust, but rather at the other sections of the tribe.

In that moment, he had realised his reading of the Krieghund was, at least partly, correct and Jordis was the one in whom he could place his trust without fear of treachery.

Varga returned the nod and then stared benevolently towards the rest of the clan. At the point where the last echoes of the howl dissipated, he began to stamp his massive fur-booted feet upon the floor, chanting "Ulfhednar, Ulfhednar" in rhythm with the pounding.

As with the howl, the invitation was taken up by the tribe and the name of the clan echoed up to the rafters.

He had descended the steps then, acclaiming the response he had received from the crowd. One by one he went to the Krieghund, shaking their hands warmly to the accompaniment of increased cheers.

Varga leant into each of them in turn, still smiling the languid smile which had appeared upon his face as he had walked down the dais towards them. Jordis had been the first of the quartet and Varga had greeted him with a salutation of heartfelt thanks. To all outward appearances, he did the same to the remaining three. However the words he bestowed upon them were nothing of the sort, though the grin remained fixed upon his visage, belying the venomous words he spoke in their ears. To each of them he repeated the exact same warning, "I have made you leaders, so act like leaders. Control your sections or you will be relieved of both your duties and your lives. I do not want to have to deal with petty rubbish like this again. Is that clear?"

The trio had nodded in mute acceptance, acutely aware that they had lost the crowd to Varga's inspiring oratory and conceding that whatever they had hoped to gain from the gathering would not be achieved.

Varga was jerked out of his recollections by a sharp bark of pain from Morten. As he was wrenched back to the present, it was clear the sound had been Jawrender's painful reaction to being cracked over the head with Beyla's staff. He yanked the twisted piece of wood from her hands and made to snap it over his thigh. The old woman started to cackle contemptuously as he tried to break it in two, for it soon became clear he could not. With murder in his eyes, he ceased his struggle and sprang across the intervening space, staff raised above his head, ready to strike at the unabashed seeress.

With a blinding flash, the death-black silhouette of the figure upon the moon overlaid the scene for a split-second and, such was Varga's shock at its appearance, he screamed "Noooo" at the top of his voice.

That, in turn, startled Jawrender who, misunderstanding the shriek, stopped dead in his tracks. Hrolfsson took a few seconds to gather himself, during which time the Krieghund had, rather shamefacedly, dropped the staff to the floor.

"Surely you cannot expect a poor old woman to bend all the way down there," Beyla smirked mischievously.

Morten made no move towards it. Instead he stared at Varga, awaiting guidance.

The leader of the Ulfhednar decided that, whilst his deputy was an undoubted thorn in his side, humiliating him would serve no purpose, save to make him redouble his efforts to destabilise Varga's regime. "Do not be so coy, Beyla. I have known you for too long to fall for your poor, helpless old woman act. Pick your staff up and apologise."

"Varga, I..." she began.

"Apologise, Beyla," he repeated in the same deadpan voice.

Everything about her demeanour screamed defiance but, at the last, she turned to Jawrender, "Forgive me, Morten."

Jawrender's face twisted for a second into a sneer of contempt but, after catching a warning look from Varga, he relented, instead sending a cursory nod in the seeress's direction.

"I hope I have allayed your worries as to my welfare, Morten," Varga said, taking the smaller man by the arm and gently propelling him towards the door.

As they got to the threshold, Morten leant in closely towards his leader and whispered urgently in his ear. "We need to speak, Varga, free from the presence of Beyla."

The huge clansman rolled his eyes in irritation.

Morten gripped his leader's arm so hard that Varga grunted in surprise at the force of it. "We fear for you, Varga. You are losing the Ulfhednar." He cast a quick glance over his shoulder at the old woman who was still standing just in front of the dais, seemingly oblivious to the two of them. "I beseech you, Varga. Seek out the Krieghund tonight and hear what we have to say," again he glanced at Beyla, "free from malign influences."

With that he was gone from the Dun.

As he walked ponderously back to his throne, Varga mulled over Jawrender's words. The squat clansman had seemed genuine enough and the fact that Jordis, the only one of his elite force who had not come whining to him when the restlessness had reached its height, had accompanied him into the Dun when they came to check on Varga's wellbeing, only served to underline the point that perhaps the warning was worth heeding.

"Lost in thought, Varga?"

A brief rueful smile flashed across the chieftain's face. "Aye, Beyla. One of the joys of leadership."

Beyla cast a sidelong glance at the giant of a man as he returned to his wooden eyrie and shook her head, "You are not the man you once were, Varga Hrolfsson", she whispered to herself.

Wincing at the arthritis which flamed in her hip as she climbed the stairs, she came to stand by the leader of the Ulfhednar, resting a not unkindly hand upon his massive shoulder. "You should spend more time out amongst the tribe, Varga. You live like a hermit when you could live like a king. The only time any, bar myself and your Krieghund, see their leader is when they bring their prizes into the Dun to put on the fire and, even then, all they are witness to is a shambling drunk, ranting and raving incoherently at them, hardly the stuff of inspiration."

Varga chuckled, "Do not sugar your words, Beyla. Say what is on your mind."

"I am glad you find it humorous. I wonder if you will find it quite so amusing when you are breathing your last as an axe cleaves your back."

"To be honest, it will be a blessed release from all the infantile bickering I am forced to listen to," he snapped angrily. After a few seconds, he held up his hand, "I know I have not been myself of late." He smiled slyly at her. "It was you who started my decline, woman. You spoke of one who will be my bane or somesuch upon the *Varulv*, do you remember? Now, ever since our destruction of Dun Eiledon, I have been getting visions of this Monkshood in both my waking hours and my dreams. Is he to be the architect of my demise? Is my fate already sealed by powers beyond my control?"

The seeress nodded sagely, "So now we come to the root of your erratic behaviour then."

Hrolfsson hawked and spat upon the floor. "It is alright for you, Beyla. You are able to see what is to come in the future. We are not all as privileged as you are with the gift of second sight. For all I know Monkshood could be

186

standing outside the Dun right now, ready and waiting to slaughter me like a pig."

Through gritted teeth, Beyla hissed her response, which positively dripped with contempt. "Will you listen to yourself, man? Are you Viking born or the offspring of a faerie and a mermaid?"

At that, Varga erupted out of his chair and grabbed Beyla's arm, unsuccessfully hiding his distaste at the dry parchment-like skin, "Watch your tongue, witch."

"Or?" Beyla made no attempt to pull away, instead leaning in closer to him, though she barely reached his chest. "Your threats are as empty as that wine-stained chalice, Varga."

For a moment, the warrior's grip tightened on the old woman's arm as if he was about to snap the stick-thin bone, but instead he released her, though inwardly he still seethed with impotent fury.

Beyla absently rubbed at her elbow where Varga had grabbed her so roughly. "What do you think you will achieve by skulking in here? The Varga Hrolfsson who led the Ulfhednar across the ocean at the behest of Fenrir HelMouth would never have cowered behind closed doors, frightened of his own shadow. He would have kicked down the doors and faced his fears head on. Even if he knew that this Monkshood was waiting to confront him beyond the threshold of the Dun, he would still march out to face him down." She stared at him with unconcealed disdain, "Your paranoia has unmanned you and, if you continue to act in this craven manner, the Ulfhednar will be lost to you and so will your father."

Her sneer softened as she saw her words hit home. "You have to get past this, Varga. You have to be a leader again."

The Viking warchief could only nod, finding himself unable to speak. Eventually he managed a strangled dismissal of Beyla, watching abjectly as the seeress departed from the huge longhouse shaking her head slowly.

He sat unmoving for an indeterminate time, mulling over both Morten and Beyla's words, staring dumbly at the flickering play of firelight upon the wall.

As he had so often recently, he sought solace in the bottom of a goblet, gulping the contents down without really tasting them. After he had hastily tipped three drinks down his throat, he became aware of a change in the atmosphere of the Dun. It had become deathly quiet and as cold as the grave, chilling Varga to the depths of his bones. He cried out in hysteria, but the sound emerged as a reedy whisper which was quickly absorbed into the breathless silence. His breath came in short, sharp bursts and did not seem to be enough to fill his lungs. In wide-eyed terror, he saw that the eternal flame of Surtr, which forever guttered underneath the macabre pile of skulls that held pride of place in the centre of the Ulfhednar's home, had stopped moving. As he crept closer to it, he saw that the hitherto eternally wavering fire had indeed ceased its constant roiling and the shadows which dotted the walls now looked wan and dead.

Suddenly there was movement to the left. Out of the corner of his eye, Varga saw a flicker of something, though what it was he did not know. As his head whipped round, his right eye caught the ghost of something else. In horror, he watched as the shadows on the wall began to flow unnaturally together like small pools of black mercury, merging into a massive, though indistinct, shape.

The blackness of the form upon the planking on the wall began to thicken into something tangible.

By this time, Varga had dropped to his knees and buried his face in his hands whimpering incoherently, certain that the figure before him would transform itself into the monk which populated his tortured dreams and despatch him to Hel into the vengeful maw of Fenrir.

"Get to your feet, you pathetic worm, before I rip your head from your shoulders," A guttural voice thundered.

Varga felt himself yanked onto the vertical plane like a puppet on a string and was spun round dizzyingly fast.

Fenrir HelMouth, son of Loki, god of mischief and Angrbooa, giantess of grief, seethed at the wretched creature who was his chief vessel of worship upon the earth. "Give me one good reason why I should not kill you where you stand, Hrolfsson?"

What relief Varga had felt at Fenrir materialising before him rather than the nightmare of Monkshood, evaporated like ice before a flame as the full weight of Fenrir's scorn came crashing down upon him.

His head dropped and he could not look the massive wolf in the eye. "I have no excuse to give you, Lord. I find my every waking hour assailed by doubts which I am unable to quell." He heaved a huge shuddering sigh and lifted his head up with a great effort. "I fear I am not worthy of the task you have set me, Fenrir."

The wolf-god continued to breathe heavily, barely keeping his temper in check. Every sinew of his body was straining, poised to fall on Varga and tear him to shreds. However, the truth of the matter was that, without the slaughter which the Ulfhednar had inflicted upon their victims, Fenrir would never have possessed the power to appear before Varga in anything other than a dream. Yet now here he was, bulking massively above the snivelling clan leader, snuffing in the tastes and smells of real life once more.

As he breathed in huge lungfuls of the air, he slowly regained control of his towering rage. "Hrolfsson, attend to my words. It is only through dint of your tribe's efforts so far that you do not lie dead at my feet. I feel my strength returning day upon day as the blood which is spilt in my name invigorates me and makes me whole once more. In some ways it is more of a torture than being wholly bereft of power, for the memories of my previous life have been awakened as I have been strengthened and my senses are now exquisitely tantalised by what was and what will be again." His pitiless blue eyes narrowed and he pinned Varga to the spot with the ferocity of his glare. "I burn for the day when I will arise from the depths of Hel and cement my dominion over the earth and all who dwell upon it."

As before, when he had dreamt of Fenrir in the mist-wreathed cavern, the passion of the wolf-god's words poured hot fire down Varga's spine and he felt the seemingly immovable mountain of doubt shudder, as if rocked by a great concussion.

"Know this, Varga Hrolfsson. I will not tolerate such spineless cowardice again," Fenrir finished.

Varga straightened up and nodded.

The Norse deity regarded his disciple. "Perhaps you need another reminder of why you are undertaking these great deeds?" he murmured.

Even as the Viking's brows furrowed in uncertainty as to what the huge wolf meant, Fenrir leapt at him so quickly that he had no time to react as the all-engulfing jaws clamped down upon him.

Suddenly Varga was everywhere and nowhere in a world of absolute darkness

His senses tried to grope at anything which resembled a modicum of reality, but all he could comprehend was that he was falling down, down to who knew where. Just when he thought that breath would never inhabit his lungs again, with a giddying swiftness, the sensation stopped.

As he sought to squash his rising alarm, Varga felt like his body was a hollow shell, flimsy and held to the ground by the most tenuous of connections. Then, as he began to regain his equilibrium, in a feeling akin to wine being poured into an empty goblet, he sensed he was somehow becoming more substantial and, as his body engorged and became more material, so the darkness began to evaporate before his eyes, slowly at first but then coruscating into a wondrous display of every hue imaginable.

Eventually, he was whole again and able to comprehend where he was.

Like funereal bells tolling their sonorous peals in his head, memories of the sagas heard at his father's knee came crashing into his mind:

'On the Nástrond is a great hall steeped in evil with its doors facing to the north. It is all woven of serpent-backs like a wattle-house and all the snake-heads turn into the house and blow venom, so that, along the hall, run rivers of venom and those who have broken oaths and murderers wade in these rivers, wailing and bemoaning their eternal agony.'

"Behold the Corpse Shore, Hrolfsson." Fenrir grinned, his face twisting into a vile smirk.

As he gaped in catatonic shock at his surroundings, Varga struggled to take in all that he saw. The ceiling and walls of the massive cavern were in a constant state of glittering chaos as the roaring flames which blazed along both shores of the river of Hel reflected off the glass-smooth scales that encompassed every inch of their surface. The cave stretched back as far as the eye could see and beyond. The Viking warchief gasped as a black mass began to move out of the shadows at the far end of the gargantuan hall towards them. Even though it was a long way away from where he and Fenrir stood, the shape gave off an impression of huge magnitude. With a grace that belied its undoubted bulk, the figure detached itself from the ceiling and twisted majestically, its wings snapping out with an audible crack. From there it glided across the hellish landscape to the accompaniment of even greater sounds of woe from the wrongdoers who suffered in the acid venom which flowed in the river.

The wyrm halted its swoop, gaining height for a moment then plummeting into the fast-flowing poison. Its equine face stabbed downwards again and again, each time gathering several unfortunates within its jaws and swallowing them whole.

As the carnage continued, Fenrir's voice rumbled in Varga's ears. "I hope that you appreciate how privileged you are, Ulfhednar. Not many get to see Nidhogg feed and live to tell the tale."

Malice Striker, as Nidhogg was otherwise known in the Viking sagas, continued to feast, grunting with pleasure as it crunched and chewed its way through the denizens of Hel, seemingly oblivious to its audience.

Without taking his enraptured eyes from the fantastical panorama before him, he spoke to his god, amazed at how even he managed to keep his voice.

"Why have you brought me here, Fenrir?"

"You have lost your way, Varga and the longer it takes you to regain your focus upon your hallowed task, the longer I have to bide in this fetid pit." As he spoke, Fenrir absently flicked out a massive paw at one of the damned who had managed to scramble free of the noxious tide of the river and penetrate the wall of flame that surrounded it. The woman, already hideously scarred by the toxins of the waterway and the white-hot flame upon the banks, had been so intent upon her escape from Nidhogg and the river that, inexplicably, she had not seen the immense wolf patiently sitting upon his haunches and skidded to a halt as she stumbled into his shadow.

The beginnings of a scream were bit off abruptly as Fenrir's massive claw destroyed the naked female, her innards exploding over the rocky floor in a torrent of blood and viscera.

After he had fed upon the remnants of his victim, the pair began to follow the meandering course of the river Hel and Fenrir continued his explanation,

"You have become so wrapped up in your distrust of everyone and everything that the quest has become secondary in your mind, behind holding on to the pitiful amount of power you have as the leader of the Ulfhednar."

Varga pondered Fenrir's words as they walked, but the wolf took his silence to show that his words were still not registering with the clan leader, so he continued relentlessly.

"Have you forgotten that, if you fail in your endeavours, not only do you doom me to this squalid existence but you condemn yourself to it also?"

Finally Varga spoke, though it was barely louder than a murmur, "No, I have not."

Fenrir stopped and jerked his head slightly towards a wooden door which led off the main hall. "Not only yourself but others too," he said enigmatically.

Hesitantly Varga walked towards the door, encouraged by another slight nod from the God of Wolves.

The ebon surface was pitted and rough and bore numerous scorch marks from the constant conflagration raging in the hall. Varga ran his hands over it gently, wondering what would confront him when he opened it. With a deep breath, he bunched his colossal muscles and brought his weight to bear against the wood. For a few seconds, the ages of rust which had accumulated on the hinges held fast but, with a pained screech, they gave way and Varga fell into the room, coughing as a cloud of dust shot up his nose and into his mouth.

"Who's there?" A cracked voice asked nervously.

It was a voice which the leader of the Ulfhednar had not heard for many years and was so unexpected that, for a moment, Varga could not find his tongue.

Shambling sandalled feet shuffled into view supporting painfully thin legs upon which a plethora of blue and purple veins stood out like an army of snakes. They were wrapped in pitifully torn rags stained with dried urine and blood. The arms protruding from the gaping holes on each side of the besmirched tunic were even thinner than the legs and looked as if they would snap in a strong wind.

It was then that Varga came to the face. Though he had steeled himself, he was still appalled by what he saw. The once bull-like neck was stretched and wrinkled and the beard was no more than a few wisps of white hair. The mouth was toothless aside from three blackened stumps and the emerald eyes which had once blazed with immense strength and power were now milky-white and blind.

Hands with broken discoloured nails reached before the old man, as he repeated his inquiry.

Varga swallowed hard but could not stop the piteous sobs bubbling to the surface as he beheld the shell of a man before him, "Father?" he quavered.

Kraaken Hrolfsson turned at the voice with a sharp intake of breath. "Varga?" he whispered, the catch in his voice making his words barely intelligible, "Is that you, son?"

Without another word, Varga stepped across the space and engulfed his father in a bear-hug, though he was mindful of the old man's fragile state and did not squeeze hard.

For a seemingly eternal moment, they stood unmoving, revelling in the overwhelming force of the emotions which had been unleashed by their reunion.

Pushing his son away, Kraaken cuffed the unashamed tears from his cheeks, a look of concern upon his face. "How do you come to be here, boy? Does this mean you too have passed over?"

Momentarily forgetting his father's blindness, Varga shook his head. "No, Father. I stand before you as the most blessed disciple of Fenrir HelMouth. It is by his arts that I am here and it is with his blessing that we have met."

"Truly? This is not some sort of cruel dream brought on by madness and isolation?"

"Yes, father, truly," Varga replied. The look of pride on his father's face filled him with such a rush, he nearly gasped at the sheer power of it. However, the look was swiftly replaced by one of despair and his father turned from him with his head bowed. "How can this be, Varga? How have you risen so high in the wolf-god's standing when you have been forced to live with the ignominy of my demise? I am surprised one so favoured would waste time seeking out one who has let him down so badly."

Varga's heart felt as if it would break at the pain in the voice and, at that moment, realised why Fenrir had brought him here. Taking the old man's skeletal chin in his massive hand, he lifted the head up and stared intensely into the opaque eyes. "Do not speak like that, Father. It is I who has let you down with my selfishness and weakness."

Kraaken wailed, "I don't understand, Varga."

The Viking clan-chief cast about for somewhere to sit. His eyes traced around the room, taking in the four walls of dull, forbidding rock. He looked to the gloom from where his father had emerged and saw a decrepit bed covered in filthy clumps of straw. He led his father over to it and, with a twist of distaste quirking his lips, sat down next to the old man.

Despite looming over his father, the huge warrior felt as if he was back at the family home in Ulfsgaard, lost in respect and adoration for his sire. He laid a kindly arm around the bony shoulders and began to speak. "Father, I have had a great honour bestowed upon me and I have you to thank for it. I am War-Leader of the Ulfhednar now and I am embroiled in a sacred task set before me by Fenrir himself. If the tribe succeed in our endeavours then it will be feted in sagas as yet unsung and the name Hrolfsson will be writ large in the tomes of history forever more. I have been charged with bringing about the second coming of Ragnarok and freeing Fenrir from the fetters with which the treacherous Aesir bound him."

The old man inhaled sharply at that, "A momentous task to be sure. But I still do not understand how you have become so favoured in His eyes."

Varga began to speak, "When I returned from my first voyage, I found you fevered and days from death. After the life you had led, it ate away at me that you would meet your end in such a manner. Beyla and I sat your final vigil as you hovered on the cusp and I prayed for you, Father. I prayed for the gods to intervene and spare you the injustice of such a demise, but they did nothing. The damnable Aesir deserted you when you needed them the most. As you breathed your last, I vowed to make them regret their inaction. I remembered the sagas which I learnt at your knee and hit upon the perfect revenge to visit on the bastard gods who forsook you so readily. Though I did not have a precise idea of how to go about it, I remembered the tale of Fenrir slaying Odin upon the field of Vigrid and decided to devote my life to him. Knowing that he was trapped upon the Nastrond, my purpose became two-fold. Firstly, I reasoned that, if I found favour with him, then it would somehow protect you from the worst of the torments suffered by those who bide here. Secondly, as Fenrir was the one who had bested the Aesir's leader the first time round, it seemed obvious that he would be the perfect vessel to exploit all the hatred and anger which I felt towards the scum of Asgard."

Throughout the diatribe, Kraaken's eyes had grown wider at his son's words, "How did the elders in Ulfsgaard react to this, boy?"

A wolfish grin flickered on Varga's face. "They did not take too kindly to it, but I was certainly not going to let their narrow-mindedness stop me on my quest. Let us just say I persuaded them around to my point of view."

Kraaken nodded sombrely. Though he would have counted the village elders as some of his oldest friends, the Viking hierarchy was, and always had been, decided by strength of arms and rite of blood so he felt no more than a small tug of regret that they had been swept aside by the tide of Varga's fervour.

193

"They were the first sacrifices to the cause. From then on, we of the Ulfhednar stripped the country bare of unbelievers, fuelling the fires both day and night with the bodies of the dead, praying to Fenrir and seeking his favour. Then, on one special night, He came to me, Father. Fenrir HelMouth came to me in a dream and, where before I had been floundering in the undergrowth, he showed me the way and planted my feet firmly on the path to greatness. He showed me the most wondrous of treasures and bid me return them to the world of men, there to create a pathway from Hel to the world above where He would claim dominion over the lands of the earth, even as the rest of his family ruled over the oceans, heavens and Hel itself."

Kraaken Hrolfsson began to speak but there was no stopping Varga in his flow of excited conversation. "Father, he showed me the skulls of Hati and Skoll, then, by miraculous means, he fused them to my body, making them part of me and enabling me to hold a flaming shard of Surtr's sword, the very weapon he used to cleanse the earth and restart the world anew. I held it in my hands, Father, and due to Fenrir's blessing, it burned me not. It lies in Dun Varulfur even now."

The old man's brows knitted in confusion. "This is all so much to take in, Varga. What is Dun Varulfur?"

"It is the Ulfhednar's new home. You see, Fenrir warned me that there were forces advancing upon us, looking to prevent us from completing our sanctified task. He told me to take the tribe across the ocean to hunt out a new home where we could lay the foundations for all that was to come. We travelled far and wide, drowning our enemies in wave upon wave of blood. For nearly two years we sailed upon the *Varulv*, all the while hoarding the severed heads of those we had overcome, against the day they would be consumed by Surtr's flame, for that is how we are to effect His resurrection. A hundred thousand skulls are to be consumed by the pyre, melting the very earth to nothing, creating a gate through which Fenrir will ascend into the world of men, taking the Ulfhednar with him to the very pinnacle of existence. And he will free you, Father. He has promised to bring you with him as repayment for the deeds I have performed in His name."

Unabashed tears of paternal pleasure ran down the ancient's cheeks as he took in his son's words. "And the reason for this began with your desire to save me?" he managed to say.

Though he knew he could not see him, Varga turned his father round by the shoulders so that they faced each other, "Yes, Father. You shaped me into the man I am today. Without the backbone you instilled in me and the values of the warrior which you implanted in my very being, I would just be another aimless foot-soldier indulging in the idle decadence of the other tribes. Instead, I am the earthbound vessel at the right-hand of our God." He paused, shaking his head almost as if *he* disbelieved how far he had risen in the ranks of his race. "It is thanks to you, father. I have undertaken this task for you but I have also undertaken it *because* of you."

A beatific sigh escaped the elder Hrolfsson's lips and he too shook his head. "Oh Varga, I have not felt as joyful as this for so long. Thank you, son," he said simply. "Thank you."

Once again, Varga's heart leapt at the expression of happiness which shone on his father's face and, for all too brief a moment, he basked in it, pleased beyond words that he had been its architect.

However, just as suddenly as the sun had emerged, clouds appeared to obscure it. A frown appeared upon Kraaken's deeply wrinkled brow, emphasising the unrelenting damage which disease and old age had already wrought upon him. "If it was anyone else telling me this, Varga, I would not believe them. It is so fantastical and I am so, so proud of you but, if all is as you say, then how could you possibly have let me down? What you have achieved since I perished is nothing short of a miracle. The very fact that Fenrir is prepared to use his powers just to transport you here to see me is testament enough to your pre-eminence."

The Ulfhednar leader laughed ironically, "Though I am extremely grateful to Him for re-uniting me with you before I have completed the sacred mission he has conferred upon me, I do not think his reasons could be counted as entirely altruistic." He sighed hugely. "Recently, I have been, shall we say, less than focussed on Fenrir's grand plan and your rescue. I have become beset by doubts, unable to make the smallest decisions for fear of failure and loss of face. I have been concentrating more on holding onto my leadership of the tribe than on my original purpose. I cannot bring myself to trust anyone, not even Beyla."

"She still lives?" Varga's father gasped incredulously.

Despite his woes, the clan-chief could not help but smile at his father's reaction. "Aye, she'll bury us all." He chuckled, before realising what he had said, "I...I am sorry, I..."

Kraaken shrugged, ignoring the rather tactless comment. "Do you trust your god?"

A look of righteous zeal appeared on Varga's face immediately, "Of course," he stated emphatically.

"Do you, Varga? Have you not already said that you are paralysed by fear of failing to fulfil Fenrir's wishes?"

The massive Viking looked very small and hunched as he nodded.

In his most authoritative parental voice, Kraaken snapped, "I am blind, boy, you have to speak for me to know what is on your mind."

"Yes, father." Varga mumbled apologetically.

195

"Why is that? Who are you to cast doubt on the wisdom of Him? He chose you to be His vessel. Out of all the warriors he could have selected, he opted for you. Are you saying His choice was wrong? That's pretty presumptuous, isn't it, boy?"

Varga fidgeted uncomfortably as his father continued to press the point.

"Who are you to dare second-guess Him?" The old man stood up and, with a strength of voice belying his frail state, began to stalk about the dusty room. "Ah, lad, if that had been me...chosen by Fenrir himself...I think I would have burst at the privilege of it. Damn it, boy. How can you even contemplate turning your back on such an honour?"

Varga moaned, "I did not say that, father. I never, ever thought about not continuing with the task until my dying breath."

"Then why are you here, boy? Why did Fenrir drag you down to this fetid hovel?"

Varga stared shamefacedly at his father, feeling humiliated by the lecture. Finally when he could bear it no more, he rose and placed his hands upon his father's shoulders. "He brought me here to remind me of what I am fighting for." For a long moment, the huge warrior stared affectionately at the old man, then pulled him into a crushing bear-hug once more.

Kraaken managed a good-humoured grunt, "Dammit, boy," he smiled, "I have died once already. Are you trying to kill me again?"

A great guffaw exploded from the clan-chief. "By the gods, I've missed you, Father." Varga sighed and returned his father to the dusty floor. "Be assured that Fenrir's scheme has borne fruit. I will no longer let my own petty inadequacies distract me from what I have been chosen to do." He shook his head with a smile. "From now on, my every waking moment will be dedicated to the cause. Rest assured, father, soon you will be free of this odious place and be breathing the free air once again."

Kraaken Hrolfsson stepped back and regarded his son with sightless eyes and, it seemed to Varga, that he now stood straighter and prouder. "Go then, boy, accomplish your destiny."

The Ulfhednar leader headed towards the door of the cell. "I will, father, I will." He promised, the emotional catch returning to his voice as he departed from his beloved father once again.

Outside of the room, he found the wolf-god waiting patiently. Without a word, they began to walk back from the way they had come. Dust and bones crunched under their feet as they strode alongside the banks of the River Hel. At length, they came to an eldritch door, carved with angular runes of a language unknown to Varga.

Fenrir turned to the Viking chief, "If you walk through this door you have merely to follow the path and you will find yourself back at Dun Varulfur."

Varga made to go through the door but halted and turned back to the Wolf-God. "Thank you for doing this, my Lord. You cannot know how much this means to me."

Fenrir's slitted blue eyes narrowed, "Know this, Hrolfsson, I will not grant you such largesse if you descend into paranoia and despair again. I hope this has been the salutary lesson you needed to continue your works on the world above. My appearance in the flesh at the Dun is a powerful sign that your deeds are having the desired effect. However, every time I am forced to use my arts in such a way, it drains me terribly. I envisage that it will become easier as more blood is spilt, but I do not intend wasting any more precious energy on you, so be warned. If we are to meet here again, it will be to make you watch as I devour your father, then keep you alive for all eternity whilst I eat you limb by limb, spit you out and begin the process again."

With a curt nod, Varga pushed the door open and stepped through without a moment's hesitation.

Immediately, he was catapulted into the same non-world which he had experienced when he had first been dragged down to the netherworld by Fenrir. This time though, the disorientation was not nearly so overwhelming and he was able to calm himself and wait tolerantly until he felt himself return to the Dun.

He gingerly opened his eyes and was grateful to see the flicker of Surtr's fire at play upon the walls once more.

He sniffed hugely to regain his breath, his nose wrinkling as he found the twin stench of death and smoke still present in his nostrils.

Getting to his feet, he stared around Dun Varulfur as if seeing it for the first time. His eye was drawn to the ornate throne atop the dais from where he had presided over the Ulfhednar. He had commissioned it built to demonstrate the potency of his position, the sharp angles and intimidating carvings intended to cow all who stood before it. When he had received it and first planted his backside upon it, he had felt like a king, looking down upon everyone from the lofty position which was rightfully his.

Now he saw it for what it truly was. An anchor which he had clung to when he had been assailed on all sides by his mistrust in both himself and others. Now though, it merely served as a reminder of how self-centred and deluded he had become. He marched towards it, then broke into a run as he took the steps of the dais two at a time. He grabbed both arms of the chair and, with a mighty heave, cast it to the bloodstained floor of the Dun where it broke into three pieces.

His eyes were ripped to the door at the far end of the longhouse as it flew open. Beyla stood on the threshold, her toothless mouth gaping and a look of absolute bewilderment upon her face. "Varga, what..." she paused momentarily as she saw the wrecked throne lying at the bottom of the platform, "what happened?" she finished.

Varga strode purposefully down the steps as he spoke. "I had my eyes opened." He said simply.

The ancient seeress stared intently at the Viking chief as he came closer to her. She was taken aback by the transformation which had seemingly overtaken him since she had walked out of the Dun mere moments before. He seemed to have physically grown back into the colossus he had been when he had first attained the ultimate authority of the tribe. He strode past her with a calm assuredness, flashing her a toothy smile as he did so.

She struggled to keep up with him as his long loping steps increased in pace. "Varga," she called. He stopped and turned to her. "Though it makes my withered heart sing to see it, you have not set foot outside the Dun for many a long night. Might I ask where you are bound?"

With a slight hardening around the eyes suggesting that the clan-chief thought the inquiry impertinent, he answered, "Though it is none of your business, Beyla, I have a sudden yearning to sniff the night air and feel the winter wind in my beard. I trust this meets with your permission?"

"Morten means to assume your mantle, you know," the seeress murmured but, as she looked at Varga, she felt that her warning would go unheeded whether he believed her or not. "You are walking into a trap."

"I do not recall mentioning Morten." He eyed the seeress haughtily, only relenting when he saw her shoulders deflate. Suddenly struck by how tired she looked, he smiled benignly at her. "Traps can always be sprung, Beyla, especially if the one who walks into them is properly prepared."

The ancient woman looked slightly happier but still placed her gnarled fingers upon his arm. "I hope you are right, Varga. Be careful."

"Have you seen the events that will come to pass this night?" he asked in a quiet voice, knowing that, even if she told him he was to die at the hand of his deputy, he would still follow the same course.

She shook her head, looking more dejected than he had ever seen her. "No, Varga, I have not. I could lie to you to try and sway you from your rendezvous, but I will not. I think your mind is set beyond my abilities of persuasion anyway." She shrugged then straightened up, seeming to brighten as she did so. "I am not sure what sort of revelation you have had, but you have the look of the wolf about you once more and that has been absent for too long. Perhaps I am just clucking over you like a mother hen when, in reality, you are ready to fly the coop once more."

"Perhaps," Varga nodded acknowledgement, not sure that he appreciated being likened to a chicken. Without another word, leaving Beyla to her thoughts, he walked resolutely along the narrow platforms which interlinked the various huts of the Ulfhednar settlement until he came to the home of Morten Jawrender. Without ceremony, he thumped on the door with his fist, immediately causing the hushed voices within to lapse into silence.

The wooden door opened and Morten ushered him in, smiling predatorially at Varga's massive back as the clan-leader strode past him. As he entered the room further, Hrolfsson nodded acknowledgment to Andrakhan Steinsson and Futhark Vermaelen, who lounged with forced casualness upon their fur-covered chairs.

"No Jordis?" Varga asked pointedly.

Morten's voice cut through the silence. "He was unable to make it."

Varga shrugged then asked cheerily. "Well then, what's on your mind, lads?"

The trio of Ulfhednar deputies looked at each other, slightly nonplussed by the apparent confidence of their visitor. With a deep breath, Jawrender began to speak, "It is what I said back at the Dun, Varga. You are losing the support of the clan. Your behaviour can only be described as erratic at best, insane at worst. You rarely venture beyond the confines of the longhouse and, when you do, you are barely coherent, though at the moment you do appear slightly less...emotional than you have been in recent months." Jawrender looked at his cohorts for support and they both nodded emphatically.

Andrakhan took up the conversational baton. "There are rumblings of unrest, Varga, rumblings which have the feel of the first signs of an earthquake. We have tried through both word and deed to quell them but still they persist."

Varga's face twisted momentarily into an expression of disbelief at that, but he held his counsel.

"The quest has fallen by the wayside and is no longer uppermost in your mind." Futhark rumbled in his unnaturally deep timbre.

For the first time, Varga's face betrayed some emotion. "And you know what is uppermost in my thinking, do you, Futhark?" he hissed through gritted teeth.

"I know that whatever it has been, it has not been the quest." The Krieghund sat up straighter, stopping just short of rising from his seat.

The leader looked from face to face, seeing nothing but distrust and cold calculation. Recognising the danger but forcing a smile nonetheless, he gestured effusively, "Well, lads, you need not concern yourselves with that any more. I acknowledge my leadership of late has been somewhat lax, but no more." He lowered his head and shook it ashamedly. "The Ulfhednar will never languish under such slack control again. I am genuinely sorry that my actions have brought the tribe so low."

199

Morten and Andrakhan looked surprised by the contrition but Futhark erupted from his chair, "So that's it, is it? Crocodile tears then a return to the status quo, as if nothing has happened. No, not good enough, Varga. You have sent the Krieghund all over these islands whilst you have skulked in Dun Varulfur picking your arse and wallowing in self-pity. Morten was wrong in his warning to you, O Esteemed Leader, you are not in danger of losing the Ulfhednar, you have already lost them." He snarled, yanking the wicked looking seax from his belt and stabbing it towards Varga's throat.

Though the clan-chief had been expecting an attack ever since he entered Morten's home, it still caught him slightly off-guard and he grimaced as he felt the blade nick him on the shoulder as he swayed back from the blow.

Without thinking, he grabbed Vermaelen's stabbing arm and spun him around. The Krieghund screamed as Varga's instinctive act placed him directly in the path of Morten's sword-thrust and it took him in the back, skewering his kidney then erupting from his stomach in a gush of blood.

As Morten tried to drag his weapon clear of his fallen comrade, Varga made a run for the door only to be blocked by Andrakhan, who slashed at him viciously, forcing him back into the room. Ignoring the pitiful whimpers of the dying clansman, the two began circling the one. Morten nodded curtly at Andrakhan, who snarled at Varga then laid his sword against the wall behind him. Closing his eyes, he began the metamorphosis from man to wolf.

Varga licked his lips nervously, knowing how much quicker Andrakhan would be once he had assumed his wolven form. Though he hated himself for it, the clan-leader found himself regretting leaving Dun Varulfur unarmed. Upon waking from the dream induced by Fenrir, he had decided to trust in his god to protect him should the Krieghund turn on him, but now, as Morten's blade glinted in the guttering firelight and Andrakhan's body twisted and contorted in the exquisite agonies of his bestial conversion, he reasoned that, at this precise moment, he would have been better placing his faith in a mortal weapon rather than an immortal shield.

Morten had moved across in front of Andrakhan to protect him because, even though his strengths would be multiplied once he became a werewolf, Andrakhan was still vulnerable to attack during the change.

Instinctively, Varga's battle-sharpened sixth sense kicked in. He knew he would have no chance once Andrakhan became wolven, so he acted immediately. He grabbed the arm of the chair which Futhark had been seated upon and threw it at Morten, who instinctively dodged it. However, the wooden furniture clattered into Steinsson's head, knocking him senseless. With Morten off-balance and Andrakhan temporarily stunned, Hrolfsson dived at his human assailant, barely dodging the desperate thrust of Jawrender's weapon. Then the leader of the Ulfhednar was upon him and giving full vent to his berserk rage. The pinched, nasty little face of Morten Jawrender was ripped from his head as Varga let free the chains binding the wolf within. Long after Morten had died, Varga continued ripping and rending at his lifeless body, his razor claws slicing through unresisting flesh and his blood-soaked muzzle plunging again and again into the bloody mess which had been his deputy.

When the red mist finally began to dissolve before his eyes and he gained a small modicum of control over himself once again, he became aware of a weak pressure on his hind leg. With a growl, he snapped at the malformed hand which gripped him. His slitted green eyes found themselves staring into the anguished face of Andrakhan Steinsson.

The Krieghund tried to speak but all that came out from his peculiarly bulbous mouth was an unintelligible yowl. His face was the stuff of nightmares. One iris had slitted like Varga's but the other remained circular and human-like. The nose and jaws had extended into a muzzle but still retained the nostrils and upturn of a human nose with a wolven mouth filled with sharp teeth underneath.

His body had also become a travesty of nature, a cross between wolf and man, arms and legs trapped in the middle of the lycan metamorphosis, covered in uneven patches of grey wiry hair. The hands possessed both fingers and claws with the feet also sharing toe and talon in equal number.

As Varga returned to humanity and his abstract thought processes became keener, he realised what had happened.

For most werewolves, the change from man to beast was an irresistible surge which the one who was changing had about as much control over as driftwood in the tide. However, though the change could not actually be halted once it had begun, a measure of human influence still remained and the one who was transforming could channel the power which coursed through them and ride the wave so that the switch from man to wolf would reach the required conclusion.

The chair which Varga had hefted must have disrupted the Krieghund's concentration to such an extent that he had lost all remnants of control over the change and, as such, it had become disjointed and lacking coherence, which resulted in the mockery of life that lay before him, tortured and condemned.

Varga straightened up and stared down at Andrakhan with contempt. "See where your treachery has left you? I have a mind to leave you like this as an example to those who might contemplate challenging my authority."

Andrakhan's head dropped and he whimpered pathetically.

With a sigh, Varga walked past the bereft Viking and, with a fluid motion, collected Steinsson's sword from the wall of the hut. In two strides, he was back at his side and, without hesitation, swung the weapon down in an unstoppable arc, taking the Krieghund's head from his shoulders with one smooth sweep.

As the severed head rolled to a halt next to the devastated body of Morten, he turned to the grievously wounded Vermaelen and dispatched him in the same ruthless manner. Despite the treachery of his erstwhile confederates, Varga was surprised at the strength of loss he felt. He was able to cull some solace from the fact that the ever loyal Jordis had obviously wanted no part of the attempt on his life, but it was still a source of pain to the hulking leader that his standing had diminished so much in the eyes of his peers. He walked over to the table which occupied half of the furthest wall and emptied two of the three full goblets of wine that sat upon it. He was about to swallow the third when his eye found itself drawn to the nearest of the two curtained-off rooms which lay off the main living space.

The end of a booted foot protruded from underneath the sheet of hide which partitioned the room off from the rest of the hut. Without taking his gaze from it, Varga put the chalice down and moved to the curtain, wrenching the velvety animal skin aside with a sinking feeling.

His feelings of loss for the fallen trio in the next room evaporated like mist in the sunshine. Jordis Rasmussen lay on his back, one lifeless eye staring sightlessly at the ceiling, the other pierced into nothingness by a small knife which jutted obscenely from his skull. The only other injury was the gaping hole in his chest where his heart had been removed. Varga looked closely at the fallen man's arms, noting the bruises which were beginning to show between elbow and hand. They described, as clear as day, the shape of fingers. As he looked at Jordis' corpse, a proud smile alighted upon his face. He knew from experience that the bruises would not have appeared so quickly if they had not been the result of a titanic struggle. He could almost picture the scene in his head, the stoic Jordis railing against the devious machinations of the others, arguing Varga's corner with his usual unstinting steadfastness, then two of the cowards restraining him as the other plunged the blade home.

"Ah, Jordis, you will never know how sorry I am that you have paid for my shortcomings," he whispered.

He turned from Rasmussen and stalked back into the main room. Without ceremony, he dragged the bodies out into the still night air, uncaring that they would be subjected to the gaze of any curious passersby. He did not fear reprisal from any of the Krieghund's minions, reckoning that the grisly tableau would serve as a pointed enough warning to any who held the same thoughts of subversion.

It was the work of minutes to deposit the dead men outside in the dirt, the trail of blood making the area outside the front door of Morten's home slippery underfoot.

A crowd of ten Ulfhednar had gathered, open-mouthed, as Varga emerged from the hut cradling Jordis in his arms. He stood there momentarily, scanning the faces of the stunned crowd, ignoring the weight of his loyal deputy and the gentle brushing of the dead Viking's golden braids against his thigh. "Remove these scum from my sight," he instructed two of the gawpers, "Now!" he yelled, as they both remained transfixed despite his order. They jumped at the roar of Varga's voice and rushed to do his bidding, sharing looks of disbelief at what they were witnessing.

The leader of the Ulfhednar then bore his tragic cargo back to Dun Varulfur without comment, silently mulling over the destruction of the remaining four Krieghund all within the space of one bloody hour.

Varga Hrolfsson stood dispassionately, ignoring the icy rain which lashed into his face in angry squalls. His expression was unreadable as he looked upon the massive pyre which had been built in honour of Jordis Rasmussen, late of the Ulfhednar.

Varga himself had laid the body in the centre of the newly-dug mound which was surrounded by jutting obelisks in the traditional manner of a Viking 'stone ship' funeral. Jordis' body was surrounded by grave goods with his weaponry, family treasures and an ornately carved shield all laying beside him, wrapped in his ceremonial cloak bearing the rune of Fenrir. The only weapon which was not enveloped in the leathery folds of the cape was Jordis' favourite weapon, Jormungandr, a schmalsax which had exquisitely carved serpents embossed upon the narrow blade. This was laid upon his chest with both of his hands positioned as if gripping the hilt.

Next to his grave were three untidily excavated holes which looked incongruous next to the carefully fashioned hollow in which Jordis lay in state. Each of these housed one of the treacherous Krieghund who had perpetrated Jordis' murder. Upon reflection, Varga had countermanded his own order and decided to condemn the trio to thralldom, the Viking equivalent of slavery, which meant they would serve Jordis eternally in the halls of Valhalla.

When the circumstances of Jordis' death had come to light, three of the Ulfhednar women had put themselves forward as human sacrifices, offering themselves up to be buried with him, resplendent in their best jewellery and garments, readied to care for his every need for all eternity, and now they laid next to him in his grave. To do this, the women each had to undergo several sexual rites. When Jordis had been laid to rest in the 'stone ship', the three sacrifices had gone from tent to tent visiting the warriors who had made up Rasmussen's section in life, each knowing they would be repeatedly violated by every warrior, who would tell them that they performed these acts for their love of the dead Viking.

Lastly, they entered a specially prepared tent, which was raised in the middle of the stone ship above Jordis' grave, and six men had intercourse with them before they were strangled and stabbed, the final constriction being performed by Beyla, who, for the purposes of the ceremony was addressed by all present as the Angel of Death. The sexual rites with the chosen sacrifices were to show that they were considered to be vessels for the transmission of life force to the deceased warrior.

In Viking tradition, death had always been a critical moment for those bereaved, and consequently was surrounded by many taboos. The ceremonies were transitional rites which were intended to give the deceased peace in his or her new plane of existence. At the same time, they provided strength for the bereaved to carry on with their lives.

Despite the war-like ways of the Vikings and the Ulfhednar especially, there was still an inbred element of fear surrounding death and what came after. If the deceased was not buried and provided for properly, he might not find peace in the afterlife and the dead person could then visit the bereaved as a revenant, with such a sight usually being interpreted as a sign that additional family members or tribe members would follow them to the grave.

All of these customs, whilst being hugely important to the tribe, paled into insignificance for Varga, who simply wanted to erect a fitting monument to his most loyal chieftain.

Now, after all the proper rituals had been observed and all the fitting tributes voiced, Varga stepped forward, placing the flaming torch as deeply as he could within the pile of wood which sat atop Jordis' grave. The heap of splintered planks, sitting as neatly as possible upon the earthwork, were a result of the industrious efforts of the clan who had torn into the homes of the three disgraced Krieghund with great gusto.

As he watched the flames begin to take and sparks begin to fizz and spit towards the sky, he reflected on the failed experiment of the Krieghund. Deciding there and then that to divide the pack in such a way again would cause more problems than it would solve, Varga turned to address the ranks of the Ulfhednar as they stood in respectful silence, each alone with their own thoughts.

"Harken to me, Ulfhednar, for I must give voice to the pain I feel at the foul events which transpired on the bloody night when Jordis Rasmussen fell. I am pained that I have lost such a steadfast and trustworthy friend to such a breathtaking act of base treachery. Know this, my children, after what has occurred, the Krieghund will never be resurrected and the Ulfhednar will never be divided in such a way again. The despicable act of Jawrender, Steinsson and Vermaelen is a heinous chapter in the history of our people and one which must never be revisited. As they are left to reflect on their crime, serving Jordis in Hel until the end of days, I command you to redouble your efforts to harvest the skulls of our enemies, for the sooner we achieve our ultimate ambition and rend the living earth in two so that Fenrir may ascend to his rightful authority, the sooner each member of the Ulfhednar will be able to descend into the kingdom of Hel and punish the perfidious scum again and again for all eternity."

A huge atavistic roar erupted from the throng as Varga threw his arms up towards the darkening sky. Behind him a vast column of smoke was beginning to snake its way heavenwards, mingling with the steel grey clouds until it was unclear where the smoke ended and the clouds started.

Despite the rain changing into sleet and then to snow in quick succession, the fire increased in its intensity and Varga was forced to move further away from the conflagration.

When the tumult had diminished sufficiently, the clan-chief of the Ulfhednar spoke again, "Let us celebrate Jordis' life for the remaining span of the night, for soon we will leave this place and strike out for new lands to pillage and new blood to let. Let us gather upon the shores of the loch when the sun reaches its zenith tomorrow and make preparations to unleash a new hurricane of domination upon these islands."

The savage howl began again with Varga's announcement and, for the first time in a long time, Hrolfsson felt his blood fired with an ecstatic passion which served as the most potent reminder possible of what he had been missing in the previous months of self-imposed isolation.

He spotted Beyla seated upon a moss-encrusted boulder slightly separate from the main seething mass of the tribe. He made his way across the uneven ground to where the ancient seeress sat. He was unexpectedly gratified when she turned as he approached and nodded appreciatively to him. "Well said, Varga." Her gaze drifted up and down his body, appraising him before settling on his emerald eyes. "I do believe the Ulfhednar have their leader back."

The clan-chief smiled then turned his stare toward the tribe, whose revelry had begun to degenerate into drunkenness and orgiastic debauchery almost as soon as he had ceased speaking. He shook his head and said to Beyla, "I have been a fool, have I not?"

The old woman shifted position with a wince, "Aye, Varga."

"How could I have even contemplated turning my back on this? This is the way of the Ulfhednar," he murmured rhetorically, breathing heavily as he began to experience the surge of a lust which had long been held dormant. "I am the Ulfhednar!" he bellowed, unable to contain himself any longer.

With his shout still echoing off the rocks, he thrust his way past a heaving heap of bodies before throwing a tribeswoman to the ground and mounting her.

Beyla grinned at the spectacle being played out before her. "Oh, Varga, you do not know how much it warms my old bones to hear you say that."

The next day, as a weak and watery sun struggled to break through a threatening thunderhead of snow-heavy cloud, the tribe gathered upon the edge of the loch, huddled around the smouldering pile of ash which marked the spot where Jordis was buried. Straws were drawn to determine which Viking warriors would stay behind as a token defence of Dun Varulfur even though the clan had depopulated the land for miles around their homestead. However, Varga's newfound attitude meant that he was prepared to leave nothing to chance in his absence.

A glare from their leader was enough to silence the grumbling from those unfortunate clansmen who lost out in the lottery and had to watch their kinsmen begin the trek southwards.

In the morning, Varga and Beyla had convened in Dun Varulfur and the old woman had cast three sacred stones which she said would provide guidance as to which direction the Vikings should follow.

When the rocks had come to rest, Varga had asked tremulously what their positioning meant. As he had stared intently at the three stones, each one inscribed with a Viking rune and shaped like a bulbous arrowhead, Beyla's gnarled index finger had pointed, "See, the tapered ends of the Wolfstones point towards the south and have landed upon the three remaining compass points. The significance is clear to all who are schooled in the reading of runes."

Varga had expected this was what they meant as they had picked clean the land and all the islands to the north, but it still did not do to second guess the seeress' sorcery.

And so, with a howling northerly wind which spoke of death and desolation at their backs, two hundred Vikings of the Ulfhednar clan struck out for the south of the islands, advancing on the unprepared natives with the inexorable progress of an avalanche tumbling from the highest peak of the *Jotunheimen*.

They began heading south-east until they hit the western edge of Loch Seaforth, at a point far south of where they had razed the McLeishs' home village to the ground. That had been the furthest place which had been touched by their pestilential hand, but now they followed the loch's winding shoreline as it meandered down the island, falling upon the settlements of

Bowglass and Ardvourlie in a whirlwind of bloody devastation. From there, they roved back towards the southwest, initially finding the small pickings of odd farmhouses dotted about the bleak landscape before obliterating the villages of Bunavoneadar and Ardhasaig.

However, they were now confronted by the expanse of the western half of Loch Tarbert which stretched before them, calm yet foreboding, as if challenging them to cross its unknown waters.

After some discussion as to which direction they should continue in, Varga decided that, as the holy stones had bid them go south, they would continue on that course for as long as they were able. Again, at this point, they drew straws, with the losers being dispatched back to Dun Varulfur with a twofold purpose, to deliver the skulls of the islanders killed so far and also to relieve those first chosen to stay behind and point them on the way to Loch Tarbert, there to join up with the rest of the tribe.

Once the numbers had been restored to their full complement, the Norsemen set off once more on as southerly a course as they were able, until, with Varga nodding knowingly, they reached a place where the seemingly endless loch narrowed to a point and they were able to traverse it without getting their feet wet, not knowing that, in fact, the vastness of water stretching off to their left was classed as the eastern half of the same loch.

Onward they advanced, immersing the islands in a flood of brutality. They tore across the land, destroying lives and livelihoods without stint. Just as the Ulfhednar domain around Dun Varulfur had now been rendered a barren wasteland, bereft of life and joy, so it was now with the countryside along the Norsemen's southerly route which had experienced the misfortune of feeling the stomp of the Viking boot.

They had been on their expedition for the best part of a month, but now found themselves at a crossroads in their plans once more.

They had just routed fifty or so Vacomagi tribespeople in a tiny community called Auchremin when a raging blizzard had blown in, resulting in conditions that even the hardiest warriors of the tribe blanched at travelling through.

The tribe had congregated in the main longhouse, huddled round a hastily constructed fire made up of some of the livestock which the Vikings had found milling about behind a partitioned off area of the domicile. In addition to this, further fuel which was heaped onto the feeble fire came in the shape of the headless bodies of the vanquished tribespeople.

Varga stared around the cramped accommodation, ignoring the rank atmosphere of stale sweat and fear. The stench of the burning detritus, mixed in with the odour of the animals, made for a particularly unedifying reek and he scrunched his nose up in a vain attempt to soften its effects.

207

To take his mind off it, he craned his neck upwards, grunting in appreciation at the design of the low rounded roof, which had been elaborately roped together, he guessed, to resist the strong winds and horrendous weather which was an accepted part of the climate.

As he pondered this, the screams of several Vacomagi women began to sound, their agonised shrieks prompting hoots of excitement from the Vikings and even more consternation among the cattle and sheep.

Varga was impressed with the warmth that was beginning to build up inside the longhouse. Even he had been taken aback by the sudden ferocity of the snowstorm, but the heat from the fire was starting to become unbearable to those within close proximity. With slowly building alarm, it became clear to the tribesmen that, in the mad initial rush to banish the freezing memory of the blizzard, they had seriously underestimated the efficiency of the insulation of the Vacomagi dwelling.

The flames were now beginning to lick at the straw-thatched wooden roof and the Vikings began to retreat towards the far end of the house where the farm animals were housed, but the noise from the distressed livestock was deafening as their panic reached its height. In line with the traditional architecture of the Pictish tribes, there was only one door in and out of the longhouse and it soon became the focus of a headlong rush to escape the engorging fire.

Some of the Ulfhednar had the presence of mind to change into their bestial forms and they raced for the opening, scrambling over the struggling group of bodies and out into the bitterness of the snowstorm which mercifully had abated somewhat, though the snow was still falling thickly.

Wafting clouds drifted skywards as both man and beast gasped for breath in an attempt to compensate for the extreme change in temperature.

After bursting through the doorway, the Ulfhednar chief turned to face the incandescent blaze. The tribe had exited the longhouse just in time, for even before Varga had a chance to regain his breath, the roof gave way with a violent concussion. The timbers hit the ground with an audible whoomph, sending a rush of superheated air over the blanket of snow, frazzling eyebrows and singeing furs.

The relief of escape washed over Varga in much the same way as the hot gust had and he closed his eyes with a sigh, bathing in the sensual emotion. Upon opening them, he found that the brightness momentarily blinded him and he squinted through streaming eyes until his vision reasserted itself. He was greeted by a sight which choked the breath in his throat. In the midst of the fire, he could clearly see the silhouette of the monk once more, sword upraised, poised to brutally cleave the life from him. He had not seen the spectral figure of Monkshood since talking to his father in Hel, two months past. The shock of the shadow's appearance rocked him to the core and he felt all his old insecurities come flooding back. He threw his hands up and let out a low, pitiful moan. Varga felt his legs giving way beneath him but, just as he was about to fall to the soaking wet ground, the scene wavered and another shape reared up above the immobile monk. The unmistakable form of a gargantuan wolf seemed to leap from the flames, devouring the ominous figure of the cleric in the blink of an eye.

Hrolfsson stood open-mouthed, rubbing at his eyes in doubt at what he had seen, for the whole tableau from start to finish had taken a mere matter of seconds.

The massive swing of emotions left Varga uncertain and disturbed. To disguise his distress, he walked away from the scene as purposefully as he could, sucking in huge lungfuls of the cold air and calming himself. When he was ready, he chanced a glance over his shoulder at the blazing longhouse, half expecting to see the two intangible figures locked in a struggle to the death.

When he saw all was as it should be, he regained his composure and pondered his options. It did not take him long to decide what course of action to take. He stalked over towards the milling crowd of Viking warriors, peering around at the group before espying the face he sought. His hand shot out and grabbed a furred collar, "Strogen, pass the word. Ensure the skulls are safeguarded, for Dun Varulfur is calling to me like a siren."

When the Ulfhednar warrior stared blankly at him, Varga threw him to the soft white carpet covering the ground and spat contemptuously, "Do I have to spell it out, idiot? We are going home."

209

Chapter 9

Sir Galahad finished his silent prayer and got slowly to his sandaled feet. He padded out of the oratory enjoying, as he always did, the calming peace of the monastery which had been his home for the past four and a half months.

Once he had left the five other postulants in the sanctified room, permeated as it was with the heavy bitter smell of incense, he stepped into the cold afternoon air, snuffing in the natural scents of the flowers and shrubs of the enclosed garden and watching the snowflakes complete their graceful descent to the ground.

As he moved along the cloister, he peered across the quadrangle at the well in the centre of the garden. He walked out from under the shelter of the colonnade, pausing to pull back the hood from his head and enjoy the frigid breeze upon his celtic tonsure.

A shadow fell across him and he looked up into the hazel eyes of Brother Adomain, one of the monks who had lived within the sacred walls of the holy mission since it was founded nearly twenty years previously.

"How goes it, brother?" the middle-aged monk asked, placing his hands into the capacious sleeves of his habit and falling into step alongside the newest member of the monastery.

Galahad inhaled deeply and found that the answer came to him straight away. "I cannot remember the last time I have looked forward to each new day as much as I do now, Adomain. I am at peace." He finished simply.

Brother Adomain nodded, warmed by the sentiment but holding his counsel. In his two decades of experience as a member of the Order he had often found that, if people wished to unburden themselves of any troubles they had, then an open-ended period of silence was a more useful tool for teasing those issues out than any amount of questions, no matter how delicately put.

When it became clear Galahad was not going to offer any further words, the monk smiled and said, "Truly then, that is a wondrous state of affairs and I am pleased beyond measure for you." Adomain stood before Galahad, placed both hands upon his cheeks and planted a gentle kiss upon the former knight's bald pate. "Praise be to God."

Galahad shifted uncomfortably before echoing the blessing as he had yet to come to grips with the surprisingly tactile monks. However, Adomain had been the one who had found him wandering lost and purposeless in the Caledonian countryside and accompanied him on the short sea trip over from the mainland to the awe-inspiring vistas of Iona, so he bore the, at times, unsettling physicality of the man with the barest modicum of discomfort.

As they resumed their walk along one of the four paths which branched from the central well to each of the cloisters surrounding the garden, Galahad's mind flew back to that first meeting.

He had been aimlessly ambling across the bleak countryside which provided the stunning backdrop to the border between England and Scotland, deep in contemplation. His new mount, who he had also named Farregas in honour of the steed he had lost on the scree-laden slopes just outside Bamburgh, plodded along docilely under his new master, responding to Galahad's directions with little more than a gentle shake of the reins. Though the former knight was vaguely pleased that his new horse had adapted to his stewardship instantly, he could not help but miss the little quirks and whims of the original Farregas' personality.

His directionless journey took him across the border in a roughly north-westerly direction until he hit the course of the River Teviot, though Galahad did not know it as such, unknowingly happening upon its origin in the foothills of Comb Hill as he led Farregas to drink from its icy clear water.

From there, he went north-east, following the rushing tide until he found himself gazing upon the confluence of the river with the much larger River Tweed.

Deciding against crossing the fast-moving waterway, he opted to strike out to the west, going back across country rather than heading on towards the coast.

From time to time, he came across evidence of the bloody conflicts which raged intermittently between the Anglian tribes of the area but his skills at concealment and, when it was required, his intimidating presence was more than enough to enable him to pass unmolested.

His first encounter with the native population came about as he was breasting the summit of one of the innumerable hills which dotted the rugged terrain. Farregas had taken the slope gingerly at first but, as it began to level out near the top, had loped into a canter. Unfortunately, he rode straight into the midst of a flock of sheep which had been gambolling innocently atop the hill.

The twenty or so animals scattered immediately, their reproachful bleats breaking the placidity of the scene with a jarring edge.

The two shepherds who were in charge of the herd had emerged from behind a collection of jutting boulders which were so haphazardly arranged, they looked as if they had been dropped from the sky and left to rest where they lay.

Galahad struggled to control Farregas as the two wild looking men approached him, shouting angrily at the interloper in their rural idyll. As they came close enough to see the expensive cut of his clothes, the finery of his livery and, perhaps more importantly, the imposing blade of Whitecleave protruding from his pack, their advance slowed considerably and their heavily accented voices dropped to a throaty whisper. Before Galahad had a chance to offer to help them round up their errant charges, the pair were gone, their long, lank hair trailing behind them and their wooden staffs describing a furious tattoo upon the rocky ground.

Though Galahad had never been this far north before, he was well aware of the ferocity of the clans who inhabited the area and, despite having no doubts as to his ability to deal with trouble, he still had no inclination to become embroiled in any unnecessary violence so he cast an expert eye over the terrain and decided to give Farregas his head for a few miles, putting as much distance between himself and the irate shepherds as he could, in case they returned in numbers to remonstrate with him. He felt another small twang of guilt as his headlong flight took him directly through a couple of knots of the scattered sheep, which only served to disperse them even further.

Trusting that the local farmers would be more than capable of dealing with a few mischievous animals, he reined in Farregas and took stock of his surroundings.

He saw a relatively thick stand of trees off to his left which started to look very inviting, given the threatening bank of clouds which was beginning to build up to the north.

Galahad made it to the shelter of the copse just as the first drops of rain began to fall. He tethered his horse to a sturdy trunk and began looking for dry wood to make a fire. Before long, he was hunkered down, blowing gently at a tentative plume of smoke, coaxing it into a flame upon which he could cook the large rabbit which he had managed to bring down with his sling.

He skewered the freshly skinned beast and balanced it on the makeshift spit, slowly turning it over and over until the vivid scarlet of the raw meat began to shade brown. Just as he was about to remove the creature from the fire, a branch snapped off to his right. Both he and Farregas jerked their heads round at the noise and, despite Galahad trying to quieten his steed, Farregas let forth a loud snort and pawed at the ground.

A black shape obscured by the trees began to resolve itself into a man on horseback carefully negotiating his way across the leaf-strewn ground. The knight scanned the immediate area and strained his senses but could not discern any other people nearby. He returned to the fire, seating himself between it and Farregas so that, if needs be, he could have Whitecleave within his grasp before any unpleasantness could occur.

The newcomer began to angle in towards the flickering flame. Galahad affected disinterest but kept one eye upon the approaching stranger as he began to set about separating succulent meat from the bone.

"Ho, the camp," came an effete, heavily accented voice upon the frigid air, "may I join you?"

Galahad looked up at the man as he walked unhurriedly into the intangible circle of the fire's warmth. The first thing he noted, as the man drew back his brown hood and cloak, was the brown scapular reaching down to his knees which, Galahad knew, meant a monk or some sort of holy man. That the man was a monk was further confirmed by the tonsure which was exposed when he turned around to tie his horse. Having said that, recent events weighed heavily on the knight's mind and he remained on his guard until he was certain the stranger posed no threat.

He gestured for the new arrival to sit, offering him a chunk of meat which was accepted with hearty thanks.

The newcomer licked grease from his fingers and introduced himself, "I am Brother Adomain," he said.

"Galahad," grunted the knight. Thrilled was probably too strong a word to describe how he felt to be interacting with another human being but, after leaving the environs of Bamburgh, in a flash of insight, he realised that he had not actually spoken to anyone other than Farregas for nearly a month. "I do not recognise your accent. I suspect you do not hail from these parts?"

The monk nodded, "You are right. I am a pupil of Clonard Abbey, which lies far to the west in God's own country."

Sir Galahad's brows wrinkled, causing the white beard of the monk to split into a warm smile,

"Ireland, my boy. Ireland." Adomain breathed with a look of ecstasy on his face. "I came over to these lands with Columba of Donegal to convert the savage barbarians of this land to the Christian faith."

The former knight of Camelot found his interest piqued by the unexpected answer. That the man was a monk was obvious by his appearance, but for him to have travelled so far and in such dangerous lands on an evangelising mission, spoke volumes to Galahad about the man's character. "We were granted one of the islands off the coast by the Kings of Dal Riata, Iona it is called, a beauteous jewel of a place, there to establish a mission from where we could spread the word of God." Adomain continued with a look of pride which seemed to light up his face from within. "The monastery there has attracted many pilgrims to its gates and has become a renowned seat of learning in these lands. The monastery is a permanent home to over two hundred men, both acolytes and full members of the brotherhood, and it provides succour and solace to many more who pass through on a transitory basis."

Galahad found the pious tone of Brother Adomain to be quite jarring, but he kept his voice even. "It seems your monastery's reputation has yet to reach these parts, for the names of which you speak mean nothing to me."

"I cannot say I am surprised. I have been on the road for many a mile riding ever eastwards so that I might find new converts and extend the healing reach of my faith." Adomain conceded. He delved into the recesses of his cloak and produced a gourd from which he drunk deeply before proffering it to Galahad. Smacking his lips, he breathed "Uisce beatha." When Galahad looked confused once more, he explained, "Water of life, my son."

The knight regarded the hollowed-out fruit warily before taking a small nip of the liquid inside. The hot fluid slid down his throat leaving a subtle burning sensation which took his breath momentarily. After the initial shock however, he found that the sharpness mellowed very quickly, leaving him with a pleasant smoky aftertaste which he nodded appreciatively at.

"Enough of me," Adomain said. "What of you, Galahad? I see by your garments and riding accoutrements that you are a man of means." He regarded his drinking companion for a few moments. "Or perhaps was a man of means fallen on hard times?"

Galahad's need for conversation outweighed his natural reticence and he laughed, "You are not shy about coming to the point, are you?"

The holy man shrugged, unabashed by Galahad's reaction. "I see little point in tiptoeing around a conversation. You may tell me the truth or you may avail me with a wondrous tale of your fantastic life which, in reality, is nothing but a concoction of your own fantasy, I will not know the difference. However, I consider myself a good judge of people, indeed it is one of the reasons I chose this calling, and I sense that you are a man to whom lying does not come easily."

The knight nodded at the compliment then sighed, "I fear that if I did tell you how I came to be here, you would change your opinion instantly, for it is a fantastical tale though, upon my oath, every word is true."

Adomain said nothing and merely raised his eyebrow slightly.

With a deep breath, Galahad began to speak, giving the monk a potted history of his life since his departure from Camelot and offloading all the unspoken thoughts which had arisen during his isolated journey of the last month in one fell swoop.

By the time he had finished, the fire had burned low and the night had closed in. Adomain added some wood to the fire to build it up once more then resumed his seat, staring across the guttering flames of the campfire. "You were not wrong in your estimation. That is indeed an astonishing amount of bad luck to be visited with in such a short space of time."

Sir Galahad shrugged and poked a stick into the fire, sending up a couple of sparks. "It has not been easy these last few months. There have been times when I have felt like I taint everything I touch." He fixed the monk with a seemingly ferocious stare and sneered ironically, "I would suggest you think about moving on, lest my bad luck afflicts you in the night and you wake up in the morning to find yourself dead."

Brother Adomain's laughter erupted into the night and, despite his mood, Galahad found that he could not help smiling at the chortling monk.

Once he had regained his composure, the holy man spoke seriously to the knight. "Galahad, you should not condemn yourself in such a manner. Your acts are not those of a man driven by anything other than the best intentions. After what you have been through, it is no surprise you feel bitter and unjustly treated, but, despite all the ill-starred twists which your life has taken, you have still never once failed to show your compassion and empathy for others. When Romney and his associates tried to waylay you and you injured him, you could have ridden away from the scene, leaving the poor man to die alone in agony, yet you stayed with him, you heard his confession and I suspect you probably prayed for him."

Galahad did not trust himself to say anything, he just stared blindly into the cavorting flames.

Adomain continued, "Were you right to leave Joyous Garde without attempting to aid this Lady Guinevere? Some would say yes, some would say no, but then what of your pledge to King Arthur? Either you are a man of your word or you are not? You were hamstrung by an impossible situation and extricated yourself from it in as dignified a manner as possible." Brother Adomain shrugged and Galahad was suddenly struck by a timeless quality in his face, an indefinable sense of peace and tranquillity which seemed to emanate from him.

"But what of the men I killed? Romney's cohorts and the soldiers from Joyous Garde?" Galahad muttered.

"What should you have done?" Adomain countered. "Lay down and died? What purpose would that have served, save to rob the world of a good man."

The knight shifted uneasily, "Granted, the two who attacked me outside of Camelot were not the most wholesome of fellows, but the horsemen from Joyous Garde were only doing their masters' bidding."

"And would have killed you in a heartbeat," Adomain spread his hands. "We could debate the whys and wherefores of your actions from now until the sun comes up, which I am happy to do if that is what you wish, but before it comes to that, what you must do, what I beseech you to do, is examine your deeds and consider your motives for doing them. If what you have vouchsafed to me is true and, from our conversation and my impression of

215

you, I do not doubt for a second it is, then I do not believe you will find that any of your conduct was stimulated by selfishness or spite."

Galahad chewed upon his lip, again at a loss as to how to respond.

"You are a good man, Galahad of Camelot. Do not punish yourself for things which are beyond your control."

For long moments, the knight held the monk's gaze unblinkingly then he bowed his head. "Thank you, Brother Adomain," he said in a voice thick with emotion. "Thank you."

After that cathartic moment, the pair talked of nothing very much. Galahad reminisced of happier times at Camelot, remembering such glories as his recovery of the Holy Grail and his assumption of the Siege Perilous at the Round Table.

For his part, Adomain spoke of the minutiae of life in the monastery, the wondrous feeling of serenity engendered within its walls and the inner peace which seemed to be afforded to both those who lived there and also to those who visited it. "Forgive me for my presumption, Galahad, but I cannot help feeling that you would benefit from a stay at the monastery. Though you are an esteemed warrior, who need have no fear as to what he might encounter on the road, it is not a conducive atmosphere in which to contemplate the problems which life has thrown at you."

If Galahad was honest, the more Adomain elaborated on existence at the monastery, the more attractive it seemed. As he had recounted the difficult journey from Camelot to the Irish monk, he found himself reflecting on all the choices he had made and all the paths he had travelled through his own volition and where they had led him.

Perhaps now was the time to find a place of serenity and peace to take stock of his life. He was tired of viewing all who he came upon with mistrust.

Upon making the decision, Galahad extended his hand. "I will take you up on your offer, Adomain," he sighed, as if a great weight had been lifted from him. "It will be nice to be able to live for a time without the need to have Whitecleave close by me every waking second."

The Irish monk clasped the knight's hand and shook it vigorously. "We will leave at first light then, my friend."

Galahad cast an eye into the darkness beyond the fire's penumbra, waiting a few seconds for his night vision to adjust itself as it tried to bridge the stark contrast between the firelight and the blackness of the trees. Eventually he noticed a tinge of colour starting to show through some gaps in the woodland and jerked his head towards it. "Perhaps we should get some sleep first. I do not much fancy falling asleep in the saddle."

With that said, they checked their horses were picketed securely, extinguished the fire and made themselves as comfortable as they could on their travel blankets. Galahad could not sleep initially and found himself staring across the embers at the shapeless mass of the monk as he slumbered. Yet another unexpected twist in my life, he thought as his eyes grew heavier and heavier. Everything about going to the monastery seemed right, a sabbatical of this sort was an ideal opportunity for him to reconnect with himself and with his god. The pessimistic side of his nature reared its head momentarily and he found himself speculating whether his need for some sort of direction in his life was overriding his innate caution but, after replaying the talk with Adomain in his head and re-analysing the man's demeanour, he could not bring himself to believe that. No, Galahad thought, this feels like the right thing to do.

And so, as the sun began to colour the sky above the horizon, with that thought comforting him, he finally surrendered to sleep.

Galahad blinked as he was brought back to reality by a huge sigh exploding from Adomain.

"My apologies," the monk immediately said, "I did not mean to disturb your contemplation."

Galahad shrugged off the apology. "I was remembering our first meeting. I came to the monastery because of how you described it. I did think at the time your portrayal of it may have been coloured by homesickness or something similar, but it has lived up to the effusive praise you bestowed upon it and has been everything you said and more. I owe you a great debt, Adomain."

"Nonsense," Adomain scoffed. "I merely gave you the option of following my chosen path. It was your choice whether you walked alongside me or not."

Galahad shook his head. "For the first time in my life, I feel a genuine camaraderie with others. Truth be told, even at Camelot, I always felt a man apart. Though most were respectful of the choices I made in my lifestyle, I always felt a certain amount of disdain towards me as if I was somehow less of a warrior because of them." He chuckled quietly. "It is not as if I have never felt the intoxication of battle or the giddying thrill of lust-filled thoughts, it is just that I hold my promises to God to be of higher importance than my own pleasures."

Adomain's laughter boomed out, startling a couple of other monks out of their prayers. "You have no need to explain that to me of all people, Galahad."

The former knight of Camelot grinned sheepishly then clapped Adomain on the shoulder. "You see, that is the sort of empathy which has been missing

217

from my life. This place, this way of living, this is what I need to complete me."

The two monks, whom Adomain had startled from their prayers, fell into step alongside the two of them as a sonorous bell sounded, summoning the quartet inside for their morning meal. As they walked along the cold, stone corridors, Galahad basked in the unforced fellowship of the moment. The four monks spoke of nothing very much but somehow the mundanity did not grate on him as it had done when he had experienced it in Camelot.

At length, they came to the communal dining room, an austere rectangle with four lines of plain wooden benches and tables bereft of decoration, apart from a crude tapestry depicting a white dove upon a blue background in reference to Columba of Donegal's Gaelic name, Colum Cille, which meant Dove of The Church.

The large double doors at the far end of the hall were both open, so that the bustling postulants who toiled in the kitchen could move easily back and forth distributing the unexciting but nonetheless nourishing vittles. Today's fare was a choice of a thick porridge flavoured with honey or freshly baked bread and cheese. Adomain attacked a small plate of bread and cheese with vigour whilst the other three opted for the porridge. Galahad took a pinch of salt and spooned the hot liquid into his mouth.

As he ate, he regarded the monk who sat opposite him. Brother Ruaraidh was a huge bear of a man with an explosion of red hair so unruly, it hid his ceremonial tonsure. Despite his impressive bulk, he was a gentle man with a quick wit who had become fast friends with Galahad due to his easygoing manner and understanding nature. They both shared a spartanly furnished dormitory with five others of the Order. There was Brother Maes, a slim hook-nosed man disfigured by a large purple birthmark which ran from the base of his left ear down his neck. He was the polar opposite of Ruaraidh, surly and reticent and had barely exchanged a handful of words with Galahad since he had been allocated a bed in the room.

In the bed next to him was Brother Walter, the youngest of the seven. He was said to be a distant relative of the head monk, Columba, though if it was true, he did not seem to be favoured because of it. He had a mop of blond curls and a bright-eyed enthusiasm which some of the other monks found slightly overpowering at times, especially Maes, who often snapped at him with unnecessary venom.

The other monk who had accompanied them to the dining hall was called Brother Paulinus, a former Roman legionary who had arrived at the monastic halls two years ago, road-dirtied and blood-spattered. As was the way with those initiated into the Order of Columba, once they walked through the wooden gates which served as the entrance to the cloistered halls of the complex, no questions were asked regarding the life of the newcomer before they stepped across the threshold. They were free to volunteer the information if they so chose, but it was by no means compulsory. However, after divesting himself of his uniform, Paulinus had slumped tearfully into the arms of Columba and, in halting tones, regaled him with tales of the horrendous savagery of the death throes of Roman rule in Britain and how as the army had retreated towards the South Coast to Gaul, he had felt progressively more and more sullied by the acts perpetrated in the name of the Empire. One night, something inside him had snapped and, under cover of darkness, he had stolen away from the encampment and begun making his way north, hoping to put both physical and mental distance between himself and the abhorrent behaviour of the other Roman legionaries. He was similar in temperament to Maes, though without the spiteful tongue, and was to be found, more often than not, staring distractedly across the glorious countryside, lost in a graveyard of memories that would not stay buried.

The other two inhabitants of the dormitory were twins, Brother Nathan and Brother Joseph. Nathan was a bull-necked man, bald as a coot and fiercely protective of his younger sibling who had been in ill-health since birth. Though they were twins, they were both very different in appearance. Where Nathan was built like he had been hewn rather than born, Joseph was a slight man, prone to sickness of both physical and mental nature. He rarely spoke and, when he did, he used a variety of tongues and languages, some familiar, others eldritch and unsettling, which, Nathan claimed, were a result of the visions and dreams which he suffered with nightly.

For all that, the seven who occupied the dormitory, though they all hailed from hugely disparate backgrounds had, over the time of their residency together, built a strong bond with each other and all felt comfortable sharing their thoughts and innermost feelings with the others.

After the meal was finished, Ruaraidh and Paulinus said they would return to the garden to finish their interrupted prayer and Adomain announced that he was to have an audience with Columba. This left Galahad at somewhat of a loose end and he found himself treading the cool corridors which led to the library of over three hundred books that had either come over from Donegal with the monks or been transcribed by Columba himself from various ancient texts.

One of the most prized items in the collection and one which Galahad had studied on numerous occasions was an incomplete vellum manuscript upon which was a copy of a psalter penned by Finian of Moville, one of Columba's teachers at Clonard Abbey in Ireland. Though the decoration of the folios was limited to the first letter of each psalm, represented as it was with ornate calligraphy, he found the intricacy of the script absolutely captivating,

219

especially as the letters which immediately followed the initial capital gradually reduced in size until they were the same size of the main body of text. It leant the words a flowing, magical quality and somehow made the Latin translation of the holy text more entrancing to the eye.

Galahad had spent many an hour poring over the musty volumes housed within the candlelit room. Whilst he had been able to read quite well from his time at Camelot, he found his choice of reading in the library heavily restricted, partially due to the damaged state of many of the books or by the complexity of some of the fonts and typefaces. However, he had become well acquainted with Brother Neville, the elderly monk whose main responsibility was cataloguing all the works which the Irish monks had brought with them on the voyage across the northern channel of the Irish Sea.

The ancient fellow was always to be found ghosting through the chaotic piles of manuscripts that dotted the cramped space in apparent disorder, yet he was unfailingly able to locate any requested book within the space of a few seconds and so, due to Galahad's voracious appetite for widening his knowledge, he had become, to all intents and purposes, Brother Neville's unofficial assistant.

As he entered the library, Galahad immediately scanned the room for the old man. As usual, he was sat at his rickety desk, hunched over a raft of unbound parchment, face locked in a fierce look of concentration as he threaded a length of twine through the eye of a bookbinding needle. Galahad cleared his throat before he approached to ensure he did not make Neville jump then strode over to the desk.

Neville finished what he was doing then turned towards his visitor. "Hello, Galahad," he said.

"Good evening, Brother," the knight replied, looking over the monk's shoulder. "That looks like a fiddly task," he smiled.

Neville returned the smile, "Aye, rewarding though. It is a journal written by Finnian of Clonard of his time spent in study under the great saints in Wales. He spent thirty years there before returning to God's country and travelling from place to place, preaching, teaching, and founding churches. It is said that, in the course of his spiritual journey, he was led by an angel to Cluain Eraird, which the angel told him would be the place of his resurrection. Once there he built a little cell and a church of clay and wattle, which formed the basis of the abbey where we all learnt scripture, and entered into a life of study and prayer. It was not long before the fame of his learning and sanctity became known throughout Ireland and beyond. Scholars of all ages and all levels flocked to his monastic retreat—young laymen and clerics, abbots, even bishops." Neville beckoned Galahad closer to the desk and pointed at another document which had been propped open so he could refer to it when required. "See here what it says about the abbey." The old man pointed a gnarled finger at the decorative lettering.

"In the Office of St. Finnian it is stated that there were no fewer than 3000 pupils receiving instruction at one time in the school in the green fields of Clonard under the broad canopy of heaven. The master excelled in exposition of the Sacred Scriptures, and to this fact must be mainly attributed the extraordinary popularity which his lectures enjoyed."

Galahad turned to the old man and was immediately struck by the pride which shone from his moistened eyes. "I was one of those three thousand who used to sit and listen to him upon the dew-sodden grass. By the holy father, Finnian had such a way with words. He could make you shrink from God's righteous wrath or leave you basking in the endless compassion of Him, such was the skill with which he sermonised." Slowly, the mist of nostalgia cleared from Brother Neville's eyes and he regarded Galahad as his visitor stood in the flickering candlelight. "Have you come to return to your study of Finian's psalter?"

"If you have no other tasks for me?"

Brother Neville chuckled as he shook his head. "I wish all the brothers in the monastery were as industrious as you, Galahad. No, there is nothing I require from you today." He gestured towards a parchment which lay open atop an unruly mass of yellowing vellum. "Please return to your studies."

Galahad nodded appreciation at the compliment and walked over to the psalter, seeing immediately that it rested upon the page which he had been reading the last time he had perused it.

He retrieved it from the pile and seated himself upon a decrepit bench running along one of the walls of the book-lined chamber. After about five minutes of scrutiny, Galahad felt a momentary dizziness. Shrugging the odd sensation off, he licked his index finger and turned to the next page only to be visited by the same unsettling feeling a minute later. As he read on, he became vaguely aware of a roaring in his ears, seemingly composed of a multitude of incoherent voices which gradually melded into an unintelligible babble. Blinking furiously, the world seemed to fall away from him and he suddenly felt as if he was unbalanced, falling forwards into the convoluted swirls of the writing on the psalter.

Everything went black.

Galahad jerked awake, his rumpled sheets sodden with sweat. It took him a few seconds to get his bearings, but he soon realised he was back in the dormitory sitting upon his bunk.

Brother Ruaraidh had rushed to his side as soon as he had seen Galahad come upright. Concern was writ large in the large man's eyes and he laid a kindly hand upon the former knight's shoulder. "Are you alright?" he asked urgently.

"I seem to be," Galahad responded after remaining silent for a moment. "I do not know what happened? How did I come to be here? I remember the library, I think...then the psalter, then..." his voice tailed off and he shrugged expansively.

Once it was clear Galahad's faculties were apparently intact, the worry fled his face and Ruaraidh sat back and returned the shrug. "The truth is I have not been in the room long. All I know is that, upon returning from my evening observances, Walter told me you had taken some sort of turn whilst in the company of Brother Neville and you had been taken back here to recover." Ruaraidh looked sidelong at his room-mate. "So you do not recall anything of what occurred?"

The erstwhile champion of Camelot dragged a tired hand over his face, "No, I have never taken any sort of faint or fit before." His eyes widened for a second, "There were...voices."

Ruaraidh ran a pudgy hand through his mane of hair and shot Galahad a glance which spoke volumes about what he thought of people who heard voices in their head. "What kind of voices? What did they say?" he pressed.

"It was not even really voices. It was a wall of sounds, agonised cries and shouts, all intermingled and garbled together."

"Perhaps Adomain will be able to unravel what happened? He has a knack of teasing out the truth from improbable events."

Almost as if Ruaraidh had called him into the room, Adomain entered through the door in a rush, his monastic robe flailing behind him. When he saw that the stricken knight was awake, he stopped abruptly and peered at him with a strange tension around his eyes. Where Ruaraidh's expression had been one of undisguised concern, Adomain's features were noticeably harder and unforgiving.

"Are you recovered?" he asked without preamble.

Galahad did not have the energy to waste on his friend's apparent lack of alarm. "I feel more myself again, yes." He nodded.

"Do you feel up to moving? Columba wishes to see you." The older man asked abruptly.

Shooting a confused look towards his room-mate, Galahad nodded once more and swung his legs off the bed.

The two of them walked down the passageway in an uneasy silence until the former knight could contain himself no longer. He stopped the older man with a forceful hand upon the shoulder. "What is wrong, Adomain? You are not normally this reticent when we walk the corridors?"

The monk stopped and stared at the ground. "I cannot...", he began to say something but changed his mind. "Do you have any idea what happened to you?" he asked pointedly.

Shaking his head in irritation at having to repeat himself again, a thought occurred to Galahad. He prodded a finger into Adomain's chest. "Do you?" he shot back. "Has something like this happened before?"

The holy man's eyes swivelled nervously in their sockets, which was all the confirmation Galahad needed that something was amiss. "You must speak to Columba, I cannot say more."

Galahad stormed past Adomain. "Then let us see him as soon as we may," he snapped. Without waiting for his companion, he strode purposefully across the flagstones so quickly that Adomain found himself struggling to keep up. As he walked, Galahad found all his familiar anxieties begin to rise within him. Emotional dread cloaked him as he felt the continuously unsteady foundations of his happiness begin to erode again. As had happened on so many occasions before, just as he appeared to be on the verge of contentment and possessed of some security in his life, some unforeseen obstacle reared up before him to baulk his designs.

With a sharp word, Adomain halted Galahad's determined walk and directed him into a rather finely appointed antechamber, though he was in no mood to appreciate the tapestries and fine upholstery of the furniture. He slumped down upon the nearest chair, ignoring Adomain as he continued on through the imposing door on the opposite wall and into the adjoining room.

He was so unsettled by Adomain's demeanour towards him that he found he was unable to remain seated and began to stalk around the room, staring at the pictures upon the wall but not taking in any detail.

"Galahad."

The knight jumped as Adomain had come upon him soundlessly. The white-haired monk muttered, "Columba will see you now," but studiously avoided eye contact.

He allowed himself to be ushered into the presence of the most exalted member of the monastery without resistance because so many questions were cannoning around his head.

Galahad had only ever seen the founder of the monastery once before and that had been in the first week when he had walked through the gates. He had been part of a weekly assembly which the head monk conducted to welcome newcomers to the claustral life of Iona. The hour-long acceptance rite had largely passed Galahad by as he was still in the initial overwhelming throes of his new surroundings and, as a consequence, he did not have many memories of what the man actually looked like.

Columba was a surprisingly, slightly built man though something about him resonated power, but not the power associated with force of arms, rather an all-encompassing benignity which seemed to leech away at Galahad's anger, replacing it with a cool detachment that still demanded answers to the questions posed but in not such an exacting manner.

He was sitting at a large desk which was covered in scrolls of parchment, some rolled and bound with twine, others arranged haphazardly in such a way as to cover most of the dark wooden surface. Half of the open sheets were blank, their unused whiteness contrasting harshly with the yellowing vellum of the ones upon which there was writing.

Columba stood up and moved around the desk, beckoning his visitor into a comfortably plush chair. In fact, Galahad found himself surprised at the richness of all around him. Even the monk's robes were of a higher quality than any others he had seen about the cloisters, being a deep sky-blue and appearing almost velvety in texture. He sported a neatly trimmed black beard which was liberally flecked with grey, though his head was shaven clean of hair. A pair of piercing hazel eyes peered at Galahad down the length of a hawk-like nose as he said, "I apologise for summoning you here so quickly after your fainting episode but I feel it hugely important that I speak to you whilst the event is still fresh in your mind." He perched himself informally on the edge of the desk and gestured for Galahad to speak.

With a deep breath, Galahad began to recount what had occurred within the musty library. "I have looked over the psalter on many occasions beforehand and nothing has happened. Even that page I have studied before." He shook his head. "It makes no sense," Galahad looked at the expression on Columba's face, "to me anyway," he said quizzically. "I suspect this is not the first time you have witnessed this phenomenon?"

A wry smile creased the monk's face. "You are nothing if not perceptive," he said calmly, seemingly unfazed by Galahad's realisation. "You are correct, something similar has happened on a number of occasions before." He leant in to the former knight of Camelot. "Tell me everything. I promise I will tell you everything I suspect, once you have told me all that transpired in the library."

Galahad held the holy man's stare for a few moments whilst he composed his thoughts. "There is not really much more to tell, to be honest. It came upon me in waves of giddiness. I felt as if I was falling forward into the words and they were rising up to meet me," he shrugged.

"What about the sounds? What did you hear?" Columba asked eagerly.

"There were no words as such. There was some incoherent shouts and..." he paused before continuing his recollection in more excited tones, "metal upon metal, swords clashing, yes, that's what it reminded me of, the sounds of a battlefield." Galahad's eyes lit up even further as if his remembrance of blade upon shield had opened up whole new vistas of his memory. "There was something else. Just before I passed out, I caught a smell, no, more than that, a stench of death." He looked up pleadingly at Columba. "As God is my witness, that is all I can recall."

The monastery's founder and leader thrust himself off the edge of the desk and walked back behind it. He slumped down in the chair and drew a hand across his suddenly tired-looking face. "This is ill news indeed. I had hoped you would say something different but...." He spread his hands and shook his head.

After a moment, Columba cleared his throat and peered at Galahad over steepled fingers. "What I am about to tell you is known only to a select band of people. I cannot compel you to keep what you hear within these four walls, for that is not the way of the monks of Iona, but I would ask you to consider all sides of the story before you divulge it to anyone else."

With a huge exhalation, Columba began to relate the reason why the monks of Iona had come to settle on this beauteous but isolated and far-flung outpost of Christendom. "As I said, of all who live within this holy place, none but myself, Adomain and Neville are aware of why this monastery was established. You would think that to be able to gaze upon this wondrous idyll would be a privilege, not a penance, but you would be wrong. This monastery was established as atonement for an act of violence which took place upon the mainland of my home country." Columba fixed Galahad with a ferocious gaze, trying to gauge his reaction. For his part, Galahad sat outwardly impassive whilst his mind wondered what revelations he was about to become privy to.

The monk continued, "Though the original psalter contains words of comfort and devotion, this particular manuscript might as well have been written in blood." Columba sneered.

Galahad blinked furiously at the heat in his words and the haunted look on his face.

"The copy that caused you to take such a violent turn is one which I made whilst I studied under Saint Finnian of Moville at the Abbey in Clonard. St Finnian was one of a kind, a more pious man you could never wish to meet. During my time of study under him, his words inspired me to heights of devotion which I thought impossible. That was what motivated me to reproduce the psalter in the scriptorium at Clonard Abbey. It was a clumsy attempt on my part to, I don't know, get him to notice me or stand out from

225

the crowd of acolytes." Columba sighed hugely and looked down at the intricately patterned rug that adorned the floor of his office. "It certainly did that," he laughed bitterly.

The former knight was at a loss as to how to respond. "What do you mean?" he asked quietly, intrigued and concerned in equal measure.

"I presented it to him one day in November," he cast a glance out of the window and chuckled ironically, "a day very like today actually, the snow was blowing in flurries and the sky was the colour of slate." Again, the sigh exploded into the room. "I do not really know what I expected to achieve by it but the reaction I got was so unexpected, it completely crushed me. Finnian erupted into a towering rage, accusing me of blasphemy and false pride in making a copy of the holy book and threw me from the premises. As you can imagine, I was crushed by this and, whether or not pride had been the inspiration for my plagiarising the psalter, it certainly governed my actions from then on.

Some of the other postulants who lived within Clonard, Adomain and Neville among them, were also outraged at this perceived injustice and gathered by my side, their blood fired by the unfairness of my treatment. To this day I cannot explain what possessed us on that winter's night, but we forced entrance to the abbey, determined to retrieve my confiscated copy from Finnian's quarters." He shivered at the rawness of the memory. "At my behest, in my name, blood was spilt in that holiest of holy places, all over a copy of a book. Soon the whole of the abbey was drawn into the conflict and it spilled into the surrounding fields. Thousands were killed, Galahad. Thousands of men became fodder for the crows, because of my injured arrogance."

Galahad sat in shocked silence, jolted to his very core by the enormity of Columba's confession.

"I have tried for years to convince myself that the quarrel over the book was the pebble which started the avalanche and merely served to galvanize the younger monks into lashing out against the established order but, in both my heart and head, I know that to be a falsehood." Columba lapsed into a contemplative silence which Galahad had no wish to break.

After a few moments, the Irish apostle resumed his recounting of events, "A synod of clerics and scholars was convened and they threatened to excommunicate me for my sins. For what it is worth, I counted myself lucky that more did not push for me to be put to death, though, in the cold light of day, I would not have opposed them if they had. But, luckily for me, St. Brendan of Birr spoke on my behalf and it was decided that I was to go into exile instead. The three of us, Adomain, Neville and myself, plus a smattering of our supporters suggested we should work as missionaries to help convert as many people as had been killed in the battle. We were despatched across the Irish Sea to Caledonia with the clothes we stood up in and not much else, although I think some of the synod thought it amusing to allow me to keep the copy of the psalter." With that, he stared at Galahad pointedly, "So now you know the shame of Columba, Galahad. Within these walls, bar myself, Adomain and Neville and now yourself, only five other people knew of this and they are all now biding with God. So, now you know, that is the crux of why I am so grieved at your reaction to the book."

Galahad hunched over as if he was protecting himself against the freezing bite of a winter's gale. The foreboding which had touched him as he had walked with Adomain bore down upon him as he whispered, "What happened to them?"

"One of the poor unfortunates was the first convert we made upon our arrival in Iona. He went by the name of Cuthbert Main and he saw us beach upon the coast of the island. Though he was initially suspicious of us, to cut a long story short, he ended up providing us with a roof over our heads and food in our bellies until we managed to build the monastery to a sufficient standard where we could take occupation of it. Once it was properly built and worshippers began congregating there, he stayed with us. He said it was out of curiosity as to what we were preaching, but I suspect that was just an excuse for him continuing his acquaintance with us, because he often commented how lonely he had been since he had lost his family."

During the tale, Columba's voice had dropped to a hoarse whisper, "Brother Neville found him in the library, raving and snarling. The psalter was sprawled upon the floor next to him. He attacked any who came near him, all the while screaming 'Cul Dreimhne, Cul Dreimhne'. It took all three of us to overpower him but it was a close-run thing. He died in Neville's arms with blood dribbling from his mouth and naught but the whites of his eyes showing."

Though Galahad was gripped by the passion in Columba's voice, he shrugged at the significance of the priest's words.

"Galahad, Cul Dreimhne is the field which surrounded Clonard Abbey. It is the field upon which so many men fell in the battle over the psalter. There is no way he could have known the name of that field, no way on God's earth. As you can imagine, the three of us were hugely shaken by the name he had spoken. After much discussion, we sent Adomain away, charging him to seek out Cuthbert's family in the vain hope that he may have visited Clonard as a young man or somesuch unlikely coincidence, but he found no such knowledge. What he did find shocked us to the core."

Without asking, Columba walked over to an ornate decanter and poured out two drinks, one of which he placed before Galahad. The former knight took a sip and immediately recognised it as the so-called 'water of life' which he and Adomain had both partaken of when they had first met.

"Adomain found no information about Cuthbert on the island and so set off across the Sound of Iona to Mull to see if he could find anything there. The first village he came to, Bunessan it was called, upon asking after Cuthbert, the clansmen told Adomain he had been chased from the area for his crimes." Columba shook his head once more. "According to the islanders, Cuthbert Main was a monster. He owned land upon the side of Ben More, one of the hills upon the island, housing himself in a huge homestead with his family. He and his kinsmen were notorious for their crimes, mainly thievery and banditry. They were also suspected of the blackest acts, murder and suchlike. Anyway, finally the people of Mull were able to unseat them and Cuthbert fled across the Sound to Iona, barely escaping the mob which had slaughtered the rest of his family. Adomain returned to Iona and managed to trace Cuthbert's passage across the island to where he came to bide when we first happened upon him. The bizarre thing is that the Ionans knew nothing of his sinful past. All they knew of him was that he kept himself to himself and never bothered anybody. There was no hint that he had committed any sort of wrongdoing upon Iona. Whether he had some sort of epiphany on the short journey across the Sound, I do not know and will never know, but he certainly seemed to have had some sort of change for the better."

Galahad placed his goblet down upon the monk's desk and fixed Columba with a sceptical look, "So what are you saying, Columba? The book is tainted by the circumstances of its creation and somehow it reawakened the bloodlust within Cuthbert which he had managed to quell since his arrival upon Iona?" he guffawed.

There was no hint of humour in Columba's face as he nodded, "That is exactly what I'm saying." He held his hands up as Galahad scoffed again. "Adomain was the one who first suggested it and, to be honest, my reaction was extremely similar to yours. But, having said that, we still could not explain the manner of Cuthbert's violent death or his recitation of the name of Cul Dreimhne," Columba shrugged. "We had no time to ponder the reasons for it. As more followers flocked to our gates, the business of running the monastery became our over-arching purpose and, though we found ourselves briefly revisiting the memory of it in quieter moments, it gradually disappeared from our minds, until it happened again." Columba drained his drink in one gulp then refilled it, "It was just over two years later. Brother Adomain had been despatched to the mainland to continue to add to the influx of visitors to our peaceful home and Cuthbert's demise was nothing but a sad, distant reminiscence. Brother Neville came running into this very office and dragged me down to the library. As I stand before you now,

Galahad, I swear the scene I bore witness to on that day was a near-perfect replica of how we found Cuthbert. The book on the floor, the same incessant chant, the same unstoppable madness," Columba's whole body shuddered, "the same tragic outcome," he finished quietly. "Again, with the aid of some research and discussion with the man's companions, we found that the victim's history was as full of death and violence as Cuthbert's, except that the horrors of this man's life had been experienced upon the streets of Constantinople. He hailed from the capital of the Byzantine Empire, fleeing from its burning ruins after witnessing riots culminating in tens of thousands of deaths. That was all we could gain from his fellow travellers as they seemed reluctant to clarify exactly what part he had played in these riots but, whatever his history was, he had been nothing but a model resident of the monastery, until he laid hands upon that psalter." Columba paused for effect. "The same story has repeated itself at times during the existence of the monastery. I hate myself for succumbing to superstition in this way but all the evidence points to that book being accursed."

The champion of Camelot erupted out of his chair and advanced upon Columba with a dangerous look. "Then why is it still housed within the library where anyone can fall under its supposed spell? Why has it not been destroyed or at least hidden away from unsuspecting eyes?"

The monk remained unmoved, "As I said previously, it is not the way of the Order to hide behind secrets and besides, the psalter is a holy book that does not affect all who touch it in the way it has afflicted you and others like you. What right have I, or indeed any of us, got to deny others the wisdom and compassion of the psalms?"

"I sense a hidden meaning in that last statement, Columba. Pray tell, who are these others that are *like me*?" Galahad snarled.

Again, Columba raised his hands placatingly, a gesture which Galahad was beginning to find infuriating. "I apologise for my indelicacy. I merely meant that the people who have been, shall we say, disturbed by the psalter all seem to have a similar thread running through their lives."

The rage which had propelled Galahad out of his chair subsided and he slumped back heavily upon it. So it would appear that his troubled past was to haunt him once again. However, to his surprise, Columba then lit a proverbial candle in the rapidly approaching darkness which his words had conjured. "Having said all that, you are the first to have reacted to the book's influence without violence so perhaps this occurrence is not as clear-cut as a simple case of history repeating itself." He got up and paced about the room once more. "This is why I am so interested in every little detail of your experience in the library, Galahad. Are you sure there is nothing more you can tell me?"

229

Numbly, the former knight of Camelot shook his head. He knew he should have been buoyed by Columba's qualification of what had happened to him, but he felt it was no more than a token attempt by the monk to soften the blow of what he was about to say.

"I have thought about this ever since Brother Neville informed me of what occurred and, if there is nothing more you can remember, then I will put my theory to you now and see if you agree with me."

Galahad shrugged indifferently.

Once again, Columba steepled his fingers and began to speak, "I think that the difference between you and the others who have been upset by the psalter is that they have been contaminated by their previous evil deeds. Though they found some semblance of peace within these walls, the spectre of their innate sinfulness was always lurking in their minds and they were not strong enough to resist it when it was re-awakened by the book's accursedness. You, on the other hand, are a fundamentally good man untainted as they were by wicked acts from a wicked past."

"So why has it affected me at all?" Galahad asked with a grating whine. "I would presume that you would view most, if not all, the others who have passed through the gates of the monastery as fundamentally good, yet they have not been touched in this way."

Columba stroked his neatly trimmed beard as he framed his response. "Tell me of your history," he said suddenly. "I know small sections of it from what you confided in Adomain on your journey across Caledonia." He quickly interjected as Galahad began to say something, "Do not worry. Nothing has been divulged beyond these walls. It is your choice what you chose to tell the residents of the monastery of your past, not mine or Adomain's. Anyway, as I said, perhaps the answer to the conundrum can be found in there? Obviously, it is entirely your own choice how much you choose to share and I will certainly not compel you if you do not wish to, but everything about your demeanour suggests to me that you wish to get to the bottom of this puzzle as much as I do."

"I cannot deny that." Galahad agreed, a sardonic smile playing on his lips. Trusting Columba's assertion that nothing he said would be revealed outside the monk's study, Galahad seized the opportunity to unburden himself as fully as he could. He briefly skated over his life at Camelot, somewhat surprisingly finding that the acuteness of the pain he usually felt when he re-examined the circumstances of King Arthur's death was somewhat dulled. However, once he got past that tragic event, he unconsciously found himself analysing his life in much greater detail, which cemented in his mind the suspicion that it was that cataclysmic occurrence more than any other which had brought him to this place.

Columba sat silently, taking in every word, dispassionately studying the man before him. As far as he was concerned, Galahad's recounting proved he had been right in his surmising, the knight's past held the key to why he had reacted so violently to the psalter.

By the end of Galahad's relating of his life story, the sun had begun to disappear beyond the horizon and Columba was forced to light a trio of candles which were set within an exquisitely ornate candelabrum standing upon his desk.

"Thank you, Galahad. I appreciate your candour." Columba nodded acknowledgement after the knight fell silent. "And, if you will permit me, I will try to answer your question." He cleared his throat and filled both goblets with water, taking a dainty sip before he spoke. "As you will recall, I said you were a good man untainted by a wicked past. Do not misunderstand me but I think that might not be strictly true. The difference, as I see it, is that it is precisely because you are such a decent man you have been affected so. The heinous things which you have seen and the heinous things which you have experienced are so anathema to you, so alien to all you stand for and believe in that, despite your best efforts, they *have* tainted you, though you may not be conscious of the fact. Also, though you will probably not thank me for saying it, from what you have told me I think there is a part of you that revels in all the people you have despatched to God's judgement."

Galahad's mind flew back guiltily to the exultation he had felt when he had killed the robbers who had assailed him within sight of the walls of Camelot all those months ago. That scene was then replaced with gut-wrenching speed by the soldiers from Joyous Garde which he had slaughtered upon the rocky slopes just outside Bamburgh. A succession of images assaulted his mind then. All those who had been unfortunate enough to feel the bite of Whitecleave lined up before his mind's eye, the awful wounds inflicted by his blade still spurting blood and gore. Gradually, Columba's voice began to permeate Galahad's troubled vision and he found himself back in the monk's office.

"I do not believe you have ever killed anyone for pleasure or for selfish motives. I merely think that this is the part of you which the dreadful nature of the book connected with." He shrugged as if he was indifferent to Galahad's opinion of his speculation, but a tightening around his eyes suggested that he was keen to win the knight's approval of his theory.

Galahad drained his goblet in one swig. "It would be easy for me to dismiss your musings as pure fantasy but I have fallen victim to the sin of pride before and it has done me no favours." He was silent for a few seconds. "As you did for me, I thank you for your honesty." He fidgeted uncomfortably before returning Columba's stare with the same intensity. "What does this mean in terms of my residency within the cloisters?"

Columba smiled warmly. "It changes nothing, Galahad. Obviously, if you were to embark on a murderous rampage, we might throw you out but otherwise I see no need for your ejection."

With an explosive breath, Galahad returned Columba's expression of mirth. "Well, I will try not to," he chuckled. His grin was quickly replaced by a sombre look. "I had feared you would chase me from the door." He shook his head. "I have found happiness here, everyone has been so welcoming and friendly. For that to end so abruptly would have been a hugely bitter blow to me."

The founder of the monastery laid a sympathetic hand upon his shoulder. "It gladdens my heart to hear you talk in such glowing terms of our Order." He hesitated, mirroring the change in Galahad's face from joyous to solemn in the blink of an eye.

Galahad's look froze in place at the sudden change in his host's gaze.

"However," Columba continued, "I am not sure you will be able to quieten your more, shall we say, aggressive nature forever. I do not doubt for a second the sincerity of your feelings but I wonder if, for one such as yourself, the claustral life of inner peace and placidity will be enough to satisfy you."

Galahad tried as best he could to sound convincing, but both men secretly thought that his voice had a smidgen of desperation about it. "You need not worry on that account, Columba. I am weary of life lived upon the road. This place has given me a chance to re-establish the roots which were so cruelly thrown to the winds by events upon the field of Camlann."

Columba's face was unreadable as he offered Galahad his hand and said, "I truly pray that that will be the case, Sir Galahad of Camelot, for you have been a more than creditable addition to our order."

"Please, Columba, just plain Galahad will more than suffice. That affectation is in the past now."

"As you wish," Columba nodded as he ushered him from his office. They stopped upon the threshold and clasped hands warmly. "I am glad we had this talk, Columba." Galahad said. "I can see now why the monks here hold you in such high regard. Your words of wisdom and compassion are a great comfort."

As he turned from the holy man's presence, he espied Adomain skulking in the corridor outside the antechamber of Columba's office. Without hesitation he strode over to him. Facing his oldest friend within the monastery, he placed a hand on the older man's shoulder. "I understand now why your behaviour as you led me to Columba's study was so ill at ease and I am sorry for the way I spoke to you."

Adomain stared over his shoulder at Columba, who gave him the merest of nods. "Do not concern yourself, Galahad. It is forgotten." The monk said warmly.

With a final smile directed towards Columba and Adomain, Galahad walked back to his sleeping quarters where he was met by a worried looking Ruaraidh.

The former knight slumped down upon his bed as his giant room-mate stared at him owlishly.

As he had walked back from Columba's chambers, he had pondered the gentle warning which the founder of the monastery had given him with regards to the divulgence of what had passed between them. He appreciated the candidness of it and also the fact that he had not been sworn to secrecy. However, that had then presented him with the problem of what to tell the monks who he roomed with, as they would undoubtedly question him about what had happened.

After a minute's silence, a voice emanated from one of the other beds. "Tell him what happened, for heavens sake. He's been fit to burst ever since Adomain came and hauled you away."

Galahad's head jerked around at the unexpected words. He had only seen Ruaraidh upon entering but now realised that Maes was also in the room.

Affecting disinterest, the newest member of the dormitory waved away the question. "To be honest, both Columba and Adomain are as unsure about what occurred as I am. I spoke to Columba and he thinks I simply had some sort of fainting fit."

Ruaraidh and Maes exchanged glances and it was clear to Galahad they knew he was withholding something from them.

"You mentioned a psalter," Ruaraidh pointed out, "before Adomain came by. Was it the one you have been studying?"

Galahad saw out of the corner of his eye that Maes had swung his legs off his bed and was staring at him intently. Again he shrugged. "It was, yes. What of it? I have read it on many occasions before and it has not affected me in any way, let alone caused me to pass out."

"I know I am a man of few words but I use the time when most others babble and chatter to study the behaviour of others." Maes said slowly. "It is clear to me you are not telling us all of what transpired within Columba's office."

Galahad looked from the disfigured monk's non-committal expression to the look of hurt on Ruaraidh's open countenance. He knew he could protest his innocence to the pair of them but he was also acutely aware that lying did not come easily to him and he doubted his ability to further deceive them. "Look," he sighed plaintively, "Columba did say some other things to me but he hinted that they might be best left unsaid outside the walls of his chambers."

Ruaraidh pulled at his beard. "Not for the ears of such lowly fellows as us, you mean," he huffed.

Galahad sat up and shook his head. "Come now, you know Columba better than that."

"All we know is that you have been here a scant few months yet you seem to be privy to secrets which are deemed too important to share." Maes sniffed. "Besides, you said Columba hinted you should keep them to yourself. Did he forbid you from sharing them with us or are you merely enjoying being the centre of attention for a while?"

Galahad threw himself back onto his bunk in frustration. He could feel his trepidation growing again. He was being backed into a corner and there was no way out of it without causing trouble. He could keep his counsel and alienate his room-mates or tell them all and risk the wrath of Columba.

Though he did not doubt that the leader of Iona would not compel him to remain quiet on the matter of the psalter, he was not so naïve as to imagine that there would not be repercussions if he were to go against the implied wishes of the monastery's founder.

As he stared at the ceiling, his innate honesty decided the matter for him. He realised the only course of action which his conscience would allow him to take was to be as open about what had happened to his companions as he had been to Columba. With unseeing eyes staring blankly at the ceiling, he told them everything he could remember about his conversation with Columba and the conclusions that had been drawn from it.

When he had finished, Maes stalked over to him with an inscrutable look upon his face. He regarded him for a few moments then nodded, "Thank you for being honest with us, Galahad," he said simply.

Galahad felt as if some sort of bridge had been crossed between him and the two monks who had listened to his tale and he was gladdened by it.

As if in unspoken unison with their thoughts, the bell for the evening meal tolled in the corridor and all three suddenly realised that they were famished. "Shall we?" Maes smiled, ushering the both of them out of the door.

Chapter 10

Craigan McIntyre found his eyes irresistibly drawn to the threatening confusion of slate-grey cloud that had been building up to the north for the last couple of hours. He was sat at the prow of the small boat which the quartet of travellers had procured from a deserted village that stood at the southeasternmost tip of Loch Seaforth.

He looked back towards the stern of the boat at the McLeish twins as they bent their backs to the laborious task of navigating the currents of the Lower Minch. A slight smile appeared as he reflected on the behaviour of the twins. Their unforced levity provided a much needed counterpoint to Taiga's seemingly unending pessimism as to the outcome of the quest. The weather had been unceasingly grim ever since they had embarked upon their crossing and, as the foursome had been buffeted by the harsh, cold winds and bitter snow-flecked weather, all Taiga's conversation had consisted of was a litany of doubt and misgiving.

To the young Venicone, the wulver was a mass of contradictions which his limited life experience had no hope of unravelling. Whilst they were in sight of the land, Taiga had seemed full of eagerness to begin looking for Monkshood but, once the machairs of the islands had drifted over the horizon, his mood had blackened like the incessant overcast that seemed to have been the staple weather for what felt like months. Craigan peered sidelong at the wolfman, watching him as he sat staring at the rough planking that formed the base of the boat, seemingly oblivious to all around him.

Shaking his head regretfully at the unwelcome change in the demeanour of his companion, Craigan went back to surveying the horizon.

Taiga's eyes continued to stare unblinkingly at the floor of the vessel, concentrating with all his being on the stained wood. His rational mind tried to make itself heard amongst the tricks which his memory was playing on him, but it was no more than a whisper in the gale. Every time he looked up he saw again the flotilla of fishing boats and currachs that his tribe had been forced to use when they had been driven from Hermaness. His ears echoed once more with the pitiful wails of those of his clan rendered injured or dying by the Picts, whose fears of the Ulfhednar had prompted the attempted extermination of his people.

Slowly he became aware of a human voice wheedling its way through the spectral clamour that sounded in his mind. With a huge effort, he looked up into Craigan's concerned face.

"Taiga, it's our turn at the oars." The youngster said carefully, unsure of the wulver's reaction to the disturbance of his contemplation.

235

He cast a glance at the two brothers, who regarded him warily as they sat stretching their backs. An awkward silence began to grow, broken only by the gentle lapping of the water against the hull.

With a suddenness that made all three humans jump, Taiga thrust himself to his feet, unsettling the boat, and snatched an oar from Tavish. As the two Taexali clansman scuttled to the prow, Taiga snarled sarcastically at Craigan, "I thought it was *our* turn or am I expected to row on my own? This voyage is going to get very boring if we are just going to sit here going around in circles."

Despite himself, Craigan snapped back, "It is boring already as we have to listen to your constant moaning. To listen to you, you would think we are defeated before we even set foot on the mainland. At the moment, you would be just as much use if you were to cast yourself over the side of the boat, at least then the three of us would not have to drag your dead weight about with us any more." With that said, he snatched the other paddle from Warren and thudded himself down next to the open-mouthed wulver with a challenging look on his face as if he dared Taiga to say anything.

The McLeishs looked at each other with widened eyes. Warren bit his lip before saying, "We would probably get further if we threw Tavish over the side. He's fatter than yon wulver."

"Hey now," Tavish feigned offence before grabbing at Warren's waist. "You're not exactly slim, boy. I dare say our speed would double if you took a dive overboard."

The two of them then began to mock-fight, slapping and scratching ineffectually at each other, making the boat rock alarmingly.

Despite himself, Craigan began to laugh at the pair's antics, at first trying to stifle the sound before letting it explode in a great guffaw. Out of the corner of his eye, he saw Taiga trying to maintain a look of steely-eyed disapproval but a slight wrinkling around his eyes suggested that the twins' capering was beginning to wear down his sour mood.

Finally, the small vessel began to pitch so violently that it threatened to capsize, at which point Taiga shouted "Enough, lads" to the two Taexali.

The warning came out harsher than the wulver intended and the pair of clansman froze immediately, Tavish with Warren in a headlock and Warren throwing a punch into his brother's midriff.

The tableau looked so ludicrous that Taiga could contain himself no longer and joined in with Craigan's laughter.

As the two tribesmen subsided and Taiga returned to his station at the stern with Craigan, the adolescent Venicone turned to his companion and said, "Damn, but it's good to see your face with something other than a scowl upon it."

236

The wulver dragged a hairy hand across his face and sighed, "I have not been good company recently, have I?"

Craigan kept his counsel, hoping that this statement would be like the first crack in the winter ice, a small indication that there was an end in sight to the unrelenting chilliness of the atmosphere. After another moment's silence, he was proved right.

"It has taken me aback how vivid the crossing from Hermaness still is in my mind. As soon as we lost sight of the island, my treacherous memory cast me back to those days of horror as if they had happened yesterday, not over a year ago. When I look across the water, all I can see are my kith and kin dying one by one without hope or salvation. It is close to overwhelming me, Craigan."

The young lad put his back into the mind-numbing task, chewing over the wulver's words. After a few seconds, he shook his head, "You are their hope and salvation now, Taiga. You are the vessel through which your race can gain vengeance for the wrong done to them." He fixed the amalgam of man and beast with a pointed gaze, "As am I for my people."

Taiga pondered the young Pict's words, inwardly startled once again by the maturity that the apparently immature tribesman showed in both word and deed.

For long moments, the two of them sat, their oars cleaving the water in perfect harmony and Craigan sensed Taiga's demeanour becoming gradually less uptight. Their conversation then reverted to the small talk of friends, reminiscing upon the mundane life they had lived before the Ulfhednar had come. A life which they had taken for granted and often belittled precisely for its tedium, but one that they would have given anything to return to.

They had been at sea for a couple of days now, surviving on a deer carcass which the twins had managed to catch and cook before the foursome set off and had then been expertly gutted and trimmed by Craigan. They supplemented this with a minimal diet of fruits and berries. The twins had also found waterskins in the village where they had acquired the boat, filling them with water from one of the glut of freshwater springs they had found flowing through the hills and woods of the countryside.

Taiga managed to catch one or two fish using a crude rod that they had found in the same hut as the boat, but as they had nothing to cook them with, only the wulver was able to eat them.

The McLeish twins were back on rowing duties when Craigan first spotted land. He and Taiga looked at each other, both exhilarated and apprehensive in equal measure whilst Tavish and Warren whooped excitedly.

"Where do you suppose we will land?" Craigan asked.

All four of the seafarers looked at each other. Of the quartet, Taiga was by far the most-travelled but that had been due to necessity rather than curiosity. The three Picts had never ventured far from their homes and certainly not undertaken any sort of sea voyage, so they had even less idea of what lay before them.

"And so we return to the whim of Fate once again," the Venicone sighed. He stared up at the slightly lighter patch of grey in the all-pervading overcast which indicated where the sun was. "Have any of you taken heed of which way the tides have taken us? To be honest, I have no idea which direction we have been blown in."

Taiga spoke, "I believe we have been moving fairly steadily south." He cast a glance at the cliffs that were beginning to dominate the horizon in front of them. "It looks pretty inhospitable though. I have heard tell that these waters are dotted with many little islands, inhabited by nothing more than birds and beasts."

"I cannot see any immediately obvious places to beach," Tavish gnawed at his bottom lip. "Can we take a chance on landing here? If we damage the boat then find out we are stranded on a deserted spit of land then what?"

The other three reluctantly nodded agreement.

"Perhaps then we should hug the coastline until we find somewhere we can land safely? These cliffs cannot go on forever." Warren suggested.

As no other ideas were put forward, the foursome continued their sea voyage, acutely aware that night would soon be upon them and, if they were not aground by then, they would have no means of determining their position as they drifted upon the waves.

The McLeishs had been rowing for a goodly amount of hours and so Taiga and Craigan took over whilst the twins strained to see if there were any breaks in the basaltic walls which reared above them.

Cursing frustratedly, they did not find a suitable place before the gloom robbed them of their vision. Taiga then took their place at the prow hoping against hope that his superior night sight would succeed where the Taexali had failed. Unfortunately it did not and the party were condemned to another night aboard the tiny cramped vessel which had been their home for the last three days.

The next morning found them bobbing gently in open sea once more with land nowhere in sight.

The twins were very quiet, fearing that their caution of the previous night had cost the party a chance of sleeping on dry land, however Taiga and Craigan were quick to dismiss that.

"Do not concern yourself, laddies." The wulver waved his hands vaguely. "We would most certainly be undone should the boat have come to grief. I am sure we will make land in due time," he said calmly. "After all, we don't even know where exactly we are bound so one landing site will be as good as any other."

Craigan held his tongue, redoubling his efforts to row because, although Taiga had insisted that the twins' reluctance to beach the boat was not bothersome, he felt it was a missed opportunity to embark properly on their hunt for Monkshood.

They continued on their southerly course finding along the way, as Taiga had mentioned, many unpopulated islands which were so small they were barely worthy of the name.

After another two days aimless sailing, during which they had beached upon two narrow islets, only to find that they could traverse them in a matter of minutes, they found themselves upon a rather more substantial expanse of sand. They managed to start a fire of sorts and the quartet huddled around it, slavering in anticipation of a hot meal, something they had not enjoyed for the best part of a week. An unlucky black-backed gull had been caught, plucked and skewered and was, even now, revolving slowly round on a makeshift spit, the fatty juices causing big chunky sparks to leap into the night sky as they hit the heat of the flame. After a while, the bird was cooked to everyone's satisfaction and the four companions relaxed as they ate. In between mouthfuls, Tavish asked what the plan of action was now they had reached a starting point for their search.

Taiga shrugged, "We undoubtedly have a huge task in front of us if we are to find Monkshood. I fear that we will have to trust to fate to a great extent," he sighed.

"Yet it seems to have served us fairly well so far. It brought us together after all." Craigan put in, licking his greasy fingers and smearing them down the front of his tunic. "Until we lie dead on the ground, we cannot give in to doubt."

Warren smirked at the way Craigan had expressed his sentiments. "But once we are dead, we can accept that there may not be much hope, yes?"

The Venicone fixed his Taexali counterpart with a steady gaze. "You know what I am trying to say, McLeish. I was merely pointing out that fate has enabled us to pool our resources together whereas, if we had not met, our chances of success would be even slighter."

Warren acknowledged the point with a nod as Tavish yawned, "Are we planning to find this Monkshood tonight, because I for one would appreciate a good night's sleep before we start searching."

Not surprisingly, that opinion met with no argument and they settled down for the night.

Craigan came awake slowly and found himself shivering as the fire had burnt itself out. He wrapped his woollen cloak around his shoulders and looked about for the others, noting the thick mist which had come in off the sea during the night. Tavish and Warren were still both asleep whilst Taiga was nowhere to be seen. Craigan was not unduly worried about this so he went over to the fire to see if there was any chance of re-igniting it. The sound of footfalls crunching on the sand caused him to turn. Taiga's head appeared over the crest of a dune that squatted inland from the beach. From his expression, it was clear that something was amiss.

He sat down without ceremony and spat upon the ground, "You know," he hissed to Craigan, "I am beginning to hate the dawn. It ushers the new day in, instilling you with promise and hope then, as it resolves into the cold light of day, it shows your hopes up for what they are, foolish and misplaced."

Another voice entered the conversation, "My, we are a ray of sunshine on a cloudy day this morning, aren't we?"

Taiga muttered an obscenity at Tavish as the hirsute Pict ambled over to the blackened area where the fire had been laid.

"What is it, Taiga?" Craigan asked, too impatient to worry about the wulver's temper.

With an extravagant wave of his arm, Taiga pointed in the direction of where he had appeared from moments before. "I have been walking since first light, trying to get a feel for where we are."

"And?" Craigan yawned.

"We have fetched up on another bloody island which you could walk round in one morning. Go over that dune and you can see the sea. Walk a couple of miles south and you will see the same as you will if you walk north. Not that you can see much anyway, because of the bloody fog."

"So it is back to the boat then?" Craigan sighed.

"Aye," Taiga agreed. "Tavish, plant a boot up the arse of your idle brother and wake him. The mist is beginning to thin out and the more hours of daylight we have, the more likely we are to find a place where there might actually be people rather than nothing but seaweed and sand."

The mood of the travellers was as gloomy as the weather which seemed to be dogging their every step. To top off everyone's despondency, almost as soon as they pushed off from the beach, an icy sleet began to scythe down, soaking them completely and utterly and even causing the normally unflappable Taiga to wrap a cloak around his muscular frame.

Unbeknownst to the quartet of seafarers, their journey south had actually taken them free of the Minches and they were now travelling through the Sea Of The Hebrides. The forbidding headland which they had avoided when they first sighted land had been the Duirinish Peninsula, which was the westernmost point of Skye and the island upon which they had spent the previous night would come to be known as Canna, the westernmost of the Small Isles archipelago of the Inner Hebrides.

They endured the horrendous weather for most of the morning and made little progress as, whoever was rowing found themselves severely hampered by the choppy waters and vicious wind that seemed to be blowing in their eyes whichever way they faced.

Mercifully, the sleet began to ease and, though there was not a break in the cloud to be seen, the temperature started to climb steadily to the point that the travellers could divest themselves of their drenched clothing without too much discomfort.

As the sleet lifted, so did their spirits and they began to make good distance over the now-becalmed sea, sharing the rowing duties equally without complaint.

The sky was just beginning to change, from the dreary grey of a cloudy day to the deeper darkness of a starless night, when they sighted land once again. It was Taiga who spotted it first, wordlessly pointing towards the endless sandy beach that was becoming more defined with every stroke of the oars.

Though there was no basis for the thought, something made Craigan cautiously optimistic that this landfall would not be on a desolate wind-blasted skerry with only rocks and a few scrubby bushes for company.

The feeling must have communicated itself to the other three as well, for they all exchanged grins with each other. It was Tavish who broke the silence with a joyful hoot, "Look," he hollered, "on the beach."

Craigan and Taiga followed the trajectory of Tavish's finger as he jabbed it towards the expanse of sand. There were indistinct figures appearing from out of the hazy mass of greenery which could just be seen beyond the shore.

"Perhaps now we can start our quest in earnest." Craigan said to Taiga.

The wulver nodded but sounded a predictable note of caution as they approached the island. "Let us not get carried away, laddies. We need to sound out the ground before we can continue inland. Those who draw near might not be friendly to newcomers." He pointed out tersely.

Craigan accepted the point whilst Tavish and Warren shifted uncomfortably as they looked at the wulver. "Is there something you wish to say?" Taiga asked levelly.

Tavish took a deep breath then plunged on, "To be honest, we were wondering how the islanders would react to you. I remember how shocked we were when we first laid eyes upon you." He looked over to his brother for confirmation and received an emphatic nod for a response. "Though it is unlikely, it is possible that these have also been visited by the horde of

241

wolves, in which case, they will be even less well disposed to one of your…appearance."

"Yes, I take your point." Taiga hissed testily. "I will swaddle myself in cloaks like a newborn baby so they may be spared my hideous countenance."

Tavish looked solemn, "Do not take it in that manner, wulver. You have proved a more than amiable companion on this voyage and you must know that, though others may view you with distrust, myself and my brother regard you as a friend and you know that young McIntyre here holds you in the same high regard."

The speech seemed to cut little ice with Taiga as he rummaged in the travelling packs for something to cover himself with.

By the time they ran aground on the pebbly beach, there was a group of ten islanders waiting to meet them. The welcoming party seemed neither hostile nor particularly friendly, they simply stood regarding the foursome as they climbed out of the boat.

All but one was dressed in traditional clan robes, their heavy woollen capes fluttering dramatically behind them in the quickening wind. However, there was something about the other one which drew the eye. His deep-blue robes seemed to be of a more expensive cut than the tribesmen's and he held within his right hand a hefty, yet ornate golden staff fashioned like a shepherd's crook. His stance was one of placid assurance and the surrounding clansmen all seemed to show him a measure of deference, though outwardly he did not appear to be one of them.

With hearts pounding, the four newcomers dragged their small craft completely clear of the tide and walked across the sand to the men who had appeared atop the shallow dune that led away inland.

Craigan walked towards the robed man but found his way barred by two of the tribesmen, who stepped in front of the youngster with their hands resting on the handles of the axes at their belts.

The Venicone spread his hands in a conciliatory gesture but addressed his apology to the man being guarded, rather than acknowledging the threat of the pair of tribesmen blocking his path. "Be assured we mean no harm to you or your fellows. We are simply seeking a man who may be able to help us. A man by the name of Monkshood," Craigan said without preamble.

The beginnings of a strange smile could be discerned amongst the heavy white beard that dominated the man's face as he said, "That is an odd name to go by. Could it be that it is a pseudonym rather than a real name?"

Craigan shrugged, "In truth we do not know. All we know is that we need to find this Monkshood as a matter of urgency."

"Well, surely it is not so urgent that you cannot accept an offer of a hearty meal after your voyage." With that said, the man and his cohorts began to walk away from the four new arrivals without waiting to see if they followed. The three clansmen and Taiga shared exasperated glances before hurrying after the rapidly retreating backs of their new acquaintances.

As they crested the dune, they saw before them an expanse of forbidding moorland beyond which reared a series of ominous looking peaks whose snow-capped summits glowed brightly against the darkening sky. The two parties walked in silence towards an ugly squat stone building, skulking in the lee of one of the mountains which overshadowed the landscape. As they walked, Craigan had to admit that, amidst the boggy terrain and biting wind, the lights emanating from the building did look hugely inviting and he found that the hunger which had been suppressed by tiredness and stress had returned with a vengeance now that the questers were on dry land.

At length, they found themselves walking through a pair of oaken gates, under an overhang of serviceable brickwork into a flagstoned courtyard, encircled by roughly twenty sconces which guttered and flickered in the wind, despite the area being far more sheltered than the surrounding moors.

The nine tribesmen had dispersed, leaving the man with the staff alone with the seafarers. He gestured expansively, "Welcome to Caisteal Uisgean, our humble home," he said in a deep rumbling voice. "My name is Brother Padraig, founder of the Order here on Mull and I invite you to break bread with us at our table."

Craigan's eyes bulged at that and he sighed gratefully, "Thank you for your gracious offer."

Padraig nodded, "That is the way of those who bide within these walls. We are pledged to spread the Christian faith throughout these lands and part of that faith is charity towards those who require it. It is clear from your haggard appearance that you and your companions have been through a sore trial. Come, let me show you to a place where you can wash away the aches and pains of your voyage."

The appeal of a hot meal and hot bath overrode any caution which the trio of tribesmen had about their host and they accepted the suggestion with gusto. Taiga hung back however, unsure what to do. Seeing this, Craigan strode to his side and propelled him into one of the pools of shadow in between the penumbrae of the torches. "I can understand your reticence but we do not want to risk offending our hosts, do we."

"It is alright for you," Taiga grumbled. "They will not shrink back from you when they see you standing in the light."

The Venicone turned to Brother Padraig who stood watching the two of them impassively. "Perhaps they will not react in the way you suspect?"

The wulver stiffened as Padraig walked towards them, "Is something the matter, my friends?" he asked.

With a jaundiced look at Craigan and, in the absence of any plausible reason not to, Taiga took the only course open to him. He slowly unwrapped the cloak from round his face, all the while holding the gaze of their host, wordlessly challenging him to comment. He was surprised and indeed gratified to see that, bar a slight flaring around Padraig's eyes, he did not react in any way to his appearance.

"I see now the reason for your hesitancy in revealing yourself." Padraig said levelly. "Still, another precept of our Christianity is that we should hold all of God's creatures in the same esteem as we hold ourselves, so do not be afeared, those who live within this place will judge you by your deeds and words, not your appearance."

With that sensitive hurdle seemingly negotiated, the foursome allowed themselves to be escorted along the cold stone cloisters and Taiga had to admit that, despite drawing several looks which ranged from mildly curious to downright startled, the denizens of the monastery were good to the word of their leader. After a few minutes stroll, the questers were shown into a small but serviceable room in which four tin baths stood, half full with steaming water. As they all descended into the liquid's embrace with contented sighs, they began discussing the apparent upturn in their circumstances.

"Do you know," Tavish began, "I have never been one for bathing but, after the last few days, this is absolutely blissful."

"Aye, that it is," his brother agreed.

Craigan ducked beneath the surface of the water, emerging with a sharp intake of breath and letting the rivulets run down his face. As he blinked the water clear of his eyes, he said, "What did Padraig call his faith? Christianity, was it?"

Taiga, sighing happily, grunted in the affirmative.

"Well, whatever it is called, I could certainly get used to it."

Again, the grunt. "That may be so, but let us not forget why we have fetched up here."

That statement served to concentrate the minds of the four bathers and they finished their ablutions in silence, each alone with their own thoughts and memories, their moods darkened by the pall which the Ulfhednar had cast over their lives.

They were just dressing themselves, in coarse woollen tunics provided by one of Padraig's underlings that covered them from neck to ankle as well as cracked, leather sandals, when they heard a bell tolling. Almost at that instant, the door to the room opened and a tonsured head poked itself into view. "If you would all follow me, I will escort you to Brother Padraig's quarters."

As they fell into line behind their guide, Taiga whispered in Craigan's ear, "Do we tell them everything?"

The youngster fixed him with an intense stare that again left Taiga reflecting on the lad's unexpected maturity. "I think we have to. If we cannot bring ourselves to trust others, then we have no hope of finding whom we seek."

Within minutes, the youthful postulant had left them in a small antechamber which was as sparsely decorated as the corridors had been. The only adornment was an ornate gold crucifix that dominated one of the four walls.

Warren walked over to it and studied it closely before observing, "Strange that he looks so happy. If I was pinned to something like that, I do not think I would look so pleased."

"He is the Lord Jesus Christ and he died for our sins," Padraig's sonorous voice resonated around the room.

"Speak for yourself," Warren shot back. "Anyway, how could he have died for my sins? I have never met him nor do I know the name."

"Surely if anyone should die for his sins, it should be Warren, not this Jesus Christ." Tavish put in. "It hardly seems fair that he should have to pay for this reprobate's degenerate behaviour."

An impish smile appeared on the younger McLeish's face. "I apologise for nothing, I am sorry but that is just the way I am."

"Warren, Tavish, hold your tongues." Craigan looked nervously from the two smirking Taexali to the unblinking eyes of Brother Padraig, expecting at any moment the patriarchal face to wrinkle in distaste at the pair's tomfoolery. Instead, to the youngster's wide-eyed surprise, the leader of the Order of Mull threw his head back and laughed heartily, "I apologise. I am unused to mixing with those who are ignorant of the Christian faith. If you wish, as we eat, I will explain some more about Christianity and all its glories."

With non-committal shrugs, the quartet followed Padraig through to a cold, airy refectory with six benches and tables set out across the middle, around which sat twenty or so diners each, some of whom Taiga recognised from the welcoming party who had met them on the dunes. Mixed in with those were men dressed in much the same way as Padraig, however, the difference in appearance counted for nothing as both sets of people intermingled freely with each other. Once again, a few glances were thrown in Taiga's direction but they merely contained piqued interest rather than any enmity.

The five of them made their way to a previously unnoticed table at the top of the room which was set apart from the sextet in the centre. Chairs were arranged all around it so that all who sat there could talk to each other

245

without difficulty. As the travellers made their way to the table, they looked about the room. The walls were all fashioned from unpolished stonework and, like the other rooms they had seen, simply decorated. There were wooden crucifixes arrayed upon each side and, in the approximate centre of three of the walls, was an alcove inside which a large, leatherbound book rested. Indeed, as Craigan walked past the nearest recess, he was rather taken aback by how elaborate the manuscript was, finding it an incongruous splash of colour in a uniformly grey place.

In the wall which sat nearest the table they were to dine at, a pair of double doors stood. Through them wafted a host of delicious smells that set the newcomers' mouths to watering. The three tribesmen could pick out fresh bread and chicken but Taiga's more finely-tuned senses also noted honey, pork and game.

As they took their seats, the doors opened and platters of food were brought out and placed liberally about on each table. After the kitchen workers had finished, Taiga and Craigan started to help themselves to the food until the wulver noticed that Padraig was sitting with his head bowed in silence. He then looked around the room and saw that all save him, Craigan and the McLeishs were doing likewise. Ignoring his growling stomach, he grabbed Craigan's arm as the youngster reached towards a steaming hunk of bread and, with a curt wave of his other hand, indicated to the brothers that they should restrain their hunger as well. All four shared confused looks as the silence in the room was broken by Padraig's resonant words,

"Nos oremus! Benedic, Domine, nos et hæc Tua dona, quæ de Tua largitate sumus sumpturi. Per Christum, Dominum nostrum. Amen."

With a deep sigh, Padraig finished the prayer. He happened to be staring at Taiga as he opened his eyes. He unconsciously scanned the food in front of his guests, nodding in appreciation at the fact that it remained untouched. "There was no need for you to be so respecting of our ways for I can only guess at how hungry you must be, but the gesture is much appreciated. Please do not resist your hunger any more." Padraig said, gesturing for them to tuck in, which they did so with great enthusiasm. As he tore the leg off a roasted chicken which had been cooked to perfection, Taiga asked Padraig, "What were those words you said before we began eating?"

Padraig finished buttering some bread and laid it down fastidiously on his wooden plate. "It was the prayer of Grace. It is but a simple entreaty offering thanks to God for the food that is laid before us."

"It certainly has a pleasing poetry to it," Craigan said in between mouthfuls.

"Indeed it does," Padraig acknowledged. "After the evening meal is finished, we will be retiring to the oratory to pray to the Lord. Perhaps you would care to join us?"

Craigan shifted uncomfortably in his chair and looked at his companions for their reaction.

Padraig waved away the lack of response, "It is of no consequence if you do not wish to." He mopped up the sauce on his plate with the last hunk of bread then patted his stomach. "So, might I ask what has brought you to the Isle of Mull? I know you mentioned the name Monkshood upon the shore, however I have no doubt that there is a good deal more to your story than just locating a single man."

Craigan nodded, and with a glance at Taiga, who returned the nod with a reassuring one of his own, began to recount his journey from the destruction of Dun Eiledon to being plucked from the depths of Loch Seaforth by Taiga. At that point Taiga took up the story, not only continuing the narrative until the point that they arrived on Mull but also availing Padraig of the history of his people and their legends concerning the Ulfhednar.

By the time Taiga had finished his account, the refectory had emptied, except for Padraig and the four travellers and the wulver found his words echoing menacingly in the hushed atmosphere.

All through the tale Brother Padraig had remained silent, although when the young tribesman had talked about the horror of Jameson's demise and Taiga had spoken of the devastation which had been wrought on Unst by the werewolves, his eyes looked as if they would start from his face.

Once Taiga had finished, he let out a huge breath and shook his head, "I see now why you braved the whims of the sea in such an ill-prepared craft. I have nothing but admiration for your fortitude and courage, especially if it is to be used to rid the world of such a heinous group of creatures but, alas I have no knowledge of anyone who goes by the name of Monkshood. From the depths of my heart, I wish I was able to aid you in your endeavours." He steepled his fingers and stared for a moment at the crucifix on the opposite wall, "It may be that no-one within this place is able to help you but the monks at Iona have a most extensive library. Perhaps the identity of this Monkshood will become apparent there."

Both Taiga and Craigan leant into the table and regarded the Christian holy man intently, "What did you say?" the wulver gasped.

"The monks at Iona might be able to provide enlightenment as to Monkshood's identity." Padraig repeated, his eyebrows furrowing in confusion.

Craigan looked blankly at Taiga and the McLeishs. "Monks?" he asked.

Brother Padraig nodded slowly, "The building in which you are sitting is a monastery, a holy place peopled by monks."

Taiga slumped back in his chair whilst the two Taexali brothers exchanged glances.

"I take it you have not heard the word before."

All four shook their heads. "No," Craigan confirmed.

"That is why, on the beach, I asked you if Monkshood was a nickname. Our robes are all fitted with hoods, you see." Padraig reached behind him and pulled his up, momentarily covering his head.

"Are there many of these monasteries? How many monks live within each?" Taiga asked, chewing on his bottom lip.

Padraig shook his head, "Not as far as I am aware, although as the faith is spread I am sure more will appear. No, the main one in these islands is the one at Iona which I have already mentioned." He tugged at his beard. "As I have said, I do not know this Monkshood, but I would guess that your best chance of locating him, or at least finding some knowledge of him, would be in the library at Iona. It is located at the southwestern tip of the island. Mull is a mountainous isle so it will be a fair trek across country or, if you remain confident in your nautical abilities, you could shadow Mull's coastline and approach it that way." He rose from the table. "Come, I will show you to your room. I suspect you will want to rest in preparation for your trip to Iona, though you are more than welcome to bide here for as long as you require."

Taiga got up from the table purposefully, "Thank you for the offer, Padraig but you are right in your assumption, we have a thread to cling to now, albeit a tenuous one. We must pursue it as soon as we can." He looked at his companions. "We will bide here tonight then depart for Iona in the morning."

Padraig nodded. "I thought as much. Rest assured you will all be in our prayers tonight."

All four rose in unison. "Thank you for the meal. It was sorely needed," Craigan said. "Hopefully, the information you have provided us with will be invaluable in our search." He tried to stifle a yawn but failed.

The monk ushered them from the room. "You are exhausted. If you intend to leave tomorrow then you will need your rest."

Without further words, the questers allowed themselves to be guided down the corridor and into a dull but functional room, made cramped by the four beds which had been laid out especially for them.

Padraig exited the room to the accompaniment of mumbled gratitude and all four were asleep within minutes.

They awoke to a hideous day. The glacial wind could be both felt and heard howling down the corridors and the incessant tattoo of rain was an eternal noise in the background of the hushed environment of the monastery.

Taiga and Craigan stalked about the cloisters in exasperation, repeatedly looking to the skies to see if there was any sign of a break in the inky cloudscape. They had both wanted to set out that morning despite the inclemency of the weather but, after Padraig's warning that there had been more than a few fatalities caused by people becoming disorientated in the mountains during bad weather and being found several days later frozen to death on the slopes, they had reluctantly acceded to his pleas for patience.

The wulver and the Venicone were also becoming increasingly maddened by the McLeishs' behaviour. Though Brother Padraig had repeatedly told them that they were welcome to come and go as they pleased about the monastery, the two of them felt that the Taexali were taking advantage of their hosts' hospitality, continually pestering the kitchen workers for food and drink or disturbing the monks as they were praying, with their boorish conduct. When they returned from the refectory for the fifth time with an armful of fruit, Taiga could contain himself no longer. "It is just as well we are going to Iona across country rather than by boat. The craft would never be able to take the extra weight."

Tavish deliberately bit into a succulent apple, letting the juice dribble into his beard and down the front of his tunic, whilst Warren shrugged disinterestedly as he drained another mug of mead. "Why should we not take the opportunity to rest while we are able?" he argued. Pointing towards the wall, he continued, "It will not be long before we are back out there in the snow and rain, getting drenched to the skin. We need all the strength we can get."

Tavish belched loudly and patted his belly, "We are merely stockpiling our energy reserves against the difficulties of the journey ahead." He smirked objectionably.

For a long moment, Taiga stood seething, his fists clenching and unclenching before stalking from the room, slamming the door behind him. Craigan stared at the twins and shook his head before hurrying across the room to follow the wulver.

As he exited, Tavish turned to Warren and said in a slurred voice loud enough for Craigan to hear, "I thought it was humans which had animals as pets, not the other way about."

The Venicone stopped as he was halfway into the corridor, wanting to turn round and berate the two tribesmen for their indolence. Whereas their inane behaviour had been a welcome distraction on the difficult sea crossing, now, in the relative comfort of the monastery, it had become jarring and tedious.

Instead he went to seek out Taiga, ignoring the insulting inference of Tavish's comment. With each passing moment since their expedition had started, he realised that he identified with the wulver and his attitude towards the search much more closely than he did with the McLeishs. It seemed a bizarre thing to acknowledge, given that they differed in species, but perhaps, Craigan reflected, the need for revenge of those who had been wronged transcended any racial differences.

He eventually found Taiga standing in the slight shelter afforded by the portico at the front gates, staring into the middle distance across the wild moorland, seemingly indifferent to the rain lashing into his face. Though the wulver did not acknowledge Craigan's presence, within seconds of the Venicone taking up station at his shoulder, he hissed between gritted teeth, "Will this bastard weather ever let up?"

Craigan was all too aware that the weather was only a part of what was upsetting his companion. "Ignore them, Taiga. They are both idiots and well in their cups."

The wulver spun round. "Do not seek to excuse their ignorance, Craigan, for they will only drag you down to their level."

Craigan held his hands up placatingly, "Do not misunderstand me, I am in no way excusing them. It says a great deal for the people here that they accept their behaviour with such good grace. They seem to have unending patience and they have been nothing but wonderful hosts to us. To be honest, if our needs were not so pressing, I would be interested in staying to find out more about what these monks do here."

Taiga regarded the youngster for a moment before returning to his scrutiny of the cloud-cloaked horizon. "Aye, I know what you mean. It seems to be such a peaceful place. Even as I stormed away from those two imbeciles, I found my temper subsiding almost immediately. There is something in the air here, even the full ferocity of the weather does not seem to penetrate the walls." He turned back to Craigan. "Perhaps once we have slain the werewolves, we can return here for some peace and quiet, eh?"

The tribesman from Dun Eiledon laughed bitterly at the remark, "Why not? Even if we do achieve our ultimate goal, there is nothing for us back upon the islands, is there?"

With that sobering thought weighing heavily on their minds, the pair of them resumed their silent vigil, each lost in their own thoughts. For how long they stood neither knew but, after a while, Craigan tapped Taiga on the shoulder and pointed to the right. "The storm is breaking," he said with a barely restrained excitement.

"Finally," the wulver breathed as he stared at the mass of lighter grey racing in from the north which seemed to be banishing the darker gloom before it at a rapid rate of knots.

They both raced back to their sleeping quarters, all thoughts of their argument with Warren and Tavish forgotten. They burst in through the door to find the two brothers fast asleep, Tavish snoring hugely with his empty mug broken on the floor at the side of his bunk and Warren lying in a pool of vomit on the floor at the base of his bed.

Craigan made to go over and rouse them but Taiga snapped, "Leave them," in a voice that brooked no argument.

"But..." the youngster began before Taiga savagely cut him short.

"Do not waste your time on them," he spat with a twisted snarl of disgust. "What kind of people are they? They have seen their lives destroyed by the wolves yet when they have a chance to exact revenge, what do they do?" He waved a dismissive hand in the general direction of the twins. "They get so drunk they cannot even stand up. If we wait for them to be in any fit state to accompany us, we lose another day." He shook his head. "No, I will not wait any longer than I have to, Craigan, especially now we are making progress."

The Venicone blinked in surprise at the ferocity in Taiga's voice. "Perhaps they are scared of what is to come in the future and seek to find some courage?" he mumbled.

For a moment Taiga ceased his diatribe and looked at the slumbering pair. Shaking his head, he turned back. "I do not doubt that they are scared, they would be stupid not to be, but the fact is they are spineless cowards who add little or nothing to our search. I would not trust them to stand with us when we face the nightwalkers."

"You don't know that, Taiga. What right have you to judge them for deeds as yet unperformed?" Craigan said evenly.

The wulver rounded on the youngster. "On the contrary, I have already seen first-hand their craven cowardice. I have not told you this before, as I do not like to dwell on such events but, when you were suffering in the forest, these two and McChirder attacked us. I was forced to kill McChirder because, if I had not, one or other of these would have murdered you where you lay."

"What?"

Taiga's rage subsided as he watched the blood drain from Craigan's face in shock. "I am sorry, lad, but it is true. What makes it even worse is that, when I managed to best them, they turned on McChirder in the blink of an eye, bowing to my orders without question, simply because I was more powerful than them." He walked over to stand next to Craigan, laying a kindly hand on his shoulder.

The Venicone shrugged it off before muttering quietly, "Let us go then" and walking from the room without a backward glance.

Taiga bestowed one last glare of disdain on the brothers before following him.

When they were gone, Tavish opened a beady eye before slowly sitting up. Warren was still prostrate at his feet, so he nudged him with his boot. "You can get up, they are gone," he said in a subdued voice.

Warren remained where he was, staring blankly at the ceiling before rising to sit on his bed with a sigh. "We are better off out of it, Tavish. That wulver chills me to the bone when he loses his temper and he is on our side. Can you imagine what these Ulfhednar are like?"

Tavish could not bring himself to answer. The scorn of the wulver had cut through him like a knife. He had wanted to spring to his and his brother's defence but, deep in his heart, he knew that the wolfman had been right. And now here he was, with the twin burdens of his fear of the werewolves and his shame at the unpalatable truth of Taiga's words, rendering him speechless. With a shake of his head, Tavish Mcleish also walked from the room without a backward glance, leaving his brother alone in his own private world of embarrassment and guilt.

At the front gate of the monastery, Brother Padraig was bidding Taiga and Craigan farewell, presenting them with food parcels prepared in the kitchens the previous night. "I notice that your party has been halved," Padraig said, "Are the brothers not joining you?"

Taiga shook his head curtly as Craigan muttered, "No, they are remaining behind" in clipped tones.

Shrugging aside the rather obvious hostility which had appeared on both his guests' faces when he had mentioned the McLeishs' absence, Padraig introduced the two travellers to one of his acolytes, Brother Lorcan, a skinny young man with wide brown eyes and a wispy beard, who was to act as their guide on the cross-country trek to the south-western tip of the island.

Brother Lorcan greeted them warmly and, after they had said their goodbyes, the three of them struck out across the island.

As they walked through the boggy moorland, Lorcan began telling them about the work of the monastery and about Christianity in general. "We worship one God, who is personified in the Holy Trinity, the Father known as God, the son who is Jesus and the Holy Spirit which is a mixture of both God and Jesus and which enabled God to send his son down to preach the gospel and go about his work upon the earth."

Craigan found the monk, who he judged to be only slightly older than himself, rather pompous, but he was rather surprised that Taiga seemed intensely interested in what he had to say.

"And these prayers are answered, are they?" the wulver asked eagerly. "Every time?"

Lorcan smiled at Taiga in a manner that the Venicone found rather condescending. "Yes, though perhaps not in the way that one would expect," Lorcan answered. "It is hard to put into words but, when I am asked questions of this nature, I always tell the story of the footprints in the sand."

Craigan stared disinterestedly into the distance, his eyes following the wide circle of a buzzard as it wheeled effortlessly in the air.

Lorcan continued, "A man had died, neither good nor evil, just a man such as your companion here, and he walked with God along a deserted beach, revisiting the events of his life. As he and God talked, the man noticed two sets of footprints in the sand next to them, following the same path which he and God were walking. They walked on, examining what had happened in the man's life and, for the most part, these two sets of footprints were a constant accompaniment to their journey. However, the man noticed that, when they talked of the hard times which he had experienced upon the earth, his father beating him as a child, his son falling ill, his wife dying, one set of footprints disappeared and only returned once his life had become bearable again. After this had happened for the fourth time the man stopped and rounded on God, berating him for deserting him in times of trouble. God took the censure with good grace and, when the man had stopped, laid a compassionate hand upon his shoulder and said, "In those times of hardship, I did not desert you."

"Then why is there only one set of footprints in the sand?" the man countered.

And God smiled benignly and said, "Those were the times that I carried you, my son."

Again, Craigan was surprised by the enthusiasm in Taiga's voice when he said, "That is a fine tale."

"It never fails to move me," Lorcan agreed.

Craigan pointed to a bank of cloud which was building up behind a forbidding mountain rising up to the south. "Is there any shelter hereabouts, Lorcan? I think we will need it soon, if we are not to get soaked to the skin again."

The monk pointed towards the craggy slope of the mount, "Aye, there are many caverns hidden upon the incline. We will have no problem finding sanctuary should the weather break again."

Two hours later, the trio were to be found huddled in the mouth of a small cave, staring out at sheets of sleeting rain. They had managed to make the shelter just as the first drops of rain had begun to fall but, after casting about the hollow for some fuel for a fire, came up empty-handed.

"Perhaps you could go out into the rain and pray for some kindling?" Craigan suggested with an innocent look on his face.

"And what would you say if I was to do that, Craigan?" Lorcan shot back with an amused smile.

"I would say thank you and light a fire," the youngster said.

"Then it would be doubly worthwhile for me to find some," the monk chuckled. Quickly hefting his hood over his unruly blonde hair, Brother Lorcan walked out into the rain.

Taiga watched the holy man's retreating back for a moment then turned to the Venicone. "Are you going to tell me what your problem is with our guide, or must he endure your sarcasm until we get to Iona?"

Craigan raised an eyebrow, "Only if *you* explain why *you* are so enraptured by him, or must I endure *your* fawning all the way there?"

The nasty tone of the tribesman's voice rankled with the wulver. "Why do you bridle at Lorcan's words so much, lad?"

Craigan stared out into the sleet for a long moment, occasionally catching a glimpse of the monk as he searched for tinder amongst the greenery of the moor. "I object to being told how I should live my life, that's all. I like to think that I lived a good life before I had even heard of Christianity. Were my actions any less worthy because they were not done to honour his God? No, yet that is what his words imply," he hissed.

"I think you are taking offence at nothing, Craigan. At what point has he said that you are less worthy than him? At what point has he taken issue with any of your previous deeds?" Taiga asked pointedly. "These Christians have taken us in, fed us, clothed us, allowed us to sleep under their roof, provided us with a guide and food for our journey to *another* one of their monasteries where, I should imagine, we will receive the selfsame treatment. I may be missing the point here, but I cannot understand why you have such hostility towards him."

"It does not matter," Craigan mumbled as he turned back to the gloomy day. He could not articulate his uneasiness at the whole idea of worshipping what, to all intents and purposes, was another human being, or at least, a god that was represented as a human being. The religion which Craigan and his tribe had followed, if it could be called that, numbered no such deities, being animistic in nature instead, its gods existing in the natural world and its places of worship being rivers and trees rather than man-made constructions like churches and monasteries.

For his own part, Craigan had never been a particularly devout follower of the various rituals and practices of his clan, regarding the ancient wisdom and knowledge that Jameson the Seer used to impart as being born from the memories and actions of his druidic predecessors, rather than the product of an intangible entity which decided the course of events on a whim.

He acknowledged that the Christians had been nothing less than the perfect hosts as Taiga had pointed out, but he had felt that, had they stayed within the confines of the monastery for a protracted time then, though there would be no explicit attempt to force the issue, the pressure to conform to the Christian manner of worship would have become more pronounced.

His mind returned to Padraig's rather condescending comment, that he was unused to mixing with people 'ignorant' of the Christian faith, suggesting that those who were aware of it were possessed of some sort of superiority over those who were not. This had been compounded by the manner of the tribesmen who had wordlessly greeted them on the beach, and also those who had been in the refectory when the foursome had broken bread with Padraig. He was unused to seeing normally ferocious and proud Pictish clansmen subjugating themselves to one not of their race and he wondered at the powers of persuasion of Padraig and his fellow monks, finding it unsettling rather than a comfort.

Whilst Craigan had been pondering this, Brother Lorcan had returned to the shelter of the cave with an armful of relatively dry wood which he and Taiga began furiously rubbing to try and ignite a fire. As the pair of them worked, Craigan found himself intrigued by Taiga's behaviour towards the young monk. The wulver seemed to be in the thrall of Lorcan's faith, hanging on his words and seeming to lap up any pronouncements which the holy man made. Perhaps the Christians did have some fey magic at their disposal which allowed them to subdue others without having to resort to means of force or intimidation?

With that worrying thought playing on his mind, he joined his two companions in their attempts at getting the bundle of sticks to light, privately resolving to speak to Taiga about his concerns at the next available opportunity.

The next day dawned with a clear sky, hinting at a rare spell of sunshine for the travellers as they traversed the island. Despite the weather, they had walked a reasonable distance the previous day and the sense of urgency that pressed down on Taiga and Craigan had subsided somewhat.

Lorcan stood in the mouth of the cave, inhaled a deep lungful of air and proclaimed, "God has provided us with a fine day, the better that we may appreciate his works."

Craigan thought about mentioning the hideous conditions of the past few days but bit his tongue as he did not wish to be the recipient of another venomous look from Taiga.

After a quick but nourishing breakfast of bread and cheese, the trio set off once more.

Lorcan estimated they still had, at the very least, three days travelling ahead of them before they reached the south-western tip of the island. From there they had to travel a further mile by boat over the Sound of Iona before reaching the Ionan mainland and Columba's monastery.

Even though the weather was set fair for a while, Craigan found himself shrouded in a black mood. He found his eyes jealously trailing Taiga and Lorcan as they negotiated the uneven tussocks and mounds of the moorland, deep in conversation. Could his antipathy for Lorcan be that simple, Craigan thought in a moment of uncomfortable insight, did he see the young monk as a threat to his new-found friendship with the wulver? However, after contemplating the thought for a moment, he dismissed it. He had found himself identifying with Taiga on so many levels that he was certain his companion would not be so shallow as to supplant him with another, in such an off-hand fashion.

He was so lost in thought that he did not see the pair of them halt in front of him until Lorcan's sonorous voice intruded upon his consciousness. He looked up to see the monk pointing to the south towards a snow-capped peak in the distance, which erupted out of the flat expanse of the moor before them. "That is Ben Molyneaux, the second highest peak on the island, after Ben More, which we will see tomorrow assuming we keep progressing at the same rate. Though you cannot see them from here, it is encircled by small lochs, which make the surrounding ground treacherous and boggy. The most trodden trail takes us around the outer shores of the lochs and will add at least half a day onto our trek. I do know of a track which will take us onto the lower slopes of the mount and will allow us to keep travelling in a more or less straight line, but it is very craggy and unforgiving." He turned to face Craigan and Taiga then looked to the sky. "I judge that, were we back at the monastery, it would be time for the afternoon observances, so I will take myself off to pray for our safe passage and will leave it to your good selves to decide which route to take."

They both watched him walk away until he was beyond their hearing, then Taiga turned to Craigan, "Of course, if we are to do that, we need to actually speak to each other." He said pointedly before his expression turned plaintive. "You have barely uttered a word since this morning. Tell me what is on your mind, lad."

Craigan checked over his shoulder to ensure the holy man was still out of earshot before he began speaking, "I just..." he hesitated, trying desperately to frame his answer in the way he wished, "it is not that I do not trust Lorcan, it is just...it is what I said before, I feel like there is an almost continual pressure being placed upon us to convert to his faith. I do not know if it is subconscious or whether it is a deliberate act on his part, but every other word he utters seems to be about how good and worthy his god is. It is incessant and insidious and makes me feel hugely uncomfortable, to be honest." With a deep breath, Craigan plunged on, the words spilling in a torrent from his mouth, "And what makes me more uncomfortable is that he seems to have you completely under his spell."

Taiga nodded slowly, digesting Craigan's words while he considered his response. "Firstly, young Craigan, I have enough about me to decide for myself what to believe and no amount of honeyed words from anyone, and that includes you or Lorcan or Padraig or whoever, will make up my mind for me.

Secondly, you may be surprised to know that, to a certain extent, I share your misgivings about Brother Lorcan's unending litany of his life within the monastery's boundaries and how fulfilling it is. Think about it from his point of view though. He has given his life up for this Christianity. These monks deny themselves many things, as they feel to do so brings them closer to their god. You have to have the flame of belief burning very brightly within you to make that sort of sacrifice. Having said that, rather than dismissing it out of hand and closing my mind to it as you have, as the three of us have walked across country, I have taken the opportunity to pose questions of him and challenge what he has said. For example, he asserted that his god created all living things and that all creatures were sacred, as they were the product of divine fashioning. I then told him of the werewolves and their wicked deeds and asked how they could possibly be blessed. He answered that his God moved in mysterious ways and, though the purpose of the Ulfhednar walking the earth was not necessarily apparent to us, we could be rest assured that his god had a good reason for creating them."

"Not much of an answer, is it?" Craigan huffed.

"From our viewpoint, no, but, if you have the strength of faith which Lorcan possesses, well," he spread his hands "it answers everything, does it not?"

Craigan shook his head irritably, "I suppose," he whined.

Taiga's face hardened at his companion's intransigence. "What you also have to remember is that he is guiding us to Iona at our behest and, even if you do not agree with his beliefs, perhaps a bit of common courtesy would not go amiss."

Craigan sighed and stared silently up at the sky for a few moments, "You are right, of course," he muttered quietly. "I think it is my impatience at taking the fight back to the werewolves which is making me so testy. I cannot help feeling that we are running away from them as they continue to rampage unchallenged across our homeland."

Taiga rounded on him, "Do you not think I feel exactly the same, boy?" he snapped.

"Of course, I..." the youngster stammered.

"You forget there are many more of you humans than wulvers dotted about the land. I could be the last of my race, let alone the last of my clan." The gaze he fixed on Craigan chilled the Venicone to the bone. "I physically ache for the day I will stare down at that giant bastard who leads the Ulfhednar and spit upon his frigid corpse."

"As do I," Craigan shot back in a tremulous voice.

Taiga turned from him with a look of disdain. "Do you?" he hissed unkindly. "When it comes to facing the wolves, will you stand or will you turn tail like those cowardly scum we left behind quivering in the monastery?"

This time it was Craigan whose anger erupted, "Do not for one moment believe I am the same as those two fools," he jabbed a finger in Taiga's face. "And, as you are so intent on singing Lorcan's praises for what he is doing for us, let us take a moment to examine exactly where you were in your attempts to thwart the Ulfhednar before you fished me out of the loch? Vaguely following them from place to place without any idea as to how to stop their evil deeds."

Taiga's teeth peeled back and his seething voice was filled with menace, but his snarl was directed as much at his own impotence as Craigan's statement. "You have only faced down one of the beasts and the only reason you killed her was down to luck." He leant in to the Venicone and his whisper was as cold as a winter's gale. "You have not seen what the nightwalkers are capable of when the pack hunts. The stench of fear goes before them and the reek of death fills their wake. They are an implacable force of nature, cunning, nigh on impossible to stop and lethal to those who stand in their way."

To the wulver's surprise, Craigan stood his ground in the face of his fury. Whereas before, when Taiga had become enraged, the young clansman had shrunk back and mumbled apologies, this time he merely stared the wulver down unblinkingly, "Your point being what exactly, Taiga? I am still here, am I not? We are making progress, are we not?"

They both stood facing each other with venomous sneers locked on their faces, struggling to contain tempers enlarged by hurtful words and unjust insults.

"I take it you are still debating which path we should choose?" Lorcan asked as he joined them, though there was a mirthful glint in his eye as he said it.

When they both ignored him, the monk stepped between them and the amusement in his eyes disappeared to be replaced by a steely calm. "I do not know what the issue is between you, but these Ulfhednar you seek to conquer will never be vanquished if you cannot resolve it here and now. Arguments left unresolved fester inside like poison until they can be contained no longer, resulting in the poison being put into words which, once spoken, can never be taken back."

"Very poetic," Craigan sneered, "Did your god tell you that or did you make it up all by yourself?"

"Dammit, boy, hold your tongue," Taiga shouted.

Lorcan thrust both his hands out, the move taking both antagonists by surprise and knocking each to the ground. "Enough!" he thundered. "What is the matter with the two of you?" He stared from Taiga's shocked expression to Craigan's face of murderous intent. The Venicone leapt up and advanced on the monk who, in much the same way as Craigan had done moments before, stood his ground defiantly.

"And what good will it do if you strike me, clansman? Will it make you feel better? Will it aid us in our search?" the monk asked placidly, his eyes never straying from the youngster's face.

Craigan drew his fist back but, at the last, dropped it to his side before stalking away from the two of them.

"I apologise for my companion's behaviour," Taiga began to say before Lorcan cut across him.

"Whilst I appreciate your concern, I am perfectly capable of defending myself, both verbally and physically, so perhaps it would cause less friction if you were to allow events to take their course." The monk sighed. "Especially as I suspect that it is my presence which is causing the problem."

Taiga looked like he was about to bridle at the unexpected chiding but instead, nodded in agreement. "I am afraid he thinks you are trying to inveigle us into worshipping your god."

Brother Lorcan blinked in astonishment. "I assure you that is not and never will be my intention whilst we travel together," he responded hotly.

Taiga held up his hirsute hands placatingly, "I realise that but Craigan is adamant."

The monk from Mull placed his hands within his capacious sleeves and turned to go to Craigan, who was standing in the distance staring at a swirl of white cloud which seemed to cling to the distant summit of the mountain. He was stopped by Taiga's restraining fingers upon his arm.

"I would leave him to his own counsel for a while," the wulver suggested.

A look of irritation flickered briefly on Lorcan's face before he continued on his way across the irregular terrain to where Craigan skulked.

The Venicone turned as he heard the monk's footfalls but quickly resumed his scrutiny of Ben Molyneaux when he saw who it was that approached him.

Lorcan took up station next to him and they both stood in uncomfortable silence for a long moment. "Impressive, is it not?" he murmured. When this elicited no response, he walked in front of Craigan, forcing him to acknowledge his presence. "I understand you believe I am trying to convince you to follow my faith." He said simply, deciding to get the issue out into the open.

The tribesman's eyes roamed the monk's face but he remained silent.

The monk sighed hugely and his composure crumbled, "Padraig has warned me of this before. This is why I was picked as your guide. He felt I had become too insular, too married to life within the monastery. He wanted me to have contact with those who do not know of the glories of God and the wonders of the monastic life."

Craigan's face wrinkled in disgust, "You see, all the time you talk of the glories of God and the wonders of life at the monastery. You never stop. It is all you talk of. It makes you sound like the life you have chosen to live is far greater than any other. You have no concept of what it is like to work the land in all weathers, scraping through the winter with an all but empty stomach, knowing that you will face starvation if the rains come at the wrong time of year." The youngster was almost shaking with anger as the words spewed from his mouth.

Brother Lorcan hung his head, "No, you are right, I do not," he whispered hoarsely. "Although," and here he looked Craigan straight in the eye, "I would be more than happy to listen to you if you wish to tell me of it."

Craigan's mouth hung open. He had been expecting Lorcan to bristle at his criticism but, as he locked gazes with the monk, he saw nothing but honesty and openness. The monk's reaction threw him completely off-guard and he found an unexpected sympathy welling within him for the distraught man.

"I promise you, Craigan," Lorcan continued, "the uppermost priority in my mind is to aid you in finding Monkshood. If you are lucky enough to come to the faith, then we of the Order will welcome you with open arms, but all whom we have taken under our wing, have done so of their own free will. We would be hypocrites if we used coercion or trickery to gain worshippers to our religion. The reason I speak in such glowing terms of the monks at Caisteal Uisgean is because I have found a great sense of inner peace there and, for people such as yourself and Taiga, who have experienced such horror and hardship, I feel sure that such a feeling of placidity and purity of life would be wonderfully beneficial to you both," Craigan began to protest, but Lorcan cut him off, "however, as I said, I would never, in all good conscience, try to push that point of view upon you. Padraig would have my guts for garters if he thought I had done so. No, Craigan, you have misread my words and intentions."

"If I might get a word in," Craigan said quickly with a half-smile on his face, "I feel I also probably owe you an apology for my conduct. I had no reason to doubt your motives and, as Taiga pointed out, your order has fed and clothed us and put a roof over our heads without asking for any sort of recompense." They clasped forearms in the manner of the warrior's handshake, although the monk looked uncomfortable as he did so. "Let us wipe the slate clean, Brother Lorcan. It is a bright sunny day which should not be clouded by black moods and dismal faces." Craigan exclaimed.

With a genuinely warm smile, Lorcan nodded agreement at the sentiment, "Well said."

They both turned as Taiga approached across the mossy ground. He had been standing back from the pair, waiting to see what transpired but, when Craigan had instigated the handshake, he had assumed that whatever problems he had with the holy man had been resolved.

By this time the sun had reached its zenith and they chose to take advantage of it, managing to find a surprisingly dry patch of grass. They ate a simple lunch of assorted fruit and berries and talked of nothing very much.

After a while, Craigan noted that the wisps of white cloud which had dappled the deep-blue sky were beginning to merge and darken.

By unspoken agreement, the three of them packed up quickly and struck out immediately for the slopes of Ben Molyneaux. After a short discussion, they decided to attempt the shorter route, hoping they might pick up some of the time which they had lost because of the storm that had hit the island before they set off from Caisteal Uisgean.

As on the previous day, the rain started to fall just as they were about to begin their ascent of the peak. However, it was not much more than a light drizzle and did not delay them significantly. The disappearance of the sunshine did seem to bring back the oppressive mood of the previous day though, despite Craigan and Lorcan's reconciliation.

The monk's observation, that the track might prove difficult to negotiate, was borne out after they had climbed roughly halfway around it. Craigan lost his footing on an uneven pile of rocks which he was climbing. With a yelp of surprise, he found himself tumbling back down the slope and knocking Lorcan off his feet. Taiga would also have been up-ended but demonstrated reflexes which bordered on cat-like.

In an instant he was by the side of the fallen men, examining them for injury. Lorcan got to his feet almost immediately but the Venicone had been less lucky. He had fallen heavily on his right ankle and when he tried to regain his feet, his leg crumpled beneath him. "Damn!" the youngster spat.

Taiga held the abused joint, noting that it had already begun to discolour slightly, as Lorcan tapped him on the shoulder. "I seem to remember there is a small grotto slightly higher up the mountain quite close to here. I shall go and look for it while you tend to him."

With a terse nod, the wulver dismissed the monk and returned his scrutiny to the injury.

"How does it look, because it hurts like a bitch?" Craigan hissed.

"There is a bruise coming out already but, whether that is a good thing or not, I do not know."

With a wince, the clansman slowly rotated the joint, gritting his teeth against the pain.

"Can you walk on it at all? I saw you collapse when you tried before but that might just have been the initial pain?" Taiga said levelly, though he was trying to keep his temper in check. Lorcan had warned Craigan of the treacherous going underfoot, but the adolescent tribesman had still scurried up the slope with careless abandon.

"I don't know," Craigan forced himself to his feet and put his arm around the wulver's powerful shoulders but, as soon as he put weight on it, the joint gave out once more, forcing him to rely on Taiga completely.

"Damn it but you're an idiot, boy." Taiga fumed as he took the clansman's weight and they began making their way further along the path at a snail's pace. "Lorcan warned you of the terrain, yet you scampered off like a startled rabbit."

"Look on the bright side, Taiga. Perhaps you will get to carry me like God did with the man on the beach," Craigan smiled in embarrassment.

"Or perhaps I will drop you on your arse and leave you to freeze on the hillside," Taiga snapped back, though he delivered the rebuke with the beginnings of a smirk playing on his lips.

They reached some ground which was slightly flatter and Craigan found he could support himself quite well if he was not required to put too much pressure on his ankle.

Lorcan's head appeared from a fissure in the rock which jutted out as they rounded the next curve. "Not broken then?" He smiled at the pair as he ushered them into the hollow in the rock. It did not retreat more than ten feet into the face of the mountain but, luckily for the travellers, the wind was blowing across the entrance rather than into it so, though it was not deep, it did provide them with somewhere dry to rest.

Taiga turned to Brother Lorcan, "Is it worth continuing today or should we bide here until the dawn to give our wounded warrior a chance to recuperate for a while?"

The monk looked back at Craigan who shrugged. With a considered look on his face, the Christian pursed his lips, "I think it probably for the best if we remain here. I have something in my pack which may help but, if it is to work, he will need to rest."

Taiga fixed Craigan with a withering look, "You had better be on your feet and dancing by tomorrow, laddie, or we will leave you here, go to the monks of Iona, find out what we need to and pick you up on the way back."

"I am sure it will be fine come the morning," Craigan replied with a confidence he did not feel. Inwardly he cursed his own stupidity, whilst hoping against hope that the damage to his ankle would not prove too extensive.

He watched as Lorcan returned to the cave with a soaking wet piece of cloth which he wrapped around Craigan's bare leg, though not so tightly that it felt restrictive. As he pillowed a spare robe under the youngster's leg, he waggled an admonitory finger. "You must keep your ankle raised as much as you can, as it seems to aid the healing process."

With his wound now bandaged, Craigan lay back and sighed as Taiga and Lorcan prepared the campfire.

The young Venicone tribesman stood in the mouth of the cave, his ankle seemingly fully repaired, for it bore his weight with no discomfort. He stared across the argent landscape, marvelling at the silent beauty of the scene. The moonlight glistened off the surface of one of the lochs which described an irregular circle around the base of Ben Molyneaux and Craigan found his breath quickening at the sheer perfection of the view.

Though the night still had the world firmly within its grip, Craigan found he could not contain his delight at the view and turned excitedly to wake Taiga and Lorcan so they might share the moment with him.

Inexplicably, his companions were nowhere to be seen and neither was there any trace of them to indicate where they may have gone. He turned back to the silver panorama with an unsettling shiver running through him. His nervous tongue darted across suddenly dry lips as a spine-freezing howl tore through the breathless silence. His eyes swept the vista from left to right, urgently seeking out the source of the terrifying call.

The breath stuck in his throat as languid black shadows seemed to ooze from the shining surface of the water. Terror focussed his mind and he counted twenty indistinct figures arrowing towards his precarious eyrie. Some moved like animals, whilst others walked upright, but all were moving with unerring accuracy towards the cave. Cold sweat drenched him and he found his legs would not move, so petrified was he by the approaching creatures.

In all too brief a time, the wolves gained the scree at the bottom of Ben Molyneaux but the change in terrain did not stay them at all. On they came and now Craigan could hear the snuffling of muzzles and the shifting of loose rock as both human and wolf drew nearer.

Craigan blinked and suddenly found he had inexplicably retreated from the precipice and now had his back pressed against the cold stone of the rock-face as shapes began to appear over the lip of the slope.

With the moonlight increasing in intensity, he was now able to make out individual features and it was a sight which would haunt him for the rest of his days. He wanted to lift his hands to cover his eyes but his arms felt like two lumps of immovable stone.

Though he would have done anything to be spared the torture of what he beheld, he found himself forced to stare at faces from his past. Faces which he thought he would never see again, save for when his memory chose to conjure up times of nostalgia and happiness. Now though, he knew with a dread certainty, that those reminiscences would be tainted forever.

The first creature to lope into the cave was a lithe wolf which padded to within inches of him before dropping to its haunches and studying him as a cat would study a small animal. However, he instantly forgot that beast as he beheld the next member of the parade of monsters with a look of absolute horror on his face.

Dana MacKendrick stood before him, naked and seductive. Her long brown hair had fallen across her breasts but, with a proud swish of her shoulders she exposed them to Craigan, licking her lips and beckoning the young man to her. He knew that the feelings which roared through him were wrong, but the ache he felt was so compulsive, it nearly brought him to his knees. He could not stop his eyes roaming each exquisite curve of her, though part of him felt horrified at regarding her in such a way. The passion died as his wandering gaze alighted upon her eyes, for Craigan found his skin crawling at the deadness which stared back at him. Shaking his head as if to try and clear away the last vestiges of lust, he returned his gaze to the others who had entered the cave whilst he had been leering at Dana's body.

With sick revulsion, he found himself looking at the twisted soulless faces of Jameson the Seer, Duncan MacKendrick and even the angelic Ffiona MacKintosh. The wolves and humans began to close in and, just as Craigan tensed himself for the agony of the claws puncturing and slicing his flesh, he saw Taiga and Lorcan, their expressions distorted by hatred like the others and he screamed and screamed and screamed.

"Craigan!" Taiga shook the clansman by his shoulders.

The young man threw a fist at the wulver, knocking him to the unyielding floor of the cave, "Get off me!" Craigan shrieked, coming fully awake and pushing himself backwards with his heels. Stars exploded before his eyes as his head cracked against the wall of the cave but, despite the pain, he realised he had been dreaming and he thrust an apologetic hand towards Taiga just as the wulver gained his feet with murder in his eyes. "I..." he winced as a fresh wave of pain rippled across his skull, "I am sorry, Taiga. It was a dream, well, a nightmare really and as I came awake, you were leaning over me. It was just an instinctive reaction. I'm sorry." He repeated.

The wulver gingerly rolled his jaw as he quelled the anger that he felt at being struck.

Craigan blinked furiously as his vision ebbed and weaved erratically. He looked at the blurred form of Taiga as he stalked over to the fire and jammed a stick into it with unnecessary force, sending a couple of sparks tumbling upwards into a sky which was just beginning to emerge from the blackness of a cloudy winter's night. His guttural voice drifted across to Craigan, "I suspected as much. You were moaning and writhing around in your sleep and the sweat was streaming off you." He paused before walking back over to the prostrate tribesman. "I will understand if you do not wish to tell me but might I ask what you saw in your nightmare?" he continued after a deep breath, "And who is Dana? Was she the chieftain's daughter you mentioned when we first met the McLeishs?"

Craigan's head whipped round, despite the agony that accompanied such a quick movement.

"You cried out the name as you dreamed." Taiga explained, keeping to himself the overwhelming anguish which had been present in Craigan's voice.

The Venicone looked past the wulver's shoulder at the flickering flames and began to speak in a dull monotone that somehow provided a poignant counterpoint to the rawness of the scene he described. "She was the eldest daughter of Duncan McKendrick, the chief of my tribe. She was a wonder to behold and a joy to know. She was the kind of person who makes you feel good about yourself, just by being near her." The beginnings of a smile had started to emerge as Craigan talked, but it melted away like the morning dew on a hot summer's morning. "She died at Dun Eiledon." He tried to continue, but remained silent for a moment.

"You loved her?" Taiga hesitantly asked, inwardly cursing himself for making Craigan revisit painful memories.

The youngster laughed, though it was a bitter sound, "I did, aye. We all did in our way. She was impossible not to love."

The wulver smiled indulgently. He personally doubted that Dana held all the Venicones under such an all-consuming spell, but he did not for a second begrudge Craigan his memories of the poor girl, "Did she love you?" he asked.

"I do not even know if she knew I existed, much less harboured any sort of feelings for me. It would not have bothered me if she had loved my worst enemy as long as she was happy." His gaze shot from the flames to study Taiga's face, "You probably think me pathetic."

The wulver raised his eyebrows in surprise. "Why would I think that, lad? I would never mock such a sentiment. I would think you weak and selfish were you to put your own happiness above all others, but your words speak volumes about your character." His voice tailed off to a whisper. "I was lucky enough to experience a love such as the one you describe."

Craigan did not know what to say. It was obvious it would cause his friend pain to speak of it and he did not wish to do that, so he held his peace, once again feeling an overpowering sense of camaraderie at how his life seemed to mirror Taiga's.

As it was, the wulver continued to talk in a similarly flat manner, "We wulvers mate for life, you see. My mate, ah Craigan, she was amazing." Taiga breathed as he closed his eyes, conjuring up a picture of his beloved in his mind, "My Anitra was everything to me. She was so graceful and beautiful and had an irresistible magnetism about her. Wherever she walked, all eyes followed. All of the clan males would have been privileged to welcome her into their lives but she chose me." As he opened his eyes and looked at Craigan, his voice took on a joyous quality and a light seemed to shine from within him, "She chose me. Of all the ones she could have chosen, she chose me and that made me walk ten feet tall every day. She gave me two sons and a daughter. My little pride and joys. Dughall, Raibert and little Mhairi." He sighed with an almost physical pain and turned away from the tribesman, lapsing into a silence which Craigan had no desire to fill. After a moment, he spoke in a voice so quiet that the young Venicone struggled to hear it, "They perished when the Ulfhednar tore through the island. I see their faces every time I go to sleep."

Craigan's stomach turned at the grief in Taiga's voice and he found his eyes filling with tears in concert with the wulver's. He stood up gingerly as he still felt slightly dizzy, tested his ankle and was gratified to find that Lorcan's dressing seemed to support it well enough. He walked over to Taiga's side and placed a hand upon his companion's shoulder. "Though I was never fortunate enough to have what you had with your family, I expect you have found yourself wondering why you were the one who was spared in the midst of such carnage and at the expense of all others. I know I have. It is a question I have mulled over every day since I left Dun Eiledon," he laughed softly. "I even asked Jameson that same question just before he died." Suddenly, he spun Taiga round and fixed him with a ferocious look. "We survived so that we could bring about an end to the werewolves and their evil reign. That is our purpose, Taiga. It has to be. We *have* to see this through, my friend. For Dana, for Anitra and your little ones and for all those who have fallen before the Ulfhednar."

Taiga looked at him for a long moment, his expression unreadable. At length, he nodded and walked away from the firelight to stand on the lip of the slope, an unmoving silhouette outlined against the lightening horizon.

Craigan was about to go and stand with him when he heard a yawn from Lorcan's direction. The monk was resting on his elbows and looking at the statuesque wulver. "Fine words, Craigan. For one of such tender years, you speak with a deep understanding of life and all that goes with it."

The Venicone found the remark slightly patronising but, after the talk which the two had conducted on the previous day, he knew it was unintentional. "To be told that by someone who must be all of five years older than me is a great compliment," he replied playfully.

"I meant that, having heard the elder members of the Order preaching to the faithful, your words fired my blood in much the same way as well as providing comfort." Lorcan chuckled.

Craigan nodded at the compliment then joined the holy man in his scrutiny of Taiga. "He has been a tower of strength since we met. He has saved my life twice and provided more than his own fair share of reassurance whilst we have been travelling. It is only right and proper that the favour is returned."

The Venicone prodded halfheartedly at the fire with a stick "I think he also feels he has some sort of responsibility towards keeping me safe. He is much older so perhaps he thinks he should not show any sort of weakness in front of me." Craigan shook his head and threw the stick over the precipice with an angry look on his face. "When we argued, before you split us up, he said to me that there were many more humans who still lived but, for all he knows he could be the last one of his kind in all the world. Can you imagine how frightening that must be?" Craigan looked once more at the wulver's immobile figure. "It is a wonder he manages to string two words together, let alone give counsel to others."

"It certainly is," Lorcan breathed. He sat up quickly and stared intently at the young tribesman. "Tell me something of these Ulfhednar," he asked urgently. "Taiga spoke of them as we trekked across the island but I would be interested to find out how you view them."

Craigan looked surprised, "I am sure Taiga told you everything that he knew. He certainly knows more about the hideous creatures than I do."

For only the second time since they had met, Lorcan's façade of cool superiority slipped and he looked decidedly uncomfortable. "Yes, but I was hoping for a more…human view of the monsters."

267

Craigan's eyes hardened at the implication, "Do you not trust him?" he spluttered incredulously.

"Do not misunderstand me," Lorcan pleaded. "You would not believe how much I have enjoyed the cut and thrust of our debates during the journey, it is just that I found it strange to be talking of such things to one who is, well, one who is so wolf-like." The monk looked so miserable that Craigan found his anger waning. "For all my talk of God and how much my faith comforts me, I am ashamed to say that, when Taiga spoke of the Ulfhednar, my blood ran cold at the thought of facing such beasts." He continued slowly as if he had to force the words from his mouth. "I do not know if I am strong enough to confront these creatures should we come across them."

"You will not know that until they are hunting you down and you feel their hot stinking breath upon your neck." Taiga rumbled.

Both Craigan and Lorcan jumped as the wulver's shadow fell across them. "The sky is lightening to the east." He said quietly. "We should make a start to our day's travelling before the weather changes."

"Are we set fine for another sunny start to the day?" Craigan asked lightly.

Without turning, Taiga muttered, "Does it matter? We have seen snow or rain every day for months or so it seems. Why should today be any different?"

On that pessimistic note, the two men gathered their belongings together and set off after the wulver as he disappeared from view around the curve of the rocky path.

Chapter 11

Galahad looked at the studded wooden door with a huge sense of trepidation flooding through him. He took a second to reflect on how often he had walked through this particular threshold without any sort of emotion at all, apart from anticipation as to what new knowledge he would discover on his visit.

Wiping sweating hands down his dull brown robe, he pushed open the library door and peered around the pitted wood, "Brother Neville?" he called out nervously.

As there was no reply, he edged past the door and shut it behind him. The recognizable smells of parchment and leather hit him immediately and he sucked in a deep breath, chiding himself for such an extreme reaction, but also trying to mentally prepare himself should the memory of his encounter with the psalter rear its unwelcome head. To his surprise, he saw the bent back of the aged librarian in its accustomed pose, leaning intently over the haphazard piles of parchment upon his small desk, his face locked in a grimace of concentration as he threaded some twine into the eye of a wickedly sharp-looking needle. He waited until the old man had finished the fastidious task then cleared his throat loudly to announce his presence.

Neville looked up quickly and smiled when he saw who it was, "Ah, my dear boy, it is good to see you back within these walls. Quite an accumulation has piled up since you have absented yourself from here."

Galahad breathed a little easier after the warm welcome Neville had given him. He had been worried that his relationship with the ancient monk would suffer after what had occurred the last time he had been in Neville's domain but, on the evidence of the monk's behaviour towards him, his fears were unfounded. The holy man regarded Galahad's constantly moving eyes and nervous demeanour and nodded solemnly. "Do not fret, Galahad. It has been removed from here."

The former knight rolled his eyes and sighed in relief. Though he had been buoyed by the knowledge that he had not succumbed to the psalter's purported spell in the same calamitous way as the others who had been affected by it, he was still wary that there might be some sort of after-effects which had not yet made themselves apparent.

"I suspect you need not have worried anyway," Neville said knowingly. "I bore witness to the other five unfortunates whom the book intoxicated. They all became madmen, delirious and altered beyond recognition. You did not." Neville shrugged, echoing Columba's theory. "You must be possessed of a stronger constitution than them." He laid a hand on his erstwhile assistant's shoulder warmly. "Let us consign that episode to the past."

269

Galahad nodded in agreement and moved his gaze to the untidy stack of vellum on Neville's work desk. "Would you like some help with your backlog?" he asked.

With the awkward moment negotiated, the former champion of King Arthur threw himself into whatever tasks Neville asked of him, finding a pleasant comfort in the mundanity of routine. Such was his enthusiasm at returning to work in the library, several candles, which illuminated the cramped room, had burned down to half-size before he was forced to stop by his aching joints and throbbing eyes. He straightened up, ignoring the protest which spread across his lower back from being sat in the same position for hours on end, and blinked in the dim light.

Just at that moment, Brother Neville returned from his evening meal, blinking in shock to find his helper still hard at work. "I thought you were going to join me in the refectory when you had finished?" he asked with an amused look on his face.

Smiling sheepishly, Galahad stretched expansively and yawned, "I did mean to come and get a bite to eat but I became engrossed in St Finnian's journal. I found it revealing that he spoke of his teachers, Saint Teilo and Hywel, in the same glowing terms as you did of him."

Neville acknowledged the observation, "Aye, he was obviously as great a student as he was a teacher, for he preached the word of God as if he was born to it. If the saints of Wales actually taught him that, then they must have been remarkable men indeed."

Now Galahad had ceased concentrating on the complicated calligraphy of the vellum manuscripts, a great wave of tiredness washed over him and the thoughts of food, which had been conjured by Neville's reappearance from the dining hall, were forgotten. He excused himself from the library, intent on nothing more than retiring to the dormitory and falling asleep upon his bunk.

After a couple of minutes walk, Galahad found himself at the threshold of his sleeping quarters. He was about to enter when he heard raised voices from within. Fighting off another tide of fatigue, he opened the door, fervently praying that the disturbance, whatever it was, would be dealt with as soon as possible so he could retire to his bed.

Brother Nathan was sat upon the edge of one of the bunks, pinning his brother down, concern obvious upon his face as Brother Walter hovered nearby. On the bunk, the thrashing form of Brother Joseph could be seen, straining against his bigger sibling's iron grip, his face contorting obscenely as he snarled curses in an unfamiliar guttural voice. Walter looked up at Galahad as he entered and, with a distressed glance at Nathan, ushered the former knight back into the corridor.

The young monk was clearly upset, though his voice remained level. "He has been like this for the last fifteen minutes or so, convulsing and fitting. Normally, Nathan is able to comfort him until he emerges from the dreamstate but he has been trying since the vision started and the madness shows no sign of abating." Walter wrung his hands and spoke in a voice halfway between a sob and a wail. "This is the worst I have ever seen him."

In the months since Galahad had been at the monastery, he had only ever been present when Brother Joseph had been in a mild delirium, so the hideous expression of insanity upon the normally cherubic face of the youthful monk had been a huge shock. "Does Nathan require any help? Is there anything we can do?"

Walter shrugged helplessly, "I do not think so. Though we have all become friendly with Nathan and Joseph, he has told us before that, when these episodes occur, the best thing is for us all to allow him to minister to his younger brother and keep our distance."

Suddenly the shrieking howls increased in volume and the crash of furniture was heard, ending with the door slamming into its frame. Both Galahad and Walter brought their strength to bear against the wood and managed to move it slightly. As they did so, through the crack in the door, they saw a large hand flop to the floor. This caused them to redouble their efforts and beads of sweat broke out on both their foreheads. Through gritted teeth, as the door edged further into the room, Galahad hissed "Nathan must be lying against it."

They were about to resume their labour when the sound of Joseph's psychotic outburst suddenly stopped. The two room-mates shared uneasy glances, for the silence had an expectant quality, like the pocket of peace which is found in the eye of a hurricane.

They both watched in horror as Nathan's arm was dragged out of view and the door creaked open. To his unspoken relief, Galahad found his battle instincts had not been dulled by the tranquillity of his monastic life as, without thought, he pushed Walter behind him and stalked cat-like into the room.

Nathan was lying unconscious in a pool of blood which oozed gradually across the stone floor. It was pouring from his face, some from his ruined nose which had been broken with brutal force, and the rest from his lips which looked as if they had been shredded against his teeth. One of his arms appeared to have been wrenched completely out of the shoulder socket and hung uselessly at his side.

Walter was at his side immediately, his caring nature completely disregarding the danger he had put himself in by breaking away so suddenly from Galahad's guard. As it was, when Galahad scanned the rest of the

271

room, Joseph seemed to be sleeping peacefully upon his bed, the only indication of anything untoward having happened being a reddening of his knuckles and the dishevelled, blood-spotted bedding upon which he lay.

Walter finished examining his patient and leapt to his feet, "I must get Columba and Adomain," he said and, without waiting for a response, fled from the room. As Galahad heard his sandals slapping down the corridor, he regarded the huge bear of a man upon the floor before turning back to the slim, unhealthy looking figure upon the bed. The stick-thin Joseph did not look capable of pushing his elder brother an inch, let alone sending him hurtling across the room like a rag doll, yet Galahad surmised that was what had occurred. He was pondering this when a sibilant voice intruded upon his ears, chilling him with its eerie tone.

He turned just in time to catch the figure of Joseph erupt to his feet in one smooth motion from his prostrate position on the bed. Though he was vertical, his body was limp as if it was hanging from his head. The young man's eyes were rolled up inside his head and his mouth was open and unmoving, yet still the words rolled out,

"Fylliz fiǫrvi feigra manna, rýðr ragna siǫt, rauðom dreyra. Svǫrt verða sólskin of sumor eptir, veðr ǫll válynd Vitoð ér enn, eða hvat?" the voice spat.

The inflection at the end of the sentence clearly indicated a question, but Galahad did not recognise the language and could only look on helplessly. There was no change in the pitch as the voice continued to speak though, so Galahad did not know if his lack of response was noticed or not.

"Brœðr muno beriaz ok at bǫnom verðaz muno systrungar sifiom spilla. Hart er í heimi, hórdómr mikill —skeggǫld, skálmǫld —skildir ro klofnir— vindǫld, vargǫld— áðr verǫld steypiz. Mun engi maðr ǫðrom þyrma."

The former knight of Camelot took a tentative step towards the being, putting himself between it and Brother Nathan and amazing himself by keeping his voice so calm, "I do not know what you are saying, Joseph."

"Ragnarok" muttered the young monk repeatedly in the unsettling voice, *"Ragnarok, Ragnarok."*

With a sigh that seemed to shudder through the length of his body, he crumpled to the bed, bouncing upon the pillows and blankets and ending up on the floor in a catatonic state.

Galahad hesitated for a few seconds before rushing to the fallen youngster's side, satisfied that the collapse had been genuine and not a ruse to tempt him within range of attack.

Though he was unconscious, Galahad lifted him onto the bed. He then gingerly pulled back Joseph's eyelids, sighing in relief as he saw a sky-blue iris upon the eyeball. As he closed the monk's eyes, Joseph jolted awake, thinking it was his brother leaning over him and staring in confusion at the unexpected face. "Nathan?" he asked plaintively in a feeble whisper.

Galahad chewed upon his lip as he delayed his answer. He knew Brother Joseph's mental state was delicate at the best of times and was unsure if the psychosis would return if he told him that he had gravely injured his brother.

As it was, the decision was taken away from him because Joseph looked down the bed and beheld the wounded monk upon the floor. "No!" he whined agonisingly. "Nathan! Nathan!" he cried, as Galahad, in a move which surprised him as much as the distraught monk, leant over and held Joseph close, rocking back and forth with him as his distress lessened. "He will be fine, Joseph. Walter has gone to get Columba and Adomain, they will see him aright."

"Did I do that?" Joseph asked in a shaking voice, still staring fearfully at his older sibling.

Galahad let go of the boy, releasing his hold to allow him to slump back on the pillows. "You did, yes, but you were not yourself. There is no blame to attach, you had no control over your actions."

Joseph seemed to accept the answer, transferring his gaze to Galahad, causing the knight to shift uncomfortably under the intense scrutiny.

"You were there," Joseph said quietly.

Galahad blinked, "Where?" he asked.

"In my vision. Were you ever a knight?"

The question took the former champion of Camelot off guard and his eyes hooded. "Yes, I was," he replied, wondering where the conversation would lead.

"I saw you, standing with your sword upraised, the red cross upon your white blazon glowing as if it was on fire, in the midst of a field of blue and purple flowers." His face became peaceful as he spoke of it. "There was a gentle breeze which continually caressed the blooms, causing the petals to part company with their stalks and surround you in a whirling cascade of constantly moving colour."

The knight's brow furrowed as he wondered at the significance of his appearance in Joseph's dream. He was not especially surprised by Joseph seeing him clad as a knight, as he had not kept his past a secret, but what had disturbed him was the fact that Joseph had described the colours of his tabard correctly, even down to the design.

At that moment, Adomain and Columba returned in the company of Walter so he did not have the opportunity to question the young monk further. The

273

two senior members of the monastery immediately began examining Brother Nathan as Walter sidled over to Galahad, all the while bestowing sidelong glances on the now becalmed Joseph.

"The seizure is passed, Walter," Joseph murmured weakly. "You need not be afraid."

"I am not," Walter blustered hollowly.

Joseph propped himself up on his elbows and stared numbly at his brother's broken body. "Will he be alright?" he asked Columba, who had straightened up and stalked over to the bed.

"I do not know in all honesty. He has taken a fearsome blow to the head and injuries of that type are always difficult to predict."

Joseph's bottom lip quivered and tears started in his eyes. "Why am I cursed with this affliction?" he wailed to the chief monk.

Columba held the young man's pitiable gaze for a few seconds before saying, "It is the way of things, Joseph. We are all special in our own way. It would be a hugely tedious world if God made us identical. I accept that, on this occasion, what has happened as a result of your fit is horrendous and dreadful, but think of the other occasions where your dreams have provided people with great comfort." He sat on the edge of the bed and laid a comforting hand upon Joseph's shoulder. "Do you remember when, in your dreams, you walked with Brother William as he lay in the infirmary suffering with fever, hovering on the cusp of death? He told me of it when he was well again. He said it was truly miraculous. He credited you with his recovery."

By this time, Adomain had come over to the bedside, "I have sent for a stretcher to bear Nathan to the hospital. His breathing seems steady and his pallor is good. Once he wakes up, we will know more of how he fares." He smiled at Joseph, hoping that his assessment would provide some sort of reassurance to the youthful postulant. "Columba is right," he said seriously. "You must not look upon your visions as an affliction any more than you should look upon them as a gift. They are simply part of what makes you the person you are."

"Normal people do not nearly kill their brothers," Joseph moaned.

"Neither do they comfort comatose people and bring them back to life," Columba countered.

Though it was clear the senior monk's answers did not satisfy Joseph, he subsided into silence as two other monks entered the room. The quintet watched as they lifted the bulky man onto the stretcher and carried him through the door. Adomain followed them out of the room as Columba turned to Joseph, "How are you feeling? Do you think a visit to the hospital would benefit you?"

The young man nodded, "I would like to be beside Nathan when he wakes and explain my actions," he said, hanging his head.

Columba smiled warmly, "I know your brother and he loves you to the ends of the earth. Though I am sure it will help you to offload your emotions, I do not think you will need to apologise to him."

Joseph stood up and Columba offered him his arm, for he swayed alarmingly. "We will see," he sniffed miserably, accompanying the elder monk from the room.

"Columba," Galahad said as the pair were about to leave. "Might I speak with you tomorrow? I would ask for your audience tonight but I am all but dead on my feet."

The founder of the Order nodded, "Of course," he said curtly and with that, they were gone.

Walter and Galahad looked around the wrecked dormitory and began straightening the disrupted furniture. Although Nathan had been thrown right across the room by his brother, due to the sparse nature of the fixtures and fittings, there was not much to rearrange and it was the work of but a few minutes to get the room straight again.

Galahad slumped down upon his bed as did Walter upon his. The former knight thought his exhaustion would see him asleep in seconds but the younger man was snoring very quickly. Rest would still not come to the unsettled Galahad and, while he lay upon his bed, the other room-mates all returned to the dormitory and were in their slumbers before him.

He lay there in the darkness, staring blindly at the ceiling, endlessly replaying Joseph's description in his head. For a reason that he could not put his finger on, he found his appearance in the midst of the young man's vision deeply disturbing, especially as it had led to such violence. Fervently hoping that Columba's words would provide as much succour to him as they had done previously when he had fallen prey to the psalter's curse, he turned upon his side, pummelled at his pillows and tried to fall asleep.

"Galahad."

The knight sat bolt upright, even though the voice which had roused him was no more than a gentle whisper. He blinked disorientatedly as he focussed on Brother Adomain's grave face. "I am sorry to wake you. Neville told me how long you had been at work in the library yesterday but you need to come and see Columba as a matter of urgency."

Galahad heaved himself off the bed and retrieved his robes from the heap on the floor. Adomain had left him to attend Columba's office saying he would meet him there. As he walked down the corridors to his appointment, the former knight was visited by the same apprehension he had felt when the

275

elderly monk had escorted him to Columba before. He tried to assemble the questions which had been rebounding around his head after learning of Joseph's vision but he found that lack of sleep was robbing his thoughts of any coherence. He was so lost in thought he nearly walked past the entrance to the head monk's antechamber.

The sound of his name being called jerked him into reality. Adomain emerged from the room to his left and beckoned him in urgently. Without further words, he led him into Columba's office.

The founder of the Order on Iona was sat poring over documents on his desk with Brother Neville, but he lost all interest in them when he saw Galahad enter with his deputy.

"Sit down, Galahad," Columba said without preamble. "Am I the only one who has noticed that I only seem to speak to you when there is a stressful situation occurring?" he said with an amused smirk on his face.

Galahad did not share the humour and frowned, "What do you want of me, Columba?" he asked, imitating the no-nonsense tone with which proceedings had started.

The three oldest monks of the Ionan order shared significant looks with one another before Columba spoke. "Whilst myself and Joseph sat vigil in the hospital at his brother's bedside, Joseph told me all of his vision that he could remember." Galahad started to speak, but Columba held up a quietening hand, "Including the part that involved you, yes. I presumed that was the reason you wanted to talk to me today which is why I pre-empted you by summoning you here. Anyway, this morning we had three visitors arrive at our door. Two travellers from the islands away to the west and one of our brothers from the monastery at Mull." In response to the confusion which planted itself upon Galahad's face, Columba continued, "They had a story to tell, that was for sure. As I have said, they had travelled hundreds of miles from the islands across the Hebridean Sea on a mission. The two travellers were seeking one by the name of Monkshood, to rid their lands of a pack of werewolves called the Ulfhednar."

At this, Galahad snorted derisively, "Werewolves?" he repeated. "They are the stuff of fairytales, surely?"

Brother Neville cleared his throat. "On the contrary, there are many documented instances of the phenomenon. The so-called 'Father of History', the Greek historian Herodotus, wrote in his *Histories* of a tribe called the Neuri, who were purported to transform into wolves. The esteemed Greek poet, Virgil, also wrote of such creatures. The Roman scribe Ovid wrote of men roaming the woods of Arcadia in the lycan form."

"You have fought demons as well, have you not, Galahad?" Adomain put in. "Do not dismiss something out of hand just because you have not witnessed it with your own eyes."

Columba leant forward, "Once I introduce you to them, your doubts will be dispelled anyway, for one of the travellers is a creature called a wulver?"

"Wulver?"

"A kind of werewolf which, before one appeared at the front gate this morning, was thought of only as a figure of folklore among the Picts." Neville explained. "We have many clansmen here, both residents and visitors and, when we asked them, those who had heard the name each described a wulver as a man, covered with short brown hair, but with a wolf's head."

The former knight of Camelot sat agape as Brother Neville took up the conversation, "Apparently, unlike most werewolves, they are a peaceable race if left undisturbed." He fixed Galahad with a fierce look. "For one of his kind to make himself known in such a blatant fashion suggests there may be some credence to their story."

Galahad held up his hands in surrender. "You are quite right and I apologise for doubting you. Aside from the werewolves, what does this wulver's tale have to do with me?"

Columba looked meaningfully at Adomain and Neville before continuing, "Did Joseph tell you everything he saw during his fit?" he asked.

"Only that he had seen me in my knightly garb surrounded by a field of flowers."

"He did not tell you that the flowers themselves were also surrounded?"

Galahad sighed irritably, "No, he did not. All he did was describe a peaceful, pastoral scene."

"He told me that the field was encircled by ravening wolves." The elder monk stated flatly. "Joseph said that the sight of you was enough to hold them at bay, aside from one who bulked larger than the others. This one approached you in his bestial guise then transformed into a massive warrior clad in wolfskin. Joseph then said this man spoke to you, though he did not understand the words."

Galahad nodded pensively, "Brother Joseph did spit out something spite-filled in my direction just before he came round. It was a vile, harsh tongue but, unfortunately, I did not understand it any more than Joseph did." He shrugged, "There was one word which he repeated, three times in fact, the last word before he awoke. Ragnarok, I think it was."

Brother Neville's eyes grew distant for a second then he shook his head. "It is not familiar to me." He looked at the others in the room who returned his gaze with blank expressions of their own. The old librarian shrugged, "It sounds Germanic or Scandinavian. I will see if I can find mention of it in any of the Old Norse texts which I have in the library."

Columba nodded curtly, "Anyway, in light of Joseph's vision of you confronting the beasts, and the fortuitous appearance of Brother Lorcan with his companions and their story, all within the space of hours, that leads me to an obvious conclusion."

Galahad's eyes narrowed, "Which would be?" he said challengingly.

"You are Monkshood. You are the one they seek."

The ex-knight stood up so quickly, his chair clattered onto the floor as the back of his legs upended it. "That is ridiculous. Of all in this room, I am the least likely to be this 'Monkshood'. I have never even worn the habit of a monk," he sneered incredulously.

"That is true, but..."

Galahad cut him off, stalking around the office, waving his arms angrily, "I misjudged you, Columba. I had thought the matter of the psalter was over and done with but it is obviously not, given this transparent attempt to remove me from the premises."

Columba's eyes hardened but his voice remained calm, "I am a man of my word, Galahad, as are all here. I have said that you would not be compelled to keep what I told you secret regarding Cul Dreimhne and indeed I understand you have divulged it those who share your sleeping quarters. Have I taken any action against you?"

Galahad remained silent, yet found he could not hold the monk's gaze.

"What I said just now was an honest opinion which, after discussion, is shared by Adomain and Neville." He looked at his two fellow monks, receiving a nod of confirmation from Neville but a more ambiguous expression from Adomain, which suggested to Galahad that perhaps the consensus had not been quite as clear-cut as Columba was implying. "You see, today is the day that marks six months since you set foot inside the monastery. Today is the day on which you would have been offered a place within our order." Columba's voice descended in volume yet seemed more powerful than ever. "Today is the day which you were to be asked if you wished to make the move from postulant to monk." He gestured to a neatly folded pile of garments on his desk. "These are your robes." Columba picked up the clothes and unfolded them, making a particular show of displaying the long hooded cowl that was the uniform of all who had taken their religious orders.

The former champion of The Round Table was at a complete loss as to how to respond. In truth, he was overwhelmed that Columba's order wished to accept him into their ranks, but immediately recognised that, if he were to take up the tunic, scapular and cowl, it would lend yet more weight to

Columba's theory that he was the sought-after Monkshood, in which case, he was sure he would be expected to leave the cloisters and face down the voracious Ulfhednar.

He was aware of all eyes upon him and that he had still not responded to the unasked question. "Might I take some time to ponder all this?" Galahad asked miserably. "Please do not think that I regard your offer as anything other than a great honour but what you have said has caught me completely off guard."

There was no overt reaction from Columba, for which Galahad was glad. He had no wish to offend the trio of monks whose compassion and understanding had been so instrumental in the happiness he had felt over the last six months, but something deep inside stopped him accepting the offer. The unnamed dread which had assailed him in the corridor returned with a vengeance and suddenly he felt the hand of destiny upon his shoulder, propelling him towards a future which he might not necessarily want but would nonetheless come to be, regardless of his efforts to make it otherwise.

"If I may retire?" he asked.

Columba nodded and Galahad left the room, his mind in turmoil.

The former knight spent the rest of the day aimlessly wandering the corridors and cloisters of the monastery. Whether it was a subconscious need for him to imprint the place upon his memory as he had found such happiness here, or just the urge to keep his body as busy as his mind whilst it feverishly worked at the choices before him, he did not know but, whichever it was, he found himself just as restless and unsettled when darkness began to descend as he had been when the sun had risen.

With little hope of a restful night, he lay upon his bunk, giving only the most perfunctory of greetings to his room-mates as they retired for the night.

Finally, in the early hours, sleep came to him but, as he had guessed, it was not a placid slumber and he found himself besieged by eerie dreams and disconcerting visions.

Snow falls as nerve-freezing howls destroy the silence of the night. He stares at the blizzard that advances towards him. His knightly attire sits upon him like a second skin and he draws warmth from it.

The thick flakes fizz as they hit the ground, yet they do not encroach into the circle that is described by the richly coloured flora which surrounds him.

He thinks he can make out shapes in the wildly blowing drifts of whiteness. Another howl sounds directly in front of him before reverberating strangely in the hostile northerly wind which whips around his legs, until he is no longer sure whether he faces a host of wolves or just one beast.

Whitecleave flies into his hands without him reaching for it and he steps forward to face his foe.

Jerking awake and bathed in sweat, Galahad stared into the blackness of the room, puffing heavily and trying to calm the rapid beat of his heart. Minutes later, he was asleep once more.

He is down on bended knee, head bowed and unmoving while a cacophony of violence rages overhead, underneath and all around him. With great effort, he forces his head up and finds his breath stolen by the awesome display of energies which rips the landscape in two.

A huge tree, bulking larger than the tallest peak rears before him and sheds leaves in great clumps.

The deep booming note of a gargantuan horn echoes through the firmament.

Waves higher than mountains erupt as a massive serpent's tail lashes into the ocean.

The savage howl of a gigantic dog raises the hairs on the back of his neck.

A ship manned by giants and forged from human nails crashes onto a tortured beach.

The tip of a flaming sword appears above the horizon, scorching the earth before it.

Massive beings do battle on the plain below and the ground quakes and heaves underfoot.

A hole appears in the midst of the melee, out of which a gust of superheated air wafts and an orange flame belches.

A muzzle appears, blood dripping from its maw and bones sticking out from between its teeth.

A sense of hopelessness overwhelms him as the titanic wolf bears down upon him.

He raises Whitecleave to protect himself.

Galahad's eyes burst open and he almost fell out of his bed, for the dream had left him utterly disorientated. He blinked furiously before focussing on the pink tinge of the dawn which was beginning to shine through the high windows upon the far wall.

The visions had been so vivid that the acid whiff of brimstone still filled his nostrils and the icy blast of breath from the wolf which had sprung from the pit, still chilled him to the marrow.

Returning his gaze to the rapidly lightening stone, he cursed the loss of another night's sleep, certain that he would not be able to return to his slumbers now that the sun was coming up.

He is down on bended knee once more but this time all is silent about him, save the mournful sough of a pleasantly warm wind which caresses him. He is praying to his

280

God and sighs deeply at the soothing feel of the breeze. His prayer finished, he begins to get up...except he cannot move. Uncertainty is rapidly replaced by an overbearing panic as every muscle of his body screams at him, demanding an explanation as to why he is still kneeling when he should be on his feet, enjoying the sun upon his face.

For how long he struggles, he does not know, but fatigue begins to envelop him even though he has not moved a muscle. His arms ache, though they do not move and his eyes feel heavy, though they do not blink. He feels the balmy embrace of sleep engulf him and all goes black.

Galahad awoke with a start, squinting in the brightness of a new day. He went to raise his arm across his eyes, because the sunshine was almost painful to behold for one who had woken so suddenly, but found it throbbing and tender. Had the exertions in his dream been real? He managed to lift his head momentarily and saw that his bedding was sweat-sodden and rumpled.

He was gradually becoming aware that his whole body was stiff and wearied and he slumped back onto the pillow.

Eventually, he heaved himself from the bed and half-staggered into the communal wash area where he doused himself with cold water in the hope of energising his exhausted body into some sort of normality.

Feeling slightly more human after the shock of the icy water, he walked purposefully down to the refectory to break his fast because he found he was absolutely famished. On reflection, as he ate a steaming bowl of porridge and nearly half a loaf of exquisitely baked bread, he realised that, what with working long into the evening at the library, then dealing with the aftermath of Joseph's attack on Nathan, and the meeting in Columba's office, he had had very little sleep and very little to eat over the last two days. He took the return of his appetite to be a signal that he had reached a decision regarding his acceptance into the order of monks on Iona.

After tidying his plate and cutlery away, he made straight for Columba's rooms, determined that, now he had resolved the dilemma within his own mind, he would advise the elders of the Order as soon as possible.

When he arrived at the fabulously appointed antechamber, he found the office unoccupied but, as he was about to walk out of the room, Brother Neville came in from the corridor, so they both took a seat to wait.

"Have you reached a decision?" Neville asked.

Nodding, Galahad sat forward and rested his elbows upon his knees. "I have but, if you do not mind, I will wait until Adomain and Columba are in attendance before I announce it to save repeating myself."

Neville returned the nod and sat back, "That seems eminently reasonable. Indeed, I have information regarding the events of the last two days but, like you, I think I will keep my counsel until the two of them return." He regarded

Galahad out of the corner of his eye. "There is one thing which you might find interesting though. After Nathan had regained consciousness in the infirmary and Joseph had spoken to him, he accompanied me to the library. Whilst we were there, I unearthed a copy of Historia Plantarum by Theophrastus, a botanist who lived in ancient Greece and, on a whim, asked Joseph to flick through it to see if he could identify the type of flowers in which he saw you standing during his vision."

"And?" Galahad asked.

"Joseph immediately identified it as aconite, a herbaceous perennial plant which is chiefly native to mountainous parts of the north."

The ex-champion of the Round Table sat back in his chair disappointedly. The way Neville had introduced the subject had led him to believe that he was about to impart some earth-shattering revelation.

Neville's face was intrigued as he replied, "Galahad, aconite is known by many names, one of them being monkshood."

Galahad knew that Neville would not try and deceive him and was rocked by the information. "Could it be coincidence?" the former knight asked.

"An understandable reaction," Neville allowed. "The trouble with that theory is that aconite is also known as wolfsbane."

If Galahad harboured any doubts about his decision, they were dispelled by Brother Neville's information. It obviously had indeed been the hand of fate he had felt upon his shoulder in Columba's office. A smirk flickered across his mouth as the supercilious face of Merlin unexpectedly reared before his mind's eye, and he remembered being at the receiving end of a diatribe about the similarities between the notion of religious worship and the notion of fate. Was it God's will that he should depart the monastery to vanquish the tribe of werewolves, or was that simply a way of justifying him taking the pommel of Whitecleave in his hand once more and partaking in one last instance of righteous blood-letting before he threw himself completely and absolutely into a life of spartan asceticism.

His train of thought was broken as Columba and Adomain entered the room followed by two young men, one clad similarly to the Ionan monks and the other dressed in the traditional manner of the Pictish tribesmen who made up a good deal of the population of the monastery.

He rose to greet Columba before stopping in his tracks and fighting down an urge to reach for the sword that, up until he took up the claustral life, had hung at his belt as a matter of course.

The half-man, half-wolf who had walked in behind them also hesitated, his eyes immediately taking in Galahad's movement.

Without preamble, Columba introduced the trio of strangers. "Galahad, these are the travellers who appeared at our door on the night of the unpleasantness between Nathan and Joseph." He gestured to the young monk first. "This is Brother Lorcan from our fellow parish on the island of Mull, to the north-east of here. The young man next to him is Craigan McIntyre from the islands across the Hebridean Sea. He is the last surviving member of his tribe. His is the tribe which the Ulfhednar," he looked to Taiga for confirmation that his pronunciation was correct, "all but exterminated."

Galahad returned the nod which Craigan had given him during Columba's introduction, then turned his attention to the final newcomer who Columba presented with what Galahad felt was a rather overdramatic flourish. "And this is the wulver, Taiga Haas, last of the Kurtadam clan, another family brought to the brink of extinction by the werewolves."

The monk who founded the order on Iona then turned to his guests and gestured towards Galahad. "Gentlemen," he said, pretending to ignore Taiga's look of weary resignation at the inappropriate epithet, "I believe this is the man you have travelled for many miles to meet. This, I believe, is Monkshood."

Judging by the trio's reactions of astonishment, Columba had obviously not told them who they were about to meet. Inwardly steeling himself, Galahad strode across the intervening space to shake the hands of all three, making a special point of talking to Taiga. "I am sorry for my reaction to your appearance a few moments ago."

The wulver acknowledged the apology with good grace as they were all ushered into the senior monk's office. After the group were seated, Columba asked Craigan and Taiga to recount in as much detail as possible what had occurred to cause them to embark upon their quest. Galahad listened intently to their words, remaining silent for the most part, but asking pertinent questions when he thought it apt.

"So all the seer gave you was a name?" he asked disbelievingly, amazed that the two had trekked for so many miles on nothing more than a few vague words. "And not even a real name at that."

"Yet hopefully our search has borne fruit," Craigan said.

"And much sooner than we ever dared to imagine," Taiga rumbled. "If you are Monkshood, that is," he finished.

Columba crossed his arms and sat upon the edge of his desk. "I agree that it does seem fortuitous you should find whom you seek so quickly but the culmination of events is too coincidental to just dismiss out of hand."

"I have something else to add to that as well, if you will permit me," Galahad said. "Last night, after spending the day pondering all that had happened, I experienced a horrendous sleep crammed full of nightmares and the strangest of hallucinations. I do not remember all of what I saw, but I had a vision which sounded very similar to what Joseph described to me, the field of flowers and the wolves encircling them. The only difference I can remember was that it was all in the midst of the worst blizzard I have ever seen, which Joseph certainly did not mention to me." He looked to Columba. "Did he mention that to you when you spoke in the infirmary?" Columba shook his head and Galahad ploughed on, "No matter. As I have said, I can only remember glimpses of the images I saw but, the one dream which stands head and shoulders above anything else in my memory, is a titanic battle spread across a vast panorama."

To the surprise of all, at the mention of this, Neville leant forward enthusiastically, "Tell me more of this."

The intensity of Neville's voice caused Galahad to stumble over his words for a brief moment before the enormity of his dream came back to haunt him and he continued his recounting, "I was standing statue-still, surveying a huge ice-gripped plain girdled by a roiling angry ocean. I saw a ship, riding upon the waves and a giant serpent thrashing about amidst the tumult. Upon the plain itself, I saw a colossal tree and all around it, figures fighting each other to the death."

"Do you remember what any of the figures looked like?" Neville breathed, his face rapidly turning a ghastly white.

Galahad considered the question for a moment, "I cannot. Even as I tell you this, I can feel the images paling into nothingness."

Galahad took a step back as Neville advanced upon him, "You must try to remember."

The former knight looked from face to face and saw that they were all as disturbed as he was by Neville's manner. "I remember hearing the howl of a dog, I am sure it was a dog rather than a wolf..." his voice tailed off as he tried to dredge his dissipating memory, "although, at the end, a wolf did appear out of a flaming pit which opened up in the middle of the fray." He shook his head miserably. "That is all I remember. I woke up after that, I think. I do not know, I cannot remember..."

Columba stared closely at Brother Neville, who had stumbled back to his seat looking sick. "What is wrong, Neville?"

The old man did not answer immediately and Galahad found himself wondering if he had even heard the question. When he did speak, his voice was troubled. "You recall the word Ragnarok which Joseph repeated at the end of his fit?"

Columba nodded, "What of it? What does it mean?"

Neville returned to some semblance of his normal self and spoke more calmly, "It is a word in the language of Old Norse that means 'final destiny of the gods'. It is a prophecy which, in Norse paganism, describes a series of events that ultimately leads to the world being consumed in flames and all life extinguished."

At the mention of flames, Galahad remembered the incandescent blade which had appeared on the far horizon and informed his audience of it.

Neville murmured, "The flame of Surtr."

"Pardon?" Columba asked.

"It is part of the prophecy. Surtr was a jotunn, a giant of Norse mythology, and the flame of Surtr refers to his weapon. According to the myth, it was his sword stroke that ignited the conflagration which incinerated the world." Neville stalked around the office excitedly, "It is all beginning to fit," he muttered. "All of this is mentioned in the work in which I found the translation," he said in a louder voice. "My reading of the prophecy leads me to believe that the tree could possibly have been Yggdrasil, the World Tree, from which the pagans believe all life on earth gains nourishment. The howl of the dog might relate to either the wolf-god Fenrir or more likely, Garmr, who is described in the text as *the greatest of monsters*. His howls are said to herald the coming of this Ragnarok event."

"What of the wolf who emerged from the pit?" Galahad asked tentatively. He had not disclosed that the hideous beast had pounced upon him just before he had awoken and found himself dreading what the answer might be. "Does the prophecy mention such a creature?"

"Unfortunately, the only allusions to wolves that I managed to find in the manuscripts on the mythology of the Norsemen, spoke of three malevolent beings who were hated by their pantheon of gods. Fenrir, who I mentioned previously, was bound in a cave deep underground as he was so feared by the Norse gods. The others were his two sons, Hati and Skoll who, supposedly, devoured the sun and moon, again, as a supposed precursor to the end of the world."

Adomain stepped forward, shaking his head, "Hold hard there, Brother Neville, let us not forget we are talking about unfounded pagan legends here," he huffed pompously. "Should we be setting such store by this sort of rustic gibberish?"

"Yet the coincidences keep mounting up, do they not?" Columba observed.

Though, as Galahad had said, the fantastical imagery of his dream was drifting away from his mind like fog in a gust of wind, he still remembered the all-consuming evil which had emanated from the massive wolf as it loped towards him across the blood-soaked tundra. Though Adomain was obviously scoffing at Neville's interpretation of the occurrences of the last three days, Galahad found himself if not wholly convinced, then at least intrigued enough by Neville's revelations and Joseph's vision that he could not put off announcing his decision any longer.

285

"What do you want of me?" he directed the question at Craigan and Taiga. He heard a sharp intake of breath from Adomain's direction and turned to him before waiting for an answer and said, "I know you have no patience with what you have heard but, with all due respect, you did not see Joseph when he was in the throes of his fit and you did not dream what I dreamt last night. I have heard enough and seen enough to be certain there is some sort of connection between myself and this Monkshood. Perhaps I am him and perhaps not, but I do not think, in all good conscience, after all that has transpired, I can turn my back on these fellows after they have walked so many miles and gone through so much hardship. Their endeavours demand that I at least hear what they require of me." He turned back to the wulver and the Venicone and spread his hands, "So what are you wanting of me?"

Galahad's offhand manner took the both of them completely off-guard and they looked at each other, open-mouthed. Finally, Craigan managed to say, "To be honest, we have no plan of action in mind, beyond returning home and ridding the land of the scum that have devastated it so heinously."

With an emphatic nod, Galahad stood up, "I suspected it would be something of that nature. Columba, I am going to decline your offer of joining the order for the time being. I will place my trust in God that He will deliver me safely back to the monastery once I have faced down this one final foe."

The sorrow evident in Columba's eyes touched Galahad deeply and he stepped forward to embrace the 'Dove of The Church'. He released his hold and moved to Brother Adomain, but the monk who had been his friend for the longest within the four walls, stepped back from him with a look of absolute disgust upon his face. "How can you have the hypocrisy to accuse Columba of wanting to get rid of you yesterday with spurious reasoning and now stand there using these ridiculous stories of pagan rubbish, as an excuse to play the sword-wielding fool once more." With those heated words hanging in the air, Adomain made for the door. Just before he exited he turned once more and hissed, "I had thought your stay on Iona had enabled you to overcome such kneejerk militaristic reactions, but obviously not. I will have nothing to do with this absurd nonsense."

Galahad made no attempt to hide his bewilderment at the bitterness dripping from Adomain's voice and moved to follow the older man out of the office.

"I would leave him be for a little while, Galahad." Columba sighed miserably. "He is too emotional at the moment. The words which he spat at you just now were borne of love not hate, though they may not have appeared so. He fears for your safety should you depart with our guests. He said as much when we initially discussed the matter."

"That is as maybe, but it does not give him a reason to speak so witheringly to me or anyone."

Columba nodded in agreement. "I do not dispute that but I think he feels some sort of special bond with you given the circumstances in which he brought you to our door. I surmise his hostility stems from the fact that he thought he had already lost you once when you reacted so violently to the psalter," the senior monk said.

"He did act extremely strangely when the episode first occurred," the former knight agreed.

"Adomain was ecstatic when he realised you would not succumb to the bloody history of the tome. I suspect he thought that, when you overcame the initial episode, you were completely clear of its malign influence."

"And do you?" Galahad asked without rancour, mindful of Columba's theory concerning why he had responded in such a markedly different way to the other unfortunates who had been affected by it.

St Columba smiled as he said, "You will probably not be surprised to know that I stand by my original speculation." His expression turned serious. "Adomain had no right to speak to you as he did but we can all be over-emotional at times. Please ensure you at least try and make your peace with him before you depart for the islands."

"I will," Galahad promised.

Turning back to the rest of his audience, who had been left fidgeting uncomfortably by Adomain's outburst, Columba spread his hands benevolently. "I suspect the lunchtime bell is not far away from tolling, so let us repair to the refectory." He ushered his guests out of the room and followed them down the corridor. Galahad was still full from his hearty breakfast, so he excused himself from the party and returned to the dormitory, ostensibly to pack his belongings for the journey ahead. However, he also wished to seek out Adomain and try to get to the bottom of whatever had triggered the unexpected animosity.

It was not Adomain who he encountered however. He happened upon Brother Maes in the dormitory.

The disfigured monk was lying upon his bunk when Galahad entered the austere room. He nodded in greeting and did not speak until Galahad began bundling his travelling clothes inside a jute bag.

"Going somewhere?" he asked in his usual sardonic drawl.

Galahad had found to his surprise, he liked Maes immensely and smiled warmly in response. "Yes, I am away to the islands of the West to fight werewolves."

Maes' face froze and he snapped, "There is no need to be facetious. I merely asked a question."

An explosive laugh escaped from Galahad's mouth which increased in volume as the colour rose even further in his room-mate's cheeks. "I kid you not, Maes. I will not bore you with the details but I am away to the Hebrides in the morning."

Maes' eyes searched Galahad's face for signs of mockery but, when he found none, his expression became more animated than the former knight had ever seen. "But they are creatures of myth and legend, are they not?"

"That is what I also thought. Apparently we were both mistaken. I have spoken to two who have seen them, even killed one of them. One is a tribesman from the Western Isles and the other, well, if you did have any doubts as to the existence of werewolves, then he is the most compelling evidence you would ever need."

Maes got up quickly from his bed and strode over to Galahad, the disbelieving look which he had sported when the monsters had first been mentioned returning to his face in an instant. "Sorry, am I understanding you correctly. Are you saying that the second one is a werewolf?"

Trying to keep his voice as even as possible, Galahad nodded, "Not as you or I think of them, though. He is a wulver."

Maes' brow furrowed at the unfamiliar word.

"Would you believe a wulver is a peaceable species of werewolf?" Galahad explained. "Even saying it to you now seems ridiculous but I have seen him with my own eyes. He walks and talks like you or I but is covered in a soft pelt of wolfskin."

Galahad went on to describe in further detail his assumption of the mantle of Monkshood and how it tied in with Craigan and Taiga's arrival. When he had finished explaining, Maes let out a huge breath, "What a fantastical tale. And you leave in the morning?"

"To return to these four walls when I have fulfilled my role in this story, yes."

Maes returned to his bunk with a sardonic expression on his face, "You seem rather sure of conquering these Ulfhednar."

Galahad grunted non-committally at the comment.

"Do not take that as a criticism, there is certainly nothing wrong with a little self-confidence, it is just that, if the islanders are to be believed, and you obviously do believe them, then these beasts will not be easy to vanquish, will they?"

Galahad stopped his packing and turned to face Maes, "You know my history, Brother. I have been privileged by so much in my life. I have seen the wondrous display of magic which the Holy Grail can conjure, I have seen the ethereal beauty of the Lady of The Lake and there have been times when I believe I have felt the gentle hand of God upon my shoulder, guiding me onto the right path. However, as in all things, there has to be some sort of balance. To counteract all the marvels which I have been fortunate enough to experience, I have also faced down a hideous demon and been consumed by the red mist of the berserker, killing my enemies without a second thought." Here, Galahad took a shuddering breath, realising with a jolt that he had not thought of Arthur and his other companions of the Round Table for a surprisingly long time. "I have also outlived too many of my friends and peers, seeing them perish upon the field of battle. There have been times when I felt like I was dwelling within the deepest pit of despair, drowning in an ocean of blood and death."

Maes digested and dissected Galahad's words in his usual considered manner before offering a response. "Excuse my lack of insight, but I do not understand your point. Surely by embarking upon this journey you are risking a return to the dark depths of slaughter and carnage that you describe?"

"You did not hear the story the travellers told, Maes. The deeds that these werewolves have perpetrated are evil incarnate, they are a death-cult themselves by the sound of it." He explained the heinous acts that Craigan and Taiga had described and watched as Maes' eyes grew wider and wider in horror.

"Could they have exaggerated the sinfulness of these creatures to try and persuade you to their cause?" the monk asked in a strangled voice.

Galahad shook his head straight away. "If you had spoken to them, seen the haunted look in their eyes and the anguish in their voices, you would know just how unworthy that question is."

"I did not mean to call their integrity into question, it is just that I sometimes find it hard to believe some of the things which are supposed to fit into God's great plan."

Galahad smiled, recognising the look on his room-mate's face as very similar to the one he wore when he was faced with such a religious conundrum. "I do not wish to sound self-important but I deem their purpose as providing some sort of climax to my life as a warrior for God." He chewed upon his lip. "I wandered the cloisters for the whole day yesterday, ruing the fact that I seemed to have been embroiled into this saga and was likely to be taken away from this place, especially after Columba offered me entrance into the ranks of the Order."

"Has it been six months since you arrived here?" Maes gasped.

"Yes," the former knight sighed, "it is true what they say about time going by quickly when one is happy and content." He shook his head to try and free it of the sudden melancholia which had descended upon him, and forced a smile. "No matter. I fully intend to return to this most holy of places after defeating the werewolves. As I said, I came to the decision as I walked the corridors. Instead of letting the pessimism of the thought of leaving depress me, I decided to look upon the chance of ridding the lands of these monstrosities as nothing more nor less than a final physical manifestation of my devotion to God. After it is done, I will sheathe Whitecleave for the last time, never to draw it in anger again and return to the monastery so that I might serve Him as you and the rest of the Order have done so well for so long."

As Columba had predicted in his office, the sonorous tone of the bell which announced lunch was about to be served, rang throughout the stone building and Maes left Galahad to finish off his preparations for the journey. The disfigured monk was discomfited by an uneasy feeling that, despite his protestations to the contrary, Galahad's words smacked of being prideful and he found himself praying that his friend did not come to regret such ill-judged pronouncements.

After double-checking the contents of his pack, the former knight of Camelot returned to pondering Adomain's reaction to his decision. He could not recall ever seeing the secondmost senior monk in Iona respond in such a dramatic way to anything. He was caught between walking down to the refectory for something to eat or seeking out Adomain to try and resolve whatever issue Galahad's choice had thrown up between them, though he could not for the life of him think what it could be.

Though he had said to Columba and his guests that he was still full from his breakfast, he knew enough about life on the road to recognise how important it was to prepare his body as much as possible for the rigours of travelling. His pragmatic side won out and he opted for the meal, reasoning that he had the best part of half a day to find Adomain and challenge him over his erratic behaviour.

He ate his way mechanically through a bowl of steaming vegetable soup and a couple of oaty biscuits. He knew he should have tried to eat more but found his appetite sadly lacking as he sat down to eat.

So it was that Ruaraidh found him, staring into space, his tongue absently trying to dislodge a shred of swede from between his teeth.

The Irish monk placed his bowl down carefully then sat opposite his room-mate, staring at him through the clouds of aromatic steam which wafted towards the ceiling of the dining room. "Good afternoon," he said with a nod. "Galahad," he prompted when no response was forthcoming.

"Hmm? Oh, good day, Ruaraidh. How are you?" Galahad blinked in surprise.

"Something on your mind?" Ruaraidh asked, his capacious beard moving in such a way as to suggest an amused smile was lurking beneath it.

Galahad shook his head sadly, "No, not really."

The grin disappeared as the monk beheld his room-mate's abject wretchedness. "I hear you are to leave us in the morning." Ruaraidh changed the subject in the hope of distracting his friend from whatever was troubling him.

"If I can resolve some unfinished business here I am, yes."

Ruaraidh's mouth formed an 'O' as the heat of the soup nearly burned his tongue. "Is it anything which I can help you with?" he asked, more out of politeness than any real desire to actually help.

Galahad laughed bitterly, "No, it is Brother Adomain with whom I need to speak."

"Well, in that case, I can help you. I saw him coming out of our dormitory just before I came here for my luncheon."

"If you will excuse me then," Galahad jumped up and was off across the stone floor at a run, nearly knocking some of his fellow diners from their feet in his rush to exit the room. A part of him did think that it was Adomain who should be doing the rushing around, as it was he who had taken such exception to Galahad's choice, but he accepted that, if he wanted a resolution to the problem before he left for the Western Isles, then he had to take the initiative.

He strode along the corridor, stopping a couple of members of the Order to ask if they had been Columba's second in command. Infuriatingly, they both answered in the negative. He reached the door to the communal sleeping quarters and walked purposefully through it, startling Brother Joseph, who was sitting on the edge of his bed, intensely studying a jaundiced manuscript.

Galahad spared a nod at the youngster before checking the rest of the room for his quarry. He was about to leave but stopped on the threshold, pausing to reflect on the fact that he was not the only person in the world burdened by problems. He walked back into the room and sat down on the bunk next to Joseph, who greeted him with a wan smile.

"How is your brother, Joseph?" Galahad asked quietly.

With great deliberation, Joseph placed the manuscript on the bed and turned back to face him.

Galahad found himself trying not to shrink back from the anguish in the young man's eyes as he spoke in a monotone, "Brother Fearghas thinks he has at least three broken ribs and the bones in his left arm are shattered."

"You must know it was not your fault, Joseph," Galahad patted his hand comfortingly. "You were not yourself," he continued on, unconsciously grateful to be able to think about something other than his quarrel with Adomain. "And what is more, I will wager that Columba was right, was he not? About your brother bearing you no ill will?" Galahad prompted.

291

To the former knight's surprise, this made the young monk look even unhappier, "That is what he said, yes." Joseph agreed.

"Then why so glum?"

"That is what he said, but his eyes disagreed with his words. It was lip-service, Galahad. He was parroting what he thought I wanted to hear." Joseph's lip trembled and tears started in his eyes, "But the way he looked at me…" The youngster's voice broke and he began to sob, "I could tell that it was only what he saw as his fraternal responsibility which stopped him from disowning me there and then."

"With all due respect, Joseph, you cannot know that for sure," Galahad held up his hands and had to raise his voice over the youth's protests. "You were obviously fraught at seeing your brother in such a state. In such a distressing situation, the mind can become confused and perceive things which are not there." He stood up and began to walk around the room. "Consider what you have just said, Joseph. When I entered the room on that night, Brother Nathan was trying with all his strength to restrain you so you would not hurt yourself and his look was of a man fearing that his heart would break at the loss of one whom was so cherished." Galahad stopped and lifted Joseph's head gently by the chin. "Does that sound like the behaviour of a man who does not care deeply for his brother?"

Joseph did not look convinced but he nodded anyway, "Thank you for your words of comfort, Galahad," he sniffed.

"It is good to know that I have a modicum of counselling skills as I am sure I will need them if I am to be a member of the Order on Iona." Galahad smiled and moved to leave the room.

At that, Joseph's head came up again, "I am glad you have chosen to take your holy orders and remain with us."

Nodding at the compliment, Galahad walked towards the open door. As he was about to re-enter the corridor, he spotted something on his pillow. Wrinkling his forehead, he strolled over to get a better look at it. It was a single stem, crowned by large and eye-catching purple flowers. "Joseph, what is this?" he asked quietly.

He heard the other occupant of the room get up from his bed and walk over to his side. "It is a bloom of aconite," Joseph answered, confirming Galahad's suspicion. "That must have been why Adomain looked in a few moments ago. He came in and stood by your bed for a time. I spoke to him but he did not acknowledge me. Perhaps it is a good luck charm for your journey to the islands, eh?"

Galahad twisted the delicate stem around in his fingers. "Perhaps," he murmured. "Did you happen to see which way he went when he left the room?"

"No, I did not. Sorry," Joseph shrugged.

Galahad returned the gesture. "It does not matter. I wished to speak to him, that was all."

With that he left the room to find Adomain, knowing time was against him as he was to depart with his fellow travellers the following morning, but praying he would be able to locate the erratically behaving monk before darkness fell. He knew from experience that he could not afford to sacrifice any sleep before journeying northwards, so he decided he would continue his hunt until the sun dropped below the horizon but not after that.

Fruitless hours came and went as Galahad visited and revisited the places he had looked in earlier in the day but Adomain was nowhere to be found. He went to Columba's offices but the founder of the monastery had seen neither hide nor hair of him either and, from his manner, was also becoming concerned over the missing holy man. He called several other postulants to his office and requested they join Galahad in the search. The group of nine split up, Galahad and Walter despatched outside into the wintry countryside surrounding the monastery, Columba and Ruaraidh going to Adomain's rooms to look for hints of his whereabouts there, Taiga, Craigan and Lorcan simply walking the corridors of the unfamiliar building and two other monks, a middle-aged balding monk by the name of Julian and a younger man, slightly reminiscent of Brother Joseph in fact, called Brother Haynes, searching the area of the refectory and infirmary.

However, after hours of fruitless searching, they called off the hunt and ended up congregating in Columba's chambers.

Once again, the founder of the Ionan monks showed his compassion by immediately trying to appease Galahad's distress at not being able to find Adomain, "You have done all you can, Galahad, all you can and more. The blame for Adomain's disappearance can in no way be laid at your door. He chose to take himself off to wherever he is biding. Do not upset yourself, rest assured we will seek him out in time. For now, you must try to concentrate on the road ahead, not the road behind. You have a hugely difficult task before you and you should direct all your attention to completing that."

He looked from the hunched form of Galahad towards the trio who he was to travel north with and beckoned them over. "I have prepared a room for the four of you to bunk in tonight." He looked piercingly at Craigan and Taiga, "Remind Galahad of the travails which face you all. Take his mind off the situation here, a situation which, I repeat, is not in any way his fault." He patted the former knight of Camelot on the back. "Get yourself a good night's sleep, Galahad. Hopefully, when you awaken, we will find an apologetic Adomain back in our midst once more. If not," he shrugged, "then do not concern yourself. We *will* find him. It may even be he has decided to embark

293

on another tour of the mainland for more recruits to the cause, although he has never done so without informing us beforehand. However, perhaps he was too mortified by his behaviour to face you, or indeed any of those present during his outburst, and is simply lying low until your expedition has departed the monastery." He stood up and returned to the plush chair behind his desk, peering at those assembled over steepled fingers. "For now, I bid you retire to your beds to sleep the sleep of the just and we will reconvene when you depart in the morning. Brother Haynes, will you take them to their room and ensure they have all they require?"

Brother Haynes escorted the quartet to their dormitory and left them to their own devices after finding that they needed nothing more from him.

The three travellers from the isles immediately started being as solicitous to Galahad as Columba had been. However, for Craigan and Taiga at least, the reason for doing so was slightly more selfish, as Galahad was the much sought-after hope for victory over their foe, though having said that, their kindly gestures were no less heartfelt than Columba's.

"Please," Galahad held up his hands, "do not think I do not appreciate your words but, for now, I just wish to retire and prepare myself for the journey." With that said, he lay back upon his bunk and closed his eyes, though the others did not believe for one moment that he was asleep.

Taking that rather dismissive cue, the three other occupants of the room slunk out into the corridor and huddled together. Craigan was the first to speak, "Could we delay our leaving by a few hours tomorrow? Give him another chance to find this Adomain fellow?"

Surprisingly, it was Lorcan who shook his head, "Personally I think it would be counter-productive to do that. What if, in those hours, he still does not find him? Do you give him further time? At what point do you draw the search to a close? No, at the moment Saint Columba has given his blessing to our departure in the morning. If you countermand that then you cannot, a little while later, turn round and demand to leave at a different time of your choosing."

Both Taiga and Craigan blinked in surprise at the passion in Lorcan's voice as the young monk continued, "The Order in both Mull and here was founded on many principles, one of which was that it would aid those in dire need if its members were able to. At the moment, it is yourselves who are in the greatest need, not Brother Adomain, therefore if Galahad is to prove himself worthy of joining our ranks, I would suggest he is compelled to depart with us tomorrow at a time of your choosing."

As Craigan pondered his words, Taiga spoke, "Well said," he nodded. "I think Columba is correct. Once Monkshood is free of this place, from the little I have seen of him and from what Columba has told me of his history, I think his mind will re-focus upon the task in hand. And, though this may sound harsh, the manner of the one who stormed out put me in mind of a petulant youngster and I for one would strongly resent having to postpone our leaving because of a tantrum from one who should know better."

Lorcan agreed, "I had heard the name Brother Adomain before. He came over with Saint Columba from Ireland and is well known within the order, by reputation, at least," his voice took on a distant quality and tailed off, "However, having witnessed that outburst, my opinion has been completely revised of him."

Inside the room Galahad turned onto his side and stared blindly at the wall. He knew his travelling companions were right and tried to mentally prepare himself for the rigours of the road. However, it was long after darkness had engulfed the room and his cohorts had turned in, that he felt his eyes becoming heavy and the last thing he remembered before falling asleep was the face of the man who had brought him to this place of worship, a place where he had felt at peace for one of the first times in his life. He still felt that he owed some sort of debt to him for that act and disliked the thought of leaving the monastery without achieving a reconciliation but he also found himself acknowledging the wisdom of Lorcan's observation.

With a suspicion that he may have another night disturbed by nightmares, albeit of a more mundane nature than his visions of Ragnarok, Galahad fell asleep.

Chapter 12

The *Varulv* hoved through the choppy waters of the Minches, having just set sail off the northern coast of Skye, the largest island of the Inner Hebrides.

They had cleaved a bloody path down the eastern side of the Outer Hebridean islands, adding substantially to the number of trophies that they would be able to bring back in triumph to the pyre which still blazed incandescently within Dun Varulfur.

When they had returned from Auchremin to their homestead, Varga had found his lust for blood reawakened by the expedition south. This was tempered somewhat though by the distance that the Ulfhednar had trekked in order to increase the amount of skulls with which they could stoke the fire of Surtr.

Though he was more than pleased with the total of severed heads which the tribe had garnered on the extended blood-raid, it was clear that they would have to widen their area of operation still further if they were to continue to add to the grisly mountain with similar frequency in the future.

To that end, some of the tribe had been charged with the task of constructing a fleet of longboats so the Ulfhednar could strike out across the waters surrounding their adopted homeland and wreak their havoc upon the unsuspecting people of the nearby islands. As Beyla had pointed out, it would be an excuse for an exhilarating return to their Viking roots when their ancestors had ridden the oceans on waves of plunder and pillage.

Since this fleet had been built, the communities on the tiny islands of Scalpay and Hermetray as well as the larger expanse of Harris had felt the slash of the Ulfhednar talon and Varga's decision had seemed to be justifying itself as the werewolf clan reaped a bumper harvest of skulls on their passage south. However, just after they had left the moors of North Uist behind them, a blizzard had assailed the fleet and the Arctic wind contained within it had separated the ships, blowing Varga's craft far to the South and it was only the intrinsic talent for seamanship, which seemed inbred within the Norsemen's physical make-up, that had saved the longboat from an unmarked watery grave in the Sea of The Hebrides.

Once the storm had exhausted itself, Varga and his clansmen found themselves floating among the treacherous currents which battered the southwest corner of the island of Tiree. Grateful to be alive and plant their feet on dry land once more, the Ulfhednar set about cleansing the island of its human population with a frenzied passion and thus, due to nothing more than the whim of wind and weather, an island which might have remained untouched for years by the plague of wolven aggression, found itself helpless in the face of such unbridled violence.

Now that the skulls had been gathered and loaded into the chests which each oarsmen sat upon on the deck of the longship, the Ulfhednar set off again, this time on a north-easterly heading, reasoning that, as they had been driven so far off their intended course, they would employ their tried and tested method of navigation by the stars to work their way back to Loch Seaforth and the home comforts of Dun Varulfur, hugging the coastlines and shores of the seemingly never-ending plethora of skerries and islands which had provided such rich pickings so far.

Varga stood at the prow of the boat, staring into the distance across the granite grey of the sea with a humourless set to his features, one hand resting upon the hilt of Varkolak, the other upon the wooden nape of the wolf carved as the figurehead of the Viking's ship.

All of the clansmen knew better than to disturb their leader when his face had such an introspective aspect but, unbeknownst to them, inside, Varga's heart was singing. It seemed to the massive Norseman that, ever since he had witnessed the astonishing tableau of the insubstantial wolf devouring the shadow of the monk in the flames of the disintegrating barn at Auchremin, every judgment he had made, no matter how seemingly insignificant, had borne great fruit, none more so than the decision to return to the inconstant permanence of the sea.

Though a goodly number of the clan had nearly perished when the blizzard had unleashed its fury upon the Varulv, Varga had stood where he was positioned now, cordage engulfed in his iron grip, one foot upon the railing at the side of the prow, either laughing hysterically as the ship heeled at a seemingly impossible angle before righting itself or shrieking curses at Thor, the God of storms, challenging him to smash the Varulv into firewood with his famed hammer, Mjollnir.

The defiance which their leader showed to one of the major figures in the hierarchy of the hated Aesir, and the tribe's subsequent survival, acted as a great stimulus to the Ulfhednar and was a masterpiece of propaganda for Varga, who proclaimed it as an omen that their work was progressing towards a successful outcome.

The clan had stood upon the beach at Tiree, aware that, as well as his fellow tribesmen, a group of the native islanders had gathered upon the machair-filled slope overlooking the beach, unaware that their curiosity would soon turn to terror as the Vikings advanced towards them with murderous intent glowing in their eyes.

However, before the Ulfhednar had delved once again into their apparently bottomless pit of battle lust, they had had their blood fired by Varga's words as he addressed them upon the windswept shore.

"My children, we find ourselves on strange sands once more, driven here by a vengeful and petty god, no doubt at the behest of his pathetic father. A god who has already fallen once to the prowess of one who was counted brother to our beloved Fenrir. This woeful attempt to drive us from our appointed course is yet more proof that our deeds are directing us upon the correct path. The Aesir are so cowed by the momentum which we have generated by our rites of worship that they seek to destroy us by underhand means, knowing that, should they attempt to bring us down face to face, they would fall to the earth dead just as Odin fell before Fenrir upon the field of Vigrid during the first Ragnarok.

Know this, my Ulfhednar kin, we are blessed beyond any before us, for we have it within us to bring about a new order to the world through our endeavours. Already the Aesir quake before us, for they can see we have it in us to bring about their end and the end of those lickspittles who refuse to accept the inevitable conclusion of what we are striving for and continue to kowtow to them, thinking they will be able to afford them protection against the coming storm. Well, they are wrong. There is nothing that can stop us from achieving our ultimate goal. Our clan will rise from the ashes of Surtr's second cleansing to sit at the right hand of the returning wolf god and, in His triumph, we will be as demi-gods among men, forever ready and willing to do Fenrir's bidding and revel in his glory. Now come with me, my sons and daughters, come with me and take but one more step upon the road to rebirth."

Varkolak came free from its leather sheath with an audible swish and Varga drove it towards the sky, screaming, "Breathe the air while you may, deceitful Aesir, for your death knell is sounding ever louder. Ulfhednar, Ulfhednar…"

The roar was taken up by the clan and, as one, they tore across the beach, gaining the rocks at the base of the gentle gradient before the Pictish farmers had even moved.

Though they did not understand the chilling battle-cries which were hurled toward them, the intent was all too clear and the natives dropped their implements to the grass of the spongy meadow and began to run from the oncoming tide of death. But, as had been the case on so many of the Hebridean islands, their flight was to no avail.

The Vikings had ripped into the fleeing islanders, their wickedly sharp weapons separating heads from necks and limbs from torsos with ruthless efficiency. They decimated the farmers of Tiree in minutes, scything through them like harvesters gathering in their crop. Men, women and children all fell before the onslaught, murdered without a second thought.

The next six weeks saw the population of Tiree completely obliterated as the Ulfhednar, impassioned by Varga's inspirational speech upon the headland, set about their task with a will, desperate to prove to their leader how devoted they were to the cause.

Varga had viewed it all with a warm satisfaction brewing inside him. However, he knew that, until the gruesome fruits of their labours were plunged into the flame at Dun Varulfur, Fenrir would not feel the benefit and they would be no closer to resurrecting him. He well remembered the beatific look upon Fenrir's face as he told him of the frisson which he experienced every time a sacrificial skull was added to the misshapen pile that grew ever higher above the eternally burning ember of the jotunn's sword.

To that end, when the scouts returned to the temporary base which the clan had set up in the ruins of a broch called Dun Mor, and reported that they had not encountered any human life during their search of the thirty miles of the island, he did not hesitate to order the Ulfhednar back out onto the Sea of the Hebrides.

So now, here the Vikings were once more, sailing north after beaching in the middle of a small archipelago of islands that, rather infuriatingly for the clan, had proved to be uninhabited.

To the west, they could see a large expanse of hills bulking upon the horizon, the lands obscured by a bank of low cloud, heavy with sleet and snow, but Varga stuck to his decision and ordered them onwards as the call of home was baying loudly in his ears now. Ever since the initial departure from Three, when he had been ecstatic at the howl aboard the Varulv, he had found a strange urgency beginning to gnaw at him, growing in power with every stroke of the oars. There seemed to be an inaudible whisper permanently caressing his ears, always on the cusp of his hearing, but never quite resolving itself into words. Curiously, he found he was not overly disturbed by the feeling, it simply seemed to cloak him in an unaccustomed melancholia which he could not shake off.

It was whilst he was shrouded in this gloom that the weather began turning once more, but he was so preoccupied he did not immediately notice the thick flakes of snow falling gracefully past him until one blew into his eye and he blinked it free.

As the wind picked up, he felt the ship heel in an easterly direction, pushing the longboat out into deeper waters. He stoically maintained his position to the left of the vulpine figurehead and watched the island of Coll recede into the distance to his left.

After no more than five minutes, from being as becalmed as it was possible to be in the choppy waters of the Hebridean seas, the *Varulv* found itself assailed on all sides by a swirling, howling hurricane of wind, snow and sleet.

The storm hit the Vikings so hard and so fast that they barely had time to reef in the single sail. A couple of the crew were injured as the ship pitched violently and the oar that they were using came free from its rowlock, smashing into their chests and snapping their ribs with an audible report.

As the ship was dragged further to starboard, the sky darkened still further and soon the only thing visible was the white tops of the waves as they erupted into the air and crashed back to the water's surface, fragmenting into a million droplets as they hit.

The chaotic clouds were so black that even Varga struggled to make out the faces of those on the deck. Those that he could see were filled with trepidation, though he was gratified to see that, when his gaze fell upon them, their expressions metamorphosed into courageous defiance.

With the stars blotted out from the sky, there was no definite way to confirm their easterly course but Varga was confident they were heading that way.

The leader of the Ulfhednar found the whole experience utterly liberating. This was what being a Viking was really all about, he felt. Confronting the elements, ploughing forwards through unknown waters, unsure of a destination but confident in the ability to deal with whatever the capricious gods threw at them. For the first time in a long time, he found his memory returning to the one and only blood raid he had participated in before his ascendancy to leadership of the clan. Hitherto, the remembrance had always been coloured by his return and finding his father in such a wretched state. Now though, he found himself reminded of the heady thrill of staring across the ocean, dumbstruck in awe at the enormity of the water, stretching from horizon to horizon without end. Then the murmur of anticipation as land was sighted. Upon hearing the call, he had immediately turned to the more experienced warriors aboard the Goksberg longship and scanned their demeanours, noting the tightening of the grip upon the weapons, the licking of lips, the intensity of the eyes, all the small but significant changes to their manner that spoke volumes of the mounting excitement of beaching upon the shores of an alien land, ready to unleash the full destructive force of the Viking invasion machine upon whomsoever lived there.

His memory then became a rapid succession of images, each one a snapshot which triggered a pleasurable recollection. His first victim, a young blond girl of roughly sixteen years of age, fleeing from him as he chased her down and planted his seax perfectly in between her shoulder blades. After taking a moment to drink in the joy of killing and look about the battlefield, he realised there were other ways of sating the volcano of emotions which roared within him. He homed in on another girl, this one older but just as attractive and, Varga realised with a rush of excitement, just as powerless to resist his advances. After violating her, he slit her throat, his expression cold and detached as the light of life fled her eyes and the warm rush of blood flooded over his fingers.

More innocent victims of his bloodletting then rushed to the forefront of his mind, men both strong and vital or ancient and decrepit, women slim or buxom, blonde or brunette, young or old, children, boys and girls, blue or brown eyed, babes-in-arms or adolescents on the brink of adulthood, in greater or lesser number, all had fallen before the Vikings' insatiable lust for conquest and domination.

As he stood on his precarious eyrie at the prow, blinking away the dense flakes of snow that were whipped into his face by the strengthening wind, he found himself musing why his memories were filling him with such pleasure in this instance rather than with the anguish which normally accompanied them. He reasoned that it could only be because he could envisage his father living and breathing once more, restored to his full impressive prime by Fenrir as but one of the myriad of favours which the wolf-god would undoubtedly bestow on his most fervent worshipper.

A shout disturbed him from his reverie and his eyes flared in surprise at the forbidding headland which reared up to his right, looming over the longship like an avalanche frozen in time.

The wind had been so strong and the darkness so absolute that even the skills of the Ulfhednar crew had been unable to prevent the *Varulv* from drifting perilously close to the coastline of the island.

For a split second, Varga wondered if Thor had heard his blasphemy upon the beach at Tiree and was exacting a fatal vengeance for it, but the thought died aborning for, at that moment, the wind dropped just enough for the longship to lurch drunkenly away from the shadow of the cliffs.

It was only a brief respite though, as the seamen soon found themselves fighting again with all their might against the snow-laden gusts which seemed determined to hurl the boat onto the rocks.

So desperate was the situation that Varga left his station and stalked the deck like a man possessed, in equal turns exalting and cursing his men into greater effort, even though they were plainly at their limit.

On five separate occasions, warriors fell victim to the destructive power of the oars as they slipped their rowlocks and cannoned into their ranks but, as always, Varga seemed to be there, arresting the apparently unstoppable momentum with the merest hint of effort, and throwing the stricken men to the side and taking their place until others were able to fill the empty positions.

After what seemed like hours but was, in fact, only a few minutes, the *Varulv* returned to something approaching an even keel and the rock face which had emerged from the gloom so threateningly had receded, only to be replaced by an improbably flat beach that beckoned to the weary Vikings like the most beauteous siren.

301

With great relief, the exhausted crew ran the *Varulv* as far up the sand as they could, then disembarked, crumpling to the sands with various prayers being offered to Fenrir for delivering them to safety and thwarting the Aesir once more.

As further testament to Varga's suspicions regarding the origin of the violent storm, the wind and snow did not strike so strongly once the longship had left the waves. "Rest here for a spell, my kinsmen," the clan leader said, "for you have earned it. Once again, the blessings of our god and your indomitable strength have seen us safe when lesser men would have come to grief."

He then went to the five injured men, who each regarded him fearfully, as they did not know in which mood they would find him, the fearsome tyrant who viewed any sort of weakness as punishable by death or the inspirational leader who appreciated the sacrifices which his clansmen had made to help him realise his dream of resurrecting Fenrir and releasing his father from the Nastrond.

As it was, they found him to be the latter, not knowing it was only the fact that Varga thought it would be counter-productive for the tribe as a whole to bear witness to his wrath so soon after praising them so effusively. They mistook his intense gaze as evidence of his concern for their wellbeing when, in actual fact, it was merely Varga filing away their names in his memory, mentally granting them a brief stay of execution, but keeping them in mind should they again fall below the standards he expected of his men.

After about an hour, Strogen sidled over to his chief, "You know we are being watched?" he said off-handedly.

Varga was sat upon the sand, his massive back resting against a huge rock, polished as smooth as glass by the continual touch of the tide. He opened his eyes and nodded, "Aye, for the last fifteen minutes. What of it?"

Strogen's eyes narrowed and Varga was struck, not for the first time, by how rat-like he looked. "Shall we get rid of them? I dislike being observed in such a manner."

A blond eyebrow arched up and the Ulfhednar chief rolled his tongue around his mouth before answering, "Do as you wish. I assume I can trust you to dispose of them without a problem? If not, we will get rid of them in due course."

Strogen coloured at the sarcasm evident in his leader's question and stood up briskly, "Of course."

"Then why are we having this conversation? Honestly, Strogen, do I have to wipe your arse for you *every* time you shit?"

The Ulfhednar clansman shook his head mutely, cutting a pathetic figure and Varga found he could not even bring himself to continue speaking to him and simply shut his eyes again.

As Strogen walked away from the withering dismissal, the war-leader peered sidelong at his retreating back, determining then and there that, if the slightest thing went wrong with Strogen's foray, then the weaselly fool would pay for it with his life. After all, he thought, with the amount of praise I have heaped upon the tribe over the last few days, I would not want them to think I had gone soft.

Strogen stomped away from Varga, outwardly calm but inwardly seething. He glanced at the two Ulfhednar who had cajoled him into asking the question and saw that they were trying unsuccessfully to stifle laughter. He swung towards them and affected a casualness which belied the rage bubbling within him.

"Well, come on then," Strogen gestured. "Hrolfsson says we can attack if we wish. For myself, I have a sudden urge to rip flesh and break heads." He stood, hands on hips, regarding the two werewolves with contempt, "or are you pair too cowardly to join me?"

One of the two thrust out a hand to restrain his snarling brother. "What did you say?" he hissed in a deceptively quiet voice.

In the normal course of events, Strogen would have shied away from provoking the two Olsen brothers, but Varga's insulting manner had angered him to such an extent that he had spat out the insult before thinking. For a brief instant, Strogen's natural character fought for supremacy and he was on the brink of mumbling an apology, but the face of the elder sibling, Tormod, was set in such an offensive expression of arrogance and scorn that, to Strogen's surprise, he found his temper undiminished and continued baiting them. "Well?" he sneered. "Of course, if you think it will be too much, I am sure I can find someone else who would be of more use to me."

Tormod's face froze as his brother, Preben, broke free of his grip and stalked towards Strogen. "Aye, we will come, Muntersson. No doubt you will need someone there to cover up the mistakes which you are bound to make."

Strogen smiled with his mouth and walked off without waiting to see if the pair followed him. When he heard the brothers padding alongside him he smiled grimly but did not acknowledge them, merely concentrating on the row of orange flames that wavered in the wind a few hundred yards away.

As the trio of Ulfhednar drew closer, it became clear there were no more than ten members of the welcoming party and Strogen's mouth split into a huge grin. Easy pickings tonight, he thought.

A change in the air to his left and his right, told him that the Olsen brothers had changed into their wolven form and he contemplated doing the same, but held off at the last minute due to a small voice inside him which counselled caution.

A cry of disbelief broke through the silence, having emanated from the gathering at the top of the slope, Strogen presumed, in response to seeing the transformation of man to wolf for the first time.

What he heard next stopped him momentarily in his tracks. One of the group had shouted something which would have been lost completely due to the language barrier, had it not been for one word that stood out like a shriek in the night.

At that moment, Strogen offered a quick whispered prayer to Fenrir, for if he had done as the Olsen brothers had and changed into a werewolf, he would never have picked out the word "Ulfhednar" as it was screamed into the sky. It was the first time he had heard anyone other than his clan use the word and it sounded strange and wrong when spoken in another accent. Intrigued by this, he held back from the headlong charge which the brothers had launched into, instead homing in on one of the torches that bobbed unevenly away from the group, which was being held, he assumed, by one who had been sent to get aid of some sort.

The sounds of flight turned into the sounds of struggle as Tormod and Preben caught up with the islanders. Strogen ignored the shouts which rapidly turned to screams as the two beasts fell upon the retreating Picts and sped up his pursuit. It took him less than a minute to reach the native tribesman and he brought him down with a flying leap. For a few seconds, the two bodies went down in a tangle of limbs before Strogen gained the upper hand, bringing his superior strength to bear as he strangled the man.

He kept applying the pressure until he felt him go limp, beneath his straddled thighs. As he brushed himself off, he noted with passing interest the different cut of the man's clothes, which were of a much better quality than the usual mixture of grubby furs and woollen tunics caked in mud and filth. His attention was drawn back to the melee off to his left, where the main group had formed itself into a circle and was fending off the attack by brandishing their flaming torches at the ferocious beasts. The blazing brands stole his night vision from him and so now he did transform into a werewolf.

Instantly, he could see the make-up of the killing ground, now that he was possessed of the acute eyesight of his kind. His head flickered from left to right as he spotted Tormod on one side of the circle and Preben on the other. He quickly saw his estimate of ten had been correct. Four prostrate forms could be seen unmoving in the short grass of the battlefield whilst five still stood, their un-coordinated movements speaking volumes of their fear and shock. Despite this, they still had enough of their wits about them to hold the brothers at bay. Three stood facing Tormod, who prowled to and fro, snapping and snarling incessantly but shying away from the heat of the torches when they were waved in his direction. The other two followed Preben as he did the same as his brother, probing, searching for a gap in the shield of flame through which he could mount another assault.

Strogen squinted again at Preben and smiled evilly as he saw the younger wolf favouring his front left paw over his right. "So, you have been hurt, have you, you little bastard?" Strogen sniggered, "Such a shame," he tutted theatrically before advancing on the group, ghosting silently through the night like an angel of death.

"Can you see him?" Gordon McKinson wailed jabbing his blazing brand at the massive wolf as it lunged for them again.

"I can see a flame in the distance." His compatriot, Duncan Watson, blurted, having chanced the sharpest of glances over his shoulder, "but it does not seem to be moving. I told you there were three of the monsters. The other one must have claimed him as he ran for the monastery." He leant back from the whoomph of the heat which was generated by Gordon's desperate defence. "Damn it, Gordon, have a care," he shook his head bitterly. "Remind me again why we have started to leave our weapons back at the cloisters, will you?"

"Padraig says it is not very welcoming if we confront all who arrive upon our shores armed to the teeth. Christianity is supposed to be based on peace and love after all." Duncan shouted above the sounds of slaughter.

An agonised shriek was cut short and Duncan choked back tears. He had recognised the voice as being that of James Carlyle, a fellow member of his tribe and, until a few seconds ago, the clansman who had stood at his back and held the group together as the wolves had rushed in.

Now though, his back was exposed and the circle tightened evermore.

As the foursome bobbed and weaved, Duncan found himself turning to the left and he noticed that the flame he had seen in the distance was growing in intensity and size. In perplexity, he began to lower the torch in his hand, remembering just in time, it was the only thing standing between him and the beast. He brought it back up just as the wolf went for his throat and was gratified to hear a hastily cut-off growl followed by a pained whine. Emboldened by this and the growing hysteria of their predicament, he snarled, "Leave us in peace or burn in hell."

For a moment, the melee lulled as both wolves were now nursing injuries. All four of the tribesmen squinted into the darkness, trying to make out the loping creatures which stalked them, but the night had gone ominously quiet.

The only noise was the soughing wind and a distant hiss and crackle.

"That should bring help anyway," a voice behind Duncan quavered.

"What should, Owen?"

Owen Patterson pointed with his free hand towards the engorging flame which had erupted approximately one hundred yards away from where the quartet fought for their lives. Inexplicably, despite the cold and damp conditions, the beacon which had been dropped by Strogen's victim had ignited the machair and the fire was spreading.

"Praise the Lord," Duncan breathed somewhat self-consciously. "Hopefully," he began to say, "...wait, what's that?"

A shadow in the unmistakeable shape of a wolf moved across the flame towards them.

"Dear God, not another one of..." the final member of the foursome, Stuart Nicol, started to speak before he was wrenched out of the group by one of the wolves.

This restored the raw panic to the situation, because the suddenness of the attack had caused Stuart to lose hold of his torch, which flew balletically up into the air and landed in the midst of the circle, giving the wolves all the opportunity they needed to pick off the remaining tribesmen.

Patterson was the first to be taken. In the chaos, a huge shape barrelled into the trio and bore him to the ground. His hysterical screams did not last for long before they subsided into a hideous bubbling groan as his throat was ripped to pieces.

Gordon McKinson lay about himself frantically with the torch, scoring a couple of blows before Preben broke through his frenetic defence and plunged his teeth into the tribesman's right thigh. As he fell backwards, Strogen appeared out of the night and took him in the throat, cutting him off in mid-shriek.

Duncan ran blindly away from the gory spectacle, flinging his torch back towards where the wolves were feeding, striking out across the meadow towards the fire that was growing ever larger and splitting the night into depthless black and eye-watering orange. Soon he was surrounded by a cloying cloud of smoke which teared his eyes and clawed at his lungs. In seconds, he became hopelessly disorientated and stumbled to his knees. He wanted to cough up the choking phlegm which the smoke had produced in his throat but he knew such a noise would give away his position, so he tried to quell it but without success. The first cough was stifled but still sounded thunderous in the supercharged silence. This gave way to an extended bout of hacking and spluttering which he could not contain and he fell upon his front, burying his face in the machair and holding his breath, tensing himself for the razor sharp pain of the werewolves' feeding frenzy.

306

After a few seconds, he let out an explosive breath and chanced a glance up into the darkness, listening with all his might for sounds of pursuit. To his relief and confusion, there were none, so he began to crawl towards the guttering flames which were now, finally, starting to dwindle in the chill wind which had picked up a little while before but had passed unnoticed by the tribesmen who had suddenly found themselves plunged into a fight for their lives.

He made painful progress, the smoke burning his lungs and the shock freezing his limbs. Eventually, he found that he had managed to get to the far side of the flames, putting them between him and the scene of carnage. After pausing once more to double-check he was not on the brink of capture, he jumped up and took to his heels, determined not to stop until he reached the relative sanctuary of his home.

Preben stepped back from the gore-spattered corpse which he had been feeding on as his long tongue snaked out to clean his whiskers and muzzle. He thought that one of the islanders had run past him but he could not be sure. The pain blooming in his belly and face was robbing him of any sort of concentration. He had taken two thrusts in the fight, one of which had brushed his chest, singeing his fur and burning his white underbelly. The other had inflicted a great deal more damage. It had hit him square in the left eye, only for a second, but long enough to rob him of sight.

As the adrenaline of the slaughter diminished, so the pain of his wounds grew and he started to yowl in agony, pawing unthinkingly at his eye with his dew-claw which only served to increase the pain.

Then the world was spinning as something cannoned into him and he was sent sprawling to the ground. Instinctively he lashed out with his claws and half-heartedly snapped at the mystery assailant.

A pain unlike anything he had ever felt before screeched through his back legs and he tried to stand, but the limbs collapsed beneath him. The last thing that his poor abused eyes made out before everything went black did not make sense. One of his own kind was looming over him, its aggressive stance leaving no doubt as to its ultimate purpose.

Strogen stared down unpityingly at the twisted form of Preben Olsen and shuddered with pleasure. His eyes narrowed as a strangled yelp sounded behind him and he took a couple of steps back to allow the distraught Tormod to limp over to his fallen brother.

In perfect unison, the two brothers transformed back into their human form and, despite his hatred of Tormod, Strogen winced in sympathy as Tormod's body went through the contortions of the change, obviously hampered by his injuries. On the other hand, Preben's transition from beast to man was something wonderfully pure. Surprisingly in all his years in the Ulfhednar, Strogen had never paid much attention to the conversion of a dead clan member before, finding it a too potent reminder of his own mortality, but now he found his eye drawn to it and his breath caught in his throat.

Whether it was because there was no resistance to it from Preben or for some other reason he did not know, the change flowed effortlessly, rippling up the dead man's body as if he had been submerged under an invisible tide.

Strogen was jerked out of his reverie by Tormod's anguished voice, "What happened to my brother? How did they kill him?" he wailed.

Still in his wolven form and taking advantage of his quarry's misunderstanding of events, he leapt at Tormod's jugular before the bereaved brother had time to react. His bared teeth closed about the shocked man's throat even as his claws raked down the heavily bleeding cut which had been inflicted during the melee with the islanders. Tormod did not have a chance against Strogen's onslaught and, within seconds, he had joined his brother upon the benighted shores of the Nastrond.

After the bitterness he had felt at his treatment from Varga, the elation of his plan of action working so perfectly was more than he could contain and he howled his joy to the stars.

"Strogen?"

The voice wrenched him from his contemplation of the murdered brothers. As he turned to face his leader, he felt gladdened that he had chosen to return to his human form as soon as he had perpetrated the deed rather than remaining as a wolf. It was so much easier to marshal thoughts and hide lies when you walked on two legs.

"What occurred here?" Hrolfsson asked quizzically.

Strogen searched his eyes for any hint of suspicion in the massive Viking's expression but could find none. "Pure luck on their part, Varga," he said, nodding at the blood-soaked islanders who lay upon the grass. "They only had torches but they fought like demons. I warned them to be careful but you know what the Olsens are...were like when they had the scent of blood in their nostrils."

Varga grunted non-committally before pointing past Strogen's shoulder, "What of that?"

The Ulfhednar clansman turned and his mouth gaped. The fire caused by the torch of the fleeing islander had diminished to a certain extent but was still burning fiercely and was sending a cloud of smoke hundreds of feet into the air. He did not take his eyes off it as he responded quietly, "One of them broke from the group. I chased him down," he shrugged. "I did not think in these conditions the flame would catch in such a way. Anyway, I thought it more important to help Preben and Tormod finish off the natives."

He was quite proud of himself as, in previous times, Varga's wildly unpredictable moods and vicious temper had filled him with fear, but his voice had remained calm and matter-of-fact and he was sure he had given no clue as to his deception.

Without a word, Varga backhanded him across the face, breaking his jaw and sending three teeth rocketing out of his mouth onto the grass. "Do not dare insult my intelligence, you craven bastard."

His head swimming from the pain and shock, Strogen tried to retreat but Varga was upon him in a second, "I am not concerned that you have sent up a beacon which will attract all the islanders nearby, because that will preclude us having to walk the length and breadth of this land for trophies. What I am concerned with is the fact you think I am stupid."

Strogen whimpered in abject terror as Varga grasped his neck and lifted him off his feet, "It is obvious you killed them, you snivelling wretch." He looked down at the prone brothers. "There is not a chance in the Nine Worlds of Hel that Preben and Tormod would have failed to overcome such a small force and, unless the islanders hereabouts have torches with teeth and claws, it is unlikely that their deaths were the work of normal men." Varga leant in and Strogen shuddered as he felt the clan-leader's hot breath upon his cheek. "I have been looking for an excuse to slaughter you like the pig you are for many a moon." He whispered in a voice so quiet only Strogen could hear it. "Now I have it."

"Varga, please…" the desperate clansman managed to gurgle.

Hrolfsson lowered him to the ground, kept his right hand on Strogen's neck and slammed his left down upon the crown of his head. Effortlessly, he jerked his two hands in opposite directions, resulting in a snap so audible that several of the watching clansmen jumped. Varga kept twisting, his muscles bunching tighter and tighter until, with a huge hiss of effort, he tore Strogen's head clear of his shoulders. With a sensual sigh, he held it up to the sky and howled, in much the same way as Strogen had done minutes before, however the fact that the sound issued from a human mouth seemed to make it all the more eerie. However, it was soon drowned out by the other Ulfhednar taking up the howl. The spine-tingling ululation went on for just over a minute before the sound was lost in the wind.

Duncan wheezed and stumbled his way across the moor, his ankles aching from the uneven ground which he had to negotiate in the dark and his lungs straining to expel the last of the smoke from the fire. For a heart-stopping moment, he froze as the chilling call of the werewolves reached his ears but, mercifully, he could now make out the monastery, which was outlined against the lightening sky.

Within minutes, he was hammering with all his strength upon the door until it swung ponderously back. He fell to the flagstones of the courtyard and vomited copiously before gentle hands raised him to his feet. Duncan found himself staring into the concerned face of Brother Eamonn and began hysterically burbling the details of what had befallen him and his fellow clansmen.

The monk tried to quieten his distress, to get him to slow down and catch his breath, but Duncan would not be stayed, "I must tell Padraig," he managed to blurt when it was clear Brother Eamonn still did not understand what his tidings meant for the monastery, or indeed the island as a whole. "Where is he?" He grabbed the shocked holy man by the front of his robe and shook him.

"Duncan, Duncan!" Brother Padraig's urgent brogue echoed around the courtyard as Watson collapsed into his arms, unable to speak from the shock of what he had witnessed.

Despite himself, Brother Eamonn looked relieved to have passed on the burden of the panic-stricken islander, "I am sorry, Padraig, I could not comfort him. He said all who went to greet those on the ship that beached, were slaughtered, murdered by wolves who walked as men or something. Even Brother Malcolm. What he said made no sense." Eamonn's hurried summary of what had transpired between himself and Duncan stopped dead when he saw the look on the senior monk's face. "Do you know what he is talking about, Padraig?"

"Ulfhednar," Padraig breathed, staring into space. Whilst the strange word meant nothing to Brother Eamonn, it was enough to jerk Duncan out of his catatonia. His red puffy eyes fixed on the founder of the Order at Mull. "That is the word Brother Malcolm used before he began to run back towards the monastery."

All pretence of concern for Duncan's wellbeing fled as Padraig's face went ashen. "Come with me," he hissed, physically dragging the stunned tribesman behind him as he nearly ran through the cloisters.

Stopping at what looked to Duncan like every other door they had bolted past, without knocking, Padraig burst in, startling the occupants out of their beds. He pushed Duncan into the room and hissed, "Tell them all of what you saw."

A cold icy pit opened up in each of the McLeishs' stomachs as Duncan Watson recounted all he could remember and they stared in horror at the grey-faced Padraig as he listened again to Watson's tale.

"It would seem that your cowardice has not allowed you to escape the werewolves' clutches, does it not," Padraig sneered.

Warren and Tavish began to protest but the monk cut them off, "I am not going to waste another second of my life listening to your wheedling. When Taiga and Craigan departed, I initially thought the wulver's judgement of you two was harsh in the extreme but, the more I have come to know you and witness first-hand your indolent ways, the more I have concluded he was not harsh enough." Padraig had gone red in the face and Duncan thought, for a second, that the leader of the monks of Mull who, as far as he was aware, had never raised a hand to another human being, was on the brink of striking the two Taexali.

With a great effort of will, Padraig dragged his temper back from the edge and continued to speak more calmly, "That said, you now have the opportunity to salvage some sort of honour from the ruins of your reputation. You know as well as any here that these monsters will not be swayed by clever words or reasoned argument. They are here to kill us all," he shook his head, sighing heavily.

"We could hole up here and try to wait out the coming storm." Warren suggested hopefully.

Padraig's face twisted into an ugly snarl, "No, we cannot. Not without betraying all the principles we have preached for the last few years. We must leave the gates open to all whom would seek sanctuary within these walls. If the people of this island are in need of us, then we cannot deny them access to the monastery just to save our own skins."

"You could not defend this place anyway. Not against the wolves." Tavish murmured despondently. He stood up and faced Padraig. "What would you have us do?"

A modicum of respect appeared in Padraig's eyes as he said, "Did Taiga or Craigan say anything of any weaknesses that this horde have? How can they be beaten?"

The twins looked at each other and shook their heads, "If they knew of any, they did not discuss them with us, but then I do not believe the wulver was particularly taken by our...easygoing manner." Tavish said with an eyebrow raised towards his brother and a sardonic smirk on his face.

Padraig said nothing, sensing that Tavish wanted to say more. His intuition was borne out as the smile dissolved from the Taexali's face and he slumped down upon his bed dejectedly. "Look, Padraig, we did not distinguish ourselves when we were in the company of Taiga and Craigan. We are sheep not shepherds. Confrontation does not sit easy with us and the quiet life is what we seek. Would you say that was fair, Warren?"

Though he was obviously uncomfortable at admitting his failings in such a blatant manner, Warren nodded solemnly, "Never had much of a backbone, to be honest," he muttered.

Looking from one to the other, Padraig found his frustration at the brothers' behaviour lessening and he nodded in appreciation of their honesty. "Well, at least you are able to admit to your faults. That is more than a lot of people would be prepared to do." He began pacing the room, aware that he did not have much time before the wolves appeared at the monastery's doors. "I can see by the set of your shoulders you are not proud of how you perceive yourselves, but I find myself wondering how you would react if your lives were truly on the line." Padraig's face became sombre again. "Well, that is the situation now, lads, Duncan's account leaves no doubt to that. Either we kill the wolves or they will kill us. Will you stand with us, Tavish? Warren?"

For long moments, the McLeish twins looked at one another in an agony of indecision. Padraig and Duncan retreated from the room for a moment and, while they waited, the monk told the clansman to go and ring the refectory bell, deeming that to be the fastest way to gather the residents of the monastery together in one place.

Duncan ran off along the corridor, his legs still slightly wobbly from the horror which he had been through in the last hour. Resolving to give the brothers no longer than a minute to make a decision, he grabbed the next man to walk past and ordered him to find a couple of other men, be they native clansmen or monks, then go and retrieve a weapon each from the cache in the cellar which was added to whenever an armed newcomer entered the building, then secure the front gates and guard them.

The monk was about to re-enter the McLeishs' room when they both came out and stood before him, "Warren and I have been talking and, well, perhaps it is time to stop running from responsibility and turn round and face whatever life throws at us."

"Nowhere to run anyway, is there?" Warren grunted. "We are stuck on an island and, such is the sum of our boating skills, I am not sure we would even know which end of the oar to stick in the water."

Tavish sighed theatrically, "Now why did you go and say that? I nearly had him convinced we had experienced an epiphany in our sad and sorry lives which had led us to put our very existence on the line on behalf of the monastery. You have just gone and spoiled it."

Padraig tried to look appropriately shocked but could not keep a smile from creasing his face and the trio shared a chuckle in the corridor. As their laughter subsided, the distant vestiges of a howl reached their ears and the mirth died instantly.

Padraig mumbled, "You had better repair to the cellar and fetch yourselves a sword each."

Without a word, and with fear written large in their eyes, the brothers dragged themselves off to the lower reaches of the building.

The Irish monk began to hurry to the dining area just as the bell began tolling its ominous summons.

Within minutes, the vast majority of the people living within the cloisters of Mull were milling uncertainly around the wooden benches and Padraig felt all eyes upon him as he rushed into the room. Without ceremony, he climbed upon the nearest table and held up his hands for silence. The strangeness of the situation was enough that he achieved his goal within seconds. For a few moments, he looked at the sea of faces before him and had to stop himself from wondering how many would be residing in heaven once the aftermath of the Ulfhednar's scourge was fully realised. Blinking away the melancholy thought, he addressed his audience.

"My friends, you will recall the wulver Taiga Haas and his companion Craigan McIntyre who visited us not two weeks hence. They appeared at our gates windswept, hungry and burdened with a tale of dreadfulness and horror which had driven them across the sea. Their abiding ambition was to bring to an end the abominable reign of terror that a tribe of god-forsaken monsters had brought to their homeland. We were able to help in a small way, by providing them with food, shelter and spiritual strength for their quest as well as the services of Brother Lorcan, then we sent them forth in the hope that we had played our part in the tale as well as any Christians could. Unfortunately, it would appear that our involvement in this narrative is far from over."

At that moment, the first pause in Padraig's speech, the baying of wolves could clearly be heard drifting on the wind and, from his elevated position, Padraig saw dreadful realisation appear on at least a dozen faces. Before the hubbub grew to unmanageable volume, he spoke on, "Yes, my friends, by some evil quirk, it appears that the Ulfhednar have appeared at our gates. They have already claimed nine of our number. If it was not for the fact that Duncan here managed to escape their clutches we would, even now, be unaware of their presence befouling this wondrous island."

Even though he was still scared beyond anything he had ever known, Duncan managed an embarrassed smile as he became the object of the crowd's scrutiny.

"As you can hear, brothers, we do not have much time. The nearness of the beasts precludes any debate as to what we should do. We have no option but to stand and fight. I realise that many of you took your orders or came to reside within these walls to escape violence and bloodshed, but these creatures cannot be reasoned with or bargained with. They live for one purpose. To kill those they meet without mercy. Therefore I ask you all to make your way down to the cellars and take up once more the weapons which you forsook when you entered our holy house."

Some voices were raised in protest at this but once again, Padraig's stern glare brooked no argument. "I know it does not sit well with our beliefs, but these creatures are spawned from the deepest pit of Hell itself and we must face them. If there are any here who feel unable to bear weapons then I will not order you to, but I would also say that, if those who do resist these beasts are defeated, no amount of prayer will stop them from slaughtering you where you kneel."

He jumped down from the table and strode purposefully out of the nearest door, closely followed by every single one of his audience.

Brother Eamonn choked back a strangled squeak as the doors shook to a fearsome pounding from without.

He licked arid lips and stared nervously at his fellow guards, a Venicone tribesman called Douglas Beath and one of his fellow monks, Brother Cormac.

Douglas was a wiry, small-built man with a shaven head and bushy ginger beard who had opted for a spear as a weapon of choice, which he now levelled at the door. "Will ye open it, brother? Or wait for Padraig?" he asked in a harsh brogue.

Eamonn's hand moved slowly towards the sliding panel which had been placed at eye height in the door before stopping inches from it. He looked at Cormac, one of his oldest friends from over the water, for some guidance, flinching again when the tattoo sounded once more on the wood.

Cormac pulled a face, "Padraig said we were to let in those in need, did he not?"

"Aye, but what if it is one of the hell-beasts?" Douglas put in.

Taking a deep breath, Eamonn placed his hand on the panel and pulled it back. "At least we can see who is there. That, at least, will not cost us anyth..."

Cormac and Douglas gaped in horror as a hairy paw with claws extended thrust through the small rectangle in the wood, then disappeared up to the knuckle into Brother Eamonn's skull.

The monk was dead before he hit the ground. The claw withdrew and the two guards watched in petrified shock as it closed around the edge of the gap, pulling it into splinters. As the hole became wider, more animal talons tore at the space, increasing its size second by second.

Cormac blinked in shock as Douglas let out a primal scream of rage and thrust his spear through the throng. He was rewarded with a pained yelp and growl of anger. Driving his weapon forward again and again, he managed to say to the monk, "Are ye going to use that bloody sword or nae?"

Cormac felt as if he had been plunged into a nightmare as he stepped to the left and saw the full horror of the werewolves for the first time.

There were five of them, their maws matted with blood and saliva, their faces contorted hideously with rage. However, the worst aspect was their eyes.

Cormac was educated enough to know that, though it would always be in the nature of the wolf to be a merciless killer, that instinct would always be mitigated by the fact that, despite popular belief, they killed to survive, a process repeated at every single level of the animal world. However, the mockeries which, even now, were gaining entry to the monastery were all too well aware of what they were doing. They had no excuse for their actions beyond a sick pleasure in violence and killing.

In a bitter irony, Cormac realised that one of the beliefs of his religion was that man was closer to God than animals due to the ability to reason and think intelligently, yet it was this very spark of intelligence which made the Ulfhednar such dreadful adversaries.

Unbidden, the words of the *Pater Noster* came to his lips even as he began to hack and slash at those who sought to send him to face God's judgement.

More and more evil faces appeared at the slowly widening gap as Douglas and Cormac manfully fought for their lives. The tribesman's face was a mass of cuts and his forearms were spattered with blood, both human and wolf. He was struggling to wield the spear as his arms grew ever more tired and it was not long before a clutching bunch of talons gripped the weapon's shaft and yanked it from his grasp, pulling him within range of the razor-sharp claws of the Ulfhednar.

Before Cormac could react, a paw sliced across the Vacomagi's face and he screamed in pain as his nose was smashed into a pulp and one of his eyes was ruined. The monk grabbed his bloodied tunic, pulled him free of the grasping claws and launched a brutal hacking swing which separated the offending extremity from its owner's arm.

To his disbelief, Douglas scrabbled on the floor for Eamonn's unused blade and tried to rejoin the fray but his injuries were too severe and he fell to the side, moaning incoherently.

"But deliver us from evil," Cormac murmured as a deflected slash left his blade embedded deeply within the wood of the door and left him momentarily unarmed. He reached down for Eamonn's weapon, forgetting that Douglas had moved it, then sensed rather than saw, a massive shadow loom over him.

His breath quickened in preparation for his death, but all he heard was a sickening squelch and the sensation of the shadow falling away from him.

He stared in confusion at the naked body of a woman prostrate on the cold stone next to him. His eyes were drawn inexorably to the gory wound which split her chest in two and the blood-drenched axe laying next to her.

Bodies rushed past him as he looked up. He caught a glimpse of Padraig in the van of the charge with the McLeish brothers at his side. More familiar faces followed and fully twenty people had stormed past him before one detached from the attack and knelt by his side. He blinked furiously and finally the face of Brother Sheridan swum into focus.

"Are you hurt?" he asked solicitously.

"I do not think so," Cormac mumbled then his eyes widened, "But Eamonn...Douglas...?" His voice rose in panic until he saw the expression on his companion's face, which was all the answer he needed.

"How am I not dead?" he quavered. "I could feel the monster rearing above me poised to strike."

A hysterical zeal lit Brother Sheridan's eyes as he spoke, "It was Padraig. He was like the Archangel Michael when he fought the Great Dragon and hurled him down from Heaven. He glided along the corridor and let loose a Labrys, which flew straight and true as if guided by God, cleaving the beast in the sternum. It was a privilege to witness it."

Cormac's brow furrowed at the enthusiasm in Sheridan's voice but put it down to the stress of the battle. He got unsteadily to his feet, helped by his fellow monk.

The weight of numbers that had joined the defenders, plus the cramped space in which the fight was occurring, swung the attack back into the favour of the monks and islanders momentarily, as the wolves found their fellow clansmen unable to join the fray.

With an unexpected suddenness, there was a lull in the fighting and the Ulfhednar pulled back from the ruined entranceway. A ragged cheer erupted from the defenders but it quickly tailed off as they took stock of their casualties. Twelve of them lay dead, all with horrific injuries caused by raking claws and supernatural strength. Of those still standing, only one remained uninjured.

Brother Padraig stumbled numbly over to Cormac, dragged an exhausted hand down his face and leant against the wall. "At least we have driven them back for a moment." He clapped his hand on Cormac's shoulder and smiled wanly, "I am amazed you held this long."

Cormac went pale as he looked at Eamonn's ruined face once more. "It was Douglas, really. Brother Eamonn was cut down in a trice then Douglas just leapt into his place. I barely did anything."

316

The founder of the Order on Mull looked closely at the many cuts on Cormac's arm and face as well as a large bruise which was beginning to show around his left eye. "Come now, I do not believe that. It is clear that you more than stood your ground."

Cormac said nothing, merely shaking his head despairingly. Brother Sheridan, on the other hand, was full of excitement. "Where on earth did you learn to fight like that, Brother? It was awe-inspiring."

Padraig sighed, "I was not always a holy man. I was once high up in the echelons of Báetán mac Cairill's army. I was sent to these lands to collect tribute from Áedán mac Gabráin of Dál Riata but, on the crossing from Ulster, we were blown off-course and beached on the coast of Iona, where we found the wings of Colum Cille open in welcome. I was converted within days, choosing to leave my military life behind and enjoy the anonymity of the order on Iona. I do not think I was ever happier than those few months with Columba." He shrugged. "However, Baetan was not the sort of king to just forgive and forget and he sent men to find me. Columba was so impressed with me that he felt I was due some sort of reward so he sent me to Mull to establish the Order here." He fixed Sheridan with an icy stare. "Do not be impressed by my prowess, for I am not proud of it. Every time I take a life it sickens me to the pit of my stomach, even if the victim is one who has ascended the steps which lead from the depths of Hell."

A spine-chilling roar cut Padraig short and a massive shape blotted out the light that came in through the hole in the door from outside.

"Dear God," Cormac whimpered as Varga crashed through the door as if it was made of paper.

He stood facing the assembled residents of the monastery with a look of absolute contempt on his face and from him emanated such a powerful aura that those who were in a position to baulk his progress were paralysed by fear.

Playing upon this, with a calculating look sweeping to and fro across his audience, he began the metamorphosis of man to wolf. Though he knew he was vulnerable during the transformation, he was supremely confident that not one of his enemies would move to attack him before the change was complete. Within seconds, Varga had assumed his wolven form and the silence in the room was such that the sound of the massive wolf's breathing was impossibly loud.

The world seemed to stand still for a moment until Varga sensed movement to his right.

Brother Padraig had retrieved the double-headed axe from the flagstones and walked slowly in front of Varga, his stare never leaving his adversary's emerald eyes.

317

A low growl started in Varga's throat and his muscles bunched at the impertinence.

"I defy you, Satan-spawn. Come, feel the bite of my blessed blade." The monk hissed as he began to swing the wickedly sharp weapon in a figure of eight.

When Varga leapt, it was so fast that he did not appear to cross the intervening space between himself and the holy man and the two went bowling over in a tangle of limbs, scattering the watchers.

Despite the speed of the attack, Padraig had managed to bring his weapon up enough to protect him from any serious harm. However, Varga was a raging mountain of fur and he did not take long to inflict a severe injury down Padraig's left arm which left it hanging uselessly at the monk's side. Somehow he managed to push Varga away from him and, at one point, forced the massive beast back a couple of steps, but it was a false dawn and, on the very next stroke of the axe, he overstretched, leaving himself open to Varga's assault.

One gargantuan paw swept round in an unstoppable arc and the horrified audience winced as they heard the sickening sound of Padraig's rib-cage stoving inwards.

The monk fell gasping to the flagstones, groping for a breath which would never come.

In an instant, Varga returned to his human form and leant in close to the dying man, a look of grudging respect upon his face.

Suddenly Padraig grabbed at the Ulfhednar leader and whispered, "Monkshood is coming for you."

Varga jerked back momentarily as if he had been stung. He was still surprised that the mere mention of the name was enough to unsettle him so but, within seconds, the arrogant mask appeared once more and he shook off his unease. He unpeeled Padraig's fingers from his furs and pushed him to the stone, causing a gush of blood to erupt from the gravely injured monk's lips. Varga picked Padraig up by his hair and snapped his neck with nothing but a swift flick of his wrists, though the report of vertebrae was loud enough to jerk all those watching out of their horrified waking nightmare.

Suddenly all the residents of the monastery realised that, whilst they had been mesmerized by the appalling violence of their leader's death, upwards of twenty Ulfhednar had slunk into the courtyard and now surrounded them, poised to fall without mercy upon the now cowering men.

Varga beckoned one of the werewolves over as he walked from the scene of carnage, turning momentarily, just as he stepped over the threshold of the ruined door and ordering, "Kill them."

As the screams of the dying fled towards the night sky, Varga looked at his companion as they walked across the machair in the direction of the rapidly dying fire which had started as a result of Strogen's ill-judged attack.

"We must make for home as quickly as we are able, Vidkun. Dun Varulfur is singing its sweet siren song in my ears louder than ever before."

Vidkun Hagelin nodded. He was a veteran of many Viking blood-raids and was regarded by Hrolfsson as one of the most experienced sailors in the Ulfhednar ranks. "Rest assured, Varga, I will wring every last drop of sweat from the oarsmen to ensure we make good speed across the seas."

Hrolfsson smiled at the statement, "Go and prepare the *Varulv* for the voyage home. I estimate we are nearing our goal of a hundred thousand skulls." He breathed hugely and exhaled with a sensual sigh, "Soon we will be exalted above all others amongst our people, for we will be at the right-hand of our God, rising above all and claiming the dominion which is ours by rite of blood and conquest."

Hagelin could not suppress the grin on his face and raced away from his leader to do as he was bid.

Hrolfsson took the opportunity for a too rare moment of privacy and simply stood watching the fluid dance of the flaming meadow. As his eyes became ever more captivated by the constant ebb and flow of the flickering oranges and yellows, he felt as if the world was falling away from him and he was being pulled forward into the flames. He knew he should be afraid but he was not. With a suddenness that was almost audible, his momentum ceased and he found himself in a cave very similar to the one in which he had first been granted audience by Fenrir all those years ago.

He stared around the mammoth space feeling dwarfed once more at the sheer scale of the fissure. A pointed cough spun him round and he found himself staring upon a wondrous sight.

The blond woman walked over to the leader of the Ulfhednar and stroked his massive chest with her left hand, whilst unclipping the brooch which held her tunic together with the other. The garment fell to the floor of the cave and she stepped back from him, slowly turning to allow Varga to fully appreciate every curve of her body. She beckoned for him to follow as she sashayed silently out of the light which bathed the cave on all four walls through an arch carved into the nearest side. It was then that a tinkling music filled his ears and he realised, inexplicably, he was as naked as she was.

Unselfconsciously, Varga strode after her, marvelling at the grace of her movement and finding his body filled with yearning.

He walked through the arch into a pitch black room, yet still fear did not touch him. Slowly, a pulsing glow began to emanate from the floor upwards,

319

washing over the grey stone in an aurora of many colours. As his eyes grew accustomed to the light, he took in the scene before him.

The centrepiece of the room was a huge ornate bed with a canopy overhanging it. The canopy itself was supported by four posts all inlaid with carvings of wolves and runic inscriptions. As he stepped towards it, the flimsy material swept aside of its own accord and revealed the mysterious woman in all her glory. She lay before him, ready to receive the leader of the Ulfhednar and Varga was not a man to turn down such an open invitation. However, as he climbed into the bed he did not feel the usual unquenchable lust that took him during the heat of battle, instead his body was suffused with an overwhelming tenderness and as the two came together as one, Varga took the time to cherish his partner and ensure that both of them enjoyed the experience as much as the other.

As he lay back he murmured, "May I have your name, lady. I feel I should know you."

The voice that replied shocked him out of his comfort with all the force of a plunge into icy water.

"You do, young Hrolfsson. You do."

Varga shot out of the bed like a bolt loosed from a crossbow. "Beyla?" he spat in disbelief, as the woman dissolved into a fit of laughter.

"Aye, Varga."

His eyes blazed in fury and he lunged for her. In an instant, the canopy of the bed became as impenetrable as a rock face. He could clearly see the seeress through the flimsy material, but he still could not reach her, try though he might. "Explain yourself, hag!" he roared.

She turned her back to him and thrust her naked bottom in his direction before peering coquettishly over her shoulder. "I feel hag is a bit unfair. Am I not pleasing to your eye, my lord?" she purred.

Varga found his rage draining away and he even forced a laugh, though he was still angered by the deception. "Come, Beyla. Even you will admit this is out of character. Why have you tricked me in this way?"

Beyla lay back again and her eyes roamed her own body, "You know, I did actually used to look like this many moons ago," she sighed and her eyes misted. "The passage of time has robbed me of many things, Varga. Family, friends, looks, memories." She smiled and the radiance almost brought tears to his eyes. "I am dying, my lord. All too soon, the future becomes a wall of absolute darkness. I am a seeress, Varga, and I am well aware of what that means. Please, I beseech you, hurry home to Dun Varulfur. You have, aboard the *Varulv*, enough skulls but one to release Fenrir from his eternal fetters. I just pray I will still be alive when you return, for I wish to be the final skull to sit atop the pyre when Fenrir comes to reclaim what is rightfully his."

With a sudden burst of insight, the mystery of the enigmatic voice that had been hovering on the very edge of Varga's consciousness came to him. "It is you," he breathed. "You have been summoning me home."

Beyla nodded in confirmation, "I have been trying to call to you for weeks, ever since I began to sense what was to come, but to no avail. I have good days and bad days, on the bad days I can barely make myself heard in my own chambers, let alone across the ocean waves but, on the good days, well," she smiled again and gestured at him making Varga's heart ache for her once more, "this has been a good day."

"Would you not rather stay alive and enjoy the fruits of our labours? Why give your life in such a way?"

"I could do that, it is true, but I have lived more years than I can remember, Varga. I could make myself look like this every day, I could weave my spells, I could take lovers, I could do all of that and more, but I would still feel every single one of my years here." She placed her fist over her breast. "I have already lived far, far too long and I am tired. I can think of no more fitting an end to my life than the one I have described."

Varga looked about to say something but instead merely nodded at the old seeress, "We are coming." He whispered, tears running unashamedly down his cheeks. "Hold on for us, Beyla, hold on."

"Thank you, Varga. May Fenrir HelMouth bless you and keep you safe," she said quietly.

He tried to move towards her again but the seeress, the bed, indeed the whole room, began to retreat from his sight until he was once again standing ankle-deep in the machair of Mull staring into the flames which still burned upon the field of battle.

He became aware that the other Ulfhednar were coming out of the monastery and making their way over to him. Clearing his throat and wiping his face, he forced himself into composure before turning to them and bellowing, "Come, Ulfhednar, we are going home."

Chapter 13

"Dammit, will this snow never cease." Taiga growled as he shook himself free of the thick white flakes which were settling with growing rapidity on his broad shoulders.

"Moaning about it will not change it." Craigan pointed out.

Galahad slid Whitecleave into the loop on his belt and wiggled his toes about in his leather boots. He had not worn them for many months, adopting the sandals which seemed to be the standard footwear of the Ionan monks, and they had started chafing him already. That discomfort, coupled with the unending snow, hinted at the journey being a hugely uncomfortable one for the former champion of Camelot.

"Well," the wulver huffed childishly, "it seems as if it has been snowing for months. Can you remember a day recently when it has not?"

Craigan chuckled at Taiga's irritation, "Why are you worried? Your temper will melt anything that gets in our way."

Galahad smiled at the youngster but also privately conceded that Taiga had a point. He was unsure how much Brother Neville had told his companions about the Norse myth of Ragnarok beyond what they had all heard in Columba's office but, as he peered into the swirling blizzard blotting out everything beyond the edge of sand which skirted the southern end of the Sound of Iona, a word came back to him again and again. Fimbulvetr.

After the meeting had broken up and during a break from his search for Adomain, Galahad had sought out the elderly monk in the library and questioned him further about the Norse texts from which he had gleaned his information.

"I will not lie to you, Galahad, what has happened in the last couple of days is unsettling, to say the least." He sighed miserably before giving a hollow laugh which was so glaringly false, Galahad's eyes narrowed in suspicion. "If I was not so devout in my faith, I would think there might be some substance to these tales of the end of the world," Neville said with a sidelong glance at Galahad.

The former knight saw straight through his friend's clumsy inference and held his gaze fiercely. "You are not giving credence to this, are you?" Galahad gasped.

When Neville could not bring himself to hold his gaze, Galahad's eyes widened further, "You are, aren't you? You believe it is going to happen."

Again, the heartfelt sigh came and Galahad felt slightly guilty at the accusatory tone in his voice. "To be honest, yes, I believe that something is happening," Neville muttered ashamedly. "There are only so many events that can be explained away by coincidence." He shook his head and gestured wildly towards the wall. "If there was a window in the wall and you were to peer out of it, what would you see?"

Galahad looked blankly at the old man as his face became more animated, "Snow, I would be willing to wager. If not actual snowfall then at least ground which is ice-gripped and white, yes?"

"I suppose so."

"And has it not been like that for months on end, ever since you came here anyway." Neville pressed.

Galahad shrugged, "I had not really noticed it, but, yes, I suppose it has."

"That is one of the alleged heralds for Ragnarok. Listen to this," Neville went to his desk and turned a couple of pages of the tome which rested there. His arthritic finger traced the angular runes written on the vellum as he translated, '*The first sign of Ragnarök will be Fimbulvetr, during which time three winters will arrive without a summer, and the sun will be useless.*' Neville looked at Galahad with haunted eyes. "It goes on to say, '*The earth and mountains will shake so violently that the trees will come loose from the soil, the mountains will topple, and all restraints will break, causing Fenrir to break free from his bonds and the great serpent Jörmungandr will breach land as the sea violently swells onto it*'."

Galahad's eyes met Neville's with great trepidation. It was his dream. The dream which had disturbed his sleep so violently the previous night, scribed in minute detail upon a yellowing page written God knows how many years ago.

"Galahad."

The former warrior of King Arthur blinked as he came back to the present.

Columba stood before him and laid a kindly hand on his shoulder, "Good luck in your endeavour. We of the Order will pray every night for the safe return of our newest brother, for, though you have not physically taken the brown robe, I feel that it is wrapped tightly around your heart."

He then turned to Taiga, Craigan and Lorcan and wished them well also, saving some special words for the monk from Mull, though they were lost to Galahad as he turned to heft his travelling pack upon his back.

As he jostled the lumpy pack into some semblance of comfort, he reflected upon the other reason he viewed the coming trek with disillusionment.

As soon as Farregas had come anywhere near Taiga, Galahad's mount had become skittish and nigh-on impossible to handle, making him a liability in normal weather let alone the dreadful wintry conditions which currently held Iona in their grip, so he had been forced to leave his steed behind.

Finally, the quartet was ready to depart across the Sound. They moved towards the small rowing boat which was to convey them across the water.

Columba walked over to Galahad once more, "I know it has been praying on your mind but there is still no sign of Adomain. You must not let his disappearance concern you, Galahad. Divert all your efforts to returning to us safe and sound. I am sure by that time he will have reappeared. God speed to you, Brother." He turned to the others. "Goodbye to you all."

With that, the foursome clambered onto the boat and set off across the mile of choppy water to the south-western tip of Mull, there to make their way across the island to the monastery and then onwards to confront the might of the Ulfhednar werewolves.

The short trip passed without incident and they did not hesitate once they beached upon Mull's sandy coast. Dragging the small boat out of the lapping surf, they set off behind Brother Lorcan as he began to walk back to the monastery he called home.

Though he had thoroughly enjoyed his time on Iona, drinking in the wide lexicon of knowledge, both oral and written, of the more experienced monks, he yearned to get back to the comfortable surroundings of the monastery and regale the elders and his friends of his journey, especially as the whole point of it had come to such a satisfactory conclusion so quickly.

The blizzard conditions which had continued without stint as they navigated the Sound meant that conversation was impossible and so they trudged silently through the snow-muffled landscape, the only noise being made by their numbed feet as they tramped across the countryside.

The four of them described a ragged line with Lorcan taking the lead, the feeling of homesickness driving him irresistibly onwards with reckless abandon. Behind him was Taiga who, on a couple of occasions, had to yell at the advancing monk to slow down as the line of travellers was becoming too stretched and Taiga was having trouble making out the advancing monk's back.

Galahad took up station very close to the shoulder of Craigan. He was still astonished at how young the Venicone was and, even though Taiga and Lorcan had both told him of Craigan's fortitude, he could still not quite bring himself to believe that this youthful lad would not struggle to cope in such trying circumstances.

After about two hours of miserable progress, Lorcan stopped to allow them to catch up with him. "If I am right, we are even now standing in the shadows of Ben More," he said, then sighed, "I really think we need to seriously consider stopping for a break."

Taiga nodded in agreement. "It is certainly draining, trying to walk through all this," he gestured angrily at the white flakes which were still falling with unfailing monotony.

Craigan forced a grin onto his bluing lips. "Struggling to keep up, old lad?"

The wulver smiled mirthlessly and went off with Lorcan to find a suitable place for them to hole up and eat.

Within half an hour, the four of them were huddled in a small cave, crowding around a small fire which Galahad had lit with the aid of his tinderbox and some of the kindling that he was carrying in his pack.

Lorcan drew some provisions from his pack and they hunkered down to eat. As the young monk shared out the simple fare of beef and cheese, he asked, "How did you fetch up at Columba's door, Galahad? I have little experience in these matters but, even one as unschooled as I can see you carry your blade with a self-assurance that is surely not borne from a religious life?"

Camelot's former champion absently prodded at the fire, sending up a couple of sparks and a waft of smoke to the stone ceiling. "You are right, Lorcan. I have lived another life, one which only ended less than a year ago." His voice tailed off as he murmured, "Though it seems to be far further in the past than that."

"I am sorry, Galahad. It was not my intention to pry." Lorcan said.

Galahad waved away the comment, "I do not mind. I do not know what the accepted practice is when newcomers arrive at the gates of Mull but the residents of the Ionan monastery have the choice as to whether to disclose their previous life or not to their fellows. I have not spoken of my life before I found Columba's Order to anyone for a while, that is all." He looked at Lorcan. "Is that the custom where you bide?"

The young monk shrugged, "I do not know, in truth. I came over aboard a ship with most of the monks who live at the monastery, so the question never really came up. Padraig is a bit of an enigma though, I must admit. He was sent by Columba to take over the running of the monastery a year or so ago." He stopped and regarded Galahad once more. "To be honest, his manner and gait put me in mind of your good self."

Taiga and Craigan looked at each other knowingly. They too had commented to each other in private on the way Galahad's eyes were always searching the surroundings, studying his audience, gauging distances, one hundred percent aware of his environment, in short, a hunter untroubled and certain of himself in whatever setting he found himself in.

The former knight chuckled at Lorcan, "I am glad you say you are not prying as I would hate to be subject to a serious interrogation from you."

Lorcan looked suitably embarrassed as Taiga and Craigan joined in the amusement. "In answer to your question, yes, I used to be a knight for a celebrated monarch in the south. His champion, in fact. Have you heard of Camelot Castle, seat of King Arthur Pendragon of Wessex?"

The listening trio all shook their heads in the negative so Galahad continued, "He was a fine man and a kind and just monarch. I was one of twelve esteemed warrior knights who fought for God and country and sat at the Round Table of Camelot. I was counted second only to the King in swordmanship and valour." The last was said without any hint of boastfulness, though the world-weary Taiga did glance at Lorcan and Craigan who were both sitting attentively hanging on every word.

Rolling his eyes, Taiga said, "If you don't mind me saying, sitting round a fire with us in the middle of a snowstorm seems to be a bit of a come-down for one who used to hold such a position of importance."

Galahad's eyes roamed Taiga's face for a moment then he sighed, "That depends on how you view such trappings. I did not undertake the deeds which catapulted me to such high regard for my own benefit, I merely did what was right according to the teachings of my faith. In fact, if I am honest, I found the opulence of the castle slightly at odds with the teachings of the good Lord, but they were part and parcel of my station as a knight and I suffered them so that I could continue in my holy duties."

Galahad looked at each in turn then spoke once more but, where his voice when describing Camelot had been a subdued monotone, now it was full of vigour and enthusiasm. "You see this as a come-down for me, but you are wrong, wulver. This is what I was born to do, fighting a hell-spawned foe with God guiding my blade. If I can aid you in your efforts to cleanse the lands of such filth then I will be taking yet another huge step upon the stairway to heaven. That is what is important to me and that is why I came with you on this journey."

Taiga nodded in approval of the answer, surprising himself by how impressed he was with the passion present in Galahad's voice.

The conversation lapsed as, after the small distraction of his description of his previous existence, Galahad's allusion to the Ulfhednar served to concentrate their minds once more on the task at hand.

After ten minutes or so of silent contemplation, Craigan got to his feet, rolling his ankle which still ached every now and again from his fall on the journey to Iona. "The snow is clearing," he nodded towards the cave's mouth.

They quickly extinguished the fire and shouldered their packs, setting off again in the same order they had been in before they stopped.

The rest of the day remained gloomy and the only snow which fell after they left the transitory shelter of the cave was no more than a dusting so they made good time, settling in one of the small caves which pockmarked the lower slopes of Ben Molyneaux, albeit one on the opposite side of the mountain from where the three travellers had camped on their outward journey.

As they moved further north, an unnamed edginess began to gnaw at Galahad and Taiga, though the other two seemed oblivious to it.

When the quartet had made camp, Taiga gave vent to the creeping uneasiness. "I think perhaps someone should keep watch tonight," he said quietly as they laid out their blankets.

Lorcan and Craigan exchanged looks of confusion. "What for?" the Venicone asked.

Galahad smiled at the youngster but there was no humour in his expression, "Can you not feel something in the air, lad?" He looked to the wulver. "You can, can't you, Taiga?"

Taiga nodded slowly then walked to the edge of the slope which fell away from the entrance of the cave, staring across the rolling dunes of whiteness that stretched to the horizon, as if searching for the origin of his disquiet.

One by one they joined the wulver upon his eyrie, gazing across the shrouded countryside, which seemed to glow ethereally as the twilight sky reflected off the blanket of snow.

With a swiftness that took them all by surprise, they found their senses being assailed on all sides.

The reek of smoke filled the air though none could be seen.

The screams of the dying were heard by all, but no-one was in sight.

Craigan stared in horror as the dying face of Warren McLeish filled his vision.

Lorcan retched as the severed head of Brother Padraig dominated his view, mouth locked in an eternal silent scream and eyes permanently frozen open in terror.

Taiga immediately dropped into a battle-crouch as the despised face of Varga Hrolfsson appeared in its full hideous glory before him.

Galahad was the only one to remain unmoved, though he was scared nearly witless, as the huge face of the Norse God, Fenrir HelMouth snarled and snapped at him.

But as soon as the visions had come, the sounds, smells and sights were gone and the quartet was once again gaping in confusion across the picturesque scenery of the island.

Barely able to keep the quiver from his voice, Galahad said quietly, "We must go to the monastery."

He looked at his three statuesque companions as they stared at him uncomprehendingly.

"Now!" he bellowed, snapping them out of their petrified trances.

Without further words necessary, they broke camp and continued their journey north, having gone from studied calm to foreboding trepidation in the blink of an eye.

The next day found them trudging through yet more snow and on the brink of exhaustion. They had continued through the night without stopping, the horrendous visions driving them onwards to the monastery, desperate to pass off what they had seen as a waking nightmare, but scared to death that it was not.

The more experienced pair, of Galahad and Taiga, knew this was the worst thing to do, as they would be fatally tired if the group happened upon the werewolves in their current state, but the pair also recognised that Lorcan had been so shaken by the visions, they could not realistically expect him to wait. Aside from that, they needed the young monk to guide them back across the island in the quickest possible time.

It was a grim-faced quartet which crested one of the innumerable hills dotting the island and found themselves gazing down upon a scene which brought their worst fears into stark reality.

The fire which had started in the machair had all but gone out but the air was still thick with cloying smoke. Lorcan wailed as the wind created a gap in the wall of greyness, revealing the bodies of the tribesmen who had been sent to seek out the identity of those who had beached upon the isle.

He ran down the slope, nearly losing his footing on more than one occasion, dreading the identity of the corpses. He fell to his knees and vomited because, to his absolute horror, he saw that all the bodies had been beheaded.

After a few deep breaths, some semblance of thought asserted itself and a great rush of relief swept through him. The blood-drenched garb of the bodies had made him realise that no monks lay among the dead and he whispered a guilty prayer of thanks.

He tore his gaze from the grisly scene and saw his companions standing around something about twenty yards away from where he knelt. He got to his feet and began to walk over, breaking into a run as Taiga broke from the trio to try and cut his progress off before he got too near.

On this occasion, the wulver was too slow and Lorcan saw the rumpled brown robe and the headless body within it before it could be hidden.

As Taiga comforted the distraught monk, Craigan and Galahad took themselves over to the scene of carnage. "I can understand them killing the tribesmen but why have they stripped these three?"

Craigan shook his head, "They are not islanders. These are the beasts themselves."

The former knight's eyes flared but he said nothing as Craigan continued, "I killed one on the shores of Loch Seaforth back up in my homeland. I was half-crazed with fear and fatigue and she cornered me." His jaw tightened as, for the first time in a while, he found himself remembering what was left of the surprisingly feminine face of the woman he had battered to death. He sighed sadly, "When I see the butchery these wolves are capable of, it just brings into focus how lucky I actually was to walk away from that encounter." He shook his head vigorously as if shaking the memory free from the forefront of his mind. "Anyway, the point is, when these creatures perish, they revert to their human form. Taiga knows more about it than I do." He waved in the wulver's general direction.

Galahad looked at Craigan with new-found respect. That one so young was able to deal with the brutality of the Ulfhednar was impressive enough, but the matter-of-fact way in which Craigan had described his deed, spoke volumes to Galahad about the young man. It would have been so easy for him to revel in the fact he had bested one of the creatures, especially after they had brought such misery and pain into his life but, it was clear to Galahad that Craigan had viewed it as a life or death struggle and had derived no pleasure from the fact he had won out, save for the initial elation that he had escaped with his life.

Galahad knew from bitter personal experience how intoxicating the adrenalin of bloodlust could be and, at that moment, resolved to try and overcome his knee-jerk expectancy that Craigan was too inexperienced and immature to cope with what was ahead of them.

Taiga ran over and indicated with a jerk of his thumb the forlorn figure of Lorcan, walking like a zombie towards the distant monastery. "We should be with him when he enters. It is unlikely that there will be anyone left alive in there." he said grimly.

Forcing themselves into a run, they caught up within seconds and walked towards the holy building. Even from a distance, there was something intangible suggesting that it was bereft of human life, though none of the four could put their finger on it.

A murder of crows wheeled and banked over the courtyard which lay just on the other side of the outer wall and their guttural calls raked across the ears of the approaching party. Their eyes were immediately drawn to the gaping hole in the wooden doors at the front of the monastery.

Taking his companions by surprise, Brother Lorcan broke into a sprint leaving the three others trailing behind him.

"Lorcan!" Craigan yelled but to no avail. The monk disappeared through the hole before any of them could get close to him.

The shriek momentarily stopped them in their tracks, so full of anguish and loss as it was. The crows exploded into the air, cawing loudly their disapproval at being disturbed in such an abrupt way.

Galahad was first through the door and, grizzled warrior though he was, even he shrunk back from the massacre which greeted his eyes.

The floor was slick with the blood which had drained from the bodies of all the decapitated corpses. Here and there he spotted the nude bodies of dead Ulfhednar but, compared to the numbers of monks and tribesmen, they were very few and far between.

The gasps he heard told him that Craigan and Taiga had joined him in the courtyard. They both pushed past him and moved urgently from body to body, searching for some sort of inkling as to who was who amongst the fallen.

Forcing his eyes to roam the room, the warrior of God saw Brother Lorcan sitting at the base of the left wall of the square, rocking back and forth and staring at some random point amidst all the gore and horror. He walked over to the holy man and crouched down next to him, unable to find any words which would provide any sort of consolation to the young monk.

Taiga and Craigan joined them, both with tears starting in their eyes. The wulver held the chain of a bloodied pendant in his hand, letting it swing hypnotically to and fro. It depicted an emblem startlingly similar in design to the shield of Galahad except that the red cross was emblazoned on a field of yellow rather than white. "Padraig" was all he said.

Lorcan's head came up with a tortuous slowness and his eyes fixed on the pattern described upon the locket, following its progress from side to side. He then looked to Taiga, his face a portrait of agony.

Without a word, the wulver handed over the pendant, turning away as Lorcan took it from him and stared at it numbly as it rested in the palm of his hand.

The trio shifted uncomfortably as the hideous realisation of the butchery that they had imagined threw them completely off-kilter for a moment. Galahad was about to say something to Craigan when the young man's head whipped round and he hissed, "What was that?"

Taiga and Galahad looked at him quizzically but, as the former knight was about to say something, they all clearly heard the sound of movement and a muffled groan.

In an instant, they were up and searching for its source. Within minutes, Taiga yelled, "Over here. He is still…damn me, it's Warren, he's alive."

Whilst the name meant nothing to Galahad, Craigan let out a sigh of happiness and raced over to join his companion. "How is he still alive?" the Venicone gasped.

As Taiga crouched over the injured Taexali, he spoke softly and urgently, "Sheer bloody luck, that's how. Perhaps he was knocked to the floor unconscious and, in the confusion, his furs rode up over his head. That is how I found him anyway. With the amount of blood and carnage in here, the accursed wolves must have thought him already beheaded."

Their looks of astonishment were dragged down to the clansman as he wailed incoherently and feebly tried to push away from the wulver. "Warren, it is Taiga," Craigan crouched next to the wolfman. "You are safe. It is us. Do not be afeared."

The look on McLeish's face ran the gamut from utter confusion, to recognition then to a brief flicker of relief at his survival, before the full impact of realisation hit him. "Tavish!" he screeched.

As Craigan tried to comfort the hysterical tribesman, Taiga and Galahad moved away and the wulver explained how they came to know the twins. "I presume his brother has perished at the hands of the wolves," he breathed heavily. "I wish I could recognise more of who lie here but we did not bide here long enough for me to remember names. The only reason I picked out Brother Padraig was the pendant he wore." Taiga shook his head and turned a fearsome look upon Galahad. "Do you see now why the world must be rid of such creatures?"

Galahad laid a hand on the wulver's shoulder, "If I did not before, I certainly do now." He pursed his lips. "What bothers me is that, even though there have been copious amounts of blood spilt here, some has still not dried, which suggests to me that this atrocity was perpetrated within the last day or so."

Taiga's eyes started at that, "That thought had not occurred to me, I must be honest, but yes, you must be right." He sucked in a huge lungful of breath, ashamed at the fear that arose within him. "How close did we come to being caught up in this, I wonder?"

They turned back to Craigan and Warren. The Taexali was no longer crying at the loss of his brother but instead seemed to have lapsed into a state very much akin to Lorcan's catatonia. His skin was a deathly grey and bathed in sweat.

"I think we missed the Ulfhednar by less than a day. When he was talking, he was not making much sense but, from what I could gather, the wolves departed from here at dawn. He is pretty groggy though." Craigan conceded.

Indeed, as Craigan said that, Warren jerked himself out of the youngster's grasp and threw up on the floor. Resting on his elbow, he looked up at his three saviours. "I am sorry," he said, hanging his head.

They looked at each other in bewilderment as Warren spoke, addressing Taiga and Craigan more than Galahad. "I am sorry we did not accompany you to Iona. I am sorry we did not put ourselves forward when you had need of us." He retched but did not vomit then, with a deep breath, continued, "I am just so, so sorry."

Craigan looked at Taiga pleadingly, knowing full well the antipathy that the wulver had felt towards the McLeishs when the two of them had departed for Columba's monastery.

Taiga looked at him reassuringly and hunkered down next to Warren, laying a tender hand upon his arm. "I am just sorry it took a catastrophe like this to change your mind."

Warren made a noise which was halfway between a laugh and a sob, "Tavish was on the brink of following you, you know, but, at the last, I persuaded him not to." His whole body shuddered. "I talked him out of leaving the monastery and, because of that, he is dead. It is all my fault," he held his head in his hands, "It is all my fault."

The three gathered around him, ostensibly to offer comfort, but he waved them away and they stepped back from the expression which blazed in his eyes. "I will have my revenge though." He got to his feet drunkenly. "I will have my revenge." He slurred, swaying unsteadily as a stream of blood gushed from his nose. His eyes rolled up in the back of his head and he fell backwards, his skull hitting the flagstones with a sickening crack.

Galahad was at his side in a second, pulling up his eyelids with his thumb. One pupil was normal but the other was slitted and, even as he looked, the white of the good eye began to turn yellow. Then the other one began to undergo the same change of colour and shape.

"What is...?" Galahad stopped speaking and shrank back from the stricken tribesman as a return to consciousness flickered in his eyes. The three of them huddled together in fear as Warren's hair began to lengthen and his face and body contorted horribly as he started to transform into a werewolf. An animal scream which froze their spines echoed around the courtyard as McLeish's body endured the agonies of transformation from man to beast.

Fortunately for the quartet, his inexperience at effecting the change was his undoing. Taiga and Craigan were upon him before he could call on the formidable advantages which would have been afforded to him by his new form.

Galahad stood back from the werewolf and was able to appreciate the economy with which Craigan and Taiga dispatched their erstwhile companion. The young Venicone came in low, sweeping his sword across Warren's legs and opening up gaping wounds on both whilst Taiga brought his blade across in a graceful arc which anticipated the man's plummet to the ground and separated his head from his shoulders before he had hit the flagstones.

The two of them stood puffing heavily, not through physical exertion, but more through the shock of the moment.

Galahad nudged the Taexali's severed head with his boot then bent down and, with a sigh, closed Warren's eyes before getting painfully to his feet with a shake of his head.

Craigan gazed at the ceiling then turned and planted a vicious kick in the ribs of the nearest Ulfhednar corpse, accompanying it with a strangled cry of pain intermingled with rage.

"He can make his apologies now to his brother, at least," Taiga muttered. "One of the beasts must have bitten him in the melee."

They surrounded the fallen clansman, each alone with their thoughts, each feeling like they were floundering in a whirlpool of chaos, each trying to make sense of something that defied sense, each wondering how they could possibly triumph against such a merciless enemy.

Suddenly they were aware of Lorcan's presence and they turned as one.

The young monk looked as if he had aged by a decade. His pinched and haggard face was still wet with tears but there was a hardening in his eyes which his companions had never seen before and Galahad found himself wondering if Lorcan's innocence had been the final casualty of the massacre.

Fingering Brother Padraig's pendant which now hung around his neck, Lorcan spoke levelly, "There is nothing more to be done here, save one thing which I will undertake alone within the hour. Once it is done, let us be away across the sea to hunt down the bastard wolves."

After a sidelong look at his cohorts, Taiga said, "We need to rest, Lorcan believe me, I understand completely your eagerness to pursue them as quickly as we may. When my clan was exterminated, I would have chased the filth into the depths of hell itself, but we have travelled through the night which is ill preparation in itself and now we have had to deal with this horrific event." The wulver shook his head. "No, if we are to have any chance against the beasts, we must give ourselves whatever advantages are available to us." He cast an arm about the grisly scene in which they found themselves. "We will be of no use to all those who fell here, and all those who fell before them, if we arrive at the Ulfhednar's den half-dead with exhaustion."

Galahad nodded in agreement. "We are physically and mentally tired, Brother." He jabbed a finger in Lorcan's direction. "We have to rest. All of us here know how passionate the flame of revenge can burn when it has been stoked by an atrocity such as this, but let us bank it for now, nurture it, let it build and build until its wrath can be held in check no more, then let us unleash a firestorm upon these ungodly creatures." He rested a hand upon the young man's shoulder, "Go and complete the task which you mentioned just now then return to the dormitories and try to rest. Even a sleep haunted by nightmares is better than no sleep at all."

Brother Lorcan looked from face to face, nodded briefly then walked out of the gaping hole in the monastery door.

Craigan took a couple of steps towards the door also, only to be held back by Taiga, "Leave him be, laddie."

"But what if he flees like Adomain did?" the Venicone asked.

Galahad blinked. He had not thought of that, but the idea did not seem to worry Taiga overly much. "If he tries to pursue them by himself, he will surely die. If that is what he feels he needs to do, then who are we to stop him?"

"Because we are to follow him into death's cold embrace soon enough, is that what you mean?" Craigan blurted accusingly.

"Perhaps I do. But tell me, could you live with yourself if you did not try to stop the Ulfhednar, boy?" The wulver responded calmly. "We have Monkshood with us, do we not?" He countered, nodding towards Galahad. "Did your seer ever steer your tribe wrong before?"

The youthful islander shook his head.

"Then we have the best chance possible to defeat these scum, do we not?"

"Yes," Craigan muttered and hung his head.

"If you go through life fearing death, then you will never truly live, son." Galahad put in. After a thoughtful pause, as both the wulver's and the knight's words registered with Craigan, Galahad cleared his throat pointedly, "Now, do you know where the sleeping quarters are?"

McIntyre nodded sombrely.

"Let us find one to bunk down in then. Once we have left our packs, we will return here. Taiga, will you stay here and keep an eye out for Lorcan?"

"Aye," Taiga said quietly.

Galahad shouldered the wulver's pack and Craigan scooped up Lorcan's, then they left the blood-soaked courtyard.

As they disappeared into one of the cloisters, thick fluffy flakes of snow began to fall once more. Taiga looked skywards and muttered a curse aimed at the weather, the gods, the werewolves and just about anyone else he could think of.

Lorcan trudged across the machair towards one of the many cliffs which encircled Mull, ensconced utterly in a world of despair. As soon as he had digested the horrifying reality of what had transpired at the monastery, he had known what he had to do.

Galahad's perception had been right. As he had stared from corpse to corpse, able to recognise too few of the victims due to the horrendous violation their bodies had suffered, something *had* died inside the young man.

He recognised that, up until this point in his life, he had existed in a comfortable cocoon which real life had touched all too seldom. He had taken the food, the shelter and the companionship for granted and, in return, all he had given back were pompous words mouthed mechanically rather than with real belief. The prayers and observances had not actually achieved anything that bettered his life. They had certainly not protected the monks when the Ulfhednar had attacked.

In a short time, he found himself on the lip of the precipice, peering over it at the white-topped surf crashing against the rocks below. As the wind buffeted him and the snow blew in his face, he looked at the grey clouds pouring like ink across the sky and bellowed, "Where were you when they needed you? How could you remain in your heavenly domain when your servants were in such peril?" He threw his arms wide like Jesus on the cross. "Strike me down now if you exist. I challenge you to show yourself and smite me for my blasphemy, for I deny you. I deny you." He shrieked above the quickening gale.

For long moments he stood in the pose, eyes tightly shut, face turned upwards toward the God who he had worshipped for most of his adult life, screeching imprecations, hoping in his heart of hearts that those years would prove not to be wasted but fearing that the wrath he was trying to call down upon himself would be as non-existent as the wrath which should have fallen upon the Ulfhednar when they had defiled the monastery with their heinous actions.

"I thought as much," Lorcan sighed sadly. "All those people in there, those good, kind, honest people gave their lives over to you. It seems they gave up their lives for a lie." He looked to the sky once more. Before, he had imagined the Holy Father and the angelic host gazing down benevolently upon him and his fellows. Now though, all he saw were thick black clouds pregnant with snow.

"If you do exist, you will not hear from me again. You are dead to me. Here and now I forsake you and all your works, just as you forsook the monks of Mull in their hour of need."

He threw off the brown robe of the Order, leaving it crumpled in a puddle of muddy slush. Though the cold wind sliced into his spine like a knife and he was shivering within seconds, he was damned if he was going to continue to wear what had been a potent symbol of his monastic lifestyle, but was now just one more reminder of what a fallacy his life had been.

There was purpose now in his stride as he ate up the ground between himself and the monastery and, as he entered the courtyard, Taiga immediately noted the change in the young man's demeanour.

335

"Is everything alright?" the wulver asked carefully. "Have you completed your…errand?"

Lorcan nodded grimly as he reached down and grabbed a bloodied sword from the scarlet splashed flagstones, hefting it for weight and slashing it inexpertly through the air. "I have ceased journeying down the path I had chosen and now wish to tread another with you and those who travel with you, if you will have me?"

Taiga held up his hands. "I cannot speak for the others but I, for one, would be glad to have you with us."

Lorcan forced a smile onto his face and continued his attempts at swordplay while Taiga regarded him out of the corner of his eye. There had been something about Lorcan's expression as he had returned to the courtyard which had immediately set the wulver's teeth on edge. When the monk had departed, his eyes had been agonised and his brow deeply furrowed, but now there was a calmness and apparent serenity to his features which simply did not ring true and Taiga found himself wondering exactly what the task was that Lorcan felt he had to complete before they continued on to face the Ulfhednar.

As he was pondering this, Galahad and Craigan appeared in the room. The Venicone made a bee-line to Lorcan, his face a picture of concern, whilst Galahad sidled over to Taiga and whispered out of the corner of his mouth, "Our wanderer has returned then?"

"He has not been back long." Taiga responded in a similarly quiet voice. "Something has changed within him, Monkshood. He is not the same man who walked out of that door scant minutes ago."

"What do you mean?" Galahad asked quizzically.

Taiga shrugged, "I think his first taste of the evils of the world has been a bit of a shock for him."

They both watched as Craigan stood at the monk's shoulder, looking from body to body before saying something to Lorcan. However, it looked as if he may as well have been talking to the wall, for Lorcan did not appear to be reacting to the clansman's words in any way, he simply continued laying about the immediate vicinity with his newfound blade.

"He wishes to come with us to the islands," Taiga said in a louder voice.

Without hesitation, Galahad said, "That is good. The more swords we have to call on, the better." He looked back at Lorcan with a critical eye and tutted, "However, we will have to teach him the finer points of swordsmanship else, when it comes to the battle, he will kill us before the werewolves have a chance to." He took one last look around the horrendous sight of the courtyard. "What should we do about the bodies? I am loath to leave them unblessed and unburied whilst we are about our business, but I also chafe at the delay which that would entail if we were to lay them to rest."

Taiga nodded at the point, "There is already a miasma of death beginning to befoul the air."

"We should ask Lorcan what to do. He is the one who has bided here for the longest." Galahad's arm swept across the corpse-strewn floor, "These were his friends. He should have the final decision."

They picked their way across the killing ground carefully and got Lorcan's attention. "I understand you wish to join us on our quest," Galahad began, "and that is all well and good. It will be welcome to have another sword-arm to call upon." He glanced at Taiga who kept his face studiedly blank. "However, before we depart, we need to lay these poor unfortunate people to rest. Taiga and myself felt it best to leave the decision to you and we will do whatever you want of us, within reason."

Lorcan ignored the qualification which Galahad had added and said, "Of course you are right. They deserve some sort of dignity in death." He chewed upon his lip and, once again, Taiga was struck by the lack of emotion in his voice and manner. "How long do you think it would take to bury this many bodies?"

Galahad shifted uneasily. He knew it would be wrong to leave the dead to the crows which, even now, were regrouping atop the walls waiting patiently for the party to leave the vicinity but, as he had confided to Taiga, the thought of postponing their pursuit of the Ulfhednar for any length of time did not sit well with him. "I have no idea," he hedged, looking at Taiga, who looked just as blank.

Then, in a move which surprised them all, Lorcan turned to Craigan and asked, "What rites do your people perform when one of their number dies?"

McIntyre blinked in astonishment at being asked such a thing, "Nothing much beyond burial, as far as I am aware." His eyebrows furrowed. "I was given to understand that your religion had ceremonies and prayers for funerals."

Lorcan's face darkened. "Words, that is all. Anyone can speak words," he spat.

Galahad gasped, "I would have thought you would want your fellow postulants to have a proper Christian burial in as much as we are able to give them such."

The former knight of Camelot coloured at the scathing look of disdain that Lorcan threw in his direction. However, it quickly dissolved and one of regret took its place. With a sigh, he said, "Perhaps that would be appropriate."

"Well, I would think so, considering the life you and they chose." Galahad suggested.

337

The scorn returned in an instant. "We all make mistakes, do we not?"

"Lorcan, I can understand that your faith is shaken. If I had found my companions murdered in such a brutal manner, doubt would assail me irresistibly also," Galahad jabbed a finger in the young monk's direction, "but do not make the mistake of thinking you are the only one who has suffered such grievous loss in your life. There is not one of us here who has not suffered this same sort of happenstance, but you must remember that, despite what revelation you may have had with regards to your God and your religion, the likelihood is that most, if not all, of those who perished here still clung to their beliefs even as they were being rent by the wolven teeth." His voice lost its accusatory quality and became softer. "Do not take your feelings of helplessness out upon those who do not deserve it."

Lorcan held Galahad's gaze for a moment then affected a casual shrug though his eyes suggested a great struggle was raging within him. "Burial it is then," he said quietly. With a jerk of his head, he indicated a door to the right. "There are shovels and other digging implements through there in the garden that…" his voice quavered for a moment then returned to its previous level, "…that Padraig had begun to cultivate when he first arrived here."

Craigan nodded, "Aye, he showed me it briefly when we stayed here. It was a bonny little plot but I fear it will be far too small to accommodate all of the bodies here."

Lorcan shook his head. "You misunderstand me. I was not suggesting we bury them all in the garden. That is just where the shovels are housed."

Initially, like Galahad, Taiga did not care for the thought of delaying their return to the islands. To him, the quest had now begun to gain momentum towards its climax. The fortuitously swift discovery of Monkshood had galvanised that feeling and now it felt like, for once, they had some sort of advantage and were moving forward towards the wolves instead of retreating from them.

However, he did not, indeed could not, begrudge the massacred monks and other native Mull residents of the monastery a dignified send-off.

Taiga knew all too well the ignorance of irrational prejudice, especially after the reaction of the natives of Unst as they drove his race from the island after the Ulfhednar's coming, but the treatment he had received at the hands of the monks of Mull spoke volumes about the sort of people they were. Beyond a few looks of alarm which he had received when they had first arrived at the monastery, he had been treated with nothing less than the usual courtesy which one would expect a host to pay a guest.

In fact, it occurred to Taiga that the same civility had been afforded him in Iona as well. What had he heard one of the monks say as he quoted from their scripture, 'Do unto others as you would have them do unto you.' The wulver nodded to himself. That was an admirably good principle to conduct your life by, he thought.

The quartet split into pairs and began the gruesome task of removing the bodies to the fields outside the building.

Craigan gravitated towards Taiga and Galahad found himself helping Lorcan. For the most part, the work was undertaken in silence as, once again, the brutality of what had transpired hammered itself home with every ruined corpse they removed from the courtyard. However, as they were nearing the end of their task, Galahad asked Lorcan where he proposed to site the cemetery for all the bodies.

"Right here in this field. We will dig the graves so that they face to the southwest, in the direction of the country we called home." Lorcan breathed, a poignant catch in his voice. "They would want that. I would like to think that, every morning, as the sun rises and kisses the land with its warmth, their shades will rise and gaze across the miles to God's own country." He turned to face Galahad with a sad smile. "Though there has been too little of it recently, when it is clear and cloudless, the sun stays shining on this field for every minute it bides in the sky."

Galahad peered across the whitened cliffs and out over the waves, though they were starting to become obscured by low clouds drifting in over the water. "I can think of no better place, Lorcan. This is a good choice." He turned back to the young man, "Will you say a prayer for them when we are finished in our work?"

The smile disappeared like the sun going behind a cloud and Lorcan shook his head, "I cannot, Monkshood. I will say something as these people were my friends and companions for a good deal of my life and, to not say goodbye would leave me empty and regretful, but I will not pray for them. I would be mouthing words which I do not believe any more and that would be doing them a disservice. No, if you wish to mouth meaningless platitudes to God then be my guest but I will have none of it."

He looked up as Taiga and Craigan emerged from the ruined doors once more with yet another cadaver. They trudged tiredly across the field, following the furrow that their boots had begun to cut into the grass, their ghastly load swinging limply between them. "That is the last," Taiga sighed, stifling a yawn, "Save the dead wolves, anyway."

"They must burn," Lorcan blurted.

When the other three just stood looking at each other, he ignored them and walked back towards the monastery, spitting over his shoulder, "Do not concern yourselves if you are too tired to aid me. I will drag every single one of the bastards out myself if I have to."

Craigan made to move after him but Galahad held him back gently. "Let him get some of the hatred out of his system under his own steam. His grief and fatigue are making him too erratic at the moment."

"We should start digging the graves then, Galahad." Taiga said wearily, though everything else about his stance suggested he was on the brink of exhaustion.

The former knight shut his eyes and shook his head, "We are all dead on our feet. The bodies are laid out neatly enough and the cold will ensure they do not putrify overnight." He waved a hand in the vague direction of the sea. "Look, there is more snow coming in. That should put paid to any attentions which the crows might think to give to the bodies."

The wulver and the Venicone followed the direction of Galahad's finger and found they could see no further than the immediate cliff-edge.

Craigan looked unhappy, but Taiga backed him up. "He's right, laddie, we need to sleep. Dammit, we have not eaten yet today either."

They each shouldered their shovels and plodded back to the desecrated building, every step a colossal effort as the tiredness began to hit them in nauseating waves. The three of them walked past Lorcan, who did not see them at first. He had managed to move two of the ten naked corpses but he was struggling with a massive male body when they entered the courtyard.

When he heard their footsteps, he dropped the body, which made a squelching thud as it hit the flagstones, and spun round. "Where are you going?" he demanded.

"We are retiring for some sorely needed food and rest, Lorcan," Galahad sighed, "and you would do well to do the same. The weather is closing in fast and we will achieve next to nothing if we try to dig resting places in conditions like that."

Lorcan looked in disbelief from face to face. "So you would leave my friends to the crows, is that the way of it?" He spat.

"If you truly think that is the reason, laddie, then you have no business travelling with us and I have nothing further to say to you." Taiga stated in a dull monotone before walking from the courtyard towards the refectory.

"We are all exhausted, my friend. We could die out there if we collapse from tiredness. I have been caught in conditions like that before. Though the bodies lie barely a hundred yards from the monastery, when the wind is whirling the snowflakes every which way, it is all too easy to become disorientated. If a blizzard hits, you are just as likely to walk off the edge of the cliff as you are of finding the monastery again." Galahad said with a sympathetic voice.

Lorcan looked to Craigan for support, but received none, "They are right, Lorcan. We would be insane to risk ourselves in such a way. I cannot believe the crows will brave such awful weather to worry at the bodies, if that is your concern. Everyone knows they are a craven species of bird."

The young Irishman looked forlorn. He turned away quickly, muttering over his shoulder, "Do whatever you see fit. I will continue ridding this place of the Ulfhednar's taint."

With a shake of his head, Galahad beckoned to Craigan to lead him to the dining hall, leaving the stony-faced Lorcan to his labours.

An hour or so later, the three were sat in the hall, forcing down some fruit and hunks of stale bread dipped in a tasteless broth which Craigan had managed to quickly make upon one of the stoves in the deserted kitchen. None of them felt like eating anything as they still felt sick to the stomach by what they had seen. Every corridor they had walked down had signs of the Ulfhednar's presence, some obvious, like a trail of blood leading into one of the rooms off of the main corridor and others subtle, like a set of four fading scarlet pawprints leading off into the distance. They had tried to cleanse their hands and forearms of blood but, even now, their fingers were tinged with redness and Taiga's fur was still matted in places.

Nonetheless, they doggedly forced the food down because they knew they had to build their strength and fortitude up as best they could for what was to come.

Galahad was seated facing the door and nodded towards it as Lorcan walked in. Taiga and Craigan both turned in their seats to face him. The young monk was grey faced and breathing hard as he made his way painfully over and took a seat upon the bench next to Galahad.

Craigan disappeared into the kitchen and returned with a steaming bowl held in leather gloved hands. "Have a care, it is hot," he said as he placed it in front of Lorcan.

The monk nodded his thanks and slowly reached across the table to one of the uneaten hunks of loaf which still remained. He dipped it in the broth and ate it, flinching slightly as the hot liquid came into contact with his tongue. "I have purified the hall," he whispered hoarsely.

Despite himself, Galahad was impressed. Every one of the Ulfhednar which he had seen lying dead upon the floor must have been upwards of one-hundred and fifty pounds and Lorcan's build was slim to the point of emaciation.

Once again, it appeared he had misjudged one of his companions on the grounds of looks and inexperience. Even though he had expressed his happiness at the monk joining them, he had privately wondered if the slight young man would be able to stay the course of such a hard physical and

341

mental journey. His deed in single-handedly removing all the accursed werewolves from the premises certainly seemed to bode well for the future.

His train of thought was interrupted by Lorcan's voice.

"You were right. I could barely see where I was going at times. Once again, I spoke out of turn. I can only apologise for my words, you have laboured tirelessly for people you barely know and I had no right to..." At that point, his voice failed him and he crumpled to the table, knocking his half-finished bowl of broth onto the floor.

Taiga sighed deeply, "There is no need to say sorry, lad. It is both understandable and entirely forgiveable that, in the absence of those who are truly to blame for this horror, you should strike out at the only targets available to you."

Lorcan dragged his head up from the besmirched wood of the table and nodded his thanks for the kindness of the wulver's words. He sniffed and cuffed away the tears from his eyes. After he had regained his composure, he said, "I am all but spent. I think I will try and get some sleep, tortured though it may be."

Taiga smiled warmly and gestured towards Lorcan, "Ah, the wisdom of youth. That sounds like a grand idea, laddie."

"What if the wolves return?" Craigan asked.

Galahad turned to the Venicone. "Why would they? They have plundered all their trophies from here now. They have nothing to return for."

The four of them made their way to the sleeping quarters which Craigan had found. They had looked in six previous rooms before finding one which had not been infected by the Ulfhednar's blight, but both Galahad and Craigan had resolved not to tell Lorcan of this.

As they all settled down on their bunks, Galahad said, "We have lost a day on the Ulfhednar but, the more I think about it, the more I believe our delay is for the best. It would have preyed upon all of our minds if we had left Mull without properly dealing with the victims of the werewolves. To that end, I think we should bide here until we have properly laid everyone to rest. Tomorrow I think we should scour the building for any remaining casualties and lay them with their fellows out in the meadow. Then we must bury them and perhaps honour them all in whatever manner each of us sees fit?" He left the last statement hanging in the air as a question. "If it takes a week to complete the task, then it takes a week," he shrugged, "Does any of us here truly believe the outcome will be manifestly different if our conflict with the Ulfhednar is put off for a few days?"

The other three shook their heads in unison.

The ex-knight clapped his hands together. "Then let us do right by all who used to live within these walls, yes?"

Murmurs of approval came from Craigan, Taiga and, more importantly, Lorcan.

"Let us try to get some rest then because, even though we have agreed to give ourselves time to take stock and bury the monks, once that task is completed and all is as it should be, we will be away across the water, ready to bring an end to the Ulfhednar's evil reign of terror."

No further words were required and all in the room were asleep within minutes, even though it was only early afternoon.

Chapter 14

Fenrir, wolf-god of the Norse pantheon and most revered deity of the Ulfhednar, shivered in anticipation of the raw power that was so tangibly close, it tasted like ice upon his tongue.

He had been wonderfully surprised by the success of Varga Hrolfsson in plundering the requisite amount of skulls in such a relatively quick time. The huge wolf had resigned himself to at least a decade of waiting on the cusp of emergence from his benighted existence on the Nastrond, but the Ulfhednar had set about their god-given task with such a voracious will that his ascendancy would be achieved in just under half that time.

He had retired from his usual perch upon the banks of the Poison River and was padding towards his place of rest, a massive nook gouged out of the forbidding rock-face which stretched away as far as the eye could see in both directions. As he swept some of the hundreds of bones that were strewn about the floor into the seething water and settled himself down to sleep, his mind drifted back to a very similar cave many moons ago.

He had known from birth that he was destined for greatness, after all, what else could the offspring of a Norse God become?

Of his siblings he knew little, save that Odin had cast his serpent brother into the sea and his malformed sister into the Abode of Mists, from where she presided over those condemned to Hel.

For himself, Fenrir had been taken into the care of the Aesir, though only Tyr, the god of victory, was brave enough to approach him and give him food.

The gods had thought to bring Fenrir up in their own way, thus hoping to mould him into less of a threat than all the prophecies suggested he would be when he reached adulthood. However, it was soon clear this stratagem was flawed and the Aesir reconvened to hatch another plan to diminish the menace of Loki's son.

To that end, they decided to prepare three fetters with which to bind him but, knowing that his cunning was great, they opted to trick him with flattery rather than force. En masse, the Aesir attended Fenrir in his cavernous home and spoke to him of the three bindings.

The first rope was called 'Leyding'. They brought it to Fenrir and suggested that the wolf try his strength with it. Though suspicious, Fenrir judged that it was not beyond his power and so, with an indifferent shrug, allowed the gods to do what they wanted with it. As he had surmised, with his first kick the bind snapped and, with a snort of derision, Fenrir released himself from 'Leyding'.

Despite themselves, the gods were impressed though also afeared by Fenrir's awesome strength and announced from thereafter that 'to loose from Leyding' would be a saying synonymous with a feat of great strength and would bring great fame upon the wolf. Still wary, Fenrir accepted their congratulations with begrudging respect.

The Aesir then made a second fetter, which they counted to be twice as strong as 'Leyding' and named it 'Dromi'. The Gods asked Fenrir to attempt to break the new fetter, and that, should he do so, this feat would bestow even greater fame upon him. The wolf-god considered that the fetter was very strong and pondered the question for a time. However, he considered his strength had grown since he had torn 'Leyding' into pieces, so he consented to the challenge, reasoning that he would have to take some risks if he were to become as famed as he wished.

When the Aesir announced that the blessed rope was ready, Fenrir shook himself, knocked the fetter to the ground and kicked mightily with his feet, snapping the fetter and breaking it into pieces which flew far into the distance.

Once again, the gods applauded the gargantuan efforts of the wolf and pronounced that to 'strike out of Dromi' would also thereafter be a saying in the vocabulary of the Norsemen.

Despite their apparent appreciation of Fenrir's exertions, the Aesir started to fear they would not be able to bind him and so Odin sent Freyr's messenger Skírnir down into the land of Svartalfaheimr to the dwarves who bade there and requested they make another fetter, this time named 'Gleipnir'.

Using six mythical ingredients, the dwarves constructed 'Gleipnir' and brought the ribbon to the Aesir, who thanked them heartily for completing the task so well. The fetter itself was smooth and soft as a silken ribbon, yet strong and firm.

The gods then took the silken twine to Fenrir and told him to tear it, stating that it was much stronger than it appeared.

The look of 'Gleipnir' was enough to awaken deep distrust in Fenrir's mind and he was not shy about sharing his misgivings with the assembled gods.

"How will I gain fame from this deed if I tear apart such a slender band? I suspect it is made with some sort of art and trickery, so though it looks thin, I decline your test."

The Aesir scoffed at this, saying that perhaps Fenrir was not as worthy as they had first thought, if he was unable to quickly tear apart such a thin silken strip. They alluded to his earlier feats of strength and added that, if Fenrir was not able to break slender 'Gleipnir', then he was nothing for the Gods to fear, and, as a result, would be freed.

To that accusation, Fenrir responded, "I am reluctant to have this band on me. If you bind me so I am unable to release myself then, rather than have you question my courage, I request one of you put his hand in my mouth as a pledge that this is not a cunning artifice and is being done in good faith. If you accede to my demand, then I will indeed let you bind me with the ribbon."

All of the Aesir looked at one another, finding themselves in a dilemma.

To Fenrir's complete lack of surprise, every one of them refused to place their hand in his mouth until Týr volunteered. As he was the god who had fed and cared for the wolf in Asgard, Fenrir was less inclined to distrust him, so when Týr put out his right hand and placed it into his jaws, the massive wolf allowed the gods to tether him.

All but Týr stood back as Fenrir kicked. To the Aesir's joy 'Gleipnir' caught tightly and, the more Fenrir struggled, the stronger the band grew. At this, the gods laughed and Týr attempted to withdraw his hand from the fearsome jaws before Fenrir bit down, but he was too late and he lost the extremity to the wolf's razor sharp teeth. When the gods saw that Fenrir was fully bound, their deceit was fully exposed to the wolf-god.

Out of the very air, they produced a cord called 'Gelgja' and attached it to 'Gleipnir'. They inserted the cord through a large stone slab which they named 'Gjöll' then the gods fastened the stone slab deep into the ground. After that, the gods took the great rock 'Thviti' and thrust it even further into the ground as an anchoring peg.

Fenrir howled mournfully, the sound echoing through the earth and reverberating around the Nine Worlds. He raged at the devious ways of the Aesir, he raged at his own towering pride which had landed him in such a dire situation and he raged at the silken strand which should have been obliterated by his fury, but was not.

When his wrath had subsided, he fixed every Aesir with a baleful glare and swore his revenge upon them.

The first Ragnarok had provided him with his opportunity and, to a certain extent, he had exacted his vengeance by slaying Odin upon the field of Vigrid, but then, in his hour of triumph, Odin's son, Vidar, had slain him and he had been condemned to skulk in the pit which he now found himself.

With a start, he jerked awake, turning to snap at the bite of 'Gleipnir' and blinking in surprise when he saw it no longer bound him. He must have fallen asleep as he dwelt upon his betrayal at the hands of the Aesir.

"Soon, all scores will be settled and all will languish under my rule." Fenrir sighed blissfully. "And the bastard Aesir will come to rue their underestimation of me."

This time, the massive wolf rested his head on his front paws and settled down to a dream-free slumber.

The *Varulv* touched upon the northwestern edge of Loch Seaforth and gently ground to a halt upon the gritty sand. With whoops of joy, the crew fairly leapt down onto the beach and began to prepare the vessel for its portage across the five miles between their disembarkation point and Dun Varulfur.

The reason for the Viking's elation was obvious. Varga had told his men of the vision he had experienced with Beyla and the knowledge that they were so close to immortality had been like hot fire poured into their veins.

Though the ecstasy roared just as loudly in the ears of Varga Hrolfsson, an apprehension still sat upon the Ulfhednar warleader's shoulders. The wintry storms had delayed them once again on the crossing and they had been forced to beach upon four tiny uninhabited islands on the way home and, as a consequence, it had taken at least two weeks longer than it should have for them to gain the waters of the loch.

In all that time, in fact since the dream of Beyla, he had not heard her any more, neither as a whisper or a clear voice. Though he recognised that, to achieve her ambition, she would have to be dead anyway, he still prayed to Fenrir that she would be alive when they got back to the homestead, so she might gaze upon his victory and know that her work of decades, even centuries, had come to fruition.

With a barked order, he commanded his clansmen to cease their capering and concentrate on the last leg of the journey. A journey which had seen them banished in disgrace from their homeland and decried by the other tribes of Rogaland and beyond. Varga's face became grimly determined as he pictured his tribe's triumphant homecoming to the Petty Kingdom. His former countrymen would be the first to pay when Fenrir was resurrected and the Ulfhednar had the full unchecked power of their god to call upon.

As the tribe swarmed over the ship, readying it for its short overland voyage, Varga took himself away from the feverish activity and tried once more to make contact with the ailing seeress, screwing his eyes tightly shut and steering all his mental effort towards that goal. Still, he heard nothing.

He was hailed from behind by Vidkun Hagelin, "Ho, Varga, she is ready."

"Then let us move as if the breath of Njord himself is propelling us." Hrolfsson said.

Hagelin nodded and moved back towards the *Varulv*. Within moments, the mainland of Lewis was once again witness to the bizarre spectacle of a Viking longship drifting through its meadows and fields as gracefully as if it was gliding across the surface of the smoothest sea.

He watched his men admiringly as they hefted the weight of the *Varulv* and began lifting it across country. It was a brief moment of reflection but, in that instant, Varga found himself wondering why, with such a proficient and effective body of men at his disposal, he had been so concerned about this Monkshood. When it came right down to it, what could one man do against a force as formidable as the Ulfhednar?

Shaking his head, the war-chief jogged to the van of the procession and began to lead his tribe towards Dun Varulfur in a manner befitting the return of conquering heroes.

As he walked, though a tiny voice of pessimism warned him of the dangers of hubris, he could not help himself from wondering how long it would be before he was embracing his father once more and they were both wallowing in the eternal gratitude of Fenrir HelMouth.

The permafrost crunched rhythmically under the clan's booted feet as they moved slowly through the many small stands of spruce and pine which dotted their route back to the Dun. He looked up at the sky, noting the granite-grey clouds bulging with yet more snow and grunted non-committally. Even knowing the very necessary reason for the incessant cold weather did not alter the fact that the interminable snow had been a lot more than just an irritant, nearly costing them their lives on more than one occasion on the various sea voyages which they had embarked upon, and losing them more time than Varga dared to contemplate.

A mist was beginning to form in the trees ahead, wheedling its way around the trunks and branches like a million insubstantial snakes, blotting out the path behind it and seeming to deaden the footfalls of the Vikings. Blinking in confusion, Varga found he was beginning to feel light-headed and he stumbled, falling to his knees as the first tendrils of the fog began to close behind him. He sniffed and shook his head, trying to clear it of the fug which enveloped it, but to no avail. A sweet smell engulfed him and he fought down an urge to vomit. Yells and shouts from behind told him that his fellow clansmen were being affected in the same way and he turned round to try and see what was occurring, but his senses were so befuddled that he lost his balance and pitched forward onto the needle-strewn ground. The concentration of fog was not so thick on the ground and, after a moment or two, he started to feel himself once more. As he lay on his back, concentrating on his breathing and calming himself down, he looked more closely at the clouds of smoke which were wafting about before his eyes. Smoke and not mist? He gaped. What manner of magic was this?

The curses of confusion turned to screams of pain and he heard running feet and the unmistakable noise of arrows flying through the air.

Varga turned his head so that he was peering along the ground underneath the main concentration of smoke. Through the banging nausea of the headache which had begun to batter at his temples, he could see the keel of the *Varulv* mere feet away, plus many Ulfhednar on their knees and throwing up, or pairs of legs stumbling clumsily about, trying to keep upright. Aside from that, there were at least three of his men lying prostrate and unmoving with crossbow bolts protruding crazily from their skulls.

He tried to think, tried to get up, but the attack had been so unexpected that, for once in his life, Varga was rendered helpless to act.

Then he saw them. Two pairs of running feet, one encased in leather boots and the other sandalled with shins bereft of adornment.

To his horror, the next sound was the swish of a sword being unsheathed and the obscene noise of blade upon bone.

Movement to his right. One of the pairs of milling legs had collapsed and fallen towards him. Varga's gorge rose as the body hit the ground and the head rolled clear, cleaved from its owner in one clean sweep. An ocean of blood began to pump onto the floor of the wood as more of the Ulfhednar followed their fellow tribesman to a bloody death.

With a scream of rage and fear, Varga forced himself to his feet and stood swaying drunkenly, trying to understand what was going on.

He just made out a figure clambering onto the deck of the *Varulv* with something in its hand before falling to the ground once more.

His lips felt numb and his throat was burning. He was seconds from unconsciousness when a breeze began to blow, slowly at first but with growing rapidity, dispersing the smoke and clearing his head.

After what seemed like an age but was, in fact, only a few moments, he felt able to stand up once more.

He felt his heart thumping in his chest and his breathing quicken as he beheld the scene.

Every single one of his men had been affected in some way by the mysterious smoke, most still kneeling and choking, some gaining their feet once more. However, fully thirty of the hundred Ulfhednar who had set foot upon the shores of Loch Seaforth not two hours before, were dead, all decapitated brutally.

As he stumbled through the ranks of his clan, moans and groans met him from every direction. He turned as a hand fell upon his shoulder.

"What in Hel was that, Varga?" Strindberg Graavsen, the helmsman of the *Varulv*, gasped.

The warleader of the Ulfhednar hawked a gobbet of phlegm to the floor. "Hjelmer," he snarled. "Do you not recognise its stink?"

Strindberg was not listening to the answer. Wordlessly, he pointed to the longship which had served the Ulfhednar from the first moment they had set out from the shores of their homeland.

Varga spun round just in time to see flames begin to catch at the mast of the ship. He grabbed a hank of Strindberg's furs and practically threw him towards the *Varulv*. "Do not just stand there gaping, do something, put it out."

Despite their dizziness and nausea, those Vikings who were able to began boarding the stricken ship, hoping they could extinguish the fire before it destroyed their vessel.

Varga roared impotently as it soon became clear that nothing could be done to save the craft. "The *Varulv* is lost. Get the skulls off, we must carry them to the Dun," he bellowed.

His anger was threatening to burst out of him like a volcano and he sought something on which to vent his fury. He kicked the nearest corpse as hard as he could then turned to another wanting to do the same. However, a moan came from the tribesman and he placed his foot back on the ground.

It was Vidkun and he was bleeding copiously from a hideous wound in his shoulder and neck. He murmured something, his voice muffled by his injury and the blood pooling in his throat.

Varga's eyes flared. He grabbed the clansman and pulled him off the ground so he might hear the words more clearly but the movement only served to worsen the massive cut and Hagelin died before he could repeat it. However, Varga had heard exactly what the dying Viking had whispered, he just did not want to believe it.

Letting the dead man fall to the ground, Varga threw his head back and screamed to the sky. "Come show yourself then, Monkshood. Show yourself. Show yourself, you bastard."

But the only sound to be heard was the crackle of fire as it ate into the wood of the *Varulv* and the shouts of the Ulfhednar as they removed their trophies from the deck.

Galahad and Lorcan ran as fast as they could through the woodland, determined to distance themselves from the wolves as quickly as possible. The plan had worked better than they had ever dared hope and, as they were joined in their headlong flight by Craigan and Taiga, the adrenaline of the moment got to the young monk and he gave voice to an elation he could not contain, the yell of joy echoing through the trees and across the snow-covered countryside.

"Quiet, you idiot," Galahad hissed angrily. "Do you want to bring the wolven horde down upon us?"

Despite the reproach, Lorcan's face was still locked in an inane smile, "I am sorry. I never thought the rush of killing those hateful creatures would awaken such feelings inside me. Damn me, it was good to take a modicum of revenge upon them." He held up his hand. "Do not worry, I think I have got it out of my system now, but damn me, it felt good." He breathed heavily as their pace began to slow, "And I will not apologise for saying that." His eyes blazed as he stared at Galahad, almost as if challenging him to comment.

Galahad opted to hold his tongue. He wanted to chide Lorcan further but, after what had happened at the monastery, perhaps the raid had acted as a catharsis for Lorcan and the initial lust for vengeance would subside.

The quartet stopped after a couple of miles and Taiga removed the cloth which he had tied around his nose and mouth. He walked back a few paces and snuffed the air whilst the others listened for any signs of pursuit.

The wulver coughed and turned round with his eyes watering, "My, but that aconite is strong. Even here I can still pick up a slight tang of it on the breeze."

The trio waited nervously as Taiga rubbed his eyes and spat onto the snow. "I do not think they are chasing us but the fumes are not exactly conducive to confirming it." He shrugged. "Having said that, if the reek is affecting me from this far away, then I would think they would not be in any fit state to do much about us anyway."

Galahad chewed upon his lip then came to a decision. "Then let us repair to our shelter and take stock."

The foursome took off across the blanketed landscape once more, their emotions veering wildly between pleasure at the success of their lightning strike upon the Ulfhednar and fear as to what reprisals it would provoke. Though the four had been intent on fleeing, each one's blood had frozen at the hatred in Varga's bellowed challenge, even if they did not understand the words contained within it.

The twilight found them huddled together underneath an overhang of rock artfully masked by a stand of trees. The elation had quickly worn off and they sat miserably in a cold camp. They did not dare light a fire for fear of discovery, so they lay together underneath a bundle of furs which they had brought with them from Mull.

When the four had gained their camp, Galahad had taken charge. "Make yourself comfortable, for this will be our last few hours here. As soon as the sun is up we must harry them and keep them off-guard as best we can." He looked to Taiga excitedly. At last, the time for action was upon them. His mind recalled the first night they had spent on the island when Taiga and Craigan had described the massive task before them.

351

The quartet had settled into their shelter on the first day they had landed and, once all was laid out as it should be, they were relaxing as much as they could on the unyielding rock and the knight had asked about the Ulfhednar's home.

Craigan had explained, "Dun Varulfur, it is called. It is the biggest of a network of crannogs located upon Loch Langavat, not five miles northwest of Loch Seaforth, where we landed."

"Sorry?" Lorcan put in. "Did you say *upon* Loch Langavat?"

Taiga nodded, "Tis a most clever system. The tribe who lived there before the Ulfhednar came, Vacomagi I think they were, built platforms of wood which bide just below the water-line and interlink between each home."

Craigan agreed, "It is well-known among my people as a most ingenious piece of design."

"And eminently defensible as well," Taiga put in as an afterthought.

The former champion of Camelot rolled his eyes, "Do you have any more good news for us before we retire for the night? This Loch Langavat, is it poisonous, perhaps, or maybe it is a lake of fire?"

"It is only right that you get as complete a picture as possible." Taiga mumbled, looking slightly offended.

"Of course it is," Galahad apologised. "I was attempting to lighten the mood." He sighed. "Though there is precious little in this whole situation that could raise our spirits."

The four had then grabbed a hunk of cold meat each from the food pack and chewed upon it, staring blindly out into the forest, each alone with their thoughts.

A sigh from Lorcan brought him back into the present. The young monk was starting to feel the after-effects of the burst of chaotic excitement which had propelled him through the brief encounter with the wolves in the wood and his eyes were becoming heavy.

Craigan was rolling his shoulders to and fro to free them of the ache which had begun to set in as soon as they had stopped moving. He had been in the same rigid position with the crossbow in preparation for the ambush upon the werewolves and was paying for it now. He reflected that they had not wholly thought that part of the plan through and it was only as the smoke had begun to waft into the air that they realised it would render Taiga's aim useless with its fumes. He looked to the right as the warmth of the wulver settled next to him.

Taiga was still suffering the effects of the aconite but the discomfort was lessening. The nausea and headache had all but gone, however his lips still felt tingly and, every now and again, a touch of dizziness unsettled him.

Galahad stood away from them, his mind working feverishly. If he was honest, the size of some of the wolves had left him in awe when he had first come upon them but his battle instinct had kicked in and he had quickly gotten over that hurdle. He then went through the ambush in his head and wondered what could have been done differently. Had they achieved the maximum amount of victims they could? If it had not have been for the wind which had sprung up from nowhere, the cloud of smoke might have lingered for longer and they could have continued their assault. Ah, well, it could not be helped. You could not control the weather, after all.

He allowed himself a smile. The actual idea had worked like a dream. The seed had been planted during a conversation between the four questers back on Mull. As the adrenaline of the attack hit him and his eyelids also started to fall, he found his mind wandering back to Padraig's study at the monastery.

It had taken three days for them to finish the solemn task of emptying the monastery of corpses and interring the dead in the meadow which Lorcan had identified because, mercifully, the snow had held off, save for one short-lived blizzard.

After they had eaten their evening meal on the third day, Galahad had determined that, as he and Lorcan still knew very little about the Ulfhednar, Taiga and Craigan should go back over everything they knew about the werewolves once more in the slim hope that an advantage, no matter how small, might present itself.

As he was detailing the worryingly small amount of weaknesses which the werewolves were susceptible to, the subject of aconite had arisen.

They were sat in the room which had acted as Padraig's study. Galahad had just lit a taper as the light was beginning to fail and Craigan and Taiga were standing by the door, two unmoving sentinels draped in twilit shadow. Lorcan was sitting at Padraig's desk, absentmindedly fiddling with some documents which lay upon it.

"What did you say it looked like?" Lorcan threw the parchment aside and leant forward intently when Taiga detailed the debilitating effects which the plant had on the monsters.

The wulver repeated his description of the flower only for Lorcan to jump up excitedly, "Ben Molyneaux!" He exclaimed. "If it looks as you say, I will swear there are fields of it upon the slopes of Ben Molyneaux."

"Are you certain?" Galahad hissed.

"I am sure, yes," Lorcan rejoiced for a moment but then his face fell, "It will surely be dead though. There cannot be many flowers which could survive such weather as we have had to endure these months past."

353

"They are hardy plants, native to mountainous regions and, even if the specimens you find are dead, they will still be potent, I believe." Taiga countered. He looked from face to face. "Regardless, there is only one way to find out if they are there. Ben Molyneaux is within a day of here, is it not?" He asked Lorcan.

The young man nodded emphatically.

"Right," Galahad said, "Lorcan, you take Taiga to the mountain tomorrow. Find something to bundle the flowers into and bring back as many plants as you can."

The wulver shook his head, "Sorry, Monkshood, as it affects the Ulfhednar, so does it affect me also. I may not handle it any more than them."

Galahad tutted, "Take Craigan then, lad, just bring back as much as you can. If it is as toxic as you say, Taiga, it could be a potent weapon if used in the right way."

The next day, whilst the two young men were away upon their urgent errand, Galahad and Taiga spent every waking second, formulating, discarding or rethinking plans. The two of them were mature enough to recognise that the power of soothsaying only worked up to a certain point and, if they were to just waltz into the wolf's den and expect to win the day on the strength of Jameson's prophecy, then they would be despatched in very quick fashion.

Galahad also worried at the amount of enemies they faced and confided this fear in the wulver. "It is fiendishly difficult to plan an assault of any kind if you do not know the numbers involved," he sighed.

"If we manage to obtain a goodly amount of aconite, it will be helpful." Taiga mused. "The effects of the plant upon those of wolvenkind are devastating."

"That, at least, is good news." Galahad rolled his eyes. "If they can find any living specimens, anyway."

The wulver waved a hairy finger, "As I said, I have a feeling that might not matter." He took a deep breath. "Perhaps if we were to burn one of the dead flowers, I will inhale the fumes and we can gain some sort of idea whether it is still potent in that state or not."

The ex-knight's eyes showed what he thought of that. He contented himself with saying, "Is that wise? What if it incapacitates you or worse?"

"I cannot believe just one flower would be strong enough to harm me too much." The wolfman shrugged helplessly. "What other way will we have of knowing? You have just said we need to plan as extensively as possible," he leant forward on his elbows. "What other way is there?"

The man from Camelot snapped his fingers, "We have a flower." He ran from the room, quickly returning with the bloom which Adomain had left upon his pillow in the monastery at Iona.

Though the plant had been crushed in Galahad's travel pack and was obviously dead, Taiga was about to ask if he was sure he wanted to get rid of the token without knowing Adomain's fate, but the knight had already placed the wilted bloom in the jumping flame of a candle, watching it intently as the small purple petals turned brown and shrivelled in the heat. "Come then, smell." He beckoned the wulver over.

Taiga was caught off-guard by the need to test his hypothesis quite so quickly but he put that aside and walked over to the curling wisp of smoke which wafted gently up from the small flame atop the wick.

He stood there in silence with Galahad watching him intently, inhaling deeply through his nose and exhaling from his mouth, until the flower had been utterly consumed by the fire.

He stared at Galahad shaking his head helplessly, as it seemed the vapours were having no effect but, as he went to retake his seat, he faltered and nearly fell to the floor.

Galahad was at his side in an instant, "What is it?"

The wulver failed to focus on the knight's face for a brief second, but when he did, a toothy grin lit up his features. "Damn me," he breathed. "And that was just one flower?"

"Taiga, what happened?" Galahad pressed.

A dull ache had begun in the wulver's temples and his eyes felt gritty and sore but still he smiled. "I feel heady and disorientated, Galahad." He laughed drunkenly. "And that was just one flower." He repeated in a giggly voice.

Already the knight's mind had begun feverishly working out schemes with which to exploit the effectiveness of the aconite's scent. However, all of them depended on being in front of the Ulfhednar and luring them into some sort of ambush.

"We must leave as soon as we are able," Galahad pronounced.

Taiga blinked the last of his giddiness away and nodded slowly, "Into the gaping jaws of the wolf it is then."

"We have to get ahead of them if we are to utilise the aconite in any sort of effective way." Galahad thumped his fist down upon Padraig's desk. "We should not have delayed so long."

"Do not chide yourself for showing compassion, Monkshood. Would we have been able to concentrate upon defeating the beasts if we knew that we had left the good people who died here to the mercy of the ravens? I know I would have felt that I had done them an injustice if we had not buried them."

355

He shook his head. "No, we did right by them, Galahad, and if that puts us at a disadvantage when we face down the Ulfhednar, then so be it." Taiga held the former knight's gaze. "Would you have done anything different if you had known about the properties of aconite beforehand?"

Galahad shook his head, but remained silent.

"I thought not," Taiga smiled. "You have a good heart, Galahad. We all have but, if we have to descend to the level of the Ulfhednar to achieve our goal, then it will not be much of a victory."

Suddenly Galahad thrust himself out of his seat and began stalking about the room. "It is this damnable waiting which annoys me."

This time Taiga laughed heartily, though the sound was also drenched in bitterness. "You talk to me of annoyance at all the waiting? You have been aware of these foul creatures for, what, two or three weeks? I have been pursuing them for a couple of years. They wiped out my family, possibly even my race. Every thought in my mind and every fibre of my body hungers to kill them all, every last one of them, but it would be suicide to rush in unprepared. You forget I have seen them in action, Galahad. You have not. And I tell you now, there is no way on earth we will be able to defeat them by strength of arms alone, so banish that thought from your mind. We have to find a way to reduce their numbers in some way because the odds are stacked far too much in their favour at the moment. At the moment, we have nothing, save yourself and the ramblings of a Pictish seer, to suggest we will defeat these bastards. However, this bloom, if Lorcan and Craigan can find it, will help us. And so fate swings back in our direction, maybe only slightly but in our direction nonetheless. Would you sacrifice that just for the sake of your impatience?" He ceased his diatribe and turned away from the chastened knight.

In an attempt to change the subject and pierce the suddenly heavy silence, Galahad looked to the rapidly descending darkness outside the window of the chamber. "They should be back soon with any luck. Let us hope they have managed to harvest a reasonable amount."

"I am sorry, Galahad." Taiga blurted. "If I am honest, I have been wrestling with the same dilemma which you spoke of. My harsh words were borne of frustration at myself, not you. As soon as we found you and began our journey from Iona, I believed our luck had turned. But now, I feel like we are standing still once more, or even worse, losing the ground that we have made up."

The former champion waved away the wulver's words, "It is I who should be apologising to you, Taiga. In my former existence, if a situation like this presented itself, we of the Round Table tended to act almost instantaneously or so it seemed. That is why the delay irritates me so." He smiled self-deprecatingly. "Once I have the bit between my teeth, I am afraid it is very hard to rein me in and stop me galloping."

The wulver laughed, and this time there was genuine humour in the sound. He poured himself and Galahad a drink and they settled down to wait for the return of the monk and the Venicone.

They did not have to wait long.

Craigan entered the room first, sweating despite the cold weather, with a tired but triumphant look upon his face. Lorcan was not far behind him and he mirrored the young clansman's expression.

"He was right," Craigan jerked his thumb in the direction of Lorcan, who had just filled a goblet with wine and drained it in three gulps. "There was aconite in abundance. We took a small wagon with us and brought back as much as we could." He broke off as Lorcan offered him a drink, then continued when he had finished, "What are you proposing to do with them all?"

Galahad told them of the experiment which he and Taiga had conducted and the astonishing results of it. It was but the work of a few moments to devise a plan of ambush but, as Galahad had said to Taiga, it relied on them being able to lure the Ulfhednar into a trap and that meant being ahead of them.

"So, to that end," Galahad said, "we leave at dawn. Agreed?" He looked to the trio of fellow travellers and received nods in return.

"Let us retire then and be glad of it, for I fear we shall be strangers to comfort for a good many days."

The next day found them navigating the Sea of The Hebrides in a boat procured from the village of Ceall Lismore, which was situated a mile or so down the coast from the monastery and had, for the most part, seemingly escaped the ransacking by the Ulfhednar. However, even though it appeared to be untainted by the werewolves, it was nevertheless deserted, so the quartet could not be sure that the horde had not visited the settlement.

The craft itself was a sturdy fishing boat fitted with two rows of oars and a mast which afforded the four of them ample room aboard, whilst not being too heavy for them to propel through the water.

Unfortunately, the mast was bereft of rope and canvas so the four of them were forced to leave for the islands under their own steam.

That made for very little conversation as they began their voyage across the choppy waters.

Taiga and Craigan were seated on the rowing bench closest to the prow as they had stowed their packs along with the bundles of aconite in the wider

357

space of the stern because, whilst the wulver was pleased with the result of the test in Padraig's study, he had no wish to recreate it whilst at sea.

After little more than an hour, the two rowing teams found themselves sharing foreboding looks with each other as the sky before them grew greyer and darker with every stroke of their wooden blades.

"Where away shall we steer?" Lorcan shouted above the whip of the wind.

Galahad stared from horizon to horizon and saw no land in sight. As he had become the de facto leader of the group, he knew they were looking to him for a decision but he had never been on the open sea in his entire life and did not have the first idea as to what to do.

Whether Taiga suspected this or not, Galahad did not know, but to the former knight's relief, the wulver pointed to the north-west and shouted, "There, it appears lighter over there. Let us make for that and hopefully we will skirt the weather which is to come."

They began to move towards the break in the cloud cover, but a swirling westerly wind kept causing them to veer back in the direction of thunderous bank of clouds.

As the foursome was blown inexorably closer to the storm, they could clearly see the swarm of snowflakes dropping to the water. They strained and heaved at the oars, trying to arrest their momentum into the maw of the blizzard. Mercifully, as the first flakes began to fall upon their vessel, the westerly lost some of its power and the inexperienced seafarers were able to pull away from the ominous clouds, manfully ignoring their protesting muscles and cutting through the waves with reckless speed.

After what seemed like hours of grim-faced exertion, Craigan pointed to the western horizon, "Is that…is that land?" he breathed hoarsely.

For a few seconds, all four stopped rowing and stared across the water, squinting at an intangible mass which hoved in and out of view as the boat was bucked up and down by the rough seas.

With relief, as they drew closer, more of the headland became visible and they saw an expanse of smooth land stretching away along the coastline of the unnamed island.

The sea had now settled down to a great extent and, after emerging intact from their close encounter with the vagaries of the maritime weather, the quartet found their confidence restored.

"Do we go on or bide here for a spell?" Craigan asked.

Galahad responded immediately. "We will stop here for something to eat. We are ill-prepared enough without arriving at the Ulfhednar's den dehydrated and malnourished. As we eat, we will keep a keen eye upon the weather and go from there."

They gained the beach and Craigan doled out some fruit and watered wine. Taiga and Lorcan managed to find some dry tinder underneath a pile of driftwood which was heaped haphazardly on the sand, but the wind kept extinguishing the feeble flame which they were trying to ignite so they gave up trying to light it.

One positive effect of the wind, however, was to disperse the thunderhead which was roiling angrily just off the shore and, whilst it did not allow the all too seldom seen sun to break through, it did lift a degree of the prevailing gloom.

The quartet stayed upon the island's shore for less than an hour before setting off once more across the Sea of The Hebrides. They opted to hug the coast as far as they were able, reasoning that, if the weather closed in once more, they would have a lot less further to row if they needed to put in to dry land again.

As it was, the mass of cloud remained a fair distance away from them to their right. However, as they passed the island's northernmost tip, they were greeted by a vast span of water with no sign of land upon it and the trepidation returned to their faces as they left the anonymous island behind and struck out for their destination.

The four continued on a northwest heading using the weak light of the sun that was trying its damnedest to shine upon their crossing to direct them. They were starting to fear that they would be adrift upon the waves when darkness fell as they had not sighted land for the previous few hours but, just as the glow was disappearing behind the granite clouds which had been a constant companion on their voyage, some snow-capped hills began to peek over the horizon and they redoubled their efforts to find land.

As the boat's keel bit into the stony sand, Galahad, Craigan and Lorcan scrambled over the side and the three men began immediately searching for shelter. Taiga elected to stay with their craft as they were not sure where they had fetched up and he did not want to alarm any of the natives, should they happen to meet any, in case the Ulfhednar had been this way and he was mistaken for one of them.

The trio slogged their way through the cloying wet sand and over the jagged flinty rocks which skirted the inlet.

As Taiga used his wolven strength to bring the boat further ashore and away from the incoming tide, Galahad led the way as they broached the steep gradient of rocks which formed a border between the sands and the fields of heather which lay beyond. The trio found themselves staring across the meadows of billowing purple flowers to a bleak landscape of rolling hills which were pockmarked with huge boulders, dotted erratically among the billowing grassland clinging to the slopes of the host of tors which broke up the line of the horizon.

"Civilisation, it seems." Lorcan pointed to a stone structure skulking halfway up the side of a large hill off to the right of where they stood.

A thin wisp of smoke was rising from a hole in the roof of the building which slowed their progress a little, for they did not wish to alarm whoever inhabited the broch.

A flock of thirty or so sheep fled before them as the three moved over the field. They were within twenty paces of the door when it opened to allow a grey-haired man out into the cold air. As he closed the door and turned round, he saw them, letting out a gasp of surprise.

They held up their hands to show that they were unarmed and Craigan stepped forward, "Well met." He said as confidently as he could manage.

The man regarded them coldly with hooded eyes. He was dressed in a dull brown woollen robe, underneath which a faded leather kilt could be seen poking out. His boots were of simple design but sturdy and well suited to the elements. Little could be seen of his features for they were encased in a wild beard which jutted out at crazy angles from his face. Atop his head, he wore a Tam o'shanter of deep blue with a pompon of a slightly fairer shade. As he stared at the new arrivals on his land, he shifted the staff he was resting upon into both hands, and they were all struck by how quickly the simple piece of wood transformed from a walking aid into a possible weapon.

"What business d'ye have upon my pastures?" He asked belligerently.

Craigan's eyebrow arched at the aggressive tone but he guessed that the dangers of living in such an isolated place were brought into very sharp focus when strangers appeared at your door.

"I am Craigan McIntyre, last of the Venicone tribe of Duncan McKendrick, late of Dun Eiledon, and these are my travelling companions, Brother Lorcan of the monastery on the Isle of Mull and Monkshood, former sword champion of Camelot Castle, far away to the south of this island."

The man's stance did not change as he chewed over Craigan's words, "Am I meant to be impressed, boy, because all your flowery rambling means nothing to me? All I care about is what business Craigan McIntyre, Brother Lorcan and Monkshood have upon the lands of Walcott Griffin." He pointed the end of his staff at Craigan's face.

"We mean you no harm, sir. We are simply seeking knowledge as to where we have landed. We were crossing the Hebridean Sea and were blown off course by a storm." Lorcan put in.

"Aye, it has certainly been a time of storms recently." Walcott murmured to himself before the rich timbre returned to his voice. "Storms and snow and the biting cold of the grave have been gripping this land for too long a time and I suspect there will be some sort of reckoning soon."

As if in response to the shepherd's maudlin statement, a wind soughed across the landscape, causing the three newcomers to shiver and huddle more tightly under their clothing.

Griffin seemed unmoved by the frigid blast and his eyes took on a mocking quality as he beheld the trio shudder. "You have landed on the island of Barra." He stared at them with a sneer before continuing, "Well, now you have your knowledge, your business here is at an end, so do not let me delay you as you leave."

"Tell me, are all of your people so polite and nice to know?" Galahad sniffed casually.

Walcott was walking away from them but he stopped and spun round, missing Galahad by inches with his outswung staff. The former knight stumbled and fell upon his backside, staring defiantly at the grizzled shepherd as he advanced upon him. "Who do you think you are, judging me within minutes of our meeting?" He stabbed the staff down between Galahad's outstretched legs. "Shall I tell you what happened the last time I allowed strangers to sit at my hearth?"

Craigan and Lorcan circled the incandescent farmer and, as he appeared disinclined to offer any violence beyond intimidation, gingerly helped Galahad to his feet.

"Three of the scum there were Not much different from yourselves, in fact. They appeared harmless and being so polite and nice to know," he sneered at Galahad, "I fed them and let them warm themselves by my fire. Well, they liked it so much they decided to stay and, when I tried to eject them, they turned nasty. The bastards knew I could wring their scrawny little necks for them so, on their way out, they grabbed a brand from the fire and decided to set light to my thatch and burn my house to the ground," he seethed, "so excuse me if you find the hand of friendship around your throat rather than clasping your own in a hearty handshake."

Galahad was seething at being dumped upon the ground in such a degrading manner but Lorcan gripped his arm tightly, "Do you have much knowledge of the islands further north of here, Walcott?" he asked levelly.

"We are seeking the way back to Loch Seaforth, where my people lived." Craigan put in, the past tense of his statement tasting like acid on his tongue.

"That is no-one's business but my own, boy." The aged shepherd spat.

Galahad threw off Lorcan's restraining arm and responded in the same aggressive tone of voice, "Look, old man, make no mistake, if I were of a certain turn of mind, I could cut you down where you stand and the first you would know about it would be when your head rolled to a halt in the

361

heather." He unsheathed Whitecleave and hefted it threateningly, "Now, I am willing to accept that your wariness of strangers is well justified but I can assure you my companions and I would not visit any sort of violence upon you unless provoked into it." He drew in several calming breaths then continued in a more composed voice, "Now, I believe Lorcan asked you a question, did he not?"

Privately, Galahad was impressed at the lack of reaction from the man. Aside from his dull-grey eyes being transfixed by the glinting tip of Whitecleave, he appeared unmoved by the threat.

Griffin's face slowly cracked into a grudging sneer. "I hail from Benbecula, forty or so miles to the north." He said in a singsong voice, though he did actually appear to be digesting what was being asked of him rather than automatically railing against it as he had done previously. "Do you know which island this Loch Seaforth is on? The name means nothing to me."

"I have heard some of the elders of my tribe call it 'The Long Island'." Craigan mused.

Walcott shook his head, "Then I cannot help you, I am afraid. I have heard of the Long Island and it is much further north than I have ever been. If my memory is not playing tricks, it is another fifty miles at least beyond Benbecula." He tugged at his beard. "You lads have another hundred miles or so before you."

Galahad nodded graciously and resheathed his weapon. "I thank you, good sir, and I apologise for drawing my sword upon you. Both I and my cohorts are involved in a mission to rid these islands of a heinous band of monsters who have wreaked havoc in this area for the last five years or so, slaughtering all before them, their victims numbered in the thousands."

For the first time since they had come across Walcott, he appeared genuinely interested in what they had to say. "What manner of beasts are those you speak of?"

"Wolves," Lorcan stated flatly. "Massive wolves that walk as men."

Walcott's gaze took on a distant look and he spoke quietly but somehow his voice carried to them above the mournful groan of the wind. "Wolves who walk as men, you say?"

The trio nodded silently, intrigued by the change in the wizened fellow's demeanour.

Griffin placed both of his hands atop the staff and rested his chin upon them, "Two months hence, during a blizzard of epic proportion, there was a ship being blown south, a ship of a design which I have never seen before or since, that skirted the coast beyond yonder hills. Indeed, it would have landed here had the wind and tide not yanked it back out to sea mere yards from the sand. I was tending my flock, you see, and some of my sheep, being the stupid lumps they are, decided that, rather than joining me in the warmth of the broch, they would take a little trip over the hills and down to the sea. Despite the weather, I went after them. I only managed to find them because they all came running back past me up the slope, bleating insanely, struggling with all their might against the conditions, scared witless by something or other. I was knocked to the ground and winded, just at the summit there." He pointed his staff in the general direction of where the trio had walked down to Griffin's farmstead, "Anyway, as I lay there, fighting to get up, the snowstorm lessened for a moment and I saw a large ship listing and rocking upon the white tops." He fixed them with a sidelong glance. "It had a huge wolf's head at the prow and the biggest man I have ever seen standing at its shoulder." He looked pensively at the crest of the hill once more. "Now I come to think of it, I heard an eerie howling as I lay upon the ground, but I took it to be the wind."

The trio of travellers exchanged meaningful looks with each other before Craigan said, "You may have had a very lucky escape, my friend," and went on to elaborate on some of the hideous exploits of the Ulfhednar.

Walcott listened agape, searching the newcomer's eyes for signs of deceit and finding nothing but saddened honesty as they described the reality of the wolves' deeds. Craigan reeled off the litany of atrocities which the werewolves had committed, but the most affecting contribution came from Lorcan as, in a dull monotone, he told the shepherd of the horrific scene that the party had come upon when they had returned to the monastery at Mull.

Grey with the realisation of how close he had come to death at the hands of the ravening horde of werewolves, Walcott beckoned them into his broch without any further words being necessary.

Being ever aware of his surroundings, as they gained the threshold of Walcott's home, Galahad took the opportunity to take in the layout of the stone construction. To his surprise, he saw there were two floors to the building, with slabs leading upwards acting as both stairs and also support which linked the three-metre thick outer and inner walls. The ground floor was made of a sturdy wood and the whole dwelling had a thatched roof overlaying a timber frame.

The main room itself was roughly ten metres in diameter and was bereft of all but the most basic furniture, a rough pitted table with a dirty bowl upon it, a pallet covered in rumpled coarse blankets and two stools which sat on either side of a fireplace, formed in a dug-out section of the inner wall. The fire was not burning at the current time but there was a slight hint of orange tinging some of the embers, meaning it had not long been extinguished. A large hanging fire pot was suspended above the glowing ashes, from which a mouthwatering smell emanated.

Walcott waved them towards the table then went to the cauldron and ladled out three helpings of the stew which was in the pot into some bowls stacked haphazardly next to the nook.

They attacked the stew with great gusto, each sighing deeply as the warmth of the food slid down their throat. Craigan was first to finish and, as he cuffed the remains of the rich gravy from the stubble which had begun to dot his top lip, he glanced guiltily towards the door. "We should tell him about Taiga," he said. "It is not fair that we should be sitting in here enjoying Walcott's hospitality whilst our friend skulks outside in the storm."

Griffin looked intrigued as Lorcan and Galahad exchanged looks before nodding in agreement. The youthful Venicone clansman turned to their host and asked, "As you may have gathered from what I said just now, there is one other in our party, one whom you might find a little unsettling, given the tales we have told you previously."

Walcott's eyes hooded and the air of suspicion which had permeated his demeanour when they had first met returned with a vengeance. To disguise his trepidation that he had misjudged the trio in the same way he had miscalculated the three vagabonds who had burnt his house down, he snorted off-handedly, "What are you telling me? You have one of these monsters in your company who has seen the error of his ways?"

When Galahad and Lorcan looked sidelong at each other with no hint of levity in their eyes, Walcott's breath caught in his throat.

"Have you ever heard of a wulver?" Craigan asked.

As Walcott shook his head in the negative, Lorcan got to his feet, "If you will permit me, I will go and fetch our friend and you may decide for yourself." With a slight nod of his head, he left the broch before the shepherd could respond.

Griffin slumped down in the chair vacated by the young monk, feeling that events were running away from him. "What in hell is a wulver?" he sighed exasperatedly.

Despite himself, Galahad could not help but smile at the despondent figure before him. "An amalgam of wolf and man, similar in appearance to the Ulfhednar but of a totally different temperament and nature," the knight explained. "I imagine you will be taken aback when you first see him but he has proved himself a steadfast companion in the dark days we have just experienced." He turned to Craigan. "You have known him the longest, lad. What do you make of him?"

McIntyre shrugged, pondering the question for a few moments. "He has saved my life twice in the short space of time I have known him. He has been instrumental in us getting this far on our quest. He and I are kindred spirits, united in our determination to vanquish the wolven scum who have

364

exterminated our tribes by their actions. Save Monkshood here, he is the only one I would trust to stand with me when the final reckoning is upon us and we have to face the beasts in their lair."

Galahad regarded the shepherd as he fiddled nervously with his beard. "You must not be afeared of Taiga when you see him, Walcott, or indeed any of us. We seek to harm only the Ulfhednar. Even if you had sent us on our way without any food or drink in our bellies and your harsh words ringing in our ears, we would not have hurt you."

Craigan and Galahad both saw the tension in the grizzled shepherd's shoulders leech away. Walcott looked at the adolescent man and nodded, "That was a damned fine testimony you gave this Taiga fellow."

Again, Craigan shrugged, "I have only known him for a short time but I would trust him with my life. Well," he chuckled, "as I said, he has saved my life twice already."

"Then I too will look past his appearance and take him as I find him." Walcott extended his hand towards the Venicone who, after blinking in surprise, clasped it in his. Galahad then shook hands with Walcott also. The light had almost completely leeched from the landscape as Lorcan returned with a clearly reluctant Taiga in tow.

To his credit, Griffin was good to his word and stood up to welcome Taiga as if he was just another member of the company, even though the guttering candlelight leant a shadowy ferocity to the wulver's appearance.

The wolfman looked startled but pleased at the farmer's lack of reaction and, after murmured greetings, set about devouring the portion of stew which the host had served for him.

Once Taiga had finished and the bowls were scraped clean, the five gathered around the small table sipping goblets of crystal clear water that Walcott explained had come from a mountain spring which rose in the hills nearby.

The talk soon returned to the all-encompassing mission which filled all but their host's future.

Walcott listened to them as they spoke of what was to come before saying, "I think perhaps you have solved a puzzle for me." He rested his elbows on the table and stared at each of them in turn. "Ever since the day that ship brushed the coast of this fair island, there has been something disquieting in the air. Though it was over two months hence, my flock has been restless and troubled, even the birds have seemed subdued. Hell, even the sun, on the few occasions it has managed to break through the clouds, has seemed watery and pallid." He fixed them with a look of monumental sobriety. "It is as if these Ulfhednar are so malevolent, so foul, they live in their very own pall of evil and it infects all who come into contact with it, no matter how fleetingly." He stood up. "Before the three bastards who burned my house to ashes came

365

along, I was a man prepared to give the benefit of the doubt to most people, believing that all I met were basically good deep down inside. The scum who wronged me changed me into a crabby, mistrustful recluse, only happy in the company of my livestock and myself."

He drained his goblet before continuing, "I look at you almost hoping to find some hint of trickery in your faces for the yarn you weave is fantastical, to say the least, yet I do not, and that forces me to believe you are speaking the truth." He sighed. "Yet you are still determined to follow through on your course of action, though the odds are immensely stacked against you surviving." Shaking his head, he sat back down and stared at the wooden entrance to his home. "I wish you all the luck in the world, for you are braver men than I." He gestured towards a small cubbyhole curtained off from the main room. "There is a spence of sorts behind that drape, help yourselves to what you need for provisions. I will be able to gather more when I require it. You, on the other hand, will have enough on your minds without worrying where the next meal is coming from."

The quartet nodded their gratitude at the gesture and both Galahad and Taiga took themselves off to harvest what they felt they needed from the store. They found meagre rations in the small niche which, to the pair of travellers, made the offer even more poignant as they knew how much Walcott would struggle to replenish what they took, especially with the wintry conditions which had gripped the countryside for months on end.

The knight and the wulver swapped looks and wordlessly decided between themselves that they would only take the bare minimum from the shepherd's stocks. They stowed a salmon and a couple of unplucked chickens in their packs as well as a small bundle of fruit before returning to the table where Craigan and Lorcan were bidding their goodbyes.

"Many thanks for this, Walcott. Thank you for your hospitality and your generosity." Galahad said simply, hefting the bag which contained the newly acquired provisions.

Walcott stood and shook each of them by the hand, "It is I who should be thanking you lads. Your nobility and courage have rekindled my faith in the human spirit. When I see a group as young as yourselves marching towards your destinies with such dignity, well, it is enough to make this old man's heart sing."

They all stood open-mouthed at Walcott's apparent change of heart and fidgeted uncomfortably until Galahad found his tongue, "I am glad we have been able to inspire such a fundamental change in your feelings."

The aged sheep-herder waved away the comment as he accompanied them back out into the brutally cold night. Walcott pulled his leather cape about his shoulders and stared intently into the darkness. "I can still feel the malevolence in the atmosphere from that ship. Anyone who is willing to face down such a foe does not need the added burden of a bitter old fool's words ringing in their ears."

Lorcan shook his head and his voice was as hard as the rocks they had clambered across to reach Walcott's home. He said calmly, "You were wronged very badly by what those arsonists did to your home. You had every right to view us in the manner you did when we first arrived at your steading, but at least you have shown the type of man you are by giving us a chance to prove ourselves and not being so set in your ways that you cannot change your point of view and admit you were mistaken." He breathed heavily and hung his head. "I have also had my home ransacked and desecrated by filthy scum recently and I know full well how the hatred eats away at you and twists your outlook on life. Your ability to get past your disgust at what those villains did does you great credit."

Griffin nodded at the sentiment contained within the words then looked left and right as clouds of breath rose into the freezing sky. "Should you not bide here for the span of the night and set off when dawn breaks?" he suggested.

Galahad hesitated at the suggestion before looking for guidance from the others. "I know little of sea travel and I think the same could be said of all of us. Personally, I yearn to be back on our journey once more but, by the same token, the thought of traversing the waters in the darkness does not exactly fill me with great excitement."

"How long do we have before there is light in the sky again, do you think?" Craigan asked.

Walcott peered upwards again but clouds covered the landscape like a cloak and neither moon nor stars could be seen. "It is impossible to say. The light was fading when we first met. I could not even begin to guess how long we have bided in the house."

"Do you have spare pallets upon which we may rest?" Taiga asked next.

The shepherd shook his head, "Only the floor, I am afraid, but I am sure we can bundle some blankets together for makeshift beds."

The wulver turned to his companions. "We should try to sleep when we have the opportunity," he pointed out. "We will not fulfil our quest if we lose our bearings in the dark and drift out to sea. I vote we take Walcott up on his kind offer and bunk down here for the remainder of the night."

With that consensus reached, they returned to the warming atmosphere of Walcott's home and tried to catch up on some of the hours of sleep they had undoubtedly lost during the last few weeks and months.

The new day dawned with a miserably cold sleet slashing down upon the fields of Barra, but the travellers knew they could not delay their departure just because of inclement weather.

They said their muted farewells and set off back to the fishing boat, having determined the night before that they would do their damnedest to keep to the rugged coastline as closely as possible as they could not rely on the sun by day or the stars by night to keep them on their desired course.

Within the hour they were, once again, moving steadily north, each one grateful for the few precious hours of sleep they had elected to take before continuing.

As the day wore on, they moved past uninhabited islets like Fuday which were little more than single rocks surrounded by the sea, as well as larger islands such as Eriskay and South Uist where they could just make out distant settlements far inland, though they saw no sign of the people who dwelt within them.

Mercifully, the seemingly ever-present wind had dropped to a gentle breeze and the only sound to be heard was the creak of the oars and the '*crex crex*' call of a corncrake hidden somewhere within the machair which stretched away as far as the eye could see. As the green of the flora receded into the browny yellow of a rock-strewn sandy beach, flocks of redshank and dunlin could be seen erupting from the damp sands of the shore and the plethora of sandbars which peeked above the ever-moving waters, executing sharp turns and death-defying changes of direction with apparently telepathic precision.

From the relatively busy eastern coast of South Uist, they continued north, flirting with the bleak island of Wiay which, though it stretched away over the indistinct horizon, somehow gave off the impression of being uninhabited even without the need for the quartet to land there and find out.

It was as they began to leave the rugged outcrops and knolls of Ronay behind them, the bulk of North Uist began to loom before them and the weather took a turn for the worse. The skies darkened and the clouds became bulbous with snow, which began to fall steadily as they came to a rest on the sandy beach.

The four clambered out of the boat and manhandled it out of the lapping ebb of the incoming tide. The countryside which greeted them was surprisingly flat and featureless compared to the other islands they had landed on or passed, though there were some small hillocks dotted about the fields.

Almost as soon as their boots touched the grass, Taiga's head came up, eyes narrowed and nostrils flared, "They have been here," he murmured. "Their stench still sits upon the land they have befouled with their presence."

The other three licked suddenly dry lips. The wulver did not need to explain who 'they' were.

Craigan stared across the meadows and nodded slowly, "At least we will find shelter here while the storm blows itself out. As long as you do not mind sharing with the dead, that is," he gestured towards the nearest mound squatting upon the grass. "These hillocks are not natural, they are chambered cairns raised by the clans to house the remains of the dead."

The flakes began falling more frequently and the surrounding land was beginning to disappear behind an inconstant shield of whiteness.

Lorcan shrugged, "There is no help for it, I suppose." His face quirked into a humourless smile, "It seems that ever since yourselves and the Ulfhednar have come into my life, I have been surrounded by death on all sides."

"That is the curse of all those who suffer contact with the bastard werewolf clan, I am afraid." Taiga said, as Galahad lit a torch which rested in a sconce by the opening to the communal grave, and they ducked into the dark entrance of the stonework.

The burial chamber itself consisted of five compartments, each containing its own intact skeleton, flanking a passageway which was almost seven yards in length. The walls rose to a height of almost seven feet and were constructed primarily of thin stacked slabs of local stone. At the end of the passageway, the corridor opened out into a circular room empty of all but a few dusty bones scattered upon the gritty floor.

After a quick exploration, which yielded nothing more interesting than a few broken earthenware bowls and some animal bones, Galahad spoke in a hushed voice which echoed queerly off the walls, "Come, we should not tarry in here. Aside from the fact that those who do reside here do not deserve to have us disturb their peace, we need to keep an eye on the weather."

The four moved towards the exit of the cairn, miserably noting the blizzard which had settled in outside. They crouched down in the narrow corridor and ate some of the fruit they had been given by Walcott, all the while studiously ignoring their grinning, unmoving audience.

In response to the silence within the barrow, they ate without speaking, the heavy atmosphere of the dank passageway further accentuated by the deadening effect of the blanket of snow which was starting to build up outside.

The four sat for an indeterminate period, each one glancing from time to time towards the snowstorm which hindered their journey. By the time the flakes had stopped their stately descent, darkness had fallen and the quartet was forced to endure an uncomfortable night with the ghoulish denizens of the cairn.

The third day since their departure from Mull began in much the same way as the previous two, with the sky a sickly yellow and the air damp and cold. However, the apparently never-ending snowfall had let up for the present, so the questers made for their secured boat without breaking their fast, so keen were they to resume what they fervently hoped would be the last leg of their journey.

As they were rowing through the northern end of the Little Minch, skirting the eastern coast of the myriad islands which peppered the waters, out of nowhere, Craigan piped up animatedly, pointing towards a small fort in the distance. "Loch an Duin. This must be Scalpay. We have little more than ten miles to go. If we keep the land on our left and simply follow the water, we should find ourselves upon Loch Seaforth before dark."

Suddenly, the sense that their expedition was nearing its climax leant an excited nerviness to their words and actions but, conversely, also led to them all contemplating their own mortality.

"Do you think we will be afforded a cairn like the one we stayed in last night?" Lorcan asked quietly.

Taiga's eyebrow arched and he glanced questioningly at Galahad as Craigan clapped the monk on his shoulder and exclaimed in a voice of forced jollity, "Aye, we'll build it ourselves, but only when we've put all the Ulfhednar in their graves first."

Lorcan forced a chuckle, but it was obvious how scared he was. Not for the first time, Galahad pondered the wisdom of acceding to the young monk's request of joining them in their hunt for the wolven horde. However, as Taiga had noted, if they had refused his companionship, Lorcan would simply have set off in pursuit of the Ulfhednar on his own.

Galahad looked sideways at the youthful holy man and reflected on the huge upheaval which his life had undergone in the space of the last few days. Perhaps a reminder of the faith he had so blatantly turned his back on during the company's return to Mull would help him through the trying ordeal which he was about to endure. "For myself, I would prefer a proper Christian burial like the one we gave to the monks on Mull." He held up a hand towards Craigan and Taiga. "Please do not take that as any sort of insult to the tribal customs of your people, it is just that I wish to go to my rest with the blessings of God accompanying me on my way."

The former knight of Camelot's idea did distract Lorcan from his doubts but not in the way he would have wished. The former monk snorted at his companion's sentiments and his face instantly changed from pallid fear to ruddy anger, "I imagine my former friends at the monastery would quite liked to have had the blessings of God at their back when the werewolves ripped them to shreds but, from what I saw, it would appear that the heavenly support was somewhat lacking," he spat.

Galahad shrugged evenly, "If that is what you truly think, Lorcan, then it is a crying shame you feel you have dedicated your formative years to what you now deem a lie and I can understand your bitterness, but before you dismiss our Lord out of hand, think on this...."

Before Galahad could continue, Lorcan cut across him, "If you are about to begin waffling about God's ineffable grand plan and how we should not try to second guess His will, then do not waste your breath."

Galahad turned back to the oars with a saddened expression. "One act of evil has brought you to this conclusion, has it?" he sighed.

Lorcan's voice was full of plaintive regret as, instead of exploding once more at the former knight of Camelot, he replied with a hoarse whisper, "When I disappeared from the courtyard on Mull to go about the task I said I had to do, I took myself away to one of the bluffs which look out to sea and I challenged Him. I challenged Him to provide me with a reason as to why he did not come to the aid of those who had given their lives over to him. I asked Him why he let the werewolves enjoy their bloody sport without intervening?" He cuffed away unashamed tears as they streamed down his cheeks. "The only answer I received was the wind and spray in my face and the crashing of the waves in my ears. If you can explain to me why He did not answer, then perhaps I will change my mind but, until that time, you will not find me worshipping a deity that can treat His subjects with such disdain."

"My words will not sway you, Lorcan, that much is clear." Galahad murmured. "You must find your own path back to Him. But, as I was about to say before you interrupted me, think on this. Do you have enough about you to face the Ulfhednar as a faithless man, doomed to end your days as food for the worms, your soul eternally tied to the bonds of the earth with no hope of ever gaining entrance to heaven?"

"Hold hard there, Monkshood." Craigan interjected. "I do not believe in your God and, though Taiga held some deep conversations with Lorcan, I do not believe he has ever expressed any actual belief in your God, so where exactly does that leave us? Waving goodbye as you ascend to paradise whilst our corpses provide sustenance for the ravens?"

Galahad's face became a picture of misery as he found himself wondering how the debate had slipped away from him so spectacularly. "But you still have your belief system, do you not? The point I was trying to make to Lorcan was that, if he has forsaken his religion and is then faced with death without the cushion of his faith to provide him succour, then what will become of him." He laid a sympathetic hand upon Lorcan's shoulder. "I fear for you, that is all."

The young monk removed Galahad's hand and said in a brittle voice, "If it is my time to die, then I will accept whatever fate has in store for me. If I am wrong and God does wish to take me into his house, then I will gladly accept his hospitality but it will not stop me asking him why he allowed the horrors on Mull to unfold." With that, Lorcan turned to his oar and began rowing

371

again, back turned to Galahad and eyes firmly fixed on the horizon, the set of his shoulders leaving no doubt that he considered the debate closed.

The former champion of Camelot cursed inwardly that he had handled the situation so tactlessly. He looked from Lorcan's back to Craigan's wide-eyed face of innocence to Taiga's carefully neutral expression and bit his lip. In the space of minutes, the mood on the small fishing boat had transformed from nervous anticipation at how close they were to their destination to funereal inevitability at their impending deaths and there was no doubt in his mind that he had caused the change to take place.

They continued their voyage in silence, their entrance into the waters of Loch Seaforth shrouded in a pall of dark contemplation.

It was not long, however, before Craigan felt his mood lifting as they drew closer to Dun Eiledon and his former home. The thought of avenging his fallen clan burned within him even more strongly and he began really bending his back into the rowing. In unspoken unison, the other three took up the increased pace and they began to cover the water at impressive speed.

After about ten miles or so, Taiga tapped Craigan on the back and gestured to the right. There, on the shore, skulking in the twilight, was the deserted Taexali hamlet where they had first run into James McChirder and the McLeish twins. Inexorably, the young clansman's head was drawn to the opposite shore where he had slain the Ulfhednar wolf-bitch in a red mist of rage and grief.

He turned to the wulver and smiled slightly at the look of empathy which he received in return. "Well, lad," Taiga beamed warmly, "we have come full circle from whence we first met. I think we should be proud of ourselves that we have achieved so much so quickly but now we need to finish the task otherwise our endeavours will be pointless."

Craigan nodded but he did not smile, "I am sorry, my friend, I will not feel any sort of pride until the Ulfhednar have been obliterated from the face of the earth."

The foursome arrowed the boat towards the western shore of the loch, their momentum taking them out of the surf and onto the shingled shore in one smooth sweep.

Immediately, the young Venicone vaulted out of the boat and started combing the water-smoothed pebbles for something. Only Taiga knew what McIntyre was looking for and he hushed the other two into silence as the youth stopped his frenzied search and simply stood silently peering down at a seemingly nondescript patch of the shore.

"Stay here." Taiga murmured to Galahad and Lorcan as he made his stealthy way over to the Venicone.

The carcass of the female werewolf was a hideous study in decomposition. As it had been exposed to the elements, the soft tissue had liquefied extensively and the insects on the shoreline had not been slow to help themselves to the banquet on offer.

Craigan's beating had obviously caused a great deal of skeletal trauma, for several broken ribs could clearly be seen poking through the putrefying mess on the stones. An area of the skull had been picked clean of hair and skin by various birds and it was indented and bloodstained. As well as that, a crack in the skull gaped open, exposing what was left of the brain to the air.

"What other choice did you have, Craigan?" Taiga asked, his voice held in vice-like steadiness as he fought down the urge to vomit.

"None," Craigan's head came up and Taiga had to stop himself taking a step back from the ferocity of the tribesman's glare. "And even if I could have, I would not change what happened," he seethed. "When I first killed this travesty, I was tortured with regret. I thought I had descended to the beast's level by murdering it in cold blood but...," the rage overcame him for a second and he was rendered incapable of continuing. After a few deep lungfuls of the loch-side air, he was able to speak once more, "You see, before the devastation at Mull I had not actually seen first-hand what dreadful deeds the werewolves were capable of. I only saw the one body over the way there in Tavish and Warren's village and I was not able to return to Dun Eiledon after the wolves attacked, so the monastery was actually the first time I had witnessed what the Ulfhednar are fully capable of. And you know what, Taiga? It made me glad I had lessened their number, even if it meant killing another living thing. He turned and began walking back towards Galahad and Lorcan who had finished emptying the boat of their travel packs and the sacks of aconite. "Some things are not fit to sully the light of day." He said quietly before shouldering his pack and walking off towards the rolling hills of the Lewis countryside.

The two men looked questioningly towards Taiga, but the wulver ignored them and copied Craigan, hefting his travel belongings and walking off without a word.

"We"ll bring everything else then, shall we?" Lorcan asked rhetorically, staring helplessly at Galahad before taking his fair share of the remaining burden.

Within hours, they had made their camp in a natural cave which skulked approximately halfway up one of the many hills which were liberally scattered over the large island. From there, they could see a great expanse of Loch Seaforth, which they assumed would be the entrance point back to the island for the Ulfhednar if, by some miracle, they had managed to get ahead of the wolves.

373

The day after that, four days from when they departed the horror on Mull, they split into pairs once more, this time Galahad accompanying Taiga to scout out the Ulfhednar's den to try and ascertain if the evil clan had indeed returned to their homestead.

Whilst the wulver and the knight were away on their covert expedition, Craigan and Lorcan were left in the camp, keeping a close eye on the fog-wreathed waters for the werewolves' longship, in equal measure hoping to see it hove into view, for that would mean they would have an opportunity to set their planned ambush, but also dreading the sight of the blood-spattered wolf's mouth which adorned the prow of the *Varulv*, because of what it would mean for their immediate existence.

This pattern of operations continued for the best part of a week though, simply for boredom's sake, once Galahad was sure of Dun Varulfur's location in relation to where they had made camp, they varied his companions. It was obvious Galahad was the most strategically canny member of the group which was why he went on every sojourn into the island countryside, but it was hoped that by changing the person accompanying him, a fresh pair of eyes would pick up on something which he might miss.

The middle of the second week of clandestine reconnaissance found Lorcan and Craigan nervously sitting in the makeshift camp, watching the too-rarely seen sun go down, burnishing Loch Seaforth in a golden hue. It so happened that it was the turn of the original pair of scouts, Galahad and Taiga, to be out measuring their quarry, but they had left not long after dawn and were still not back.

The two young men were beginning to worry at this turn of events but neither wanted to show it.

"Should we go and look for them?" Craigan asked querulously, chewing on his bottom lip.

Lorcan shrugged absently, eyes still fixed as much as possible on the sparkling waters of the loch. "We should stay here, really," he murmured, though the set of his body suggested he did not necessarily believe that.

"But what if they have been taken?" Craigan blurted, finally giving vent to the unspoken dread which they had both been feeling.

"Then our chances of success have considerably lessened," Lorcan stated in deadpan tones, amazed that his voice had remained steady. With a sigh, he turned to the young Venicone, "Look, Craigan, I admit my experience of battle situations is hopelessly limited, but there is something about Monkshood and Taiga that instils me with, I don't know, not optimism exactly, but..." he tutted, annoyed at himself that he could not articulate what he was trying to say, "They seem so assured, so aware of their environment, it is reassuring." He threw his arms up in the air. "I do not believe they would allow themselves to be taken, that is the upshot of what I am trying to say."

He resumed his scrutiny of Loch Seaforth and continued speaking quietly, "When we were returning to Mull, I feared for you three, embarking on a quest with very little hope of success. If I am honest, I pitied you. I am ashamed to say I did not understand why you would throw your lives away on a cause you could not possibly win." He hung his head. "I resolved to pray for you but it would not have occurred to me in a million years to offer any physical help to you. I thought I could stand atop the moral high ground looking down upon you as you gave up your lives." Lorcan's voice became a hoarse whisper. "Then when I walked into the monastery, I was overwhelmed by the horror which confronted me. I saw the unbridled brutality and implacable wickedness and, to be honest, it was a revelation to me." He fixed Craigan with a look of maturity that belied his tender age. "It was only then that I understood. If the Ulfhednar had not attacked and I had stayed in the cosseted comfort of the monastery and waved you on your way, it would have been you who would have been looking down upon me." Tears formed in the monk's eyes as he wailed, "Why did it take the murder of all my friends for me to realise that, Craigan? Why did they have to die for me to understand?"

Craigan felt hopelessly unable to answer such a profound observation. He picked up one of the three crossbows they had salvaged from the weapons cache in the cellar at Mull and polished the stock for what seemed like the thousandth time while he thought about his response. A flash of insight hit him and he laughed ironically, "Why do you think I am here, Lorcan? Do you honestly believe if the bastard wolves had not descended upon Dun Eiledon and slaughtered my clan I would be here?" He gestured into the twilight in the general direction of the Ulfhednar's home. "Up until recently, I was just a young nobody drifting along, daydreaming in the fields without a care in the world. And that is still what I would like to be, but destiny has placed my feet upon a different road. Now I am the final hope of my clan. If I die, the Venicones die with me, our history, our line, everything, obliterated by those accursed beasts. Believe me, the responsibility sits heavily upon my shoulders. If I had fled without at least trying to make a stand against the evil of the Ulfhednar, then the Venicones would have died with me anyway and I would not have been worthy of either the name or their memory." He smiled at Lorcan. "Like it or not, adversity is the best forge in which to form your character. Until the wickedness of the world beats a path to your door, it is easy to detach yourself from others who have not been so lucky." His hand stretched across the space between them and Lorcan half turned at the comforting pressure on his shoulder. "It is said that the only thing necessary

375

for the triumph of evil is for good men to do nothing," Craigan continued, "The point is, you might have been thinking about doing nothing to aid us beyond sending positive thoughts on our behalf, but when it came to the crunch and you were faced with the starkest of choices, you chose to stand up and be counted. Nothing else matters, Lorcan, not a thing. That act in itself is a measure of the man you are."

The sound of approaching footsteps cut their conversation short and they both tensed, Craigan settling the crossbow against his shoulder and Lorcan snaking his hand around the pommel of his sword and dragging it into his grasp.

With a sigh of relief, they both laid their weapons aside as Taiga came running into the small hollow, closely shadowed by Galahad.

"What has kept you so long?" Lorcan hissed irritably.

Craigan studied the faces of the new arrivals with a quizzical look. "Why are you smirking?" He asked Galahad intently with a slight smile of his own starting to twist at the corners of his mouth. The mirth soon disappeared though, as the next question occurred to him. "Why are you running? Are you being pursued?" He inquired urgently, staring out into the rapidly darkening evening, his imagination filling the fields and hills with rabid wolves.

Galahad shook his head, "I doubt it. Those who live within the wolven village will likely as not be far too distracted to worry about us."

"What have you two done?" Lorcan wondered aloud, itching to join in with Taiga and Galahad's good spirits but hesitating to nonetheless, until he found out the reason.

Galahad bowed floridly in Taiga's direction. "I will let our hirsute friend explain," he said good-naturedly.

Taiga grinned and spread his hands wide. "Let us just say the first blow has been struck."

Craigan dropped the crossbow and studied the wulver's right hand closely. The hair was singed and the skin cracked and sore and when the Venicone reached out to touch it, Taiga drew it back as if he had burnt himself. The wulver shrugged the injury off with a blasé gesture, "A small price to pay." He waved for Craigan to sit down as the adolescent clansman began to speak. "Hold your tongue, laddie and I will tell all."

Craigan subsided with an impatient look on his face and seated himself next to Lorcan with his back to the cave wall, so keen to hear the tale that he ignored the harsh cold of the stone through his tunic and furs.

"I will stand guard," Galahad said, peering out into the dusk, "though we have barely an hour of light left."

The trio watched him take up station in the mouth of the cave then Taiga turned and began his tale.

"Myself and Galahad were skirting the borders of Loch Langavat, keeping out of sight, but getting a good idea of the number of Ulfhednar who still lurked within the boundaries of their homestead. We counted twenty milling about the loch-side but we could hear more within the main crannog. To be honest, the odds did not seem very attractive at that moment, so we," and here he cast a glance towards Galahad's unmoving back as he strained his eyes and ears out into the gloom, "decided to try and reduce their number a little."

Lorcan and Craigan stared open-mouthed at each other, "How the hell would a company of two manage to do that?"

"By the skin of our teeth, that's how," came Galahad's voice, floating eerily through the frigid air.

Taiga smirked and went on, "We had to bide our time and wait for the main Dun to empty, that is why we have been away so long, but as that seemed to be the main gathering point, we knew that was where we had to strike if we were to make any sort of impression. Luckily, Monkshood had brought some aconite with him in his pouch. He mashed up some flowers and petals with two rocks and managed to get a good deal of it in his water bottle. We waited for one of the patrolling wolves to come close enough to our place of concealment so we could kill him without being noticed." Taiga's face took on a peculiar twist of disdain as he explained how Galahad had fluttered the wolf with one blow of his mailed fist. "I know what evil the wolves have visited on all of us, but I still felt a slight distaste when I snapped the bastard's neck." He held up his wounded hand as Craigan's eyes flared angrily. "Please do not take that as a criticism of what you said on the edge of Loch Seaforth. I would never presume to lecture you on how you should feel towards the werewolves. Perhaps if you had shown some sort of enjoyment at your deed, I might have taken issue but all I saw when you spoke of the incident on the shore was rage at the injustice of what had happened to your clan and a yearning to try and put things right and that, my friend, is a feeling which burns in all of us." He waved his hand in a dismissive gesture and returned to the main thrust of the conversation, "Anyway, as I said, I snapped his neck. It had to be that way, as we could not take the chance of his blood being scented upon the breeze." He pulled at the furs he was wearing with a look of revulsion. "We stripped him of his robes and I put them on, the better to disguise my presence within the Ulfhednar's midst."

"You went in amongst them?" Craigan blurted incredulously, "By yourself? Are you insane?" he growled.

"Perhaps," Taiga conceded, then shrugged, "Whatever gathering had been taking place at the Dun had broken up which is why we chose to make our move when we did. I slipped across the thin strip of grass which skirts the rim of the water and walked unmolested into the wolven crannog." He caught their amazed looks and pulled a face that was every bit as disbelieving as his audience. "It really was as simple as that, I do not know if the dominance of their immediate surroundings has left them overly complacent but their patrols seemed very lax." He chewed upon his lip as if pondering the lack of security once again.

Lorcan breathed quietly, "So you have been in the jaws of the wolf?"

"Aye, and believe me, it will be a blessing to destroy that benighted place. The stench of death and blood is appalling and the twin aromas of stale sweat and burnt flesh fill the air. There is a spectral atmosphere in there which sent shivers down my spine." The half-light of their hideaway lent the wulver an infernal look as he continued, "It is almost as if the gateway to the next world is but a hair's breadth away." He shivered as if shaking an evil cloak from about his shoulders. "But by far the worst aspect of it is a mountain of skulls piled up in the centre of the crannog."

The two men inhaled sharply and the colour drained from their faces.

"There is some sort of fire burning underneath the mound, one with enough heat to melt its fuel, for the bottom of the mass is an obscenely twisted bulge of off-white bone," Taiga shuddered. "About halfway up you begin to see the parts of individual skulls, eyeholes and jutting jaws and the like." He gritted his teeth as if he did not want to say any more but he forced himself to continue, intent on expanding on the full dreadfulness of the scene he had beheld, "But on the top section," his breathing became quick as he blurted the words, "some of the skulls still had hair and flesh encasing them and..." his voice cracked and tailed off into silence.

"What is it, Taiga?" Craigan breathed, wondering what the wulver could possibly say that would be worse than the mental picture he had already painted.

"They were not all adult skulls. Some were no bigger than babies. I...I am sorry, I..." he shook his head and re-lapsed into horrified silence again.

The shock of the wulver's recounting was such that it took a little while for Taiga's words to sink in. "There is no need for any sort of apology, Taiga." Lorcan muttered hoarsely.

The wulver hung his head and snivelled, "Like it or not, those...things are my kin, distant kin no doubt, but kin nonetheless." His expression was of such abject misery that Lorcan and Craigan found their hearts aching at the agony which their companion was enduring. The difference between the wulver's expression now and the mirthful quirk to his features when he and

Galahad had returned to the camp, served to remind Craigan of how they had got onto the subject of the werewolves' Dun and the horrors inside, so he returned to the original gist of Taiga's story, hoping to drag the wulver free of his self-inflicted but thoroughly undeserved pit of despair. "You still have not told us what you have done to them, Taiga."

The wulver could not bring himself to look at the two young men for a moment, but he finally took a huge breath and finished his story in a flat monotone voice which seemed to make the horrible scene he had just described even more poignant. "Along one wall, there was a table lined with goblets. Each one was about two thirds full of some sort of drink, a brew from which arose a bitter but pleasant smell. All I did was top them all up with our little concoction. In my haste, some splashed upon my hand, hence this." The wulver held up his wounded appendage. "Still, as I said, it is a small price to pay. I find every wave of pain a comfort when I think of the same agony tearing down the throat of each one of those bastards. I just hope each one of those evil fiends took a nice long draught and it choked them all."

"And you managed to do all this without detection?" Lorcan gaped.

Galahad joined them and nodded at the last remark, "As far as my instincts and Taiga's senses are concerned, we were not pursued after we fled, however, as the wolves are abroad at night we would do well to keep alert. To be honest, the adrenaline which today's escapade has brought has left me fatigued." He held up placating hands. "I realise you two have been sat here all day waiting for the rest of the Ulfhednar to emerge from the fog, but both myself and Taiga have had a draining day. If you two take first duty, we will take over when we awaken."

Lorcan and Craigan shared irritable looks but acknowledged the point. After all, Monkshood was their great hope and it would surely be better for their cause if he was sufficiently rested before battle was joined. Lorcan nodded tiredly and stood up, stretching fatigued muscles and aching bones. He was closely followed by Craigan, who turned to the wulver and the knight and said, "Rest your heads and relieve us as soon as you feel able, for sometimes anticipation of the deed can be just as exhausting as the deed itself."

Taiga nodded and lay on his rumpled bedroll without any attempt to straighten it. Galahad did the same and, just before he turned his back, said, "You and Lorcan can go out tomorrow. I sometimes forget your youth belies an attitude which is far more mature than it has any right to be."

Craigan shrugged off the compliment and took up station next to Lorcan in the mouth of the hollow, contemplating the change of scene which he and Lorcan would experience the following day.

However, he and the monk never had the chance to scout the way to Loch Langavat for they were both woken by the urgent voices of Taiga and Galahad rousing them from their slumbers.

The *Varulv* had hoved into view upon Loch Seaforth.

With the two slumbering men now instantly awake, the quartet had set off across country immediately, Taiga carrying two crossbows, one for him and one for Craigan, plus a sword for Lorcan. The young man from Mull had been practising with the bow whilst they had been encamped upon the hill but had proven to be more of a danger to his fellow bowmen than to any target he happened to be aiming at. The wulver had offered to lash Whitecleave to his belt, but Galahad had baulked at being separated from his trusted blade and waved away the offer.

They had arrived at their destination within the hour and settled down to wait for the wolven clan to walk into their trap. A goodly amount of their strategy relied on the Ulfhednar taking a certain route from the loch to their Dun and, fortunately for the questers, the complacency of the werewolves did indeed lead them in the anticipated direction and they walked straight into the false fog which the foursome had induced with the fumes of aconite.

Galahad jerked awake with a start. He blinked away his confusion as the reality of where he was and the vividness of his memories from the last few days clamoured for equal attention. Painfully lifting himself up onto his elbows, he stared around the small hollow which had been the group's shelter for the last week and a half. Taiga was snoring quietly to his right as was Lorcan to his left. They were both wrapped tightly in their bedrolls, gaining what little warmth they could against the intemperate conditions. Craigan was sitting with his back against the left hand rock face staring out into the gloomy morning with a stern expression on his face. The young Venicone half-turned when Galahad seated himself next to him, "I did not think it was your duty to guard us tonight?" the former knight of Camelot asked.

McIntyre shook his head. "It wasn't. I could not sleep so I relieved Lorcan about two hours ago."

Galahad shrugged diffidently. He knew the value of rest in a situation like this, but he also knew there would be no use chiding the youngster for his eagerness to engage the enemy.

"How much longer will we give them before we are away to try and press the advantage we have garnered from yesterday?" Craigan asked, trying to keep the bloodthirsty zeal of revenge from his eyes.

Galahad waggled a warning finger in the youngster's direction. "I think advantage might be too strong a word, lad. What we have done will be an

380

irritation to the Ulfhednar, nothing more. You heard that monster in the clearing, did you not? Any hunter worth his salt knows that any animal, no matter how powerful or timid, is at its most dangerous when it is wounded and that is all we have done, we have drawn blood not severed a limb."

"My, what a ray of sunshine you are." Taiga smiled as he and Lorcan joined them.

Craigan got to his feet and the four stood in silence on the threshold of the hollow, contemplating the next few hours, surprisingly not with dread or terror, but with a healthy pride as to the task they were about to undertake. The thought that they were about to stand against such a depthless evil fired their blood and filled them with a strange elation, given they each privately acknowledged that this day would, like as not, be their last on earth.

"Now, lads, is that not a sight for sore eyes?" Taiga nearly laughed for, as they stared across the snow-covered landscape, the bright yellow semi-circle of the sun began to crest the horizon, bathing an inexplicably cloudless sky in a radiant wash of vibrant yellow.

In unison, the travellers stared at one another and each clasped the other's forearms in the traditional handshake of the warrior then, without words, gathered their packs and began descending the gentle slope towards the shore of Loch Langavat and the capricious whims of destiny.

Chapter 15

Dag Kennetson, an Ulfhednar clansman of less than twenty years of age, stood in a clump of trees that sprouted a few yards from the edge of Loch Langavat, staring in disbelief at the headless body which lay crumpled underneath a makeshift pile of leaves and pebbles.

The breath caught in his throat as he saw the distinctive scar which raked across the right palm of the corpse. That immediately identified the body as Knut Hungargunn, who had failed to return from his patrol and had been missing for the best part of the last day. The remains were not well hidden and Knut's body would undoubtedly have been discovered earlier had it not been for the chaos which had erupted in the Dun the last evening.

As the moon had risen in the sky, as had happened every night since the wolves had made Dun Varulfur their own, all but a few of the clan gathered within the fetid atmosphere of their homestead to partake of the mystical concoction which aided the transformation from man to wolf, the better to indulge their debased lust and orgiastic pleasures.

Dag had been stood on the perimeter of the loch, cursing his luck at being one of the unfortunate minority deprived of the nightly debauchery in the Dun, when the howls of pain had begun to sound.

The young Ulfhednar had been one of the first to arrive upon the scene and had been greeted by his kith and kin writhing in exquisite agonies upon the filth-caked floor of the crannog, clawing at their throats and struggling to breathe. He had watched in horrified fascination as his closest friend, Tomas Klemperer, had fallen at his feet, trying in vain to speak but raking at his throat, drawing blood with the ferocity of his actions. As Dag had tentatively reached out, Tomas fell to the wooden boards, eyes rolling up in his head, the whites rapidly turning red as they filled with blood. When Dag had finally snapped out of his shock and dropped to his knees in despair, Tomas' tongue had lolled free of his open mouth. In horror, Kennetson had drawn back, for the Ulfhednar's mouth and tongue were blistered and burnt.

As he looked around the Dun in stupefied terror, the same fate was being experienced by other members of the clan, both female and male, young and old, wolf and man. His head jerked round as one of the ceremonial bronze goblets clattered to the floor, falling from the stricken hand of one of his compatriots. He stumbled over to the table and grabbed the nearest one. He gingerly sniffed at it, his nose wrinkling at the familiar scent. He was just about to take a sip when he caught a slight after-tang in the heady aroma. He stood up too quickly, the giddy mixture of the aconite and the shock of what he was seeing making him unsteady on his feet. "Do not drink," he yelled in a slurred voice, "It is the Bleidwein," he wailed using the traditional clan name for the narcotic-laced beverage, "it has been poisoned." He swept his arms drunkenly across the table, sending as many untouched drinks as he could crashing to the floor, but something was playing havoc with his senses and he lost his balance again. Eventually he managed to drag himself out into the freezing night, gulping huge lungfuls of the refreshing air and feeling the fog that shrouded his mind begin to dissipate.

Though the Ulfhednar's chosen lives meant they were used to seeing the twin agonies of pain and death, Dag had never witnessed it occurring to so many of his clan at one time and it shook him to the core as fully fifty of his fellow Ulfhednar lay dead in attitudes of dreadful anguish. The other guards had been so traumatised by what they had seen that they had even braved the disease-ridden stench of Beyla's home in the hope that the stricken seeress would be able to offer some sort of advice but Dag had found her in a deep-rooted delirium which no amount of cajoling could retrieve her from.

It was as the unaffected Norsemen were milling about uncertainly that Knut's absence was first noted, but, by that time, the countryside was in the grip of darkness and though the Ulfhednar in their wolven form were the undisputed rulers of the night in these parts, none of the inexperienced clansmen showed any sort of inclination to transform and investigate Knut's disappearance, especially as this was one of the few nights in recent times the moon had failed to remain visible in the night sky.

It was not until the first indications of dawn were beginning to colour the sky that Dag and his fellow guards were able to re-enter the Dun without feeling any ill-effects.

They all viewed the devastation in silence, each privately wondering whether their reign of dominance had just been tested or whether the poisoning, if that is what had caused such mayhem, was just a one-off instance of dreadfully inexplicable bad luck.

Once they had cleared the crannog of the cadavers and poured some of the loch's water over the floor to dilute the congealing puddles of Bleidwein, they returned to the matter of Knut's disappearance and set off to hunt out the errant clansman.

And so it was that Dag had found him, laying on his front amongst the leaves and pine needles, his eyes staring sightlessly at the whispering canopy overhead.

"What in the nine worlds of Hel is happening?" Kennetson whispered tormentedly.

The youngster had always been an anonymous member of the wolven horde, keen to indulge in the decadence and debauchery which was always on offer, but not so eager to partake of the violence which enabled it to happen. He was by no means a coward though and had killed his fair share of victims, as indeed had all the tribe, but he had no wish to be part of anything that would draw the attention of the chilling ice-green stare of his war-chief because, though he had nothing but the greatest respect for what the leader of the Ulfhednar had achieved, it was a respect borne of fear at the giant's unpredictable moods and his capacity for unexpected violence. In short, Varga Hrolfsson scared the life out of him.

Therefore, it was Dag's bad luck that Knut's body had been deposited directly on the route from Loch Seaforth to Dun Varulfur. His heart began to thunder in his ribs as he heard the sound of movement in the woods and Varga stepped into view, his face reddened both by rage and the effects of the trap set by Monkshood and his allies.

He checked his stride and angled over towards the horrified youngster, eyes flaring momentarily when he saw the corpse at Kennetson's feet. "Monkshood?" he snarled, eyes narrowing as Dag's face creased at the unfamiliar word.

As such an unimportant member of the tribe, Dag was unaware of the small but significant threat of Monkshood which had hung over the ambitions of the Ulfhednar since before they had established themselves at Dun Varulfur. "I am sorry, my lord, I do not understand." Dag wheedled in an unprepossessing whine which irritated Varga.

"How did he die, idiot?" Varga growled.

Kennetson tried to keep his voice level but instead it quavered unevenly, "I do not know. He went missing on patrol last night and I have only just found him."

Varga grunted then looked at the corpse once more. "He has been dead for most of the night, I would guess. Why was he undiscovered until now? I see no sign of burial so presumably the body was left to the mercy of the elements above ground?"

Dag nodded dumbly, "What happened at the Dun occupied most of the night, we have only just been able to resume the patrols," he croaked.

Hrolfsson's head whipped round and he advanced on the hapless clansman, "The Dun? What happened at the Dun?"

The Viking warleader could feel a volcano of rage begin to build inside him as Dag stammered his way through an account of the pandemonium in the Ulfhednar's homestead.

However, Varga was acutely aware that what was fuelling his fury was a tight ball of fear at how easily the clan's defences had been breached. He had come to view Dun Varulfur as an unshakeable foundation upon which the Ulfhednar could always rely, an impenetrable fortress which served as a potent symbol of their dominant status upon the islands. Now, though, that assumed security had been compromised and, on top of the assault in the woods and the loss of the *Varulv*, Varga found the doubts he had felt previously clamouring for attention in his head once more. What made those misgivings even graver was that he had now seen the power of Monkshood with his own eyes. How was he able to inflict such harm upon the clan with such little effort when all who had attempted it before had been swept aside like seeds in the wind? How could one man halt the unstoppable progress of the Ulfhednar and thwart Fenrir's ascent to godhood?

The questions hammered into his brain one after the other and he stood before Kennetson wild-eyed and breathing heavily, struggling vainly for calm and clarity of thought.

Suddenly, through the maelstrom of jumbled ideas and fractured contemplation, a welcome familiar voice sounded, its soothing tones gently banishing the doubts from his mind.

"Varga," it whispered, "I feel you are near. Come to me. Come to me."

"Beyla!" He exclaimed and set off towards the wolven settlement, leaving Dag shivering with relief that he was out of the warleader's presence without any injury being bestowed upon him.

Varga ran like a man possessed, ignoring the uneven terrain underfoot and the battering his boots took as he gained the pebbly shore of the loch. He arrowed through the settlement, drawing surprised looks and a few shouts of recognition, but he paid them no heed.

The massive Viking did not bother knocking upon the door of Beyla's home, he just barged into the dank two-roomed dwelling and made his way over to the threadbare curtain which separated the useless bedchamber from the rest of the house. As he reached out for the soiled material, a reedy voice muttered hoarsely, "Varga, is that you?"

"Yes, Beyla, it is me," he hesitated as he laid his shocked eyes upon the brittle stick-thin shell that Beyla had become, "...come to see that you fulfil your destiny."

She sighed painfully before plunging into a bout of tuberculotic coughing which left her weeping and gasping in agony, "Take me to the Dun, Varga," she wheezed once she was able to speak again. "Carry me to the mountain of skulls and spill my blood upon it. Place my head atop the heap and resurrect Fenrir HelMouth as is *your* destiny but do it quickly, for Monkshood draws nearer even now." Her breath came in short sharp bursts as the ebb and flow of pain careered around her entire being. "He or one who follows him has already despoiled the Dun with their unholy presence." She sighed once more, but this time it was a sound of contentment. "Once I have assumed my rightful place at the summit of the skulls, no power on earth will be able to resist the resurgent power of the wolf-god. No power on earth...." Her voice faded into silence and Varga's heart began to ache with loss. A moment later

385

though, her eyes fluttered and she fixed him with a surprisingly ferocious stare considering her proximity to the afterlife. "Do not stand there like a helpless pup, Hrolfsson. Bear me to the Dun," she barked.

Despite Beyla's condition, the massive clan-chief of the Ulfhednar could not prevent a smile forming upon his lips. That clipped command had rolled back the years and cast Varga's memory back to when the Vikings had first been harried from Ulfsgaard and Beyla had been full of vim and vigour, able to cow all who challenged her into silence with naught but a piercing stare.

With that nostalgic sight pleasantly nestling in his mind's eye, he peeled back the sweat-drenched coverlet and lifted the old seeress free of the indistinct indentation which her tortured writhing had described on the soiled sheets. The pleasing reminiscence was blotted out immediately as, in shock, Varga nearly overbalanced due to Beyla's miniscule weight. Manfully holding onto the memories and overlooking the unpleasantness of the old woman's dry papery skin against his, he walked effortlessly back through the settlement, the mental burden outweighing the physical a hundredfold.

Along the way, he acquired a respectful snake of Ulfhednar warriors as they joined the death march of the ancient seeress. Within minutes, he found himself upon the threshold of the Dun. Without hesitation, he planted a hefty kick upon the heavy door, sending it crashing back against the wall.

As the pair of them went from the cooling air of the wintry day to the close, stale atmosphere of the Dun, Beyla sighed deeply and snuggled her wrinkled head into Varga's shoulder.

Varga stood as near to the ossified pile of skulls as he could, waiting patiently for Dun Varulfur to fill up with Ulfhednar for, even though Beyla's warning of Monkshood's closeness still rang loudly in his ears, her sacrifice would be the culmination of everything that the Ulfhednar had striven for ever since Varga's initial railing at the Aesir for their betrayal of his father and he felt it would be both disrespectful and unlucky to try and rush through it.

By this time, the voyagers from the *Varulv* had made it into the village and deposited their cargo upon the warped heap which rose above the flame of Surtr. They then joined their fellows in the assembled throng which hissed with a sotto voce susurration as the seafarers caught up with those left behind to tend to the wolven community.

In unspoken unison, the whispers dwindled into nothingness as Varga climbed awkwardly to the summit of the mound and placed Beyla's limp body reverently down upon it. From his precarious eyrie, he turned to the crowd and caught the attention of one of the nearest clansmen. He did not immediately recognise the face as it was one of the most recent converts to the werewolf tribe but, as he studied the features, an evil smile creased his own craggy face. "Yes, you will be a perfect guard." He picked another two clan members and told them to go and join Dag Kennetson on guard duty at the door of the crannog.

An undisguised look of misery settled on the original tribesman's face, an act of insolence that, in the normal course of events, would have resulted in the complainant's violent demise, however, given the identity of its wearer, Varga decided to let it go.

Satisfied all was as it should be, Varga hushed the room into utter silence then drew Varkolak from its sheath, advancing towards Beyla with a sad but proud look upon his face.

The foursome of questers watched warily from the branches of a sturdy tree that sat on the fringes of the wood which overlooked the eastern side of Loch Langavat.

They had borne witness to Varga's headlong sprint into the settlement and then his more sedate progress towards Dun Varulfur with Beyla.

They watched as the majority of the denizens entered the crannog behind the massive clan-chief and his poignant burden.

After a minute or so, the village was deserted and the quartet made their move. "This is what we came here to do." Galahad said calmly. "Let us cut this cancer from the flesh of the world."

Lorcan and Galahad dropped from the low-lying canopy and began running implacably across the space between the trees and the loch, causing confused consternation among the quartet of guards stationed at the end of the hidden wooden causeway which led to the entrance of the Ulfhednar's gathering place.

The two men sent a volley of crossbow bolts slicing through the air and two of the guards dropped like stones with feathered shafts dipped in a mixture of water and crushed aconite protruding from their unseeing eyes.

The two remaining werewolves stood transfixed and, it was not until the attackers were nearly upon them, that one of the guards snapped out of his shock and began to scramble back across the wooden path to warn those inside of the assault.

The adrenaline of revenge infusing his being lent breakneck speed to Lorcan's feet and he was the first to gain the bridge. The remaining guard threw himself out of the way so the young monk left him for Galahad to deal with while he ran down the other one. However it soon became clear that Lorcan's insane rush would not be enough to bring him within striking distance and prevent the werewolf from warning those inside.

He halted as the crazy-eyed Ulfhednar pounded frantically on the door then jogged back to Galahad's side wondering why, as he approached him, he had not killed the still prostrate Norseman and, in actual fact, appeared to be just as shocked as the wolves had been when the pair of them had first advanced.

"What are you doing? Kill the bastard!" Lorcan snarled. When the former knight did not respond, he hefted his sword and spat, "I will do it myself then." To his utter disbelief, as he brought his blade down, Whitecleave shot into view and blocked the stroke. "What the…" Lorcan began to say before Galahad cut him off.

"Lorcan, wait," Galahad breathed hoarsely.

The move was so unexpected that Lorcan actually took a step back. "What? Why? Has fear unmanned you, Monkshood? At the last, will you desert us just as your God deserted those who perished at Mull?"

"Hold your tongue, Lorcan," Galahad hissed back and reached down to the supine man. "Adomain, is that you?" he whispered in horror.

Brother Adomain hid his nodding head in his hands and wept.

"Adomain?" Lorcan gaped, "Adomain of Iona? But how…" the young monk began before the melancholic voice of the elderly monk interrupted.

"I went to Mull," he stated flatly, glaring at Galahad. "I went to Mull in the hope of dissuading you from embarking on your ridiculous sword-wielding fantasy. Little did I know I was walking straight into the jaws of the Ulfhednar." He got to his knees and crawled over to the statue-still Galahad. "I did not believe that such evil existed. I thought the clansmen's tale was some sort of ruse to spirit you away from Iona, from me." Tears welled in Adomain's eyes as he wailed, "Now you can witness the harvest which my selfishness has sown. They fell upon Padraig's house like the Great Flood, unstoppable and leaving only destruction in their wake," he shuddered and lapsed into silence.

"You were there?" Lorcan breathed.

Taiga and Craigan watched in confused dismay as the young werewolf who had retreated before Lorcan and Galahad fell back from the door of the Dun as it opened.

Adomain nodded miserably. "I saw it all. The slaughter, the violations, the atrocities that were perpetrated…I am sorry I doubted the wulver and the Venicone." He absently looked around. "Where are they? I wish to apologise to them face to face."

Galahad ignored the question. "How was it you survived, Brother?" he whispered.

An ironic snort of laughter sounded from the monk, "I told them I knew of you, Galahad. I told them I knew of Monkshood."

"So you did not fight?" Lorcan spat. "You did not seek to avenge Padraig or Cormac or any of the others?"

"What the hell are they doing?" Craigan hissed under his breath as the Ulfhednar began to file out of the crannog and approach the three men who stood in a seemingly frozen tableau at the end of the wooden causeway.

Taiga grabbed his arm as he moved to erupt from their hiding place, "Wait, laddie. You know the plan. Keep your focus on what we have to do and let them concentrate on what they have to do. I am sure Monkshood knows what he is about."

"There seemed little point." Adomain shrugged then fixed Lorcan with a look of guilt. "You have not seen what they are capable of. It would have been like trying to keep back the tide with a dinner bowl." He shook his head and began to weep, "It made little difference for they took my life anyway."

The Ulfhednar now had them surrounded on the shores of Loch Langavat but something stayed their attack. The two questers' heads shot up as Varga Hrolfsson emerged from the darkness of the Dun.

"What does that mean?" Lorcan snapped irritably, as he realised they now stood in the centre of a circle of wolves. He momentarily wondered how such imposing creatures could move so silently.

Galahad's cheeks ran with tears as the implication of Adomain's words sunk in, "He is one of them, Lorcan."

As he said this, a barked command from behind him cut through the electric atmosphere.

"No, please, no." Adomain moaned.

The order jerked Galahad out of his misery-filled contemplation and he gasped, "You understand their language?"

Sweat flooded Adomain's forehead as he struggled against some unseen force. "Once they inveigle you into their tribe, some sort of mental link... is established and... his words...make...sense. Nooooo..." the monk screamed as Varga repeated his demand in a harsher voice.

"We must do something." Craigan whined. "They will be ripped to pieces."

Taiga was at a loss to explain what was unfolding before him. "Have faith in Monkshood, laddie," he said with an assurance he did not feel.

Galahad and Lorcan watched in petrified horror as Adomain's face and hands elongated and coarse hair began to sprout all over his body.

"Monkshood?"

Galahad jumped as a huge shadow fell across him. Varga Hrolfsson stood before him, eyeing him up and down with an apparently friendly smile, "Monkshood?" he repeated.

Galahad found his gaze ripped from the toothy grin and inexorably dragged back to the ghastly torture which Adomain was enduring, his body contorting in agony and his shrieks ripping the peace of the evening asunder.

And then it was over. Adomain had transformed into a wiry slavering wolf and the anguish in his eyes had been replaced by a bestial fury which would only be sated by the blood of his former friend.

The wolf made to snap at Galahad but was restrained by another command from Varga.

"You see," Varga spun round, pointing at Galahad, whose shoulders had slumped in despair at the travesty that Adomain had become. "This is the famous Monkshood, supposedly prophesied to bring about the downfall of the Ulfhednar. Let our supposed conqueror instead be the first sacrifice given to Fenrir HelMouth when he returns to us, yes?"

Through the tumult which greeted Varga's words, he turned to Galahad, "You come?" the Viking chief said pleasantly, ushering the knight towards the entrance of the Dun.

As if in a trance, Galahad followed him in apparent dejection. However, he was still aware enough to rumble a warning to Lorcan when he saw the young man's hand snake down to his sword. "Unsheath your blade and you will surely die, Lorcan. Stay by my side, lad, and control yourself."

Lorcan was about to roar defiance, ignore Galahad's cowardly surrender and launch himself at the wolven horde, though it would surely mean his death, but something in the knight's tone suggested to the monk that perhaps Galahad was not quite as despondent as he seemed. Still expecting to be torn to pieces at any moment, Lorcan did as he was bid and fell into step next to Galahad.

This did not seem to worry Varga unduly and, with an extravagant gesture, he waved the Ulfhednar and their uninvited guests back into Dun Varulfur.

As the door to the werewolves' gathering place closed with a slam of death knell finality, Taiga and Craigan looked askance at one another. The wulver looked for signs of movement in the settlement for a time but the crannogs and huts appeared lifeless and silent. He shrugged, "We can only do what we have been charged to do and just hope for a miracle to occur inside the wolves' lair."

The pair of them dropped to the ground from their hiding place amongst the branches of the tree and made their stealthy way across the now-deserted sixty or so yards of open space between the woods and the Dun.

The Ulfhednar fanned out around the diameter of the crannog, leaving Galahad and Lorcan standing opposite Varga and the wolven form of Adomain who was still snapping and snarling at them but seemed to be restrained by some sort of invisible leash.

Lorcan chanced a glance at the pile of skulls which Taiga had described in such vivid detail then wished he had not. The open mouths of the heads near the top seemed to be calling to him, their woe hitting him with an almost physical force. For some reason, there was an ancient woman sprawled naked across the top of the grotesque pile but Lorcan had no time to ponder the significance of this because one of Varga's massive hands had spun him round to face the drooling maw of Adomain.

"You fight," the huge Viking gestured at the wolf. "You fight to the death."

Lorcan's eyes swivelled like caged animals and he licked suddenly dry lips. The sounds of a scuffle broke out behind him and he glanced over his shoulder to see Galahad straining against the iron grip of five Ulfhednar.

A sensation of movement tore his gaze away from his companion just as Adomain leapt. The young monk threw himself to the side and drew his sword, slashing it in the vague direction of the former holy man of Iona.

The pair circled each other as the baying from the mob of werewolves increased in volume. As Lorcan took a step to the left, someone in the throng thrust out a leg and sent him tumbling to the wooden boards. Within a second, the wolf was upon him, his teeth closing about the youngster's left arm. Adomain shook his head vigorously, tearing the limb free in a gory spray of blood and muscle. Lorcan's shriek raked down Galahad's spine and he redoubled his efforts to break free from his captors.

As the young monk lay dying, staring in anguished horror at the bloodied stump of his arm, Varga said something to the beast which Adomain of Iona had become and, at once, the middle-aged holy man began to resume his human form. As the bestial ferocity fled him and his humanity began to reassert itself, Adomain's face became a nightmare of sorrow. He took a faltering step towards the rapidly failing Lorcan but stopped in his tracks when he heard Galahad's roar of wrath.

The former knight of Camelot was so blinded by rage, so intent on avenging the dreadful wound inflicted upon his companion, he did not see Varga nod at the beasts who held him.

In an instant, he was free with Whitecleave in his hand and murder in his heart. Adomain moaned incoherently, Lorcan's blood dribbling onto his naked torso.

Galahad raised his famed blade above his head, ready to decapitate his former friend as he cowered before him but stopped as Varga's hand clamped upon his arm like a vice.

"Translate," the clan-leader said calmly to Adomain, the authority in his voice dragging the Ionan back from the brink of madness. Varga turned to Galahad. "Your friend, "he gestured at Lorcan, who had passed out from the pain but still had an erratic tell-tale flutter about his chest, "need not pass into the next life." He paused for a few seconds while Adomain translated. "However, if you kill this one, he will." Varga arched an eyebrow, gesturing towards Adomain, as the older man whimpered his way to silence.

Even as they spoke, Galahad could see a noticeable change begin to take hold of Lorcan's ravaged body. "But he will be one of you," Galahad spat, "and that is no life at all." He threw an elbow towards Varga who took the blow in his stomach though he did not move. He did, however, release the knight to complete his bloody work.

"You do not know what it is like when the change is upon you, it cannot be contained, it is a compulsion. You cannot control your actions. Please, Galahad, please." Adomain wailed, scrambling backwards, away from the advancing knight.

King Arthur's champion was torn in two by the wretched entreaty. He knew in his heart Adomain would not have committed such a foul deed had he been of sane mind, but how could he let such a heinous act go unpunished? His gaze rebounded from Adomain's bloodstained face and chest, to Lorcan's much-abused body which was on its way to transforming into a wolf, to the arrogant expression of the massive clan-leader who stared at the unfolding scene with a carefully neutral face.

That did not help him in any way as he realised whichever course he opted for would cause him great pain. Kill Adomain for an act over which he had no power and he would be killing both him and Lorcan as well as shouldering the guilt for the act itself. Spare him and he would condemn them to the travesty of life which was the existence of the Ulfhednar, as well as adding one more to the number of voracious beasts.

Varga's emerald eyes followed the tip of Whitecleave as Galahad lowered it to the ground.

"I will not…I cannot…." The knight mumbled.

The war-chief looked to Adomain for a translation then, when he received it, allowed a brief flash of anger to cross his face. He had hoped to goad Monkshood into slaying his former friend but, with his plan thwarted, now felt the need to lash out himself. "Tell him it makes no difference as we would not be able to support such a lame clansman anyway."

As Adomain began to repeat Varga's words, the huge Viking strode over to Lorcan's body, grabbed a hank of hair, lifted the whole body up and, with his muscles bunching in effort, ripped the youngster's head off.

Galahad fell to his knees and vomited as Varga carelessly threw the two parts of Lorcan's body into the baying crowd, who fell upon them with great gusto. The knight staggered to his feet and contemplated a strike at the gargantuan Norseman but Lorcan's death had been so matter-of-fact and effortless that he was plunged into an abyss of despair from which he had no hope of emerging.

Varga saw the look of despondency on his supposed nemesis' face and laughed hugely. "To me, faithful hound." He chortled at Adomain, who dragged himself reluctantly to the Viking's side.

Varga stood in the middle of the arena of noise and lifted his hand up high for all to see. He felt so in command, so certain of his victory, so in possession of his faculties that he allowed himself a little indulgence. His fingers began to elongate and darken and claws emerged where his nails had been until, within a few seconds, his whole hand down to the wrist had become a large paw.

In two strides, he bounded to the edge of the crowd and jabbed his hand into the face of an Ulfhednar clansman, the razor sharp claws entering the luckless werewolf's head through the eyes. The mob was instantly silent as the grievously injured wolf slid from Varga's fingers and crumpled to the floor.

"Feed, my children," he purred.

The nearest wolves knew better than to pause for any length of time after an order from their leader so they tore into the corpse, rendering it unrecognisable from the clansman who had been standing in the throng mere seconds before howling fictitiously and enjoying the blood-soaked spectacle.

As Hrolfsson walked past Galahad, he muttered something that was lost in the newly returned furore.

The knight looked numbly at Adomain as the bereft monk, who seemed to have aged by twenty years since he had slaughtered the youngster from Mull, recited what Varga had said, "The one he killed was the one who tripped Lorcan before...he died." As Galahad stared uncomprehendingly at Adomain, Columba's former deputy blurted a pain-filled laugh and finished his translation, "He said he did not think it was right that Lorcan died because of an act which was so underhand."

Galahad's narrowed eyes immediately sought out the figure of Varga Hrolfsson as he climbed the pile of skulls, gaining the summit in four strides. He was the architect of all this misery and evil and Galahad yearned with all his being to race up behind him and separate his head from his shoulders but he knew he would not get close.

By this time, Varga had ceased his ascent and stood astride the puny body of the nude old woman who lay atop the ossified heap.

393

"Ah, my kinsmen," he breathed huskily. "The conclusion of our journey is finally here, the destination within sight. Our work is at an end and we are on the brink of concluding the task bestowed upon us by our god." He stooped and swept Beyla up in his arms easily. "Fittingly, it will be our seeress who will provide the final step upon the stairway and open the door through which Fenrir will emerge triumphantly into the moonlight. I cannot think of a more apt end to a life dedicated to nothing but the advancement and triumph of our god and our tribe. We have all, at times, been enriched by her wisdom just as we have all, at times, felt the bite of her acid tongue but, with this selfless deed, one of so, so many she has performed throughout her life for the Ulfhednar, whatever memories we have of her will be forever dominated by this scene. I bid you emblazon this moment upon your minds, Ulfhednar, and reflect on the fact that you will never see the like of Beyla again."

With his speech finished and the clamour of the Ulfhednar reverberating from the rafters of Dun Varulfur, Varga laid her reverently down once more and unsheathed Varkolak, his seax. As the blade came closer to the old woman's throat, her eyes fluttered open and she whispered, "A most fitting send-off, Varga. Thank you."

With unbidden tears falling unabashedly, Varkolak's blade sliced into her papery skin and Beyla the Seeress, wise-woman to the Ulfhednar clan for century upon century, died.

Varga took the headless body over to the specially prepared shroud which had been unfolded on the dais where his throne had formerly stood. As he laid her upon it, he heard a gasp from the crowd and glanced up to see the source of the susurration.

He gaped in disbelief at what he saw.

A white mist had begun emanating out of Beyla's skull, cloaking the whole mound in its insubstantial grip. As Varga looked, Beyla's eyes opened and her features began to change.

Her face lost its myriad wrinkles and took on a timeless quality, making it impossible to place in terms of age. The right side became blackened as if burnt though, aside from the colour change, it remained unmarked in any other way. The other half remained the same, however.

The mist then emanated downwards and continued across the floor, lapping around the legs of the mystified Ulfhednar. However, the cloud which had wrapped itself around the mound of skulls writhed strangely and lost its transparency, hardening into a cloak of the purest white. The cloak then began to contract, crushing the mass of hitherto implacable bone into a smaller, thinner shape until it finally resolved itself into a tall woman.

"Beyla?" Varga whispered in the absolute silence that greeted the unexpected display.

"Do you not recognise me, Varga Hrolfsson of the Ulfhednar?" An echoing voice barren of warmth and pity replied, "Do you not recognise the sister of the one you have given your life over to?" the woman said as she pulled back the hood of the ethereal cloak. Her eyes were bone-white and colourless as was her hair, which fell about her shoulders in an elegant cascade.

Varga dropped to his knees in instant supplication, completely thrown off-kilter by the sudden appearance of the goddess Hel. "I apologise for my ignorance, mistress. I took you to be ministering to your charges in the Abode of Mists. Though it is an honour beyond imagining for you to have graced us with your presence, I confess I am confused by it."

She beckoned Varga to his feet, her unlined, frigidly beauteous countenance touched by the slightest of smiles at the giant's honeyed words. "I am here because my brother seems intent on exiting my realm with a battering ram when he need only ask for a key."

The goddess closed her eyes and pointed to the flame of Surtr which now lay exposed upon the floor of the Dun, glowing powerfully through the all-encompassing fog which still whirled and heaved in eye-watering fashion. She began twisting her finger round and round with increasing rapidity and the mist parted, leaving a perfect circle in the centre of which sparkled the shard of the jotunn's enchanted sword.

The floor beneath fell away as if it had been built over the gaping maw of a bottomless pit, but the flame floated on open air. As Varga looked down the vertiginous hole, something moved on the edge of his vision, then there was a sensation of onrushing movement and, within the blink of an eye, the grinning face of Fenrir HelMouth, eldest son of Loki, most revered God of the Ulfhednar, was snapping and snarling at the threshold, ravening and crazed, yet seemingly unable to progress past the tiny obstruction of Surtr's flame.

Varga wept in ecstasy as he saw the culmination of his life's work come to fruition. He screamed an order and all the Ulfhednar, save himself, dropped to their knees and touched their foreheads to the floor, their heads disappearing below the curling mist. There was a brief tussle as Galahad tried to remain standing but he was forced to adopt the same position as all the others in the room by means of several vicious punches to his stomach.

Hel glided across the portal which she had created and reached down towards the shining beacon that pinpointed its centre, "Calm yourself, brother mine. I do not wish to be knocked to the ground by you in your eagerness to be free."

The massive wolf grinned toothily, snaked his tongue across his lips then subsided for a moment.

The goddess picked up the flame of Surtr and placed it within her cowl. "Never again will the fires of Hel diminish once the flame of Surtr has been added to them," she said, withdrawing to the side of the hole to allow her brother passage into the realm which had been denied to him for so long.

Fenrir HelMouth exploded into the Dun, his massive presence dwarfing even that of his goddess-sister.

"At last," he howled with ear-shattering volume, "I am free of the accursed Aesir's prison."

Despite his best efforts, Galahad found himself dragged to the floor by his werewolf captors and his head plunged into the mist. Almost immediately he felt the grip slacken as the pair who held him began coughing and spluttering as the coils of mist wormed their way down their throats and into their lungs.

He smirked evilly as he straightened up and a cacophony of strangulated moans and whines came to his ears. It seemed that Taiga and Craigan's part of the plan was working better than they had dared hope.

During the often tedious wait for the return of the Ulfhednar aboard their longship, the foursome had been formulating schemes and plans of how they might do the greatest damage to the Viking cause. From what they had witnessed over the recent period of reconnoitring, they had rightly guessed that the wolves were complacent to the point of stupidity by the perceived strength of their reputation and would not bother to keep any watch on the surrounding area once their leader had returned, because they simply could not comprehend that any force could possibly topple them from their position of power.

Therefore, as per the plan, once Galahad and Lorcan had been frogmarched into the Dun, the wulver and the Venicone had taken the stockpile of aconite which they had gathered from the slopes of Ben Molyneaux and encircled the whole of the crannog with it, heaping it in larger piles beneath each window and at the front entrance. With Taiga's hands rather incongruously encased in Galahad's gauntlets and his face swaddled in one of Craigan's spare tunics, which left only his eyes showing, the two of them methodically set light to the purple petals and rich green stalks, then retreated to the end of the cunningly concealed causeway where they both stood like unmoving sentinels.

Craigan was poised to let the bolts of his crossbow sing across the water and Taiga was grimly clutching a brutally sharp sword garnered from the accumulation of weaponry in the cellar of the monastery on Mull.

Galahad shook his right arm free of the loosened grip and brought the side of his hand down on the base of the werewolf's neck, feeling a rush of vicious joy as he was rewarded with a loud crack. He stared quickly around the fetid crannog and found himself unobserved. Here was his chance, he thought, and he hefted Whitecleave and got to his feet.

But as he turned back to the muscular form of Varga Hrolfsson, the joy leeched from him immediately and his mind was catapulted back to the nightmare he had experienced on Iona, the fevered dream that had made up his mind as to whether he would accept the responsibility of being the vessel of final hope for two clans, one human, one inhuman. And here it was before him, an impossibility made reality, in all its horrifying magnificence.

The gigantic figure of Fenrir HelMouth leapt free of his God-forged bondage and screamed his challenge to Asgard, home of the Aesir and the Norse pantheon shook at its ferocity.

After the initial rush of pure unfettered elation at his successful resurrection, Fenrir fought to calm himself. It had worked. The plan which had been in the making for longer than he could remember had worked beyond his wildest dreams. Right up until his sister had removed the flame of Surtr and permitted him ingress into the domain that was rightfully his to rule, he had expected some sort of trickery, some sort of betrayal perpetrated by the Aesir, to snatch the heady glory from him at the last second, but the anticipated trap had not materialised.

At length, after breathing the true air for the first time in an age, he finally took note of his surroundings. The mist from his sister's appearance and the smoke from the aconite intermingled into an all-enveloping fog which rose from ceiling to floor. All but three figures in the room were prostrate on the floor and, to the rose-tinted eyes of Fenrir, they were all locked in attitudes of dutiful worship though, in reality, they were all suffering the effects of the cloying fumes from the enchanted plant which crackled and burned outwith the Dun.

He recognised two of the three who remained on their feet. His Goddess-sister, timelessly beautiful and totally unmoved by the earth-shattering events which she had helped bring about. Then his gaze turned to Varga Hrolfsson, main architect of his release from eternal detention, a true-born Viking, a credit to his god and a credit to his race. There had been many times when, in the privacy of his own mind, Fenrir had doubted that Varga possessed the wherewithal to complete the task appointed to him, but now he had fulfilled his destiny and, though the wolf-god's father was notorious for his capricious moods and lack of gratitude, Fenrir HelMouth would not be found wanting when it came to bestowing just reward upon his most favoured disciple.

The third one who stood was an enigma though. Fenrir felt he should know him, but he was at a loss. Something about the man's stance and naked hostility unsettled the Wolf-God and, though he knew he should merely squash the insolent fool like an annoying insect, he hesitated in doing so.

Varga, once he had ridden the overwhelming wave of accomplishment and pleasure which had engulfed him when his God had emerged so spectacularly from the pit, found himself following the trajectory of Fenrir's gaze. When his stare alighted on Galahad, the breath stuck in his throat, "Monkshood?" he bellowed. "It is not possible."

Fenrir's head jerked sideways to look in horror at his minion an instant after he had spoken the name. "Monkshood? The bane of wolves which Beyla warned you of? The only creature capable of thwarting my plans?" The God actually took a step back, "How has he come to be in my presence?" He yowled as all his doubts about the deceptive Aesir returned with an irresistible vengeance.

"I…know not, I…." Hrolfsson coughed and peered through tear-filled eyes at his enemy just as the sickly sweet aroma of the aconite reached his nostrils. He gaped in terror as he realised the clan, which he had led across trackless oceans and countless islands, were dying all around him, overcome by the floral smoke.

"Get up," he screamed. "Cease your worship and serve your God with deeds, not words." Spittle arced from his mouth as none of the other clansmen and women moved. Motion caught his eye and he saw Monkshood begin to stalk towards Fenrir. "No," he yelled and put himself between the grim-faced knight and the disconcerted deity.

The whine of fear which Galahad had heard in Fenrir's voice when his identity had been revealed, leant him a newfound confidence and he spat venomously. "You stand there snivelling like a newborn pup and you purport to be a God?"

"I am the God of Wolves and all will quake before me when I am ruler of this world." Fenrir shot back.

Galahad raised Whitecleave and pointed it at Fenrir's face, "Yet I stand before you right here, right now and it is not me who is doing the quaking."

"Do not seek to deny me what is rightfully mine, human." Fenrir roared.

"Rightfully yours?" The knight yelled back just as loudly. "This world is no more yours than it is mine. The only right you have to claim dominion over all on earth is one dreamed up by yourself and your delusional lap-dog." He dropped the point of his sword for the briefest of seconds to thrust it towards Varga. "You claim omnipotence, yet you refuse to even face me in combat. One man, that is all. I can understand that you would be scared to act, as I am, after all, the one man who has been prophesied to best you, but it hardly becomes a being trying to attain godhood to cower like a castrated puppy before one who he intends to dominate into venerating him when he reaches his exalted position."

"I am scared of no-one!" Fenrir shrieked, causing a concussion which shook the dust from the rafters.

"Then prove it, hellhound." Galahad began to swing Whitecleave in a figure of eight and advance upon the two wolven beings. "Stop hiding behind your lickspittle and face me."

"Stand aside, Hrolfsson." Fenrir's voice was as cold as the Fimbulvetr which had held the world in its clenched freezing fist for so long.

"My lord, I…" Varga began before Galahad cut in.

"See, even your most loyal follower doubts you." He snarled.

The Wolf-God's eyes swivelled to Varga and the Viking shrunk before the insane rage which burned within them. "Move, Hrolfsson, or feel my wrath."

Varga fell back before the tangible wave of evil which emanated from the God.

Fenrir leapt at his nemesis.

Galahad dropped to one knee, sword clasped in his hands, pointing straight upwards to heaven.

The massive wolf bore down upon him, mouth agape, razor-sharp teeth gleaming, tongue snaking out, eyes narrowed, vengeance complete.

At the last second, just as the beast's muzzle began to engulf Galahad's head, the knight appeared to surge upright, and he was launched bodily into the maw of the wolf-god.

Varga had been knocked onto his back by the force of Fenrir's passage, but he quickly scrambled to his feet and stood in shocked silence. Had it really been that easy? After all the bravado of Monkshood, he had thought to vanquish Fenrir by placing his faith in an intangible God, rather than a flesh and blood deity like the wondrous being before him. He was suddenly filled with an overpowering love for Fenrir and he wept unashamedly, feeling blessed beyond words to have witnessed events whose repercussions would be felt around the world.

He finally found his tongue and dropped to one knee. With head bowed, he breathed, "My lord, I am privileged…."

A strange sound came to his ears. At first, he wondered if the fumes of the wolfsbane were confounding his senses as the initial triumph of his deed wore off. However, the next few seconds toppled him from the summit of the mountain into the deepest trench of horror that he had ever and would ever experience.

Fenrir's eyes were pain-filled and looked as if they were about to burst forth from their sockets. The sound which had jolted Varga from his worshipful words was the wolf-god reaching for a breath that would not come.

As Varga watched, Fenrir's neck bulged obscenely, then split in a shower of blood as the blade of a sword punched through the skin and began slicing its way upwards. The spinal cord snapped with a juddering report and the Wolf-God's head began to loll to the side as blood gushed forth from the huge mouth and life fled from the huge mournful eyes.

Fenrir HelMouth's head fell to the floor and Galahad emerged, caked from head to foot in scarlet gore, with Whitecleave held victoriously towards the sky.

The tableau remained frozen for a moment before the whisper of Hel's robe could be heard sliding across the wooden floor.

Galahad stepped aside as the magical rope Gleipnir appeared in the goddess' hand and she looped it over the severed head of the dead god. Time seemed to stand still as the soul of Fenrir rose from its earthly dwelling and once again became the insubstantial creature which Varga had first met in his dreams all those years ago.

The ghost tore at the dwarven binding with all his might but Hel remained unmoved by the struggle. "It appears it is not your time, brother." The Goddess observed evenly and began to walk towards the gateway she had opened mere minutes ago.

Fenrir extended his claws and tried to embed them in the wood of the crannog's floor but they simply passed through it and he was dragged inexorably towards the yawning entrance of his sister's realm.

He snarled and turned to Varga, who watched, petrified by dread at what he was seeing. "This is your fault, you dim-witted idiot. You allowed him ingress to your domain. You have cost me everything."

"My lord, I...." Varga stammered, rocked to the core by the venom in Fenrir's sneer.

The massive wolf lunged for the Viking and the last thing Varga heard before darkness engulfed him was his God's hideous promise, "You will spend eternity on the shores of the Nastrond with your father, each watching the other die again and again at my hand."

And then Hel began descending into the portal, pulling her immense brother behind her without any apparent effort.

With a sensuous sigh rather than the earth-shattering concussion which Galahad had been expecting, the doorway to Hel disappeared in the blink of an eye.

Absolute silence cloaked the Dun. Even Galahad found he was holding his breath. He was an island in a sea of corpses, the wolves all remaining in their positions of prayer, their leader having condemned them all to death with his command that they should kneel before their god.

He hesitantly walked to the edge of where the entrance to Hel had been mere seconds ago and stared intently at it, but the wooden boards were all in place, scuffed and dirty, as if they had been there since the dawn of time.

Shaking his head in awestruck wonder, Galahad stumbled towards the exit of the Dun, groping his way gingerly through the thickening smoke. Halfway to the door, he stopped, resheathed Whitecleave, then bent to the ground and lifted Lorcan's body onto his shoulder.

Galahad's expression was unreadable as he wound his way through the maze of fallen Ulfhednar, shielding his face with his free arm as he neared the flaming door. He raised his boot and kicked it open, squinting his eyes in preparation for the light that he assumed was about to flood in.

He carried the body of the young monk out under a star-blasted sky, confused at the passage of time within the crannog. He laid Lorcan's corpse on the causeway and was about to re-enter the Dun to retrieve Adomain when a shout brought him up short.

Taiga and Craigan pounded across the narrow walkway until they were by his side. The Venicone gasped in anguish at the remains of the young man from Mull, and even the normally non-committal visage of Taiga winced when he saw the still-vivid injury to Lorcan's arm.

Galahad cut off the myriad questions which were queuing up on the wulver's tongue with a curt hand gesture and jogged into the crannog, returning moments later with the slighter form of Adomain.

The trio carried the two bodies to the loch's edge, Taiga and Craigan sharing bewildered glances at the unexpected reappearance of Brother Adomain.

"Is it over?" Craigan breathed. "Did we...you kill them all? How did...?"

Taiga waved his young friend into silence, whilst staring all the while at the swaying figure of Galahad. The former knight was staring numbly at the pair of unfortunate monks who had lost their lives so needlessly. He was cloaked in a scarlet shroud of blood which coated him from head to toe and his eyes had a wild look of madness about them.

"Leave him be for a few moments, laddie. Let him come to terms with what has happened. He will tell us all in his own good time, I am sure." The wulver muttered.

Galahad found himself staring at the silvery circle of a full moon which bulked hugely in the sky, shaking his head at the irony of such a sight dominating the skyscape on the night that the God of Wolves and his evil underlings fell. After a moment, he felt a great calm settle upon him and he came back into himself. The knight pulled at his sodden clothes with a gasp of disgust. He turned to his two companions and said, "Let me cleanse myself in the loch and then I will answer all your questions, I promise."

The middle-aged wulver and young Venicone watched Galahad strip and submerge himself in the cold water, both involuntarily shivering in sympathy as the freezing liquid closed about his body.

He emerged blue-lipped and quivering but feeling like a new man, purified by the banishment of the blood which had covered him so absolutely.

Taiga held out a change of clothes for him, which he had retrieved from one of the packs that lay on the skirt of the woods whilst the knight had been bathing.

As he finished dressing by looping Whitecleave in his belt, in a measured voice, he related what he could of the momentous events which had transpired in the werewolves' crannog, not needing to embellish anything as he felt the facts of the matter were fantastical enough in their own right.

He had just finished describing Fenrir's and Varga's descent into the realm of Hel, as his voice dwindled into silence and he stared up at the sky with an anguished look upon his face.

His two rapt listeners shared looks of utter incredulity at what they had just heard. Neither could quite believe that their quest, their mission to avenge their kith and kin, was over and had come to a successful conclusion. Despite the unexpectedly wondrous outcome, Taiga could not help but feel slightly cheated that he had not been in at the death, had not been able to stand and gloat over Varga Hrolfsson as Fenrir had consumed him and returned him to his rightful place, skulking like the animal he was in the lowest, filthiest pit of the underworld.

Galahad murmured something, breaking the wulver's train of thought and he leant in towards the man who had fulfilled his appointed destiny so fully, "What was that you said, Monkshood?" he asked.

The knight's head came up and, to Taiga's horror, his pupils were slitted and the whites of his eyes flashed yellow. "Run." Galahad snarled hoarsely.

Craigan had been lying on the grass, enjoying the busyness of the night, the constant chittering of insects, the swish of bat's wings, the sounds of life being lived, but Galahad's tone jerked him out of his placid reverie. His eye was immediately drawn to a long dappled line of red which stretched from the middle of Galahad's back to the top of his britches.

Taiga had scrambled to his feet, looking nervously at the knight, "What is…".

"Run!" Galahad screamed, fighting the near-irresistible urge which pounded in his blood, compelling him to leap at the wulver and rip him to pieces.

Taiga looked at Craigan, still unsure of what to do, but then the Venicone pointed wordlessly to the wound on Galahad's back and realisation dawned, "Oh, Monkshood, no," he cried.

The knight writhed in agony as the call of the wolf assailed every cell of his being, demanding that his body change into a murderous monster, commanding him to kill all those who would stand before him. "Dear God," he wept, "run, you must....run, I cannot....stop this".

Taiga grabbed Craigan and pulled him away from the agonised man, breaking into a run and cursing the twisted whims of fate.

"This is not right," Craigan wailed. "It cannot end for him like this. He has done all that we asked of him and so much more, he is..."

A gut-twisting howl shrieked its way skywards and seemed to fill the world with its aching grief.

Taiga's face was set in a fearsome mask as he and Craigan continued to cover the uneven ground as fast as they could. "He is Ulfhednar now, lad. He must have been bitten in the melee and not realised it until now. Damn, but that is unfair...," another howl sounded, this time much closer, "but it has happened and cannot be helped. Enough talk now, lad. He has spared our respective clans from extinction but, in this guise, he will not hesitate to change that. Come, lad, we must go."

With his improved night vision, Galahad could clearly see Taiga and Craigan standing roughly twenty yards off to the right and silently beseeched them to resume their flight.

He had managed to maintain a modicum of humanity despite the all-encompassing change which was violating his body so forcibly

His mind was so full of aggression and murderous intent that he could not marshal his thoughts sufficiently to rage at the injustice of his predicament. All he could do was try to cling to the tiny molecule of humanity which still existed within him.

Faces from the past lined up before a mind on the brink of insanity. Arthur Pendragon, Merlin the magician, Sir Lancelot Du Lac, Lady Joanna Dubin, Saint Columba...a candle-flame flickered in the blackness of his despair...the face of Taiga hoved into view, sitting in Columba's study on Iona, mouthing something which Galahad could not quite comprehend, "What are you saying?" The cursed knight shrieked in his mind.

In a moment of clarity, the wulver's rich voice intruded on the cacophony and the garbled gibberish became intelligible words,

"If you are bitten yourself then the curse may be removed by receiving three blows on the head with a knife or by kneeling in the same place for a hundred years."

And then, it was all too clear what he had to do.

403

With a last look at the rapidly retreating backs of Craigan McIntyre, last of the Venicone clan of Picts and Taiga Haas, last of the Kurtadam clan of wulvers, and a warm feeling suffusing him as he recognised his actions had ensured the temporary survival of two clans, Sir Galahad of Camelot, former champion of King Arthur Pendragon, dropped to his knees, thrust Whitecleave towards the night sky and began to pray, trusting that the flame of faith, which he had felt in God for most of his life, would consume utterly the disgusting poison coursing through his body, attempting to drag him down to its own evil level.

Epilogue

"Over there, supposedly," The young man pointed an index finger towards the sparkling water and then traced the same digit down the page of the book which he held in his hand.

"What, that wee island there?" His companion snorted disbelievingly.

He tapped her playfully on the shoulder. "That is what it says," he protested and referred to the book again for confirmation, "and don't laugh at me like that. I believe in this stuff and mocking people's beliefs is not nice." He huffed, a warm grin robbing the reproach of any sort of venom.

The young woman rolled her eyes, then a mischievous smirk appeared on her face and she yanked the man's bookmark out of the volume and ran along the shore, screaming in mock alarm as the man took to his heels after her.

She cut across to the long tussocks of grass which marked the transition from beach to meadow.

He caught up with her and swept her off her feet, swinging her round and round in his arms until they both fell to the damp ground, breathless with joy.

They lay there for several moments, drinking in the glory of each other's love.

"I know how important this stuff is to you, darling. I'm sorry I laughed," she sighed.

The man stared at the white clouds scudding across the blue sky high above them. "That's alright. I know I can get a bit intense sometimes." He lapsed into one of his brooding silences for a time and she privately wondered if she had offended him.

Suddenly, he jumped up, pulling her to her feet, "Come on, I want to show you something."

They walked quickly through the grass until they came to a bizarrely shaped boulder standing all on its own in the middle of the field. "Weird, isn't it?" he said. "It's supposed to be the petrified body of a great hero." He jerked a thumb over his shoulder. "Apparently, he was the one who vanquished the werewolves who lived on the loch."

"What, all of them? You said according to the legends there were at least a hundred of them. How can one man do all that?"

He shrugged, "That's what heroes are supposed to do, isn't it? Triumph against overwhelming odds." He said, walking round the strangely fashioned rock.

As she looked at it, in the same way that pictures suddenly appear in clouds, the lines of the rock seemed to flow for a moment and she caught a glimpse of a man kneeling with his head bowed.

She blinked bemusedly as her boyfriend's voice broke the momentary spell, "It's better if you look at it from this side."

She walked round, immediately seeing what he meant. There was the leg stretched out behind, the other foot planted firmly on the ground, the hands clasped in prayer, the noble nose pointing to the grass...she hesitated, were the hands praying or were they holding something?

Her eyes travelled up the long, slim protruberance of rock which arrowed towards the sky. Something glinted momentarily at the top and it took her a few seconds to realise what it was.

"Oh, Craig, yes, yes, of course I will." She squealed delightedly as she retrieved the diamond ring from the top of the rock.

Craig McIntyre's heart sang. Ever since he had seen this place in the course of his research, he had felt a strange pull drawing him to its picturesque scenery. He had snuck away the month before and had known as soon as he had seen it in all its beauty that this was the right place.

"Damn, it's good to be alive," he said, kissing his soon-to-be wife and idly wondering what the future held for them both.

Lightning Source UK Ltd.
Milton Keynes UK
UKOW031808211012

200935UK00003B/5/P